PENGUIN BOOKS

BOOTS OF LEATHER, SLIPPERS OF GOLD

Elizabeth Lapovsky Kennedy is Professor of American Studies and Women's Studies at SUNY, Buffalo.

Madeline D. Davis is Chief Conservator and Head of Preservation for the Buffalo and Erie County Public Library System.

BOOTS OF LEATHER

Chorus

For she walks in boots of leather
And in slippers made of gold;
She will be a child forever
And forever, she'll be old.
She's the heroine of legends;
She's the eagle and the dove.
She's the daughter of the moon;
She's my sister and my love.

She was born in winter's fury,
with the wind about her ears.
She was raised on strife and sadness,
and the city-dweller's fears.
She was nursed on wine and bloodshed
and she cut her teeth on steel;
and she wept alone in darkness
for the pain she was to feel.

Chorus

Many nights can fill a cavern;
many days can dry the seas;
many years will dull the longing
and erode the memories.
Ever more the granite forests
make a place for her to dwell.
And the streets of sleepy dreaming
Make a story she can tell.

Chorus

—Madeline Davis c. 1974

Boots of Leather, Slippers of Gold

THE HISTORY OF A LESBIAN COMMUNITY

Liz Lapovsky Kennedy

Madeline D. Davis

Elizabeth Lapovsky Kennedy
Madeline D. Davis

PENGUIN BOOKS

PENGUIN BOOKS
Published by the Penguin Group
Penguin Books USA Inc., 375 Hudson Street,
New York, New York 10014, U.S.A.
Penguin Books Ltd, 27 Wrights Lane,
London W8 5TZ, England
Penguin Books Australia Ltd,
Ringwood, Victoria, Australia
Penguin Books Canada Ltd, 10 Alcorn Avenue,
Toronto, Ontario, Canada M4V 3B2
Penguin Books (N.Z.) Ltd, 182-190 Wairau Road,
Auckland 10, New Zealand

Penguin Books Ltd, Registered Offices: Harmondsworth,
Middlesex, England

First published in the United States of America by Routledge, Chapman and Hall, 1993
Published in Penguin Books 1994

1 3 5 7 9 10 8 6 4 2

THE LIBRARY OF CONGRESS HAS CATALOGUED THE HARDCOVER AS FOLLOWS:
Kennedy, Elizabeth Lapovsky, 1939–
Boots of leather, slippers of gold: the history of a lesbian community/
Elizabeth Lapovsky Kennedy and Madeline D. Davis.
p.   cm.
Includes bibliographical references and index.
ISBN 0-415-90293-2 (hc.)
ISBN 0 14 02.3550 7 (pbk.)
1. Lesbians—New York (State)—Buffalo—History—20th century.
2. Lesbians—New York (State)—Buffalo—Social conditions.
3. Working class—New York (State)—Buffalo—History—20th century.
4. Women's studies—New York (State)—Buffalo.
5. Buffalo (N.Y.)—History—20th century.
I. Davis, Madeline D., 1940– . II. Title.
HQ75.6.U5K47   1993
305.48'9664—dc20   92–43420

Printed in the United States of America

To the women who have gone before us, brave women, outlaws, who sought only to find a life of love and dignity, and some of them did.

CONTENTS

ACKNOWLEDGMENTS

Many people and institutions have been invaluable in helping with this project through the years. We wish to acknowledge and thank them.

Because of homophobia the material support of lesbian and gay research was, and in many cases still is, controversial. It was difficult to find financial support for this work, and, therefore, those grants that we did receive were particularly important. In 1979 the Division of Graduate and Professional Education of the State University of New York at Buffalo awarded us a small grant for beginning the process of transcribing tapes, and in 1986 the Faculty of Arts and Letters Research and Development Funds gave us a small grant to continue transcriptions and travel to archives. In addition, in 1981, we received a small grant from the Astreia Foundation to help us establish links with the African-American lesbian community. With such modest support, a good deal of the money that went into the transcription of tapes, our major expense, came from the honorariums paid to us by college, university and community groups that invited us to speak throughout the country, and we are grateful for their support.

The Rockefeller Humanities Fellowship program at the Southwest Institute for Research on Women, the University of Arizona at Tucson supported Liz for the full academic year 1988–89 to complete the first draft of this book. All of the Women's Studies faculty, especially Myra Dinnerstein and Sheila Slaughter, provided an exciting and supportive intellectual atmosphere that encouraged steady writing. Both authors are grateful for the Fellowship's monetary and intellectual support and see it as a turning point in the evolution of the project.

Several colleagues have been enormously helpful in the shaping of this manuscript. We are extremely grateful to them for reading significant portions, offering comments and criticism, and expressing belief in the importance of our work. We are particularly indebted to Esther Newton and John D'Emilio for sharing their knowledge of lesbian and gay history in their comments on a major portion of the first draft. Ellen DuBois gave a close reading to the majority of the manuscript and was invaluable for pushing us to articulate our ideas precisely and to place them in the context of U.S. social history. Joan Nestle offered helpful commentary and criticism on the entire manuscript and was a consistent source of encouragement throughout the writing process, reminding us of its worth and insisting that it be finished. Also, both Ellen and Joan have given constant emotional support throughout the years. Lillian Robinson also read the entire manuscript, paying particular attention to issues of style. Since our use of extended narrators' quotes was quite controversial in academic circles, her knowledge of and sensitivity to working-class voices made her an important advocate with the publisher for their inclusion in the book. In addition, Margaret Randall was an important advisor on the use of oral history narratives and the best way to edit them.

Other colleagues have read shorter, more discrete portions of the manuscript, and were extremely helpful. At different stages of the book various chapters have benefited from the comments of Lisa Albrecht, Katie Gilmartin, Ron Grele, Susan Phillips, David Schneider, Sheila Slaughter, Bev Sorenson, and Rose Weitz. The book has also profited from ideas and research tips offered by colleagues in conversations and correspondence. Although the list is too long to be inclusive of everyone, we want to attempt to name at least a few: Allan Berube, Libby Bouvier, George Chauncey, Janet Cohen, Tee Corrine, Chris Czernik, Myra Dinnerstein, Frances Doughty, Lisa Duggan, Deb Edel, William Fischer, Estelle Freedman, Michael Frisch, Linda Gordon, Pat Gozemba, Amber Hollibaugh, Nan Hunter, Jonathan Katz, Ruth Meyerowitz, Gayle Rubin, Judith Schwarz, Henry Louis Taylor, Jr., Carole Vance, and Monique Wittig. Contact with the San Francisco Lesbian and Gay History Project, the Boston Area Lesbian and Gay History Project and the Canadian Gay Archives were also stimulating and inspirational for our continuing work, and time spent at the Lesbian Herstory Archives in New York City was invaluable for providing a national context. Further we wish to acknowledge the research help given us by Ruth Willett and the staff of the History Department of the Buffalo and Erie County Public Library, and by Mary Bell and the staff of the Buffalo and Erie County Historical Society.

Buffalo residents, Joan Rzadkiewicz and Joan Laughlin, read the entire book in order to give us feedback from a local perspective, and we are grateful to them. We would also like to thank Bernice, who has read a substantial portion of the manuscript, and whose clarity of thought has been invaluable regarding Black community history and traditions, and Madeline's co-workers Jeanette Perry and Willie Whipple, who gave unique insights into Black community social life. We are also indebted to Bonnie Danielson and Pat Gonser who searched photo collections and located some wonderful images. In addition, we are grateful to Julia B. Reinstein, whose life story does not appear in this book because she was not a member of the bar community. However, she was an invaluable resource for placing that community in a larger context and for illuminating the relation between photographs and memories.

The prose style of the book owes a great deal to Liz's writing group. Together, its members, Betsy Cromley, Hester Eisenstein, Claire Kahane, Carolyn Korsmeyer, Suzanne Pucci, and Carol Zemel, have an awesome sense of what constitutes engaging prose. Their time and sharp attention are greatly appreciated. We are also deeply indebted to Beverly Harrison who singlehandedly transcribed the many hours of oral history tapes with skill and accuracy.

In the past five years, work with graduate students at the State University of New York at Buffalo, particularly Melissa Ragona, Claudia Friedetzky, Sue Aki, the late Lucho Carrillo-Molino, and all the students in the Fall 1991 Gay and Lesbian Community History course, have helped to crystallize our thinking. We also want to thank Candace Kanes and Bonita Hampton for their excellent research assistance. We especially appreciate Candace's sharp wit and eye which were invaluable for tidying up the manuscript in its last few months of preparation. Thanks to Kathleen Haggerty who took over some of Liz's work obligations, and in a pinch did some final computer work, freeing us to finish.

The inclusion of photographs in the book presented numerous challenges because of the need to camouflage some images. We thank Christine Eber for several years of work exploring different ways to disguise narrators' faces, although in the end our joint efforts did not produce a satisfactory solution. We are particularly indebted to Fred Kwiecien, supervisor of photography at Academic Services, Computing and Information Technology at the State University of New York at Buffalo, for contacting us about the use of computer technology for solving our problems, before we even realized we should ask him for help. His professional expertise has been invaluable for producing the final images used in this book. We cannot praise enough his artistic sensibility, his technical skill, and his consummate patience while we negotiated with narrators for their approval. Thomas Headrick at the State University of New York Law School gave generously of his time, advising us on the legal implications of the use of photographs. We also wish to thank Donald Watkins, assistant for instructional resources, and Nancy MacDonald, graphic and computer artist, of Academic Services, Computing and Information Technology at the State University of New York at Buffalo for designing a clear map of lesbian gathering places. Nancy was particularly attentive to details and extremely tolerant of changes. In addition, we are pleased to have worked with Renee Ruffino on cover art and are appreciative of her many creative ideas.

In a process as long as this one, friends and family have been essential for offering the support needed to keep going, even if they have no direct relation to the book. For Liz, Angela and Charles Keil, Sherri Darrow, and the late Gail Paradise Kelly constantly validated the importance of the work as an academic endeavor. Isabel Marcus was always generous with her legal expertise, and Peggy Baker and Margaret Small provided sound advice about the use of computer technology. Members of the Buffalo and Tucson Re-evaluation Counseling Communities offered Liz persistent help for overcoming writer's block, particularly Pauline Mendola, Jean Ann, and Cindy Cox. Liz also appreciates the consistent encouragement her parents, Dr. Arthur Lapovsky and the late Martha Lapovsky, gave her to finish this book and her entire family's tolerance of her consuming commitment to the work.

For Madeline, the emotional and spiritual support of Spiderwoman Coven has been invaluable, as has the unfailing concern and encouragement of her mother Harriet, her sister Sheila, and her brother Mark. Madeline would also like to thank Bobbi Prebis for thirty-seven years of friendship and advice on how to survive and thrive in Buffalo's gay community. She is also grateful for the enduring friendship of Elizabeth Stone who provided quiet respite and numerous back adjustments. Madeline wishes to give a special thank you to her grandmother, Rose Morris, who passed away in March 1991 at age ninety-five. For Rose, Madeline's lesbianism and her involvement in community work were always a focus of interest and pride. She was a consistent source of strength, good humor, and love and told great stories about lesbians who came to the Chippewa Market where she had a stand. Rosie would have loved this book.

Both Liz and Madeline are thankful to our dinner group for their reliable companionship and terrific meals. We are also indebted to the Buffalo lesbian community for the constant support of our work. Most every year during Gay Pride they sponsored us to give a talk that was often attended by over one hundred people. The enthusiastic response gave us the energy to continue, and the questions asked helped us keep in touch with the concerns of contemporary lesbians.

Finally, to state the obvious, the success of a project like this depends primarily on the cooperation of the narrators. And it is to them that we owe our deepest debt of gratitude. They not only shared their life stories with us, but allowed us to return to them repeatedly to clarify points and ask more questions. A substantial number actively helped us shape the project by sharing ideas about how to interpret lesbian history and by introducing us to other narrators whom they thought it would be important to interview. Many also helped us locate photographs and gave valuable comments on computer camouflage. In addition, several gave generously of their time by coming to presentations and/or reading portions of the manuscript.

As will be explained in chapter 1, we have chosen to use first-name pseudonyms in identifying people throughout the book. Most narrators wanted to be associated with the project in this manner. But a significant minority of narrators spent their entire lives refusing to hide, and therefore were not completely satisfied with our decision to use pseudonyms. In these acknowledgments it seems appropriate not only to thank the narrators in general but also to specifically mention those who are able to be visible: Marge, Andy Wares, Butch Pat, Mary, Buff Fisher, Joan, Pat Gilbert and Randy. We particularly want to thank two narrators who have worked tirelessly for the project. Bobbi Prebis was a constant resource throughout the thirteen years of the research. She was always thinking about people we needed to interview and how we could meet them, as well as serving as an advisor on fine points of community life. Terry Morone read the manuscript at two different stages, offering us detailed feedback on both versions. We sorrowfully acknowledge the death of four narrators before the publication of this book. Known in the book by their pseudonyms, Joanna, Dee, Cheryl and Lonnie, their words are a valuable legacy.

As we complete this book we want to thank Avra Michelson for her excellent thinking during the period she was co-director of the project and Wanda Edwards for her helpful insights as advisor to the project. We are especially grateful for the enthusiastic support we have received from our editor, Cecelia Cancellaro. She has thought creatively about how her office can make this the best book possible, and has been very understanding about missed deadlines.

The process of writing a book like this requires the support and understanding of the authors' significant others. They need to pick up the slack at home, and put on hold their personal desires. Liz gives her love and gratitude to Bobbi Prebis for her tenacity over fourteen years, particularly when the going was rough. Bobbi's humor and pride were constant reminders of the importance of telling this story. Madeline is grateful to Leslie Wolff who read and criticized parts of the manuscript, commented on language and style, and consistently provided laughter, patience, and a sustaining love.

PREFACE

Boots of Leather, Slippers of Gold: The History of a Lesbian Community has been fourteen years in preparation. When we began this research in 1978, there were only a few published works on gay and lesbian history.[1] But there was a ferment in the air generated in part by the searching questions of a movement of gays and lesbians who had only recently rid themselves of the idea that there was something terribly wrong with them—be it sin, sickness, or criminality—and had come to understand that they had been oppressed like other social groups; and in part by the probing research of women as they threw off sexist blinders and looked for less domesticated and more powerful forms of womanhood. Participants in the women's and gay liberation movements would no longer accept the medical profession's model of "deviance," that dominated the discourse on gays and lesbians during the first half of the twentieth century. They envisioned a world without oppression, where homosexuals lived side by side with heterosexuals and sexuality was not dichotomized. With this impetus, we taught ourselves to research and write lesbian history, drawing on our previous training and experience.

Liz Lapovsky Kennedy: "During the 1960s, I trained as an anthropologist and completed two years' field work with the Waunan, an indigenous people living in the Pacific Coast rain forest of Colombia. The Waunan revealed to me the potential for human beings to live in harmony with one another and with nature, and the importance of political economy and culture for creating such possibilities. With the help of the antiwar movement and later the Black power and women's liberation movements, I became painfully aware of the limitations of studies of small communities in faraway places that focus on one moment in time and ignore the context of colonial domination. While building the program in Women's Studies at the State University of New York at Buffalo, I resolved to use my skills to do useful, woman-centered research for a local group. At this time my interest in the history of working-class lesbian community was piqued by the wonderful tales graduate students told about older lesbians in the bars. After coming out in the context of the feminist movement in 1976, I felt optimistic that I could design a research project with older, working-class lesbians that would focus on their culture of survival and resistance in the context of twentieth-century U.S. history, and would meet my new standards for ethical and useful research. I was hoping to correct the assumption of my students that lesbian history consists of Sappho, Gertrude Stein, and gay liberation."

Madeline Davis: "As an early gay and lesbian activist, I had co-researched and co-taught the first course on Lesbianism in the U.S. and had become intensely involved in local, state, and national gay politics. In 1972 I was elected the first open lesbian delegate to a major political convention (Dem./McGovern) and afterwards worked in party politics as an out lesbian feminist. I had been writing and singing gay and lesbian music for many years and had been working as a librarian for more than a decade when I decided to return to school for an interdisciplinary degree in American Studies/Women's Studies. As a result of the influence of a burgeoning women's movement that gave me a new understanding of the confluence of economics, sexuality, oppression, and consciousness in the lives of the women with whom I had been associating since the late 1950s, I became interested in lesbian history. I also wanted to write an accurate and compassionate chronicle of the lives of these brave women who had cared for me so generously when I came out in the mid-1960s."

Each of us was unaware of the other's interest in this topic until Liz served as faculty supervisor when Madeline taught a course on lesbian history and politics. After sharing our research dreams, we turned the class requirement that each student conduct a taped interview with an older lesbian into a pilot for testing the amount of material available for writing a history of Buffalo's lesbian community. These interviews became part of the present study.

At first, there was little room in the university for such bold research. As a result, the movement generated community-based lesbian and gay history projects which supported one another, and began to uncover evidence of gay and lesbian resistance, strength, and happiness in the past. These projects did exceptional work.[2] In 1978, we founded the Buffalo Women's Oral History Project and made contact with the many similar projects nationally. From the beginning, the project had three goals that we have maintained over the years: first, to write a comprehensive history of the lesbian community in Buffalo, New York, using as the major source, oral histories of lesbians who participated in a lesbian community prior to 1970; second, to create and index an archive of oral-history tapes, written interviews, and relevant supplementary materials; and third, to give this history back to the community from which it derives; the last to be done in the form of public presentations. Several months after the project began, Avra Michelson joined and was an equal participant for three and one-half years, contributing to the early conceptualization of the interviews and the outline of the book. In 1981 Wanda Edwards joined the project as a paid researcher for six months and stayed on for several years as a consultant who advised us on the best ways to conceptualize Black lesbian history.[3]

Although we adhered from the beginning to strict rules of thorough and responsible research, our connection to the community made the work more than just a research project. Uncovering our hidden history was a labor of love, and restoring this history to our community was a political responsibility. This level of commitment to the project provided the patience and stamina needed to solve the problems that emerged over the years of research. But it also created frustration and impatience when the project became protracted. How could we respond to questions from narrators about when the book would be ready? Could any end product justify the time spent? Was this really the best place for our energies?

Emotional involvement in the subject also raised ethical questions about whether narrators were receiving enough back for their contributions. Is the emotional bond of the interview and the final book a sufficient return? We remain unsure. Sometimes people would share so much of themselves that we wanted to respond beyond the confines of the interview. Our policy was to hold off involvement until a set of interviews was finished; then, if we wished, we could establish an ongoing relationship. We also decided early on that a major share of any profit made from the book would be given to a fund to support services for older lesbians and we have structured our contract to designate this.

Since we envisaged the research as a project of the lesbian and feminist movements, we began with high ideals about collective work. But as the research and writing evolved, we were often faced with the difficult dynamics caused by divergent personal needs, and differences in approach and method as well as in interest and ability. In time we modified our expectations. For the last six years, Liz and Madeline have taken joint responsibility for the research while Liz had the major responsibility for drafting and revising the book. Both of us have actively worked on refining the ideas and polishing the prose. We have enjoyed working together, drawing strength and laughter from our often startling differences in character, knowledge, and preparation. Liz's thinking is informed by a passion for understanding oppressed peoples' resistance in history and Madeline's by a powerful intuitive sense about emotional life and personality. Liz bristles with the desire to confront injustice directly while Madeline seeks to defuse injustice and render it impotent with drama and humor.

Over the past fifteen years, the amount of research on lesbian and gay history has increased to the point where we can now speak of it as a new and growing field. More and more, this research is being produced by scholars connected to colleges and universities, and as a result it has begun to gain some acceptance.[4] Although we have benefited from and contributed to this process of legitimization, we did not give up our original roots, but instead tried to encompass the orientation of both the community and the university. We aim to give this research back to the community at the same time that we incorporate and further the analytical perspectives of the best scholarship on lesbians. We hope that this work will inspire others to look at their own cities and begin to uncover the richness of their local histories. We can only build a strong future with knowledge of the past.

1

"TO COVER UP THE TRUTH WOULD BE A WASTE OF TIME": INTRODUCTION

"Things back then were horrible and I think that because I fought like a man to survive I made it somehow easier for the kids coming out today. I did all their fighting for them. I'm not a rich person. I don't have a lot of money; I don't even have a little money. I would have nothing to leave anybody in this world, but I have that—that I can leave to the kids who are coming out now, who will come out into the future. That I left them a better place to come out into. And that's all I have to offer, to leave them. But I wouldn't deny it. Even though I was getting my brains beaten up I would never stand up and say, 'No don't hit me. I'm not gay; I'm not gay.' I wouldn't do that. I was maybe stupid and proud, but they'd come up and say, 'Are you gay?' And I'd say, 'Yes I am.' Pow, they'd hit you. For no reason at all. It was silly and it was ridiculous; and I took my beatings and I survived it."

—Matty

Working-class lesbians of the 1940s and 1950s searched for and built communities—usually around bars and house parties—in which they could be with others like themselves. Like the woman quoted above they did not deny their lesbianism, despite severe consequences; and today many of them judge their actions as having contributed to a better life for gays and lesbians. Their self-reliance and dream of a better world placed them solidly in the democratic tradition of the United States. But what happened to that independent spirit and hope when it was awakened in working-class lesbians whose very being was an anathema to American morality? *Boots of Leather, Slippers of Gold: The History of a Lesbian Community* tells that story. We document how working-class lesbians—African Americans, European Americans, and Native Americans—created a community whose members not only supported one another for survival in an extremely negative and punitive environment, but also boldly challenged and helped to change social life and morals in the U.S.[1]

Popular culture, the medical establishment, affluent lesbians and gays, and recently, many lesbian feminists have stereotyped members of this community as low-life societal discards and pathetic imitators of heterosexuality, and therefore hardly self-conscious actors in history.[2] Our own first-hand acquaintance with some older working-class lesbians, who told lively and dramatic stories about the joys and pains of their experiences, led us to question this view. We suspected that they had forged a culture for survival and resistance under difficult conditions and had passed this sense of community on to newcomers; in our minds, these were signs of a movement in its prepolitical stage.[3] Our research has reinforced the appropriateness of this framework, revealing that working-class lesbians of the 1940s and 1950s were strong and forceful participants in the growth of gay and lesbian consciousness and pride, and necessary predecessors of the gay and lesbian liberation movements that emerged in the late 1960s.

John D'Emilio points out that the ideology of gay liberation was based on an intriguing paradox.[4] It was a movement that called for an end to years of secrecy, hiding, and shame; yet its rapid growth suggests that gays and lesbians could not have been completely isolated and hidden in the time period just prior to the movement's inception. Gay liberation built on and transformed previously existing communities and networks. In his own work, D'Emilio explores in detail how the homophile movement, a network of organizations formed in the 1950s advocating peaceful negotiation for legal change and social acceptance, laid the groundwork for gay and lesbian politics of the late 1960s and early 1970s. The homophile movement, however, was very small and held itself separate from the large gay and lesbian communities that centered in bars and house parties; its history, therefore, can tell only part of the story. D'Emilio's work suggests, but does not itself explore, that bar communities were equally important predecessors.

Boots of Leather, Slippers of Gold is the first book-length study of a mid-century bar community. Focusing on Buffalo, New York, the book aims to explore how the culture of resistance that developed in working-class, lesbian bars and house parties contributed to shaping twentieth-century gay and lesbian consciousness and politics. Our approach is that of ethno-history: a combination of the methodology of ethnography—the intensive study of the culture and identity of a single community—with history—the analysis of the forces that shaped how that community changed over time, using as our primary sources oral histories of Buffalo lesbians.

We have chosen to focus on working-class lesbians because we view them as having had a unique role in the formation of the homophile and gay liberation movements. Like virtually every other aspect of modern social relations, lesbian social life and culture differed according to social class. Lesbians who were independently wealthy and not dependent on society's approval for making a living and a home could risk being open about their lesbianism with few material consequences. But this privilege also meant that their ways of living had limited benefit for the majority of working lesbians.[5] Middle-class lesbians who held teaching and other professional jobs had to be secretive about their identity because their jobs and status in life depended on their reputations as morally upstanding women. So, they, too, could not initiate the early effort to make lesbianism a visible and viable opportunity for women, nor develop a mass political movement that could change social conditions.[6] By contrast, working-class lesbians pioneered ways of socializing together and creating intimate sexual relationships without losing the ability to earn a living. Who these working-class lesbians were and how they developed forms of community that had lasting influence on the emergence of the homophile, gay liberation, and lesbian feminist movements are central issues in this book.

The focus on community rather than the individual is based upon our assumption that community is key to the development of twentieth-century lesbian identity and consciousness. Even though lesbians or gays did not live in the same areas, or work at the same place, they formed communities that were primary in shaping lesbian and gay culture and individual lives by socializing together. In the 1960s, sociologists and psychologists already had come to realize that what many had taken as the idiosyncratic behavior of gays and lesbians was really a manifestation of gay and lesbian culture formed in the context of bar communities.[7] But the ideology characterizing gays and lesbians as isolated, abnormal individuals remains so dominant that the importance of community in twentieth-century working-class lesbian life has reached few people and has to be affirmed and explained regularly to new audiences.

For the purpose of this book, we define the Buffalo working-class lesbian community as that group of people who regularly frequented lesbian bars and open or semiopen house parties during the 1940s and 1950s. Such a definition raises problematic issues about boundaries. Were those who went to the bars once a year "members" of the community in the same way as those who went once a week? Was there a single national lesbian community, since some Buffalonians regularly visited other cities and experienced a shared culture? Was there more than one community in Buffalo since it definitely had subcommunities with somewhat different cultures? Did African-American lesbians have more in common with African-American lesbians in Harlem in the 1950s than with European-American lesbians in Buffalo? We have no easy answers for such questions, but they are explored recurrently throughout the book.

By focusing on working-class lesbian communities that centered in bars and open house parties, we are highlighting the similarities between lesbians and gay men, since gay men and lesbians socialized together in such locales. Nevertheless, we decided to focus primarily on lesbians in order to ask questions from a lesbian point of view. Our aim is to understand the imperatives of lesbian life in the context of the oppression of homosexuals and of women. Later in the book, in the context of information on patterns of socializing and then again in the conclusion, we will consider the extent to which gay men and lesbians can be considered a single community.

Boots of Leather, Slippers of Gold covers a crucial period in the development of lesbian community, slightly more than two decades from the late 1930s to the early 1960s. Since our method is oral history, we are forced to start in the 1930s because that is as far back as our narrators' memories reach.[8] We believe, however, that World War II was a critical period for the formation of the Buffalo working-class community, and, therefore, the late 1930s is an appropriate starting point. The study ends before the rise of gay liberation and feminism.

Within this period, significant changes occurred in lesbian life. In Buffalo in the 1930s, the public lesbian community was small and fragmented. Lesbians had a difficult time finding others like themselves and felt extremely isolated. During the 1940s and in the context of World War II, the lesbian community stabilized and began to flourish. There were approximately the same number of gay and lesbian bars in Buffalo during the 1940s as there are today. In the 1950s, despite the witch-hunts of gays and lesbians, the rigidification of sex roles, and the general cold-war atmosphere, the lesbian community became more defiant and continued its pursuit of sexual autonomy for women. The community also became more complex. The relatively autonomous African-American and European-American communities became integrated to the extent that each had some contact with the other, and certain bars and house parties were frequented by a racially mixed crowd. In addition, the community became class-stratified with a more upwardly mobile group and a rough and tough blue-collar group each going its separate way. Each of these groups developed a somewhat different culture and different strategies for carving out space and respect in a hostile heterosexual world.

The concern of this book is to document these changes in detail, to understand what they meant for lesbian culture, consciousness, and identity, and to explore the connection between particular kinds of consciousness and the homophile movement on the one hand and gay liberation on the other. We also seek answers to why particular changes occurred at particular times. One of our underlying questions is, Who makes lesbian history? Although as oppressed people lesbians were deeply affected by the dominant social system, the degree to which they acted on their own behalf needs to be understood. To what extent did the activities of lesbians shape their developing social life and politics? Toward this end, we examine the activities of lesbians within their own community as well as their interactions with the larger society.

At first we were swept away by the exciting interconnections between socializing in bars and developing lesbian culture and tended to relegate sex and relationships to a position of lesser importance in the formation of identity and consciousness. This impulse was based in part on the conceptual division between the public (social life and politics) and the private (intimacy and sex), which characterized nineteenth-century society, and has remained deeply rooted in modern consciousness. With women's move out of the home and the eroticizing of social life in general, the twentieth century has seen a realignment of the public and the private. The emergence of gay and lesbian communities was related to this shift and contributes to a more subtle understanding of the relationships between these two spheres.

The life stories of our narrators as they talked freely about sexuality led us to what should have been immediately obvious: Although securing public space was indeed important, it was strongly motivated by the need to find a setting for the formation of intimate relationships. By definition, this community was created to foster intimacy among its members and was therefore built on a dynamic interconnection between public socializing and personal intimacy. This study therefore encompasses social life in bars and house parties and sexual and emotional intimacy, and the interconnections between them. It asks such questions as: How does women's sexuality develop outside of the restraints of male power? What was the role of community socializing in the development of lesbian sexuality? How did lesbians balance an interest in sex and a desire for emotional closeness? What was the impact of community social life on the longevity of lesbian relationships?

All commentators on twentieth-century lesbian life have noted the prominence of butch-fem roles.[9] Before the 1970s, their presence was unmistakable in all working-class lesbian communities: the butch projected the masculine image of her particular time period—at least regarding dress and mannerisms—and the fem, the feminine image; and almost all members were exclusively one or the other. Buffalo was no exception. As in most places, butch-fem roles not only shaped the lesbian image but also lesbian desire, constituting the base for a deeply satisfying erotic system. Beginning this research at a time when the modern feminist movement was challenging gender polarization and gender roles were generally declining in importance, we at first viewed butch-fem roles as peripheral to the growth and development of the community. Eventually we came to understand that these were at the core of the community's culture, consciousness, and identity. For many women, their identity was in fact butch or fem, rather than gay or lesbian. The unique project of this book, therefore, is to understand butch-fem culture from an insider's perspective.

Why should the opposition of masculine and feminine be woven into and become a fundamental principle of lesbian culture? Several scholars have addressed this question. Modern lesbian culture developed in the context of the late nineteenth and early twentieth centuries, when elaborate hierarchical distinctions were made between the sexes and gender was a fundamental organizing principle of cultural life. In documenting the lives of women who "passed" as men, Jonathan Katz argues that, in the context of this nineteenth-century polarization of masculinity and femininity, one of the few ways for women to achieve independence in work and travel and to escape passivity was by assuming the male role.[10] In a similar vein, Jeffrey Weeks holds that the adoption of male images by lesbians at the turn of the century broke through women's and lesbians' invisibility, a necessity if lesbians were to become part of public life.[11] Expanding this approach, Esther

Newton situates the adoption of male imagery in the context of the New Woman's search for an independent life, and delineates how male imagery helped to break through the nineteenth-century assumptions about women's natural lack of sexual desire and to introduce overt sexuality into women's relationships with one another.[12]

We agree with these interpretations and modify them for the conditions of the 1930s, 1940s, and 1950s. During this period, manipulation of the basic ingredient of patriarchy—the hierarchical distinction between male and female—continued to be an effective way for the working-class lesbian community to give public expression to its affirmation of women's autonomy and women's romantic and sexual interest in women. Butches defied convention by usurping male privilege in appearance and sexuality, and with their fems, outraged society by creating a romantic and sexual unit within which women were not under male control. At a time when lesbian communities were developing solidarity and consciousness, but had not yet formed political groups, butch-fem roles were the key structure for organizing against heterosexual dominance. They were the central prepolitical form of resistance. From this perspective, butch-fem roles cannot be viewed simply as an imitation of heterosexual, sexist society. Although they derived in great part from heterosexual models, the roles also transformed those models and created an authentic lesbian lifestyle. Through roles, lesbians began to carve out a public world of their own and developed unique forms for women's sexual love of women.[13]

Like any responsible ethnography, this book aims to take the reader inside butch-fem culture and demonstrate its internal logic and multidimensional meanings. We will document the subtle ways that lesbian community life transformed heterosexual models, pondering the inevitable and fascinating confusions: What does it mean to eroticize gender difference in the absence of institutionalized male power? Is it possible to adopt extremely masculine characteristics and yet not want to be male? In addition, in writing this history, we consider the context of the severe oppression of women and homosexuals that generated and reproduced butch-fem communities, showing the way that butch-fem roles changed over time as part of lesbians' resistance to oppression and their attempt to build a better life. We explore butch-fem culture as an historically specific form of rebellion that facilitated the building of communities, that supported women's erotic interest in one another, and that contributed to women's general struggle for entrance into the public sphere and for sexual autonomy.

In an ethnography, the precise use of language is a significant part of conveying a community's culture. In this context the use of the term "lesbian" is problematic. We use the term "lesbian" to refer to all women in the twentieth century who pursued sexual relationships with other women. Narrators, however, rarely used the word "lesbian," either to refer to themselves or to women like themselves. In the 1940s the terms used in the European-American community were "butch and fem," a "butch and her girlfriend," sometimes a "lesbian and her girlfriend." Sometimes butches would refer to themselves as "homos" when trying to indicate the stigmatized position they held in society. Some people, not all, would use the term "gay girls" or "gay kids" to refer to either butch or fem, or both. In the 1950s, the European-American community still used "butch" and "fem"; however, slang terms became more common. Sometimes butches of the rough crowd were referred to as "diesel dykes" or "truck drivers." They sometimes would refer to themselves as "queer" to indicate social stigma. In the African-American community "stud broad" and "stud and her lady" were common terms, although "butch" and "fem" were also used. Many used the phrase "my people" to indicate a partner. The term "bull dagger" was used by hostile straights as an insult,[14] but was sometimes used by members of the African-American community to indicate toughness. For both communities the term "gay" was more prevalent in the 1950s than in the 1940s as the generic term for lesbians. Still, language usage was not consistent and a white leader in the 1950s says that she might have referred to lesbians as "weird people." In attempting to use the terms appropriate to each group and each time period, our prose became very muddied and difficult to handle. We therefore have chosen to use the term "lesbian" as the generic to make our writing clearer. Inevitably, however, this leads to a distorted understanding of our narrators' consciousness and renders lesbian identity too elemental. We try to account for this in chapter 9 when we discuss identity in detail. We ask the reader to keep this problem in mind as she/he progresses through the book.

PLACING BUFFALO WORKING-CLASS LESBIANS IN THE CONTEXT OF GAY AND WOMEN'S HISTORY

Writing working-class lesbian history is still a new undertaking that demands the intersection of gay and women's history. Together these two fields have had a profound impact on the questions we asked and, therefore, on what we learned.[15] In framing our study of Buffalo's butch-fem community, we have been particularly influenced by gay history's discovery that the homosexual person—one who defines herself as different primarily on the basis of sexual interests and who desires to congregate with others like herself—is a modern, Western phenomenon. This insight freed us to ask questions about the changing forms of identity and community, and how these were related to lesbian resistance. In addition, the insights of feminism have constructively informed the entire book; we have been influenced particularly, however, by having to rethink lesbian feminism's marginalization of butch-fem communities in lesbian history.

Together, the fields of gay and women's history have complicated the definition of lesbianism by documenting the existence of four distinct kinds of erotic relationships among women in the late nineteenth and early twentieth centuries. First, a number of individual women passed as men, some engaging in erotic relationships with women. These "passing women" lived separate from one another in the heterosexual world without the distinct identity and consciousness that comes with community.[16] Second, many nineteenth-century, middle-class married women had intense passionate friendships with women. These did not disrupt their wifely or motherly duties, but rather supported them. While many of these relationships were unquestionably erotic, they were rarely, if ever, explicitly genital.[17] Third, in the late nineteenth and early twentieth centuries, middle-class, unmarried women built powerful lives around communities of women defined by work, politics, or school. They too had intensely passionate but not consciously sexual relationships. They saw themselves as women outside of marriage, not as women who had a form of sexuality different from others; it was not primarily erotic interest in women around which they chose to come together.[18]

Fourth and finally, there were the women like those who are the center of this book, who socialized together because of their explicit romantic and sexual interest in other women. These communities mark the beginning of modern lesbian identity. Those who participated in these communities experienced themselves as different and this difference was a core part of their identity.[19] The new gay history argues that this form of lesbian identity, which prevails now in contemporary Europe and America—and parallels gay male identity—is unique to this culture and time period.[20] Homosexual behavior certainly existed in earlier times and in other cultures, but it was a discrete part of a person's life, not something around which an individual constructed his or her identity. In the twentieth century, however, being lesbian or gay became a core identity around which people came together with others like themselves and built their lives.

There is some disagreement about when this modern gay and lesbian identity emerged, but most scholars place its origin at the end of the nineteenth century.[21] There is also significant disagreement about the radical discontinuity implied by the view that modern lesbian and gay identity has little in common with that of other cultures or historical periods, for instance, Ancient Greece.[22] Nevertheless, the identification of distinct forms of homosexuality in different periods of history and different cultures has indelibly shaped gay and lesbian history. It has also marked the study of sexuality in general, by implying that all sexuality and sexual groupings, including heterosexuality, are socially created.[23]

Our study of the Buffalo lesbian community is in this interpretive tradition. In order to understand the growth and transformation of modern lesbian identity, we look at how lesbians came to identify as such, how they socialized together and built a community in bars or at house parties, and the kind of culture and consciousness they developed. We also assume that what we discover is relevant beyond the lesbian and gay community. The lesbian community was forged in the context of the larger society and had a dialectical relationship with that society, the history of which provides valuable insights into heterosexuality.

Buffalo's public lesbian community is one of many to form and flourish in the U.S. and Europe in the twentieth century. A variety of factors contributed to the emergence of lesbian communities and a distinct lesbian identity at the turn of the century.[24] First, the development of large industrial cities inhabited by migrants—both individuals and families—offered the opportunity for gays and lesbians to congregate more or less anonymously. Second, the movement of women from the domestic sphere into the public realm in education, work, and politics allowed them to function somewhat independently of their families. The availability of jobs for women was particularly important because it gave them the opportunity to support themselves. Third, the increasing eroticization of the public realm through the development of a consumer society, which promoted sexual pleasure and leisure to sell products, created a culture that separated sex from reproduction and valued the pursuit of sexual interests. The earliest manifestations of commercialized and eroticized leisure were late-nineteenth-century amusement parks where young working people met one another and socialized with sexual intentions. By the early twentieth century, most high school students participated in a distinct youth culture that centered on the excitement of erotic tension. Fourth, intellectuals of this period made sex basic to their interpretive and artistic frameworks, as typified by the ideas of Freud that claim erotic interest as central to a person's being. This period was unquestionably one of change for emotional and erotic life. Historians of sexuality identify the turn of the century as a period of transition from the sexual system of the nineteenth century, based on sexual self-control, to that of the twentieth century, based on sexual expression.[25]

The first evidence for lesbians socializing together in public places comes from fiction and memoirs about Paris and New York City in the last two decades of the nineteenth century.[26] By the turn of the century, lesbian communities were developing in all large metropolitan centers of Europe and America.[27] Ample evidence indicates the existence of an upper-class, artistic lesbian community in Paris during this period.[28] From the turn of the century through World War II, members of this Parisian community, many of whom were expatriate Americans, explored in their lives and in their art what it meant to be women who were erotically interested in women, and began to develop a lesbian consciousness.[29] To the best of our knowledge, this upper-class Parisian community had little contact with working-class lesbians of the time, about whom there is little documentation except for the passages in Colette's memoirs.[30] Furthermore, at this stage of research, it appears that the ideas of this upper-class community had negligible impact on succeeding generations of middle- and working-class lesbians who read Radclyffe Hall's The Well of Loneliness but little else.

In the U.S. during the Harlem Renaissance—1920 to 1935—Black artists and working-class Black lesbians and gay men came together, joined sometimes by white lesbians and gay men, in communities that centered around buffet flats, house parties, speakeasies, drag balls, and entertainment clubs.[31] Because of the class mixture of people involved, some written sources in the form of novels and memoirs have survived, though more for men than for women. The prominence of gays and lesbians in Black culture during this period is indicated by their appearance in a number of blues songs. For instance, in "B.D. Women Blues" by Lucille Bogan, "B.D." refers to bull daggers.[32] It is our guess that this powerful culture was formative for working-class lesbian culture for the rest of the century.

Precisely when lesbian communities formed outside of large, sophisticated cities is hard to determine, because they rarely appear in memoirs or in creative work. From a Salt Lake City woman's diaries about her participation in a middle-class lesbian community during the 1920s and 1930s, we can safely deduce that some forms of lesbian community existed in all regions of the U.S. by this time.[33] By the 1940s and 1950s, working-class communities that formed around women's explicit sexual interest in other women existed in most sizable cities in the U.S. Interviews with comedian Pat Bond document lively lesbian bars in San Francisco immediately after World War II.[34] Several women in Lowell, Massachusetts, have shared their memories with the Lesbian Herstory Archives about their strong community around the lesbian bar, Moody Garden, in the mid-1950s.[35] In fact, for the 1950s, documented evidence of working-class lesbian bars for cities throughout the U.S. are too numerous to list.[36] But all this evidence is fragmentary, offering only glimpses of a more developed lesbian working-class community and culture.

The history of Buffalo working-class lesbians as portrayed in *Boots of Leather, Slippers of Gold* is probably similar to that of other thriving, middle-sized U.S. industrial cities with large working-class populations, such as Minneapolis, St. Louis, Kansas City, and Cleveland, except for the fact that the racial/ethnic composition would vary according to region.[37] In the first half of the twentieth century, Buffalo had all the characteristics that would permit the growth of lesbian community. It was large enough to allow the anonymity necessary for lesbians to separate their social lives from work and family. In 1900, Buffalo had a population of 352,387, and it continued to grow for the next fifty years, peaking in 1950 at 580,132.[38] As a major railroad nexus for shipment of grain and manufactured goods on the Great Lakes, and as the terminus of the Erie Canal, Buffalo was a prosperous industrial center.[39] Its industry provided lesbians with the jobs needed to support themselves outside of marriage.[40] As an active player in the development of consumer capitalism, Buffalo was part of the trend toward commercialized and eroticized leisure and amusement that provided the base for a working-class lesbian sexual culture. In addition, the African-American population in Buffalo increased dramatically during this time period, from 4,511 in 1920 to 70,904 in 1960, making possible a semi-independent African-American lesbian community.[41]

The choice to focus on a proudly role-defined and explicitly sexual community, and to place it in the context of developing gay male communities, had political implications we had not expected. In reclaiming the history of a working-class, butch-fem lesbian community, we were not simply challenging the homophobic assumptions and stereotypes of the dominant society, but also the political ideas about lesbians' and women's sexuality held by many feminists and lesbian feminists. From its very beginning in the early 1970s, lesbian feminism defined these butch-fem communities as an anathema to feminism. Our work, therefore, emerged in opposition to the dominant feminist discourse of the late 1970s and early 1980s. In order to listen to and represent our narrators' voices, we had to clear space for them on the feminist landscape. Many questions we asked were shaped in the context of this task.

The inclusion of working-class lesbians in lesbian history is essential because of their role in shaping history and the issues they raise about gender, sexuality, and agency. On the surface, lesbian feminists in the early 1970s dissociated themselves from butch-fem communities as a reaction to the gender-defined roles of that community. From their perspective, butch-fem roles reproduced the patriarchy and institutionalized hierarchy in women's relationships.[42] In our minds, the underlying issue raised by their approach is the degree to which we understand working-class lesbian culture as distinct, its own creation, versus the degree to which we understand it as integrated into the dominant society. Drawing on the tradition of anthropology, we began by attempting to understand lesbian culture on its own terms, distinct from the larger society. As useful and necessary as this was, it was also somewhat suspect because so much of the lesbian community's behavior and symbols were embedded in the dominant society. Butch-fem roles were both like male-female roles in the heterosexual world and different, just as lesbian relationships were like heterosexual marriage but also very different. Lesbian feminism tends to subsume butch-fem communities in the dominant society, seeing them simply as reproductions of heterosexual gender. To go beyond the approach of lesbian feminist writing, we were pushed to address the distinctness of lesbian culture while at the same time examining how it was affected by and in turn influenced changing forms of sexuality and women's struggle for freedom in the general society. In this context, the question of the extent to which butch-fem roles were a reproduction of patriarchy and the extent to which they transformed gender to create a specifically lesbian culture in an extremely oppressive environment became central to our work.

Lesbian feminism's negative valuation of butch-fem communities also seems to be a response to the explicit sexuality these communities expressed through butch-fem roles. From the beginning, lesbian feminists tended to downplay sexuality between women in an attempt to free lesbians from the stigma of sexual deviance.[43] They separated lesbians from gay men, primarily with respect to the place of sexual expression in men's and women's lives. This trend, which became fully elaborated in the 1980s, was central to the identity around which lesbian-feminist politics was built and to the debates that developed around sexuality throughout the entire feminist movement.[44]

In 1980 and 1981, the publication of two works had a powerful impact on the shape of lesbian feminism and on research about lesbian history, Adrienne Rich's "Compulsory Heterosexuality and Lesbian Existence" and Lillian Faderman's *Surpassing the Love of Men*.[45] Both works privileged passionate and loving relationships over specifically sexual relationships in defining lesbianism and explicitly separated lesbian history from gay-male history. Rich's work is not intended to be an historical study; nevertheless, it proposes a framework for lesbian history. She establishes a "lesbian continuum" that consists of woman-identified resistance to patriarchal oppression throughout history. The lesbian transcends time periods and cultures in her common links to all women who have dared to affirm themselves as activists, warriors, or passionate friends. The place of sexuality in this resistance is not specified and the butch-fem lesbian communities of the twentieth century, because of their use of gender roles, are considered, at best, marginal to women's long history of resistance to patriarchy. Thus, in this formative work for lesbian feminism, the only group of women in history willing to explicitly acknowledge their erotic interest in women are not central to the definition of lesbian.[46]

Lillian Faderman's book, an explicitly historical study, resonates with the themes of Rich. Faderman emphasizes the historical continuity of women's passionate friendships in the middle and upper classes throughout history. She reclaims this hidden dimension of the lesbian past, which is particularly important in the late twentieth century, when the dominant culture admits little possibility of connection between women. At the same time, she gives minimal attention to the explicitly sexual lesbian communities of the turn of the century, treating their sexuality as problematic. She argues that the sexualizing of relationships between women was the result of the medical profession's diagnosis of love between women as pathological. In her analysis, the nineteenth-century women's movement's achievement of some autonomy for women in the public world, coupled with the tradition of female passionate friendships, gave women the potential for self-sufficiency. Patriarchy responded to the severe threat by characterizing close ties between women as sexual and therefore suspect.

These works have been criticized for focusing on similarities in relationships between women, ignoring changing historical conditions that create different kinds of relationships, and for their valorizing of nonsexual relationships. For instance, Martha Vicinus shows that boarding-school "passionate friendships" in nineteenth-century England were not without strife and difficult power dynamics.[47] Others have shown how the developments of urban life and the rise of consumer capitalism, combined with shifts in the organization of male supremacy, created new conditions that allowed for the development of explicitly gay-male and lesbian communities.[48]

In the early 1980s a feminist sex-radical position reemerged that validated sex as a source of pleasure as well as danger for women and recognized butch-fem roles as an erotic system that fostered and shaped women's desire.[49] In the mid-1980s, the feminist movement became embroiled in a debate about the place and meaning of the erotic in women's lives.[50] Historical evidence about women's erotic relationships was marshaled for each side. On the one hand, the prominence of women's passionate friendships in the late nineteenth and early twentieth centuries corresponded nicely with and even buttressed a position that equates sexuality with maleness, perversion, and violence.[51] On the other hand, the history of explicitly sexual, butch-fem communities validated the view that sexual expression has been a source of autonomy and pleasure for women. As feminists studying the development of a women's community formed around sexuality, we were influenced by and contributed to this debate concerning women's erotic relationships.[52] We were identifying sexuality as an essential ingredient in lesbian life. In its final form, our study intentionally continues to invite a reconsideration of reductive judgments about butch-fem lesbian communities of the mid-century and reevaluation of the place of sexuality in working-class women's lives. We also aim to understand the ways in which the lesbian community is like that of gay men, particularly in regard to the place and expression of sexuality.

The hostility of lesbian feminism to butch-fem communities has far-reaching and subtle implications for lesbian scholarship, including the understanding of lesbian agency in history. The stigma attached to working-class, butch-fem lesbians by most commentators has meant that there is not yet a strong tradition for understanding working-class lesbians as active forces in history. Even Lillian Faderman's new work on lesbian history, *Odd Girls and Twilight Lovers: A History of Lesbian Life in Twentieth-Century America*, which provides an informative and comprehensive picture of the varieties of lesbian experience in the twentieth century, still treats the working-class bar subculture as passive and therefore tangential to developing lesbian consciousness and politics. Faderman views butch-fem roles, which were so central to working-class lesbian subculture, as originating with the sexologists and medical doctors of the turn of the century and as continuing due to lesbians' uninspired imitation of heterosexuality. She characterizes working-class lesbian social life primarily in terms of oppression.

> They tolerated the smallest crumbs and the shabbiest turf in their desperation for a "place." And even that was periodically taken away, whenever the majority community wanted to make a show of its high moral standards. But in their determination to establish some area, however minute, where they could be together as women and as lesbians, they were pioneers of a sort. They created a lesbian geography despite slim resources and particularly unsympathetic times.[53]

Faderman's version of lesbian history does not assign agency to lesbians unless they are involved in explicitly political institutions, and therefore excludes a good portion of working-class lesbians of this century. From our own perspective, this approach cannot explain how lesbian identity was formed in the twentieth century, and how the lesbian feminist and gay liberation movements so quickly became mass movements.

Scholarship on all oppressed people faces the challenge of assessing the degree to which they are actors in shaping their own history or mere victims of larger historical forces. This is particularly hard with lesbians and gay men. The dominant Western intellectual tradition, which has understood homosexuality as an individual's illness, sin, or crime, has been challenged but not yet replaced by a strong counterconceptualization of the way that oppression relates to gays' and lesbians' creating a better life for themselves. In addition, not being born into the community with which they come to identify as adults, gays and lesbians share a culture based on survival and resistance that is not passed on from childhood. Each individual has to work out her own balance later in life, albeit with some help from the community. Furthermore, the fact that gays and lesbians have built their culture out of the symbols and meanings of the dominant society makes it difficult to distinguish which characteristics it has created and which have been forced upon them.

Joan Nestle, Audre Lorde, and Judy Grahn, all of whom related to some aspect of working-class lesbian communities in the 1950s, give us the beginnings of a new tradition, one that portrays working-class lesbians as creating lesbian culture and resisting oppression in the context of a severely oppressive environment.[54] Our work builds on this tradition. The phrase "Boots of Leather, Slippers of Gold" captures the duality that lies at the core of lesbian communities of the past—the toughness required to endure and struggle against severe and often violent homophobia, and the light and joy gained from the quest for the perfect love and the faith that a safe and respected place in the world was possible.[55] Throughout the book, in chronicling the history of the Buffalo lesbian community, we attempt to balance this duality. Without a developed tradition for representing the character and quality of lesbian life, it has not been easy. We found ourselves swinging between the conventional poles of seeing lesbians as heroes bravely building their own lives and as suffering victims of extreme social hostility.[56] Our narrators were key in pointing us toward a more complicated reality that encompassed both.

The most common criticism we heard from narrators as they listened to or read our work was about the weight we gave to either suffering or happiness. After reading an early draft of the chapter on relationships, Vic, a European-American narrator commented:

> "It sounds like it was pretty much the good side of the whole thing. It didn't sound like there was as much on hard times or heartaches, or whatever you want to call it that really happened. I don't know how you took your interviews, if you just took certain things out. It sounded like it really was a nice life to live, and it wasn't. I don't think it was. It wasn't for me anyway. It didn't tell all the hard times, really. Unless people didn't talk about them."

When we asked her what she meant—had we left out how bad people felt over breakups or how badly people treated one another—she replied, "Mostly how society treated you when you were out and things like that, not so much the people you were with." Conversely, Jodi, an African-American narrator, commenting on an early draft of the chapter on social life in the 1950s, said that we didn't adequately convey the good times and fun African-American lesbians had on an evening out. The bleakness born from oppression and the energy that emerges from resistance were at the core of their lives, and they wanted us to convey this as fully as possible.

CONSTRUCTING LESBIAN COMMUNITY HISTORY USING ORAL HISTORY

Documents on working-class community, culture, and identity are always difficult to find and this problem is compounded by the stigmatization of lesbians, which forces them to remain hidden or live at the periphery of society. Upper-class and/or artistic lesbians are likely to leave creative work, diaries, letters, or memoirs for posterity, while ordinary lesbians usually do not. Even if they do, their work is unlikely to enter the public realm to be found by historians.[57] To address this situation, we and other lesbian and gay history projects have turned to oral history, an invaluable method for documenting the experience of the invisible; it allows the narrators to speak in their own voices of their lives, loves, and struggles.

In our research and writing, we experiment with constructing a detailed community history using oral-history narratives as the primary source.[58] Oral history has been criticized as a basis for historical study, on the grounds that memory is too subjective and idiosyncratic. Whether the more conventional sources for historical and sociological studies—letters, newspaper accounts, court records, or observation—provide a sounder base than rich oral narratives for the constructing of community history is in our minds a moot question. Although such sources do not introduce issues about the distortion of memory, they do raise other kinds of problems, such as the limited representation of community participants' own views, or the lack of multiple perspectives.

We are writing at a time when most scholars are conscious of the contingent nature of all historical and anthropological studies. Built from limited data and shaped by the researchers' perspectives, such studies need to be open to revision when new information appears. This is an atmosphere that liberates all sorts of possibilities for the researcher and the subjects of study. At one extreme we could argue, following the discourse theorists, that all history is memory, and that powerful representations of human life and society are not dependent on verifiable fact. We are uncomfortable with such a position, however. Although not believing that we can present the "objective truth" about society in history, we do assume that some interpretations reveal more about the past and about different cultures than others, and that research should try to achieve the best approximations of "reality."[59] We aim in research, analysis, and writing to find the appropriate balance between recognizing that our results are constructed—that they are shaped by our own culture's questions, and our personal perspectives, as well as the consciousness and position of our narrators—while offering them as part of the historical record about the lesbian community of the 1940s and 1950s.

In all, we have collected oral histories from forty-five people, whom we call narrators.[60] Ten of them entered the bar community in the 1930s and 1940s. Of these, nine were European-American and one African-American; seven were butch and three fem. Twenty-three of the narrators entered the public lesbian community in the 1950s. Of these, sixteen were European-American, five African-American, and two Native-American; nineteen were from the rough and tough crowd and three from the more upwardly mobile crowd; seventeen were butch and five fem. The remaining twelve did not participate in the public lesbian community of this time period but provided information about or perspectives on it. For instance, we interviewed a woman who participated in a more middle-class community during the 1930s, a man who knew some of the women in the bars of the 1940s, and one Hispanic woman who entered the bars in the mid-1960s.

The first women we interviewed were friends of the authors. Although these women consistently said things like, "I have nothing to say" or "My life isn't very important," they had a flair for storytelling, and invariably showed awareness of community structure and strategies for resisting oppression. After these initial oral histories, we began to map out whom we needed to interview for a full understanding of the lesbian community in the 1940s and 1950s. Some narrators made suggestions about key people and helped us locate them. The oral histories themselves also gave us clues. When we began, we assumed that we were studying one racially mixed community, but as we listened to the narrators we came to suspect that the public lesbian community during this period consisted of two subcommunities, Black and white, and that integration began to take place only in the middle 1950s, and did so without undermining the separate identity of each.[61] Some Blacks and whites might have functioned in both, and some Black women might have participated more in the white community than in the Black, or vice versa. Nevertheless, two semiautonomous communities with distinct histories existed.[62] Indian women socialized in either community, but usually in the white community, and we know of no Hispanic or Asian American women in the pre-1960 Buffalo lesbian community.[63] To gain a full perspective on the working-class lesbian community, we tried to make sure that our narrators came from different racial/ethnic groups. We also looked for members of different social groups, so that we would have a variety of views on the community. Furthermore, we attempted to include the respected leaders.

In general, white women who came out in the 1950s were not difficult to contact through our network of friends. Those who were more obvious or more openly rebellious were quite easily convinced to participate in the project, while those who were more upwardly mobile, and therefore had more invested in camouflaging their lesbianism, were more hesitant to be interviewed. As a result, we have many more oral histories from the former group.

We also were easily able to make contact with and gain the cooperation of Indian and Black women who socialized with white women during the 1950s; we had great difficulty, however, in locating Black narrators who socialized primarily with other Black lesbians, even though we had introductions from young Black women, and from white women who had moved in the Black community at different periods.[64] Two factors seem to account for our lack of success. First, we were unknown quantities in this community, and racism in the society at large made Black lesbians generally suspicious of our goals. They had no reason to trust our seriousness or want to help us. To what end were we picking their memories? Could we be trusted to present Black lesbian culture of the past in an acceptable manner? Second, the depressed economy in Buffalo aggravated the situation, as many Black women were unemployed and scrambling for survival, making it hard to give priority to a project like ours. Several Black women mentioned directly that they were unemployed, and they would speak to us another time when they were doing, and therefore feeling, better.

Finding narrators who were part of the white lesbian community in the 1940s also was extremely difficult; in the case of Black narrators it was nearly impossible. We attempted to contact members of a group that had stayed together for many years. Even with introductions from friends of friends, several people turned us down, claiming that they had nothing to say. We telephoned another woman monthly for about a year and a half and every month were put off with an excuse about how busy she was that month. It was ironic that we could not establish even minimal contact—not to mention trust—with members of our own society, while one of us (Liz) had spent two harmonious years with Native Americans in the rain forest of Colombia. Finally, we gave a copy of one of our papers documenting bar life to a younger woman who knew this older crowd, and asked if she could help us inspire interest in the project by sharing the paper with them at a party. This strategy worked. One woman was so appalled by the mistakes we had made and the things we had left out that she decided to "set us straight." She agreed to come to an interview session and to bring a friend, who was in fact the woman we had been calling for a year and a half. They did indeed correct some significant errors. They also had such fun reminiscing about old times that, after they left us, they continued swapping stories at a local tavern, and thought of many more things to tell us in two subsequent sessions. Over the years we have been able to go back to them as further questions arose. They enjoyed the interviews but manifested the general reticence we had found among other women who had come out in the 1940s. They would not allow their interviews to be taped, and they did not actively introduce us to other women in their circle of friends. Even though they were pioneers in the formation of lesbian community, the caution required of them to minimize the risk of exposure had continued to be a way of life forty years later. With persistence however, we were able to locate several more narrators for this period, some of whom felt comfortable using a tape recorder.

Finding fem narrators in these subcommunities was difficult, and therefore we have the stories of significantly fewer fems. Many fems of this period became butch, others went straight, and others claimed to be too shy to be interviewed. In the beginning, we had decided that we would only interview women who were still lesbians. At the time we didn't realize how many fems we were excluding. Whether women who were no longer lesbian would have agreed to be interviewed is hard to know. One woman we were able to contact turned us down.

Although we did not participate in the community during the 1940s and 1950s, we do participate in the same general community in which our narrators now function today and our paths variably interconnect, depending on age, friendship groups, class, race, ethnicity, and culture. This apparently helped us in identifying narrators and convincing them to participate in the project, for groups with which we had the least direct contact were also the ones with which we had the least success in finding narrators.

Our contact with the community, however, also had its pitfalls. The main drawback to researching a community where we carried on our social lives was that we could not make a clear separation between work and personal life, placing tremendous demands on our moral character to meet high ethical standards for research. We felt—rightly or wrongly—the need to be models of respectability and sensitivity in order to convince people that we were trustworthy and that the project was worthy of their participation. We also had to manage our personal lives carefully so that we did not inadvertently become involved in community tensions and rifts, thereby limiting our access to those who might help us find narrators. It was also essential to guard against using the research to personal advantage in our social lives. As we collected oral histories, moreover, we came to know a great deal about the lives of members of the community; yet because we had guaranteed our narrators confidentiality, we had to develop a discipline for digesting information without using it or sharing it directly in our lives.[65] And when narrators who were not held to our standards as researchers might use an interview to vent a grievance or manipulate one of us, we had to learn to ignore it.

Research in the lesbian community—finding narrators, archiving oral histories, or writing a book—raises immediately the problem of protecting the narrators' identities. We had to be extremely careful in order for people to feel comfortable about introducing us to others and supporting our work.[66] But also for our own peace of mind. Although the lesbian and gay movements of the past fifteen years have achieved a less repressive social climate, the recent rise of right-wing social movements and their homophobic positions, in the context of knowledge about the persecution of gays and lesbians during the 1950s, convinced us that we did not want a file with the names of our narrators.[67]

We not only had to worry about protecting the identities of narrators, but also the identities of those people who were mentioned in the interviews. Many narrators considered this to be of the utmost importance, for they felt that they could make decisions for themselves but not for others. The extraordinary sensitivity our narrators had for protecting others, rarely giving the name of someone who they had not decided in advance it was all right to mention, educated us about how important this issue was in their lives. In one set of interviews lasting more than eight hours, a narrator mentioned only three people by name; they were the three women with whom she had had long-term relationships. In each interview, one of them "casually" stopped by for a visit. Initially, such coincidences puzzled us, but then we realized that the narrator had invited them to meet the interviewer as their names were being mentioned on the tape. We, therefore, developed a policy of respecting narrators' reluctance to mention the names of others on tape and agreed to erase the names that came up inadvertently; as a result we often had trouble analyzing community relations—tracing friendships and relationships—because people's identities were not immediately apparent.

In the writing of the book we have been scrupulous about concealing the identities of narrators and their friends. Although the statements by narrators offer insight into the life experience, character, and philosophy of particular people, we have been careful to subtly disguise individuals. We use pseudonyms for everybody.[68] In addition, all identifying features of a particular person—distinctive physical features, city of birth or place of work, or activism in a particular organization—have been altered. Even nicknames have been recast. Furthermore, some faces in the photographs have been modified to camouflage identity.[69] We do not think that this undermines the validity of our study because it is a community history and therefore not dependent on the exact details of individual lives.

Knowing from the beginning that we wanted to write a community history based on oral histories meant we had to be sure that narrators gave us comparable information about the details of their lives in the community. We were faced with the challenge of asking detailed questions that would help us understand the social and cultural life of the Buffalo lesbian community without destroying the narrator's control over the direction of her story. In order to help the narrator take control of her own story, a necessity in oral history, and to give us some understanding of her perspective on lesbian life, we opened our interviews with some variations on the following three questions: 1) What is important for us to cover in a book about the lesbian community of the past and lesbian lives? 2) What do you see as turning points in the history of the lesbian community? 3) What do you see as the turning points in your own life? The first question allowed a narrator to say what was on her mind, and let her know that we were interested in what she had to say. The next two questions helped us and the narrators to think historically.

Beyond this opening, we did not have a set interview format. The interviews were organized by a combination of the flow of our narrators' memories, the periods a narrator had delineated in her discussion of turning points, and the topics that concerned us. For instance, one narrator identified her own turning points as life in the Army, life as a bar dyke, life in and out of mental hospitals, and life as a participant in an active gay organization. (Her language of course was more specific, naming the mental hospitals and the gay organization, but we have generalized these as we do throughout the book to make her less identifiable.) We then used these segments to provide an historical framework for the interview. If people could not identify turning points, time periods were based on the narrator's progression of lovers or on the obvious historical developments in the gay and lesbian community.

Topics we expected to cover in the course of an interview included: bars, relationships, socializing, coming out, family, motherhood, aging, butch-fem roles, racism, work, gay men, the gay and women's liberation movements, oppression and resistance, sexuality, and how these changed over time. Early in our work we had what we called "hunch sessions" on each topic to determine why a topic might be important to our study, what other people had said about it, and our own hunches about what we expected to find and why. From these we were able to develop a thorough list of questions that we needed answered. For instance, our hunch sessions on bars generated the following kinds of questions: How does a bar become a gay bar? Recalling the first gay bar you entered, what was the physical layout? What kind of music was played? Could lesbians dance together? Was the bartender male or female? Was the owner male or female? Did straight people frequent the bar? Did gay men and lesbians frequent the same bars? How did you get to meet someone who looked interesting at the bar? For each topic we were interested in how narrators learned about appropriate behavior. On the topic of sexuality, for example, our hunch session generated the following kinds of questions: How did you learn about making love to a woman, and was the way you learned common in the community? How did you learn the language that surrounds lovemaking? Have you ever passed this information on to another lesbian?

Despite the specificity of these questions, they were only generated to help us think creatively about the issues likely to arise during an interview. Each of us reworked these questions as an interview progressed in order to make them appropriate to the individual narrator, the flow of her own memory, and the topics she considered important. Before an interview, we refreshed our memories on these topics; then we listened carefully to the narrator, developing particular questions from what she said. Only when there was a definite lull in an interview and a narrator had finished what she wanted to say might we interject one of our own questions.

Ideally, we had more than one interview session with a narrator.[70] Since memory often improves with use, we encouraged narrators to prepare between interviews, and often at a second interview people would say, "I remembered something I haven't thought about for years." We also encouraged narrators to bring photos and other souvenirs, since physical memorabilia often serve as points of departure for discussion. In addition, we would come prepared with as much specific information as possible about the events a narrator mentioned, because specific names of places and facts about events often stimulate memory.

Oral history as a method involves a personal relationship between the narrator and the researcher; in any successful interview there is a bond of affirmation and understanding that can be very rewarding for both parties. The narrator has a chance to reflect fully on her life with the interested attention of another person. The interviewer has the benefit of learning valuable and exciting information that may be relevant to her own life. The nature of the lesbian community meant that the memories shared were often very painful, because narrators were public about their lesbianism at a time when this was a very difficult thing to do, and they suffered severe consequences. At first we considered not encouraging people to explore these painful memories, but then came to wonder who was really protected by such a move.[71] One of the values of doing an oral history for a narrator might be the chance to air some of these painful experiences. Although some narrators would not talk about aspects of their past, precisely because they were too painful, others told emotional stories about being thrown out of school in their youth and ending up in reformatories, about losing jobs, or about brutal beatings, or they reflected on the loneliness in their lives due to the scars of past treatment. We had to learn that being good listeners was an adequate and respectful response.

Narrators' memories are colorful, illuminating, and very moving. Our purpose, however, was not only to collect individual life stories, but also to use these as a basis for constructing the social structure and culture of the lesbian community. To create from individual memories a useful analysis of this community's social life and history presented a difficult challenge. The method we developed was slow and painstaking. We treated each oral history as an historical document, taking into account each narrator's particular social position and how that might affect her memories. We also considered how our own point of view influenced the kind of information we received and the way in which we interpreted a narrator's story. We juxtaposed all interviews with one another to identify patterns and contradictions and when possible checked our developing understanding with other sources, such as newspaper accounts, legal cases, and labor statistics. From this close work with the data, we reexamined our original hunches and developed new or more precise interpretive frameworks. Some analytical perspectives were unquestionably better than others, in that they illuminated more of the data at hand, explaining cultural patterns, contradictions, and seemingly unrelated facts. They let the data sing, revealing deep cultural resonances and elegant themes.[72]

As mentioned earlier, we first focused on understanding and documenting lesbian bar life. From the many vibrant and humorous stories about adventures in bars and from the mountains of seemingly unrelated detail about how women spent their time, we began to identify a chronology of bars and to recognize distinctive social mores and forms of lesbian consciousness that were associated with different time periods and even with different bars. We checked and supplemented our analysis by research into newspaper accounts of bar raids and closings and actions of the State Liquor Authority. Contradictions frequently emerged in narrators' accounts of bar life, but, as we pursued them, we found they were rarely due to idiosyncratic or faulty memory, but to the complexity of bar life. Often the differences could be resolved by taking into account the different social positions of narrators or the kinds of questions we had asked to elicit the information we received. If conflicting views persisted, we tried to return to the narrators for clarification. Some contradictions existed in the community at the time. For instance, narrators consistently told us about the joys of bar life as well as the pain. We came to understand that both were part of the real experience of bar life during the 1940s and 1950s.

Using memories to trace the evolution of sexual norms and expression is, at least superficially, more problematic than using them to document social life in bars. There are no public events or institutions to which the memories can be linked. Thus, when a narrator talks about butch-fem sexuality in the 1940s, we must bear in mind that her view and her practice of butch-fem sexuality was likely to have been modified in the 1950s, 1960s, 1970s, and 1980s and that this might color her memories. By contrast, when a narrator talks about bars in the 1940s, even though social life in bars might have changed over the last forty years, she can tie her memories to a concrete place that existed during a specific time period. Although not enough is known about historical memory to evaluate fully information derived from these different types of reminiscences, the vividness of narrators' stories suggests that the potential of oral history to generate full documents about women's sexuality might be especially rich in the lesbian community.[73] Since one of the reasons for building public communities was to facilitate the pursuit of intimate relationships, lesbian memories about sexual ideals and experiences were not separated from more public or social activities. In addition, when the oppression of homosexuals marked most lesbians' lives with fear of punishment and lack of acceptance, sexuality was one of the few areas in which many lesbians found satisfaction and pleasure. This was reinforced by the fact that for lesbians, sexuality was not directly linked with the pain and danger of women's responsibility for childbearing and their economic dependence on men. Memories of sexual experience, therefore, might be more positive and more easily shared. But these ideas are tentative. An understanding of the nature of memory about sexuality invites further research.

Memories about sexual or emotional life do present special problems with respect to precision about dates. We cannot identify specific years for changes in sexual and emotional life, such as when sex became a public topic of conversation in the Buffalo lesbian community or when role-appropriate sex became a community concern. We can talk only of trends within the framework of decades. In addition, we are unable to find supplementary material to verify and spark narrators' memories. There are no government documents or newspaper reports on lesbian sexuality. The best one can find are memoirs or fiction written about or by residents in other cities, and even these don't exist for participants in working-class communities of the 1940s.[74]

Even more surprising to us than our success in learning about sexuality was our ability to trace changes in lesbian identity from narrators' life stories. Originally, we had not intended to address this issue, thinking that it was too psychological for this kind of community study. But the words of narrators drew us to it. They made apparent that being lesbian, being butch, being fem, had different meanings over time. Although we had always believed that sexuality was historically con-structed, we had not understood how identity changed in the context of community formation. The fact that we could analyze such complex phenomena as what it meant to be lesbian, butch, or fem is a testimony to the fullness of narrators' life stories, and the generosity with which narrators shared their memories and perspectives on the world.

Our experience indicates that the number of people interviewed is critical to the success of our method, whether we are concerned with analyzing the history of bar life, emotional and sexual life, or identity. We feel that between five and ten narrators' stories need to be juxtaposed in order to develop an analysis that is not changed dramatically by each new story. At the present time, our analysis of the white lesbian community of the 1950s is based on oral histories from more than fifteen narrators, while that of the white community of the 1940s is based on seven narrators. We are therefore fairly confident in our analysis of the white lesbian community of this period. Unfortunately, we have only five narrators for the Black community of the 1950s and only one from that of the 1940s, and therefore we are somewhat tentative about our generalizations concerning the Black lesbian community. We do not have five fems for any subcommunity of a specific time period, so our analysis of the butch-fem dyad is likely to need further modification.

The most important check we have on our data and our analysis is from the narrators themselves. Several narrators have attended our public presentations and others have read written drafts of chapters. In both situations, narrators have been generous with their feedback. Their criticisms have ranged from the correction of minor factual details to evaluation of our general framework, tone, and emphasis, all of which we have attempted to incorporate in this book. The narrators have been a powerful force pushing us to tell the most comprehensive and accurate story possible about their lives. For instance, when we presented a draft of chapter 8 to a Buffalo audience, some members of the audience said they were uncomfortable with the way we insisted on uncovering the negative aspect of lesbian relationships in the 1950s. One narrator, Bert, rose and said, "But this is oral history. This is our lives. This is the truth." She was followed by a second, Matty, "What do you want them to do—spend ten years working on a book, and then have it cover up the truth? That would be a waste of time."

We also have confirmation that our analysis has validity for the community beyond the lives of particular narrators. When presenting our work in other cities, we have frequently heard from women in the audience who participated in similar communities during this time period that we had captured their lives. After a reading from a draft of the chapter on relationships, a woman we had never seen before told us that she felt weird listening because she felt that the quotations were coming from her. Some of the experiences were exactly like her own, even down to the number of years she had been in a relationship and how long that relationship had been good before turning sour.

Although we are confident that our analysis of lesbian community history is revealing and reliable, we also recognize that it has definite limitations based on who agreed to be narrators. First of all, it is built on the accounts of those who survived this very rough way of life. Socializing publicly with other lesbians in the severe oppression of the 1940s and 1950s took its toll. Many did not make it, going back to the straight life, suffering illness, succumbing to alcohol, or committing suicide. Often someone would suggest a possible narrator and then say that she is not sober for long enough periods in the day to do an interview or her mind has been turned to mush by alcohol. Some chose never to enter the community in the first place because of its liabilities. Second, the analysis is biased toward lesbians who felt good about their contribution to the community and what the community gave them in return. We believe that those who were completely negative about the lesbian community would not think it was worthwhile discussing and would not want to give their time to such a project. When we asked one woman if she would share her memories on the lesbian community of the past, she quipped, "What community?" before turning us down. This woman was a close friend to a woman who did agree to be interviewed, but their paths in life gave them very different perspectives on their pasts. Our desire to understand how working-class communities were forerunners of gay liberation implicitly made a positive evaluation of these communities, leading us toward the survivors, those who felt good about their participation in this community. Third, our analysis privileges the views of white rough and rebellious butch lesbians, primarily because they were the easiest for us to contact, but also because of the cultural baggage we brought with us to begin the study. As a result, the stories of African-American lesbians and more upwardly mobile white lesbians play second and third fiddle rather than emerge strongly on their own. A study that made either one of these other groups central would look somewhat different, as would one that was able to give the same weight to all three, as we had originally intended. Similarly, the story might have a different perspective if we had oral histories from an equal number of fems and butches.

In writing this community history, we experiment with interweaving the narrators' voices and our own. We give a primary place in the book to extended quotations from the oral-history narratives, which have been minimally edited.[75] These convey the courage, dignity, and pain of individuals' lives, as well as the perspectives, concepts, language, and texture of lesbian community and culture, all of which have been rendered invisible in the historical record. Cumulatively, the stories comprise an oral tradition that helped lesbians hone their wit and strengthen their will for survival and change.[76] We set these narratives in the present tense, e.g., Matty remembers, "Things back then were horrible. . . ." Although sometimes awkward, this format serves to remind the reader that the book is built from oral histories, that is, from narrators' contemporary memories about the past.

Our voice always stands separately, synthesizing the wisdom of all forty-five narrators as well as the written sources that exist. Despite our confidence in the analysis, out of respect for the narrators, and contemporary readers, we leave visible the seams by which the story is constructed. The end result aims to create for the reader a dialogue between the narrators' reflections and interpretations of their lives, and our own desire to find the best way to understand lesbian history.

The book is organized to encompass the two basic aspects of public community life that emerge repeatedly in narrators' memories: first, claiming, defending, and enjoying public space, and second, "finding the love of your life." It explores social life, butch-fem roles, intimate relationships, and identity as they intermeshed in this prepolitical era of lesbian resistance. Each chapter builds on the previous one so that intimate life is placed in the context of community life and butch-fem roles, revealing a multidimensional understanding of lesbian consciousness and identity and the forces that created them.

Chapters 2, 3, and 4 explain the growth and development of lesbian community, culture, and consciousness in the bars and open house parties of the 1940s and 1950s. Chapter 2 documents the expansion and stabilization of lesbian culture during the 1940s, and conveys the risk and benefit to lesbians who left protected social lives to establish public communities. Chapter 3 examines the emergence of lesbian pride during the 1950s, focusing on white and Black tough bar lesbians' efforts to expand their public presence and control their environment. Chapter 4 continues the discussion of the profound changes that occurred in lesbian social life during the 1950s, analyzing the desegregation of the bars and the emergence of class stratification.

The next two chapters explore butch-fem roles as both a code of personal behavior and a social imperative and speculate on why gender should be so central to the fabric of lesbian culture. Chapter 5 documents the elements of dress and mannerisms that composed the butch-fem image and analyzes visibility as a critical factor in the formation of community, identity, and consciousness. The meaning of gendered sexuality in the lesbian world is the subject of chapter 6.

Chapters 7 and 8 focus on the social forces shaping lesbian relationships. Chapter 7 identifies serial monogamy as a distinct pattern of lesbian relationships and analyzes the role of love both in bringing lesbians together and causing breakups. Chapter 8 documents the dynamics of committed relationships, attempting to reclaim them as a valuable part of the lesbian heritage. Our concern is to understand the underlying tension between the mutual cooperation of butch and fem and the tendency toward butch control.

Chapter 9 looks at the nature and content of lesbian identity, documenting the change from a gender-inversion construct to one of sexual attraction between women. Furthermore, we consider the different ways butch-fem communities and gay liberation draw the line between heterosexual and lesbian life. The Conclusion pulls together our complex narrative about the development of lesbian consciousness in communities based in bars and open house parties and its connection to the emergence of lesbian and gay politics. We also reflect on the implications of this narrative for gay-male history, for feminist understanding of butch-fem roles, and for the future of identity politics.

Hockey fans line up for tickets in front of Eddie Ryan's Niagara Hotel, 1945.
Courtesy of the Buffalo and Erie County Historical Society.

The Chesterfield and The Mardi Gras, Eagle Street corner Ellicott, 1950s.
Courtesy of the Buffalo and Erie County Historical Society.

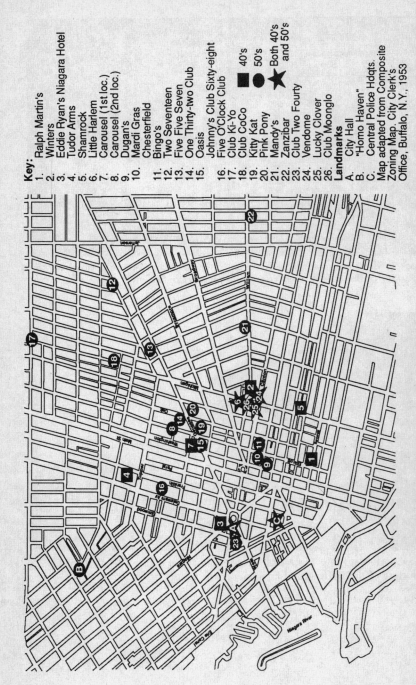

Key:

1. Ralph Martin's
2. Winters
3. Eddie Ryan's Niagara Hotel
4. Tudor Arms
5. Shamrock
6. Little Harlem
7. Carousel (1st loc.)
8. Carousel (2nd loc.)
9. Dugan's
10. Mardi Gras
11. Chesterfield
12. Bingo's
13. Two Seventeen
14. Five Five Seven
15. One Thirty-two Club
16. Oasis
17. Johnny's Club Sixty-eight
18. Five O'Clock Club
19. Club Ki-Yo
20. Club CoCo
21. Kitty Kat
22. Pink Pony
23. Mandy's
24. Zanzibar
25. Club Two Fourty
26. Vendome
27. Lucky Clover
28. Club Moonglo

Landmarks

A. City Hall
B. "Homo Haven"
C. Central Police Hdqts.

Map adapted from Composite Zoning Map. City Clerk's Office, Buffalo, N.Y., 1953

■ 40's
● 50's
★ Both 40's and 50's

Lesbian and Gay Gathering Places 1940's and 1950's, Buffalo, New York

"I COULD HARDLY WAIT TO GET BACK TO THAT BAR": LESBIAN BAR CULTURE IN THE 1930s AND 1940s

---

"To me there was nothing greater than a gay bar years ago."
—Vic

"Sure we had good times, but they were making the best of a bad situation."
—Little Gerry

In the 1930s, 1940s, and 1950s, lesbians socialized in bars for relaxation and fun, just like many other Americans.[1] But at the same time, bars (or, during prohibition, speakeasies) and public house parties were central to twentieth-century lesbian resistance. By finding ways to socialize together, individuals ended the crushing isolation of lesbian oppression and created the possibility for group consciousness and activity. In addition, by forming community in a public setting outside of the protected and restricted boundaries of their own living rooms, lesbians also began the struggle for public recognition and acceptance. The time lesbians and gays spent relaxing in bars was perhaps sweeter than for other Americans, because they were truly the only places that lesbians had to socialize; but it was also more dangerous, bringing lesbians into conflict with a hostile society—the law, family, and work. Thus, bar communities were not only the center of sociability and relaxation in the gay world, they were also a crucible for politics.

A small, though significant, body of writing exists on the complex nature of lesbian and gay bar life, but little, if any, considers changing forms of lesbian resistance. Due to the popularity of Radclyffe Hall's *The Well of Loneliness*, its depressing image of bars as seedy places where lesbians went to find solace for their individual afflictions has become embedded in the Western imagination.[2] Lesbian pulp novels, as well as journalistic fiction of the 1950s and 1960s, were the first to convey the centrality of bars to lesbian life, portraying both their allure and their depressing limitations.[3] In the 1960s, pioneering research in the social sciences established that bars were the central institution for creating lesbian and gay culture, and for teaching gays about their identity. Nancy Achilles shows that bars provide a place of socialization, a means of maintaining social cohesion, a context for each individual to confirm gay identity, and a setting for the formation of alliances against the police.[4] Ethel Sawyer documents how Black lesbian behavior is shaped by the norms and values of the bar subculture.[5] Although this research has been invaluable for subsequent scholarship, it is limited by an aura of time-lessness and the lack of a framework for understanding resistance.

The new social history of lesbians and gays, despite its emphasis on changing forms of gay politics, has tended to extend these earlier approaches and treat bar communities as an unchanging part of the gay landscape. When we began re-searching how the bar culture of the mid-twentieth century contributed to the formation of gay liberation, we also held a static model of bar culture. Our discoveries led us to tell a significantly different story: In the context of the changing social conditions of the twentieth century, lesbians acted to shape the possibilities for their future.

The turn of the century was a time of transition for leisure-time activities. The nineteenth-century community and family-based forms of entertainment and relaxation were replaced by commercialized leisure. At the same time the homoso-cial forms of socializing, such as quilting parties, were supplanted by heterosocial forms, which brought young men and women together in movie houses, dance halls, and amusement parks.[6] Kathy Peiss argues that this new leisure culture, while offering women some independence and autonomy in the pursuit of pleasure and romance outside of the strictures of their families, also institutionalized a restrictive heterosocial culture.[7] Thus, while working-class lesbian culture of the 1930s could draw on a tradition of working-class women's independent pursuit of fun and pleasure, it also by definition had to counter the powerful forces creating an exclusively heterosocial environment.

For lesbians to establish a public social life was a challenge; each opportunity had to be created and persistently pursued. Bars were the only possible place for working-class lesbians to congregate outside of private homes. They were generally unwelcome in most social settings. Open spaces like parks or beaches, commonly used by gay men, were too exposed for women to express interest in other women without constant male surveillance and harassment. This was a time when it was still dangerous for unescorted women to be out on the street. In addition, many working-class lesbians could not even use their own homes for gatherings. If they were young they often lived with their parents, and once mature and living alone, most could not afford large apartments. Those who had apartments of an adequate size ran the risk of harassment from neighbors and/or the law should they entertain a large gathering.

Even the use of bars by lesbians was dubious. Bars have been profoundly men's dominion throughout U.S. history, to the extent that the active social life of single working-class girls at the turn of the century did not include bars. The temperance movement, the most significant women's campaign in relation to bars, fought not to allow women in, but to get men out. In New York City before the First World War, working women increasingly entered saloons particularly to avail themselves of the reasonably priced good food available to men, but their presence was still controversial. Often saloon owners would not allow women, single or escorted, at the bar, but would serve them in a room in the back.[8] The fragile relation of women to bars continued through World War II, when several cities, including Chicago, passed laws prohibiting women's entrance into bars, in an attempt to limit the spread of venereal disease.[9] (Buffalo seriously considered such a move but did not undertake it.)[10] In this situation, most bars which catered to lesbians were usually located in areas known for moral permissiveness, and the availability of women for male pleasure. Such areas were therefore extremely dangerous for unescorted women.

That lesbians were able to come together and build community in bars is a testimony to their tenacity, their drive to find others like themselves, and their desire for erotic relations with other women. In the 1930s gay and lesbian bars were already well established in New York City—in Harlem and Greenwich Village—but not throughout the country in smaller cities. John D'Emilio and Allan Berube identify the 1940s as the turning point when gay and lesbian social life became firmly established in bars in most cities of the U.S.[11] In part this change has to do with the general trend in U.S. capitalism toward the increasing commercialization and sexualization of leisure culture and the concomitant increased acceptance of sexual expression. But the immediate catalyst for these 1940s changes was World War II. "By uprooting an entire generation, the war helped to channel urban gay life into a particular path of growth—away from stable private networks and toward public commercial establishments serving the needs of a displaced, transient, and young clientele."[12]

John D'Emilio and Allan Berube argue that the bringing together of sixteen million men in the armed forces radically transformed gay-male social life in the U.S. Even though the armed services excluded homosexuals, most gays and lesbians who applied were already expert at hiding their gayness, and were not detected. The discussion of the military's exclusionary policy in newspapers, books, and pamphlets and the routine questions about homosexual interest in the physical examination combined with an intensely same sex environment to heighten young men's awareness of their homosexual potential. Soldiers explored these new interests on leave in major cities, where the fervor of the war made many people anxious to support and help servicemen, and their numbers were too large to be controlled by the Military Police. As a result male gay life became firmly lodged in commercial establishments. This same analysis cannot apply directly to women since they did not join the armed forces in significant numbers—in 1943 the number of women in the armed services was less than 300,000—and therefore enlisted women never had a powerful presence in civilian life.[13]

The story of the impact of the war on lesbian social life still needs to be told and is the subject of this chapter. Moving from the fragmented lesbian culture of the 1930s to the well established bar culture of white lesbians in the 1940s, we explore the kinds of culture and consciousness that lesbians created in bar communities, paying particular attention to the strategies they developed when their new culture increased the risk of public visibility. We reflect on the reasons for the changes in lesbian social life, delineating the role of lesbians in shaping their own history.

SEARCHING FOR LESBIANS IN THE 1930s

Narrators identify the 1930s as qualitatively more difficult than any period to follow. They consider World War II the turning point in lesbian life and judge it impossible for anyone who did not live through the 1930s to imagine what they were like. Arden and Leslie, two white butches who are well-known from their many years in the bars, console themselves about the difficulty of having had to live through such hard times by reflecting on how much harder it must have been for those who came out before them.

> "Can you imagine what it was like in the 1900s when all the women had to wear those long skirts. How could you show it? How could women live together? I guess only a few could do it, who had an independent income. But even so how could they leave their families? It was hard to leave when I was young."

At this point in the interview, we share a bit of women's history and describe the intense friendships between married women in the nineteenth century. But this does not strike the narrators as part of their lesbian heritage. They are unquestionably modern lesbians, who identify themselves as different from other women because they desire to build a specifically sexual life with women outside of marriage. Leslie responds, "There must have been some who didn't marry." Arden then worries, "Those who didn't marry would be stuck at home." But her faith in the indomitable spirit of the modern lesbian wins out: "Some must have run away. But if they ran away who could work? . . . There must have been a lot of masturbation and repression in those days."

Despite the severe oppression, narrators took for granted their ability to create independent lives as lesbians during the 1930s based on opportunities for work and housing. For them, the painful difficulty of the 1930s was the intense isolation. "When I finished high school, I knew who I was and that I was attracted to girls, but I didn't know another person on earth like myself. That would not happen today" (Leslie). Arden had two gay friends, a man and a woman, while growing up in her neighborhood, but this did not significantly lessen her feelings of being alone. Lesbians knew that society did not approve of or accept who they were, and that they should hide it. "I can't imagine how we knew it, but we certainly knew it," Leslie states emphatically, and gives the following example:

> "I was very rough on my shoes and they had to be replaced every two weeks. My father worked at the railroad, and was tired of buying me shoes so frequently. So he took me to where he bought his shoes, and told the man, 'Put a pair of shoes on her that she can't wear out in two weeks.' The man felt sorry for me and would bring out the daintiest shoes and my father said 'no'. He thought he was punishing me. I couldn't let my father know that I liked them. Inside I was elated, absolutely elated. But I knew I couldn't let my father know, because he thought he was punishing me. I lived in those shoes. My mother did not like them. She would say, 'Why the hell do you always have them on?'"

Debra, a respected Black butch who grew up in the South, expresses her intuition of the need for secrecy about the sexual affair she had begun in school at the age of thirteen in 1934 in Virginia, with a woman who was three years older.

> "I [was] thirteen. And I [was] going to school, and it was a very beautiful young lady in school, but she was about three years older than me. And I used to ask her to let me take her books home, carry her books for her. And I was very much interested in that girl. So finally when I was fourteen we went out. And after we went out I knew then that was what I wanted. I really wanted her. And finally I got her and we stayed together for about three years. We weren't living together now, we were seeing each other, and it was kept from my family and also kept from hers. Because at that time, well we felt that . . . we actually felt ourselves that it wasn't a natural thing to do. . . . We had heard it somewhere, as kids, you know how you hear people talking. And we felt that it was something wrong with us."

When asked if she and her girlfriend were scared, she replies, "No I don't think so. But I often think what would have happened if they had a caught us. Because she was white and I was Black. And at that time, Boy! It would have been *very* bad."

Some narrators were less fortunate and were caught for expressing their sexual feelings as adolescents during the 1930s and were chastised and punished. Leslie recalls:

> "My mother and I had a room in a rooming house. I was doing my homework with the girl downstairs, and people in the neighborhood had clued this girl's mother in to the fact that I was 'kind of funny' and they were watching me.

I leaned over and kissed the girl, and the mother was looking in the window. She came in and made a fuss. My mother came and kept calling me 'a dirty rotten thing,' and whacked me around, and told me to get upstairs. That kind of thing cooled me down."

The isolation, punishment, and ignorance did not deter narrators from acknowledging in their teens their preference for women.[14] Arden remembers how people talked about her in her neighborhood, but it didn't change her. "I did not conform and had no intention of it." Debra took a little more time to fully accept who she was: "And I guess I was about eighteen before I found out it wasn't anything wrong with me. It was my preference. If I wanted a girl that was my business. And I carried it like that throughout life. I didn't go around broadcasting it, but I didn't try to hide it either."

The process of knowing oneself, admitting one's difference, generated the desire to find others like oneself. This was difficult because Buffalo's few gay bars were both hidden and short-lived. Also, cultural references to lesbianism were extremely limited. The only literary source on lesbianism known to narrators was Radclyffe Hall's *The Well of Loneliness*, which was published in the U.S. in 1929 and read by several narrators during adolescence in the 1930s. Therefore, the search for other lesbians required initiative and persistence, not to mention courage. For white narrators, this meant primarily finding gay and lesbian bars; for Black narrators, it meant finding a community that socialized together at parties.

Arden, the narrator with the longest experience in the gay community, went to her first gay bar, Galante's, in 1932 when she was eighteen. Galante's was a speakeasy in the downtown area behind City Hall on Wilkeson Street, a rough area that was dark and forbidding even then. This was right before the end of Prohibition and Galante's served wine and home brew. The clientele was mixed— gay men and women with a few straights straggling in. Her gay male friend from childhood had told her she would find lesbians there. When she first went, she felt some animosity directed at her.

"You know how it is when a new lesbian comes in. The boys were sitting downstairs. The women were upstairs. There was a big round table. If you were in, you sat at the round table, otherwise you were an outsider. Then someone came over to me and said, 'You look like a nice kid,' and helped me to join. One woman was the leader of this group. She would say things like, 'Get these kids out of here. There are too many kids.' The leader insulted me several times and I would answer back, and then we became friends."

Arden went back every Saturday night, became a part of the group, and learned appropriate butch behavior. For instance, on the first trip to Galante's she wore a skirt and sweater and no hat, but afterwards she "learned how to dress." The starched shirt was an essential part of a butch's attire. They didn't starch the blouses they wore to work, but "starched shirts were for Saturday night." She socialized with this crowd long after Galante's closed; many of them remained friends until relocation or death caused separation.

A lesbian bar by definition was a place where patrons felt relatively safe, otherwise they would not go. Arden remembers that her crowd stopped going to Galante's before it closed shortly after Prohibition. "It lost its glamour." There were a lot of raids, and people no longer felt comfortable there.[15] Being caught in a raid could be very dangerous. She, however, was never caught in one at Galante's although she knew people who were:

> "It was the first Saturday night I missed. I was sick with the flu. Otherwise I went out every Saturday. People's names were in the paper. [The mother and father] of a gay friend of mine saw it in the paper. It was serious. God help you if you worked in a small factory, it would go around and you would lose your job."

Leslie remembers hearing a story about this raid. Even a straight couple was treated brutally by the police:

> "I know there were some straight stragglers at [Galante's] because one Saturday night there was a raid. A friend of mine was in it. The cops were roughing people up, and she knew this one cop. He asked her what she was doing there. She said that she had just come for spaghetti and she didn't know anything about the place. He let her go. But there was a straight couple there who really didn't know anything about the place. They were sitting there eating spaghetti and the cops came over and the man said he was just there for spaghetti and that he didn't know anything about the place; then he introduced his wife and the cops knocked him in the mouth with their clubs, breaking all his teeth. He sued the police and eventually won but they drove him out of town. Wherever he parked his car he was bothered."

Narrators are not sure why Galante's became the target of frequent raids but guess that the owner was not making an adequate payoff to the police.

Leslie, who came out in Buffalo in the 1930s, had no gay acquaintances while growing up and took longer to find a lesbian bar. After years of isolation, she was introduced in the late 1930s to the Hillside, a bar on Seneca Street, far from the center of town, beyond the streetcar line. A woman who "got around" told her about this bar, which was a farmhouse. After a few unsuccessful tries, the two of them finally bought gas for the car and kept going until they found it.

> "When we went in, there was a straight couple dancing and we didn't really see anything else. We bought some drinks and then the straight couple left and some boys went up to the juke box and started dancing. Two men together dancing. I had never seen this before. I couldn't stop looking. My friend had to tell me to close my mouth, I was standing there with my mouth wide open, like a hick, I was so excited. I met several women there."

The Hillside lasted about a year, and Leslie did not become part of a stable social group there. But, by the late 1930s, other gay bars began to open, all of which lasted well into the 1940s. It was in one of these that she established friendships that would continue for years.

Dee, a reserved white narrator who participated erratically in the public lesbian community, had less trouble finding a bar. She didn't think of herself as different or interested in women until she was twenty and fell in love with a woman at work. Her lover was slightly older and had some lesbian friends she had met through work, who invited them to Eddie's (see photos after p. 190).

> "We used to go down to a little tavern on Sycamore and Johnson, which Eddie was very kind to gay women. Our whole crowd would gather there on a Saturday night and we'd take up the whole back room, and could dance when women dancing was rather frowned upon. We used to spend thirty-five cents for a half of fried chicken with french fries and ten cents for a glass of beer and for under a dollar had a great time. . . . [It was called] Eddie's Tavern. [Eddie] would not let any of the bar men, straight men, come back and annoy us. And we used to do a lot of things, our crowd, which I might add, I am friends with some of these gals even today."

We know from other sources that Eddie's was a gathering place for women involved in amateur and professional sports teams, which were very popular at the time.[16] However, if these women were lesbians they did not openly acknowledge it.[17]

Black lesbian life in the 1930s seems to have been somewhat different.[18] Debra, who came to Buffalo in 1938, met her first lesbian friends through her church group, which was racially mixed. They socialized at parties:

> "We didn't go to bars, we usually went to someone's house, if we wanted to do any drinking at all. She [her first partner in Buffalo] knew quite a few gay people, but at the time, they didn't go out and broadcast it. There would be quite a few of them like maybe [on] a Friday night or a Saturday night like that."

The parties were fairly large with usually more than 20 people. "It was almost the same as the bar life, but . . . going out to the bars, they couldn't do the things that they wanted to do like dance and stuff like that, so they would meet at someone's house where they could let their hair down." White lesbians also socialized at parties during the 1930s, particularly during the middle of the decade, when for several years there were no gay bars in Buffalo. The leader of Galante's social group was a well-paid private secretary and used to have parties, a tradition that lasted into the 1940s.

Narrators remember that the bars—and we imagine the same would be true of parties—made a tremendous difference in their social lives. Before locating the bars, they ran around with one special friend and went back and forth to each others' houses, because they didn't know other people. Once they went out to the bars, Leslie and Arden reminisce that they met other people and "things started to happen. . . . There was quite a bit of exchange. The bars were important for meeting people. How could you approach someone in a straight bar? You couldn't." Debra concurs on the difficulty of meeting people at this time.

> "Well yes, it's different from now, because now you go out there and you meet one of them, and you like her and you figure that she likes you, you're going to let her know that. Well at that time you wouldn't because you didn't know exactly how she felt. You didn't know whether she was the type that was going to broadcast it and other people would find out. Do you understand what I mean? So you would be a little leery. At that time it was always best to let them hit on you first, then you know where you stood. . . . But it was plenty of gay people at that time, but as I said, they kept it in the closet and they were more careful about exposing [themselves]."

Going to the bars also made a difference in lesbian consciousness. Butches who regularly frequented the bars understood the value of proclaiming themselves and had definite opinions about those who did not.[19] Arden captures this distinction in her reminiscing about women she knew in her bowling leagues during the 1950s. "I never saw such a bunch of gay girls who would not admit it."

Lesbians of the period were highly motivated to go out. They were pushing beyond the limitations of socializing in their own houses with close friends. In addition to frequenting parties and gay bars, when they were available, they went to the entertainment bars—the Little Harlem, the Club Moonglo, the Vendome, Pearl's, and the Lucky Clover—in the Black section of Buffalo. They were all located close to one another on or near "the Avenue," as Michigan from Broadway south was called. Many famous Black entertainers of the time, such as Billy Eckstine and Lena Horne, performed at these bars. Since it was expensive to get into the back room, lesbians would sit in the front and try to hear the music. These were not gay bars, but they were hospitable to lesbians. They had a mixed Black and white clientele that included gamblers, call girls, and lesbians, as well as people who went primarily to enjoy the show. Arden, who frequented these bars in the 1930s, explains why lesbians were welcome: "Because it was free and open and there was no pretense. Remember, there was not too much money around. They were only too glad to have you buy drinks." The easy acceptance of lesbians suggests that the cosmopolitan culture of the Harlem Renaissance had extended to the Entertainment Clubs in Buffalo's Black section.

This neighborhood and these bars remained important for lesbians' good times, at least through the 1940s. Debra, who used to do most of her socializing in these bars during the 1940s, characterizes them in much the same way as Arden. She remembers that they had a mixed Black and white clientele and were popular with gays. "I knew it wasn't [a gay bar] but you did meet a lot of gay people there.

Remember, entertainers and stuff coming in at all times. . . . Naturally if you didn't know anything about gay people you wouldn't know if they were gay or not. . . . That's how I met a lot of gay people."

Lesbians have warm memories of "the Avenue," and unquestionably felt at home there. In the 1940s, Arden used to go up and down "the Avenue" at night, and on weekends she would even go in the daytime. She remembers the owner of the Little Harlem, Ann Montgomery, tossing mail out the window, and asking her to take it to the post box. Ann Montgomery would then say, "Go into the bar and ask George [the bartender] to give you what you want." Arden, a gallant butch, who was more than willing to please a distinguished lady, would always say "it wasn't necessary." Ann Montgomery was a dynamic woman with a colorful reputation. One night she even referred publicly to Arden as a lesbian, indicating that she was fully aware of who patronized her bar. Arden still remembers this event vividly with pride and embarrassment forty-five years later.

> "There was a whole slew of people at the bar and Ann came in and told the bartender to give everyone a drink. They were all Black at the bar. I was the only white. The bartender hesitated when he got to me and Ann said, 'Yes, give that lesbian a drink too.' I nearly died. There I was with all those Black racketeers. They never bothered you though."

The special place of the Little Harlem and the other entertainment bars in lesbian life in the 1930s and 1940s can be seen in the way narrators distinguished these bars from straight bars. When asked if a bar we had seen advertised in a 1940s newspaper was gay, Arden and Leslie concur: "It was not gay. It was mostly men, straight men, and not a place for us, not for homos. You'd be better off in the Little Harlem" (Leslie). Although the entertainment bars were not gay space in the sense that gays and lesbians could not be open about who they were, they did provide a space where lesbians were comfortable and could have a good time, without having to fear being ridiculed or harassed.

THE FLOWERING OF LESBIAN BAR CULTURE IN THE 1940s

Narrators remember World War II as having a tremendous impact on lesbian life, offering lesbians more opportunities for socializing and meeting others. Before doing this research, we had assumed that the war's major influence was to allow more lesbians to be self-supporting by opening up more and higher paying jobs for women. But according to narrators, jobs for lesbians were not a result of the war. They and their friends had been working since their teens in offices, shops, and factories, and had never doubted that they could find work. In their minds the important effect of the war was to give more independence to all women, thereby making lesbians more like other women and less easy to identify.[20] Women working in defense industries were out on the street going to work, alone or in groups, at all hours of the day and night. In addition, it was no longer unusual for women to have money to spend or for women to go out to bars or restaurants alone. Many women even went out to gay bars for an evening of fun; some became regulars at the bars and entered lesbian relationships until their husbands returned. Leslie remembers wisecracking, "Here come the war brides," when groups of straight women would come into Ralph Martin's, a popular bar of the period.

Finally, and in narrators' minds most importantly, the dress code for women changed, allowing lesbians to more openly express their erotic interest in women through their clothing. Since all women were now able to wear pants to work and to purchase them in stores off the rack, butches who only wore pants in the privacy of their homes in the 1930s could now wear them on the street. Arden recalls how when she used to work the afternoon shift during the war, she would go into Ralph Martin's after work. "A woman used to come in who worked on the railroads. She would come in her work clothes, with her lantern, her overalls, and cap. She would look real cute. Some of the girls would go out of their way to come into the bars with their work clothes on."

Joining the armed forces was not a priority for narrators or their friends. One woman thought about it but didn't want to join alone. She couldn't get any of her friends to go with her. "They said, 'We can't leave our girlfriends.' " Others never seriously considered the armed forces. "I didn't want to go. I was making a lot of money; having a lot of fun. I didn't want to go into something I didn't know anything about" (Arden). For most Buffalo lesbians, the armed forces had little to offer. Since Buffalo was a thriving industrial center made even more so by the presence of war industries, lesbians had ample opportunities for high-paying jobs.[21] They had active social lives in the bars, and with men away in the war, they had more opportunity to be with women in the public world. They were no longer easily identified when they went out together dressed in trousers without male escorts.

The changes in the 1940s manifested themselves in the proliferation of bars and the extensive social life that developed around them. The bars tended to be in or adjacent to the downtown section, although a few were in residential neighborhoods, and a few on the outskirts of the city (see map, p. 28). "You know how gay bars were in [not nice] parts of town; they were looked down on so they never opened in halfway decent neighborhoods." Two bars spanned the entire decade and were central to the growth of lesbian community: Ralph Martin's, a large mixed gay and lesbian bar, and Winters, a small lesbian bar. In addition, Down's, which catered to a discreet men's crowd, opened in the late 1930s and continued into the mid-1940s. Polish John's and the Shamrock were rougher men's bars which catered to laborers and sailors. All of these men's bars were sometimes frequented by women. Eddie Ryan's Niagara Hotel (see p. 27), in the heart of downtown, had primarily well-dressed and discreet lesbian patrons in the evening and was a hangout for show girls who performed at the nearby Palace Burlesque.[22] The Tudor Arms, an elegant downtown mixed bar, and the Six Seventy, a neighborhood bar, both started in the late 1940s and lasted into the 1950s. Although neighborhood bars were not too common because of local residents' hostility toward gays, the Six Seventy stands out in narrators' memories. "It was the only neighborhood bar like that where the neighborhood people were nice to you. The men treated you well. If a man bought me a drink, then I would buy him the next drink. It worked well" (Arden).

In addition there were many short-lived bars. The Roseland, in an Italian neighborhood, discouraged lesbian patrons after the neighbors complained. And the Del-Main sponsored a women's softball team and hosted an after-game lesbian clientele; it closed when the "girls" stopped playing softball. Finally, there were bars that were not primarily gay but which gay people frequented. In addition to the entertainment bars on "the Avenue," Grogan's was popular because it had gay entertainment. Hahn's also stands out in narrators' memories because it had a girls' band—all butches. Some narrators met and had drinks with the members of the band; they also danced to the live music. "It was a lot of fun with the orchestra. . . . The foxtrot was very popular, and you did a lot of dipping. If you were any kind of butch in those days, you had to do a lot of dipping" (Leslie).

In the 1940s, gay bars were opened primarily as business enterprises, rather than from sympathy or concern for the gay clientele. Some started as gay while others became gay, often with some negotiating on the part of lesbians. Narrators think but are not certain that Ralph Martin's opened as a gay bar, and that Eddie Ryan opened the Niagara Hotel shortly after, when he saw how much money Ralph Martin's was making. "He probably said, 'Listen, jump on the band wagon,' you know, and Ralph was making a lot of money at the time" (Joanna). Other bars became gay more gradually, however. When business was bad, a couple of lesbians would go in, and if they were accepted a few more would, until eventually enough people would be going that it would become gay.[23] For instance, Arden speculates that the woman who was the leader of the group in Galante's discovered Winters as early as 1938. "She was a groundbreaker and had a big following," and found many bars. Although Arden and Leslie did not take leadership in this process, they do recall bars that gradually became gay and bars that rejected gays. They remember running around "the Avenue" when a group of people started going into a bar and the bartender realized there was quite a bit of revenue there, so decided to "let it go." They also recalled once going to a place on Niagara Street on the West Side and meeting a lot of hostility, so no one went back. Seeking new bars meant taking chances. Leslie recalls, "It was kind of like being out and stepping in [somewhere] and not really knowing, but guessing."

In some cases, the negotiations were more direct, although this did not necessarily mean greater success. Arden remembers that a woman who was dissatisfied with Ralph Martin's went out looking for another bar.

> "She went into neighborhood bars on the West Side and talked to the owners. The Roseland agreed to it, but it didn't last long. It was where it is now, and the owners began getting flack from the neighborhood, all those Italian men. She wasn't nasty about it; she rather politely told us she could do without our business. She was an old lady, and explained that she didn't want us girls getting hurt."

Lesbian and gay bars had an ambiguous relationship to the law in the 1930s, 1940s, and 1950s. The section of the state law that was most relevant to the existence of gay bars read: "No person licensed to sell alcoholic beverages shall suffer or permit any gambling on the licensed premises, or suffer or permit such premises to become disorderly."[24] In the 1940s the mere presence of homosexuals was interpreted by the State Liquor Authority as constituting disorderly conduct.[25] Gay bars, therefore, had to constantly walk a fine line between allowing gays to express themselves enough to be comfortable and want to spend time at the bar, and not allowing so much obvious gay behavior that it would attract special attention from the public and the police. They struck a successful balance during the 1940s in which there were very few raids or police closings.

Narrators are unanimous that the Mafia did not protect these 1940s bars.[26] The prevailing wisdom is that the owners paid off the local police when necessary.[27] Ralph Martin's was the only bar narrators remember being raided, and this happened rarely. In fact, we have unanimity about only one raid that occurred at the end of the decade shortly before Ralph Martin's closed.[28] Some feel he must not have made his payoff while others feel the police had to do such things to keep their credibility, particularly around election time, since Ralph's was a most notorious club. Its reputation came from the presence of flamboyant gay men, and the raid narrators remember was on the night of a drag show. "The boys were doing a drag show and someone tipped the police off. It had to be a tip-off because the boys didn't come in drag" (Arden). This raid did not adversely affect all the clientele. D.J., an amiable white butch who has been a regular bar patron since she found Ralph Martin's, remembers the evening as a high point.

> "The best time I can remember, and Pepe and I still talk about it. They had a drag show in there one night for his birthday, when they raided the joint. In fact, the cops were all on the outside, you know, the detectives or whatever you want to call them. They let the show go on all the way right up to the end, you know, with the girls . . . in their drag and everything. And then they waltzed in, so everyone started diving under the tables. There was only one that got out of it. . . . He dove under our table; so we all pulled the thing down and got our legs close together and got 'em under there [so they] didn't

see 'em. But the rest of them they all took down. . . . [They] just [took] the drag queens, the ones that were putting on the show. . . . At that time you weren't supposed to have drag shows and all this without a license or permission or some dumb thing. So they all got hauled in. But it was a beautiful night though. They used to make their own costumes, and they were gorgeous."

Raids were more common in the after-hours clubs, but, again, lesbians were not the main target. When asked if she had ever been in jail, Arden responds, "No, I don't know how I missed it. I certainly was in enough after-hours clubs. But usually when they came in they were not after the people, only the owners. That would take too much writing up for them to get them all."[29]

Even though the owners made some kind of peace with the law, the threat of police intervention was always present. The law, therefore, loomed in the background, shaping the boundaries of what was permitted and standing guard against "going too far." It even affected plans for renovation and decoration of bars. Reggie, a white butch who was underage when she entered the bars and developed close relationships with the older butches and Ralph Martin, remembers his discussing the frustrations of owning a bar: "So we [Ralph and I] used to sit and talk quite a bit. He used to look around and he'd say, 'You know, I wanna do this and this and this with this place but the cops won't let you.' I never asked him really what he meant by that, but he did pay a good buck."

The clientele of these gay bars was primarily white, with a few Indians and even fewer Blacks. Some Indians were regulars at the bars. In fact a leader of the core group at Ralph Martin's was of Indian descent. Narrators cannot remember any Blacks who were regulars in the bars. Debra is sure that there were not any Black gay bars in the 1940s. After prodding she recalls that she had been to a few white gay bars—Ralph Martin's, Eddie Ryan's Niagara Hotel, and the Tudor Arms—more than once. On the one hand, this indicates that she could and did go to these bars. On the other hand, it suggests that they were not central to her life. Although this was only one woman's experience, it does coincide with some white narrators' views that there were few, if any, Black lesbians in the lesbian and gay bars of the 1940s. Black lesbians continued to socialize primarily at parties throughout the decade.[30] They also frequently visited the entertainment bars and Black straight bars, and occasionally went to white gay and lesbian bars.

The absence of Black lesbians in the bars is particularly striking, since one of the popular lesbian bars, Winters, was in the Black section of the city, on "the Avenue", and was owned by two Black women.[31] Several factors seem relevant in explaining the Black lesbian community's preference for house parties over bars in the 1940s. First, the Black community was not yet large enough to provide anonymity for a Black lesbian social life. Although the Black community in Buffalo dates from before the turn of the century, it was relatively small. It began to increase dramatically during the 1920s, due to migration from the South. During the 1940s, the Black population of Buffalo more than doubled.[32] Debra, who socialized in Buffalo during the 1930s and 1940s recalls the need for discretion to prevent the Black community from knowing she was a lesbian. This would make it unlikely that Black lesbians would want a bar in their own neighborhood. Leslie, when queried about Black lesbian bars, doubted if they existed in the Black section. She describes it as the "old ethnic problem . . . that you can't be funny in your own neighborhood." For this reason the majority of gay and lesbian bars were downtown. Second, at this point in the history of race relations in the U.S. in general, and in Buffalo in particular, well before the Civil Rights Movement, there was little possibility of a Black lesbian bar, or a fully integrated bar, in the downtown area of the city.[33] A primarily Black gay and lesbian bar would have been too vulnerable to racist attack. And the process of integration of gay bars did not occur in Buffalo until the 1950s, and still caused tension well into the 1960s.[34] Third, Black urban culture has a strong history of house parties; rent parties and buffet flats are noted in most Black community histories of the first half of the twentieth century.[35] Thus in having regular parties Black lesbians were adapting their ethnic culture to their own specific needs.

The lesbians who patronized bars in Buffalo were not only white but working-class.[36] They came primarily from working-class families, and they themselves worked hard to earn a living, as beauticians, sales clerks, secretaries, or factory and hospital workers. Some sacrificed a lot to pursue an education and became skilled workers or technicians. A few with luck and effort were able to go into business for themselves.

The homogeneity of the lesbian bar population makes a striking contrast with gay-male culture, which has a long tradition of explicitly erotic cross-class socializing.[37] In general middle-class women did not go to the bars, because they were afraid of being exposed and losing their jobs. Charlie, a chic and competent white fem, remembers how rarely a gym teacher friend would go to the bars: "Once in a while she would go. She was very nervous about her job. And I can understand it now because that many years ago, and sometimes even now, people want to make problems. They feel that somebody might attack their children." However, upper-class lesbians in Buffalo were more public about their behavior. Working-class lesbians knew about them through gossip—for instance, from a gay man who worked for them, or a friend who sometimes went to their parties—or through newspaper stories, particularly about an older group that had been quite prominent in the social life of the city in the 1920s and 1930s. But the upper-class lesbians did not socialize with working-class lesbians in the bars or any other settings. Joanna, a popular and worldly white fem who socialized in several groups, remembers:

> "The people [they'd] hang around with were all like professionals, and [their] families were influential, very affluent, and I don't think that [they] would have considered even hanging around with us, say at the bars. . . . Maybe they did go slumming once in a while, but they sure never came to the bars when I was there. And I used to always think, gee, where do they go? Then I found

out . . . to the Westbrook and the Park Lane . . . can you imagine? and Beatrice was very butchy looking. Wish I had a picture of her, cause you would have died when you [saw] her. Very very masculine woman, and I mean really masculine looking. . . . They could get in anywhere, are you kidding. They wouldn't have turned her away. Probably spent a fortune in these places."

In addition to noᵗ going to working-class bars, the upper-class women did not welcome working-class women into their own parties. Arden remembers going with a friend to one of the parties, and the hostess asked? "Who the hell are you and how did you get in here?" Arden took the question in stride and had a pleasant evening, but did not go back frequently. All narrators are adamant that these upper-class women had little impact on their lives, and the fact that they were known lesbians did not make it easier for working-class lesbians. They think the difference was greater in the old days between those with money and those without. They were more concerned with making ends meet—working everyday, setting up an apartment—while the upper-class women had the money they needed and could concern themselves with more leisure activities.

Several factors seem to account for this lack of contact between different classes of lesbians. First, the location of bars in rough sections of the city made it too risky for upper-class women to patronize them. Their money bought them space to be lesbians in much safer environments, but did not provide them protection in less reputable sections of the city. In addition, we can deduce that lesbian culture did not eroticize power differences; there was not an erotic force bridging the gap between the classes.

Those going to gay bars for the first time in the 1940s did not have to search for them in the same way as during the 1930s. Gay and lesbian bars were relatively visible, with reputations that extended far beyond their regular clientele. Ralph Martin's, in particular, was known by many people in the city. "Ralph's was notorious. It was one of the hugest, biggest. Anyone came from out of town right away knew where Ralph's [was]" (Reggie). In fact today straight, white, working-class women who have had no contact with the lesbian community over the years remember going to Ralph Martin's in the 1940s as part of an evening out with friends.

Two narrators went to Ralph Martin's, without consciously looking for it. Reggie, who knew she had liked girls from the time she was six but never suspected that there were others like her, had started dating men in her teens. She went to Ralph Martin's with a man who almost became her fiancé, and his brother, at their suggestion, and then came to realize that there was a category of person like herself, a homosexual.

"His brother came home on furlough. . . . [He says] 'I've got to make the best of my days that I'm in town,' so he mentioned some queer place to me. And of course, inside I was very excited, I wanted to go, but I couldn't afford to let them know how excited I was. And Jimmy [my boyfriend] would give me my way, anything I wanted, and I said, 'Let's go to Ralph Martin's'. It used to be one of the biggest places here, and he said, 'O.K., why not.' And of course all the girls I met were my future [friends]. . . . And this one gay boy, Bobby LaRue floated by . . . and [Jimmy's] brother makes a crack, 'That no good queer, look at him.' And I got red and I got mad and I says, 'You're in their territory, why don't you leave them alone, why did you come?' So he turned to Jimmy and he says, 'What, are you going to get married to a queer lover?' Jimmy said, 'Shut up, she's right.' So when they wanted to leave, I wouldn't leave with his brother, I wouldn't get in the car. . . . Of course I didn't have a license or a permit, you know, big shot, fifteen, right. So Jimmy left me the keys, he said, 'Do you need any money?' And of course I needed a couple of dollars, I wasn't working, I was only fifteen, and they left. . . . So this little Italian girl [came over] . . . and she went in a circle with her finger, 'Do you want to dance?' "

This experience transformed her life. "I wasn't concentrating on my school work, cause I was so enthused and so happy, I don't know, it's like you're in a cocoon." And in time she broke off with her boyfriend because she felt she couldn't accept the engagement ring after she had started going to Ralph Martin's regularly.

Joanna, who went to Ralph Martin's completely unaware that it was a gay and lesbian bar, was also enthusiastic about her experience, and couldn't wait to return. She was brought by a female high school friend who had been once before, but didn't tell Joanna until they were inside.

"Like I said we were supposed to go out bowling, right, so we wound up at this bar. Now previous to this I had never been to a gay bar. I didn't even know they existed. It was a Friday night and that was the big night you know, bigger than Saturday. And we walked in and I thought, my God, this is really something. I couldn't believe it. . . . [I] don't think there were any straight people in the bar that night. . . . There were an awful lot of lesbians.

So we . . . sat down. We had a drink. Oh maybe about twenty to twenty-five minutes we were sitting there. We were talking and watching, you're really in awe of all this. . . . And she and a friend wandered over, same thing, another lesbian. Asked if they could buy us a drink and I said, 'Sure', didn't have that much money anyway. Actually if anybody asked us we would have had the drink because at that time money was scarce. I guess some people were making good money at the defense plants. We were too young to work in the defense plants. They sat down and started asking what our names were, you know, the first time we were there, blah blah blah. Well I could hardly wait to get back to that bar! We left in about an hour. . . . But I think it was only like a couple of days later we went back. Now it was a dull night so there were only a few people in the bar, a couple of gay boys and a couple of girls. . . . But, on Friday, we went back again. And there were the same two people, and they were so happy to see us, it was really funny."

Leslie, one of the women she met on this first night, soon became her partner for the next eight years.

D.J. found Ralph Martin's by herself, having heard about it from friends in Syracuse. She already had had lesbian relationships in a girls' reform school. When she went to Ralph Martin's for the first time in 1945 at the age of nineteen, it was a refuge, offering her a safe place where she could be herself.

"And then when I really got down and out and I said, ah, the heck with that, just traveling. . . . So I ended up right on the corner where Ralph Martin's was, when the Decos were going full blast.[38] Well I went in there one night and I was tired and I was sleeping in the booth. And I had gone in the place a couple of times during the day, just to feel it out. This one night I was sleeping in the booth and Pepe, he's a Black boy, but he worked there nights as a porter, and strictly gay, and he asked me if I would like a bed to sleep in, and I've never forgotten him since. So he took me up to his place and he lived almost right above Ralph Martin's. Oh I hit that bed and I was out like a light. So he says, 'Don't worry about nothing, nobody will bother you.' 'Cause he's down portering, cleaning and everything. Then I started getting to know a few people, and then I started getting a few jobs, oddball jobs, dishwasher and that kind of stuff, you could find it then. Now that was a fabulous bar; there'll never be another one like it."

No matter how or why butches and fems found the bars, once inside they embarked on an exciting and fulfilling social life. Part of the exhilaration came from the dramatic contrast between the acceptance and warmth found in these gathering places and the isolation and hostility lesbians experienced in their daily lives. They met and socialized in relative safety in the bars and felt as if they belonged. On weekends, butches and fems regularly went out with lovers and/or friends, and enjoyed themselves flirting with women who often became affairs or serious partners; they also established new friendships, many of which lasted for life. They would usually frequent several bars in one night, always ending up at their favorite. Sometimes butches might first go to a bar that served cheap beer, "get a bun on and go out and pick up their girls for the evening" (Leslie). Narrators remember starting Saturday afternoon and staying out all night. Fems also looked for a good time in several bars, as Charlie, reminisces: "I can't imagine that I missed many of them. . . . I would sit with other women that I knew that were feminine friends." Some bars rented rooms for those who were living at home, or were visiting from out of town, to stay the night. "I think we were kind of wild then. We would go out to the bars, have a good time, and after they closed, go on to the after-hours clubs." All the narrators—those who first came to the bars in the 1930s, and those who became regulars during the 1940s—still remember these times vividly and with affection. "They were good years. They were great; they really were" (Charlie).

Of the many lesbians who participated in bar life, some came erratically, due to temperament or fear of exposure, while others came regularly. Even for those whose attendance was irregular, the bars meant a lot. Dee remembers, "I guess it was the novelty of having a place of your own to go to that was strictly gay." Those women who came to the bars frequently, usually had one bar where they spent most of their time, and developed a close circle of friends. Winters and Ralph Martin's both had a core group whose consistent presence made them instrumental in building a bar community. The culture of each group was slightly different due to the patrons and the atmosphere of the bar.

Winters was a small and intimate bar, and felt like home to its steady clientele. However, like most bars of this period, it was not particularly well kept. Arden, who liked it better than Ralph's for many reasons, is quick to mention that it was not cleaner.

> "It had a long narrow bar with a room on the side with booths, and then in the back was another room with a big table and couch. There was a bathroom off of it, and in the back was a kitchen. What a terrible kitchen, with rats running around up on the stove. Things can't be as bad as that today. They have to be more glamorous, though you still do see some dirty johns."

The bar also had rooms upstairs where people—most usually "gay girls and show girls"—could spend the night.

The core crowd at Winters was the group of women who had been together since Galante's in the 1930s. Leslie remembers that the women at Winters were two or three years ahead of her. "Probably if I had stuck it out I would have been accepted. The [people at Ralph Martin's] were much more friendly." In addition, the Winters clientele had the reputation of being "a way-out group." "They did things that gay people didn't do at the time" (Leslie). They were older than the Ralph Martin's crowd, with some married women in the group. They had lively parties and talked about and experimented with sex. Leslie, who was familiar with the conversation and activities of the group at Winters reminisces, "It was ahead of its time. Gay life by itself was outrageous enough. When you think of it between parents and religion, by the time you wake up in the morning you think you have already done ten wrong things."

Winters was the closest thing to woman-defined space that could be imagined for a public bar of the 1940s. Sometimes a few of the Black "racketeers" would come in, but they got along quite well with the lesbians. Leslie even recalls a friend leaving her fem in their care for a few hours. It wasn't that gay men weren't allowed or weren't wanted, they just did not come in any numbers. "They didn't like it too well. They wanted to cruise and Winters was predominantly women" (Arden). Thus in the 1940s lesbians and gay men, consciously or unconsciously, created some separate space from one another. This is curious, particularly given narrators' unanimous and emphatic statements that in the past, unlike today, gay men and lesbians always mixed easily. The difference they perceive might be that in the past there was no ideological commitment to separatism, and no overt hostility between the two groups. The separation might have been due as much to economic factors as social preference. Perhaps Winters was not a large enough or high-class enough bar for men to want to frequent. Perhaps the owners discouraged men, given that at this point in history they were viewed as more troublesome; more likely to get into fights or to attract the attention of the law.

It is important to clarify that although Winters was primarily a woman's bar, it was not refined or discreet. Arden remembers, "There were quite a few rough butchy girls . . . they were older than me. . . . They swaggered around. They used foul language." Leslie confirms this, remembering how she used to be uncomfortable when many of the butches at Winters would make passes at her young girlfriend.

Ralph Martin's was also loved by its regulars who often refer to it as "the club," and recall it with reverence.[39] "There'll never be another like it, fabulous bar." It was larger than Winters, "the biggest gay bar in the city of Buffalo," with two big rooms, "a nice big back room, a nice front bar and two entrances." During the week, the atmosphere was "dull, but weekends were hopping." With a capacity for about two hundred people, it was usually "packed to the gills" on weekend nights. There was dancing—Jimmy Dorsey on the jukebox and people dancing the Big Apple—and entertainment such as drag shows. The atmosphere was very congenial. Typically, patrons remember, "I made half a million friends there." The clientele consisted of both gay men and women. Narrators emphasize, "Everyone got along beautiful. . . . We were never segregated like they are now. There was never any question about a gay guy's bar. There was no such thing. Really! We always went to the same bars, this is how we got to know so many gay boys" (Joanna). In addition to gay men and women, since Ralph Martin's was such a well-known bar, it always had some straight spectators.

Ralph Martin's was unquestionably the most open gay bar of the 1940s. At Ralph's, gay men and lesbians could be themselves and develop their own ways of living. Reggie captures the distinctiveness of Ralph's when she explains why she preferred it, and always finished her evening there, even though she considered "the action was still at Ryan's" where she waitressed and tended bar. At Ralph's, "you could do more, you could dance. Your friends were there." Women could be openly affectionate, and slow dance together. Most other bars required more discretion. Ryan's for instance did not have dancing. It was part of a hotel, right off the lobby. During the day it served lunch and had a primarily straight business crowd. At night its patrons were primarily well-dressed women, including show girls and strippers, who gave the bar its distinctive reputation for action.

Fems remember Ralph Martin's particularly because they loved to dance there:

> "They did so many different [dances] that I can't really remember all the names. However, I'll try. They did a double-time step which is similar to the lindy. . . . [What] the heck are the other things? I guess they called them the Big Apple or crazy names . . . and the Shag. . . . That's what I think really got to me was watching the dances. They're cute. . . . [A] lot of different little steps that [they'd] improvise, variations of the boogie type things." (Joanna)

Although gay men and women danced together both for enjoyment and as a kind of protection for the image of the bar, men also danced with men and women with women. Since women dancing together sometimes alarmed straight spectators and endangered the bar's liquor license, Ralph Martin relegated all dancing to the back room.

Ralph Martin himself had a colorful and controversial reputation. Some narrators, including those who were regulars at his bar, are absolutely adamant that he was not gay, "I knew his girlfriend." Others, again including regulars, claim that he was. Everyone agrees that he "looked" gay. He was always beautifully dressed, had a "characteristic" walk, dyed his hair and wore makeup. Regulars such as Reggie have fond memories of him.

> "Ralph, oh God, I used to choose his suits for him. I used to like to pick out his ties and shirts, it became a habit. Sportscoats. What to wear, you know, for the weekend. He was an older man Ralph, and wore an awful lot of makeup. He was a good businessman. Very kind, when you needed anything he was always there, helping you out. You know he'd help the fellows out, and the girls. He just loved his job, he loved his business, and he was happy to see that his dream came true."

Ralph Martin definitely extended himself for his patrons and tried to be supportive. Reggie continues:

> "And he knew how old I was and he kind of took me under his wing. He called me one afternoon and he says, 'You don't have to answer this if you don't want to, [but how old are you?]' He was very direct, he didn't like liars. He always said, 'I'd rather have a thief, they steal then leave, but a liar and you don't know whether to believe them or not.' As long as you never lied to Ralph, well I didn't know this at the time. And of course right away I had to stop and think, he owns this place, should I tell him the truth, I won't be allowed in here. Because he could lose his license, even though I didn't drink. So I debated and I said, 'Yes, I'm only fifteen.' He said, 'Well I knew that, but I wanted to hear what you were going to say.' He said, 'If you had lied to me, I wouldn't have let you come back in.'"

Ralph Martin also helped his clients who became entangled with the law. Leslie recalls that he facilitated her release from jail, when she was picked up by the police before going into an after-hours club.

> "They put me straight into the clink. Oh what a feeling that was when they closed the door behind me. There was a woman on the floor who kept asking for a cigarette. They had taken everything, my wallet and all. Meanwhile [my lady friend] called [somebody] who called Ralph who came down and got me out. They were nice to Ralph. I got my wallet back. I was never charged, nothing happened, what did I do? . . . I sure was glad to see Ralph Martin that night."

In addition, Ralph Martin protected his clientele; if anyone started trouble they were put out. Joanna distinguishes Ralph's from bars existing concurrently in Greenwich village on exactly this point:

"I was very uncomfortable even in Greenwich Village, because there were an awful lot of degenerate type people that I thought were nutsy acting. It just seemed there were an awful lot of straight people in these bars. . . . Tourists used to come in. . . . Like let's watch the freaks, you know. . . . No, I never found that in Buffalo. Well, don't forget, in Buffalo, as I said Ralph . . . protected people. If anybody came in, they didn't stay too long. Because he didn't encourage it. In fact he discouraged it. . . . New York was a little too fast at that time. There was an awful lot of servicemen getting out and . . . we were deluged. One particular night we were in a gay bar. And we had a whole bunch of, I don't know if they were coast guards or sailors. . . . [A] couple of the guys had come over to us and said something and . . . you know you don't want to be bothered. . . . 'Just leave us alone.' They were waiting for us when we got outside. . . . We were really frightened. . . . They were asking us all kinds of things. Oh it was awful. Really . . . horrible . . . not so much hassle in Buffalo. A little but not that much. As I said, most of the bars, they really protected the kids. . . . A lot more than they do now."

Ralph Martin did not keep order himself, but had bartenders who carried weapons.

Not everyone had such positive experiences at Ralph Martin's. Narrators remember Ralph Martin's being picketed in 1945, the first gay picket we have found in Buffalo. A fem had a run-in with Ralph Martin and she was banned. Arden remembers clearly, "She was six feet tall, rather an imposing figure." People weren't sure what caused the banning.

"[She was] a mouthy woman and could have said anything. It might have been as simple as her saying, 'Why do you wear all that powder?' And he was the major domo there and didn't like anybody talking fresh to him and that was that. She hadn't been out long. It was all new to her. She was quite a woman and could get to be quite a leader." (Arden)

Narrators remember this fem's boldness with affection. Rumor has it that she later fell in love with a masculine-looking woman from a small town in the Midwest—about fifty people—left Buffalo to live with her, and was subsequently appointed sheriff by her girlfriend who had been elected mayor.

The picket is a testimony to the developing sense of solidarity among lesbians. Even though it was not successful and could not attract a significant number of women over an extended period of time, it was certainly a significant first step. This woman organized the picket with a group of friends. The picketers carried placards, front and back saying, "Gay people, do not frequent this bar" (Leslie). The picket was small. Many people didn't join because they were afraid of being banned themselves, or as Arden, who was not a fan of Ralph Martin's, says, "I was not about to be walking in front of the place and have one of those hoodlums [bartenders] hit me on the head." Narrators remember going into the bar while the picket was going, and the organizer saying:

> " 'Don't go in there, don't go in there, I'm picketing.' The picket didn't last long. It fell flat. It went for about a week. It started with twelve women and then got smaller. Her group diminished as people became afraid that it would hit the paper or that Ralph would call the police." (Arden)

Some lesbians who were not involved in the picket also disliked Ralph Martin's. Arden does not remember Ralph Martin with affection. Although she went to his bar, she disliked it. She considered it a depressing gay bar and filthy. She feels he was a fake, "a south Irish dummy who knew money." What the regulars viewed as protection, she views as brutality. She remembers that he did terrible things to people. "He threw a woman out and she hit her head on the pavement. Brutal. His bartenders were Italian hoodlums and carried clubs. Ralph Martin would not do these things himself. He would just raise his hand and they would go into action." She is also of the opinion that Ralph was involved in a prostitution syndicate. "If a young girl would come into his bar and was pretty and didn't have any money he would coax her into thinking about prostitution and would send her to work in [other nearby states.]"[40] Arden thinks that Ralph did these ugly things on week nights so that the regulars would not see them. This must have been the case because some of the Ralph Martin's patrons claim to be ignorant of such goings-on.

However, others confirm that there was a lot of prostitution and violence connected with Ralph's. The regulars at the bar did not consider Ralph primarily responsible for them.

> "Like Ralph [was surrounded by] young guys . . . and the one was a nut. His name was Danny. And when I'd walk in he'd say, 'I'm gonna get you.' And of course my two great big butch 'friends,' Lee and Barb, if I wanted to go next [door] to Deco, and get a hamburger or something I'd walk between them. And another time he showed his thing in the window. I saw him rape his girlfriend he was supposed to be engaged to. He had two guys hold her down in the car. And many a time he was reported to Ralph . . . and Ralph, well, he just couldn't believe it, until he found out, then you never saw Danny again. But I used to be afraid of him [Danny] to a certain extent, that I would never walk out of there alone." (Reggie)

This level of violence against women was not surprising for bars which sheltered illegal activities in the 1940s. They assumed and encouraged male control of women's sexuality.

The disparate views about whether Ralph Martin established a protective or brutal environment grows from the contradictions of the bar environment. Protection did not mean a completely safe environment that respected women and was fully accepted by the law. It was often gained by the use of force, and other illegal means, and also linked lesbian and gay life with other sexually stigmatized groups in society. Thus, each perception is probably correct, and whether one approved of Ralph's or not, is related to what one expected was possible in a gay bar. Those who felt most at home in Ralph's appreciated what he could do given the bar's popularity and inevitable notoriety, even if they knew of the brutality involved, whereas Arden, who was a regular at Winters, appreciated that bar's less blatant use of force to establish a protected environment, an approach allowed perhaps by the absence of men, and by its relatively limited reputation.

Just as in Winters, some of the regulars at Ralph's formed close-knit groups or cliques that socialized together outside of the bar, and continued to see one another for years. One group in particular stands out as central to the social life at Ralph's. Reggie remembers this group with affection: "Leslie, Terry, Denny, Barb, the whole group was there, much older than me, naturally. . . . And like I say, they were a different bunch, they didn't have to act tough, they could if they wanted to when the circumstances arose, but they weren't, they were very good girls. . . ." This group had strong ties to one another.

> "I'm talking about a [tight-]knit little group you know. Where you went to each other's homes and that sort of thing. . . . They did a lot of home entertainment then too. Especially during the bad weather. . . . These were close people. These were not just people that you saw in the bar. . . . I'm saying twenty-five to thirty people, not couples." (Joanna)

Friends in this group helped one another solve the daily problems they faced as lesbians. For Joanna, this meant that gay people were concerned about each other and wanted life to be as easy as possible given the circumstances.

> "It was a good life when they discussed things openly with people that they were good friends with, I don't mean acquaintances. . . . They talked about their ups and downs and how, when they first started working how tough it was. . . . Because I remember listening to these discussions. . . . Like what they looked like [on their job] and how they went in, and they felt funny."

The butch who was more or less the leader of this group was particularly known for her supportiveness.

> "She was unique. . . . I've never known anybody who encouraged people more. Especially for education. Or even if they didn't want to go to school, she'd make sure they read good things and were aware of like everyone that was appearing, like a lecturer. And it was really interesting. As I said, there were a lot of things that I said, 'Oh I don't want to go to that,' she'd say, 'You'll enjoy it', and I did." (Joanna)

The core group at Ralph Martin's was cohesive enough to develop some of its own distinctive customs. "I mean they had a thing called Butch Night Out where they went out like the boys go out. That was Friday night. . . . That was the busy night. But . . . [you] very seldom ever saw a lesbian there with her girlfriend on Friday night. Isn't that odd?" (Joanna). Every Friday night at least ten butches of the Ralph Martin's core group went to the bar to meet single women and begin a flirtation or something more serious (see photos after p. 190); if they were in a couple they went without their girlfriends. D.J., who claims to have always been monogamous, conveys the romance and sexual interest of these evenings, when trying to explain that only twenty percent of butches were monogamous like her: "Cause when the butches went out, any girl at the bar, you know." A lady's equivalent to this practice did not exist. Butch Night Out was not part of the social life at Winters. Although the Winters regulars followed butch-fem roles and would sometimes join Butch Night Out at Ralph Martin's, they would finish the evening at Winters, and never initiated the practice there.

A lively social life in the bars, be it Winters or Ralph Martin's, did not substitute for other types of leisure activity, but rather seems to have encouraged lesbians to do things together in various settings. In an interview when we ask Arden who had described herself and a friend as having been active for twenty years, the 1940s and the 1950s, what she means by active, she answers, "To be out barring, having fun, going to parties in homes." Large parties are not prominent in narrators' memories, but they did occur. The woman who stands out for her initiative and gumption in picketing Ralph Martin's was also known for her parties, and was the only white woman to have given pay parties:

> "[She] had a big house and her parties were wild. . . . She was quite an aggressive woman, nothing fazed her at all. She was a very forceful person. She used to have parties on Saturday night. They were pay parties; you would pay two dollars for the whole evening, and could have all the beer you wanted. One time I asked her, 'What does your family think of all these people traipsing in?' She said, 'It doesn't matter, I'll get rid of them.' She would send her daughter out to her aunt's." (Arden)

These were open parties for lesbians and gay men. The Winters crowd went regularly, whereas the Ralph Martin's crowd did not. Perhaps the Winters crowd attended because they had been together a longer time—since Galante's—and had gone to these kinds of parties during the period in the 1930s after Galante's closed and when, for several years, there were no gay and lesbian bars. This suggests that the younger Ralph Martin's crowd had already adapted to the social life of the 1940s, and made commercial establishments the central place for public socializing with lesbians.

Narrators all went to private parties, which were smaller and limited to a close circle of friends. They also played cards together. In addition they went with their friends for outings to the country and parks. "Drives were big in those days." Their photos show them relaxing out of doors and included such activities as sleigh rides (see photos after p. 190) and summer picnics.[41]

> "Oh we had a lot of picnics together in the summer. We used to, in fact I wonder if she still has any of those pictures. They were really good. You know we had a lot of fun and everybody would bring their own food and bring extra stuff and we, we'd go to like Letchworth Park or Chestnut Ridge. The ones that were really close. Or else we'd go to Detroit, Chicago, Cleveland. Like sometimes the softball games were on in different places, and [we] went to see [them]." (Joanna)

In the late 1940s going to summer resorts became popular. Arden began to spend her summers at Sherkston, a recreation area in Canada less than an hour from Buffalo. She recalls, "I first went there because I liked the area, it was near the Quarry and the Lake." At the time, she and a couple of friends were the only gay people in the colony. The others were couples and families. She would rent for the whole summer, and continued to go every summer for twenty years. She was not the first lesbian to spend her summers at Sherkston. She remembers how even before this in the 1930s, an older woman "who was gay but kind of closety," had one of the first cottages. "Her lady friends would come over and have a good time, telling stories. They would have too many beers and do funny things, like one time they dumped the outhouse over. . . . You would go over there and they would be giggling." These women were twenty years older than this narrator. Over the years, Sherkston became more and more of a gay resort, so that by the 1960s, when Leslie began to rent, the area was predominantly gay, with a lively social life centering around parties.

HANDLING THE INCREASED RISKS OF EXPOSURE

Hostility and social disapproval from the straight world defined the context for all lesbian social life. Narrators assumed danger as the setting for good times. This is vividly reflected in narrators' attitudes to introducing newcomers to the gay life. Despite the good times people had in the 1940s and the friendship groups they developed, narrators were notably reserved about introducing people to gay life. They were hesitant to do it, either in sleeping with a newcomer, or in taking newcomers—men or women—to their first bars. They felt that it was something people had to come to by themselves, "since at times it is not the happiest life" (Arden). They don't remember being role models for anyone or anyone being role models for them. Arden remembers a younger butch who would keep asking her questions, and she would always tell her, "I will not tell you anything, anything you find out will be on your own. Do what you have to do."

The nature of lesbian oppression was such that as lesbians and gays came together to end their isolation and build a public community they also increased their visibility and therefore the risks of exposure. Lesbians had two basic strategies for handling this situation: one, separation of their lesbian social life from other aspects of their life; and second, avoidance of conflict when confronted about being lesbian. And although these might not be the approaches that lesbians would choose ten years later, or for that matter today, they were effective strategies of resistance for the time.

Women were concerned about losing their jobs should they be identified at work as lesbians. They were also worried about the effect of exposure on their families, either because of what the family might do to them, or what having a lesbian relative might do to the family. In addition they had to be prepared to meet harassment on the street from strangers who suspected their sexuality. Finally, they had to deal with harassment by the law, the worst effect of which was not so much going to jail or having a police record, but suffering increased visibility due to being named in the newspaper, or to dealing with the courts, or to having to ask someone, often family, for help in getting out of jail. The primacy of the concern for family and work and also the willingness to fight the unfair and unrestrained arm of the law are expressed concisely in Leslie's recollections of her dealings with the police when they picked her up on the way to an after-hours club: "I told him, 'I have nothing to lose, I don't have my family here, if I lose my job over this, I will make this all public, going to the papers, because then I'll have nothing more to lose.' "

Work was considered essential by 1940s lesbians; it was a necessary complement to having a good time, because their social lives required money. As Arden aptly responded when asked whether she ever had fears that she wouldn't be able to find work, "I always thought I had to work. I wanted a social life and I needed money." Social life was organized around work schedules and relegated to weekends. "During the week, we would go to work, come home, do the food shopping and such. We went out strictly on weekends" (Arden).

In order to remain employed, lesbians had to keep their sexual identities hidden. They handled the greater visibility they gained as a result of participating in bar culture and community by creating as clear a separation between work life and social life as possible. All narrators for the 1940s emphasize how discreet they were at work. Leslie was hired in the late 1930s by a large Buffalo factory, where she worked for five years, until she moved on to a more skilled job during the war. She never had any trouble, but she was very cautious. "I would dress alright and be quiet and polite, and there was no trouble. There were two other gay women that I knew, and then I recognized [another one], and got to know her. We would sometimes eat together and talk together, but we wouldn't carry on conversations that would single us out." She didn't have to learn to be this careful, she just knew it was essential. "We were smarter than we thought. How did we know that people were going to scorn us if we weren't careful? I wonder how we knew these things." Arden who started working at a large Buffalo factory in 1936 and held the job for thirty years until retiring, emphasizes a different aspect of discretion required at work, restraint on flirting. "In high school I was more free to make passes; that was before we went out to the working world. Then I knew I needed money and I had to tone things down to keep a job."

Continuous contact with people at work sometimes made it very difficult to keep work life separate from social life. Leslie remembers a very uncomfortable situation with her boss.

"He and these two women were my riders to work and back every day. He would sit in front and gradually told me his story and dropped hints about what he was interested in. The girls sat in the back. He said there was this widow who owned a grocery store in his neighborhood and she used to lure him to the store and they had oral sex. He liked it lots, but would never think of taking his new interest in sex home because he was afraid his wife would divorce him and take his kid. He thought I might know girls who would like someone to have oral sex with them. I don't know why he was looking for other partners . . . if he was getting tired of it with the woman in the deli or not. One night I was convinced to lead them all to Ralph Martin's for an evening of a few drinks. I was very uncomfortable about this but I didn't know what to say to him. He was my boss. Once we were there it was very difficult. They were just sitting there and not even a floozy walked in that I could introduce him to. After we had drunk a bit, I and this guy were dancing with the two girls, who were having a great time. The guy took me aside and said, 'Both of these girls like you.' I didn't want either of them. That was the last time I went out with them. I didn't like mixing work with play."

In general the strategy of careful separation of work life and social life, and discretion about identity was effective. Only one narrator, Debra, lost her job because she was gay; in fact she lost two jobs. Based on our knowledge of the history of discrimination in the Buffalo workforce, we suspect that lesbian oppression was worse for Black women.[42]

"I lost a job one time when they just got suspicious and thought I was gay. They didn't actually know, and I got fired. In fact I got fired off [of] two jobs for the same reason. . . . One was an elevator operator and the other one was . . . right after the war, and I was working in a plant. Those were the only two jobs I lost because of that, because after then, whenever I would get a job I would never let anyone on the job know. I didn't trust them that well because I had trusted someone before and they had carried it back in the plant and gave it to the personnel manager you know. And so for that reason I kept my mouth shut. I just kept it in the closet as it was."

Her strategy of greater vigilance on future jobs was her only option at the time, but had its limitations. The separation of work and social life was ultimately not entirely within narrators' control, a fact that kept some people from ever socializing in the bars. Going out inevitably entailed the risk of meeting people from work. Arden remembers meeting a man at Ralph Martin's with whom she worked. "He never said anything, but always had that smirk, . . . 'Remember where I saw you,' . . . when I used to see him at work." In her case she was lucky; there were no further repercussions. Straight people were not the only ones who could cause trouble at work. Another lesbian could be indiscreet. Arden also recalls, "When one of the gay girls I knew came to work, I was nervous because this woman was mouthy and talked a lot and said she knew me. But she only lasted there a week and a half."

As in work life, discretion was the rule for family life. However, the goal of keeping employers and fellow workers completely ignorant of one's lesbian identity, and the strategy of absolute separation between work life and social life, were not directly applicable to family life. By definition, family takes an active interest in its members' social life, and expects its members to participate in the same activities. For a lesbian to separate her social life and family life inevitably raised suspicion at the same time that it offered protection. This was particularly true in the 1930s and 1940s when unmarried working-class women were expected to live at home with their families rather than developing independent lives. Joanna thinks this is the reason her family couldn't accept that she moved with a friend to New York City: "In the short time, couple of years I was gone, my family was still kind of angry because I left my mother. Because, you know, being Italian and all that you don't leave the house until you get married." While leaving home aroused consternation, and focused family attention on narrators' friends and the partner with whom they were living, staying at home was no better; it drew family attention to where and with whom a daughter went out every weekend.

As a result of the contradictory demands of family life and of lesbian community, all the narrators' families suspected that they were gay. They experienced varying degrees of disapproval ranging from avoidance of the topic to violent beatings. However, none were completely rejected by their immediate families, nor were any warmly accepted. Within several years of coming out, each established a truce, so to speak, with their families, and maintained contact. The goal of discretion in family life, therefore, was not so much to keep members of the immediate family ignorant of one's lesbianism, but rather to avoid further disruption of family relationships and to protect one's immediate family from general social disgrace and from ridicule by fellow workers, neighbors, or relatives. Another distinct aspect of discretion in family relationships was its reciprocal nature. For extended family relationships to be maintained over time, members of a lesbian's immediate family had to be cautious about pursuing the topic of sexuality and causing repeated confrontation.

The families of more than half of these narrators did not explicitly know that they were lesbians. The fear of being discovered was always present. Leslie and Arden both lived with their immediate families for a long time after they became involved in bar life. Arden lived with her aunt who had raised her, and Leslie lived with her mother [the father had left when Leslie was a young adolescent]. Each one's strategy for dealing with family was to be as discreet as possible without eliminating participation in lesbian community. And, in both cases, it is fair to say that not only were they discreet, but so were their families, for they never pushed a confrontation. For example, Arden was always respectful of her aunt's values but never gave up her own social life. She reminisces, "In those days the only real suits they had for women were really tailored white linen suits. My aunt used to work ironing them for hours, then they would be such a mess when I came home covered with stains." But she would not go too far. "I stayed away from fights. I didn't like fisticuffs. If I got a marred face, how could I explain it when I got home?" Her lesbianism was never mentioned; "it was kind of an undercurrent thing." She has been able to maintain this kind of close but discreet relationship with her family until this day. Although this type of relationship avoids any direct confrontation, it nevertheless takes a toll on both parties. Leslie, who had the same relationship of mutual discretion with her mother, felt awkward about that relationship. "My mother never mentioned it, but it was the kind of thing that was held over my head, so that I would feel that I owed my mother something."

Some mothers were a little more direct in questioning their daughters. But even they did not push too far. Dee remembers vividly a difficult moment with her mother:

> "I was working at the war effort and everybody wore pants, as she [my mother] called them. . . . We were driving down River Road. . . . And she said, 'You have some strange friends these days'. And I said, 'Oh, I work with them.' And she said, 'Yes, but everybody's gonna think you're one of them.' And I was very tempted to say, 'I am,' and my common sense came to the fore and I said, 'Well, all I know is they're my friends.' So we never discussed it . . . from that day on."

This mother came to accept her daughter's friends; some even stayed for periods at her house.

D.J. managed to keep her family's awareness of her identity at the level of suspicion by participating in lesbian life in a different city. Family pressure was so great that several narrators left home for a few years shortly after coming out. D.J., however, was the only one to leave home permanently. She was from Syracuse, a smaller city, with a smaller lesbian community. For ten years she moved back and forth between Buffalo and Syracuse, but relegated most of her lesbian social life to Buffalo. Finally, in 1953, she decided to move permanently. Her explanation of this decision emphasizes the desire to protect her family and also conveys the mutual discretion that family members followed during this time period.

> "I myself, being gay and all this, I have a very high standard of morals, depending on how people look at it but I do. I have my sisters, their children, I have great nieces right now. I came right out and told my sister last year, first time she ever heard . . . the reason I really left, I would never have thrown it to my family that you got a queer for an aunt. Now this is hard for any kid to swallow, I don't care whose kid it is. And I just come out and told her, 'cause she always figured why I was never around. 'Cause I used to come up on holidays or whatever, and I even used to bring a few of the women that I lived with. And there was never any conversation, you know, 'honey,' and all this garbage over the table. She would sit there, I would sit there. My nieces and that would come around, especially Christmas time, cause I'd always give them two Christmases. And my sister always accepted my friends and I have never thrown it up in their faces. . . . So I figure well, they live their lives, I live my life; we still are together as far as sisters are concerned, but that's one of the reasons I left."

A few narrators' families knew explicitly that they were lesbians. They had not told their families themselves; rather their relatives had heard or deduced it as a consequence of narrators' activities in a public community. In a manner characteristic of the courage of lesbians who participated in the public lesbian community of this period, they made no attempt, when confronted, to deny that they were gay. For two women, Reggie and Joanna, the consequences were severe, highlighting the risks that everybody faced when joining a lesbian community at the time. In Reggie's case she was beaten by her father and eventually was sent to reform school. Her mother had died when she was young, and she was raised by her father and siblings. Somehow, her father learned that she was a lesbian, and he came after her. She had only been going to Ralph Martin's for a couple of months.

> "And he followed me, and he kicked me, literally kicked and punched my fanny all up Main Street on the way home. He said, 'No daughter of mine's gonna be queer.' And he'd never argue this one point, like I said he was very strict. He'd hit first, ask questions later. You were lucky if he asked a question later. . . . It [Ralph Martin's] was a huge place, big back room and bar, had another door on Seneca Street, and if he came in one door they'd warn me and I'd either run in the john or go outside."

People in the bars protected her so her father did not catch her often. However, one day due to a misunderstanding, she did not come home at night when her father expected her. Her brother, while on furlough, had rented a cabin. He was recalled suddenly and offered Reggie and her friends the cabin for the remainder of the weekend.

"So I told my brother, 'Don't forget to tell Dad where I am, that I'll be home Sunday.' Well in the rustle and bustle of my brother packing and being shipped out so fast, he forgot to tell my father. Meanwhile, like I said, my father is strict and strong-headed, he swore out a warrant. I came home, I had to go to court Monday. . . . The lady, [who] worked on the courts for years, she begged my father, she said, 'You don't know what you're doing 'cause she's not bad; she didn't run away. . . .' But he was very defiant. She said, 'Well why don't you put her maybe six months in Good Shepherd,' which was on Best Street. 'No, I want her out of town, I want her away.' So again you're grouped, he's gonna bring me out of town, shove me away, because he feels that I'm getting in with the wrong people, but yet, where he can shove you, there's all kinds of people. . . . So you're thrown in jail like a common criminal, you have to go before a psychiatrist which is court ordered."[43]

Reggie spent her sixteenth birthday in jail and then the next two years in New York State Reformatory. When she came out she lived with her father only a short time before getting an apartment with a girlfriend. Her father did not continue to harass her.

Joanna was beaten by her brothers and then kept by her family as a sort of prisoner at home; never allowed to go out by herself. She, along with her butch, devised an elaborate and successful plan of escape and went to New York for a few years. Her family did not pursue her, perhaps because she was already eighteen years old. She did not take any chances, however, and changed her name while she was away.

The family was alerted to the fact of her lesbianism by an anonymous call to her widowed mother. It could have been anyone because part of going out involved making oneself vulnerable to many people. "I wished I did [know who did it]. . . . I mean I'm glad they told her because it saved me from telling her . . . but . . . I didn't want her to find out that way, but I never found out who told her. She said it was a woman. Nice, huh?"

The mother then told Joanna's brothers, who waited for her outside of the bar one night.

"They caught me outside. I was coming out of the bar. . . . They didn't do anything to [my friend], thank God. . . . I said, 'Just go. Right away.' Well I wasn't living with her then. I was living at home. Don't forget if I had been a little older I'd have been smarter. Maybe I should have had them arrested for assault and battery."

In later years, Joanna discussed this with her brothers, and they explained that it was the ridicule they received from others that bothered them. Thus, her problems stemmed from much more than one phone call to her mother. Unfortunately, her participation in the lesbian community had become known throughout her brothers' circle of friends.

"Oh they die when I talk about it. Never even want to hear about it. My one brother said that 'the only reason why I did it, when I came out of the service, I went to this bar, first thing I heard, this guy told me your sister's a lesbian. Your sister's queer.' I think this is what riled him. So he talked to my other brother, and they knew where I was hanging around by then. So they waited outside the bar till I came out. They didn't come in the bar. They had a long wait, too, I think that was even what made them madder."

Going to New York didn't immediately resolve Joanna's conflicts with her family. But over the years they came to accept her.

"I called my mother many times from New York and she'd always cry, and wanted to know, 'Why did you do this to me, blah blah blah.' You know, I felt horrible. But when I came back I didn't go to see her right away. I think maybe a couple of months passed and I finally said, 'Well I've got to go see her.' And I went to see her. She was all right. She was not as bad as I thought it would be, and I went there for dinner and sat around and talked with her and of course I had to leave. That didn't set too well. She wasn't really too happy about that, but she kind of came around, accepted [my friend]. . . . Yeah, she came to my house for dinner. She had to accept her. She got to know her, she liked her. My family still likes her. It's amazing."

Of all the narrators, Debra's family treated her the most positively after learning about her lesbianism.[44] She went to New York City for several years to get away from a marriage that did not turn out well. Soon after she returned, in the late 1940s, her sister asked directly if she was gay.

"So after I went to New York and came back my sister said to me one day, I guess I had been back about three months, something like that, she says, 'You know I well understand now why you married him, [and it] didn't last but one day.' I said 'Why?' She said, 'You're not interested in men at all, you seem to be more interested in women than in men.' I said, 'So well you know, so let's forget it, hear. . . .' I told her, 'No more conversation concerning women or me or my private life. I live my life to suit myself, you live yours to suit you.' "

The sister did accept her life to the extent that they never talked about it further, although they continued to see one another. From her one-day marriage, Debra had a child whom a cousin raised for ten years. Her concern was always to protect her family from any trouble her being a lesbian might cause them. She did this by maintaining a clear separation between socializing in the gay community and socializing in straight society. This was not an impossible feat since she was not so much hiding from her family as presenting a proper image to those who knew her family. A most effective way of carrying this off, and one often used by lesbians in this era, was to use gay men as a cover. She and a gay man would go to social functions as a heterosexual couple.

"I know when I was out there in the life that I had gay men friends. Not the swishy kind, no, I couldn't afford to do that because I had a [child] and I didn't want it to get back. . . . I mean the guys that knew how to act. See I have a family, and as I said, most of my family is in government or state or county, working. And I didn't want all that to go back, so the fellows I went out with was gay but you['d] never know they were gay, not unless you were gay yourself. Then they would let you know. But out among straight people or like that, they weren't known as gay guys."

This concern to protect the family was unanimous among the narrators. It is as if their own suffering from social rejection and ridicule made them more sensitive and they did not wish to create more suffering for others. Perhaps they had to insure this kind of protection to earn minimum acceptance by their families and continue contact.

The danger of increased visibility for lesbians, brought about by creating a social life and culture with its own dress codes, extended beyond the loss of jobs and difficult family and work relations. Lesbians were generally stigmatized by straight society, and rarely, if ever, accepted as "normal," valuable human beings. Narrators remember vividly the harassment and insults from strangers on the street who suspected them of being lesbians, particularly because of the appearance of butch-fem couples. "There was a great difference in looks between a lesbian and her girl. You had to take a street car, very few people had cars, and people would stare and such" (Leslie).[45]

Harassment on the streets and in one's neighborhood was more severe than in gay and lesbian bars, which were by definition somewhat safe. However, most bars, particularly one as well known as Ralph Martin's, had straight observers. Lesbians used humor to deal with the inevitable objectification and were successful at deflecting the tension.

"In other words, back then you had an awful lot of your soldiers, sailors, straights come in, it was like going to the zoo and seeing the monkey's dance. So we'd put on a show for them. . . . And half of the women that used to walk out with their boyfriends would come back. But you know they're eyeing, it's a gay spot in town, 'Oh boy, look at that, look at that.' So we'd put on a show. . . . Oh I'd probably grab my girlfriend, . . . and the gay boys would flit around more so, gab and carry on. But basically when they came back in again they were very nice." (Reggie)

Relationships with the straight women were sometimes difficult to handle, as evidenced by a humorous incident Leslie recalls. She was in the bathroom.

"There was no door in the john so [people] would go in together and block the view for one another. If there were gay kids coming in they would all come around but sometimes straight girls would come in. This night they were in there Tee Heeing at this and that. Suddenly there was banging on the door.

It was their boyfriends shouting that we should let their girlfriends out. Even
the girls assured their boyfriends that we had done nothing."

Although usually in the bars and on the streets men did the harassing, sometimes
"women too could cause trouble; they might feel that you would follow them into
the bathroom and attack them" (Leslie).

The general strategy of creative passive resistance was used outside of the bars
as well. During the 1940s lesbians did not respond to harassment with physical
violence even when provoked:

"It was always trouble if you went out for breakfast. There would be guys
standing in front waiting, and you would be scared to leave. . . . One time a
guy came over to me and said, 'Don't worry, I'm watching you.' He was trying
to be helpful. The guys would invariably say something. There was no point
in fighting them. What can you do against hoodlums?" (Arden)

However, their strategy of passive resistance should not be confused with passivity
in relation to the straight world. As we have indicated, the act of going out
increased visibility and involved risk. The ways lesbians found new bars typifies
the initiative required for participating in bar community life.

The fights narrators do recall during this decade were between lesbians, and
even these were not that frequent. Leslie, the sole narrator who fought during this
period, can recall only two instances of physical confrontation. She felt that her
reputation far exceeded her performance.

"One was in the middle of Michigan Avenue. It began at Winters. [My friend]
was young and used to be bothered at Winters. Normally she wouldn't go
there because women wouldn't leave her alone. She used to ask me to go to
the bathroom with her because people would pester her. This night [Denny]
yanked her up on the floor, and I took [her] home and told [Denny] I would
come [back]. When I came back they [Denny and her sidekick, Jamie] followed
me out, they thought it would be two on one, I suppose. And there we fought
on Michigan Avenue. Soon some gay guys came by and they took us off two
by two, two took me and two took Jamie. We got into their cars. It was a
good thing because we would have run into trouble. Pretty soon we could
hear the sirens coming, the police."

Unquestionably, these women could fight, but did not do so as a regular part of
socializing and going out, except for the occasional conflict among themselves.

Public socializing as part of the process of community building inevitably
increased chances for exposure to and confrontation with some aspect of the legal
system. Despite the fact that raids were infrequent and very few lesbians were
involved, everybody was always aware that they were a possibility, and that they
were unpredictable; even private large parties were occasionally raided. Only
Leslie, of all the narrators, was actually picked up by the police and jailed because

she was participating in lesbian social life. Her memories of the arrest convey the unpredictability of police action.

> "It [the after-hours club] was a lively place, wide open, all the lights were on, but I never got inside. [My friends] went in, but while I was parking my car a cop came over to me and said, 'Park your car and go home. . . . Who's with you?' I said, 'Nobody,' because my friends had already gone in. He said, 'If I come back and find you in there you'll go to the clink.' So after he left, I said to [my partner], 'I think we had better not go in there' and I drove off. As I pulled around Broadway there was the same cop. Two cops came over to me and one pulled me out, and the other guy who had harassed me to begin with got in the car and drove it off with [my friend] to the police station. I said to the cop I was with, 'What is the matter with him? Would you leave your car here? What the hell is the charge?' . . . The cop suggested that the other had a problem and took me to the police station. I got there, and I had no [chance] to say [anything]. They put me straight into the clink. [My friend later] said that while she was in the car with the wild guy she figured he wanted a payoff. But she didn't have the money."

The random nature of police harassment served the purpose of controlling lesbian activity. The consequences could be severe, due to the exposure that inevitably followed. Leslie sympathetically remembers the problems of a friend who was busted: "He was at an attic party and it got raided. His parents had to go and get him out of jail. They didn't let him forget it for a while." Joanna comments on having avoided the raid at Ralph Martin's: "I was thinking, . . . thank God that you weren't there, because I guess it had been embarrassing. They dragged a lot of people downtown and took photographs of them, and just made it kind of rough for them." The power of the law was not likely to be underestimated or idealized by this group of women, since some of them had spent time in reform schools before turning eighteen.

Lesbian history provides a new perspective on women in the 1930s and 1940s. It highlights that World War II not only provided jobs for women, but created a social atmosphere which encouraged women's independence. More women could socialize together outside of the home without endangering their reputations. They also could decide how they would spend their money, using it for leisure as well as necessities. In addition, the absence of sixteen million men actually made work and neighborhoods safer and more congenial for women. These changes were instrumental in the movement of white lesbian social life from private networks to bars in the 1940s.

In a middle-sized, industrial, northern city like Buffalo, the Black lesbian community did not make the shift into bars until later, and then never completely. However, the meaning of the categories "lesbian," "homosexual," or "gay" crossed racial boundaries. Individual Black lesbians occasionally went to predominantly white lesbian and gay bars in Buffalo. But the power of racism and of their own ethnic traditions interacted to keep their social life more based in private networks. For the development of a public lesbian community, a city has to be large enough to provide some form of anonymity to lesbians when they are out socializing. Until the surge in growth of Buffalo's Black population in the 1940s, the city could not offer anonymity to Black lesbians. Because of this, many Black lesbians spent time in New York City, where they went to bars in Harlem and Greenwich Village. Though Black lesbians in Buffalo during the 1940s, like white lesbians, were not unaware of nor unaffected by the changes occurring nationally in bar life, Buffalo was not yet safe enough for taking the risks to either patronize white bars or have their own.

White lesbian community in the 1940s already had many of the characteristics we associate today with lesbian social life. Distinct from gay-male social life, it was located primarily in bars and did not make extensive use of public parks and beaches for meeting others and making sexual contacts. In our view the concentration of lesbian social life in bars derives from the danger lesbians faced as women in a patriarchal culture based on the sexual availability of women for men.[46] Lesbians required a protected environment to pursue sexual relations with women, otherwise they would be assumed to be prostitutes looking for men, or would risk being raped by men for stepping out of line. The need for protection is a central theme in lesbian history and will emerge repeatedly throughout this book.

In addition, lesbian bar life was notably homogeneous, giving little encouragement to cross-class sexual or social interaction. The lack of eroticization of class difference is particularly striking given that lesbian sexual culture was based on the eroticization of the difference between masculine and feminine as will be discussed fully in later chapters. It is perhaps the lesbian interest in relationships as well as sex that makes the eroticization of class difference less compelling.

During the 1940s lesbians began to develop a common culture, community, and consciousness, as evidenced by their working together to find new bars or to picket Ralph Martin's, and by their formation of strong friendship groups which lasted a lifetime. These groups explored what it meant to be lesbian, talked about the difficulties they faced as well as the fun, and supported one another to develop plans and strategies for working and maintaining relationships with families while still socializing as lesbians. Lesbians whose social life was based completely on private networks, did not have to consider these issues.

By coming together in public places, lesbians began to challenge the sexist and homophobic structures of U.S. society. They expanded the possibilities for women to live independent lives away from their families without men. They made it easier for lesbians to find others like themselves and to develop a sense of camaraderie and support. They also increased public awareness of the existence of lesbians, as more people became familiar with gay bars. This movement for acceptance was nevertheless limited. The strategy of complete separation of work and family life from social life did not challenge the attitudes and behaviors of employers, and only gave families a minimal awareness of lesbians' existence. As working-class women who grew up in the Depression, they were painfully aware of the ravages of unemployment and felt the need for family support. Their strategies pushed to the maximum what was possible at the time while still maintaining the means to earn a living, and the connections to their families. Although they did not dramatically change sexism and homophobia, they did begin to mitigate the disastrous effects of individual isolation and feelings of worthlessness. In doing this they laid the groundwork for increasing solidarity and consciousness that could lead to a political movement in the future.

"A WEEKEND WASN'T A WEEKEND IF THERE WASN'T A FIGHT": THE TOUGH BAR LESBIANS OF THE 1950s

---

"The Mardi Gras was a very dangerous place for any human being to hang around in. . . . And when I went in there I seen things I never seen in my life; I mean I had been to straight bars and I never seen what was going on in these bars. For the first time in my life I seen really butchy-looking dykes walking around with shirts on and crew cuts, and—it just psyched me right out."

—Ronni

"We'd have to bounce 'em [straight men] out, especially down at the Mardi Gras. They'd come in and start with remarks—then they would start to make out with one of the butches' women, and then all the butches would get together and pile him out the door."

—D.J.

The 1950s have long been recognized as a pivotal time for the development of the gay and lesbian rights movement in the United States because of the founding of the homophile movement: the predominantly male Mattachine Society formed in Los Angeles in 1951 and the all-female Daughters of Bilitis in San Francisco in 1955.[1] These first gay and lesbian political organizations made a radical break with tradition by bringing lesbians and gays together to improve the conditions of their lives. They shepherded gays and lesbians into the political process and initiated a dialogue between gays and lesbians and the rest of the society. However, their goals and style were deeply affected by the values of the dominant society. Rather than claim distinct lesbian and gay identities and confront the negative consequences, the homophile organizations attempted to prove that lesbians and gay men were no different from other people.[2] Their primary concerns were education of the public, the adjustment of the homosexual to society, the participation in research projects by professionals, and revision of the legal system. Both the Mattachine Society and Daughters of Bilitis remained relatively small during the 1950s; Mattachine had a mere two hundred and thirty members with only seven stable chapters and Daughters of Bilitis, one hundred and ten members with only four chapters.[3] In the case of Daughters of Bilitis, they consciously tried to separate themselves from bar lesbians whom they saw as vulgar and limited.[4]

Neither the Mattachine Society nor Daughters of Bilitis existed in Buffalo during the 1950s; nevertheless, profound changes occurred in the Buffalo lesbian community. Lesbians expanded their public presence and became more explicitly defiant. They expressed increased pride through their willingness to welcome newcomers and their desire to end the double life. In addition, they more frequently resorted to violence in conflicts with the straight world and within the community. These acts of resistance, although not part of traditional political institutions and very different from those advocated by the homophile movement, can helpfully be viewed as prepolitical because of the challenge they presented to the repressive social order.

The changes in the 1950s Buffalo lesbian community are best symbolized by the appearance of a new style of butch, a woman who dressed in working-class male clothes for as much of the time as she possibly could, and went to the bar every day, not just on weekends. She also was street-wise and fought back physically when provoked by straight society or by other lesbians; her presence anywhere meant potential "trouble." This new butch—Black or white—played a key role in the history of the lesbian community. Like her predecessors in the 1940s, she would not deny who she was. But she went even further: she aggressively created a lesbian life for which she set the standards. Although the tough butch was not the only participant in the public lesbian community of the 1950s, she was certainly the central actor. By the end of the decade, she was found in all the lesbian bars, and by the early 1960s, she was the leading force in all the bars that opened. To document the history of the lesbian community in the 1950s and early 1960s is to write her history.[5]

These new style lesbians did not have a distinct name. Sometimes they referred to themselves as bar people, or they distinguished themselves in class terms. A tough butch might refer to her friends as "us riffraff" and to a more genteel group as "those elite lezzies." In current usage, as a consequence of gay liberation's strategy to redefine past terms of oppression and reclaim them with positive meaning, the tough and rebellious butches could appropriately be called "dykes," and some narrators use "dyke" when talking about themselves and their friends. However, in the 1950s, "dyke" was not a word that these rough butches would have used. It had three meanings, all of which were derogatory. First, it was used by straights to stigmatize lesbians as social misfits.[6] Second, it was used by more upwardly mobile lesbians to indicate the crudeness of rough bar lesbians. Third, it was used by tough bar lesbians to indicate a woman who only engaged in "dyking," a slang term for tribadism.[7] Therefore, in the interest of historical accuracy we have decided not to use the term "dyke." Instead we use some combination of descriptive phrases like the rough, tough, street-wise, bar butch. We use "tough bar lesbian" to include butches and fems. Although the fems who associated with these rough and tough butches considered themselves feminine and certainly not rough, they were tough in the sense of being street-wise and able to handle a difficult environment.

On the surface the 1950s seem a most unlikely time for dramatic steps forward in the struggle for gay and lesbian rights, either in the founding of the homophile organizations in major metropolitan centers, or in the expansion of lesbian bar culture and the growth of lesbian pride, as occurred in Buffalo and most likely in other middle-sized industrial cities with large blue-collar populations. The ideology of the period was monolithic in valuing the nuclear family as the building block for a strong society and in promoting rigid gender roles—the man as breadwinner, the woman as homemaker—as the basis for social harmony. Those who came of age during and after the war married more than any other group in U.S. history. In addition, they married at a younger age, and had more children, again at a younger age, than the generations that immediately preceded them.[8] Having lived through the difficult years of the Depression, World War II, and the threat of nuclear war, the majority of Americans of all classes were committed to creating a happy and secure domestic life. Viable alternatives to marriage did not exist, and single women were subject to social disapproval if not ostracism.[9] Elaine Tyler May's analysis of this period of family life suggests that it does not represent a passive continuity of traditional values but rather an aggressive pursuit of a new way of life, "the first wholehearted effort to create a home that would fulfill virtually all its members' personal needs through an energized and expressive personal life."[10]

The 1950s were also a time when the persecution of homosexuals and lesbians was stronger than in any other period of U.S. history. The decade was characterized by extensive witch hunts against gays and lesbians as typified by the McCarthy investigations. John D'Emilio writes:

> Homosexuals and lesbians found themselves under virulent attack: purges from the armed forces; congressional investigations into government employment of "perverts"; disbarment from federal jobs; widespread FBI surveillance; state sexual psychopath laws; stepped-up harassment from urban police forces; and inflammatory headlines warning readers of the sex "deviates" in their midst.[11]

Such active persecution of lesbians and gays stands as an indisputable testimony to the development of lesbian and gay subculture during the 1940s. Without the increased presence of lesbians and gays in U.S. social life, there would not have been any need to target them. In addition, the aggressive harassment of lesbians and gays was connected to the glorification of the nuclear family and domestic life. On the simplest level virulent antihomosexuality was a way of reinstitutionaliz-ing male dominance and strict gender roles which had been disrupted by the

Depression and the War. But also antihomosexuality and the veneration of the family were connected as part of a cultural response to the Cold War. As Elaine May argues, the U.S. was not only committed to containment of communism abroad, but also, the containment of all forces which could disrupt home life—the cornerstone of American character and strength.[12] The culture of the Cold War promoted the idea that the best defense against the enemy abroad was controlling the enemy at home, including moral and sexual deviance.

John D'Emilio has argued that the increased repression helped to encourage greater group consciousness and fostered a more defiant response from lesbians during the 1950s. Although this is unquestionably true, it can't fully explain the profound changes for lesbians in this period. Why would some lesbians react by founding homophile organizations which emphasized the need for discretion, while others would become increasingly bold in their confrontations with society? As we analyzed the depth and complexity of the community's transformation, the picture became even more complicated. It was also at this time that the bar community became desegregated, and class divisions emerged (both issues which will take center stage in the next chapter). We had to discard our assumption that lesbian community changed simply in response to outside forces and develop a more dynamic analysis that not only took into account the structures of society at large, but also paid attention to changes in the community. We began to explore how the activity of lesbians themselves shaped their own community. Did the culture forged during the preceding decade shape the key developments of the 1950s? Did the continuity of the 1940s bar culture help develop the solidarity and pride necessary to aggressively challenge the repressive society of the 1950s?

With the assumption that the structure and culture of the lesbian community itself helped to establish the possibilities of and directions for change, this chapter begins to tell the story of tough bar lesbians and their powerful role in the 1950s lesbian community. After introducing the various 1950s bars and their relation to the law, we examine tough bar lesbians' eagerness to reach out to newcomers, their desire to stop hiding, and their willingness to defend lesbian space and physically confront the straight world. Our goal is to understand the forms of community solidarity and consciousness that developed as tough bar lesbians spent increasing amounts of time in the bars and entered new and dangerous territory.

THE LESBIAN AND GAY BARS OF THE 1950s

Bar life continued to flourish in the 1950s, and became more racially mixed. Buffalo remained the regional center for gays and lesbians and our narrators remember that the bars were always full. Matty, a loquacious and respected white butch who was an experienced bartender, recalls:

"Nobody worried about getting them [lesbians] in [to the bars] or getting them out because the bars were all crowded. . . . All the time, every night. . . . The Carousel was busy, Mardi Gras was busy, Bingo's was busy. Dugan's was, you know, an in and out thing. The One Thirty-Two was busy. They were all busy."

People came from Niagara Falls, Rochester, and Toronto. In order to be able to stay late, lesbians often spent the night in a nearby hotel. Whitney, a graceful Canadian fem, remembers several popular hotels in the area:

"For the first month we stayed in the Tourraine. And then [through] a few other people that came from Rochester we found out about the Genesee Hotel. And it was five dollars a night, and their kitchen was open all night, and it was super, scrambled eggs and what have you after the bars. So we stayed there."

Some of the new dimensions of the 1950s community were reflected in the location and nature of its bars. The major lesbian and gay bars of the 1940s, Ralph Martin's and Winters, did not remain open in the 1950s.[13] The new bars—with only a few exceptions—were more centralized, located within several blocks of one another, in the downtown section close to the main thoroughfares (see map, p. 28). This concentration of bars led to the area's being known as the homosexual section of Buffalo.[14] However, lesbians did not claim it as their own. They considered it a rough and inhospitable area. Marla, a Black narrator whose contagious good humor was widely appreciated, tells us: "The downtown area wasn't anything anybody wanted to hang around in, you know, especially the bars. Those were like the bars you'd get winos and people you just didn't want to associate with at the time; it wasn't as bad after you got used to it, after you'd been there."

Lesbians patronized a variety of bars during the 1950s. The Carousel and Bingo's were the two most popular until the One Thirty-Two opened at the end of the decade.[15] Although it changed locations, the Carousel spanned the entire decade, and is the only bar narrators refer to as a "true" gay bar, meaning that it catered primarily to gay men and lesbians. It was well-kept, and was the favorite bar of the more "elite" lesbians. Bingo's was about four blocks away from the second Carousel and was quite different. Its principal patrons were the tough bar lesbians. It served only beer and wine and was often referred to by our narrators as "a dump." The One Thirty-Two, which was popular for dancing, opened near the Carousel about the time that Bingo's closed.

Dugan's and Pat's—the latter having been remodeled in the mid 1950s and renamed the Mardi Gras (see p. 27)—were also important bars for the tough and street-wise lesbians for most of the decade. One was three blocks from Bingo's, the other, one block. They were rough bars with hookers and pimps among their regular patrons in addition to their substantial lesbian clientele and lesbian bartenders. The Chesterfield (see p. 27) was a similar, even seedier bar, which opened in the late 1950s three doors away from the Mardi Gras and continued into the next decade. Although our narrators consider these three bars their turf, they are always quick to point out that they are not lesbian bars in the sense that we use the term today, because straight people constituted a substantial part of their clientele. Sandy, who was unquestionably the most admired white butch of the late 1950s, patronized these bars. "Well like you'd call, like say the Mardi Gras, actually a straight bar. A lot of us went there, so you could call it a gay bar, if you wanted to, cause maybe it was the only one open at the time that we could go in, but it wasn't a gay bar. It was mixed. But they would let us in." We call these bars "street bars" to indicate their distinctive clientele.

In addition to the bars in the downtown section, in the early 1950s lesbian bars opened in the Black section of the city—the Five Five Seven on Cherry Street, and a few years later the Two Seventeen. Both bars had a sizable Black clientele, although neither was exclusively Black. The Five Five Seven was owned by a white man and served laborers during the day and a lesbian crowd with a few gay men at night. It was a modern bar with two rooms and a kitchen that served food, and it offered nightly entertainment. One of the most popular performers was Jacki Jordan, a good-looking local singer and male impersonator, who joined a traveling show in the early 1960s. The Two Seventeen also had a laboring crowd during the day, but was a small bar, the size of a living room. The appearance of lesbian and gay bars in the Black section of the city was related to the growth of the Black community. It was now large enough to allow Black lesbians to maintain some anonymity while going to bars in their own neighborhoods.[16]

Lesbians also went to gay men's bars, like Johnny's Club Sixty-Eight and the Oasis in the homosexual bar area as well as the Five O'clock Club, which was the elite of the male bars and in a better neighborhood. In general, the decor in the men's bars was much nicer than in lesbian bars, sometimes even plush. This may be attributed to the fact that men earned and spent more money. On any one night, a few lesbians could be found in these bars, and every one of our narrators had socialized in them at some point. The dominant feeling, however, was that lesbians were not welcome. Several reasons surface as explanations, primarily that lesbians in the 1950s, particularly the tough street-wise lesbians, had a reputation for fighting. A marked shift had taken place from the 1940s when men were the primary source of trouble in bars due to their drag shows or other explicit homosexual behavior; now women also brought trouble to the bars. Bert, a thoughtful and peaceable white butch, occasionally went to the men's bars.

> "There was one that opened, on Chippewa, that was all gay men and they didn't let gay women in. But I was allowed to go in. And I think it goes back to, that gay women were fighters. Wherever there was a group of lesbians, you could be sure that there was always going to be fights. A lot of bar room brawls."

Also, the nuances of socializing differed for men and women. Gay men and women even preferred different kinds of music, the former fast, lively music, the latter slow love songs. Sometimes tension erupted between men and women on the dance floor. Toni, a handsome white butch who actively sought out the bars while underage, remembers some of these incidents:

> "And where men and women [were] drinking together where there was a dance floor, there would often be trouble on the dance floor because the men would dance and take up a lot of space, swing their arms and move real fast, and they'd tramp on the women sometimes, so there would be trouble. And maybe the men got a lot of their energy out through their dancing. But it seemed that the bar owners favored the men."

In keeping with the expanding presence of the lesbian community, lesbians frequented several different kinds of straight bars. The "entertainment bars" in the Black section were still very popular. In addition to the clubs on Michigan Avenue, lesbians went to the Zanzibar and Mandy's, located on William Street, another major thoroughfare in the Black community. These clubs featured Jacki Jordan as a regular performer and MC, and drew a steady Black and white lesbian crowd. White women felt welcome at these shows. Sandy, who socialized in the white and Black communities, remembers.

> "She [Jacki] used to work at Mandy's on William. We used to go down there, because like I said, you could go in those bars, because colored people didn't bother you. They didn't bother you if you were gay. We'd go to floor shows. When you went out and wanted to go to a nice place and catch a show you mixed with the colored people, cause you weren't bothered."

Lesbians also went to straight bars such as the Midtown, the Kitty Kat, and the Pink Pony, which were in the neighborhood of the lesbian and gay bars. The owners and bartenders at these places tolerated lesbians, at least in small numbers. Bert explains, "You went there if you were fighting with your lover because it would take her a few hours to find you there." In addition, lesbians could be found in "Beatnik bars." Although gay men were more central to the beat scene than lesbians, individual lesbians did find a niche in the beat world. Little Gerry, a charming white butch, was a regular at a beat bar, only occasionally frequenting gay and lesbian bars, until she was banned in the early 1960s supposedly for not wearing a skirt, but more likely because she had slept with the owner's wife.

After the bars closed at 3 a.m., lesbians and gays might end their evening with a spaghetti dinner at Dante's Inferno, a small storefront restaurant about six doors down the street from the Carousel. The restaurant had only ten checkered-cloth-covered tables, and often on a weekend night a line would form at the door. Dante's great bread and lively atmosphere attracted a large clientele from the Carousel, Bingo's, and the street bars.

Finally, lesbians frequented a variety of after-hours clubs, the majority of which were in the Black section of the city including the Lucky Clover, Cherry Reds, Big Eyes, and the Lincoln Club. Some were racially integrated, others completely segregated. All illegally served liquor beyond the normal closing hours of bars, and a few had gambling. Piri, a smooth Black butch who always went dressed in masculine attire, rarely had any trouble, and remembers the Black after-hours places as much nicer than those today: "You could go there—at the time the bars closed at three o'clock—and stay for two or three days if you wanna.... You could just go in an after-hours joint and buy your drinks, and it cost you just about the same thing it would in a bar." At the very end of the decade, Jacki Jordan and Sandy opened a gay after-hours club that lasted for only a short time. It carried the name of the bar whose space they took over, the Club Co Co, but was referred to by the lesbian community as the Key Club. Jan, a self-assured Indian butch, went there often:

> "You would enter the first door with a key and then there was this real bull dyke, which you wouldn't even know she was a girl, right, was standing on the second door, and she'd look through the peekhole to see if she recognized you, and then she would let you in the second door.... I don't think they had a liquor license. So you'd go in and you'd order your drinks and then there was a lighting system in the back, and when this light would go on, whatever you had in front of you, [you] had to down. And then the waitress would come and clean up the table real quick, and then the cops would come in and look it over and it just looked like a social club, so they'd leave."

Just as in the 1940s, lesbians were aware that people ran gay bars because they were lucrative.[17] Even the street bars made significant money from the addition of their lesbian clientele. "They remodeled [Pat's], put in a circular bar, made it really nice. Because the guy was making money on the girls and could afford to do this for them" (Matty).

In the 1950s there were even fewer raids on lesbian and gay bars than in the 1940s. Not one narrator can remember a raid during the 1950s. When asked whether she wasn't concerned about being caught in a raid in the Carousel, Bert replies, "No, I never was. Particularly the Carousel, because they had been there so many years. It was a well established bar." Only the Canadians remember any harassment in the bars, and this was from the border patrol, who would come in and check for I.D.'s. Whitney had a male friend who spent the night in jail because he didn't have proper identification.

Narrators assume that bars were protected by their owners paying off the police just as in the 1940s.

> "They had to be, some places just had to be to get away with the things that were going on ... you know, when you're in a bar and you see police coming

in all the time without saying anything to you and getting drinks or getting a bottle. . . . They walk in and they hand them a bottle, you know darn well somebody [is paying them off]. It's the guys who patrol the place. They would hear a call and [say] I'll handle it, and they would go and [report], 'Aw, it was nothing.' " (Marla)

Printed sources confirm the narrators' impressions. The 1950s were a notoriously corrupt period for Buffalo police, particularly on the precinct level.[18] When Nelson Rockefeller became the governor of New York in January 1959, he initiated a statewide crackdown on vice and gambling. By the end of his first year in office, Rockefeller's New York State Investigation Commission probed vice in Buffalo. Daily reports on Commission hearings, as published in the newspapers, revealed a dark cloud hanging over the city's vice squad. For instance, gambling, vice, and liquor violation statistics for the entire city in 1958 indicate one hundred and twelve complaints made, but only two arrests completed by the Buffalo police.[19] Impropriety was alleged in Commission testimony by an individual who had complained about a certain establishment and specifically requested that police from one particular station not be called in because officers from that precinct often were seen drinking there.[20] Further, vice complaints had apparently been buried in a highly organized fashion by use of what was referred to as the "Pittsburgh Book."[21] These complaints and investigations routinely failed to enter the official record. Finally, in testimony, the Buffalo police commissioner himself was at a loss to explain the discrepancy between the vice and gambling known to exist within the precincts and the lack of any police action. What can be surmised from these hearings is that a period of police corruption existed in Buffalo, at least during the 1950s. Police payoffs seemed to have been an institutionalized aspect of Buffalo vice. In this situation, bar owners, and their bartenders and bouncers, were fairly lax about monitoring lesbian and gay behavior. Their main concern was running an operation that did not draw undue attention to the bar.

Dancing, which was very popular—"either you danced slow or you were jitterbugging"—was permitted in the gay men's bars and the Carousel, and at the end of the decade in the One Thirty-Two.[22] Fast dancing with minimum body contact was more accepted, although Toni remembers times when women boldly danced suggestively.

"Women [like men] may have been able to dance fast dances with each other. I don't think you were allowed to slow dance. Although I remember being in the Oasis one night, I was in there with my girlfriend, Arlene, and maybe we had gone in there with some gay men, 'cause I knew a lot of the gay men, and after a while Sandy and a woman she was with came in. And they had been drinking and they were dancing, and I remember they were doing exaggerated dips and grinding and stuff like that, and I don't believe anyone said anything to them. And Sandy had quite a reputation at the time, but they were quite a spectacle on the dance floor, they were like doing romantic dances for the time, and maybe 'cause they were drinking they just didn't care. 'Cause women weren't really allowed to dance like that, no."

If the police were in the bar or close by, all dancing was forbidden.

REACHING OUT TO NEWCOMERS

For those coming out in the 1950s, finding lesbian community was easier than for the preceding generation. None of the narrators remembers a long search to become connected with lesbians. They learned about gay life and the bars through family or friends, or just knowing about the existence of a homosexual section of the city. The community itself also reached out to newcomers. This ability and desire for lesbians to reach out was a new development of the 1950s and although it seems like a small matter, in the context of severe oppression, it suggests a significant transformation in lesbian consciousness.

Those already in the bars were not shy about letting others know about them.

"I was recalling my first, I guess you'd say, finding of a gay bar in Buffalo. I can still see it. 1953, Dugan's, at North Division or South Division and Ellicott. I don't know where I found out that was possibly a gay bar. And I remember walking by it. Of course with a skirt on. We didn't wear slacks, at least I didn't wear slacks then. And I didn't have enough nerve to go in. And I walked back and forth a couple of times, and this woman came out and said, 'Are you looking for' . . . I don't remember the terms she said, if it was gay or not, and I said 'Yes,' so she said, 'Come in.' " (Bert)

Because fems are often less visible in lesbian history, it is important to underline that fems as well as butches actively reached out to newcomers; the woman who invited Bert into the bar was a fem.

Marla, who was working as a dispatcher for a taxi company, was even more aggressively helped by other lesbians to enter the bars in the late 1950s. She already knew she was gay from being in the service, but on returning to Buffalo had not yet gone to the bars:

"I was sitting at the switchboard one day, and the light lit up. It was coming from Bingo's, and they asked for a cab. . . . So, I don't know what made me get into conversation with them, oh, I know, they were surprised that it was a woman at the other end, 'cause men had always been dispatchers. . . . Then I turned around and [saw] the light [lit] up again, and I answered the thing again. And I started talking to them and found out that the woman on the phone and I had been in the same branch of the service. And then I'm trying to find out where the bar was 'cause I was going to go down and meet them, not knowing what kind of bar I was going to go into right away. Well, we figure we knew each other because we had been in the service together and we just started . . . 'cause I didn't even know that there were any bars. All I was doing was trying to get friends, you know. I need to find other people, meet people, so the next thing I know they were telling me how to get there."

Sandy, who spoke to her on the phone still remembers actively encouraging her to come to Bingo's.

"And we kept talking and talking. I said, 'Well this is a gay bar,' really come right [out]—I says, 'This is a gay bar, I dare you now to come down.' She says, 'Well, just what I've been looking for, I don't believe this.' . . . And she said, 'Will you be there when I get there?' And I said, 'I'll be here.' She was getting done maybe at midnight or whatever. And she says, 'How will I know you?' And I says, 'I'm tall and thin and have blonde hair.' I says, 'How will I know you?' She says, 'I'm Black with black curly hair.' And of course, if you've ever talked to anyone over the phone, it's never what you visualize they look like. So I'm picturing when I'm talking for two hours to this girl on the phone and I'm thinking, my God. . . . Then when she come in, cause Blacks weren't around that much then you know, [she says,] 'You got to be Sandy with those golden curls.' I said, 'Yeah, come on have a drink.' Then we go to the bar and we—we've laughed about that ever since because she was looking for the place, but she was also a butch.[23] It was so funny when she did come, she was not only Black but she was butch. But we ended up being all right. She says, 'If I had never took that call that night I'd have never found my way.' "

The Black lesbian community during the 1950s did its own active outreach to newcomers. The performances of Jacki Jordan as a singer and male impersonator were known throughout the Black community and made it particularly easy for Black lesbians to identify others like themselves. But Jacki also went out of her way to introduce young lesbians to the bars. She took Jodi, a stylish young Black butch, to a white bar in the late 1950s.

"When I was, guess I was a junior in high school, do you remember Jacki Jordan, well she used to give these, what do you call um's at the Little Harlem. So me and my friend, we used to go over to her house. This was when I was wearing lipstick, oh my god! So we went over to her house one night. . . . She took us [to this bar] and it was a white bar. And this was before I was even gay, so I knew there was some white folks somewhere doing the same stuff."

Many narrators who came out in the 1950s, unlike those who had come out in the 1930s and 1940s, met their first lesbians when they joined the armed services. The appeal of the military for Buffalo lesbians in the 1950s seems to be related to two factors. In the absence of high paying defense industry jobs, the armed services became an attractive source of income for women.[24] In addition, the increased social emphasis on isolated nuclear families and rigid gender roles made it hard for young women to spend time together except in single-sexed institutions like the military.

Those who joined the Army and Air Force at the beginning of the decade found lesbian community both in the U.S. and abroad and for a while had a generally positive experience (see photos after p. 190). "In fact one of my best friends was in the Air Force, who went over on the ship with me, and she was gay. In fact, right in the middle of the Atlantic Ocean I chummed around with gay people going over" (Bert). As the decade progressed the armed services became more and more hostile to lesbians. The antilesbian witch-hunts cast their nets widely affecting all narrators who had developed lesbian connections.[25] Despite their strategies to minimize the damage of exposure, some received general discharges and others dishonorable discharges. Those who entered the armed services in the middle of the decade did not even attempt to make contact with lesbians. "And so then I went in the service [in 1955]. . . . There was a lot of gay there, but not as much as they claim there is. . . . And I didn't get involved there. . . . Because there, anything like that, out you go . . . dishonorable, my God, your whole life is fucked up" (Sandy). But even in this case she had learned enough about lesbian life to know what she was looking for when she reentered civilian life.

Although the bars in Buffalo were fairly easy to locate, entering them was still a momentous step in most lesbians' lives because they were the only place to be with other lesbians.

> "I just felt that I was looking for lesbians. I had to find lesbians. And I went with a school friend. And I was drinking then too and she was someone who would go out and drink with me. I had a crush on her, so we went together the first time. I was frightened and I was real excited, both, about being there. Some of the women frightened me, they were older and they looked real tough, some of them, and that kind of scared me a little bit. And I was pretty young [sixteen], so probably most people there were older than me. But I just knew with all the questions in my mind and the conflicting feelings about it, it was like I was home, even though it was strange territory. There was something about it, there were all women and immediately I saw the roles, the butches and the fems. And that's what I wanted." (Toni)

Similarly, Sandy, who invited Marla to Bingo's, describes this as a homecoming:

> "It was so cute. And here she comes, she's bouncing and bubbly right today like she was then. And she was so happy. She looked around you know, she couldn't believe it 'cause Bingo's, oh my god, the only ones that had the nerve to go in there were the queers. The place was infested. And she said, 'Oh I'm home.' God what a homecoming that was."

And since there were few places where tough lesbians could be with their own kind, the bars, elegant or sleazy, were captivating.

"After I found Bingo's, that was it. From the company [where I worked] I used to take my lunch break, get in my car, go down to Bingo's and have a drink . . . turn right around and get back in my car and go right to work. And at one o'clock [a.m.] I'd go right back down there and stay there until the bar closed." (Marla)

Women who were just coming out usually found easy acceptance in the bars. Many narrators of the late 1950s remember being under the legal drinking age (eighteen in New York State) when they first entered the bars; one as young as thirteen. Some people had forged identification. Although they lived in fear of being found out and thrown out, most managed to remain undetected.

The method of introduction was different for butch and for fem. As in the 1940s, fems became familiar with the community and its expectations by dating butches. "If she was your girl, and people liked her, they just knew you would take care of her and everything would be fine—she would be accepted." Not one fem narrator remembers another fem's playing an important role in welcoming her to the community. Butches were more than delighted to have this responsibility. Bert explains that if a fem came into a bar alone, she was looking, "and all the butches started looking too."

During the 1950s, the more experienced butches also helped the younger butches catch on to gay life. This had never happened in the 1940s, and therefore suggests that lesbians had a greater sense of solidarity and took more pride in being part of a community. After her first visit to a bar, a butch would often leave with an invitation to visit someone's house, or a phone number of someone with whom she could go back to the bars. Iris, a witty Indian butch, left with a phone number.

"I didn't know what to expect, it was really a trip, I really didn't know what to expect. . . . But I went down there, I met this Sandy, her name was Sandy. . . . She said, 'Why don't you give me your phone number?' and I said, 'Well, why don't you give me yours? because at present I live with my [family]. I'd rather call you than you call me.' So she did. So I called her and arranged to meet her, and I started—got to know a few of the people, and started going in Bingo's."

Toni found that receiving a phone number from someone in this unexplored place was very helpful for dealing with her fears.

"I did that night get the phone number of a woman who was about six years older than me, who defined herself as a butch, and she knew that I was just coming out. I was afraid they would think that I was spying on them, that they wouldn't know I was like them. . . . I'm sure I had a few beers, I had a few before I even went in there to get the courage up to go in. I was talking to this woman, and she told me where she lived and gave me her phone number, and encouraged me to get in touch with her. I guess she knew that I was just starting to come out. She was extending her friendship to me, and I did get in touch with her and we were friends."

The woman who was so helpful to Toni was Iris. Reaching out to newcomers had become a tradition. Older butches would talk about gay life with the younger ones, explaining its rules and etiquette. Toni describes one of her early and very influential conversations with her new friend and another older lesbian in 1958.

> "They were two of the, I guess, the star dykes around town, and I remember one time the three of us were together, we must have been standing at the bar, because I remember when [the older one] pounded her fist on the bar or table, we were talking about being gay, and she said, 'If you want to be butch you gotta be rough, tough and ready' boom! She pounded her fist on the bar. And well, it scared me, I didn't know if I could measure up to all of that but I figured I would have to try 'cause I knew I was a butch, I knew that's what I was."

Older butches of the 1950s were aware of their important role. D.J., who came out in the 1940s but was comfortable with and part of the tough bar lesbian crowd, remembers their gentle kidding of young butches. "They were still wet behind the ears. They walked in like they were big butches and we'd call out, 'Here comes the Panty Brigade.' " Stormy, a leader who came out in the early 1950s remembers, "With new butches you [tried] to befriend them. It ain't easy bein' alone . . . you wanted to take them in for their own protection."

The trend toward reaching out and educating others that began in the early 1950s continued throughout the decade, and by the late 1950s the concept and practice of role modeling became a part of lesbian culture. Most tough butch narrators who entered the community after 1958 include descriptions of the women who were their role models as an integral part of their memories of early days in the bars. Little Gerry describes Stormy: "She was loud and big, and it took me a while to learn that I wasn't afraid of her. She was wonderful to model oneself after—rough, tough and honest. She talked rough like a cowboy. But didn't hit people over the head for nothing." Stormy claims, and this is consistent with the fact that she came out in the early 1950s, that she was not consciously aware of being a role model for anyone. Nevertheless, when she shares what she thinks she would have offered to someone who had chosen to model themselves after her, it is amazingly similar to what Little Gerry claims to have learned, and this despite the fact that they have not seen one another in twenty-five years. This suggests that the educational process was very effective. "A lot of people had fantasies about me. . . . I had to straighten them out. If they modeled themselves after me, they would have been honest, kind, gentle. . . . Some made up stories that were just the other way." She emphasizes that she had to let people know all the time that she wasn't mean and tough, just competent at protecting and defending herself and the people around her.

Although the 1950s tough bar lesbians reached out to newcomers, lesbians did not consider that society was less hostile to lesbians than in the 1930s and 1940s.

Stormy mentions that she would encourage them to think seriously about what they were doing before entering the gay life.

> "Many times when young people would come in I would tell them to go home and think about it. Because if they thought they were having a good time, they weren't. I would say, 'If you follow this, you may think you're having fun here, but it's a dog-eat-dog world'. . . . It's real hard having a child ask, 'Mommy, is that a man or a woman?' Lots of gay women who weren't really gay wanted to try it out. The life was dangerous. Straights would beat you up, just come down to the bars looking to beat up queers, persecution and harassment. You had to walk down the street in pairs. And then there were the fights between the women, petty jealousies."

The view that lesbian life was very difficult because of the severity of oppression was pervasive and had direct continuity with the 1940s. The same tragic images appear in Matty's memories about the way her sister, a lesbian who came out in the 1940s, had described the gay life to her in 1951. Matty was just coming out, and she and her sister had gone to the Capri, a gay after-hours club in New York City. A friend of her sister's asked Matty to dance, and after two or three dances she returned to the table and noticed that her sister was crying. She asked why and her sister said:

> " 'I don't like the way you're looking around here. . . . This isn't the life for you.' I said, . . . 'If it's good enough for you, why isn't it good enough for me?' And she proceeded to tell me, she said, 'Look around at all these people that are laughing, and they're joking, and they're having a ball—you think they are. . . . Inside they're being ripped apart'. She said, 'Do you know what it's like to live this kind of life? Every day when you get out of bed, before your feet hit the floor, you've gotta say to yourself, come on, get up, you may get smacked right in the face again today, some way, somehow, but it might be a good day for you, you've got to take your chances.' She said, 'If you can get up every day not knowing what this day's gonna bring, whether your heart's gonna be ripped out, whether you're gonna be ridiculed, or whether people are gonna be nice to you or spit in your face, if you can face living that way, day in and day out, then you belong here; if you can't . . . get the hell out!' "

The new ability to reach out and support newcomers under these difficult conditions was a subtle though significant development. Because of the extreme homophobia of the 1950s, we think it is unlikely that this positive change could have come about simply in response to the persecution of gays. It must have also been rooted in the preceding decade's cumulative experience of building lesbian culture and community in bars, which strengthened lesbians' feelings of self and community worth and created the consciousness necessary for bolder action in an oppressive society. These new feelings of pride, even with reservation, shaped the development of lesbian community life in the 1950s. For the tough bar lesbians it was actualized in their desire to end hiding and to defend lesbian space.

CHALLENGING THE DOUBLE LIFE

The 1940s strategy of separating social life from work and family life as much as possible was no longer acceptable in the 1950s. Although a few individual lesbians in the 1940s had challenged the double life, they were loners, unappreciated by the others. By the 1950s, the tough bar lesbians as a group would not divide their lives in order to maintain a steady job and to placate family, and they became less and less willing to do so as the decade progressed. They were in the bars every day, not just on weekends, and the butches appeared masculine as much of the time as they could, not just when they went out to the bars. The consequences of this behavior were severe. By not denying who they were and looking "queer" as much of the time as possible, or associating with those who did, tough bar lesbians drastically reduced their options for work and their chances of partaking in the American dream of upward mobility. The tough bar butches did not conform to the code of dress required for success at most jobs, particularly white-collar jobs, nor did they conform to the moral values of the middle class. And it is this which gives the unmistakably working-class character to their way of life.

The older tough butches, those who came out in the early 1950s, unlike their predecessors, had not been raised during the Depression and were not terribly worried about losing their jobs. In the expanding economy of the 1950s they rightly assumed that they would always find another, and in between could hustle for money in the street bars. All of them changed jobs several times during the 1950s and 1960s, not because they were fired, but because they didn't like the constraints.

Bert's succession of jobs and her attitudes about them were quite typical. After the Army her first steady job was at the phone company, which she left after six years because she was tired of their rules and regulations.

> "I was a long distance operator. And I didn't like it because it reminded me too much of the military. . . . It was really discipline. I can remember the Buffalo snow storms, and having to take a bus to work, and I would wear a pair of slacks under my skirt because it was cold, and the telephone company is down by the City Hall, and you went down there by that wind. I took them off as soon as I got to work. They told me I could not wear slacks to work. And you couldn't look to your left, you couldn't look to your right, you couldn't do anything. . . . I remember one time I was sick and I called in sick, and they came around the house to see . . . if you were really sick. And after almost six years of being told when to get up and when to go to bed, I had had it."

While she was unemployed, someone at an employment agency took an interest in her and placed her as a counselor in an agency for retarded children. With just a high school equivalency certificate she had no formal training for this kind of work, but her medical and physical education work in the Army, combined with a natural inclination for working with young people, led her to do very well.[26] She adapted her dress just enough to meet convention. Her strategy was that of most of these older tough butches. She conformed minimally when necessary.

> "Well, as I was telling you, in the bar . . . when I worked for the child-care center I used to wear men's shirts but I wore skirts. . . . Had a D.A. haircut, but you know if you put lipstick on that was all right. . . . It was part of my way of life. Nobody ever accepted me for [queer]. If they thought it they never told me, it never interfered in my job."

She left the job due to tension and regrets the decision. When she was once again unemployed someone at the bar told her that she was eligible to work as a medical records clerk because of her training in the Army. She is proud of her ability to consistently find good jobs.

> "[My friend Alice] said that I was kind of unique. I would get down, down on my luck and down in my life, but I would never stay there. And whenever I came up I always came up higher, and I still do that. Like you know I'd be down on the money and I'd be out there hustling, next thing you know I had a good job and I was doing all right."

Another older tough butch has a similarly varied work history, except for the fact that each new job allowed her more and more freedom to dress as she wished. She first worked as a supermarket cashier starting in the mid-1940s as a teenager. After thirteen years she got tired of that, and traveled out West. When she returned she took a job in a factory, which went South after six years, and she decided not to follow. Then she worked in the bars and drove a cab, two very common occupations for the tough bar lesbians because they interfered minimally with living a lesbian-centered life. These jobs did not pay well, making it hard for lesbians to make ends meet.

The fems of this group did similar kinds of work, but in general they tended toward white-collar employment. Marla, who had some college education, had a lot of different jobs—dispatching, cooking, and cleaning at a bar—until finding one that she liked which entailed working with young people. This job required her to be quite discreet and she soon found herself having a lot in common with the more upwardly mobile lesbians.

The visibility of these tough bar lesbians made it inevitable that their families would find out about them. Despite the anger or unhappiness this may have caused, they all managed to retain regular contact. Some, like Marla, continued the 1940s pattern of mutual discretion. "Here I got discharged from the service, what was I gonna do, I had to go home and face my parents. And all my father did was two days later chased me out of the house and made me go look for a job. . . . They knew about it, but. . . . We just never sat down and discussed it, 'cause I never talked to them." Others actually achieved an open and accepting relationship with their parents.[27] The ability of some families to handle the visibility of their lesbian daughters suggests that working-class families were not monolithic centers of repression during the 1950s.

Matty directly told her parents, because she did not want the constant pressure of discretion, and the continuous worry of whether her lifestyle would get back to them. Her older sister was gay and her parents had accepted her to the point that they had gone to see her as a male impersonator at the Eighty-Two Club in New York City. When Matty came out, her sister was very worried about what it would do to their parents when they found out.

> "And [my sister] said, 'Do you know what this would do to Mom and Dad? They had to contend with me and now they're going to have to contend with you.' And I said, 'I just won't tell them.' And she said, 'Well eventually you'll have to if you want to live your life without having to look over your shoulder.' . . . And when I got back to Buffalo, the very next weekend I was sitting in the Carousel and I was having a drink with some friends of mine and that came into my head, what she said about having to look over my shoulder. . . . I turned to this girl that I was sitting with, I said, 'Listen, I'll be back as soon as I can.' She said, 'Where are you going?' I said, 'I have to go home for a minute I'll be right back.'
>
> And I went home and my mother and father were watching television and I sat down and just looked at them and my mother said, 'What's the matter, is something wrong out there you're home so early?' I said, 'No, I have to tell you something.' And my father said, 'What is it? . . .' And he got up and shut the TV off. And I said, 'I don't know how to say this without just saying it, and I don't want to hurt you.' And I told them that I was gay. . . . My mother started to cry and she said, 'Why is this happening to me? I raised two daughters and a son, I didn't raise three sons.' . . . And my mother cried and she said, 'Just think, you're going to be like your sister, you're going to dress in boys' clothes.' I said, 'No, it doesn't mean that, it just means that I'm different, it just means that I want to be with people who are like myself.' . . .
>
> And my father, who was from Italy, he had a violent temper, said, 'Come into the kitchen, I want to talk to you.' My first impulse was that when he got me into the kitchen he was going to beat the hell out of me. I sat there and my mother said to my father, 'Don't hit her, let her get out what she's trying to say. . . . Don't scare her into not being able to confide in us.' And when I got into the kitchen my father was putting the coffee pot on and he poured us a cup of coffee and he said, 'Sit down.' He said, 'Now let me understand what you're trying to say . . . you're trying to tell me you don't like boys, you like girls instead.' I said, 'Yeah, that's it exactly.' He said, 'You don't want to get married and you don't want to have children?' I said, 'No.' And then he got tears in his eyes, and he said, 'Is it our fault?' And I told him, 'I knew you were going to say that, I just knew because it's the first thing everybody, all parents say, where did I go wrong?' I said, 'No, it's not your

fault . . . you couldn't have brought me up better. . . . And my father said, '. . . I don't understand this life. . . . I don't care what life you live, if you go with women, if you go with men, I want you to be happy. But let's get something straight right now, no matter what kind of life you live, there's a right and a wrong way to do it. You live this life as right as you can. Don't do anything that's going to kill your mother, or embarrass your mother. And we love you, you're our daughter and you're always welcome.' And that was it.

It was never mentioned again. I went in and my mother was sitting there and I got on my knees . . . in front of her and . . . I said, 'Please don't cry any more.' And she put her arms around me and said, 'I love you. Be a good girl and don't let people hurt you . . . because of what you are.' . . . And my mother said, 'Is that why you're out all the time?' I said, 'Yes, to be around people who are like myself.' 'Well why didn't you bring your friends home?' I said, 'Because I didn't think you'd understand.' 'Well now you told us, I want to meet your friends.' From that time . . . Sunday was not a complete day unless my mother had two or three gay people sitting at the dinner table. And if so-and-so didn't have a place to go, they were from out of town for Thanksgiving, they were welcome at our house. Christmas Eve was open house and you brought your friends in, and after Sunday dinner we all went bowling, my mother and father included. And it was really just great, I didn't have to hide things. . . . I'll never regret telling them."

This rosy memory is in fact only slightly distorted. We know from other parts of Matty's life history that her father was angry at her for a short period of time and he beat her once or twice. But her relationship with her parents did work out just as she describes and continued to grow. "There wasn't anything I couldn't tell my mother, even sexual problems. I always loved my mother and we were close, but we never became as close as we were after I told her. I could tell her anything."

In the 1950s it was extremely rare for a daughter to sit down and discuss her gayness with her family. Bert says she never heard of it happening, which is possible because she wasn't close to Matty. None of the other older tough butch narrators ever told their parents. The common way for family, particularly parents, to learn about a person's gayness was for an aggrieved party, usually an angry lover, to take revenge by speaking to parents. This happened to two of these older tough butches. Bert's mother who learned in this way was furious at her daughter for a while.

"An irate lover of mine called up, and I went out the door flying, it was one of her tantrums. That's when I went off to live with Pearl. And the ironic part about it was that she had a gay friend when she was in her young twenties. A man that traveled with her and her group of friends, who any of the old-timers of Buffalo would remember, and his name was Tangara, he was a female impersonator. But when it comes to one of your own that's another story."

But Bert did work things out with her mother. When they were on good terms she not only brought her partners around but also her mother sometimes went out with them just to be sociable. Her mother had been single since Bert was young and had worked hard raising her children. In turn Bert put a lot of energy into developing a good relationship with her mother.

> "One of my problems . . . was I always loved my mother and wanted her to love me and didn't feel that she did. I always worked hard at getting along with her. There were periods where we got along good, in fact she used to go to the gay bars with me after she learned to accept it, with Gail and I on weekends. And she knew a lot of my gay friends."

Her aunts and uncles also accepted her "mates" at family occasions, although Bert is not sure whether they realized she was a lesbian.

The rough and tough butches who came out in the late 1950s, particularly the admired leaders, made even fewer adjustments in their way of life for work and family. As a result they were generally underemployed. Some managed to go out every night and keep a steady job; others cut back socializing during the week in order to work; "I always had to get up so early in the morning, I didn't go out too much during the week. It was too hard for me to get up and go to work. . . . But lot of times you'd meet, have a couple of drinks with four or five of the butches that went with somebody" (Iris). And others had frequent absences which led to their being fired.

In addition, the pressures for women to wear a skirt to work made them uncomfortable in the work environment. Sandy explains the difficulties her friends faced, when reminiscing about one who was forced to wear a skirt while tending bar at the Mardi Gras, despite the fact that this was a bar with a large lesbian clientele.

> "You had to wear a skirt. The guy that owned the Mardi Gras was afraid to let her behind the bar in slacks. See, women couldn't wear slacks in those days. That's what I've been trying to tell you. All these things were job [related]. How do you think she felt back there making out with a girl with a skirt on? That was still the same time when you couldn't wear pants in a profession. You couldn't go into an office and be a typist and wear pants."

When asked whether being a barmaid was a profession, Sandy responds: "You're damn right it was. There [were] laws, liquor laws and everything, on how you were presented. I promise. Yes, and you can't have an undesirable behind your bar. She could have worn slacks, and you got a charge. She would have been fired. You'd a got a charge as an undesirable."

No butch narrator was actually fired for not conforming to a feminine dress code. It was as if the rule was so pervasive they did not even challenge it. They left the jobs that required skirts and sought jobs that would let them dress the way that they wanted. They worked in factories—the two most popular were the Wax Factory and the Buffalo Envelope Company—that did not care what women wore to work. They also drove cabs, and tended bar, and a few pimped.[28]

Sandy has a typical work history for those who felt they would not conform to the female dress code. After leaving the Marines she had a good job as an accounts clerk which she left because she did not want to wear female clothes.

"Right. And I had another job, I got a job in a factory, where it was—Oh Jesus . . . a dollar an hour, a dollar five an hour . . . it was a plastic factory, lower Main Street. Quite a drop in pay, but I had to pay board at home, had to have money. But I could dress there the way I wanted to. You suffer for it 'cause you couldn't make the money, and you couldn't demand more money. And they worked the hell out of you. If you didn't like it, get out. That was the way it was. . . . [My next job], there was a lot of them. I just bounced around. . . . Oh yeah, [drove cabs] dress the way you want there too. Well my mother was on me a lot, like you can do this, you can do that. . . . I went down and I took [the] civil service exam . . . [for] secretarial, because [my mother] said, 'You got it, you got it.' Well I knew I did, but I didn't really want it, but to please her I went and I took the test. Naturally passed it of course. No problem at all. And was offered a number of very good positions, which I'd also have about twenty years in now, if I could have went to work the way I wanted to. I refused, I wouldn't even go for a job interview. Refused to get dressed, refused. So that went. And then eventually into the bars to work."

Since these were low paying jobs with a high turnover many of these tough young butches didn't care whether they kept them, and quit when they felt like partying or attending to their personal lives. Lack of concern for separating social life and work life led to a new problem at work: Angry lovers not only called family but also in the late 1950s might inform employers and even make an appearance at work. This could be very disconcerting at a respectable job. "Worked there four years until my girlfriend came in and rearranged about four million charts in the middle of the floor. Can you imagine how embarrassing that was?" (Vic). Shortly after this she left the job.

Most of these extremely tough butches felt that their decision to be open about their lesbianism radically affected the opportunities available to them throughout their lives. The leaders had done very well in school and had expected to have good jobs: one wanted to be a legal secretary or assistant, another a medical technician. They are bitter that society's prejudices prevented them from doing the kind of work they wanted.

"I could never do anything and make it. I couldn't go out and use my education or my training. I pay taxes, I serve my country, they didn't mind that, but I can't go in a bar and drink of course, and I'm arrested on sight.[29] So I had to just show that, fuck you. If I'm not taking this good job what the fuck can you do to me, what can you do to me? You can't threaten my job if I'm making a dollar five an hour instead of four fifty, five an hour, what can you do to my dollar five an hour job? Get me fired? Saying 'That's a queer working for you?'

And I could go to work the way I wanted to, I could pick up a piece of machinery or I could set a tool or a die. I learned a whole lot though, I have to say that much for that. And not taking the office jobs and things that were available to me that I couldn't get, I mean I could of if I switched around, but I went and I learned another trade." (Sandy)

Vic, a white butch who was looked up to for her romantic looks and good sense, strongly believes that she deserves Social Security payments. She feels that she has not been treated fairly by society, and therefore, she should be reimbursed for all the opportunities she was denied.

"I always wanted to get into the thing like buying a home and things like that. And then, I don't want to do that. Well first of all, lets break it down to the fact that I'm not gonna work, except maybe little part-time jobs like I did for seven years . . . 'cause I'm one of the few that went down and said, 'Look pal, this is where I'm at and somebody's gonna have to support me because I can't get a job. . . .' God damn right, ask Gloria. Gloria marched me right down there, and I was as butch as butch can be. . . . I was sitting there, they directed all their questions to her. . . . And they said, 'Well Victoria, what seems to be your problem?' Never had looked at me once. And I'm sittin' just like I am now, and [Gloria] says, 'Oh that's Victoria there,' and they says, 'Oh oh.' And they just, 'Oh well alright.' I've been on it since I lived on [the West Side]. They'd bring me down for recertification every year, they don't say a word to me. I've had some very nice little case workers. When I say nice I mean they don't question, they believe your situation's the same and that's it. I'm homosexual and until the law changes don't expect me to work, because I'm not going to be ridiculed. That's how I feel about it. . . . And I think the other six hundred thousand or however many there are around in Buffalo, should march right down there. No I mean if they aren't working or something, yeah. Now you figure it out yourself, if I'm collecting that and I've been collecting it almost ten years now. It sounds stupid to you but it's just the name of my game and that's how I have to play it. If you won't let me work at what I'm qualified to work at, support me. If I can go to work like I am and you can guarantee me that I'm not going to be ridiculed, then I'll go. And I'm qualified to do a lot of things. I didn't spend part of my life going to school to empty bedpans. Well I worked in the medical library at [a research institute] for over four years. . . . It's not a lot, but it's money that I think a lot of people should be getting that they're not."

Many of the tough young lesbians were not this bitter, and by the late 1960s when heavy industry began to hire a few women, they entered previously male jobs, and settled down to steady employment, or at least as steady as the economy would allow.[30]

Most of these younger tough butches were more concerned about keeping their social lives separate from their family lives than from employment. Even the leaders made some adjustments to maintain at least minimal contact with their families.

Once Vic had found her way into the bar community, she did not completely cut her ties with her parents, but she only saw them rarely. These visits were some of the few times she would wear more feminine clothes.

"I've never tried to hide what I am. I hide it from my family, maybe I'm a hypocrite, 'cause like I told you, when I go to see my father, I can not drag it to my house. I don't go in T-shirt and my high ridin' shoes. I turn it all around and I have to be fairly presentable to him. Now if he came to my house, this is how I would be. But when I go to his I got to respect him a little bit."

All of the families knew that they had lesbian daughters, and the relationships varied from distant to warm, with some daughters being discreet enough to ease tensions and others being quite open. When they were young and living at home, many were careful not to look too extremely butch. Toni remembers copying the appearance of her new butch friends, ". . . but [I] couldn't go quite as far as they could go because I was living at home and my mother didn't really accept me being gay." Others made fewer adjustments and were nevertheless able to preserve ongoing relationships. At first, Little Gerry was fairly discreet around her parents in order to maintain an amicable relationship. But in the early 1960s she began to project a more masculine appearance; yet her mother never made her feel uncomfortable. One time Gerry's friends were visiting in the house, and she remembers her mother saying to somebody on the phone, "There are three girls standing in my kitchen and they all look like boys." Jodi's family was even more accepting of her and her friends: "There is no Black dyke that I know that was coming up when I came up that couldn't go to our house. And then it was like some heavy studs, with men's shoes and shirts and all that kind of stuff. You know, no big deal." Jodi kept close contact with her parents until they died.

The fems who were part of this younger generation of tough bar lesbians worked at many of the same kinds of jobs, but also worked as secretaries, clerks, waitresses, and prostitutes. Their more typically feminine appearance did not conflict with the dress code of these jobs. Since their stigmatization as lesbians came mainly from associating with butches, something which they could easily prevent from happening on the job, they could work at most jobs that employed women except those that required entertaining or other forms of integration of home and work life. However, in the late 1950s the time spent with other lesbians in the bars affected a fem's relationship to work in the same way that it affected butches. Annie, a fem, got married and left gay life for fifteen years, because she felt being in the bars all the time was an irresponsible way of life.

"At that moment while you're doing it you don't really look at it whether it's right or wrong, it's a necessity. Because you're in with a crowd that wants to drink every day. It was just out for a good time. And then all of a sudden one day as you start getting older you sit there and you think, where have you

been and where are you going. And this is where a lot of kids, a lot of fems
go straight, 'cause they want security."

The tough bar lesbian's desire to stop hiding was a new development in lesbian
history, one which grew out of the 1940s community, but was a distinct departure.
(We will return to this theme again in chapter 5 to suggest connections between
the tough bar lesbian's consciousness and the ideas of gay liberation.) Decreasing
the double life of lesbians had profound implications for the social life of 1950s
lesbians. By limiting their options for class mobility, it marked these rough and
tough lesbians as indelibly working-class. In addition it increased their stigmatization and heightened their conflict with a hostile heterosexual world.

USING PHYSICAL VIOLENCE TO DEFEND LESBIAN SPACE

In contrast to the 1940s, all narrators of the 1950s have vibrant memories about
lesbians fighting on the streets and in the bars. The tough bar lesbians were the
active fighters, and in some sense physical conflict was part of their good times.
The more refined lesbians saw these fights as crass and attempted to avoid them
as much as possible. But the tough lesbians were an expanding presence, and
therefore, violence had an increasingly prominent place in 1950s bar life.

A multitude of factors contributed to the escalation of violence on the part of
both lesbians and straights in the 1950s. Because of their tough, masculine appearance and the fact that they were more visible than lesbians of the previous decade
due to the frequency with which they were on the streets and in the bars, lesbians
were easier targets for vicious attacks by straight men. At the same time, ten to
fifteen years of a common culture gave lesbians the support necessary to respond
aggressively and with pride. Two aspects of 1950s culture encouraged violence.
The antigay fervor which was central to the McCarthy era fomented the kind of
hatred and defensiveness in straights and gays that was conducive to violent
conflict. Simultaneously, the rough, tough, rebellious working-class male who did
not hesitate to resort to violence became a central character in 1950s mass culture.
Marlon Brando in *The Wild One* or James Dean in *Rebel without a Cause* captured
the public's imagination, influencing rough and tough lesbians' and their male
adversaries' visions of themselves.

Tough bar lesbians recall physical conflict as part of gay women's constant battle
for their own territory and their right to occupy it. "In those days, you were a
survivor. You had to know how to handle yourself. . . . These bars were notorious,
and you'd get the straight man who would come in looking to go to bed with a
gay woman. We were in many a fight, many a fight" (Bert). It was generally
accepted that straight men constantly invaded what they knew to be lesbian
territory out of a sense of sexual competition.

"See, it was a man's ego. Now you've been around yourself for a long time and there's a lot of beautiful gay women. And this kills a man, because she will want another woman instead of wanting him, and it knocks their ego right down to the floor—and this is when they come in drunk and wanting to start fights." (D.J.)

Sandy points out that straight men mistakenly assumed that it would be easy to take women away from the butches. "They didn't have a woman, that's why they were staring at us. They had nothing to do with their time. . . . 'This girl has to be really [desperate] . . . if she's with a queer. I've got it made.' That's what they thought."

Although most of the fighting, especially with men, was done by butches, fems were often called upon to defend themselves against wisecracks and passes. D.J. recalls: "They [fems] would get into it too because if the guy would make a smart remark or something like this, something she didn't like, well, then maybe she'd make the first hit and then we'd take over from there." Sometimes fems might even instigate the fight.

But fights were not simply defensive. They often were rooted in a desire to claim and hold bar space. Matty relates that "A weekend wasn't a weekend if there wasn't a fight . . . they threw chairs, they threw tables. It was like an old western." She tells us that women would get together and plan, "Let's go down to the Mardi Gras and see who's ass we can kick tonight." And she comments with pride, "As much as we didn't like it, there was a lot of gratification afterwards. We fought for what's ours and we still have it." Most narrators agree that they fought in their own defense, but beyond that, they were creating gay space for the safety of other lesbians as well as themselves.

Although physical fighting was a way of expressing pride about being a lesbian and required bravery, it also grew out of conditions of severe oppression and had its destructive elements. Toni captures this duality. She affirms how hostility from straights caused real provocation for fights. "[Fighting was] the only way we could act then. We just didn't have any ground except what we fought for. Especially butches on the street. . . . People just stared at them. Out on the street you were fair game." She also emphasizes how drinking and self-hate created an atmosphere in which lesbians were bristling for a fight.

"When people would drink the hostility sometimes would erupt into fighting, or at least verbally, saying things back and forth, you know, taunting one another. . . . I know in those days I didn't feel O.K. about myself and if someone said something abusive to me I had nothing inside to say that I was O.K. so I would of course react to what they said."

This destructive element was an ingredient in all fights of the period, and particularly important in lesbians' relationships with one another. Alcohol, insecurity, and repression, in combination with the tough butch image, made fights among rough and tough lesbians a prominent part of the 1950s landscape. Couples most often fought over somebody's flirting with, dancing with, or kissing someone else. Butches also fought with one another, most frequently over girlfriends. For some these are painful remembrances and indicate the "no holds barred" attitude that had to be adopted for survival. Bert speaks of a particularly disconcerting but informative experience. The fight was over her first lover. A rival butch began the argument. "And it was a case of she didn't want me to be involved with this woman and so forth, and she started a fight with me. It was in Pat's and it was very early in this game. I thought you fight clean. I had these values. Ended up with two black eyes, and broken glasses, and a few bruises." After learning the ropes however, she was able to settle her grievance. "I walked up very quietly behind her, tapped her on the shoulder, took her glasses off, stomped them into the ground, and started swinging." She had learned her lesson in the ethics of bar conflict. These two women, by the way, became good friends over the years.

As a consequence of their aggressive stance toward the straight world, most tough bar butches had been arrested at least once for skirmishes with straight men, or even the police. Since the police did not generally exert their authority in the bars, and since bystanders would intervene in bar fights to prevent them from attracting undue attention, arrests rarely occurred in the bars themselves. They were more likely to occur on the streets, especially in the area around the bars. Black lesbians in particular were targets of police harassment even in their own neighborhoods.[31]

The tough bar lesbians' participation in physical violence had significant implications for the development of lesbian community. Most importantly, the fighting with straight men engendered feelings of lesbian solidarity. These street-wise lesbians knew how to band together to clean up their territory.

> "Back in that era we were a very close, tight-knit group. If any guy would start something we would just make a circle around him and just walk right in. We wouldn't beat him up or anything. We would just walk that circle to the door . . . and we would say, 'Do you want to fight or walk while you still can?' and they would walk!" (Matty)

Most tough bar lesbians have similar memories about working together: "I think by the time they left they knew we weren't going to be pushed around. . . . There were too many of us compared to them, so they knew they'd better get on their way" (Iris). They worked together so well that Bert recalls a bar fight at Pat's in which her backup team completely took over.

> "There was this guy who was standing at the bar and he kept patting my butt. And I can't remember the words but I probably said something pretty foul and loud enough so people would hear it, and a fight started, and I stood back by the juke box and watched it. Instigated it and stood back and watched. People would fight at the drop of a hat."

The fights between lesbians didn't really undermine these feelings of solidarity. Bert explains: "But you know even though there was all this fighting there was still a lot of solidarity there. It was sort of like, 'I can say what I want about you, but don't let anybody else do it.' People band together for this." Thus, lesbians would band together against the outside world, and friends would band together in fights with other lesbians. "Your friend watched your back so that you weren't jumped from behind" (Toni).

In addition to promoting solidarity, willingness to engage in physical conflict gave lesbians more control over their environment, and allowed them to protect the central institutions of their community, particularly the bars. In the 1950s unlike the 1940s, all the bars with a significant lesbian clientele employed lesbians as either bartenders or bouncers and gave them responsibility for keeping order. This innovation was successful enough to continue in Buffalo through the present. This change can be attributed directly to the rough and tough bar lesbians, either butch or fem, because, even in a more refined bar like the Carousel, it was always the tougher women who tended bar, letting it be known that they could take charge. As women taking responsibility for protecting themselves, their activities had a definite feminist dimension.

EXPANDING INTO DANGEROUS TERRITORY: THE STREET BARS

The desire to end their double life plus their ability to defend themselves led the tough bar lesbians to expand their territory, pushing them to associate with the perilous world of prostitution. The street bars—Dugan's, Pat's (which became the Mardi Gras), and the Chesterfield—were a meeting ground for diverse elements of the sexual fringe. Their clientele was mixed. "There was everything there, there were straights, colored, pimps, whores, and gay people" (Sandy). Due to the constant presence of straight men, these were the bars in which fighting was the most prevalent. Violence was routine and most lesbians came prepared, even Ronni, a sweet and ingenuous white butch. "I used to carry a knife around . . . a switchblade, or else I'd carry a club in my pants, because there was an awful lot of competition with men coming in there [the Mardi Gras] and always trying to start trouble with you all the time. And you had to let these guys know that that was your girl and nobody could stop you".

Toni, who never got used to fighting, and in fact was only in two fights in her life, graphically captures the volatile relationship between straight men and lesbians.

"The one time I remember being in a real big brawl, the only time, a real out-and-out barroom brawl, was in Dugan's. . . . I was about twenty years old, and I was in there with a woman I was in a relationship with, Ellie, and the two of us were with Sandy and her girlfriend Annie . . . and when it got close to the time the bar was gonna close there were between ten and fifteen young men that came into the bar in a crowd. Some of them were standing behind us, and something was going back and forth between [Annie] and one of these young men, and at one point Annie took her empty beer bottle, walked over to the guy and hit him on the head with it. And then she just went back and sat on her chair. Well the guy turned around and went to hit Sandy, and when I saw him going after my friend I was gonna help. I was very idealistic, so I guess I went after one of these guys and the next thing I knew everybody in the place was hitting the floor. I jumped over the bar and on the way jumping over the bar was throwing whatever was on the bar, glasses, big heavy ashtrays, and the guys on the other side were flinging things. The whole place was just glasses, full bottles, everything being flung through the air. And everybody was hiding on the floor and . . . I felt blood coming down my neck . . . and I touched it and the first thing I thought was my jugular vein was cut and I started yelling. Two guys dragged me out and got my girlfriend out of the phone booth where she was being protected, and they took me to the hospital to get my head stitched up. We went out the back door and we had to pass around by the front door to get in their car, and the bar owners had got this crew of guys out of the bar but they were trying to break the door in. But when they saw us passing they followed us but they didn't catch us."

The men who helped her were straight men who had a grievance against those who had been harassing Toni and her friends.

Whether a person enjoyed fighting or not, she had little choice about going to the street bars if she wanted to know lesbians. "The first time I ever went in [to Pat's Cafe] there was a fight. Glasses were flying and everything. I remember I went under a table and thought, 'Oh God! what is this?' But I kept going back because this was the only way that I could get to know people that were like myself" (Bert). The owners of these bars did nothing to prevent the fights or protect their clientele. They expected those who came to take care of themselves. "They didn't have any bouncers in these bars in those days. In those days you were a survivor, you had to know how to handle yourself" (Bert).

Most tough butch narrators were ambivalent about these bars, as typified by the memories of Ronni, a regular at the Mardi Gras.

"I had to completely drop out of sight in my straight circle, because I was so involved in this whole new scene and I loved it so much. I really didn't love the sordidness of it, and I didn't love all this constant conflict with all these men that were coming in—because basically it was a straight bar, a prostitute's bar, a pimp's bar, a dope pusher's bar. It was everything and anything. It was really a dog-eat-dog situation. I had to be very tough. I had to beat people up—any girl—other dykes that used to come in and try to make out with my girl I'd have to floor her, or politely warn her to stay away. 'That's my girl.' And guys that would come in—I'd have to be willing to defend myself, and to sometimes fight for my life. Because two or three guys would come in at once and would be wanting to start something with me. I just had to go through all kinds of means to protect my relationship."

Given that lesbians had safer bars like Bingo's and the Carousel, why did they frequent these rough street bars? One reason narrators articulate was the desire to expand lesbian territory.

"If you're saying if they had a bar why fight for another bar, it's like your saying to me, well you have one set of clothes, why go out and try to find a job to make money to buy another, just be satisfied and keep wearing the ones you got. You always want to better yourself, always. I've seen some really holes that the kids hung out in." (Matty)

Sandy conveys the drive to take over the entire street bar area.

"And then we were like cockroaches, from [the Mardi Gras] we weaseled out of there and went right next door into the Chesterfield. Then we weaseled around the corner and went down to Division and we hit Dugan's . . . that was behind the Stage Door.[32] That's when we went in and we started taking showgirls then; we got to that bit. And then we went around the corner there to the Midtown, we hit that. We took over that, just about. And we just had that whole facility; we had all the corners. All the corners were ours."

In their push for more space, lesbians were most likely to be successful in the seedier bars.

"The space we were allowed to occupy was limited as far as the bars went. And the bars were our only territory. It was exciting when the prospect arose to occupy a new territory. We were all acutely aware of our stigma as homosexuals, both women and men. But the men had the cream of the crop as far as the bars went. Johnny's Sixty-Eight, The Oasis, and the plush Five O'Clock Club. Women were either admitted reluctantly or refused admission. And although Bingo's was exclusively a lesbian bar it was a dump compared to the Five O'Clock Club. The only avenue left for women to push into was the sleazy bars—unless a bar specifically invited women as patrons." (Toni)

In addition, some lesbians were specifically attracted to the clientele in these bars, excited and pained by the opportunity to be with other outcasts.

"Being a homosexual in that time slot meant you were already in the 'low life.' I felt anger at being relegated to the category of degenerate. . . . I figured as long as I was on the outskirts, on the fringes of respectability, I may as well explore this place I was in fully. My family would have been horrified. . . . Drinking in public bars was bad enough, but I was drinking with Blacks, which was taboo—along with the other people—homosexuals, pimps, prostitutes. It wasn't like, 'O.K., I'm queer, so now I'll get on with my life and become something wonderful.' Being a butch meant I was limited if it was only for

how I dressed, what I looked like. I was already an outcast and here in these
bars—this was my world. . . . It was a world that was unfamiliar and exciting."
(Toni)

Conflict with the straight men in these bars was also appealing. "I was even
attracted by the idea of fighting with men, and the violence, it attracted me, it
frightened me too" (Toni).

In Buffalo, lesbian ties with diverse elements of the sexual fringe extend back
at least into the 1940s. A prostitution network had coexisted with gay and lesbian
socializing at Ralph Martin's, although few, if any, lesbians had been involved. In
addition, lesbians had sought romantic liaisons with show girls who performed at
the Palace Burlesque. In the 1950s, it was not simply the prospect of dating
prostitutes that attracted the tough bar lesbians to the street bars. Lesbians and
prostitutes became integrated into a complex sexual subculture. Many butches
hustled money from straight men who came looking for sexual encounters; many
fems supported themselves by turning tricks.[33]

The most important reason for going to the street bars, and the one narrators
mentioned the most frequently, was the economic benefit to be gained from
contact with straight men.

> "I don't know if you've heard the story of back in those days, a lot of gay
> women were hustlers. They went out to get their drinks bought and roll these
> different guys. We used to always say if you've got entrance fee you could go
> out, 'cause all you had to do was sit and listen to some nongay man's B.S.,
> and he'd buy you drinks all night." (Bert)

Hustling was prevalent in street bars throughout the decade. Bert's statement is
similar to Sandy's who is of the next generation.

> "Now if you went to the Carousel you had to buy your drinks. The[re] was
> no one there to hustle a drink from. Lot of times we'd be in the Carousel,
> maybe we've got a couple of dollars, we'd go in there and we'd have a good
> time. . . . We're getting low, we'd look at our money and then three or five
> of us left. 'Let's go down to the Chesterfield see what we can hustle up.' So
> we'd go down there, make our money and go back to the Carousel. Or if we
> had a girl hustling, we'd go down to see if she's all right. . . . And go back to
> the Carousel. 'Cause like the Carousel at that time was all gay, you couldn't
> make any money there. All you could do was spend money."

Since society's prejudices undermined opportunities for steady work, the potential
for extra income at the street bars was very helpful.

Both fems and butches could manage to drink free for a whole evening in
exchange for listening to a straight man's line and acting interested and sympathetic.
Annie, a pretty blond fem who was knowledgeable about the world of prostitution,
remembers fems being key in this process.

"Oh the fems would more or less hustle the guy. . . . If the guy thought he was taking you to bed, you'd sit there and play up to the guy and get him to buy the drinks . . . [for yourself] and the butch. Not all guys would do that. And then a lot of time—I think the straight men, their curiosity was aroused. But they were more interested in the butchy girl than in the fem girl, 'cause maybe in their mind, they felt, maybe this girl's—just for her dressing and acting like a guy—well maybe her problem is she hasn't had a good lay." (Annie)

When asked how fems reacted to that Annie replies: "Nothing . . . let them get the drinks for a change." How did the butches react? "Nothing, and if then the guy tried to get too pushy as far as the guy's ego, and in his mind thinking, 'Well Jesus, I bought you a few drinks, aren't I gonna get anything?' Then the butchy girl would get a little on the nasty side with him" (Annie).

What is unique about this situation is the role of butches who became the object of straight men's interest and who learned to use that interest to their own advantage. Annie explains, "Some men took to them, not to have sex but they just—their ego, their curiosity." Always wise to the dangers these situations created, butches manipulated the considerable economic possibilities presented. Some even remember enjoying their conversations with the straight men who were buying drinks. "Yeah, if they [men] wanted to buy me drinks I'd let them buy me drinks, 'cause that meant money you saved. Sometimes I'd enjoy talking to these people, these nongay men, and end up becoming friends with them, when I wasn't out to take advantage of them" (Bert). When butches were out of work, they did not hesitate to use bolder tactics. Quite a few survived in between jobs by conning money from careless male patrons who had gone to the bar to purchase a good time.

"One of the things that was extremely prevalent during that time, and I became guilty of it too, was hustling the nongay man that came around looking. I hate to put it blunt, but, they used to say, they came in looking to eat pussy. Say, 'O.K. sucker, I'm going to get you but you're not going to get me.' There was a couple of women that I knew that actually went out and slept with the guys, but I never did. My little trick was to get 'em drunk enough and then get their money. And I'm not proud of these things, but these are the past and they're over. There was this one guy, and he was flashing all this money, and of course . . . everybody was trying to get this dude. So I thought up this idea, well I'll go home with him, and I'll let him think that he's gonna sleep with me, but I'll tell him I got to go take a bath first, meanwhile he'll pass out. And that happened and I got over five hundred and some dollars from the guy. Went home, showered, changed my clothes, and went out that night, and he came in; he started screaming at me in the bar that I rolled him and all that, and I said, 'I've never seen you before in my life fucker, get out of here.' I said, 'You keep this up and I'm going to call the police.' Looked at him right in the face. . . . And I did that on three occasions and I was confronted twice by the guys. But I was never frightened, because it was me and him and he couldn't prove it. It was a little game . . . take the money and run." (Bert)

Most takes were neither as big nor as dramatic as this. Sometimes the bar fights with straight men could produce a little money for the woman who was astute and agile. Bert also mentions hustling money in numerous skirmishes at Dugan's.

"Dugan's was really known for fighting, that's when it was mixed and there would be a lot of these kind of guys going up there. They'd get into a barroom fight or a street fight and I would pretend that I was trying to calm them down and while the guy was fighting I'd lift his wallet. Because they would be getting hit and pushed so much they didn't know the difference." (Bert)

Since the street bars were hangouts for prostitutes, these bars, by definition, also provided ample opportunity for lesbians to earn money by tricking. Many fems of this crowd earned their living this way.

"If you wanted to survive, and [you] didn't want to work, [you] didn't want to get up in the morning and go to work, 'cause maybe you were, the night before, drinking too much, or an everyday habit of drinking, and going down to the bars to hustle, which we did. That was your bread and butter." (Annie)

Bell, another fem who worked as a prostitute, remembers that the money was quite good. "Well if the man just wanted to be there for a short time it would be thirty to forty dollars. If he wanted like, figured a long time, it would be seventy-five or a hundred dollars. A long time . . . would be maybe twenty minutes."

In general, prostitution was an accepted occupation for fems, although the community was not completely free from self-righteous judgment, which angered Arlette, a stunningly beautiful and extremely competent Black fem:

"Then a lot of people had a lot of things against me, 'cause I had been a prostitute. But I tell them quick like this, I find a lot of gay ladies have women that are married. I said what's the difference. Dummy, you're going behind a man anyway. So don't put me in a category because I have gone out with a man for money. That you don't want to touch me. You don't want me doing anything but you're not gonna help me. So don't put me down 'cause I'm trying to live and look out for myself. But yet still I've seen gay ladies that have women that are married, and have to wait for her to sneak out. Well I mean after all, she is going behind a man still. What is the difference?"

Some fems worked out of the street bars and although they gained the protection of a lover and friends they also had to manage the tension of a lesbian presence while making connections with prospective Johns. On the whole they negotiated these conflicts well, keeping appropriate distance when necessary. However, every now and then the underlying tensions would erupt and a butch might become too possessive, or a fem might make the mistake of calling a butch a derogatory term in front of a straight man. Matty remembers being furious about the way a fem put her down:

> "I remember this one girl was leaning against the bar and this bunch of guys had a flashlight and were looking up her skirt. She turned to me and said, 'What are you looking at, cunt-lapper?' I got furious, I said to her, 'Are you talking to me?' She said 'I don't see any other cunt-lapper here.' I jumped over the bar and had her against the wall by the throat. One of the guys came up behind me and I hit him in the gut with my elbow and he went flying. I said, 'Don't you ever say anything to me again.' She said to me, 'I'm gay, I'm gay.' I said, 'I don't care if you're gay, you disgust me. If you're gay, for the first time I'm ashamed of it.' "

Some fems preferred not to work where they and their butches socialized, and some worked in several places. A few were higher class prostitutes who worked in quite different areas.

> "Let's say some would be very private about it. Now like I had a straight girl friend which I hung around, and there was times when I did my separation bit between the gays and then being with her. 'Cause, [she was] strictly a hustler. And then when you make your money then you come back, you go back where you want to be. It was that type of thing." (Annie)

Although many of the fems were prostitutes, they by no means constituted the majority of the prostitutes at these bars. A close tie existed between the straight and gay prostitutes. They often worked together and exchanged information. The straight prostitutes also socialized with butches and sometimes had affairs with them on the side. " 'Cause a lot of those girls really did, the hookers, 'cause they got their affection [from butches]. They didn't get the mistreatment and things like they had. They'd sit there and buy you drinks just because you were nice to them" (Sandy). Jan reminisces with pleasure about the time she spent hanging out with hookers.

> "But like I said, when I was younger I used to hang around with a few of the hookers. We'd either have a couple of drinks and stuff or I'd drive them to their apartment . . . and I'd take their car. Or we'd go away for weekends, which they had no connections or no ties, where other women in the area either had boyfriends or married and they couldn't just take off and go away for a weekend. And I felt they were freer . . . and that's what I wanted. . . . In fact, some of the guys involved with them approached me, like I was a pimp or something, say, 'Where's so and so? I'd say,' 'Gee, I don't know.' "

Not surprisingly, given this complex relationship between butches and prostitutes, male pimps had mixed feelings about butches. "Some [pimps] disliked us very much, but a lot of them did like us because they knew their girl was [safe] when they were with us" (Sandy).

Street bars not only offered sex for hire, but had reputations for catering to a wide variety of tastes, which were enhanced by the presence of lesbians.

"If, say, a fem, or even a butch was the—as they say—the bisexual type, turning tricks, the [straight men] would be there, and it would be a money situation. They would like to do the same thing as the butches would do—[oral sex]. Where they wouldn't be able to do it with a regular girl. See, they used to have these little quirks and they figured they could do it with the gay people. . . . So, this is why a guy would come in and buy drinks like crazy and if he found someone to go along with his ideas, that would be it." (D.J.)[34]

Bell, a white fem who was ambivalent about working as a prostitute, but never able to solidify other options, remembers that the interests of the straight male clientele were not limited to oral sex.

"One thing that you hear most of the hookers speak about is going down on a guy, I never did this. . . . I don't care what anybody says, I just refused to do that. I had different guys during the course of this thing that wanted weird things like being tied up and beaten with a belt and one guy that wanted you to walk around with your underwear on. Some that just wanted to be jerked off. . . . Some of them would like the sadism bit—in other words, you'd like to stand there and get beat with a belt and your wife wouldn't do this. She'd think you're some kind of nut, where he would get his kicks from the girls doing this." (Bell)

Although Bell was paid well for her services, the work sometimes left her emotionally raw. Beating a male client was an ambiguous experience, filled with feelings of satisfaction at being able to hurt, but disgust with the pleasure it brought.

"Yeah, I love[d] it. I thought it was great. . . . Because I felt like I could beat the shit out of him, and he couldn't do a damn thing about it you know. Here a man and that dirty thing between his legs, I sure didn't want it in me. So he said to me, 'We're gonna do this and that.' I said, 'That's fine,' and he brought the belt and stuff with him and I beat the fucking shit out of him. Because I just couldn't—I've never really, from the time I was small, have liked anything about a man, their looks, their actions or anything. I just felt that within me so strongly. . . . Yes, and I felt like I could just beat him to death. But he loved it, and he got a pleasure out of it, and that's the only way that some of these crazy assholes would come. . . . Certainly he did [come], and ugh, it was sickening though. . . . I insisted on at least a hundred dollars, I didn't care if it took five minutes. . . . I wouldn't do it for anything less. . . . Well, it was a lot of work, very strenuous and mind boggling, because at the same time I'm knocking him with the belt and he's all 'Ohh,' and I'm ready to puke my guts out."

Although it was known and accepted throughout the tough bar lesbian community that many fems were prostitutes, the same was not true about butches.

Whereas all other ways of hustling money from straight men enhanced butches' reputations as bold survivors, turning tricks met with strong disapproval from other butches. Nevertheless, occasionally butches did capitalize on the street bars' reputation for providing sex for hire, taking a small share of the business for themselves. Sandy remembers how she wanted nothing to do with such butches; they couldn't be in her crowd.

> "Well, I didn't like it too much, 'cause I always felt it was a reflection on us, on all of us. Which it was. . . . 'Cause one or two might go and really be the worst, you know, maybe even do it for nothing, who the hell knows, I don't know. What do you expect, the guy would come in and think you're all like that. A lot of shit came down over that."

Fems agree that it was rare for butches to engage in prostitution but affirm that it did happen. "There's a few, there's a couple, but they were very private on that and very discreet on it. I know one or two. I know of one, I mean when the belly started getting bigger" (Annie).

Contrary to what has been fully documented for the gay male community, and what has been hinted at about the lesbian community, almost all prostitution was heterosexual.[35] With very few exceptions female-female prostitution was not part of this culture. Many butch narrators had been propositioned by women while driving cabs, or walking the streets, and most turned them down, except for the rare occasions when they accepted the opportunity as an adventure to show off their sexual prowess. Fems do not recall ever being propositioned by a woman. "But for a woman to come and offer to pay, strictly just another woman, no. No. Usually it would be like a husband and wife team together" (Annie). And that was rare.

Pimping was another way of making money in the street bars. It was not as taboo as butches turning tricks, but was controversial for this lesbian community. Male pimps were an established part of the street bar scene. Female pimps were not institutionalized in the same way, but a few definitely existed. Of the three fem narrators who were prostitutes during the late 1950s, only one, Bell, had a pimp, and she was female.

Bell's experience was very unpleasant. Once she freed herself from the relationship, she never had one again, although she remained a prostitute for many years. Bell was lured into the life by her first lover.

> "I wasn't working at the time and the idea of what she was telling me sounded really good to me. Not in terms of going out with the men, but in terms that I would have money in my pocket and we would do this and we would do that. . . . She told me that she had a bunch of friends that she would like me to meet, and these friends were interested in parties. They would be interested in seeing a nice girl, and they wouldn't be rough with me or they wouldn't be unkind with me, but that they would pay me well, and I would not have

to go through any bullshit, I would just have to do what these guys wanted and it would be over with. . . . Well the first time I did have a date and these men were Black. . . . There were two of them, and the guy, I went into the room with him, and he just totally couldn't be pleased in any way, he was just impossible. And I . . . came out and I told her, 'I just can't go through this type of thing.' And she just insisted, so I took care of the first guy and then there was another guy there and he wanted a party. He wanted her and I to go together in front of him. And she refused. She said, 'You can go to bed with my friend, but I will not be a part of it.' And I thought, 'God this all stinks, it's good enough for me to do but not for her to do.' . . . I felt like a piece of shit, really. Like a damn piece of rotten shit. And the more I thought about this, and it was making me more bitter and more bitter. This didn't end incidentally, it ended up that I was going into hotels, seeing guys, turning a lot of tricks. . . . I would have to get that money in the beginning, in front as they would call it, before I would even take my clothes off. I mean she explained all these things to me, really taught me the ropes by sitting down and telling me each and every detail of how to do this."

Bell didn't like the situation, but had a hard time extricating herself. Her pimp sometimes resorted to violence to keep her working. Bell finally broke away after she was raped by two men who offered her a ride late one night. Her pimp not only did not offer her adequate protection, but was also the reason she was out alone so late. Bell had been afraid to go home with so little money. From this devastating experience she knew she had to change her life.

Arlette claims that there were very few female pimps, and in fact, she could think of only one, Jacki Jordan.[36] Arlette knew Jacki quite well and disapproved of her behavior.

"I got curious about Jacki Jordan and soon found out I didn't like her idea of being gay at all. Because she wanted to be a pimp. I find that a lot of these gay studs want to be so much man that they figure that a woman got to get out and hustle for them. And I never went for that, 'cause I say, 'Hey baby, what you think, I'm gonna wear myself out and save you. You're crazy. . . . We both get out here together. I got what you like. You the one that likes women. Now what the hell I'm gonna pay you to be? Nooo. What the hell I'm gonna hustle for a woman for? You got the same thing I got, I'm not gonna wear myself out to save yourself for. You walk around half virgin or what not.' "

Arlette makes a clear distinction between pimping—having a stable of women—and "having some women on the street," that is, taking care of a girlfriend who is a prostitute. For most people, but not all, in the community, the latter was acceptable. Piri remembers resenting that many people characterized her as a brute because of her economic relationship with prostitutes. "I did have girls that was hustling and what not, but hey, that was my business. They wanted to work and

I wanted to do my thing, I did my thing and they do theirs. But don't look at me as no big brutal thing because I'm off into this other thing."

Butches had various ideas about pimping, some choosing to trick with men in order to keep the favors of their fems for themselves as Arlette recalls.

> "Then you find some that don't want you to have anything to do with a man. Then I've had some studs that hustled for me, and didn't want nobody touching me. They would go out on the corner. Yes, they would go out on the corner and hustle and I stayed home. And they would bring me money every day. Nobody touched me. If anybody had to go they would go. And I had that happen. Say well, O.K., I didn't mind staying at home at all. Get fresh money every day, why not. It made more sense to me than me going out there for them. If you can't get a job, you can't support me, then fine. I like it better that way then me having to go out there and take care of you. You're supposed to be the fella."

The way of life of the lesbian street bars makes real the saying that to be butch you had to be "rough, tough, and ready." Lesbians learned to survive and, to the extent it was possible, master this difficult environment, which historically was organized to exploit women. In some cases women exploited women, but in the majority, butches and fems used this environment to women's advantage.

The lesbian presence in street bars was due to the convergence of the many factors that distinguished the period. The tough bar lesbians became bolder about confronting straight men and had no hesitancy about engaging in physical conflict with them; when necessary they worked together to defend their space. Their experience on the street prepared them to take advantage of straight men's sexual interest while maintaining the upper hand. They were also constantly looking to expand their territory, to take over, or at least find a niche in what was not yet established as lesbian space. Furthermore, the hustling environment fraught with danger and daring, easily accommodated both Black and white women, and built bridges between them.

Besides the challenge the bars provided, they were also economically beneficial. For the younger tough lesbians, who wanted to socialize as lesbians as much as possible, and in the case of butches who felt compelled to dress in a masculine style all the time, and therefore had trouble holding on to jobs, survival was made possible for long periods by the money they made in the bars. For those who had more or less steady employment, a supplement was always welcome, and between jobs, the money came in very handy. When asked whether the challenge to hustle came from herself or peer pressure, Bert replies, "I think myself. . . . My rationale for doing it was, well if I don't do it somebody else will. 'Cause they'd come in and set themselves up for it." Conning men who were out to take advantage of women was what it was all about. It gave lesbians a feeling of power, and often revenge.

Narrators' memories of this period are predominantly those of pride in having handled such difficult situations. In many cases there is also an undercurrent of resentment at having been forced into this environment because they were lesbians. None of them regrets her toughness, or her hustling. They felt they did what they had to do to survive. "But you know something, when I talk to my counselor I can't tell her, I can't look at her with a straight face and tell her that I was ashamed of it, because I wasn't exactly at that time" (Bell). Even those who have changed their lives radically accept their having hustled straight men. "I tell the people where I [work now], 'You think you know me now, I have cleaned my act up so much, you don't begin to know' " (Bert).

CONTRADICTIONS IN THE SOCIAL LIFE OF TOUGH BAR LESBIANS: BINGO'S

If lesbians had only patronized the street bars, they might have been mired in a completely dead-end existence. Little Gerry remembers the depressing nature of these bars. "Nobody was inspired to rise. At that time there was a sleazy bar called the Chesterfield that was for women, and it was usually a tough group of women that went in there, and that's where you were going to stay forever." But the street bars were simply one aspect of the tough bar lesbian's social life. Those who were out and about participated in other arenas and built different environments.

Because of the proximity of the bars, "a night out might mean that you and your friends would go from one bar to the other." All the tough bar lesbians, butches and fems alike, remember "circling" among the bars. In addition to Dugan's, the Mardi Gras, and the Chesterfield, they went to Bingo's and the Carousel, and all the other bars that were hospitable to gays:

> "If you went out on a Saturday night you hit every gay bar that was going. You went in one bar and had a few drinks and went in another and had a few drinks then you went back to the first bar to see if anyone was there. You just kept circling all night long. You never got bored, because everyone was circulating and every time you went in there was different people in there."
> (Matty)

People were the key to a good time. Bert recalls that she didn't go to every bar every night. "It depended upon the night, I guess, how many people there would be. You'd want to be where the people were, where the action was, so to speak." Action meant bars that were busy and crowded.

Although very small, Bingo's was central to the social life of the tough lesbians. It could accommodate about fifty people and had a capacity crowd on weekends. "Bingo's . . . I used to get off from work and I'd go down there, especially on a

Friday or Saturday and you would wonder if they were holding the crowd upstairs on the roof or something and pressed a button and let the elevator down because it would be that packed as small as the place was" (Marla). Another narrator remembers, "On the weekend it was so jammed you could hardly move. I went on a Friday night and it was just wall-to-wall women." To newcomers the scene was awesome: "There were so many different kinds of women in there, women I had never seen anything like before in my life, real out-and-out lesbians in men's clothing" (Toni).

Bingo's was located near the street bars; in fact, for its first several years it was a street bar, but for reasons unknown to us it changed. Its appearance was that of an ordinary dive as Iris recalls: "It was just a scrubby little bar, and I mean a scrubby little bar." Toni still remembers its appearance with distaste and resentment: "[Bingo's] was an awful dump. Nobody cared because it was a woman's bar, but it was just kind of one big rambleshack room." The bar was one room with a few booths and bar stools. Two features distinguished it sharply from the street bars. First, it served no hard liquor, only beer, which made its atmosphere thoroughly working class. Second, its patrons were primarily lesbians. The few men who frequented the bar were friends of the owner, or regulars who "got along with the girls."

Narrators all agree that Bingo, the proprietor, liked lesbians and that lesbians were welcome at his bar, at least as early as 1953. "You have to understand . . . people go where they're treated good, regardless. Bingo's was a dump but he treated the girls really good . . . so you went there" (Matty). Bingo maintained good relationships with his customers. He would make parties for people's birthdays or holidays. And although he officially condoned no overt homosexual behavior, this was easily gotten around. "There were booths that had high backs and I know people would sneak in there and neck or maybe—oh in the bathroom, people would follow you into the bathroom or in the back where the owner couldn't see, people would come back and start kissing and stuff" (Toni). Bingo was never harsh with his patrons.

To maintain a primarily lesbian clientele in this area during this time period required a bouncer. "Sometimes five or six guys would come into Bingo's looking to beat up the girls. . . . You could tell by the looks in their eyes, by the way they walked in that they were looking to fight" (Stormy). Bingo hired lesbian bartenders who could also function as bouncers. Stormy, who worked this job, reminisces about her prowess: "I was a natural bouncer. I broke up fights all the time. I never hit anybody. I used to just pick them up and throw them." She adds that she had learned judo in the Marines. Sometimes the lesbian clientele helped to keep order. Stormy remembers a time when "somebody went from Bingo's to Dugan's and got the girls" to take care of a fight. On the whole, Bingo's was successful in keeping out straight men. Their minimal presence meant that there were fewer brawls and less tension and pressure than in the street bars. "[At Bingo's] I can't ever remember being afraid for my life or afraid anybody was gonna hit me in there" (Toni).

In Bingo's the tough bar lesbians continued the 1940s tradition of creating a fun-loving and supportive environment where lesbians could meet one another in dignity. They met prospective lovers, had fun with their current partners, and hung around with their friends. Their lives were multidimensional, able to encompass humor and romance as well as violence. One butch narrator articulates precisely why gay women needed a place like Bingo's; hanging out in street bars could never have been enough because they were not conducive to romance. "You were always looking for someone that was going to be yours, that you're going to find someone. So like we went to Bingo's because it was known as a gay bar, so you kept saying, well somebody will come in" (Sandy). Bell confirms how central Bingo's was to her social life:

> "It seemed like most of the things that were happening to me then were centered around Bingo's. I went to the Carousel, I went to many other bars, Chesterfield, Dugan's, the Mardi Gras. I sort of circled around, but the main things that were happening to me were happening from Bingo's bar, the people that I was meeting and seeing and socializing with were at Bingo's."

Good times with friends are prominent in narrators' memories: "At Bingo's people would sit around and sing, harmonize. It was like family; there was a camaraderie you don't find today" (Bert). Often people would play pranks, such as in this story, variations of which we heard from several narrators:

> "It was funny at Bingo's—the bar was small. You went through a little room into the back room which was his kitchen, it had a sink and a refrigerator. The ladies room was there. His beer was there. So, maybe there would be four or five of us waiting to go to the ladies room, and he'd have all these cases of beer sitting there, and we used to sit there on the cases of beer and drink his warm beer. We'd go to the ladies room, and we'd come back out and we'd be half-smashed on warm beer. We really had a good time though. We never really hurt him, or anything. We'd just drink his warm beer." (Iris)

Friends would relax together and shoot the breeze.

> "I didn't think about this in a long time, but I remember when I went [West] I missed this. We used to sit in the bars and tell, I guess you'd call them dirty stories, by the hour, that was part of the pastime. You'd tell jokes back and forth and then one would remind you [of another]; you'd sit there for a whole evening." (Bert)

Iris expands on these memories: "Sometimes you'd laugh so hard the tears would be rolling down your face. Your stomach would be hurting from laughing so hard."

Most narrators remember the atmosphere as warmer and more congenial than the bars of today. "Everybody was everybody's friend, and you walked in and said 'hi' to everybody, walked up to the bar. It wasn't real cliquey. Like now they come in groups and they stay in their groups" (Matty). In the bar, lesbians usually sat at a table or a booth with friends. Generally, fights did not occur between butches of the same friendship group. " 'Cause they wouldn't have remained friends very long. If there were people that you would tend to fight with, then you would stay away from them, you stayed your distance" (Bert).

The tough bar lesbians spent as much of their free time as possible in the bars. "The biggest part of our life was the bars—because there wasn't any other alternative" (Bert). They rarely socialized in other settings. After the bars closed they might go out to eat, or go to an all-night bowling alley, or on a few occasions to someone's home. They had very few house parties. "There weren't as many house parties. Where there were house parties, they were usually after hours, at least of the people that I traveled with" (Bert). Furthermore, they hardly ever made special outings with small groups of friends, or invited friends to their homes. Their culture deemphasized the importance of home life. Also, the general tightness of money, due to the underemployment of many of these lesbians made them have to set strict priorities about how they spent their money, and socializing in bars was at the top of the list, particularly since some of the bars afforded an extra source of income.

The social life of these tough bar lesbians, which encompassed the good times of socializing in gay and lesbian bars, the dangers and hostility of the street bars, and the oppressive forces of straight society, was fraught with contradictions. Community solidarity had a strong undercurrent of individualism and competition. Leadership, although concerned about the well-being of lesbians, was increasingly defensive. And friendships, though many, were limited in their intimacy.

Tough bar lesbians had a definite sense of community solidarity as well as powerful feelings of belonging. "Barrooms were a way of life; that's where you were among friends. I think it's a place where you could let your hair down; could really be yourself" (Bert). The camaraderie that built up in bars through the good times and the fights was very strong. It supported each individual lesbian's right to be who she was and live in community with others, and it reinforced the daring necessary to defend such a community. Many narrators emphasize the solidarity of the times, and like Bell, think it is one of the most important things that this book can convey: "Back then in the fifties when I came out, everything had really a togetherness, things were so much different, and it's important, I think, that people know that we were for one another, not against one another, and we shared many things."

The solidarity offered tremendous support in a society which was hostile to lesbians:

"Well, you know, what I really think it was, it was our own form of an
extended family during that time, but [we were] not aware of that was what
it was. I think of an extended family in the terms of people that we felt
comfortable with that we could be ourselves. There was no phoniness there,
you were yourself and that was that." (Bert)

Bert had attempted suicide in the early 1950s while in the Army, and again in the
mid-1960s when she left Buffalo. She attributed these attempts to low self-esteem.
When asked if she hadn't had low self-esteem when she was part of the bar scene
in Buffalo, from the mid-1950s to early 1960s, she responded, "Not really. I guess
it was the sense of community in the fifties that prevented it. There was a sense
of community."

Community solidarity was developed enough to give rise to well-known leaders
whose influence extended beyond a small circle of friends. Narrators' memories
are filled with references to leadership, such as, "They were two of the, I guess,
the star dykes around town." The leaders themselves were aware of their role, and
were not shy about remembering themselves as being "on top." Bert reminisces,
"Well I always say that I've considered myself kind of on top, I don't know, I was
always a leader." Sandy, who emerged as a leader at the end of the 1950s, a period
of flamboyant toughness, was renowned as one of the best or more perfect butches.
"Being the best" was important to her, particularly because of lesbian oppression.

"Well, even growing up I wore a cowboy outfit. It always had to be Roy
Rogers. I was king of the cowboys. See he wore the white hat—I never
outgrew that. . . . To this day, I want to be the best. And I still am in my time,
for my time era I am. I'm not the best but I mean I'm on top. . . . It was
respect. You didn't go out and work your ass off for respect. And nobody
would respect you being queer. . . . My role was, and at that time it was always
a more aggressive role. I had to be good at it, because everything else about
me was . . . knocked down. I could never do anything and make it, I couldn't."

Sandy still takes a lot of pleasure in her leadership role during this period. "It was
fun being top, for a while you know. At least, if I don't have anything, I have
beautiful memories. I've got those."

In this dangerous environment, leadership was primarily concerned with effective survival. The bar community valued a person's ability to protect and defend
herself and the people around her in the bars and on the street. Since these were
butch characteristics, leadership was limited to that role. These were also the
qualities required by people tending bar at the time, and many, though not all,
leaders did such work. (As will be discussed in the next chapter, the community
that centered around house parties offered more opportunities for fem leadership.)
At first the leaders were strong individuals who liked challenges and could hold
their own in any situation. "I was . . . strong, individualistic. I can't tell you that
was what they respected, but I would have a feeling that would be about it" (Bert).

These early leaders were not averse to physical fighting, but only fought if it became necessary. They took care of others in a variety of ways. They were effective mediators. In addition they might offer someone a place to stay. Bert recalls the tension her generosity would cause with her lover:

> "I was notorious for bringing people home after the bar closed . . . [for] something to eat or a place to stay. In fact, Gail used to tell me she knows of people who bring home stray animals and I was always bringing home stray people. . . . I just felt sorry for people and tried to help them. . . . Maybe their family found out they were gay and they didn't have a place to go."

As the decade progressed, the tone and style of leadership became both more aggressive and more defensive. The leaders of the younger tough bar lesbians were poised and ready to fight. Sandy describes her comrades: "They called a spade a spade. There was no pretending. We were what we were, and we fought for what we wanted, where half of them wouldn't. We didn't take any shit, from men or women. And of course we were always on the defensive, because at that time you had to be." Prowess in fighting was the hallmark of this group, but always in the context of concern for the entire community. Little Gerri recalls the qualities she and others respected in Vic and Sandy: "Whether they liked you or not, if someone came into the bar and started trouble with any lesbian, you would know they would be messing with [the two of] them. If there was any trouble they would back you up. They were the people people asked questions of."

These younger leaders began to set and defend the standard for appropriate behavior in the late 1950s, introducing new elements of competition. Sandy affirms that her group "ruled" other butches. When asked what that meant, she replies:

> "Oh it meant like——oh geez, I'm trying to think, so it won't sound stupid. At the time I was out, naturally, you'd always talk about your time, so that was my time. So we had a certain place set, we had the bar that we went to, whether it was Bingo's or Mardi Gras or any of those dives down there. We had a place there. And if we didn't like some[thing] . . . we took care of it. . . . And the worst thing I know that always bothered me, and I know it bothered Vic, it bothered Ronni, bothered all those that stood more or less for our image. . . . These other ones that would come in and turn a trick, and are dressed like we are, and are supposedly butches, and they would go out and turn a trick. . . . Then pretty soon you might be in there, myself, with whoever I'm with, it could be my . . . girl . . . you try to make an impression. You take her to places, you're saying, 'Well this is my friend,' you want to introduce her to say your best buddy, a bunch of people, or your pack or whatever. And some guy [says], 'Hey want to go?' and he says, 'You know, twenty to get laid and thirty a blow job or whatever,' and it's her [the one who turns tricks], and you say, 'Get the hell out of here.' [He says] 'What are you acting so funny tonight? I know your type, I was with you last night and you laid and you laid my buddy or you sucked, you blowed, whatever they

were doing.' And so that was a reflection on us. And we didn't put up with
that too much, and . . . [we] were not with those people. And if we saw enough
of them outside getting a slap in the mouth we didn't help. . . . It had to be,
it had to be. You can't be out there fucking around and then come in there
and say well I'm——and stand up next to us and be with us, we don't fuck.
We want women. And if we don't have any money then we go broke for a
while. Or maybe our girlfriend helps us, but we give it back. We don't go out
and fuck for it. And that was high standard. I mean you could kick my ass on
the street, kick it and stomp it and pour acid on me and disintegrate me right
there but you can never say I was out fucking." (Sandy)

These leaders both energized the community, by establishing goals that fostered
lesbian pride, and undermined it, by provoking internal conflict and competition.

The confrontational style of the tough bar butch in this hostile environment
affected their interpersonal relations. Although they formed an amiable comradeship and were allies in protecting their world against outsiders, they did not
develop friendship groups that lasted through time. Their friendships were neither
intimate nor close. "I know a lot of people but I have very few close friends. I
mean I have a lot of friends but very few close friends" (Vic). When asked whether
she considered Sandy her friend, Vic replies: "No, not friends, as you'd call. We
were probably comrades, butches or things like that, but not friends. I don't have
any gay friends. . . . I don't spend any time with anybody, any one person other
than the person that I'm with [that is my lover]." Sandy views the two of them
as friends, but also emphasizes the distance between them.

> "Vic, I consider about like a pretty trustworthy friend. I've known her for
> years, we've gotten along about everything. We almost think alike, her and I.
> Yet, she has a different way, different way entirely than I do, different
> conception of life. Like her——I don't really know what hers is, but I know its
> not my way. Because that's why——oh I wouldn't have said I've seen her once
> for the first time in ten years if we were so much alike. I just have my way,
> everybody's different."

Even though they express respect for one another and acknowledge some similarities, these butches rarely see one another more than twice a year, and many not
even that often, now that they don't go to the bars together.

Fems did not develop "comrades" like butches, and tended to be more isolated.
Stormy recounts, "We [butches] were a gang. Maybe there were fems who would
attach themselves to a butch gang, but there was no fem gang." Bell remembers
spending time primarily in the company of butches.

> "But it seemed to me more of my friends were like butch types. . . . I don't
> know how to say that, let's see, it was like sometimes the fems at that time
> . . . they depended on their butches for so many things. The butches were so
> strong and strong looking. I felt like in sitting down and talking to them I just

felt more at ease about things and more satisfied to have more butch friends than I did fem friends."

Although fem friendships were not institutionalized like those of butches, they sometimes did occur, and in such cases they tended to be both close and intimate. Annie remembers being inseparable from her fem friends, who were prostitutes like herself, but even these friendships did not last.

The dramatic difference between the friendship forms of the tough bar lesbians of the 1950s and the lesbians of the 1940s seems to be related to their socializing completely in a bar environment. The defensive stance and the related competition for lovers and for positions of control did not encourage the vulnerability necessary for intimate friendships.

Although these tough lesbians had little regard for straight men beyond economic benefit, they had various degrees of relationship with gay men. The older butches and fems developed friendships with gay men and enjoyed their company in the bars. "Back in those days I traveled mostly with gay men, my closest friends were gay men, and I used to go into some of the men's bars" (Bert). The younger lesbians had little or no association with them and considered their presence in the women's bars at best a passing pleasantry, at worst an irritation. Jan never completely trusted them: "I really basically believe that there is no such thing as a gay man. I mean I think they're mostly all bisexual. . . . Oh you can have good buddies that won't think of you as sexually [available]. . . . I have had some real good gay friends in fact, I still have a few, but I don't bother with them too much." In general, relationships were limited to those occasions when public interaction was inescapable. Because of the great differences in ways of socializing between the tough bar lesbians and the bar-oriented gay men of this decade, contact was usually amicable but distant and both groups found the situation appropriate.

Tough bar lesbians made a radical break with their predecessors of the 1940s. Their visibility unquestionably expanded the presence of lesbians in the world of the 1950s. As they affirmed their right to live as lesbians, they made it easier for other lesbians to find them, and more difficult for the heterosexual community to ignore them. The shift in public attitudes towards gays and lesbians during the 1960s, as typified by the press's move from silence about gays to its fascination with the exotic and unknown, required at its root a persistently obvious bar culture.[37] In addition, by spending as much time as possible in the bars under difficult conditions, tough bar lesbians created a strong sense of community solidarity and belonging that included women of diverse ethnic and racial groups. They also developed strong leaders, including bartenders and bouncers, who actively worked to expand, protect, and defend the community. The tough male image represented lesbians taking care of themselves. Together these changes laid the groundwork for considering lesbians a distinct but worthwhile group of people. Because tough bar lesbians used a direct confrontational approach in dealing with the powerful straight world, their forms of resistance were fraught with contradictions that limited their effectiveness. Nevertheless their culture unmistakably left the 1940s behind, having as much in common with the forms of lesbian resistance which were to emerge in the following decade, as they did with the past.

To the best of our knowledge, we are the first researchers to note these changes in working-class lesbian culture and social life during the 1950s and recognize them as part of lesbian political history. Such an analysis raises interesting questions about whether the 1950s was indeed a more repressive decade for lesbians than the 1940s.[38] From the point of view of aggressive acts of the state against lesbians, the 1950s is unquestionably more repressive than the 1940s. But from the point of view of individual working-class lesbians looking to end their isolation, the 1940s were perhaps more difficult. Lesbians in the 1940s had to find and build community without much tradition. Although they were not aggressively persecuted by the state, the repercussions of being identified as lesbian were severe in terms of work and family. Just to socialize together on weekends pushed to the maximum what was possible without losing the means of earning a livelihood, or the emotional support of family or friends. Despite state repression, working-class lesbians in the 1950s continued developing lesbian community and culture and were able to break new ground toward ending secrecy and defending themselves. The effect of state repression and violence on the street was to make lesbian resistance more defensive, but it did not disrupt the expanding presence of lesbians.

This new history of tough bar lesbians also suggests the need for revision in the general history of the 1950s. Lesbians should be placed alongside civil-rights and labor activists as forces representing a strong radical resistance to the dominant conservatism. In fact, lesbian resistance during this period was more complex than that represented in this one chapter. Our perspective, which focuses on working-class culture and the internal developments in lesbian community as well as external forces in society at large, reveals other angles—the desegregation of the bars, the emergence of class divisions—some of which were catalyzed by the tough bar lesbians, others of which developed independently; these need to be understood to convey the fullness of lesbian resistance and are the subject of the next chapter.

4

"MAYBE 'CAUSE THINGS WERE HARDER... YOU HAD TO BE MORE FRIENDLY": RACE AND CLASS IN THE LESBIAN COMMUNITY OF THE 1950s

---

"And we found some that really broke down and liked us. We ended up going with some of them. And we found some, the next thing that came out, you're a nigger lover and all that stuff. We ran into that quite a bit. I thought, hey, you're gay, it doesn't make a difference what color you are. If you're gay, you like somebody, you just like somebody."

—Arlette

Lesbians were probably the only Black and white women in New York City in the fifties who were making any real attempt to communicate with each other; we learned lessons from each other, the values of which were not lessened by what we did not learn.

—Audre Lorde, *Zami*

"Well there was always cliques as far as that goes. You had your snooties and dooties, and people that were down to earth, and it's mixed. If they want to talk to you they talk to you. And if they didn't, well, there's always somebody else to talk to. That's the way I always looked at it."

—D.J.

The emergence of the tough bar lesbian was only one aspect of the changes in the lesbian community during the 1950s. Black lesbians expanded their house parties to last the entire weekend and began the process of desegregating the bars. At the same time a group of upwardly mobile white lesbians carved out a space for themselves at the Carousel. As a result, the lesbian community became increasingly complex with an underlying tension between the unity of one large community in the face of common oppression as lesbians and the integrity of separate subcommunities each with its own strategies of resistance. Throughout the decade the tough bar lesbians—Black and white—represented the expanding consciousness of solidarity between and among lesbians.

Gloria Joseph and bell hooks both write that the Black lesbian, unlike the Black gay man, has been culturally invisible in the Black community.[1] When she was acknowledged it was always in a derogatory manner. Despite this fact, there has been a substantial presence of Black lesbians in Black communities in cities such as Buffalo at least since the 1950s, as there probably was earlier.[2] For most Black lesbians their roots were firmly established in their Black communities and, in the 1950s, their social lives were led within these communities. Drawing on the strong Black tradition of self activity to resist oppression, they created lively house parties, reminiscent of the rent parties and buffet flats of the 1920s and 1930s, where lesbians could socialize free from the bother of straight men.[3]

The separateness of the Black lesbian community was partially due to racial prejudice which made segregation the unofficial but pervasive custom of tavern and neighborhood life in the North. When Black lesbians initiated the desegregation of white bars during the 1950s, the step was part of the general twentieth-century struggle of African Americans for a better life. Landmark events, such as the awarding of the Pulitzer Prize for poetry to Gwendolyn Brooks and the Nobel Peace Prize to Ralph Bunche in 1950, brought to national prominence the contributions of African Americans to U. S. cultural life. In 1954 the Supreme Court issued its momentous decision, Brown vs. Topeka, which mandated the end to segregated schooling.[4] In Buffalo, the struggle for racial justice was slow and painful, and lesbians were among the pioneers. Tensions erupted on Memorial Day weekend in 1956—the same year lesbian bar desegregation began—when a fight broke out on the Canadiana, the ferry that took people from Buffalo to Crystal Beach, Ontario, a popular Canadian amusement park and summer community across Lake Erie.[5] Some people remember the fight as a full scale race riot. After this event, racial violence became common wherever Black and white youths came together for public events—rock concerts, movie theaters, and even street-corner gatherings. The ability of lesbians to achieve a more multiracial social life than most other social groups at that time suggests that tough bar lesbians, Black and white, created a lesbian consciousness that crossed racial divisions and projected a unity to the outside world.

Once the bars were desegregated, the Black lesbian community continued to maintain its relative autonomy just adding the bars as one more place to socialize. By giving parties in their own neighborhoods, Black lesbians could escape the restrictions of white bar owners and remove themselves temporarily from the racial tensions that accompanied desegregation. A variation on this same pattern of Black lesbian social life existed in New York City, suggesting that it was a national phenomenon. In her biomythography, Audre Lorde describes socializing in the Greenwich Village bars, as well as in Black house parties in Brooklyn and Queens.[6] Although the bars offered the company of other lesbians which she needed and desired, ultimately she always felt alone in these settings because there were so few Black women, and the structures of racism prevented them from connecting with one another. At house parties she felt nourished by the shared culture. Going to both house parties and bars was a way to cultivate being both Black and gay.

At the same time as desegregation brought two relatively distinct lesbian communities into regular contact, creating, in some contexts at least, one larger complex community, this larger community now developed class divisions. In the bars, the primarily white, upwardly mobile crowd was distinctly uncomfortable associating with the tougher, more obvious crowd.[7] Its culture and strategies of resistance were entirely different. As the tougher lesbians moved in the direction of ending the double life and being more open about who they were, the upwardly mobile lesbians—Black and white—gave more and more emphasis to discretion. They wanted to be less obvious in order to achieve acceptance in society. At a time when lesbianism was severely stigmatized, this strategy, which had already been articulated in the 1940s by writers such as Robert Duncan, Jo Sinclair, and James Baldwin, allowed a lesbian to reclaim and affirm her humanity.[8]

Nationally, the expansion of white-collar work for women after the war created increased opportunity for achieving success and fulfillment without the support of husbands.[9] Many working-class lesbians took advantage of this opportunity and were in fact able to succeed. Although this upwardly mobile group was relatively small in Buffalo, which is predominantly a blue-collar town, it is our guess that in more cosmopolitan cities like San Francisco and New York, it had the numbers to generate the politically conscious leadership of the homophile movement.

This chapter will continue exploring changes in lesbian culture and consciousness during the 1950s by focusing on issues of race and class, and by identifying their effect on forms of lesbian resistance. We analyze the desegregation of the bars, the social life of Black lesbians in house parties, and of white upwardly mobile lesbians in the bars, and consider the implications of class and race divisions for community solidarity and consciousness. We attempt to understand whether, as a predecessor to gay liberation, this complex community is best understood as one, or as several. To better place the 1950s community in history, we document the forces that destabilized bar life during the 1960s and brought to a close this era of lesbian history in Buffalo.

DESEGREGATING THE BUFFALO LESBIAN COMMUNITY

By the mid-1950s groups of Black lesbians began to patronize Bingo's and the street bars in the downtown section, and soon after, whites went to the bars which opened in the Black section of town, thereby ending the racial homogeneity of the lesbian bar community. After years of separate socializing in the context of a racist society, Black lesbians had difficulty achieving acceptance, but the reward of new places to socialize seemed worth the effort. Arlette, who took leadership in breaking the confines of segregated lesbian society, recalls when she and her friends first started hanging around Bingo's.

> "Bingo's was the first gay place that really we found. . . . And somebody, I don't know who it was, came to say, 'Listen, I found a gay spot,' because the gay kids, really at the time, Black ones, had no bar to go to. Most of the time somebody would give a house party and we would go to that, but as far as a bar there was none that I knew of in Buffalo until I ran across Bingo's. So a whole bunch of us got together and went to the place. And it ended up we just kept going, we made friends with quite a few. And then there's still some that . . . don't let one of the white girls like the Black girls and she was considered a nigger lover."

In the beginning, the Black lesbians by their very presence challenged racial barriers and had to find ways to ease their acceptance.

> "When we started going in there, we found out how really prejudiced other white gay kids were. They didn't even want to talk to us, and they looked at us with resentment. . . . Well at Bingo's we would always sit in a booth. They would have the bar, a lot of them would look at us and roll their eyes. So we decided that we were going to get some of these to be our friends no matter what we had to do. One thing that drew them was the fact that we would get up and dance. Then some of them would say, 'Hey, I like that, teach us how to do that." (Arlette)

As we mentioned in chapter 2, individual Blacks and Indians had participated in the white community without difficulty during the 1940s. What distinguished the 1950s was that Blacks entered the predominantly white bars in groups. Indian women who continued to patronize bars as individuals, without ties to a larger Indian community, did not have to break through racial barriers.[10] Indian narrators insist that they experienced no discrimination in the lesbian community of the 1950s. One whose bar friends called her "Indian Iris" claims:

> "There didn't seem to be any prejudice. They just knew I was Indian. Like a lot of them, they would refer to me as Indian Iris. . . . It was just a title. Because there was a couple of other girls named Iris around. And so if they wanted to know who they were talking about they'd say 'Well, you know, Indian Iris,' and then everybody'd know who they were talking about. No, there was no prejudice because there was a lot of Black girls around and we all . . . nobody thought nothing of it." [11]

Positive and negative racial incidents run through all Black and white narrators' memories and make it difficult to assess the success of desegregation. On the one hand, a definite change in race relations occurred. Black lesbians now had the opportunity to go to lesbian and gay bars in the downtown section of the city if they wanted. Black and white lesbians began to interact on a regular basis and to participate in a shared culture. On the other hand, this was true for only a small segment of the community. Racial tension was always close to the surface, because desegregation coexisted with continuing prejudice. Black lesbians felt they were taking a risk when they entered a bar, and preferred to go in groups.

Some Black and white tough bar lesbians interacted with one another frequently. Melanie, a white fem who has had several relationships with Black women, goes as far as suggesting that Black/white relations were better in the past than today. In the interview when we ask her our standard question—what is the most important thing this book should tell about the past—she replies:

> "Well, I would say that years ago there was much more communication between the Black gay people and the white gay people. Now they're more separated. . . . Before the Black kids used to come to the white gay bars all the time. . . . Black people used to have parties, after the bars would close. . . . And a lot of white people used to go to their houses and drink and that. Some of them had pay parties and some of them had free parties. Like you did find some of the Black people that were real friendly with the white, and they'd say 'Well come after the bar, come to my house and we'll have some drinks.' Just socialize. It was more of that. Now everything's separate. . . . Years ago we used to dance with the Black kids and everything. We'd sit with them."

Piri confirms this impression of the mixture, but does not see it as complete, pointing out the hesitancy of many whites to go to Black neighborhoods. In keeping with their less powerful position in the racial hierarchy, Black narrators are more aware of and more frequently mention the problems and tensions, but not to the exclusion of the successes of desegregation.

> "When Arlette had parties there was a lot of whites that came. Vic used to go. And I was going with Lila too, and she's white. . . . But I think a lot of the white kids didn't come to Black parties more because of the neighborhood. I guess people in the neighborhood, guys would bother them, say different things to them and stuff like that. And they would have them scared to come."

Many white tough bar lesbians, throughout the decade, felt good about interracial socializing and expected it as a part of gay life. Stormy remembers, "We went into Black speaks with Black friends and ate in Black restaurants. Let's face it, we were still all one." Toni, like other white lesbians who came out into the bars after integration took place, particularly appreciated the racial mixing as something special in the community.

> "I remember some period of time there where the Black women would come in and sometimes there were tensions. But in a lot of respects, I mean it certainly couldn't eliminate all racial tensions because they're there in the world. But I think we let those barriers drop quite a bit in the gay community, where we would see Black and white women relating in relationships as lovers.

I had never really seen interracial couples before, and here I would see two women in a couple, one was Black and one was white. . . . I was raised with all the prejudices against everybody and then here I was in an environment where there were whites and Blacks. It was a new world and I knew the old rules didn't apply. I came with the prejudices ingrained into me. It was strange to me. But I liked it."

Another strong indicator of the degree to which Black/white social relationships became part of the tough bar lesbian culture is that the leaders who emerged in both communities toward the end of the decade were women who functioned well in both cultures. Melanie remembers Jacki Jordan in the following way:

"If she can [come] back to Buffalo she'd have it jumping again. . . . Because Jacki'd come in the bar, even the white people would come over and talk to her. Because I told you, it's just her way, she was very attractive. To me she was, I guess she was to a lot of other people too. And [a] . . . lot of white kids used to go watch her sing at the bar, Mandy's down on William."

Piri, who was younger than Jacki Jordan but also a leader at the time, says of herself: "And I've always associated with mixed, once you go to the bar. I knew more white gay kids than I did colored, but when you get to the gay bar there's a mixture of everybody." When asked whether there were any Black gay bars in the 1950s she replies: "I've never known it to be just strictly a gay Black bar. Probably if there was I wouldn't have went anyway. No, I don't know, I was always raised to get along with everybody. I don't think prejudice. It's just not in me. I don't care what color you are." Her photo album verifies that she always hung around with a racially mixed group (see photos after p. 190).

Two important leaders of the younger generation in the white community, Vic and Sandy, also had the reputation of going everywhere, mixing with everybody. Piri comments: "Unless like Vic, Vic would go anywhere. She wasn't scared of nobody. And there was a few, . . . but not that many, like it didn't bother them to come in the Black neighborhood, but some of them like were afraid. And I wouldn't blame them, at that time." Sandy worked with Jacki Jordan in the bar and after-hours club, the Club Co Co. She was one of the first white butches to go with a Black fem, and still remembers the difficulties this caused her and the responsibility she felt to make this acceptable in the white community.

"It was, as far as the affair, that was all right, but I was constantly thinking of what are people going to say about me. And here I was before, I don't give a shit, so I couldn't turn around and be a hypocrite and be ashamed to be seen with her. . . . So I thought, 'Fuck it. Walk with me.' That was it. Pretty soon, when the other ones seen us, 'Hey Sandy, we're with it, oh, that must be the in thing, I'll follow.' Because we were, like I say, very top ones then.

. . . If we walked with them then everyone, 'Oh, look what they're doing,' like it was a big deal. Which it was."

Interracial couples became quite common. A good percentage of Black and white narrators who were part of the tough bar culture and came out after the mid-1950s had at least one interracial relationship within ten years of entering the bars.[12] Since most lesbians spent social time with their sexual partners, like Sandy they had to prepare themselves to take the consequences of breaking racial taboos. Therefore, we suspect that the rise in interracial couples is related primarily to the overriding of racial boundaries by lesbians. The eroticization of racial differences was likely present, but it was not a prominent part of the culture.

Interracial dating maintained an undercurrent of tension within the community. Jodi remembers that the presence of Black studs made many white butches nervous: "Some of the stuff that happened was so typically racist, it was so ridiculous. I mean it was like Black studs were coming into the bar, people would just kind of put their arm around their women . . . [as if] they were just coming in there to snatch up their women."

The most powerful evidence of the strength of Black lesbians in pushing for desegregation and the receptivity of the white tough bar lesbian was the lack of overt racial conflict in the community. The undercurrent of tension rarely erupted into open confrontation. Sandy remembers that people would silently disapprove when she first appeared with a Black girlfriend, "Boy, did we ever get the look from our own people. 'Who is this Black chick?' y'know." Melanie, one of the first white fems to have a Black butch lover, Jacki Jordan, in 1958 does not recall white people harassing her. The criticism she received was due to the fact that Jacki was a pimp, rather than from racial issues.

"No, they never had no arguments or no fights that I know of. . . . If you were white and you were around the Blacks and some white person didn't like it they'd more or less tell you, but they'd tell you in a quiet, nice way. They didn't broadcast it all over. If they didn't like you hanging around with a Black person they would tell you, 'cause some of them didn't. . . . But I don't think it was mainly 'cause Jacki was Black, because see Jacki used to—some of those young Black girls used to be prostitutes and give her the money, and I think that was mainly why [they didn't approve]."

Melanie has similar memories about how Jacki's friends kept quiet about their objections if they had any.

Many narrators are emphatic about never having engaged in fights about racial matters. Piri reflects thoughtfully:

"I've never had a squabble in the gay life with somebody that was white, solely for the reason of color. If I had a disagreement with them it was over something else. 'Cause like I said, I was raised up around whites and Indians, Puerto

Ricans and everything, so I've never had that in me to be prejudiced against
people. And I think it's a good thing."

Arlette remembers how she used to resist the pressure to take sides in a conflict
simply on the basis of race, particularly when she was involved in an interracial
relationship.

"People would say, 'You sure ain't prejudiced.' I said, 'Well I'll tell you the
truth. I can't be too prejudiced because of the fact that my great grandaddy
was German-Irish and my grandmother is Indian, so therefore if it hadn't been
for them, I wouldn't be here. So I'm partially white too.' I felt like this: There
are white people I can't stand, and Black people I can't stand either. . . . Like
they say, when they started that racial stuff, 'Well, I hope when they start a
riot . . . I hope they protect you.' I said, 'Well I tell you this, if the white girl
is in my neighborhood and you all start that mess, you gonna have me to fight
too. I hope she'll protect me in case I'm in the white part of town and it
starts. . . .' But I felt like this, whatever side you're on, if you're wrong there's
no color. If you're wrong you're wrong, I don't care what color you are."

Narrators remember no racial fights in the 1950s, and only remember one in
the early 1960s in the Senate. This fight stands out in everyone's memory which
suggests that such incidents were indeed unusual.[13] Little Gerry was there that
night.

" '62, '63, somewhere around in there. It was a huge fight. It was really
uncalled for, because it just got out of control. There was a fight between
Sandy who was working behind the bar and this young Black woman, Linda.
Linda didn't have proof of age and she was asked to leave. She pulled a knife
on Sandy and Sandy took the knife away from her and threw her out. And
there was no incident over that. Linda was wrong. She shouldn't have been
in there, and she certainly shouldn't have pulled a knife. And what she did
was come back later on and she brought, I don't know how many, two or
three or four straight guys back with her, and she was after Sandy. By then
more Black women had come into the bar, and I don't know what the reason
was, the bar would segregate. Black women would be in the back room and
whites would be up front. And there'd be some mixing because people knew
one another. I didn't know many of the Black women at that point. And all
of a sudden everything just sort of exploded. . . . The whole place just started
turning over. You have no idea what it was like. And people were trying to
stop it, both Black and white were trying to stop it. You know, I'd go up to
you and say, 'Why don't you back off?' and somebody would see me with my
hands on you and I would get grabbed, and then you'd be saying, 'Wait a
minute, it's not what you think it is.' And then before that somebody'd grab
you because it looked like two on one. And in the events of that night Linda
was up on the bar walking back and forth on the bar screaming. And then she
saw Sandy, and threw a beer bottle at her, and this other woman, Nancy,
walked into the beer bottle and lost her eye."

At a later date, Little Gerry remembers what set off the actual fighting. When Linda came back, looking for a fight: "Garvey interceded; she also bridged the gap between Black and white from hanging out with Sandy. People were listening to her. Then someone put their hand on Diane [Garvey's girlfriend] and all hell broke loose." Protecting her girlfriend overrode intentions to mediate.

But even this incident did not end up polarizing the two subcommunities. The older Black lesbians, with whom Sandy held a place of respect, felt strongly that Linda shouldn't have done what she did.

> "It really wouldn't have made any difference who would have thrown the bottle at Sandy. Sandy was as well received in the Black community as she was in the white community. Her working there was one of the things that made Black women feel comfortable going all the way into the center of what was the West Side [a white Italian neighborhood]." (Little Gerry)

One of the Black leaders found out information about Linda and shared it with her white friends. And she herself wanted to find Linda and turn her in. Linda was not caught by the white lesbian community, nor was she prosecuted by the law. "They never caught her. One time later they chased her from the Havana Casino, Garvey and Sandy went after her. They ripped windshield wipers off cars to get her with. At a light she got into a car saying people were chasing her, and they let her in" (Little Gerry). The infrequency of racial fighting in the lesbian community of the 1950s and early 1960s is particularly remarkable in view of the tough bar lesbians' propensity toward physical conflict, and the overt racial conflict that erupted in Buffalo at the time.[14]

These accomplishments in creating interracial social relations were limited to a small group of tough bar lesbians: the majority of Black and white lesbians had minimal contact with one another. Even though the bars were desegregated they never reached the point of belonging to both Black and white lesbians. The bars in the downtown section of the city, which were originally white, continued to be thought of as white bars by the majority of Black lesbians, whereas they generally viewed the bars in the Black neighborhood as their own. Arlette recalls the Two Seventeen:

> "It was gay, but it was mostly all Black. None of the white kids hardly came in. Unless it was a white girl going with a Black girl, then she would be there, but it was mostly all Black. After we got to the point where there were a couple of clubs that didn't mind us coming in, we didn't patronize too much the other white places."[15]

White lesbians remember the bars in the Black neighborhood as predominantly Black bars that were not their regular haunts. Only certain white women who were open, adventuresome, and social might be likely to stop in. Whites remember the bars in the downtown section simply as lesbian bars. Their position in the racial hierarchy does not require them to specify color; however, when asked if there were many Blacks present, they say, "No."

Feelings of solidarity between Blacks and whites, while describing mutual support, can at the same time camouflage the distinctness of Black experience. Audre Lorde writes about how her friends' assumption of being "gay-girls" together in the 1950s was supportive and comforting and a source of her sanity, at the same time rendered her invisible.[16] Her friends never really understood that her life and consciousness were different because she was Black and gay, and they could not even contemplate that this might be an issue for discussion. This was likely true in Buffalo as well. White narrators, even those who had the most contact with the Black community, seemed to have a stereotyped understanding of Black life. For instance, Sandy regularly comments that the Black community is more tolerant of gays than the white.

> "Like, Christ, we wouldn't dare walk into just a regular bar, much less a speakeasy. We'd get our ass kicked. I don't care what you say, colored people are cool. They are the coolest. There's a lot like that, believe me. They don't care if you're white or what you are, if you're butch or fem or straight. They don't care, do your thing."

Although such a view can be supported by her own experience, it does not take into account the pain and suffering that many Black lesbians, some of whom she knew, experienced due to the homophobia in the Black community.

Interracial socializing did not extend significantly beyond the culture of the tough bar lesbian. The upwardly mobile lesbian crowd that was identified with the Carousel never included Black lesbians in any number. Black lesbians did not enter the Carousel until somewhat later than Bingo's because they did not feel welcome. Marla recalls: "I didn't want to go in the Carousel from Bingo's—the kids would go back and forth—'cause I was told at the time that the Carousel didn't like Blacks, or something, or didn't want them there, and I never went for a while." One night, a white friend met her at the door and took her into the Carousel, which she frequented from that time on. Even though Black lesbians began to go to the bar, as a group they never became an integral part of the more "elite" lesbian crowd. This crowd remained predominantly if not completely white; few of its members had interracial friendships or were part of interracial couples. Melanie suggests that the Carousel crowd's prejudice against Blacks was part of its general disapproval of the tough bar lesbians' way of life:

> "They [the Carousel crowd] were more the people that were—well I guess they didn't like seeing the prostitutes and talking to the straight men, and how should I put it, they just wanted to be around gay people. They didn't want to have nothin' to do with any other type of person. . . . But to me, I was always more open, I like to be around anybody, I don't care who it is. 'Cause everybody's different, people aren't the same. . . . They were like set in their ways, they didn't want to be around Black people or they didn't want to socialize with prostitutes or like I said, straight men or hustlers. They were people that worked, that had a job, and I guess they just wanted to be around their own kind of people."

The desegregation of the lesbian community was affected by the forces that propelled the struggle for racial justice in the United States in general. However, the fact that it happened only among tough bar lesbians suggests that integration was also shaped by internal developments in the lesbian community. The tough bar lesbian's emphasis on survival under difficult conditions, and her familiarity with the harsh realities of street life, seem to have created the bridges necessary for interracial socializing. Several narrators express the view that life was so difficult for lesbians at the time that Black and white lesbians had to work together. During the interview when we ask Melanie, who thought that there was more communication between Blacks and whites years ago, why this should be the case, she replies, "Oh Jesus . . . I don't know, maybe 'cause things were harder years ago. You had to be more friendly with other people. . . . Times were harder. Like everybody more or less had to work together. Black people worked just as hard as white people did. Could be that." Jodi explains the situation that existed between Black and white lesbians years ago by saying, "Racism was a given; it was there, everyone knew it, but you felt the more active oppression as a lesbian. . . . A Black man after your girl was more oppressive than feeling out of place in a white bar."

But history shows that the severity of oppression does not in itself create solidarity. Rather it often leads people to turn on one another. From this perspective, the absence of physical conflict suggests that the tough bar lesbian's adamant assertion of being "queer" created a consciousness of lesbian solidarity that was usually strong enough to override racial divisions. This is one further verification of the sense of unity in tough bar lesbian culture and consciousness and its power to influence the shape of lesbian history. It also provides an interesting perspective on race relations in the contemporary gay movement. The record of limited but definite Black and white socializing and of a lesbian consciousness that overrode racial division suggests that there has been little, if any, improvement in Black/white lesbian relations—indeed they might have even deteriorated—since the rise of feminism and gay liberation, despite these movements' emphasis on sisterhood and solidarity. Although the reasons for this are unquestionably multiple and in need of further research, we can't help but wonder if gay liberation's and lesbian feminism's emphasis on gay and lesbian identity doesn't by definition give second place to ethnic and racial identity rendering invisible one important aspect of Black lesbian identity. This could also make it difficult for different racial and ethnic groups to socialize and work together.[17]

BLACK LESBIAN HOUSE PARTIES

The social life of Black lesbians of the 1950s and early 1960s focused on being out and about as much as possible.[18] Black narrators, like the white tough bar lesbians, remember "partying" seven days a week.

"And Arlette and I were living together. There was a bunch of us all living in the same building, not in the same apartment but in the same building. So we [were] always partying, like seven days a week. And I don't know, I mean it had its bad points, but it had a lot of good points about it at the time too. . . . I seen it as A-O.K., 'cause by me being so young. And I found that by hanging with the older crowd I could get into places maybe I wouldn't have been able to get in by myself." (Piri)

If there wasn't a party they would get together anyway.

"People just came out, it was so great. That's like when I graduated from high school I went out, there was a couple of years before I got a job, the same people hung out every night, we went out every night, to some bar every night. There was a party every weekend, the same people. It wasn't all these cliques and stuff. If somebody was going to go out like you made twenty phone calls, and twenty people came out, or we met on the corner. That's when we used to walk up and down the street three and four o'clock in the morning. You didn't worry about mugging or something." (Jodi)

The hostile police force (which we will discuss later) did not deter them.

The combination of racism in the society at large and the distinctive traditions of Black culture acted to keep this community localized. Correspondingly, its images of community were often based in the neighborhoods where people lived. When asked about how she met others, Jodi mentions her neighborhood as well as the bars and house parties.

"Well, those people who were our age now right, who we used to call forefathers, and we met them at the bars and we started going to parties, and they also lived around too, like on the next street. People that you had seen around; thought they were kind of strange. [But they were] just the local yokels."

The community's move toward desegregation suggests that Black lesbians had developed the support, confidence, and pride which would allow them to initiate and follow through on the steps necessary to foster interracial socializing. Other changes in the Black lesbian community confirm this. Even though Black lesbians regularly patronized the Two Seventeen and Five Five Seven in the Black section of the city and went with increasing frequency to the "white" bars in the downtown section, they did not give up their tradition of partying in people's homes. Instead, the parties expanded: they became more open, sold food and drink, and lasted all weekend. In this new form they were generally referred to as "house parties."

"It just started all of a sudden. Just out of the clear blue sky somebody decided to have a house party. I can't even remember who it was. I'm trying to think who really—I think Mabel Jensen was one of the first that used to have 'em. And the next thing somebody else decided they would do it, and then it became, well I'm gonna have one, and that's the way it just started. Because it ended up it was so much fun I guess. And then you had a chance to make you a little dollars." (Arlette)

In the late 1950s and well into the 1960s a weekend for many Black lesbians would consist of going to the bars and to house parties.

"Like we finally had a nice little place on Cherry Street, the Two Seventeen, and they would have a house party a few doors down, so everybody wouldn't come out till twelve or one o'clock. And we would go to this bar. . . . We would have a couple of drinks, and by that time the bars closed at three. . . . Then we'd go to the party, and that's where we would have our fun. We bought drinks and we bought food and we would dance till all hours of the morning. In fact, we really had a good time. And then we didn't have that confusion of anybody else coming in and bothering us. We had our own little set of friends. New people could come in, you could bring a guest, and they'd find out what was new. . . . And then somebody would have one this weekend, somebody would have one the next weekend, and somebody would have one the next weekend. It was constantly rotating." (Arlette)

Black lesbians also went to Black after-hours clubs, but house parties were always more popular.

People learned about house parties by word of mouth. Lonnie, an imposing yet warm stud describes the grapevine.

"Well word spread fast, pass along word. Like maybe I know she's having a party, I see somebody else I say, 'Hey, Arlette's having a party tonight.' . . . Then it get passed on down, on down, and pretty soon she has a houseful. Because every gay is looking for something to [do], where to go to when they get out of the bar if they're not ready to go home. Like four o'clock in the morning the bars are closed, you want to go someplace else besides coming home. Years ago they used to have many parties. Fortunada and all of them they used to have those parties. . . . We used to go to their parties you know and meet a lot of people. You might have saw me a lot of times at parties."

This method of recruiting was invariably successful. "On a good night it would be like roaches in the house that hadn't been sprayed; you couldn't hardly move. But you found room to dance, and had a good time" (Arlette).

Gay men also came to these parties. "Mixed parties, girls and fellows, whatever. It was all like sisters and brothers, whatever. It was all just one big family" (Lonnie). White lesbians also attended but not in large numbers. This was resented by those Black lesbians who wanted a racially mixed community. "White kids started coming. Now they come up with, 'that neighborhood,' which I resent. Because there's no such neighborhood that anybody's gonna attack you. I get mad at that. 'Well where do you live? I don't want to come over there.' What do you mean you don't want to come over there?" (Arlette). In addition, straight people were regular guests.

"And there was some straight people that came too. Straight people that knew you, knew how you lived, they really enjoyed the parties. They would come and they would really have a good time, and dance, and admit that they had more fun at the gay party then they did at other regular house parties. . . . They found out that all they say about gay people wasn't true." (Arlette)[19]

The parties lasted for several days.

"That one house would have it for the whole weekend. Like if I have a party it would start Friday and would run till Sunday. You could go home [and] whenever you left, there would always be somebody there. You had all types of people, different sets. Like you'd have a set that comes early, twelve o'clock, they have to go to work Saturday in the morning. Then you have the latecomers that didn't have to work Saturday so they'd come at three and they might stay till eight or nine, ten o'clock in the morning. Then you had some that . . . they'd come at twelve o'clock and stay till two or three in the afternoon. And then you had another group that would come in when they got off work, they'd stop by. And they kept it going." (Arlette)

Saturday was the biggest night because most people didn't have to work on Sunday and could continue partying. Some women would take off a couple of hours to go to church.

"You know what kills me about this, plenty of gay people go to nice devout church. And they would leave to go to church, then when they came back from church they would stop by. Then you had some that came by for a drink before they went to church. And then they would go to church and come back with their church attire on, have a couple of drinks, say, 'I've got to get out of this,' and they'd go home and put on a pair of slacks and come back that afternoon, and stay around till six or seven, nine o'clock that evening. And then everybody, by nine or ten Sundays, it would be just about fizzled out. Everybody would be going home because they had to get up Monday and go to work." (Arlette)

Food and drink were amply provided for a modest fee by the hostess.

"You didn't have to pay to come in, but if you wanted a drink, it was fifty cents a drink . . . but it was a dollar for dinner if you got hungry. You had a half a chicken and vegetables. That was for a dollar, and anything you wanted to drink was fifty cents. I have spent thirty-five and forty dollars, fifty-centing!" (Arlette)

Because of their size, house parties were quite visible, inviting harassment from hostile straights and from the police. Giving parties, therefore, required leadership skills for handling the community's relations with the outside world. Managing outsiders was as important as preparing food, drink, and music. In an interview with Arlette, who had given many parties, we comment that women must have done a lot of cooking and she immediately adds, "And answering the door," giving this task a place of equal prominence. The hostess had to either take care of the door herself or delegate the task to make sure no intruders came in.

"Usually there's somebody on the door that monitored the door, 'cause you would find people . . . trying to crash. They can't come in. . . . There are people and guys that find out, 'Oh, we hear music, must be a party.' Some people would stand out and try to wait for somebody to come in and make like they're with them. And then, if you know your crowd, 'Who are you comin' to see? Sorry, it's a private party.' They turn around and leave. . . . A new face that popped up, we'd ask them 'Who told you to come here?' 'Cause sometimes people gave out the address." (Arlette)

Remarkably, hostile neighbors were relatively rare. Writing about homophobia, bell hooks criticizes the contemporary feminist view that homophobia is stronger in the Black community.[20] She argues that, if this is the case today, it is a relatively recent phenomenon. When she was growing up in the South, poor Blacks, who were struggling for survival in a society fraught with racial hatred, did not ostracize their gay and lesbian brothers and sisters. Tolerance, if not acceptance, was the norm. This would appear to be true of Buffalo in the 1950s. Few, if any, Black narrators remember being physically attacked and beaten by Black men. Most white narrators confirm that they felt more accepted in the Black straight world than in the white. This is not to say that homophobia was absent from the Black community in the 1950s; it simply took different forms and it did not generate as much aggressive physical harassment of lesbians.

The police, however, were an ever-present danger. Black narrators, unlike white narrators, recall the police as vicious during the 1950s. Racial prejudice seems to have magnified hostility toward lesbians and gays to the extent that Black lesbians risked arrest for "disorderly conduct" just by walking in their own neighborhoods.

"To me, back in the '50s bein' gay was brutal. I don't know how it was at the time [for whites]. I think it was worse for Blacks, being gay. Because I've got a brother that's gay too, and he wore women's clothes. Like on weekends and stuff he'd go out and he'd be dressed and the cops used to lay some brutal beatings on him, you know? I mean they used to beat him, throw him in jail . . . and sometime he'd get away from them, and sometimes he wouldn't and it was really chaos then. And like, I have been stopped. I was ready to go upstairs, me and two other girls. And the police station was right in the next block and they walked up, poked us in the back . . . they like hit us in the back with their night sticks. 'O.K. you spooks, walking the street all times of the night.' They took us to jail. And I was right on the corner where I live at, right?" (Piri)

The police would use any excuse to arrest a group of Black lesbians. Lonnie remembers trying to break up a fight and being arrested: "And this particular time, first time I got arrested was on the corner, I was stopping two friends of mine from fighting, and the police was that time just grabbing about every homosexual out there. And they grabbed me too, and I was just trying to stop them." She was treated very badly, even for the short time she was in jail.

> "[They treated me] cold, very cold and cruel. Very much so. . . . Got hit in the stomach. I'll never forget it. That's why I don't like cops, I hate them. I'd rather die than go to a police to help me. I mean that. . . . It [hasn't] changed much. If you're not gonna be a nigger you're gonna be a bulldyke, and I hate those words. I'm a lady lover myself."

Police harassment of house parties was frequent and had to be handled with dignity. Arlette's most successful tactic was to invite police to the party.

> "When I started with house parties I had trouble with the police, and I told them, 'Well hell, you want a chicken dinner or you want something to drink? Because it's just a private party.' And they tried to hassle me, and then after a while they left me alone. I had house parties for seven years and never had any trouble. . . . I guess its because where I lived—there was a dead-end street, it wasn't too much action, there was places for them to park. And [police] didn't run up in there too much, wasn't that many houses on the [block] anyway. And I really didn't have too much problem."

Behind her boldness was a conviction that gays and lesbians had the right to socialize together and that she had the right to have a party for them. She did not feel apologetic about herself or her friends.

> "I had one girl left a party that I had on William Street and called the police because she was mad at a girl, and had the police come there. Scared everybody, but I felt as though I don't care if they are the police, they have no right telling me I can't have a party. They either tell me to lower the music, it's too loud or whatever. Everybody panics. I said, 'What are you panicking for? There's no law says you can't have a party in your flat.' In fact I found out that you can absolutely have two parties a month in your flat if you choose, so you don't have to be hassled by police."

Her tactics were successful and some officers came to like the parties and made themselves at home.

> "I'll tell you what happened to me and Vic one time. We went to Mabel Jensen's place on Monroe. And we had caught a cab from the West Side. Now Vic dressed manly. The police spotted us and followed us all the way to the house. When we get to the house they found out that Vic really wasn't a white fellow, I don't know what they thought me and this white fellow was going to do, and ended up those same two cops came to the party every week. They would meet me there, 'Hi, how you doin?' I had a fire one time when I was having a house party, and the detective came and drank and we couldn't get him out of there. And I was afraid to charge him anything, so he drank free, but when he left he threw fifteen dollars on the bar. I just left it there.

I said, 'No, you don't have to do that.' He says, 'I want to.' And the thing that tickled me was, he left the house with another guy. Later, his partner came looking for him. 'I have no idea where he was.' But I knew he had left with another gay fella."

Party guests also took care to maintain amicable relations with the local police. They cautioned others that loud, raucous behavior could bring repercussions.

"No, we didn't have too much trouble with fights. . . . Once in a while. Most of the fights were at bars. Very seldom. I've only known of one or two that really jumped off. But otherwise there was never any fights. You're gonna have a fight anywhere, really. But if people heard somebody arguing or something, whoever's house it was would go over and say, 'Try to straighten it out. If you're gonna fight you have to leave, and please don't be in front of my door, go up the street, around the corner or go home.' Because everybody's gonna jump you if you start a fight, because they don't want it either. Because that draws the police and problems. Naturally the cops gonna [pull] up, then they're gonna notice there's a lot of cars here, then they'll start watching." (Arlette)

House parties were an attempt to provide a better social life for Black gays and lesbians. Lonnie explains: "Since everybody is so prejudiced against you being gay, you just make up your own gay thing. So the Black kids started having house parties." Most narrators see them as a way to be in the Black community, yet have a gay social life. Some, like Lonnie, also mention that they were necessary because of the poor treatment Blacks received at the white lesbian bars.

"All the older women used to have a party, if there wasn't a party at this place this week, there was a party at another place next week. We always had some place to go because the bars wouldn't accept us. At that time the Black and the white gays didn't get along, they fought every chance they got."

Regular weekend house parties continued through the mid-1960s. A small number of people, including for a while a gay man, regularly gave these parties, and took them in rotation. When throwing house parties became no longer compatible with the lifestyles of the people involved, the parties virtually disappeared. Arlette recalls with resignation:

"Every weekend somebody had a house party from Friday to Sunday. For years. In fact, I was the last one with them, 'cause the rest of them kind of dropped out, became Christians. Some of them became ill, seriously ill to the point, you know, it's just too much. A lot of them called themselves getting older, the big money spenders got into different bags and started buying homes. Then the younger set started going to school and just didn't have time. And they still have parties but they would have private ones that was invitation."

The increasing acceptance of Black lesbians in bars made the need for such parties less pressing. Also, Arlette thinks that the onset of drugs affected the viability of parties. "The younger set got into buying that and not buying food and drink. No sense having parties."

The tradition of house parties had a significant impact on leadership in the Black lesbian community. Like the tough bar community, with which it overlapped, it respected those butches who could take care of business in the difficult environment of the street. But unlike the white bar community, it recognized and respected fem leaders. One reason for this may be the structural significance of home life in the Black lesbian community. Home-based parties gave fems, whose role was associated with domestic life, an arena for contributing to the social well-being of the community. They were key organizers for the house parties, dealing with problems internal to the community as well as relations with the outside world. In addition, fems opened their houses for visitors, nurturing those who needed a place to stay. Arlette, who was an important leader in the community, had the nickname, Mother Superior. When asked how she got this name, she explains, with a mixture of embarrassment and pride, that she always took care of people.[21]

"It was because of the fact that young kids liked to hang around me, and they were doing things, and I would try to tell them, 'Look, if you work, go to school, [fine]. If you're not gonna do that you got to get out of here and do somethin' to support yourself.' And I was always feeding kids, letting them stay someplace. But I stayed on their case to the point I would actually jump on them. And rather than call me a Mother Fucker they called me Mother Superior. . . . But the name just stuck. 'Cause I'm always trying to call myself lookin' out for somebody. I would tell them point-blank, 'Look, I'll feed you but I'm not gonna take care of you. Now if you want to find a job, go look for a job, and if you're not gonna work you going to have to get out there and do something. Ain't nobody gonna take care of you, 'cause I'm out here breakin' my balls trying to exist and I'm not gonna work myself to a frazzle to support you. And you're in my house and I'm tryin' to give you something to wear, a place to lay down where nobody's gonna bother you while you're sleeping. You got a place where you don't have to worry about nobody bothering you in the middle of the night. You can sleep, you can get up and eat and you've got someplace to be out of the cold, so you better try to do somethin' to help yourself 'cause after that you're gonna have to leave here.' And it got to the point where some mothers actually came to my house to jump on me. The daughter was working in a bar. I thought she was at least eighteen. She was underage and was seeing a gay butch that lived at my house. I had to let the mother know she was working and wasn't coming to see me. It angered me for her to think I was a bad influence on her child. Then after they found out how the situation was . . . they'd call me, 'Is my daughter there, send her home.' O.K., 'your mother wants you, go home.' But they found out that I wasn't making any kids do anything. I always felt like whatever you did it was a nice way of doing it and a bad way of doing it. If you're gonna do something, if you're gonna be a prostitute, be one with class. Don't be a bum in the street. So that's why I got the name Mother Superior."

In the context of Black culture's long tradition of organizing to resist racial oppression, the Black lesbian community took responsibility for creating its own social life. They increased the public presence of lesbians and developed a strong sense of community solidarity by supporting lesbian and gay bars in the Black section of the city, gaining access to the lesbian and gay bars in the downtown area, and developing house parties explicitly to create the best possible environment for their people.[22] Their approach to building a better life had the confrontational elements of the tough bar lesbian style, as well as a concern for building bridges with the larger society. The Black studs were tough on the street and in the bars, demanding respect and fighting to defend what was theirs. At the same time, the fems, or sometimes butch-fem couples, gave parties which they handled with great pride and diplomatic skill, welcoming gay men, and reaching out to sympathetic straights. They forthrightly negotiated the boundaries between Black and white, heterosexual and lesbian and gay, and at times temporarily neutralized the power of hostile straights and the law.

THE CAROUSEL AND THE UPWARDLY MOBILE LESBIANS

The Carousel was widely known as the "true" gay and lesbian bar of the 1950s. The management consciously cultivated a lesbian and gay clientele and required that they act in an orderly manner. In fact, the younger tough bar lesbians had a hard time gaining admittance until the late 1950s when the standards of the bar changed.[23] Similarly the management did not tolerate straight "spectators" who misbehaved. Marla recalls vividly the advertisement on the bar's matchbooks. "On the front cover of the matchbook, it gave the name, The Carousel. . . . It might have been Carol's Carousel, and the address. On the back cover there was a picture of a Carousel around which was printed, 'The Gayest Spot in Town.'"

Carol, the owner of the Carousel, reputedly liked gay people and in turn was respected by them.[24] She came from a family of hotel, restaurant, and bar owners and handled the business professionally. Carol often worked in the bar herself, particularly in the daytime. Marla, who was a regular at the bar in the late 1950s, reminisces about the good times she and Carol had together.

"She'd be down there too, she'd walk in there and be working behind the bar sometimes and would talk to people. On a Saturday sometimes I would leave home at like two o'clock in the afternoon, just take a ride down there and Carol, myself, and sometimes her husband that was in there and some other people, we'd start playing . . . blackjack, or something, you know we weren't supposed to but we'd do it. I'd stay there the Saturday and wouldn't get home till four or five o'clock in the morning. When the kids would come in she'd even take the card game upstairs in one of those empty rooms."

Most Carousel patrons still remember with affection, "Carol's famous line at 3 a.m., 'You don't have to go home, but you can't stay here' " (Leslie).

The Carousel opened in the late 1940s and closed in the early 1960s. Early in the 1950s it changed locations, moving from Chippewa Street to Ellicott near Chippewa. The second Carousel was larger than any of the lesbian street bars or Bingo's. It was also the best kept. "I remember the bar at the Carousel in those days to me looked like a fancy cocktail lounge, because the first place I had gone into, Bingo's, was a horrible dump" (Toni). Nevertheless, other narrators remind us that it was still "a typical bar. It was nothing to write home about. It was, I would say, probably comparatively small to what I see opening now" (Bert). The bar was on the right of the entrance, and booths were on the left against the wall. The back room was separated from the front by a narrow vestibule which also housed the stairway to the upstairs rooms. Opposite the stairway on the north wall was an exit to an alley which lesbians ducked into when someone they did not want to see entered the bar, or when they were in danger of getting in trouble with the management. The kitchen was located off the back room.

During the day the bar also served as a restaurant. People from neighborhood businesses would come in for lunch; gays might come in too, but they would not predominate. Joanna remembers the Carousel at its first location: "I went to the Carousel with Leslie more too, cause it was always open. . . . You know, it was on Chippewa and the market was open then, and a lot of people would stop in for a beer that had been shopping."[25] In the evening the kitchen was closed and the bar became fully gay.

Upstairs, the Carousel had rooms for rent. Some of these were occupied by permanent residents who regularly took their meals in the restaurant. In addition, some rooms would be rented to Canadian gays who would come to Buffalo for a lively weekend.

> "I think it was five dollars a night, and Arty and I stayed there once or twice. But it was clean, and there was a common toilet with a bathtub in it, in the hall, that everyone used. The only thing was it was weird in the morning when you'd get up and go downstairs and you were in a bar, in the bar you'd been in the night before. It wasn't like a real hotel." (Whitney)

Whitney ended up preferring a nearby hotel. Some local gays also rented rooms, especially since many of them still lived with their families. This afforded them a way of being out of their houses on weekends. Matty describes her room in the following way: "I had the nicest room—two couches, a bed and a chair. And you'd wake up to find twenty-five people in your room, six to a bed, two on the couches, and a bunch on the floor."

Of all the 1950s bars, the Carousel most resembled the bars of the preceding decade. It was run for gay people and attempted to protect them; therefore violence did not predominate. The majority of the 1940s crowd became its regular patrons. Dee remembers what she liked about the Carousel.

> "It was clean, it was orderly, it was well kept. As I said, I only saw two fights and those were stopped right there. If anybody acted up they were banned. I used to know some of the bartenders, both the boys and the girls, and boy if they banned you, that was it, you were out. You were out if you tried to start anything that was not in accordance with good practice. Or good social behavior."

She, like most, but certainly not all, of her age group, felt very uncomfortable in the rough atmosphere of Bingo's.[26] "I was in Bingo's once and I hated every minute of it. . . . It was a dirty place, it was a crowded place, it was a noisy place, it wasn't the sort of place I enjoyed. There was arm-to-arm, wall to wall people and I don't like that closeness."

For several years after it opened the Carousel had mainly these older patrons, but in time, particularly after its move, younger lesbians started going there. Although it developed a varied clientele, it became the preferred spot for the younger, more upwardly mobile lesbians. These lesbians mixed easily with the older crowd and in many cases joined their friendship circles. They organized their social lives similarly, making a clear separation between their lesbian social lives and work and family, something which they felt their work required. But unlike those of the 1940s the demands of work took priority over socializing in the bars. Anchoring the bars as a place for lesbians was not as important as their careers, and many even felt ambivalent about social life in the bars. Nevertheless they continued to go out to bars on a regular, if limited, basis.

These upwardly mobile lesbians of the 1950s had white-collar jobs, such as teacher, technician, secretary, or shopkeeper, where dress and/or moral reputation were considered part of the employee's job performance. Although this correlation between white-collar work and a distinctive lesbian lifestyle was high, it was not one hundred percent. Some factory workers associated with the more "elite" lesbians, either because of preference or because of the requirements of their specific jobs or families, just as some tough bar lesbians had white- and pink-collar jobs. However, there were certain limits on the mixing. It was quite unlikely that one could hold a professional job and hang out with the tough bar lesbians. Their entire way of life was in direct conflict with what was required to maintain such a job and the related community position. Similarly, we doubt whether a prostitute would have been accepted in the more upwardly mobile crowd. Cheryl, an athletic butch who was a younger member of the group remembers that they were very cautious about who could come to parties. She was not even allowed to bring a new lover unless they had met her first.

"And their reason is that you don't just bring somebody new into this party, after all, they don't know her. And I said, 'How are you going to know her if I don't bring her?' . . . So maybe they're from the crew where . . . you're still hesitant about who you meet, where you're gonna see them again after that party, are you going to be embarrassed? . . . And I feel it is their loss. Because they will never expand their group."

We call this group upwardly mobile to distinguish them from the many middle-class lesbians who did not go to the bars at all.[27] Despite their emphasis on discretion, these upwardly mobile women did go to the bars. They unquestionably felt a pull to public, working-class lesbian culture particularly when they were younger. "When they're eighteen, nineteen, twenty, twenty-one, they'll wear their college jackets into the bars, they announce who they are, they don't care. Give them two or three years in their job and they're back to conservative like the rest of us" (Cheryl). Most of these upwardly mobile women were part of larger friendship groups with middle-class women who never ventured into the bars. Cheryl remembers: "There were no professionals [in the bars]. That's what I was saying, the nearest we got were the two teachers. I mean lawyers didn't go in there, doctors didn't go in there, and yet they were all around. Nurses were in there and obviously ball players from the teams if they were gay."

The actual divisions between the upwardly mobile and the tough bar lesbians were not quite as sharp as our categories imply. Although for convenience of description we, and narrators, have talked about two groups, the upwardly mobile and the rough and tough, "the elite" and "the riffraff," the Carousel crowd and the Bingo's crowd, in fact there were social sets between these two extremes. There was one circle with a collegiate appearance that looked like they were part of the upwardly mobile group but spent a lot of time in the street bars and Bingo's, attracted by the exciting social life. They not only didn't look like tough bar lesbians, but also weren't able to take care of themselves in the rough environment. However, despite the fuzziness of the boundaries, the two extremes were significant points of definition in lesbian culture.

The upwardly mobile lesbians' social life and culture was quite different from that of the tough bar lesbians. Because of the importance of their careers they emphasized discretion and limited most socializing to weekends.

"I mean they didn't go out during the week. Renée usually had things after school, activities. She had cheerleaders and she had water ballet, she had intramurals. They were things that took up a lot of her time. So it was difficult for her to go out and drink. You can't drink. [She had] to go to work the next day. Weekends we went out." (Joanna)

They also avoided physical confrontations with a hostile world as much as possible. In addition, the more affluent lesbians spent as much time socializing outside of the bars as inside, going with their friends to parties, cultural events, and picnics. Their homes became valued places to entertain friends.

Friendship groups were the primary reference point for social life. "Where you hung around with so many people, I think you became closer to that one particular group. I mean you went out and you saw other people, but there was just one particular group that you'd invite to your home. I mean it wasn't everybody that you met in the tavern" (Joanna). Friendship groups tended to form around age or occupation; one group might have more hospital workers, another more teachers. Even at special occasions, when more than one group would be together, people would stay within their own group. Joanna explains, "Yeah, I was invited to a lot of things. As I said like Christmas things and oh somebody's birthday or just like a backyard party or beach party or something. But you knew it was separate. When you got there, [there] were like separate little groups." Each group had slightly different patterns of socializing. For instance, the older butches from the 1940s continued their practice of Butch Night Out in the 1950s, but it was not picked up by others. "It was an entirely different group. Because even like when I was living with Renée, [the older] set was still doing their thing on Friday. Like they'd all meet you know . . . that was their night and they always said this was their night you know" (Joanna). Couples of the younger set often went to the bars together on Friday night and then to peoples' homes on Saturday night.

These more affluent lesbians, no matter the group, shared their social lives with gay men. Although the Carousel's patrons were primarily women, it was the only bar of the 1950s that had a steady mixed clientele. "[It was] mainly women. But men would come in. There would be a nice contingency of men, maybe about twenty men at any time, in the front bar—and they were quite welcome there. . . . They'd mostly come with other men" (Whitney).[28]

For the upwardly mobile women, socializing with gay men was part of the fun of the Carousel.

> "I like to go to parties where gay boys are at. They're fun and they're enjoyable. I like to go to bars where they are. I wouldn't seek them out, but I'm glad when they're there. And I think they're an important part of a gay woman's life. . . . They can be good friends, if they like you. They're not as catty and dishy as some of the women. I think they have a lot less hang-ups than women." (Joanna)

Whitney used to come from Canada with a male friend, and they used to dance together at the Carousel. "Arty and I were dancers. So people would enjoy seeing us dance. We always would dance in the front . . . because all the men were in front so for Arty there was his audience of the men. And that was where our friends were."

In addition to enjoying one another's company, gay men and women provided some security for one another. Having gay men and women at the front of the bar provided protection against immediate labeling by casual visitors. It also allowed gays a chance to meet people of the other sex whom they could take to family and work parties as a heterosexual cover. Marla recalls:

> "It was mostly girls until you went down to the Carousel where you had girls and guys. And then the guys were gay. You could relax with them. And also you know, there has got to be some time in everybody's life that their parents want you to go to a wedding; some family affair, and yet they kept asking, 'Where's your boyfriend?' There were some guys down there who weren't that nellie; and in fact a lot of them that you could take. They'd get all dressed up and act right and you wouldn't have a problem; your parents wouldn't know the difference. They say, 'Where did you meet him at, when you gonna bring him around?' If they only knew, that when you got through you'd both go your own directions."

Gay men were fully included in the rich and varied social activities of upwardly mobile lesbians.

> "When Renée and I were going together we had a cottage for about five years in Sherkston, and Leslie and her friend had a cottage in the same area. And this went on for about five years, we commuted, we went to work from there. And there were, two, four, six, buddy guys that had a couple of cottages also, four in one, two in another, and we had one of the best times, for those summers. 'Cause we went around May, like Memorial Day, until Labor Day, and we really had a lot of close contact with them. We had dinner together, we had cocktails together. We did a lot of crazy things, we took trips to Toronto, just like for the day, we really had a good time with them. And I don't think we would have had that good a time if there had been all women there all the time. I really enjoyed them. And everybody else did." (Joanna)

The different conditions of social life between the more affluent group of lesbians and the rough and tough lesbians generated different patterns of friendship and leadership. In contrast to the brittle, or limited, friendships of the latter, the friendships of the former, made in these small circles which were not in open confrontation with society, were intimate and long-lasting. All narrators from this more upwardly mobile group of lesbians have continued to see their friends from this time period and socialize with them regularly, if at all possible.

Leadership roles in the upwardly mobile crowd were much more muted than those of the rough and tough lesbians. There were few if any women whom everyone acknowledged as important beyond their small circle of friends. However, there were some women who were particularly well respected. The qualities that were admired were dramatically different from those appreciated by the tough bar lesbians and crystallize some of the differences between the two groups. The upwardly mobile valued individual development, career success, and a well-appointed home, suitable for entertaining, rather than asserting lesbianism in the straight world and helping others survive under hostile conditions. One woman who had a leadership role in the 1940s continued to be known as a well-educated person who helped others reach their potential by encouraging them to take a class or read a particular book. Whitney, her partner of many years reminisces about her.

> "She was vitally interested in people, and that's what they picked up. And even if one wasn't particularly motivated, the fact that she was interested—I'm making her sound like a saint, Liz, but I don't mean that. She really was interested. So you might even do something just because the next time you saw her she would say, 'Well did you do so-and-so?' You wouldn't want to disappoint her because she was so nice about it."

Joanna reminisces about the woman who was central to keeping their circle of friends together because of her flair for entertaining. "I think she is the one that holds them. She is the nucleus of, like anybody gathering together, she is great for that. She likes groups of people, she likes to have them to her home, likes to entertain."

Patterns of alcohol consumption also differed between the upwardly mobile and tough bar lesbians, although alcohol was equally important to both groups. The upwardly mobile did not usually drink socially during the week, although they might have imbibed alcohol in the privacy of their own homes. On weekends heavy drinking was commonplace and though they did not usually evince as rowdy or as pugnacious behavior as the rough lesbians, their social life centered around alcohol and many were dependent on it.[29]

Overall, the strategies of lesbians in the upwardly mobile group for resisting oppression were distinct from those of the Black and white tough lesbians. They attempted to lead lives that were acceptable to and even successful in the straight world, while still taking the risk of socializing publicly as lesbians by going to the bars on a regular, if limited, basis. It is easy for contemporary lesbians who have had the benefit of twenty years of the gay liberation movement to belittle this accomplishment and focus on the lack of willingness of the upwardly mobile to be identified as lesbians. But this viewpoint overlooks the difficulty of what they attempted: to diminish the stigma associated with lesbians, and integrate themselves into mainstream society; to have good jobs while never giving up their social life with lesbians. These lesbians, despite their fears, were not the same as those who never socialized with any but a few close friends and never set foot in the bars.

In Buffalo, which was a predominantly blue-collar city at this time, this upwardly mobile group of lesbians was not a strong catalyst for change. They achieved a precarious balance between work and a respectable home life, on the one hand,

and a lesbian social life on the other hand. This solution which was individualist and unstable could not be of use to future generations. However, on an individual basis it laid the groundwork in Buffalo for convincing society that lesbians and gays are "normal," and opened up possibilities for dialogue and discussion between the gay and heterosexual worlds.[30] Although no homophile organizations formed in Buffalo, we think that this more upwardly mobile community throws light on the conditions that gave rise to and shaped the homophile organizations in cities like San Francisco, New York, and Philadelphia. The Buffalo evidence suggests that the lesbian homophile organizations grew out of a working-class lesbian tradition—women who were conscious of lesbians as a group, from socializing in the bars—rather than a middle-class tradition of isolated individuals and couples.[31]

CLASS DIVISIONS IN THE BAR COMMUNITY

Class divisions, which crystallized around the distinctions between the Carousel and Bingo's, or the Carousel and the street bars, were woven throughout 1950s lesbian culture and imprinted firmly in its participants' minds. Stormy, obviously of the Bingo's set, reminisces: "The Carousel crowd wouldn't be caught dead in Bingo's. They would look down their nose at us. They drove better cars; we drove wrecks. . . . If you went into the Carousel with white pants on, they would stay white, in Bingo's you'd come out gray" (Stormy). After further thought, she adds that the Carousel crowd was "more quiet and reserved. They'd come in with gay men. They had more gay men friends. They sat with them; this protected the bar. They sat in the front and us riffraff would sit in the back."

Those in the Carousel distinguished the Bingo's set as "dykes" or "bull dykes." Whitney explains, "A dyke was generally a very masculine appearing, acting woman." When asked why the women of her crowd who were also masculine looking wouldn't be called "bull dykes," she explains, "Because it was also a status thing. Society was lower-class and middle-class and what have you; no, it was generally, as far as I know, it was always used for people that were not as affluent." When asked what made the difference she adds: "Well, I think to work, say in a plant, you have to have a certain amount of crassness about you, just for survival. And so I think the less privileged people were the more they assumed those type of roles just for protection."

The prominence of class-based distinctions within the bar community is puzzling given their absence in the preceding decade, and also the strong impulse toward unity as manifested by the attempts toward desegregation and the lack of ethnic divisions among white lesbians. In fact, up until now we have not mentioned the place of ethnic distinctions because they had little meaning in the Buffalo lesbian community of the 1950s. Each subcommunity consisted of women of a variety of ethnic groups—Italian, Polish, German, Irish—with no one predominating. What is particularly striking to us is that throughout hours of recorded oral histories, we have no mention of ethnic divisions or tension. Rarely, if ever, do narrators even mention the ethnic background of others, despite the fact that Buffalo has a history of strong ethnic groups. This indicates an overriding consciousness of lesbian solidarity at the time.[32] Yet it was not enough to supersede class divisions.

From the perspective of class distinctions, the community cannot accurately be described as one or several.[33] As was the case with racial divisions, in some contexts the impulse toward unity, of being lesbians together, predominated, but in others, the tendency to divide on the basis of culture came to the fore. Why should class division emerge and be so tenacious throughout the 1950s? The evidence suggests that at this period of history, in the absence of concrete political institutions— organizations, newsletters—for lesbians, the meanings of different strategies of resistance were expressed through class differences, that is they were embedded in the language and culture of class relations. Recognizing this interconnection helps to explain why when the rough and tough lesbian emerged in the 1950s, she was not given a distinct name. Rather she was referred to in class terms, "riffraff " as opposed to those "elite lesbians." Resistance had not yet been separated out as a distinct political process.

The forces that transcended these class distinctions, creating a unified lesbian community and consciousness, were many. As in the case of the desegregation of the bars, the tough bar lesbians were in the lead in bringing lesbians together. Although the majority of the Carousel set was not interested in going to Bingo's or the street bars, the Bingo's crowd did go to the Carousel. A goal of the tough bar lesbians' culture was to increase the number of places where lesbians could be themselves. They were willing, even eager, to go where they weren't initially accepted. The tough bar lesbians were particularly attracted to the Carousel since it was a "nicer" bar, one to which a person might take a date and have a quiet evening.

From the early 1950s the rough and tough bar lesbians included the Carousel as part of their circling during an evening out.

> "I think most of them went into the Carousel during the course of an evening out, but it was just a deviation to get away. Like I said, if you're sitting in the same place looking at the same people. Well see, you can take ten minutes and walk down the street and go into another bar that's full of different faces. Because back then, everybody used to come out and the gay people really stuck up for each other. They really, really stuck up for each other." (Matty)

The older tough bar lesbians were completely at home at the Carousel, and some, like Matty, even designated it as their favorite bar because in it they were treated with dignity.

> "I would say the Carousel [was my favorite]. I had a lot of fun in the other bars, but yeah, I would say the Carousel. . . . Mostly because the Mardi Gras

and Bingo's and Dugan's, they had a lot of straights going in where the
Carousel didn't. And it was easier to sit down in the Carousel and just carry
on a conversation with someone, get to really know somebody. The Carousel
was the kind of a bar where if it were here now, today, would fit right in.
They had dancing just to the juke box in the back."

Marla remembers how it was so nice she could even bring a member of the family
there without feeling ashamed.

"It was a lot cleaner; there was more offered, more things to do, more people
coming in. Then I really got to know guys and all. I used to just go and relax.
. . . It seemed to be more friendly. 'Cause I remember one time during the
parade that was downtown, I even took my sister by there and introduced her
to the people working there. . . . The atmosphere around Bingo's was tougher."

At first, the younger rough and tough lesbians were not welcome at the Carousel
because of their unwillingness to conform to the conventions imposed by the
management. By the late 1950s, perhaps due to their constant pressure, they too
became regulars, but they had mixed feelings about it. They wanted to meet the
women who went to the bar but at the same time they looked down on the
discreet lifestyle required. Although their confrontational behavior frequently
caused them to be barred, they always attempted to get back in.

The Carousel itself encouraged a sense of unity among lesbians, and between
gay men and lesbians, by the activities it organized, and by its aim to create a safe,
respectable place. The people who worked behind the bar organized parties in
which the clientele took an active part.

"I remember they also had a piano in the back. They used to do talent shows
there . . . people who wanted to do something would do it; she would have
the guys on Halloween and stuff, drag shows. She used to have parties down
there like on Saint Patrick's day, for the parade, and then she did have corned
beef. I remember that. Around Christmas time, everybody would go down
there and also at New Years. One time they had a Valentine's party. They had
a box set up, just to be funny, just to give out Valentines like little kids. You
would put them in the box and they had the box decorated up and they would
pass out the Valentines." (Marla)

The Carousel was the only bar which lesbians frequented regularly where they
could dance. The juke box was in the front room, but for the protection of the
bar, most of the dancing took place in the back room where there was a speaker.
The popular dances—the jitterbug and slow dances—demanded hand and body
contact. "It was a while yet before you started dancing when you could get out
on the floor and dance with a partner you never touched" (Marla). Allowing two
women or two men to dance together always put the bar at risk in relation to the

law. "If they thought there was a cop in the place or one coming in, they'd tell you to stop dancing. It was done, it was done" (Bert).

The distinguishing feature of the Carousel most mentioned by narrators was the absence of fights. Even though rough and tough lesbians went to the Carousel, they respected its calm atmosphere and felt a responsibility to maintain the larger community. Sandy captures the demands and benefits of a protected environment: "And in the gay bar you had to sort of be cool, because they'd bar you right away. Then the straight bars, naturally there's bound to be fights, so they wouldn't bar you.[34] They figured you're gonna get killed anyhow, so what's the difference."

The more affluent lesbians wanted a bar with no fights and expected it to be this way. Dee recalls:

> "You talked at one point about the number of fights at the Carousel. From about '54, '55 to around, well until the Carousel went out of business, and I've forgotten the year, actually there was only two fights that I had ever seen in there, and I was in there quite frequently. I mean, definitely I was on a Saturday night, and once in a while during the week. And the only time there were these two fights, I remember very distinctly that the gal I was with said, 'Oh, there's a fight,' and we ducked out the side door and went home, because we didn't want any part of it. I'm not a fighting or an aggressive person."

Since the bar was known as a gay bar, it did attract a straight clientele who went to observe; however, they were required to behave. Straights who caused any trouble were not allowed in, and the same rule was applied to lesbians, particularly the tough lesbians. Bert remembers: "The Carousel, if anybody fought there they got barred. No real stupid drunken behavior was allowed. If you were trouble there were certain people whose reputations preceded them, that when they came into the bar they would be told to leave." Since one of the main causes for conflict, the need to claim lesbian territory, did not exist in the Carousel, there was less pressure on the tougher lesbians to fight. The skirmishes that did occur in the Carousel were between lesbians. Since such behavior was forbidden, the parties to a disagreement usually stepped outside to the alley behind the bar to take care of business.

The responsibility for keeping order fell primarily on the bartenders and the bouncers. Since the older tough lesbians had gained a reputation for being able to handle difficult situations, they as well as gay men tended bar, adding yet one other way that the upwardly mobile and the rough and tough lesbians were interdependent.

> "Back then if the bartender said something, boy, you listened. Because the next thing was 'Get out and don't come back.' That's the way it should be, and the owners always——if the bartender did something and the person went to the owner and said, 'Hey, they said I'm barred,' well then you're barred.

That's very important in a bar, because a lot of time the owners weren't there." (Matty)

Dee remembers the effectiveness of the woman who usually tended bar: "Boy, she could bounce anybody on their ear out of that place faster than anybody you know."

Although the Carousel provided a relatively safe and congenial atmosphere in which lesbians could socialize, it was still a gay gathering place in a heterosexual world. Therefore it had its dangers for all groups, though they had different strategies for resistance. Just as in the 1940s, going to a bar made lesbians vulnerable to being identified by hostile outsiders. Serious repercussions were always a possibility should a neighbor, co-worker, or family member discover someone was gay. Ironically, this risk was the greatest at the Carousel, since it was known as a gay bar, and straights would come for an entertaining evening of observation. Since physical confrontation was not allowed, all lesbians at the Carousel used humor and passive resistance, tactics similar to those employed a decade earlier at Ralph Martin's, for dealing with being objectified by straights. Marla remembers that she and her friends poked fun at heterosexuals' curiosity about "strange" people. "We had our little entertainment show for people that'd come in and think they were going to see a sight. We used to sit there and put on a show. Say 'Ooh, did I leave my other hand at home,' or 'Hey, is my head on crooked or something?' "

Such tactics of course could not eliminate the risks of exposure, which were particularly worrisome for the more status conscious lesbian who maintained distance between her lesbian life and her work and family. Joanna remembers how anxious her girlfriend, a teacher, was about going to the bar. " 'You shouldn't go to gay bars.' This was what she said. And if we went, [she was] always worried about somebody seeing her and this kind of thing. I said, 'What are they here for?' you know. 'Why should you worry about that?' But she did." The exposure was unquestionably frightening. Bert remembers how difficult it was for her to come to terms with being seen at the Carousel.

> "I can remember back to the Carousel days, a lot of nongay people would come in there, to see the gay people. We'd get a little drunk and carry on and say, 'Well they're here to see the fairies, if they stick around they'll see the fairies fly at midnight.' I can remember the experiences that I went through when you'd see somebody walk through the front door that you had grown up with, that you went to school with, or they lived in your neighborhood. Should you run out the back door? What should you do? Usually everybody ran to the ladies room or out the back door. And I came to grips with that by saying, 'Well, if they're not gay'—of course we didn't use the word gay then—'how can they point a finger in here at me being here, if they're here?' And that sort of was my rationale, so that I stopped running."

Despite the varied forces working toward lesbian unity, class distinctions remained prominent in bar life. The differences were represented spatially in the Carousel. The more affluent, status-conscious lesbians tended to stay in the front, at the bar, where the men also congregated. The younger rough and tough lesbians were in the back room, if they were not barred, while the older ones were comfortable in both areas. Class-based distinctions were elaborated by a discourse which heightened the differences in all aspects of culture—appearance, manners, sexual expression—and encouraged distance. Those in the front of the Carousel were not interested in getting to know those in the back. "I mean they weren't appealing. They weren't appealing to me. So I didn't want to get to know them" (Whitney). A primary objection was to their violence. "No, I never particularly got in with the rough, tough crowd, bottle-swinging and bat-swinging bunch. I'm not a violent person" (Dee). But it was more than this, it was their overall manner—their style of being butch-fem, their appearance, their overt sexuality.

> "Oh well the back room, the back room was bad news, 'cause it was all people shuffling around in their pants. I can't think what they were wearing, it wasn't jeans I suppose, it was chinos. . . . All the women [were] back there, and hugged and kissed. I used to hug and kiss, but I did it at the bar. I only did that with [friends] when we would get in the cups, and just be so delighted with one another. It wasn't a sexual thing, it was just a love sort of thing." (Whitney)

The tough bar lesbians had equal disdain for the upwardly mobile crowd, in particular their refusal to publicly acknowledge being lesbians. Vic remembers the Carousel with some animosity:

> "That's where I spent most of my time, was at Bingo's. . . . There was Mardi Gras, Chesterfield and them, that's where I spent most of my younger life. The Carousel was open then, but that was more your elite lezzies . . . and I was never into that crowd. . . . You see in those days there were also women that didn't like the role-playing game, even though the role-playing was the majority of the gay people's life. There was your—I don't think you'd call them professional people, but they were people that had pretty good jobs that just couldn't show their colors, that hung in there. This is early in the Carousel days, not at the end where it was where anybody went in. . . . For a while there they didn't even want you in if you had pants on, they wanted the girls to wear skirts. 'Cause there was a lot of hassles about that. And they would never come down to the lower-class bars."

Even in relation to men the two groups could find little common ground. The tough bar lesbians were not interested in the kind of protection gay men offered and spent little time with them. The back room where they gathered was all women. "A lot of girls even to this day won't associate with them. . . . The guys would come in and most of the girls would go in the back and stay back there by themselves" (Marla).

The younger rough and tough lesbians, most of whom were barred from the Carousel at one time or another, some permanently, remained fundamentally ambivalent about the bar. In deference to a community larger than themselves, they respected the need to maintain order in a lesbian and gay bar. "In the gay bar you had to be careful, if you fought in there they wouldn't take any—which is the way it should have been" (Sandy). At the same time they did not feel that their behavior was wrong, and looked down on those who weren't as willing to stand up for who they were. Their memories of being barred sound like Robin Hood tales, with the rough and tough lesbian creating justice in the end. Sandy relates a humorous story:

"Oh yeah, Jamie was working there. I punched her out so that didn't go over too good. So I was barred. That really pissed me off. Because when the Canadians and all that would come over they would go there. It was a little nice, they'd go there and I'd wanted to be in there too. The girls would be there. So I got really mad about that. Who the hell was I with, I think it was Ronni. We were down at the Chesterfield, I'm pissed off. I says, 'I'm going up to that Carousel,' and I already had a plan. So we go up to the Carousel, I says, 'Pull in the driveway,' there was a driveway right beside the bar, so she pulled in there and I got out of the car and I went to the back of the Carousel where these windows with screens on them was where the kitchen was. So I ripped the screen off, opened the window and I get in. Now I'm in the kitchen. 'Course, out of the kitchen is the back room, the bar naturally is to the front. So I went in the kitchen and I'm looking around, the big cooler, so I open up the cooler; I'm looking in there. There was all these cream pies and butter and all this shit. So I go to Ronni, here, we're loading the car up, with this butter and cream pies. So now, she says, 'Come on Sandy,' she was chicken, she says, 'Get out of there, get out of there.' I says, 'Wait a minute,' I seen these big trays of chicken, all cooked. It must have been for some party or something, I don't know. So I said, 'I'll be right with you.' So I get out one of these trays, there was some towels there, put a towel over my arm, take the tray and I went in the back room from the kitchen. I had a good time then. Now nobody really knows that I'm barred, but they got everything, right? 'Chicken tonight.' I'm going around giving all this out to all the kids in the back room. About two trays of chicken I handed out. Of course I didn't go to the front or anything. Somebody had to go out to the front, and they were eating chicken. He goes, 'Where'd that chicken come from?' 'Why Sandy's back there.' 'What?' They're yelling 'That God damn Sandy.' I dove out the back window. And I was barred for good then. There was no way of ever getting back in there. And Ronni says, 'But I got so sick of those God damn cream pies.' It was better than starving. Pulled the old waiter bit."

There were many associations between class-based culture and lesbian strategies of resistance. The expanding economy of the 1950s allowed tough bar lesbians to risk exposure because they did not have to worry about keeping any one particular job. In blue-collar work, if they lost one job, they could always find another. At the same time, the more upwardly mobile seized the new opportunities available to women in the 1950s for careers in white-collar work, and emphasized discretion even more strongly than in the past in order to keep good jobs. In this context the tough bar lesbians reinforced class divisions by challenging the double life and defending themselves physically when threatened, a trait associated with working-class culture in general. In particular, only working-class women had the tradition of strength and ability to defend themselves in extremely difficult and violent conditions. The desire to be more obvious was multidimensional and included being more physical and more explicitly sexual when socializing, both characteristics associated with the working class. Similarly, the strategy of discretion fit closely with the values of the 1950s middle class, which aimed to contain all that was disruptive and troublesome.

Just as in racial desegregation, the 1950s lesbian community cannot be accurately described as either one or several. The tension between unity and division was built into the culture and characterizes this period of prepolitical resistance. At the same time that the rough and tough lesbians projected an expanding lesbian consciousness and a unified community, their very tactics set them off from the upwardly mobile and strengthened divisions in the community. In some contexts the strong impulse toward unity, of being lesbians together, predominated, but in others the tendency to divide on the basis of cultures of resistance came to the fore.

THE END OF THE BAR ERA IN THE 1960s

All the bars that were important hangouts for lesbians in Buffalo during the 1950s closed at the end of the decade or the beginning of the next, and were not easily replaced. Rockefeller's antivice campaign in Buffalo led to constant harassment of bars by the State Liquor Authority, and created a grim period for lesbian social life. Within a twenty-one-month period between 1960 and 1961, we have been able to document at least six license revocations for bars frequented by homosexuals: Johnnie's Club Sixty-Eight, Club Co Co, the One Thirty-Two, Leonard's, the Pink Pony, and the Carousel.[35] From this point on until the 1970s no bars managed to stay open for more than several years. In this hostile atmosphere the rough and tough lesbians became the leading force in the bars.

Bingo's was the first to close in 1959.[36] It was not involved in the vice raids, rather it lost patronage to the newly opened the One Thirty-Two, and to the

Carousel which had become more hospitable to the rough and tough lesbians. This marks the beginning of a contemporary pattern of lesbians changing their preference for particular night spots rapidly and often, leading to the demise of former favorites. The tough bar lesbians did not forget the years of good times at Bingo's and most returned for a raucous last night with Sandy bartending.

> "I think I was the last one working there when he [Bingo] closed. I closed a lot of bars. . . . He had an open house that night. We did anyhow, you better believe. . . . I know when he was going to close that night, I says, 'This is it.' So everybody mobs in there. I gave the bar away. I didn't take a dime and I says, 'What the hell. We've got to have this juke box, we got to have money— break it open, who'd give a shit?' Played it all night."

Governor Rockefeller's crackdown on vice, although not directed specifically against gay and lesbian bars, nevertheless resulted in closer surveillance of gay bars in the search for police impropriety.

> "It seemed like Buffalo was a real swinging city, the gay people from Toronto would come to Buffalo and from Rochester. And I can remember when the change was made, it was when Rockefeller got into office as governor, that he starts having a lot of State Senate investigations. And they sent vice squads in to those various bars. And the Carousel, which had been open for [many] years, was one of the bars that got closed." (Bert)

Under scrutiny, the police charged a bar owner with multiple violations, until the bar's license was revoked. Buffalo police raids and license revocations were often accomplished with state and federal assistance and even direction.

The Carousel was closed by the State Liquor Authority, which charged that it was "frequented by homosexuals and degenerates."[37] Matty, who is knowledgeable about bar operations in the 1960s, attributes some of the problem to management's failure to curtail increasingly obvious gay-male behavior in the face of escalating police repression. "But in my opinion, as soon as they let the guys start coming in they got careless . . . and let a little bit too much go on."

The more short-lived bars, where it would be hard to make an historical case about serving "degenerates," were charged with other infractions of the liquor law like serving minors.[38] Matty recalls that often such charges were trumped up, as was the case when she was arrested as the bartender at the Club Ki-yo.

> "Sure, just like they tried to close the Ki-yo, when I was working there, when they came in and arrested me. . . . They came in and they said, 'Are you, Matty?' Two of the biggest vice cops I've ever seen in my life. And I said, 'Yeah.' He said, 'You're under arrest.' And I started to laugh, I said, 'You're kidding me.' And I knew them. And he said, 'No you're under arrest.' I said, 'Well, what for?' He said, 'Serving a minor.' But I didn't serve a minor. We had like a cop on the door, or one of these rented cops or whatever the hell it is, checking proof. I said, 'Now if they got in here go arrest him, don't arrest

me, he was checking the proof.' They said, 'You served the drink.' They said, 'The girl was sitting at the table with the drink in front of her.' "

According to Matty, the girl had not been served the drink but had table hopped and was sitting in front of someone else's. Matty was not badly treated by the police, because they were after the owner and the bar not her.

"When they took me out of there and got me in the car they said, 'Hi, how you been Matty?' and all that. [I said], 'This is pretty nice, you pull me out of there,' and they told me, not to worry about it. . . . They didn't fingerprint me or they didn't take my picture. . . . It was just a thing to get a mark on the bar and I'm the one they picked. . . . I didn't get the lawyer, they got the lawyer for me, the owner. Because he had more at stake than I did. I wasn't really arrested, but he knew they were out to get him, to close his bar. Which eventually they did."

Most narrators remember that the law was harder on gay men than on lesbians.

"I've said this many times, Gay men have always gotten it sooner and faster than we have. The man who owned the One Thirty-Two told us about the different things, when he had to go to investigations, the things that were said. And the majority always pointed at the men. Even before that though, I do remember men being harassed into situations. Vice-squad officers would come in and, because of loss of a better word, seduce the gay men and get him outside and say 'You're under arrest.' And that wasn't done to women. Women have always been able to dance together, in gay bars or nongay bars, but let two men try to get up" (Bert).

Matty agrees but also feels that gay men were partly responsible for attracting police attention. "It was always boys who would close the bars down, propositioning guys in the john. A woman would never do a thing like that, you know, go into the bathroom for a sexual experience. I mean, at least, I'll say I don't think a woman would. There are probably some who would but—"[39]

With constant surveillance and harassment gay bars stayed open for relatively short periods during the 1960s. Some bar owners were persistent and kept opening gay bars. In addition, the rough and tough lesbians took the lead in finding new bars. Immediately after Bingo's closed, the rough and tough lesbians spent their time at the Carousel and the One Thirty-Two, as well as in the street bars, with some also going to house parties and bars in the Black community.[40] In time they became instrumental in finding and fighting for the bars of the early 1960s, including Leonard's, the Havana Casino, and the Eagle Inn. When a bar's business was slow, someone would approach the owner and negotiate with him to turn it into a gay bar. "We used to go to the bars and say, listen, you're dying here, you want to make some money and we want to come here and spend our money; we'll behave" (Sandy). This was often a very attractive proposition, particularly for bars that were already in trouble and knew that they would have to close anyway, allowing them to make money in their last few months. Sometimes negotiations weren't enough and people had to fight for the bar.

"That was a tough part of town. Well, first of all it was a straight bar and this one guy started bartending over there and told the kids, 'Come on down'; and so some of the kids started going down there, right? So the straight guys that were in there sure as hell didn't want all these dykes coming in because when I first came out you were a bull dyke or a fem, whichever—fortunately I missed the fight, but for three or four weekends in a row there were constantly fights. And I mean fights, beer bottles flying, a few knives here and there, you know, to take over the bar, fights between the bull dykes and the straight men. This is what we had to contend with; this is the way we took over a bar in those days. In fact, you never went out by yourself; you'd always go out with four or five and go in the bar to protect each other; and finally we took over. It opened up and they left us alone." (Jan)

Even when the owner intended to make a bar gay, a fight might occur, as happened at the Club Ki-yo in the mid-1960s.

"Shortly after [the Eagle Inn] closed, [the owner] kept saying, don't find a job, hang on, I'm gonna get another bar for you. One of the Radice brothers owned the Ki-yo and he went in with him to make it gay. But it was on North and Michigan in the Black section, it was a rough bar. And we had to fight for that bar but we had to fight the Blacks. I mean, I can't really blame them. It was their bar, we went in we took over. And when I say fight, I mean fight, clubs, sticks, bats. They would come in on the weekends, there would be real battles. . . . The bar was mixed [men and women]. . . . The women and the guys fought . . . every weekend for the longest time, it didn't stay open that long." (Matty)

Under these conditions, the leadership of the rough and tough lesbians was necessary if there were to be any lesbian bars at all, and therefore they set the tone of bar life. They even defended the men who patronized the mixed bars.

"The mixed bars used to be really funny because if a fight broke out, all the guys used to jump on the tables and all the girls used to do the fighting. . . . If there was, like if some straights came in and they started to pick on a particularly effeminate boy, the girls would stick up for him and fight his battles for him." (Matty)[41]

The more affluent lesbians, although most continued to go out, did not find a place where they felt comfortable. Cheryl, who moved to Buffalo in 1960, considers Buffalo bars "awful" compared to those of other cities. Her description is somewhat exaggerated but captures accurately the tone of the bars.

"Well, see now when I said awful about the bars, I compare them to Chicago, Miami, Jacksonville, Baltimore. Now those were well decorated, they were kept clean . . . like in Baltimore . . . you couldn't get in if that owner said no, because they looked every person over. They dressed better, they were better looking, and they were calmer. I never went to a bar in Buffalo that there weren't fights going on every night, and that to me was dumb. What kind of people [were these]?. . . . The language was abusive, everybody was on the make, everybody got so drunk they couldn't stand up, that didn't make any sense to me. That's what I mean by awful, they weren't having a good time. They were all in there and depressed."

The constant turnover in bars gave a new dimension to the job of gay and lesbian bartenders. They not only had to maintain order in a very difficult situation, deal with the police, and endure arrests, but now they were key figures for indicating that a place was a lesbian and/or gay bar. The community knew that bars where particular people worked intended to have a lesbian and gay clientele, and these bartenders were sought out by those who wanted to run gay bars (or turn their bars into gay bars). Matty remembers:

"When a bar was closing, like say Saturday night was going to be its last night, sometime that weekend the owner of the bar would introduce me to somebody and say, 'He'd like you to work for him when you leave here.' And I would just go from bar to bar. Everybody would just know, that if I'm in the bar, it is all right to come in there."

This particular narrator was so well-known to the bar owners, that she was referred to as the Queen Bee.

"There was one incident where I was going over to my mother's house, and my brother was there. And when I walked in the door my mother says, 'Here she comes now, the queen bee.' And I said 'What's this all about?' And my brother told me that the night before he was out with some of his friends and a guy was thinking of opening a bar, and he says, 'You know where the money is now, in the gay bars.' And my brother was sitting hearing these words, men that he knew. And [the guy] said, 'Money is in the gay bars now. You open a bar and turn it gay, you'll make a fortune.' And [my brother] said, 'This other guy pipes up and says, "Yeah, but to do that you've go to get the queen bee. I don't know her name, she's a short, dark, stocky kid, wherever she goes the girls just seem to follow.' And my brother knew that they were talking about me and he just sat there and he wanted to die. And I says to him, 'What do you mean you wanted to die, you should have proudly stood up and said, oh that's Matty, she's my sister.' And he said, 'Yeah, sure.' So that's why my mother said, 'Here she comes now, the queen bee.' I don't know how I felt about being labeled a queen bee. If it's doing good for the gay community I love it."

The pressure on gay bars was so great during the 1960s that at times there were periods without any bars at all. During one of these "dry" spells in 1969, the first Buffalo gay and lesbian organization was formed, the Mattachine Society of the

Niagara Frontier. This began a new era in Buffalo lesbian history. Hereafter, lesbians and gays had alternatives for public socializing and political activities.

The juxtaposition of the three Buffalo subcommunities reveals the political ferment in working-class lesbian life during the 1950s. In the context of a developing understanding of lesbians as a distinct group, each subcommunity developed its own strategy of resistance, and therefore brought a different prepolitical consciousness to the era of gay liberation politics. Together they provided the basis for a powerful movement. The rough and tough bar butches—Black and white— with their male appearance and manners, were brazen rebels against injustice, defying society to accept lesbians for the "queers" they were. They, and the fems who associated with them, projected a vision of a single community that could take care of itself. Those of the more upwardly mobile white group believed that they could bring about the acceptance they were entitled to by living "normal" lives, and carrying on an individual dialogue with the world. Black lesbians effectively protected their own institutions through both diplomacy and physical confrontation. Black and white lesbians together created a pattern of interracial socializing that has perhaps not been matched by gay liberation, and certainly not improved upon.

Because Buffalo was a working-class city, the rough and tough lesbians—Black and white—were a strong force and their contribution was most apparent. Of the women who, alongside men, founded the Mattachine Society of the Niagara Frontier, and brought gay liberation to Buffalo, the largest constituency were rough and tough lesbians.[42] The steady harassment of the bars by the police and the State Liquor Authority, plus the developing activist politics of gays in other cities, combined with bar culture and consciousness to create a gay and lesbian political organization.[43]

This perspective suggests that both the homophile movement and gay liberation had their roots in the working-class culture of bars and house parties. The kernel of the idea that lesbians were a distinct kind of people that deserved a better life, when combined with the expanding opportunities for women's white-collar work, provided the conditions for the development of the homophile movement. Similarly, the rebellious element of gay liberation was rooted in the bar community's own prepolitical forms of resistance. To understand this fully requires a multi-faceted exploration of butch-fem roles, which were the central institution of resistance and are the subject of the next two chapters. Here it is sufficient to suggest that the confrontational and defiant spirit of gay liberation did not derive solely from external forces like the student and Black power movements. Toni, on reading a version of this chapter, comments: "Finally, the truth is spoken. The strength of gay liberation did not originate in the classrooms of middle-class students. Its strength came from those who were tired of being kicked around. The ones who took the chances and the bruises. The ones who had been out there getting their bodies and psyches battered."

"WE'RE GOING TO BE LEGENDS, JUST LIKE COLUMBUS IS": THE BUTCH-FEM IMAGE AND THE LESBIAN FIGHT FOR PUBLIC SPACE

"I don't think that now they differentiate as much. . . . Then it was very cut and dried. It was a butch or a lesbian. And the girlfriend, the ladies. . . . And they dressed differently, they acted differently."

—Joanna

"In particular, I remember a woman who was Black, or she might have been Black and Spanish, but she was brown skinned, and had short curly hair, and in those days we put grease on our hair when we had it cut short and she had like grease on her hair and it was close cropped and real curly. She was kind of short. She was leaning up against the juke box, and she was swinging a key chain; and she had on men's spade shoes, black leather dress shoes, and maybe like a suit, or a vest, and a pair of trousers and a trench coat. She frightened me 'cause she looked so tough to me, but she intrigued me too."

—Toni

Butch-fem women made Lesbians visible in a terrifyingly clear way in a historical period when there was no Movement protection for them. Their appearance spoke of erotic independence, and they often provoked rage and censure both from their own community and straight society. Now it is time to stop judging and to begin asking questions, to begin listening.
—Joan Nestle, "Butch-Fem Relationships: Sexual Courage in the 1950s"

Although narrators differ on the importance of roles, or the ease with which they followed their prescriptions, they all agree that butch-fem roles predominated in the public lesbian community of the past.[1] They also agree that in today's world, roles take a different form, and are not immediately apparent, if, in fact, they exist at all. As they look around the bars these days, old-timers are likely to quip, "You can't tell the players without a program," or, "Look at those two. When they go home they'll toss a coin to see who will be on top!"

Our research reveals that the salience and tenacity of butch-fem roles in the pre-1970s public lesbian community derives from their functioning as both a powerful personal code of behavior and as an organizing principle for community life. As the former, they dictated the way individuals presented themselves in daily life, particularly in regard to image—appearance and mannerisms—and sexuality. Butches affected a masculine style while fems appeared characteristically feminine. Butch and fem also complemented one another in an erotic system in which the butch was expected to be the doer and the giver; and the fem's receptive passion was the butch's fulfillment. Appearance and sexual expression were the primary indicators of butch-fem roles.[2] Sometimes narrators would also refer to personality—being more or less domineering—but not consistently.

Butch-fem roles, however, entailed much more than a personal code of ethics. They were also a powerful social force. They were the organizing principle for this community's relations with the outside world. The presence of the butch with her distinctive dress and mannerism, or of the butch-fem couple—two women in a clearly gendered relationship—announced lesbians to one another and to the public. Butch-fem roles established the parameters for love relationships and friendships within the community. Two butches could be friends, but never lovers; the same was true for two fems. The importance of visibility and erotic difference for the organization of the community explains in part why appearance and sexual expression were key elements in the butch and fem guidelines for personal behavior.

Roles as the basic organizing principle for the community and roles as a code of personal behavior were inseparable throughout this period. Whether or not someone wanted to follow the code of personal behavior, the community's relations with the straight world and its methods for developing love relationships depended on roles, and therefore, to be an active member of the community a person had to adhere to the rules to some degree.[3] As a result no matter what a particular lesbian personally thought or felt about the butch-fem *code*, whether assuming a role identity felt like a natural expression of her being or something imposed, she needed to adopt a role. They were a social imperative. Only then could she participate comfortably in the community and receive its benefits. For lesbians coming out in the 1970s, 1980s, and 1990s this is a very difficult concept to grasp, because we can imagine roles only as a code of personal behavior. As a result, we make the mistake of considering the social pressure for roles as simply arbitrary, negative pressure. But in the 1940s and the 1950s, the social pressure came from the way roles functioned in building community. If they required individuals to compromise their identity they offered the reward of participation in a community which effectively resisted the oppression of gays and lesbians.

Butch-fem roles have been the subject of significant controversy in the feminist and lesbian feminist movement. Coming from a theoretical framework that associates masculinity and males with evil—violence, rape, exploitation, and destruction—some feminists have scorned butch-fem communities for their imitation of the patriarchal system of gender.[4] Others, recognizing the entrenched nature of gender in twentieth-century Western industrial culture, have explored the ways that lesbians have appropriated gender roles as a tool of resistance. As early as the 1940s, Simone de Beauvoir, in her chapter on lesbians in *The Second Sex*, recognized the power to be gained by lesbians adopting masculine characteristics.[5] Joan Nestle makes this argument historically specific, articulating how the butch-fem couple in the 1950s boldly expressed the sexual interest of women in women at a time when such love was outlawed and there was no political movement for protection.[6] Our research has been influenced by and in turn supports this tradition, revealing the complexity of gendered resistance for lesbians during the 1940s and 1950s.

Butch-fem culture unquestionably drew on elements of the patriarchal gender system; but it also transformed them. On the simplest level, butches were masculine, not male, and fems were attracted to masculine women, not men. Butch-fem roles, therefore, expressed women claiming their difference, their right to love other women at a time when few, if any, other such opportunities existed. The masculine appearance of butches distinguished them and their fems as different, thereby serving as a badge of identifiability among lesbians themselves and to the general public. The possibility of recognizing one another was essential for the building of a distinct culture and identity.

Butch-fem roles crystallized the varied possibilities for resistance and stimulated people to carry them out. The extraordinary resistance that was documented in the past three chapters was highly gendered. It was accomplished by butches and fems.[7] The core group that built the lesbian bar community of the 1940s were the severely masculine yet gentle butches who were willing to be identified as different, as "homos." The Black and white tough lesbians continued this tradition in the 1950s, pushing to be identified as lesbians, or "queers," twenty-four hours a day. They not only endured the hostility of the straight world but they defended themselves with physical force if necessary. The fem contribution was radically different, though no less important. Fems' public resistance centered around support for their butches, being seen with them on the streets or in restaurants, or bringing them to family dinners. They also validated their butches' existence by acknowledging and respecting butch identity.

To begin the process of illuminating the place of the butch-fem dyad in prefeminist lesbian communities, this chapter explores the butch-fem image as a code of personal behavior and as a social imperative and the connections between the two. (The erotic dimension of the butch-fem image, with its attendant aura of excitement, is not explored fully until the next chapter.)[8] The concept of the butch-fem image is somewhat misleading because it suggests that we are focusing strictly on the visual, when we are in fact considering personal inclination, social rules, community pressure, and politics. It is our experience that all language for talking about butches and fems is inadequate. For instance, the concept of butch-fem roles reduces butch-fem behavior to role *playing* and does not take into account the depth and complexity of butch and fem as an organizing principle which pervades all aspects of working-class lesbian culture. We, therefore, use the concept of the butch-fem image as a way of entering this complex culture, rather than as a way of simplifying it. We document the elements of dress and mannerisms that composed the butch-fem image during the 1940s and 1950s, and explore the social meaning of this image. In the interest of creating a comprehensive view of the development of twentieth-century lesbian consciousness, we consider the relationship between the prepolitical forms of resistance expressed through the butch-fem image and the rise of gay liberation.

THE BUTCH-FEM IMAGE OF THE 1940s

Narrators who entered the bars in the 1940s all have vivid memories of the striking appearance of butch lesbians. When asked how she could tell that Ralph Martin's was a gay bar on her first visit, Reggie replies: "You could tell by their dress, you could tell the boys when they walked—the butches were very butchy, very, ties, shirts." Joanna conveys a similar impression when reminiscing about her first night at Ralph Martin's.

"At that particular time there were many more lesbians who came out and didn't worry about having their hair curled, or long; or their ears pierced. Those kinds of things to look a little [feminine], because they really didn't care. . . . But at that time almost every lesbian was dressed in men's attire."

Not all butches of the time cultivated this exaggerated masculine appearance, but it was certainly the style of the core group of bar patrons.

White butches remember devoting a great deal of care—not to mention time and money—to their dress when preparing to step out on a Saturday night in the 1940s. In this culture, it was not just fems who paid attention to their looks. Butches wanted their image to be admired by others in the community and wanted to appear handsomely attractive to fems. They did not simply wear masculine clothes, but rather developed a definite style for dressing up. A distinctive part of their attire was the heavily starched shirts which contrasted with their softer everyday blouses. Leslie remembers, "They would starch them until they would break. If there was a wrinkle in them, they would put them back in the water." They wore big cuff-links in their shirts and jackets over them. In the 1930s jackets were an optional part of dressing up, since not all butches could afford them. By 1942 when they had more money, due to the economic recovery from the end of the Depression and the onset of the war, jackets were regularly worn for an evening out.

During the war, pants became more acceptable in general for women, and butches started wearing them when they went out on weekends. Previously they would wear boys' pants indoors but not outside. "You had to travel in a street car and you would run into flack from men. Women too would cause trouble, they might feel that you would follow them into the bathroom and attack them" (Leslie). Arden recalls that finding suitable pants took initiative. "You could get pants to wear for work but you got dressed up on a Saturday night. That was the night you went out," and dress pants for women were unavailable.[9] They had to have them custom tailored; despite their masculine appearance they did not wear men's dress pants. Joanna reminisces: "There was a place on Chippewa Street that used to make girls' [pants] without the fly in the front. The zipper was on the side. But they had to be tailor made. They didn't sell them in the stores, on racks, like now." Even Dee, who felt ambivalent about projecting an extremely masculine appearance, went to this shop. She loved her tailor-made slacks of fine material, which she kept until recently.

> "During the war years, everybody wore pants. They were not known as pant suits as we have today, they were not as feminine as the pant suits are today. We even, at that point, we had heard about this place on Chippewa Street where they would tailor the slacks for girls. We went in there. As probably just a sentimental thing I still had them, I threw them away when I moved [three years ago]. But at that point I had had these tailor-made slacks and I was very proud of them."

Although Black lesbians did not regularly frequent the bars during the 1940s, their dress code for house parties was not radically different from that of whites. "If you want to know how I dressed, well I had on slacks. And some of the best kind. And my hair was cut short" (Debra).

To go with their pants, butches got "the most masculine-style shoes you could find, flat shoes, like oxfords" (Leslie). White butches usually went to Eastwoods, a Buffalo specialty store for sensible, sturdy shoes. Arden remembers making excuses for her masculine shoes. When she was young she would come home with shiny, laced up shoes with thick soles. Her family would say, "It's a wonder you can't get something with a strap." She would respond, "I can't walk in them."

Their short haircuts were also consciously created for their image. Arden recalls, "It was worn very extreme, not like today; it wasn't until later that they softened it." In her case it was cut short, up over the ears. She would often wear a hat. "In my own neighborhood, I might wear a knitted cap, but when I went downtown I might wear a masculine-like hat." Unlike items of clothing, haircuts could not easily be changed between work and socializing, so not all butches could wear such a severe cut. Leslie remembers that she and a butch friend adopted the "pineapple look." They had curls all over, and therefore, didn't look so butch at work. Since long hair was traditionally associated with femininity, the cutting of hair was symbolic in the process of achieving an extremely butch appearance. "I was going through that stage, you know where well, I'm gonna cut my hair real short and do what I want to do. . . . Very mannish" (Reggie).

The fem dress code of the 1940s was not distinctive to the lesbian community, but rather copied that of fashionable women in the heterosexual world. Fem narrators like Charlie remember always having a keen interest in clothes and style. "I enjoy clothes, clothes make me happy. And it makes me happy to dress my friend too. . . . I always wore what I wanted to." When asked how she knew she was a fem, Charlie replies:

> "Well because I wore makeup, I wanted to wear makeup and I liked clothes. I never went to butchy clothes or . . . like a librarian, they wear a certain kind of clothes, you know, they don't go in with a low cut dress. Probably because of the way I wanted to dress and then I just never felt any other way."

Pearl, also a fem, remembers her appearance:

> "Well I would dress with high-heeled shoes and skirt or a dress. That's the way I usually dressed. . . . Once in a while I'd get real, I don't know if you'd call it brave or what, but I would put on . . . I don't know if you remember when the zoot suits were in style with the long jackets and the chains and the pants that had the real tight legs and you had to take your shoes off to put them on. . . . I had long hair but I wore it up. I hardly ever wore my hair down. It was usually up in a bun or french twist or just with a ribbon [in a ponytail]."

Although fems liked to dress up, some also were comfortable in casual clothes. Sometimes, they even wore pants. Joanna remembers how much she liked her first pair.

> "At that time slacks weren't really that popular. . . . And to wear a pair of slacks was really kind of looked down on because they just weren't worn for everyday attire. That wasn't part of the wardrobe. That was part of somehow, say you were going riding, or you were roughing it. But if you went out you didn't wear them. My first pair of slacks I thought were the greatest I ever had in my whole life."

Even when they both wore pants, there was a definite difference in the appearance of a lady and her butch. Joanna mentions the distinguishing features of fem appearance while remembering a time when in the late 1940s she and her butch were harassed by some men after leaving a bar in Manhattan. "I was wearing pants too but I had, like I had a blouse on. I had makeup on. So evidently we did look a hell of a lot [like a gay couple], well my hair was [done-up]."

Butch narrators' memories of the 1940s emphasize the glamorous appearance of fems. "They would wear high heels and makeup and have their hair done in the highest fashion of the day" (Leslie). Or, "The girls used to be dressed in all their finery, dresses, high heels" (Arden). Leslie, like most butches, remembers with affection and humor any difficulties fems had in achieving these high standards. "[She] dressed ultrafem, gloves up to here, and a hat with a veil, and high heels and Kolinskys [a fox-fur neckpiece], and would drink too much. The Kolinskys would fall on the floor." Leslie of course, would pick them up for her and the evening's fun would continue. Butches' appreciation of glamour was such that show girls who were flashily dressed and heavily made-up were easily accepted in the community.[10]

As visible as dress was in the presentation of a role-defined lesbian, it was not the sole determinant of image. Mannerisms were also cited by narrators in their definitions and descriptions. The significance of mannerisms is evident in the way old-timers attempt to identify roles in the current bar scene where there is no longer a role-defined dress code. D.J. explains:

> "All their appearances are all the same. There's a very few that you can really say, 'Now that's a butch, whee, there's a fem.' You can't do it no more, 'cause they're all dressed on the same order. The dungarees, the T-shirts, long hair . . . unless . . . it's the way they pick up a drink . . . if you're really watching that hard. . . . Or the way they hold a cigarette. . . . Then you can distinguish. But as far as appearance, clothes-wise, no one can tell any more."

Butch and fem mannerisms were modeled on male-female behavior as portrayed in the Hollywood movies of the period. They included all the little details of presenting one's self—manner of walking, sitting, holding a drink, tone of voice. Most butches were expert mimics who had mastered the subtleties of masculine nonverbal communication. It is particularly noteworthy that during the 1940s, despite the extreme of masculine dress, but in keeping with the lack of physical violence in the community, these butches did not project an aggressive tough image. Narrators describe their image as "severe," never tough. Reggie goes as far as to describe her friends as gentle and kind, most likely an implicit contrast to the tough bar lesbians of the next decade. She found them willing to accept her for who she was, and most importantly, restrained in their use of physical violence:

> "Your fems were very feminine, your butches were butchy but they were kind, you know. . . . They weren't the macho type and they didn't go out and want to fight right away. You know, 'You're talking to my girlfriend.' I never had to ask any of them. I asked their girls to dance. I never got a dirty look or 'Hey, out of due respect you're gonna ask me.' "

Since 1940s lesbians did not actively introduce people to gay life, they did not instruct people in how to dress or carry themselves. Newcomers picked up what they wanted. When asked if everyone was into roles in the old days, Leslie responds, "For at least ninety-five percent there was no mistaking." Then she wonders out loud, "If we did it to them, push people into roles?" She answers herself, "No, they preferred it that way. We didn't do it." And Arden concurs. Reggie remembers the 1940s lesbian community as very tolerant. She felt fully accepted by the older butches, even though with her long hair, she didn't look as severe as they. However, just the existence of admired social groups created some social pressure to conform. Dee still remembers feeling ostracized from the core group of butches at Ralph Martin's because she and her fem went to the bar one time dressed in evening gowns, with their gay male escorts, after a company dance. Furthermore, gender polarity pervaded the whole culture and was therefore difficult to escape.

An important part of the 1940s butch and fem images was not only the way each appeared and acted separately, but also the striking contrast between the two. Every narrator at some point made a comment on the difference between butch and fem appearance: "Well see there was quite a distinction" (D.J.), or "The so-called butches were really masculine looking, dressed masculine, and the fems were the same way, dressed feminine" (Phil). Joanna remembers, "There was a hell of a difference. . . . [Ladies] looked like girls . . . with the makeup and earrings." The contrast within the butch-fem couple was part of the community's aesthetic sensibility. As narrators reminisce about events or friends of their past, their flashes of memory about a particular couple regularly capture the distinctive appearance of butch and fem: the lady with "the ultrafem look" and her butch wearing "a stiff shirt with a jacket that came down to her hips" (Leslie). The fashionably feminine and intriguingly masculine communicated excitement and pleasure to partners in a couple and to the entire community (see photos after p. 190).

THE BUTCH-FEM IMAGE IN THE 1950s

The basic elements of the 1940s image for butches and fems—the importance of dressing up, with butches wearing masculine clothes and fems appearing glamorous—continued into the 1950s, but the details of presentation changed (see photos after p. 190). Part of the change simply reflected trends in male and female dress styles in the dominant society. But part of the change reflected developments in the lesbian community and the social climate for both straight women and lesbians. White tough bar lesbians, Black tough lesbians, and the primarily white upwardly mobile lesbians projected different images.

White tough bar butches cultivated an extremely working-class masculine look. They generally wore more articles of male clothing than butches in the 1940s or in the more upwardly mobile crowd of the 1950s, but not more than the tough Black butches. Although they modeled themselves after the more experienced butches, they were often influenced by the style of some of the more popular musicians of the emerging rock and roll scene. Buddy Holly, Richie Valens, and later in the decade the young Elvis Presley, with their slicked back hair, pouty lips in a slight sneer and a smoldering look about the eyes, all became models. Many butches developed a style that was at once tough and erotically enticing; simultaneously careless and intense.

Since they went out to bars every night, not just on weekends, tough bar butches had to have appropriate clothes for both casual wear and for dressing up. Stormy, a regular at Bingo's in the mid-1950s, remembers white butches on the weekend wearing sports jackets, chino pants or sometimes men's dress pants, and men's shirts—button downs, western shirts, or tuxedo shirts with ties. When they went out during the week, they dressed more casually in shirts and chinos. Penny loafers were common, and they were often worn with argyle socks. But tough butches also wore cowboy boots and low-cut men's dress boots. Despite the requirement of men's clothes, white butches in the early and mid-1950s had quite a bit of leeway in how they constructed their image. Bert recalls her partiality to colors: "Even though I wore men's clothes I always wore colorful type clothes. I can remember in the summertime one time I had a lavender top, light yellow [pants]. Just regular men's clothes."

For the younger tough white butches in the late 1950s the dress code was more restrictive. The image is captured by Ronni's description of herself: "I played a very dominant, possessive, butch, truck-driver role at that time. I wore a crew-cut and shirts. I used to have my pants tapered at the bottom. I'd have my cuffs taken in. I'd go have my hair cut at the barber." Chinos had gone out of style and blue jeans were in, so that during the week, butches wore T-shirts and jeans, a uniform popularized by the movies of James Dean and Marlon Brando.

On the weekends they still dressed up, but strictly in men's clothes. Toni remembers having to acquire the right clothes:

> "I did not have the clothes at first. On Friday night I would meet [these older butches] dressed in men's shiny shoes, men's dress pants—they were pegged at that time—white shirts and thin belts. . . . I copied these butches. I bought my first pair of men's shoes, loafers, men's slacks, men's shirts and started dressing like the others."

Absent from this memory are sports jackets, which were no longer essential in the white community by the late 1950s. Instead, butches wore sweaters—cardigans and V-necks. Little Gerry suggests that the reason for this was "TV and the growing influence of the Perry Como look."

Greased back D.A.'s were the popular haircut of the white tough bar crowd.[11] Some had other men's-style hairdos including a few crew cuts, but narrators explain that those were mainly worn by people who did not have to go to regular jobs. As in the 1940s the act of cutting hair, whatever the style, was often a personally meaningful step in acquiring the butch image.[12] Vic remembers her haircut as central to achieving her identity: "I had my first butch haircut in the back room at Bingo's bar. My hair was about down to here. Rose her name was,

I don't know if she is even still living. . . . Yeah. That was the best thing that ever happened to me though. . . . Cause that was me, that was me."

And of course purses were not part of the butch ensemble. "Back to the image, you know, the butch doesn't carry a purse." They didn't need them because unlike ladies' pants and dresses, men's pants had pockets.[13] The butch's lack of familiarity with a purse was an assumed part of the culture, and often added humor to difficult dealings with the heterosexual world, as in Matty's reminiscences about her arrest in the mid-1960s for allegedly serving a drink to a minor.

> "The guy that was bartending [with me], he was a gay guy, he was cracking up when they took me out of there. Because when they were taking me out, the girl I was seeing at the time . . . [worried that] I had nothing of a girl on. Well, underpants and a bra. But she comes running up to me and handed me her purse, she said, 'Here Matty, you forgot your purse.' And she handed me this huge purse, and I didn't even know how to carry the damn thing. There I stood looking at this purse wondering what the hell to do with it. He said [later], 'So [you] held it like you would a football if you were running with a football.' And I thought, what if they look in here, this isn't even my purse. But they didn't."

Certain items of male clothing acquired a special meaning among white tough bar butches. The T-shirt symbolized the daring of lesbians wearing male clothing, and is recalled with particular fondness.

> "This is very funny but it's really the truth; if you think about it, butches, we've always worn T-shirts. That was our thing, right? And most of the time why did we wear T-shirts, because we didn't wear a bra. We came way before the ERA movement. When did they start this big thing about fifteen years ago? We had thrown those away. We just threw them away and put on T-shirts. And boy, when you wore a T-shirt—Wow! They didn't look to see where your tits were. Oh, you have a T-shirt! We were the Original." (Sandy)

Sandy went on to explain why T-shirts were usually worn backward, a point that is vividly remembered by most narrators.

> "Do you know why? I will tell you; it's the most, the simplest thing. A lot of things I've been telling you are really simple, but this is really simple. When they made T-shirts, now, of course, they make 'em more for the contour of the body, . . . but in those days, you got the T-shirt, the neck this wide, that you could put on King Kong, right? Now what is always the highest part of the T-shirt is the neck. So you'd put them on backwards, so it would be higher up, you got it? Your T-shirt was down here in the back, but it was here [in the front]. That's why we wore our T-shirts backwards in those days. 'Cause it was higher in the back. It came out nice; it made it really crew neck, and you looked really swift. If you came out and here was your T-shirt down to here, and it was all wrinkled too, from hanging off your shoulders. Oh, you'd

look like a jerk. So you put 'em on backwards. And most of the time you cut the label off. That's why if you ever found our T-shirts lying around on the floor, you'd say, which was which, cause there was no label. We'd cut it out cause you wore it in the front. All right, some of these things I wouldn't say to a lot of people."

Toni emphasizes slightly different reasons for wearing T-shirts backward. "We wore white T-shirts. The necks sagged in the front so we wore it backwards. It covered you more. It would be more feminine to have it go down in the front."

Sandy, who talks about not wearing bras, was small-breasted. Not all butches were. Little Gerry, a full-breasted butch, remembers fems of the time joking, "Butches have all the cleavage, and they don't even want it." Breasts unquestionably presented a problem for the butch image. Fuller-breasted butches would have to choose clothes that camouflaged their bosoms. Little Gerry later explains the popularity of cardigans instead of V-necks in the early 1960s as related to this: "I had gotten a new camel-hair V-neck sweater that I liked and was quite proud of. Then [Vic] said to me, 'It's a beautiful sweater, but I myself, prefer cardigan sweaters, because they don't emphasize the breast.'" She gave her V-neck sweater away to a more flat-chested butch.

Fuller-breasted women would often modify the cups of their bras so their breasts wouldn't look so pointy.

> "But I always used to sew my bras in. Because in the '50s the two big bras were Maidenform and Exquisite Form bras. They were pointed. You sewed your bras so they weren't pointed. I did that myself. They [looked] similar to the bras they are wearing in 1982. It gave that same kind of free kind of look."

Butches might also wear binders, strips of cloth, or Ace bandages wrapped around the chest. They were not tight, but gave the appearance of a smooth front so that men's shirts would fit better.

Purchasing the men's apparel that was so critical to the butch image was often a difficult task. Some butches handled the situation by camouflaging their identities while shopping in men's stores. According to Stormy, "We didn't try them [pants] on. A lot of women at the time bought clothes for their husbands." She did try on her sports coats and covered for this by telling the salesmen, "I was buying it for a boyfriend who was a similar size to me." Other butches, particularly those who came out in the late 1950s, did not develop a cover while shopping and risked exposure and ridicule. Toni remembers that she wanted the clothes enough to endure the tension.

> "I would go into men's shops, men's departments of department stores; it was always awful. I hated it, but I wanted the clothes so I went through with it.
> . . . They either thought I was a boy and called me 'he,' which was always a real funny place to be because I never knew if at any moment they'd find out any different, and then I'd be embarrassed, or if they thought I was a woman

buying men's clothes for herself, which just was not done then. It was very embarrassing, but I wanted the clothes bad enough to put up with it. It was humiliating always to me, very embarrassing. I felt awful about myself, 'cause I felt like I was being watched."

Toni adds that there were certain stores where other butches went in which it was easier to shop.

"There were a couple of stores that some of the women would go into. I remember there was one store on Grant Street where [several butches] bought clothes, so that was like a little more comfortable. He was used to lesbians coming in there and buying pants; it wasn't like he'd look at you funny. There was one tailor that you could have your pants tailored at, if you got dress pants. [He] was used to the lesbians and he didn't, you know, make you feel embarrassed about yourself."

The fem image in the white tough bar crowd was not significantly different from that of the 1940s, except for the differences brought about by the inevitable changes in the fashion world. Fems, dressing according to the latest styles, adapted a more overtly sexy look, like the sweater-girl style popularized by Lana Turner, Jane Russell, and Marilyn Monroe. The invention of new fibers helped to create this image. Nylon and Dacron were used for sheer stockings, diaphanous materials for blouses and undergarments, and Orlon and Banlon for inexpensive, body-hugging sweaters.[14] One of the authors, Madeline, remembers being intimidated on one of her early forays into the bars in 1957, several years before she came out fem, by the sophisticated and sultry appearance of the fems.

Fems wore pants as well as skirts. Annie describes her costume of the late 1950s.

"When I first started coming around and hanging around in those bars I used to wear skirts, high heels. I used to wear my heels all the time. And then I started getting into the habit where we were wearing slacks and jerseys. Dungarees weren't really in for girls then. It was slacks. And then on occasion you'd wear a dress; you'd dress up."

A few fems in the late 1950s wore only pants. This defiance of the feminine dress code did not bring censure from other butches and fems, but it did get Bell in trouble with her probation officer.[15]

"I was a very rebellious person, I didn't like the officer because, she insisted that I wear skirts to report for probation. One time I went there and I had jeans on and she said, 'I thought I told you to wear a skirt here.' I said, 'Well I don't happen to own any skirts and I don't have the money to go out and buy any.' She said, 'Well borrow one then.' She made me go home. Somehow I had to go and borrow a skirt. I came back and I had a skirt on. And she was just so nasty. I said 'damn,' in my heart, I was just so aggravated and angry about everything, I said, 'I think I'd rather just go and do the six months rather than have to come down here and report to this asshole.' "

Whether in pants or a skirt fems usually wore makeup and had their hair done in a feminine style.

As in the 1940s, butches still appreciated a fashionably dressed fem. They went out quite frequently with show girls, and with prostitutes whose work required at least a touch of glamour. Ronni recalls the thrill of seeing her first love: "She was behind the bar with this real strapless dress on. And she looked to me like Elizabeth Taylor."

The basic content and meaning of the butch-fem image in the tough Black lesbian crowd was similar to that of the tough white lesbians. Studs wore as many items of male clothes as white rough and tough butches, if not more. However, the butch-fem image was constructed in the idiom of Black culture and therefore had a distinctive flavor. Black studs remember modeling themselves on older lesbians whose mode of dress was severe yet stylish. When asked if she dressed like a man when she went out in the 1950s, Piri responds, "All the way, all the way. . . . I just started over the last I'll say one and a half, two years toning it down, wearing women's slacks, women's clothes. I mean I don't wear no dresses. . . . Hey, I got grandkids, and I can't go around lookin' like a man in front of them." Some studs wore all men's clothes, including underwear. Others modified them: "I never went into wearing any men's underclothes. I sleep in men's pajamas, men's bathrobe. But it's just like some of them wear jock shorts and T-shirts. I wear a silk T-shirt with sleeves, but not sleeveless. Lot of them into that too" (Lonnie). So important were men's clothes to a stud's identity that some wish to be buried in them. "And I have lots of friends say they want to be buried in men's clothes. . . . I have a friend say she want to be buried in a three piece suit" (Lonnie).

Studs had high standards for dressing up, and often cut an elegant image in three-piece suits. Lonnie recalls:

> "I used to wear ladies clothes a lot, heels and stuff like that. After my grandmother died I went all the way. I started wearing three-piece suits, had my hair chopped off. And we went to—a friend of mine that's in gay life, it's a he and he always wears dresses. So we was at the Holiday Inn one night, and he had on a long gown, wig and all this, and I had on a three-piece blue suit; we blowed their minds. One woman say, 'That's the handsome man there; he don't even shave.' After my grandmother died. I got rid of my other clothes and just put them out for the garbage pickup."

Black lesbians adopted this more formal look even on week nights. Jodi does not recall them ever wearing casual clothes. Whenever they went out they wore starched white shirts with formal collars and dark dress pants. Their shoes were men's Florsheim dress shoes worn with dark nylon socks. They had their hair processed and wore it combed back at the sides and cut square at the back. Studs put a great deal of money and energy into their clothes, buying the best. Piri remembers having clothes made in Toronto or shopping in the boys' departments at Seeburg's and Kresge's.[16]

The striking appearance of studs helped lesbians identify one another, as can be seen from Arlette's description of the first woman in man's clothes she saw in Buffalo:

> "The first time I saw really gay women, mannish-looking women was here in Buffalo, New York. And I didn't know what they were. I really thought that they were men. . . . The first gay lady I saw here . . . to me she was fascinating. I kept looking at her, and I said, 'That's a good-looking guy, but it's a funny-looking guy. . . . ' I could never tell if she was a man or a woman cause I never got close enough to her, but there was one strange thing, she would have on lipstick. I said, 'This woman's different.' She's got on men's clothes, her hair was very nice, cut short. She treated a lady like a gentleman would with a lady out, but I said, 'Is that a man or a woman?' So I made it a point to get close enough to hear her voice, 'cause I knew if I could hear her talking I could tell. Then I found out, this is a woman. And I said, 'Golly, got on men's clothes and everything, what kind of women are these?' Then I started seeing more women here dressed in stone men's attire. I said, 'Well, golly, these are funny women.' Then they kind of fascinated me. What could they possibly do? Everybody want to know what can you do. I got curious and I said, 'I'm going to find out.' "

In keeping with the formal style of their studs, Black fems wore skirts or dresses, rarely pants, and aimed to achieve the highest standards of feminine beauty (see photos after p. 190). Arlette, who even now is conscious of looking stylish, remembers that they modeled themselves after entertainers and movie stars. She loved the fashions in *Vogue*. "I was *Vogue* crazy." At that time she made the majority of her clothes so she could simply create whatever suited her fancy. Black fems also had their hair styled according to the latest fashion. This required having their hair straightened and then curled. Although Arlette recalls one stud who wore her hair "natural," she remembers that during the 1950s the majority of both studs and fems hated this look.

Mannerisms continued to be an important ingredient of the butch or stud image in the 1950s. When asked what distinguished a stud, Piri gives a typical reply: "Mannerisms . . . the way they was dressed . . . the way they talk, the way they acted." "Rough" and "tough" describes the comportment of the Black and white tough butches, adjectives that were never used for the 1940s butch.[17] The style they projected was based on working-class men, who knew how to take care of themselves and did not back away from physical confrontation. D.J., who came out in the 1940s, but was at home with the tough bar crowd, identifies willingness to fight as a distinctive mark of the butch manner. "It used to be strictly the appearance of the person, the way you handled yourself. In other words you had to knock about sixteen people around to let them know you were [butch]." Their often-elegant attire did not deter studs from cultivating this rough-and-ready style.

> "Oh yeah, you have to be ready. To me, if you act all meek and humble you gettin' ready to be stepped on. I still have a tendency to be that way, 'cause to me that's the way I was brought up. If you weren't ready and rough you couldn't make it, not one bit. . . . A lot of people figured they could take advantage of [you]. . . . I've been put in a position where I was raped two or three times, 'cause I was gay. If you don't really just hang out there and you just sit back, and you don't struggle for it or fight for it then you might as well hang it up." (Piri)

The tough image prevailed not only in fighting, but in one's entire presentation of self. For instance, Toni recalls learning, "If you were in a bar, and someone called your name, you never turned around smiling. I remember Sandy objected to that kind of friendliness." For those who were hesitant to fight, the appearance of being unafraid and able to handle themselves was important. "Lots of us had to look real tough because underneath we weren't really secure about ourselves. We were scared" (Stormy). Even those who felt inadequately prepared, thought it necessary to look tough.

> "Well, see there were fights, people would fight, and I was always afraid of actually fighting physically. But I never wanted anyone to know that I was afraid so I guess I put on a real tough front. And an interesting thing was about two months ago I was at a friend's house, and I've known this woman, she's a gay woman, since those days, and she was sort of teasing me about how tough I was in those days, and how everyone was afraid of me. And I thought she was kidding me, because the thing was, I believe her now, but I was so scared that all of that was motivated by fear. But I guess I put on a pretty good front. I only really got into two fights and those were fights that I wanted to get into myself. I never usually had to fight with people, I guess, I talked my way out of things. Either talking nice or talking to scare people" (Toni).

When she was in a rough situation, Toni would make sure she was near one of the leaders who had the ability to take care of business.

Since the 1950s lesbian community was willing to educate newcomers, the butch-fem image was easily attained. Older tough butches might speak directly to younger butches and fems about their appearance and behavior, and were not shy about influencing them. In addition, newcomers energetically modeled themselves after the old timers when entering the community. Among tough bar lesbians there was strong pressure for people to conform to the butch-fem roles, as Vic remembers:

> "Well, you had to be [into roles]. If you weren't, people wouldn't associate with you. . . . You had to be one or the other or you just couldn't hang

around. There was no being versatile or saying, 'Well, I'm either one. I'm just homosexual or lesbian.' You know, they didn't even talk about that. It was basically a man-woman relationship. . . . You had to play your role."

All narrators agree that the butches and the fems of the more upwardly mobile circle looked different from those in the rough and tough bar crowd. Toni explains the difference this way. "Those [butches] in Bingo's modeled themselves on the Italian men of the West Side neighborhoods [of Buffalo] while those in the Carousel had a more collegiate look."[18] At another point she characterizes it as a more waspy, middle-class look. Others make the distinction by describing those in the Carousel as having a sporty look; still others characterized it as a more discreet look.[19]

Many of the women, who had frequented Ralph Martin's and Winters in the 1940s, continued the tradition of dressing up when they started patronizing the Carousel in the 1950s. The younger patrons, those who entered the bars for the first time in the 1950s, however, adopted a more sporty or collegiate look. Cheryl, an upwardly mobile butch, captures this image in her impression of butches on her first trip to the Carousel in 1960, "They all looked alike. They all dressed alike. Their slicked back D.A.'s, white belts, white bucks, chino pants, shirts with pockets on the side and button-down collars." Carousel butches also wore crew necks and pullovers, a definite mark of the collegiate style. If there was a pop musician of the period that might characterize this look it was Pat Boone. With his white buck shoes, button-down shirts with crew-neck or V-neck sweaters, his clean cut hair and open smile, he was the acme of the sporty boy next door, a more acceptable image for the socially conscious butches of the Carousel.

Although more sporty than that of the white or Black tough lesbians, the appearance of the upwardly mobile crowd was equally cultivated. Whitney remembers a friend of the late 1950s:

"[She] would have her old pants on, and she would have a pair of chinos that were pressed. She'd get out of the car, she'd stand at the side of the car, she'd pull on her chinos, and then she'd stand in the bar all night with that crease. She would not rest. She might rest her buttocks a little bit, but she didn't bend her legs."

Just as in the white and Black lesbian communities, time, energy, and self-consciousness went into creating the appropriate image for the butches of this more elite crowd.

The fems in this crowd adopted the same sporty or collegiate style as the butches so that the difference in the appearance between the two was less striking. Nevertheless, there was a difference. Although fems were not expected to be glamorous in the manner of movie stars or show girls, they were still expected to look feminine and pretty. Whitney recalls her early days in the Carousel in the late 1950s. "I would wear dresses; I would wear pants. I would wear like toreador

pants and things. I think that was the style then and high heels." In further
clarifying the difference between the appearance of butches and fems, she adds,
"And another thing too in butches, butches weren't as apt to wear makeup. In
fact they didn't wear makeup. . . . And another thing was, butches would have
their hair cut in a kind of butchy style, where fems would have curls and bouffant
type of things."

   In mannerisms as well as clothing the difference between the butch and fem
images of the upwardly mobile crowd was definite but muted. The butches
cultivated a masculine presence without the rough and rowdy mannerisms that
prevailed among the white and Black tough lesbians. They looked down on such
behavior as crude and aimed to be more refined and genteel. When asked why
she didn't socialize with the tough crowd, Whitney responds that she disliked
"their mannerisms, their manners. They were into a lot of the role stuff of being
tough." As in all other aspects of their lives, the butch-fem image of the upwardly
mobile crowd was more discreet than that of the tough lesbians. Neither the butch
alone, nor the butch-fem couple were immediately and necessarily recognizable as
lesbians. The butch-fem image typified and reproduced the class distinctions within
the lesbian community and was central to shaping and expressing lesbian politics.[20]

THE SOCIAL MEANING OF THE BUTCH-FEM IMAGE IN THE 1940s AND 1950s

   As much as the code of personal behavior for dress and mannerisms was modeled
on heterosexual society, it was not simply imitative. Butches of the 1940s and
1950s actively worked to create a unique image. Their goal was not to pass as
men. Although many of them knew passing women or might even have passed as
men for short periods in their lives, as part of the lesbian community they were
recognized on the streets as women who looked 'different' and therefore challenged
mainstream mores and made it possible for lesbians to find one another.

   Passing women usually had a male identity, complete with false identification
papers and were known as men at least at their work place. Leslie pithily contrasts
herself with a passing woman of her acquaintance who wore a binder and looked
like a man. "[Perhaps] this was the lesser of two evils, rather than be in the middle
like us, not looking like men or women. . . . But we weren't trying to fool the
public." In the 1950s women who passed were also known to the lesbian community, but they were not considered an integral part of its daily life. Butches chose
to look simply—and dangerously—like butches or "queers." As Stormy put it,
"We all knew we were women, let's face it." Vic remembers the terrible pressure
of the butch role: "When I was young I was made so queer conscious that I don't
ever want people to call me queer. So now wherever I go I'll either look like a

man or a woman, but I won't look like a queer. I don't want the label any longer. I had it all my life and I hate it."

From the perspective of the 1980s and 1990s it is difficult to separate being butch and passing as a man, but for members of this community, the difference was significant. Many narrators, like Vic, are resentful about this modern confusion. "People don't relate to me as a gay person, Madeline. Wow how can I even try to talk to somebody? Because people, gay women look at me and say, 'Oh she thinks she's a man.' Which I don't, but that's how they relate to me. So should I sit there and run it to 'em?"

Language usage concretized the difference between being butch and passing as a man. While passing women were referred to as "he" by everyone, including their partners, the community of the 1940s and 1950s only rarely used male pronouns to refer to butches.[21] Bell who went with a passing woman for several years remembers feeling uncomfortable with using the male pronoun: "Yes, she was, very masculine-looking and acting. . . . More times than many, I didn't like it at all. Because when we would go places she would want me to call her 'he.' [I would say,] 'But, you're not a man you're a woman. . . . '" Occasionally, in the Black lesbian community, an older stud might address a younger as "son," and might be addressed by others as "pops," but this was not institutionalized.

Although most butches had a nickname which was appropriate to their presentation of self, and served to camouflage their connection to family and jobs, these names were not exclusively male. In the 1940s, many women had nicknames that were related to particular personality characteristics or habits and were not gender-based. Leslie, who took inordinate pride in her stiffly starched shirts, was nicknamed "Arrow" by her friends. Arden, who always dressed in the immaculate taste of a corporation president, was called "the Executive." These nicknames were a sign of affection among close friends but they also provided a degree of anonymity for those who took risks by socializing in an open gay society.

In the 1950s, consistent with the fact that tough bar lesbians (Black and white) socialized primarily in house parties and bars rather than with a small group of intimate friends, such personal nicknames were rare. Most of these butches, despite their developed male image, took on unisex names, usually derived from their own names. Roberta and Barbara were shortened to Bobbi, or Margaret to Marty. Such names were advantageous because they could be used by friends in front of family without causing disruption in the daily routine. At one time, there were so many Gerrys in the community, they had to be distinguished by other attributes, such as Big Gerry, Little Gerry, Jamestown Gerry, Raincoat Gerry, Crazy Gerry, etc. A few took on unisex names that were completely unrelated to their own names. Ronni describes how she acquired her nickname on her first night out at a gay bar.

> "When I was at one of these gay bars I heard a guy call another guy Ronni. Well, being guilty and feeling like I was, I didn't want anybody to know my name. I wanted to remain anonymous, so the first [person] that walks up to me and says 'What's your name?' I said, 'Ronni,' so that popped right out of

me and I just thought, well . . . that sounds all right to me. So I became Ronni that day, that evening, at the age of twenty-one, in the first gay bar I ever walked into."

Both the commonness of unisex nicknames and the space for individual variation, at least in the Black lesbian community, are seen in Arlette's story about a woman she met at a dance in New York who became a passion in her life.

"And I looked at her, I said, 'What's your name?' She said, 'Susan.' I laughed, Susan! She's so hard looking. Most of them have a kind of [name like] Jo, anything like that. It tickled me. Well she said, 'What did you think I was gonna say, my name was Gerry or Jo, or something?' Well. I started laughing because I knew [those names here in Buffalo.] It really tickled me. 'Well,' I say 'That would have been a little more appropriate.' But Susan really floored me. She was very pressed and extremely neat."

In the 1940s and 1950s being a butch or part of a butch-fem couple on the streets meant claiming the identity of difference, of being a "homo" or a "queer." "Homo" was the term commonly used to designate their difference by those who came out in the 1930s and 1940s while "queer" is the language of those who came out in the 1950s, particularly at the end of the decade. Although both had derogatory connotations, implied stigmatization, and were used somewhat ironically, the former is more clinical, and the latter more judgmental, reflecting the increased confrontation between society and the late 1950s butches.

Most narrators were fully aware of the social meaning of the butch-fem image: To announce, or in narrators' language, "to not deny," to the straight world that one is different, is a "homo," a "queer," a "gay," or a "lesbian," and through this to find community with others like oneself. "I would not deny it" is a phrase which appears somewhere in most butch narrators' life stories.

"I mean, I don't think I'm any different now than I was back then. . . . I don't go around advertising or trying to advertise what I am . . . to so-called straight society, but yet if I was approached and they asked are you a lesbian, I wouldn't deny it either. I wouldn't wear a sign saying I'm a lesbian, but on the other hand, if a person came up to me, which it has happened, and said, 'Are you gay?' I wouldn't deny it. I wouldn't say, 'Oh no. God no, not me,' I'd say, 'Yes I am.' Because I feel I have every right to live in this world as anybody else." (Matty)

Matty's distinction between "not denying" and "advertising" draws attention to the fine line separating defensive and offensive behavior. The old time butches did not see themselves as taking the offensive. In their minds they were minding their own business and were forced to defend their right to live differently. However, it is the nature of the butch-fem image that what is seen as "not denying" by one person can be viewed as provocative flaunting behavior by another.

LIVING THE BUTCH-FEM IMAGE IN THE 1940s

During the 40s, when lesbians were discreet about separating work and family from social life, the butch appearance was particularly powerful. Those who achieved it took tremendous risks. Butch narrators vividly remember being identified as different when they went out.

> "Fems didn't look like homos. When they were walking on the street they didn't get any harassment so gay life was not that difficult for them. The only time they had any trouble was when they would go to the bar on Saturday night. There might be some straights making comments there. And afterwards when you would go out to eat at a restaurant. That got so bad that I stopped doing it. It wasn't worth it to have to deal with all the men making comments and poking fun. The biggest problem is going out on the street, and who bothers a fem when she goes out alone. She doesn't have to face that kind of thing."(Leslie)

Both butches and fems agree that the former bore the primary burden of public exposure, and therefore had a special role in the community. However, butch-fem couples on the way to bars, in the bars, or going out to eat after the bars closed drew the same kind of negative reaction as butches alone, because the couple's presence made the meaning of lesbianism explicit. Leslie finds the butch-fem couple more challenging to men than today's unisex couple. "That is perhaps why there is not so much trouble today. If a man should go into a modern bar and look around he would not be so interested in the women there. Most of the women are in pants and look alike."

Given the repression of the times, there was significant disagreement among lesbians of the period about the wisdom of being "obvious." Those who felt comfortable with the butch-fem image were the women who were out in the bars every weekend and were the core builders of community. Those who disliked the degree of visibility demanded by the butch-fem image were not concerned with the formation of community and spent long periods away from a public social life. Their discontent helps to reveal the butch-fem image as a prepolitical form of resistance.

Reggie was fundamentally ambivalent about the butch image. She was attracted to it, because it expressed pride and ended hiding, but she felt the stigma caused too many problems in her life. Her identity was always butch, but from the beginning she presented a less severe image than the core group she first met at Ralph Martin's. Her reasons were complicated.

"I had family, you have your school, later on I had my job. And I don't feel
you have to broadcast. And I have found the nicer women wouldn't want the
real butch type either. Not because you're ashamed, but again they have, say
special jobs in society, and we can't expect every straight one to recognize us
or to like us and to accept us. Just like we can't accept their ways a lot either.
That's the way I feel about it. But mainly I'd get the shit kicked out of me by
my father, which I did."

When she was young her major concern about her appearance was to keep her
identity hidden from her father. She was not able to do this, despite her caution,
and she paid dearly for it, three years in a reformatory. But her view today is based
on her total life experience, and is fairly typical of the community's understanding
of the problems associated with "broadcasting" one's lesbianism. An obvious butch
had trouble with all of society. She also would have less success with fems who
did not want to be exposed by the butches they were with.

At one period in her life, Reggie was drawn to the obvious butch image and
gave it a try, but she found it too limiting. She had taken a job at the One Eighty-
One Club in New York City where butches were part of the show as waiters and
were required to present an extreme image. She felt that image was "her," but:

"I just felt that as much as I wanted to be me, at the time I found that I was
confined too much, to the Village. 'Cause I had tried to go up to see some gay
girls I knew up in the Bronx, and my girlfriend and I almost got beat up on
the train. Another time . . . [friends and I had] just got back from shopping
and were carrying the bags and five guys went by with a car and started calling
us names. Well, I made the mistake, which it was my fault, I made a sign and
of course they went around the block. And they came back, jumped out of
the car, and they formed a circle around me. And my friends walked on, they
didn't call for the police or nothing. . . . No one on Sixth Avenue, it was in
the midafternoon, did anything. . . . So I wound up two weeks in the hospital
and I came out. I think between that and the Club, and then not being able
to see friends—I mean good friends. They were straight, but I just couldn't
bring them to town, understanding me and accepting me, I couldn't force that
on them. So I let my hair grow again, not quite as long. I just felt free. I just
felt that I'm not confined any more."[22]

The combination of harassment on the street, distance from straight friends,
and problems at the Club led her to return to being less obvious. In her experience,
the benefits she received from being obvious did not outweigh the limitations.
This decision did not stop her from being an active lesbian. She still went to bars
and dances in the Village and in Harlem and expanded her horizons, riding
motorcycles with a straight male group and visiting her friends from the reformatory in Harlem. She says of herself at the time: "You had a lot of gall when you
were younger, I guess." But she was relatively free of the public stigma of
homosexuality. This stance toward the straight world seems relevant in shaping

future developments in her life. During the 1950s, she married and went on to live with her husband for twenty-three years and raise two children. Now she is again living as a lesbian. At no period in her life was she central to the building of a public lesbian community.

The meaning of the butch image was and is so powerful that to this day, Reggie remains fundamentally ambivalent about it, attracted to the pride it represents, but uncomfortable with its confrontational aspect.

> "But, you still cannot force the issue on people, you can't. Yes you want to be proud you're gay. . . . At one time I wanted to, but I couldn't. O.K., maybe I gave up too easy, I don't know, but I still knew you had to deal with society. I can't go to my boss and say, 'Hey, [I'm gay],' because it's male ego you're dealing with one. 'Hey, what do you mean? Get that pretty girl, what the hell has she got?' I've had that, I've seen it. Not only for this reason, but just people that are hardheaded, that don't want to know anything but what they live by. There's something wrong with them, they're crazy, they're queers."

Not all fems of this period would agree with Reggie that they preferred the less-obvious butches, but some certainly did. Charlie, for instance, preferred not to associate with women who were extremely masculine and felt, in fact, that her butch lovers would be more pleased with themselves if they looked less extreme and less obvious.

> "I don't think I've ever gone out with anybody that's been very butchy, and if they are, I try to change them. . . . I think they're happier with themselves. . . . I think that they see the difference in how they look and they'd say, 'Gee, I look better this way.' That's how I feel. But I've never had a problem with anybody."

Charlie always had relationships with butches, preferring women who were more aggressive than herself, but she set clear limitations on the extent to which they could cultivate a masculine appearance.

Dee, whose role identity was not clearly defined in the sense that in some relationships she took the more masculine role and in others the more feminine, was also opposed to the obvious butch appearance. For long periods of time she did not go to the bars, particularly when her feminine lovers were hesitant about associating publicly with other gays. She was strongly against lesbians drawing attention to themselves.

> "Well some of the ones that went to extremes I thought it was rather ridiculous. Again, I always found it repugnant to wear a sign on my forehead. 'Cause to me, we live in a straight society and we should have to conform. We can be gay when we're in our own crowd at a house party, when we're out in public we should sort of not flaunt gaiety. I never went for that idea. Maybe because Heloise drummed it into me so much at the beginning."

She did not like the hostility that "flaunting" elicited.

> "I didn't think it was too good, because everybody that looked at them would sneer and scorn and be critical. . . . I at one point went with a gal who was very, very butch, she's never had a dress on in her life. Used to come to work in coveralls, and this was before this day and age, I'm talking '42, '45 with a lunch bucket. And at one point I was pretty enamored of her . . . and I know if we went into a restaurant or a tavern or anything I would sort of cringe the way people would look at us. 'Cause obviously she wasn't, so-called, norm, and was frowned upon."

Her memories of what it was like to be the more feminine partner demonstrate the way butch-fem mannerisms as well as appearance announced lesbianism. When asked what made her more feminine when she went with more masculine women, particularly since she claims to have still done some "masculine" things like repair machines, Dee responds, "And she would sort of carry me on a silver platter, so to speak. Like opening car doors, which I tried to get her out of, 'cause that's in the early 1950s or late 1940s, girls just didn't open car doors for other girls. It used to embarrass me. I said 'Don't do that.' There's a good deal of me that is conventional, even today."

Her objections to the obvious butch-fem image go beyond that of her personal discomfort. Dee did not and does not think it wise for lesbians to approach the straight world in this manner. When asked if there wasn't a positive side to butches asserting or claiming their difference, she replies, "Not necessarily, not if they're being scornful. They could make their way as a lesbian, without, shall I say, shocking the general public. I think there's other ways to attain that end of lesbianism. Such as some of, like GROW now, or Country Friends now, and you have different organizations."[23] She returns to the subject later, of her own accord, recognizing the way the butch-fem image expanded the presence of lesbians at the time, but affirming her position that it was not helpful for improving the situation of lesbians.

> "I'm not meaning to ridicule those girls. As you said, they might have had a point in educating the public, but I feel sometimes they did more harm than good. . . . Like the criticism, the sneering glances at those that were separate from the norm. And even today I think you see some of that. I mean lesbianism isn't accepted yet."

Dee remembers that she not only objected to the extreme obviousness of butch roles, but also had questions about roles per se. She disagreed with women, lesbians, identifying completely with masculine or feminine characteristics. "Actually, basically I have never bought the fact of being butch or fem, because I think all of us have some masculine tendencies and all of us have some feminine tendencies, whether it's the boys or the girls, or the men and the women." She had the beginning of a feminist critique of polarized heterosexual gender roles. In her own life she acted on this view, not always taking the butch role, and in her lasting relationships roles were not particularly important. She is the only narrator of the 1940s who raised these issues. For that group, the primary tension surrounding the butch-fem image was about the way it publicized or announced lesbianism, not the way it imitated heterosexuality, the concern of contemporary lesbians. On the whole 1940s lesbians were not critical of male and female roles; they just didn't want the power to rest solely with men.

These critiques by those who struggled with the butch-fem image vividly convey its impact. The core members of the bar community were the obvious butches and butch-fem couples who could endure stigma and scorn, while announcing the presence of "different" women, of "homos." Their visibility allowed them to build a social life that furthered the growth of a distinct lesbian culture and consciousness. The women who were uncomfortable with the obviousness of roles lived a significant portion of their lives as relatively isolated individuals or couples. They came to the community when they wanted it and needed it in their lives, and certainly appreciated its importance. But, without regularly risking identification as lesbians, they of necessity played a marginal role in community development.

LIVING THE BUTCH-FEM IMAGE IN THE 1950s

In the 1950s the butch-fem image continued to assert lesbianism in an extremely hostile world. Many of the 1940s lesbians mixed with the younger upwardly mobile crowd in the Carousel, who also socialized in bars on the weekend and maintained a firm distinction between social and work life. The pioneer spirit of breaking new ground for a public lesbian social life, however, was not continued by this group, but rather by the tough lesbians (Black and white). If anything, the lesbians of the "elite" 1950s crowd were a little more cautious than those of the 1940s. In most situations, these upwardly mobile 1950s butches wanted to underplay the butch image, and were less wedded to their butch attire than those of the 1940s. Joanna compares Leslie and Renée, her girlfriends from different decades.

> "I think Leslie and Renée dressed differently too. Like Leslie dressed very butch, you know, slacks and suits, but Renée wore dresses for different occasions. She had to. . . . But it didn't bother her. She just took all that in her stride. And I thought that was great . . . [not] that she was any more feminine. She wasn't. She just was from a different generation. . . . She did things differently. Didn't bother her to put on a dress. Leslie would never put on a dress, I don't think if they chloroformed her."

The "elite" crowd was careful about where they announced their lesbianism. Butch women were subject to criticism by other members of their group, sometimes even by their own fems, if their dress and mannerisms exposed them to the heterosexual world. Whitney speaks of her butch of many years:

> "She was a butchy looking woman. . . . I would be embarrassed. We would go downtown and I could be embarrassed when I would see people look at her, but I was also sort of . . . defiant, maybe to stick out my chin. And I was hurt and I knew she was hurt by some of the women in the community who would, if they saw her with say one of their business associates or whatever, or if they had a business . . . I was welcome to go there, but she was not."

This woman who was easily identifiable as butch had been central to the 1940s community. The 1950s elite crowd discouraged this degree of obviousness.

It was the tough butches and studs who continued the bold spirit of the butches of the 1940s. Throughout the 1950s, these butches were open about their appearance, aiming to diminish the division between their work and family lives and their lesbian lives. They forcefully defended their right to be different. This trend toward asserting one's lesbianism intensified so that the leaders of the late 1950s and early 1960s were still more "obvious" than their predecessors of the early 1950s.[24]

Tough butches and studs of the period shared a particular attitude toward their clothing that was notably different from that of butches of the 1940s or of the elite 1950s crowd. Butches and studs felt it was important to dress butch as much of the time as possible. This was in part an adaptation to the fact that they went out to bars during the week as well as on weekends. Beyond this, butches had a drive to express their difference, and rebel against the conventional standards of femininity. Before she entered the public community, Sandy had worked at an office job and was required to wear a skirt to work. She remembers, 'I hated it,' and explains how, once she found the bars, she would not do this any more.

> "I wasn't in the gay scene, so it didn't matter if someone saw me, 'cause they didn't know me anyhow. And then after I started going around—found the gay bars, the gay people—I just went the way I felt like going, and that was . . . my butch way. And then after you meet different girls, well, you couldn't meet them after work. You'd have to go home and change, and then you couldn't leave the house. It was daylight and the neighbors would see you, so you couldn't go out until it was dark, and then sneak out. And then if you were working and went out for lunch you wouldn't want anyone from the gay crowd that thought you were wow, saying something, to see you prancing around in a little skirt, why that would just blow the whole shot. So that ended the job."

The desire of butches to be seen by their gay friends only when dressed in masculine attire was fostered and reinforced by the community culture. Vic also remembers community pressure as the major reason she quit her white-collar job:

"There were a lot of butches around, if you remember, that the woman took care of them. 'Cause they couldn't work or didn't want to because they looked so butch so the woman supported them. . . . When I worked at the lab, I was living really two lives. I had to go in as a, what would you say, a woman of record. . . . And I had a little makeup on, or whatever. Because I was dealing with people and you had to have a little curl in the front here to look halfway decent. So when I came out, when I came home I was a different person. That's why I resigned. Because I couldn't lead the two lives any more. I'd run into people that I'd see at the bars, and I took more ridicule for that. You had to wear a uniform and all that. I'd go in, I couldn't do it any longer. . . . I went to work every morning for seven years, while I'd have five people sleeping on the floor at my house . . . and I just said the hell with it."

Butches took other extreme measures to appear butch as much of the time as possible. Arlette remembers how studs who lived at home would change their clothes in the car. This allowed them to look the way they wanted when they were out without offending their parents:

"Yeah, I knew girls would go out, and they would have to change clothes in cars. . . . [This one girl] didn't want her parents to see her in these men's type of clothes; so she would change clothes in the car; or in somebody's house. Then before we could take her back home, she'd have to change clothes again, to get back to the girls stuff, before she could go home."

Black and white tough lesbians had created a culture that valued asserting their difference through appearance. They looked down upon those who wouldn't take such risks, particularly the more upwardly mobile lesbians. By the late 1950s white lesbians had become competitive about butchness and set the standard that to be truly butch, the best butch, you had to look butch all the time.[25]

"The ones that were butch were butch. Now there might have been the butches that were still the sissies, they'd come and order a drink and hide in the bathroom all night, . . . afraid someone would see them. And they couldn't have short hair like us, they couldn't wear clothes—if they didn't want to I mean that's a different story, but most of them wanted to, but they were afraid to. Candy asses you know. And of course, the butches that were butches, like myself, the rest of us that were, we ruled them, because we didn't give a shit. But those candy asses took their girl, 'Shut up,' you know. They had no say so." (Sandy)

Not all tough bar lesbians achieved the ideal of looking butch all the time. Many still modified their appearance as required by work, family, and partners. The respected leaders of the late 1950s and early 1960s, however, did not alter their appearance on very many occasions. They were butch all the time and that was part of their charisma.

As the pressure to look butch all the time increased, the nonconformist character of butches came to the fore, and led them to defy the rules which they had created. Most narrators of the 1950s remember with glee when the renowned butches would come into the bars dressed in feminine attire. Bert remembers going out all dressed up just to cause a stir:

> "Talking about the butch and the fem era, I remember one time when I went with Barbara, to blow other people's minds, every once in a while on a Friday or Saturday night we'd dress up, in heels and the whole bit. . . . At first they were probably surprised and shocked, but after a while didn't seem to make any big deal about it. It probably underlying was a way of getting attention, to be noticed."

Iris remembers dressing up for diversion, but also as a way to assert her independence.

> "I used to have silver blonde hair and get dressed up. I used to run around with one of the gay boys and, on Saturday nights, just to get away from all the monotony of it all, we used to go to Cole's, Foster['s] Supper Club, the Stuyvesant, Victor Hugo's. We'd just go around and have a drink or two in each place, you know, for a change of atmosphere and that, and then we'd go down to the gay bars. . . . Right, but it was fun and I enjoyed it. Of course there was a lot of remarks, but I didn't care. I mean I just don't let people bother me because I just always felt, hey, they're not paying my bills and keeping me. When they do, then they can tell me how I live my life. . . . Yeah, I guess it was radical, but I enjoyed it. I really just never cared, I did whatever I wanted."

She remembers that in the late 1950s, some of the real "butchy butches," including herself, would plan to go out for an evening wearing slinky dresses, high heels, stockings, makeup, and jewelry. Iris still delights in recalling how they would present themselves at the bar for an evening of drinking, dancing—often with each other—and high hilarity.

> "Every once in a great while, we'd all get dressed up in dresses and go down to the Carousel. Just for something different. And we'd sit around in our dresses and talk and laugh and get up and dance with each other. Some of the people would really be confused by this time, but we had a good time."

Marla remembers being shocked by the "turnaround" and enjoying it immensely.

> "All the girls that were supposed to be big bad butches, right, turned out for some reason—was it one Thursday a month or once a week or something? They all would get dressed up, and I mean heels, dress, and everything else, and come down to the Carousel just for kicks. And you should see, some of those girls turned out to be some beautiful women really, when they got dressed up."

Sandy now remembers with incredulity dressing up for these occasions, because it was so contradictory to her identity: "I had [a dress], mine had the slits up the side. Looked like it was sort of leopard print. Trying to walk in high heels, you've got to be kidding!" Such masquerading, however, did not question the masculine identity of butches, but instead reinforced its "rightness." The fun and humor came from the attention caused by known butches taking on a feminine appearance. Other gay and lesbian patrons treated them as if they were in drag.

The importance of clothing and appearance in establishing social identity was not unique to lesbians. Assumptions about the correlation between dress and behavior pervaded 1950s culture.[26] A good deal of the objection to juvenile delinquency focused on appearance.[27] In 1955, the Buffalo Public School System developed the Dress Right program, which established strict standards for what young people could wear to school, based on the philosophy that the schools could change students' attitude toward authority by changing their presentation of self. By 1957, the program had achieved national attention, suggesting that the approach was perceived as relevant throughout the country. It was presented at national conferences of educators and discussed in the national media, on the *Good Morning America* show, in Chicago and New York newspapers, and in *Newsweek*.[28]

The increasingly masculine appearance of the tough butches and studs made their appearance fundamentally ambiguous. On the one hand, their clothes could serve as a cover, and allowed them in limited situations to pass as men. Alone on the streets, when butches did not have the protection of their group of friends, they sometimes exploited the possibility of looking like men on the surface, in order to draw less attention to themselves. Stormy reminisces about why some women would tape their chests to achieve a flat appearance: "It was easier to walk down the street if at first glance people thought you were a man." At another point in her interview, she states, "It was the local core butches who usually looked more butch. Sometimes it was a matter of what neighborhood you came from. You might feel safer if you went out dressed more like a guy so people wouldn't hassle you late at night."

On the other hand, their clothes also dramatically exposed them as "queer." Although butches cultivated a "male" cover, they did not rely on it, other than for moving through difficult situations. The ambiguous possibilities of looking male/looking queer were ever-present and appear in most butch narrators' memories: "Well I was always a tomboy, so I more or less just fit right in with them. You know, had the short hair, the D.A.'s. . . . We looked like little boys, like walking around with a sign on your back" (Iris).

Narrators emphasize that the 1950s dress code for women was very strict, so that aberrations were easily noticed:

> "Well today the trend of clothes is unisex, what a guy can wear a girl can wear in mostly anything now. It's not as bad as it was then. Now today the kids run around in Levis and shirts and all this and nobody thinks anything of it. Back then they would have said, 'Ha, ha, queer.' Today nobody thinks

anything of it. You look out this window you see all these kids, and they got boys' pants' on, boys' Levis, and nobody thinks anything of it anymore. Back in those days, boy they fingered you right out." (Matty)

Toni, when trying to describe how different the 1950s were from today, emphasizes how much lesbians stood out because of their clothing:

> "People looked at me a lot . . . either they weren't sure if I was male or female or I looked like a lesbian to them. And then there were dress codes. . . . And most women wore skirts and dresses, more female clothing. . . . And so maybe the fact that more women wore feminine clothing then, there weren't the hippies yet and there weren't the students with the long hair. People were more conservative then, and most people either looked like a man or a woman or male or female. And I looked either like a woman in men's clothes or they didn't know what the hell I was."

As in the 1940s, it was primarily the butch image that indicated difference. Even their fems, the women who chose them as lovers, were not always comfortable with the obviousness of these tough butches. Their insistence on appearing butch as much of the time as possible was a recurrent source of tension in relationships. Annie, who always went with women whose appearance was particularly masculine, felt that such obviousness made life harder. In her criticism of butch appearance she singles out the T-shirt as symbolizing the problem.

> "Well, because all they had to do was write the name queer across their T-shirts. They didn't even have to do that you know. But it's just they were dressed in drag, so butchy looking and they weren't accepted then. In fact a lot of times I would tell Sandy, 'You walk behind me.' [Because] if I didn't want someone to know, you had to keep it more to yourself."

She adds that although she was never harassed on the streets when she was alone, "because I really didn't look queer," she was harassed when she was with her butch.

> "Well not that I looked queer but the person I was with looked queer. And I mean they used to go and get the really D.A. haircuts that looked like a guy's. And Sandy and I, we have a very close attraction to one another. And it's a good thing that I didn't meet her when I was sixteen or that, and then take her home and say, 'Ma, would you like to meet my lover?!' "

Arlette, who also preferred masculine women, nevertheless feels that they often went too far: "I never cared too much for that hard man's clothes. I don't like that to this day. I never have liked that, cause I don't think you have to dress that way; to me it's advertising. And you don't have to advertise to be gay." She later clarifies that it is not the men's clothes that bother her but the insistence on wearing them all the time, rather than when appropriate for gay affairs. She recalls how she used to try to convince her butch not to wear men's clothes when she went to a club in Manhattan where Arlette worked.

"But I always tried to get her then to put on something different if you want to come in those places. 'Cause to me you're asking for trouble. 'Cause a lot of people are really sick in the head, really think, oh here come one of those— some people really get violent and want to hurt you. 'Cause some people are really that messed up in their mind."

Public reaction to the butch and the butch-fem couple was usually hostile, and often violent. Being noticed on the streets and the harassment that followed dominates the memories of both Black and white narrators. Ronni gives a typical description:

"Oh, you were looked down upon socially. When I walked down the street, cars used to pull over and say, 'Hey faggot, hey lezzie.' They called you names with such maliciousness. And they hated to see you when you were with a girl. I was the one that was mostly picked on because I was identified. I was playing the male part in this relationship and most guys hated it. Women would look at me in kind of a confused looking [way], you know, straight women would look at me in kind of wonder."

Piri remembers how the police used to harass her for dressing like a man:

"I've had the police walk up to me and say, 'Get out of the car'. I'm drivin.' They say get out of the car; and I get out. And they say, 'What kind of shoes you got on? You got on men's shoes?' And I say, 'No, I got on women's shoes.' I got on some basket-weave women's shoes. And he say, 'Well you damn lucky.' 'Cause everything else I had on were men's—shirts, pants. At that time when they pick you up, if you didn't have two garments that belong to a woman you could go to jail . . . and the same thing with a man. . . . They call it male impersonation or female impersonation and they'd take you downtown. It would really just be an inconvenience. . . . It would give them the opportunity to whack the shit out of you."

Many narrators mention the legal specification for proper dress, although some said it required three pieces of female clothing, not two. If such a law did in fact exist, it did not dramatically affect the appearance of butches, who were clever at getting around it while maintaining their masculine image.[29] The police used such regulations to harass Black lesbians more than whites, however.

Given the severe harassment, the butch role in these communities during the 1950s became identified with defending oneself and one's girl in the rough street bars and on the streets. Matty describes the connection between her appearance and her need to be an effective fighter. The cultivated masculine mannerisms were necessary on the street:

"When I first came out in the bars it was a horror story. You know they say that you play roles. Yeah, back then you did play roles, and I was a bit more masculine back then than I am now. That was only because you walk down the street and they knew you were gay and you'd be minding your business and there'd be two or three guys standing on a street corner, and they'd come up to you and say, 'You want to be a man, let's see if you can fight like a man.' Now being a man was the last thing on my mind, but man, they'd take a poke at you and you had to learn to fight. Then . . . when you go out, you better wear clothes that you could really scramble in if you had to. And it got to be really bad, I actually had walked down the street with some friends not doing anything and had people spit at me, or spit at us, it was really bad."

Toni explains how there was no choice but to defend oneself:

"I think that's the only way we could act then. We just didn't have any ground except what we fought for. Especially like Iris and Sandy for instance, on the street people just stared at them. I would see people's reactions, I would see them to me if I was alone too, but I would see reactions when I was with my friends, and the only safe place was in a gay bar, or in your own, if you had your own apartment. Out on the street you were fair game."

If the world was dangerous for butches, it was equally so for the fems in their company, whom the butches felt they needed to protect. Some butches state that they did most of their fighting for their fems. Sandy describes how confrontational men could be.

"Well you had to be strong—roll with the punches. If some guy whacked you off, said, 'Hey babe,' you know.[30] Most of the time you got all your punches for the fem anyhow, you know. It was because they hated you. . . . 'How come this queer can have you and I can do this and that. . . . ' You didn't hardly have time to say anything, but all she would have to say [is] 'No,' when he said, 'Let's go, I'll get you away from this.' He was so rejected by this 'no' that he would boom, go to you. You would naturally get up and fight the guy, at least I would. And we all did at that time, those that were out in their pants and T-shirts. And we'd knock them on their ass, and if one couldn't do it we'd all help. And that's how we kept our women. They cared for us, but you don't think for a minute they would have stayed with us too long or something if we stood there and just were silent. . . . Nine times out of ten she'd be with you to help you with your black eye and your split lip. Or you kicked his ass and she bought you dinner then. But you never failed, or you tried not to. . . . You were there, you were gay, you were queer and you were masculine."

The aggressive butch role was the most developed in the leaders of the late 1950s. They expressed their ability to defend themselves and their friends in the most macho terms. "It was strictly, you go in the bar and whoever was the baddest butch then that survived and if you didn't you got your face broke and that was it. So you had to be there" (Vic). Sandy emphasizes how she would do anything to prove herself:

"Yeah, I was trying to prove and show that I was tough, I could take it. . . . It really came down to . . . 'If you're gonna be here, then be what you are or I'll knock the shit out of you. You think you're tough, let's see how tough you are, I'll show you how tough.' Well that's what you had to be. I would kill in those days, I would kill."

Piri describes her reputation as so bad that she didn't even recognize herself:

"I've had like confrontations with people and we wind up arguing and there might not even be a fight, and again it might be. I didn't have too many people bother me. Like at one time I had a reputation that's so bad, I used to go home and cry about it. It was like, 'Hey, that's Piri, don't fool around with her. She's got some prostitutes and what not, and she'll cut you up.' And I wasn't like that. And I used to hear it all the time. And I used to get really upset and cry about it a lot. I just sit around and say, 'Well, I know I'm not that rough, I'm not that tough; I'm just defending what I want to do, what I want to be.' Like I don't want nobody up in my face, like talking a lot of bunk to me. They nag. Then I get into it. Other than that, if you leave me alone, I don't bother nobody. I used to just sit and wonder, why is my name floating around like this. Piri this, Piri that. But like I said after a while you get used to it."

Annie concurs that these leaders were strong and effective fighters, a match for any man: "You went like into a straight bar, especially with the butches, and they had strength, they was no one to mess with. Some guy would start a fight with them, or call them, 'queer' or 'lezzie' or whatever, then . . . too bad for the guy. He'd better be strong."

As macho as the tough butch and stud leaders were as fighters, they were always aware that they were not men. Ironically, if they had been men they would not have had to be such expert fighters because they would not have been under attack. In tough situations, they thought strategically and used all their resources including their femaleness. In a confrontation with the police, if they thought it would help them, they would bring up that they were women. They regularly appeared in the court as women in order to play on the judges' prejudices about women's capabilities and receive a lenient judgment.

"I didn't have any [court clothes]. I borrowed them. . . . That was the one, great advantage of being gay, was you beat the court. I beat 'em every charge. . . . Beat all of my cases. . . . [They were for] assault. One was on a police officer. . . . He could [identify me] but they didn't believe I did it to him. They didn't believe I could do it. He was in there, his head was all wrapped up, he had a concussion, broken nose, eyes, and, about a six footer. And there I am, looking as pathetic as I could. And I remember the judge, he says, 'You did that? . . . Why you couldn't weigh a hundred pounds soaking wet,' he said to me. I says, '98.' He says, 'I don't believe you did this, no I have to throw this out.' " (Sandy)

In their interactions with men in the bars, butches did and did not want to be treated as men. Although they expected men to respect their physical prowess they did not want men to include them as part of their degrading conversations about women. Vic summarizes her philosophy on this subject:

"As butch as I am, I demand respect from men, straight men. You know, not to opening doors and giving me their bar stool. But there is a definite limit drawn to what they can say to me. Even though they talk to me as a butch or a man, however they relate to me, they will not talk to me the way they talk to their locker-room buddies or something, I don't want to hear that. Can't talk and sit around, 'Well how are you doing with your old lady?' and this and that. They would never talk to me like that. I wouldn't allow it for a minute . . . but I demand that little bit of respect. I am a woman, and you're gonna treat me like one regardless of how I am dressed. Don't treat me like I'm a butch queer, 'cause I won't allow it. Then you're gonna have to hit me or I'm gonna hit you. Because I get very physical along those lines with [guys]. I'll have to go down, you know, if its over my woman or over myself.[31] Or *you*, whoever I would be with, 'cause I can't allow that."

The pressure on butches and studs not to deny their difference and to defend themselves generated an extraordinarily complex and confusing relationship to maleness, which is vividly expressed in Sandy's statement quoted above: "You were there, you were gay, you were queer and you were masculine. Men hated it." These 1950s butches, particularly the leaders, were extremely masculine, and often thought of social dynamics in terms of male and female roles and relationships. At the same time, they were not men, they were "queer." Throughout their life stories they counterpose acquiring masculine characteristics with not being male. The prominence of masculinity in their vision of themselves and in their understanding of the world is perhaps responsible for the contemporary confusion between these butches and passing women, and the assumption that these women must have been trying to be men. But to recognize their masculinity and not their queerness distorts their culture and consciousness and negates their role in building lesbian community.

Judy Grahn helpfully and creatively handles the complexity of the butch role by positing that butches are magical, ceremonial figures who develop their personae by patterning themselves after other butches, rather than by imitating men. We do not agree with Grahn that the butch role has existed and had the same meaning throughout Western history. But her argument does aptly capture the way that twentieth-century butches as announcers, protectors, and inspirers of community transcend the mundane and take on mythical proportions. This view does not exclude or belittle the fem, but enhances her as butch and fem associate together in the same life.[32]

THE BUTCH-FEM IMAGE AS A PREPOLITICAL FORM OF RESISTANCE

The butch and butch-fem image, as projected in this community, contained three explicit elements of resistance. First, butches, and the butch-fem couple, by "not denying" their interest in women, were at the core of lesbian resistance in the 1940s and 1950s. By claiming their difference butch and fem became visible to one another, establishing their own culture and therefore became a recognizable presence in a hostile world. Second, in the 1950s the butch, who was central to the community's increased boldness, had little inclination to accommodate the conventions of femininity, and pushed to diminish the time spent hiding in order to eliminate the division between public and private selves. Third, butches added a new element of resistance: the willingness to stand up for and defend with physical force their fems' and their own right to express sexual love for women.

This culture of resistance was based in and in turn generated a great deal of pride. Narrators are fully aware of how powerful their visibility was, challenging gay oppression and thereby creating a better world for lesbians today. Joanna, who was active in the community of the 1940s, sees the harassment endured in the past as freeing her from the responsibility to be active in gay liberation now:

> "I didn't want to get involved that much [in the gay movement]. To me, it wasn't worth it because I figured, let some of the kids that are just coming out, they have to learn. We paved the way for them don't forget. We were the ones that took all the slurs and insults and everything, in bars and this kind of thing. And I thought, well, there's a lot of young kids coming out, with a heck of a lot more knowledge than I had when I was a kid. And had broader shoulders, you know, they could accept a lot more."

Butch narrators of the 1950s are particularly proud of their ability to assert and defend who they were. The theme of making history, of making the world a better place for lesbians by being out, being visible and being willing to fight is explicit throughout the life story of Matty who came out in the early 1950s.

> "I'm not the type that will put a sign around my neck as I said earlier and parade around and say, 'Hey, my name's Matty and I'm gay.' But I won't deny it, and if I have to proclaim it in some way to make it easier for the gay people who are going to come along I'll gladly do it. Because my life's half gone, maybe more than half, who knows, and I think I've made it a lot easier, just as some other people that I could name, Vic, Sandy, Stormy, you yourself. In years to come I believe that we're going to be talked about and we're going to be legends, just like Columbus is. I'm serious."

The women she singles out, except for the interviewer, are the aggressive masculine butches of the late 1950s and early 1960s. Although these women are not as eloquent about their roles in shaping a better world for lesbians, their stories reflect similar understandings of having made significant contributions to gay history. Vic recalls:

> "Well Marty used to call me a crusader. 'Get off the street and stop crusading.' You don't know the time I've put in behind lesbians, defending and pushing and putting it in people's face, you don't know. You know how straight people

were about it, you'd get bopped. 'Cause I run it to them almost the same way that you're running it to me now. . . . I'm more of a crusader than you'll ever be, because I'm right there where it counts. . . . That's why my nose is crooked, 'cause I've never tried to hide what I am."

Sandy, however, conveys a lack of clarity about what she was doing at the time. On the one hand she says of the fights, "It started there. Rebellion right there." On the other hand, when asked explicitly about the goals of the rebellion, she doesn't recall having a vision of a better world for lesbians; she didn't believe such change was possible. "No, I just figured well this is the way it is and if I want to be this way just roll with the punches." Although she lacked a consistent social vision, she nevertheless had the dignity and conviction to stand up for who she was, which is the essence of tough lesbians' resistance in the 1950s.

Whether or not these butches and butch-fem couples consciously understood in the 1940s and 1950s that their appearance and actions would have the effect of making the world a better place for lesbians in the future is a moot question. The importance of these statements is not that they indicate the "true" consciousness of the past, but rather that they direct outsiders to the culture of resistance in these bar communities. For no matter how narrators chose to interpret their past actions, by any criteria, participants in these communities affirmed their right to be who they were against tremendous odds.

The developments in 1950s lesbian culture moved with accelerating force toward ending secrecy. In the context of severe repression, the forms of resistance became a dead end. By the late 1950s, the butches' constant confrontation with the straight world, and the unmitigated disapproval it generated, led to extreme stigmatization and, therefore, isolation. Narrators' sentiments of pride were commonly accompanied by equally powerful feelings of self-hate. This is especially true of the leaders of the late 1950s.[33] Vic remembers her embarrassment during a summer picnic in her backyard during the 1960s:

"Now Dana comes in, she's got tattoos runnin' up and down her arms, and size eighty-four boobs, and Jamestown Gerry and then my landlord comes out. Should I be embarrassed at my friends? I was. I say, 'Never again will that happen.' Y'know I've been embarrassed at myself, many times, but if I have to be embarrassed at the people that are around me . . . and I was. . . . And my landlord goin' . . . he's checkin' arms, he's checkin' tits, then he's lookin' at flies, he don't know what to make of the God damn [whole thing]. This is never gonna make it then."

The pain and degradation has stayed with her and is perhaps even heightened by the lack of appreciation for who she was and is in today's lesbian community. "Like people say to me, 'I could be a butch, I could do this. I could do that.' Anybody could be, y'know, for a weekend or a week. But go through life . . . dressing the way I dress, being with women who are [fem, and] men pick on you because you are with them. This is a different story." At another point in her story she explains:

> "Well, it's like I have to low-grade myself, don't have to but I do, because of what I am. . . . Well because it's been in my head. You have never had your face broke for being a queer, I have. For like twenty years of my life. And now, because you can go to a gay dance or something I'm supposed to say, 'Oh wow, now I can go there.' . . . But I can't even go there and do that cause I'm a butch and they don't want me either. Where do I go, I don't have where to go? I had to stay right where I'm at."

Sandy, whose leadership was undisputed in this period still carries great bitterness with her as the legacy of this struggle to build a lesbian life.

> "You know it pisses you off, because like today, everything is so open and accepted and equal. Women, everyone goes to where they wear slacks, and I could just kick myself in the ass, because all the opportunities I had that I had to let go because of my way. That if I was able to dress the way I wanted and everything like that I, Christ, I'd have it made, really. Makes you sick. And you look at the young people today that are gay and they're financially well-off, they got tremendous jobs, something that we couldn't take advantage of, couldn't have it. It leaves you with a lot of bitterness too. I don't go around to the gay bars much any more. It's not jealousy, it's bitterness. And I see these young people, doesn't matter which way they go, whatever the mood suits them, got tremendous jobs, and you just look at them, you know, they're happy kids, no problems. You say 'God damn it, why couldn't I have that?' And you actually get bitter, you don't even want to know them. I don't anyway. 'Cause I don't want to hear about it, don't tell me about your success. Like we were talking about archives, you know where mine is, scratched on a shit-house wall, that's where it is. And all the dives in Buffalo that are still standing with my name. That's it, that's all I got to show."

The complex culture of resistance in the public lesbian communities of the 1950s and early 1960s provided a heritage from which gay liberation could draw. Although in its youth gay liberation did not have a sense of the past, and therefore did not consciously draw on what had existed before, its ideas were likely influenced by the bar communities. In turn the bar communities provided an environment conducive to igniting a mass movement. And in cities such as Buffalo, members of the bar community formed political organizations at about the same time as the Stonewall Rebellion that became active in the gay liberation movement. In fact visibility, standing up for one's rights, and ending the double life were core issues for both the tough lesbians and gay liberation, though they approached them differently.[34] The prepolitical tactics of the tough lesbians were immediate, spontaneous, and personal. They lacked gay liberation's long-term analysis of and strategy for ending the oppression of gays and lesbians in America and changing the world. The similarities and differences between the politics of these overtly butch-fem communities and that of gay liberation can be seen in the somewhat ambivalent relationship the Black and white tough lesbians had to the founding of the Mattachine Society of the Niagara Frontier (M.S.N.F.) in which many of them participated. Many narrators felt that M.S.N.F. did not have much new to offer them because they had already achieved visibility and had asserted the right to be themselves. Matty joined M.S.N.F., at first thinking it was a good idea, and then withdrew. She remembers going to a picnic at Madeline's house and being offended by a member of Mattachine's comments about people who thought they were too good for Mattachine.

" 'It isn't that we think that we're too good, you have nothing to offer us.' And so she [a Mattachine member] said, 'What do you mean we have nothing to offer?' I said, 'Well, you tell me what you really want and what you're really fighting for, and if you're fighting for something that I don't already have I'll gladly pay another year's dues and get in.' She said, 'We're fighting to be able to work where you want to.' I said, 'I work where I want to.' She said, 'To be able to live where you want to without harassment.' I said, 'I live where I want to without harassment.' You know, 'To be able to have your neighbors know what you are and not have them,' . . . I said, 'My neighbors know what I am.' "

Jodi expresses similar feelings about how little Mattachine had to offer.

"In terms of how I've lived my life it [gay liberation] really did nothing actually, it's almost zip for me because I was never in the closet. And wherever I went I looked like this and every job I ever got I went like this, and I went to school like this. I got my present job looking like this. I go to work now looking like this, I mean there's some compromises I will not make, no matter what."

Gay liberation took the offensive, so that image was no longer the sole expression of lesbianism. Speech became paramount; visibility became more than the individual person's presentation of self. Gay liberation pursued publicity about gays on TV and in newspapers and organized demonstrations and marches. These new elements of visibility made some narrators uncomfortable. Even though they were used to being known for who they were, they were hesitant about broader publicity. They didn't feel the necessity of pushing beyond individual politics to TV appearances or marches. As a result, many narrators had mixed feelings about the tactics of M.S.N.F., as was the case of Matty who withdrew from the organization.

"The only thing I could see is every time I picked up the paper they were in trouble. At that time I don't know if they were all affiliated with the Mattachine, but they were all gung ho on the 'let's put on a sign I'm a lesbian and if you don't like it you can just,' you know, 'take it wherever you want to and march down the street.' To me that wasn't getting the right thing. It isn't that I wasn't interested in what they were trying to do because I was very interested in what they were trying to do."

A key element in the new forms of visibility was the explicit discussion of lesbianism with the heterosexual world, including the appropriation and transformation of derogatory words like "dyke" and "queer." Narrators of the 1950s asserted their lesbianism through appearance alone. Although they had words to describe their distinct identity, they did not usually talk about who they were to the heterosexual world, especially to the media. The topics of lesbianism and homosexuality, and the words themselves, did not become part of common conversations until gay liberation. "I get along with people and with neighbors. I don't hide what I am but I don't walk around with a sign on my back. Everybody knows that sign, if they don't know, it doesn't bother me one way or the other. My whole family knows and all our neighbors, mostly everyone knows" (Matty). Bert explains that hostility and oppression kept them from telling people. "I had never heard the terms [coming out, closets]. No, no. You didn't go around telling people that you preferred women instead of men, 'cause you were afraid of the oppression, how you'd become ostracized."

Narrators disagree about whether the expression "coming out" was used in Buffalo before gay liberation. However, those who remember using it indicate that its meaning was significantly different from today. Today it means telling others that you are lesbian or gay, then it meant having a first sexual relationship with a woman, or recognizing in oneself the desire for such a relationship. The narrators who are sure that they did not use "coming out" focus on the contemporary political meaning.[35] Several narrators agree with Bert's view, that although being seen by straights at the Carousel was like coming out, she never thought of it that way. "I guess it's sort of like coming out, in a way you're coming out to the people that came in [to the Carousel]. And we didn't even know about coming out. We didn't even know about closets in those days. That we felt more comfortable, you know, one more person knew you and accepted you." In her mind, coming out is about consciously and explicitly sharing one's lesbianism with the heterosexual world. It is a political process in which she did not engage until the 1970s.

> "My real coming out probably in my life was [out West] after the civil-rights rally. I was going to . . . [a] community college, and I became aware that I had gotten caught up in a life of where I associated with nothing but gay people. So of course I was comfortable with my gayness. And in sociology class one day, we were broken up into groups to work on a project, and somehow one of the gay bars . . . came up, and the people were talking very freely. They didn't say 'queer' though, you don't hear people using that word so much any more. And I all of a sudden realized that I was a minority and that they didn't think I was gay. So that human-rights rally made me so angry that I went back to all my classes and said [I was]. And nobody even reacted. I was totally shocked."

Another key difference between the prepolitical forms of resistance and the politics of gay liberation was that gay liberation worked through organizations to accomplish social change. Although many narrators from the 1940s and 1950s became members of Mattachine, none of the bar-culture leaders became political leaders. Gay liberation captured the imagination of those who entered the community in the late 1950s at a young age. Ten years later, they went on to give their best energy to gay politics.

> "I was involved first in the gay movement in '71. I guess I started with the Mattachine Society here in Buffalo. Being involved in gay liberation gave me some positive feelings about being gay, working with other gay people, not being just confined to the bars. We were doing something; we were trying to make some changes in the world, some changes in our immediate environment. We were all working together. It gave us a sense of ourselves as having some power of togetherness. And it wasn't centered around alcohol and partying And we did, we did bring about some small changes in our very immediate environment, because of the work that we did." (Toni)

In distinguishing the prepolitical forms of butch-fem culture from the politics of gay liberation, we do not mean to create an absolute division. In the 1950s bar culture there were many indications of different approaches to resistance, but the times did not allow them to coalesce into politics. Bert, for instance, who had decided she was going to relocate to Florida, was arrested during a raid on a bar in 1960, six months after her arrival. She wanted to fight the case but could not interest a lawyer: "And I remember getting out, and I went to a lawyer . . . my civil rights were imposed upon, and he said, 'Who do you think you're kidding?' He wouldn't even touch it. Which nowadays somebody would have."

During this same time period, the cultural push to be identified as lesbians—or at least different—all the time was so powerful that it generated a new form of identification among the tough bar lesbians: a star tattoo on the top of the wrist, which was usually covered by a watch. This was the first symbol of community identity that did not rely on butch-fem imagery. We can trace this phenomenon back to an evening of revelry in the late 1950's, when a few butches trooped over to "Dirty Dick's" tattoo parlor on Chippewa Street and had the tiny blue five-pointed star put on their wrists. Later, some of the fems of this group also got their stars. Bert thinks it was worn as a sign of defiance. Others claim they just got the idea one night and did it. The community views the tattoo as a definite mark of identification. Bert, who did not get the tattoo, experienced it as a dare: "And they tried to get me to do it but I wouldn't do it, and the main thing that I can think of that held me back was because of the job that I had at the time. There was the pressure, worried about them finding out why." She adds that one of her friends had told her: "The Buffalo police knew [that] the people that had the stars on their wrists were lesbians, and they had their names and so forth. That it was an identity type thing with the gay community, with the lesbian community."

The fact that the star tattoo was created by those who were firmly into roles, in fact, by the group that was considered the butchy butches and their fems, suggests that the force to assert lesbian identity was strong enough to break through the existing traditions of boldness based in butch-fem roles. The stars presage the methods of identity created by gay liberation. In fact, the mark has become something of a tradition in local circles and has seen a revival since the 1970s.

In contrast to the familiarity most narrators felt with the ideas of gay liberation, they thought that feminism offered something new and important. Some were particularly excited by it like Jodi who felt it opened up new ways for her to be in the world and realize her goals.

> "Well it made me aware that I didn't have to do or be some ways to live my life how I choose to live my life, as far as being a lesbian. . . . I mostly changed how I dressed. Some people still think I'm a boy, what can I say? And I changed some attitudes, but I'm still who I am mostly. But those changes were positive changes, and hopefully I'll always be able to change. I'll always be flexible so that good things, I'll be able to incorporate in my life, and change so that I make many more of what I'd like to be."

Ironically although lesbian feminists judged these traditional, role-defined butches and fems as an anathema to feminism, many butches, from years of claiming male privilege, and many butches and fems, from building their lives without men, were actively poised and ready to learn about feminism.

The butch-fem image both symbolized and advanced the assertion of lesbian distinctness during the 1940s and 1950s. Central to the major issues facing lesbian community—to be able to safely congregate with friends and find a romantic and sexual partner—it pervaded the entire culture. By definition this culture was never simply an imitation of heterosexuality, for butches did not completely adopt a male persona, and fems were aware that they were not with men. Rather, butch-fem culture indicated that lesbians existed, that women could live without men, that women might usurp the privileges of men, and also that women had sex with one another. In this sense, butch-fem roles were the primary prepolitical institution of resistance against oppression. This aspect of roles gave them their power and their ability to endure.

Members of the 1940s and 1950s butch-fem community struggled to determine the degree of "obviousness" appropriate and necessary for lesbian life, a debate that still continues in contemporary gay and lesbian politics. Is it better for lesbians to mute their difference and attempt to assimilate or should lesbians blatantly affirm their difference from heterosexuality? Because these butches and fems came down on the side of asserting difference, despite the consequences, they were instrumental in the development of a distinct lesbian consciousness and identity, one that profoundly influenced the development of gay liberation.

1.   Friends at Eddie's, late 1930s

2.   Butch Night Out at Ralph Martin's, 1940s

3.   Saturday night at Ralph Martin's, 1940s

4.   Butch-fem couple, 1940s

5.   Butches showing off, 1940s

6.   Sleigh ride in the park, 1940s

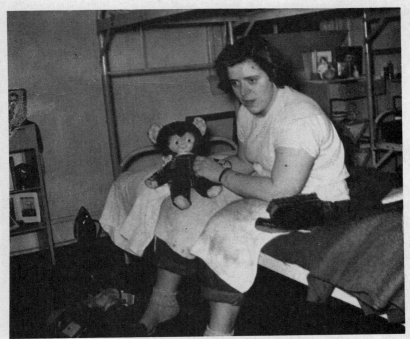

7. Lonely at boot camp, early 1950s

8. Livening up barrack life, 1952

9.   Young stud, 1950s

10.   Fashionable fem, 1950s

11.   Young Lovers, 1956

12.   It's all in the eyes, 1950s

13.   Birthday party at Duffy's 1950s

14. "Clowning around in front of our apartment," 1950s

15.   Just friends, early 1960s

16.   The kiss, early 1960s

"Now You Get this Spot Right Here": BUTCH-FEM SEXUALITY DURING THE 1940s AND 1950s

Women who were new to the life and entered bars have reported they were asked: "Well, what are you—butch or femme?" Many fled rather than answer the question. The real questions behind this discourse were, "Are you sexual?" and "Are you safe?" When one moved beyond the opening gambits, a whole range of sexuality was possible. Butch and femme covered a range of sexual responses.
—Joan Nestle, "Butch-Femme Relationships: Sexual Courage in the 1950s"

. . . all they had to give was themselves & they gave that. Judith felt the tension in the butch's body—she wanted to release that tension. And the butch's only thought was that she wanted to please her femme.
—Red Jordan Arobateau, *Jailhouse Stud*

The meaning of butch-fem roles during the 1940s and 1950s was multidimensional. In addition to the political implications embedded in butch-fem appearance, butch-fem roles organized lesbian intimacy, creating and expressing a distinctive lesbian eroticism.[1] Intrinsic to the butch-fem dyad was the presumption that the butch was the physically active partner and the leader in lovemaking. As D.J., who has given this much thought, explains, "I treat a woman as a woman, down to the basic fact it'd have to be my side doin' most of the doin.'" Insofar as the butch was the "doer" and the fem was the desired one, butch-fem roles did indeed parallel the male-female roles in heterosexuality. Yet, unlike what transpires in the dynamics of most heterosexual relationships, the butch's foremost objective was to give sexual pleasure to a fem. It was in satisfying her fem that the butch received fulfillment. "If I could give her satisfaction to the highest, that's what gave me satisfaction." As for the fem, she not only knew what would give her physical pleasure, but she also knew that she was not the receptacle for someone else's gratification. Charlie remembers her pleasure: "I really didn't do anything, just laid there and enjoyed it." The essence of this emotional/sexual dynamic is captured by the ideal of the untouchable butch, or the "stone butch," that prevailed during this period. A stone butch does all the "doin'" and does not ever allow her lover to reciprocate in kind. To be untouchable meant to gain pleasure solely from giving pleasure.

The erotic was as important as the political in the system of meanings created by butch-fem roles. When explaining how they recognized a person's role, narrators regularly referred to sexuality as well as image, even though sexual posture was less immediately apparent. In most instances, although not in all, image and sexuality were congruent, in the sense that the more masculine appearing woman was also the more aggressive sexually:[2] "You can't tell butch-fem by people's dress. You couldn't even really tell in the '50s. I knew women with long hair, fem clothes, and found out they were butches. Actually I even knew one who wore men's clothes, haircuts and ties, who was a fem" (Reggie). In these exceptional cases, sexual posture was usually taken as the primary indicator of a person's role. This is consistent with the fact that sexual posture had the most important implications for daily socializing in the community, indicating with whom a person might find sexual satisfaction.

The key to understanding the butch-fem erotic system is to grasp that it both imitates and transforms heterosexual patterns. The obvious similarity between butch-fem and male-female eroticism was that they were both based on gender polarity: In lesbian culture, masculine and feminine imagery identified the objects of desire; aggressiveness and passivity were crucial to the erotic dynamic. There were also more subtle parallels. Even the butch's concern with pleasing her fem was not an idea original to lesbian culture. The middle-class marriage manuals of the 1930s and 1940s emphasized the importance of husbands pleasing their wives.[3] On the whole, these books treated women's sexuality as something mystical and hidden, which had to be awakened by a committed and loving man. They urged husbands to please their wives and extolled the joys of mutual—especially simultaneous—orgasm. In addition, the ideal of the untouchable bears a striking resemblance to male sexuality as it was characterized during most of the twentieth century, in which the focus was exclusively on the penis's sexual prowess, ignoring the sensuality of the entire male body.[4]

Despite these similarities, other features of lesbian erotic culture sharply distinguished it from that of the heterosexual world. First and foremost, gendered lesbian eroticism was rooted in the similarity of two female bodies, and as such was not governed by the demands and rhythms of the penis.[5] Second, the butch-fem erotic system did not consistently follow the gender divisions of the dominant society. The active or "masculine" partner was associated with the giving of sexual pleasure, a service usually assumed to be "feminine." Conversely, the fem, although the more passive partner, demanded and received sexual pleasure and in this sense might be considered the more self-concerned or even more "selfish" partner.[6]

Third, the butch's pleasure was defined solely in terms of pleasing her fem. Her activity was first and foremost directed toward giving pleasure. This was not true of men. The heterosexual advice books and columns were "taming" the "true" male sexuality by foregrounding the woman's pleasure. The unique sexual desire of the butch opened the pathway for the exploration and enjoyment of the fem's sexual potential. Fourth and finally, butch-fem erotic culture contained few sanctions against women's expression of sexuality. Sexual expression was associated primarily with pleasure. The dangers inherent in sex for heterosexual women in a male supremacist society—loss of reputation, economic dependency, pregnancy, and disease—did not exist and the community did not develop substitutes.

Lesbian culture, while drawing on heterosexual models, unquestionably transformed them into specifically lesbian interactions. Through role playing, lesbians developed distinctive and fulfilling expressions of women's sexual love for women. On the one hand, butch-fem roles limited sexual expression by imposing a definite structure. On the other hand, this structure organized and gave a determinant shape to lesbian desire, which allowed individuals to know and find what they wanted. Despite the dominant society's taboos, the vitality of lesbian sexual expression was such that members of the community developed rich and satisfying sexual lives.

Butch-fem erotic culture was in the process of creation and change during the 1940s and 1950s. Two somewhat contradictory trends in lesbian sexual expression emerged. The community became more open to the discussion of sexual matters, the acceptance of new sexual practices, and learning about sex from friends as well as lovers. The language used to discuss sexuality expresses this change. Narrators of the 1940s seem most comfortable using the word "intimacy" for the discussion of sexual matters, while those who came out in the 1950s use the words "sex" and "sexuality" with freedom and ease. At the same time, the rules of butch-fem sexuality became more rigid as community concern for role-appropriate behavior increased.

These contradictory trends in attitudes and norms of lesbian sexuality parallel changes in the heterosexual world. Movement toward open discussion of sex, acceptance of oral sex, and teaching about sex took place in the society at large, as exemplified by the publication of and the material contained in the Kinsey reports.[7] In *Intimate Matters: The History of Sexuality in America*, John D'Emilio and Estelle Freedman identify the 1920s as the turning point in which a system of sexual liberalism—one that values the heterosexual expression of sexuality in its own right, at least inside marriage—came to predominate over the nineteenth-century emphasis on sexual control.[8] From this point on, there was a consistent trend toward valuing heterosexual sexual expression in all segments of society, despite minor setbacks during the Depression and the postwar return to domesticity. The movies and other media explicitly conveyed the importance of heterosexual expression. Youth culture encouraged heterosexual petting. Birth control became more acceptable and more readily available, allowing the pursuit of sexual pleasure without the fear of pregnancy.

Similarly, the lesbian community's stringent enforcement of role-defined behavior in the 1950s occurred in the context of the postwar retreat to a stricter gender division of labor and the specifically sexual ideology that accompanied it.[9] Like heterosexual society, the lesbian community experienced a temporary step backward in a trend toward less rigidly defined gender roles. These parallels indicate a close connection between the evolution of heterosexual and homosexual cultures. Our research suggests, however, that it is misleading to assume that the heterosexual world unilaterally determined the culture and behavior of the lesbian world, or that the lesbian world was simply a reflection of the heterosexual world.

As an integral part of lesbian life, lesbian sexuality developed as one facet of the community's changing resistance to sexism and lesbian oppression. The lesbian community had to forge its own sexual culture, defying social norms about heterosexuality and gender. Even though society was becoming more liberal about heterosexual expression, it continued to condemn homosexuality, even instituting new prohibitions.[10] But it was not only lesbian sexual identity that was difficult to achieve. Despite the new sexual liberalism, the sexual identity of women was fragile. Developing sexual subjectivity, therefore, was a harder process for lesbians than for gay men, because, in the heterosexual world, male sexual expression was unabashedly recognized and in many cases glorified. The heterosexual double standard toward women discouraged women's sexual expression, not to mention its celebration. Women tended to be less precocious sexually and learned about sexuality through men.

The evolution of the lesbian community's sexual mores was integrally related to its move toward pride and defiance. In the community of the 1940s, which was just beginning to support places for public gatherings, the majority was reticent about sexuality. As bar culture became more elaborate and open, lesbians gained pride and consciousness of kind. They exchanged information about all aspects of their social lives, including sexuality, more freely. Discussion of sex was one of many dimensions of an increasingly complex culture. The instruction of newcomers even came to include sexuality. This public recognition of sexuality gave lesbians the support to affirm their own sexuality and explore new horizons. At the same time, the community's growing public defiance produced an increased concern for enforcing role-appropriate behavior. To deal effectively with the hostility of the straight world, and to support one another in physical confrontations, members of the community developed rules of appropriate behavior and forms of organization and exerted pressure—particularly on butches—to live up to these standards. Because roles organized intimate life as well as the community's resistance to oppression, sexual performance was a vital part of these 1950s standards. For the tough butches, being able to please a woman more than a man could was as important in the defense of the community as were their skills in fighting.

The sexual revolution of the 1920s had a mixed impact on women. Although it affirmed the existence of women's sexual desire, the result was to define women's sexuality in the service of men, the family, and the state. Atina Grossmann concisely characterizes this legacy:

> We are only now beginning to pick up where they, our grandmothers, left off. We are confronting the multiple ways in which their sexual revolution (like ours of the 1960s?) freed women only to please men or reject them, liberated women in terms women themselves did not determine, and finally subordinated women's freedom to the interests of family and state. They provided us with no solutions. They did, I think—if we find and listen to them—identify the terms of the argument and raise the essential questions.[11]

Like most scholars writing on women's sexuality in the twentieth century, Grossmann overlooks the contribution of lesbians during the 1940s and 1950s in affirming and defining women's sexual desire. Essentially, as lesbians came to their sexual subjectivity, they were pioneers in women's struggle for sexual autonomy—that is, their ability to decide what they want and their power to obtain it—as well as in the struggle of homosexuals for the right to a decent life. They embodied the new ideas that women had sexual desires, that sexual pleasure was separate from reproduction, and that sexuality could exist outside of marriage. Above all, in lesbian culture, women's sexual expression was something powerful and pleasurable.

To illuminate the connections between lesbian sexuality and the cultural and political developments in lesbian community, this chapter explores the changing dynamics of the butch-fem erotic system in the 1940s and 1950s, paying particular attention to the social meaning of the "stone butch." Since coming to sexual subjectivity was such a major step for women of that period, we also document the way lesbians learned about sex and examine the place of sexual pleasure in lesbian culture. This chapter on sex and sexuality, like those which follow on relationships and identity, is not organized around distinctions between the Black and white communities; nor around the distinctions between the upwardly mobile and rough and tough communities. From our narrators' life stories we were unable to discover significant differences between subcommunities on these topics.[12] This has the effect of homogenizing the social positions of narrators, and in an inherently racist society this creates the illusion of whiteness. We ask the reader to remember that narrators who are identified by name and known, therefore, from preceding chapters, are Black and Indian as well as white, and we will restate this occasionally throughout the text.

LESBIAN SEXUALITY IN THE 1940s

During the 1940s, the forms of sexual expression for butch and fem were expected to be different, with the butch being the more active or aggressive partner. This difference was part of the moral fabric of lesbian culture, as D.J. explains: "There can always be a change of love, the caressing, but only to a certain degree. Not the same as a butch, there would be a limit. . . . As I say, my morals are high, and what a butch does and what a fem does is . . . a different thing." When asked if other butches would agree with her, she replies:

> "Yeah, if they had any respect for the woman they were with. I mean this is the way I look at it, I treat a woman as a woman, not as, I don't know how the hell you put it. I mean there had to be love on both sides, but I mean down to the basic fact, it still had to be my side doin' . . . most of the doing. [Fems didn't do the same things] not right down to the last nitty-gritty. Oh a few things, you know, but . . . see a true fem at that time really didn't do things [that] sometimes the butches do. How they do it now I have no knowledge of that at all."

In the 1940s most butches—Black, white, and Indian—were "aggressive" and did not allow their partners to "reciprocate" in lovemaking. (This was the language used for butch sexual behavior at that time. The terms "stone" and "untouchable" were not yet part of common usage.) Their satisfaction came from pleasing the fem. "Oh yeah. If I could give her satisfaction to the highest that gave me satisfaction. And her putting her arm around me and the necking back and all this, to a certain degree, it was beautiful" (D.J.). The language other butches use to explain their sexual behavior is strikingly similar. In response to our question about why her sexual relationships were not reciprocal, Arden says: "For me satisfying women was very important."

Joanna, who had a long-term, nonreciprocal relationship, tried to challenge her partner's behavior but met only with resistance. Her butch's whole group—those who hung around Ralph Martin's—was the same. "Because I asked her one time, I said, 'Do you think that you might be just the only one?' 'Oh no,' she said. 'I know I'm not, you know, that I've discussed with . . . different people.' [There were] no exceptions, which I thought was odd, but, I thought, well, this is how it is." For Joanna, the sexual restrictions were a source of discomfort. "It was very one-sided, you know, and . . . you never really got a chance to express your love. And I think this kind of suppressed . . . your feelings, your emotions. And I don't know whether that's healthy. I don't think so."

Although Joanna was interested in being more active, contradicting D.J., many fems did want to be the less aggressive partner. When asked if butch and fem had different roles Charlie replies:

"Years ago, definitely. . . . But I haven't been around that much either, like fifteen years with one and eleven years with the next one. That takes care of a quarter of a century. But I haven't tried enough of them probably. . . . The [butch was the] aggressive person, just their attitude I guess, 'I am boss. And you do what I tell you.' There's a stronger want that a butch would have years ago for a fem, to just try and overpower you. . . . [In my first relationship] she was the aggressor and liked it. . . . I guess I was having too much fun to ask her [how things were supposed to be]. I never asked. Nobody told me anything. . . . I didn't understand how she could have such great desires for me without me having some act in this except to be on the other end I guess you call it. I enjoyed it. . . . I didn't ask questions, I just went along with the whole thing."

She did not try to reciprocate: "No, I was scared to death of that part. . . . Making love to her. Yeah, I was scared to death, 'cause it wasn't in me. It wasn't me to do this and she never let me do anything." Pearl has similar memories: "The fem didn't do anything at the time. . . . I didn't want to and I didn't." She characterizes the attitude of butches: "Just don't touch me. Let me do what I want with you but don't you do anything with me, except maybe kiss you, and hug and stuff like that, but not anything very personal. . . . If you would do anything that they didn't want you to do they would kind of let you know in the way they acted that you shouldn't do that." Although fem narrators, including Joanna who had been interested in taking a more active role in lovemaking, understand the butch as the more aggressive partner, especially in regard to the expression of sexual interest, in their minds butch aggressiveness is related to erotic desire and pleasing, and not to violence or pain.

Butch and fem sexualities were strongly internalized and were not easily discarded as times changed. Even though in the 1960s and 1970s more and more lesbians practiced mutual lovemaking, most butches who had been active in the 1940s did not alter their patterns. Fems were more likely to make some changes, especially when going with younger women. Joanna, who had been interested in more reciprocal sex in the 1940s, was in a relationship, twenty years later, based on mutual lovemaking. Charlie, when requested, hesitantly began to make love to her partner.

"[I did] not for a long time. . . . 'Cause I was told, you just don't do that. . . . That's a tough question. I don't know, I never changed, I was always scared. But then I met someone that was a little more commanding, more demanding, you know, 'This is the way you do it.' And I guess I just went along with that too. But I mean as far as for myself to go out and look to find somebody to— I never have. That would have to be a very rare occasion. In fact, all occasions, when we get older, get rare."

Although difference between butch and fem in intimate life was the norm, deviation was neither censured nor stigmatized. The underlying reality of two women together made reciprocal sex an ever-present possibility. Two butch narrators did not strictly follow the butch-fem pattern, which means, of course, that there were fems who did not follow it either.[13] Reggie questions whether there really was a difference between butch and fem sexuality. She is ambivalent, affirming that lovemaking was mutual, while at the same time stating that one person had to be more aggressive. "You distinguished the difference of the two people . . . [by] the parts you played. But what part is it? Because basically if you want to get technical when you hit that bed you make love to one another. But I guess there's always got to be someone to be a little more aggressive, so to speak."[14] Her memories suggest that while there was a cultural logic to butch-fem behavior, there was also a compelling logic of the similarity among women. Dee claims that her relationships were mutual except for one. She guesses that for most women at the time sex was reciprocal but she is not sure because sex wasn't talked about that much: "As far as the gang I knew at that time . . . it was equal. But of course that was not discussed too very much at that point, in the '40s and '50s. It was quiet then. There would be . . . much more [discussion] in this more modern day and age, you know, with freedom of information." The reticence about discussing sexual matters made it difficult for the community to inculcate or enforce sexual norms.

When divergence from the social norm was noticed, it was not considered problematic. Leslie and Arden, who had strict standards for butch sexuality, reminisce fondly about a friend who they described as being "comme çi, comme ça." "She had a great social life and was more like the kids today." They remember asking her, "What the hell are you?" She responded, "A lavender butch." This meant she was a butch, but "femmy." The term was not pejorative; it was self-descriptive rather than a stigmatized community label. Such persons were easily integrated into community life.

The 1940s was a transitional time for lesbian intimacy in Buffalo. Within the common framework of butch-fem sexuality, the community contained significant variation in sexual mores—attitudes about sex as well as actual techniques of lovemaking. The patrons of Ralph Martin's adhered to more conservative sexual values, while those in Winters were more radical, presaging what were to become the sexual norms of the 1950s.[15] Since Ralph Martin's was the biggest and most popular bar of the period, it is fair to say that most people held conservative values. However, since the attitudes and values of the Winters' patrons came to predominate in the next decade, their importance in the culture of this period was greater than their small numbers would suggest.

The lesbian patrons of Ralph Martin's did not discuss sex openly. "People didn't talk about sex. There was no intimate conversation. It was kind of hush, hush. . . . I didn't know there were different ways" (Leslie). By contrast, this narrator recalls a visit to Winters, where other women were laughing about "sixty-nine." "I didn't get it. I went to [my girlfriend] and said, 'Somebody says "sixty-nine" and everybody gets hysterical.'" Finally, her girlfriend learned what the laughter was all about. At that time Leslie would have mentioned such intimacies only with a lover; and even then she would not discuss the actual experience of sex. It wasn't until later that she got into bull sessions about such topics. D.J., who was a regular at Ralph Martin's, also emphasizes how sexuality was never discussed.

> "In fact this is the first I've ever really talked like this even about it. 'Cause I've always figured what I did with a woman, and this is why I always respected the fem, what I did with her was with me. I kept it that way. I wouldn't go out and broadcast, 'Oh geez, I had Nelly Belly last night and we did this.' That would be showing no respect for the woman you were with. And I never talked about what I did when I was with someone. I always figured that was personal; something between us that no one could talk about, knock her, or anything else about it."

The predominant form of lovemaking, at least for the core group of patrons at Ralph Martin's, was what clinicians called "tribadism" or what most narrators for this period call "friction." Another narrator remembers women from this period calling it "banging." (Not all narrators from this group could easily come up with words for their sexual practices, which must be a function of not discussing them with one another at the time.) Most narrators who frequented Ralph Martin's did not engage in oral sex and Joanna says it was never discussed.[16] Some may have practiced it, but her butch of the time certainly did not:

> "Oh my God, [she] wouldn't even discuss [oral sex]. Would never discuss it. . . . The group she hung around were very straight laced. . . . Bet she thought it was a little more heterosexual in making love her way. Maybe she, maybe she thought it was her way of, you know, her way of expressing her [self]. I don't think she in fifty million years could ever have oral sex. Really. I know she couldn't."

Becoming a sexually active lesbian did not mean that a person cast aside other sexual prejudices. This group of friends had a reputation for sexual conservatism that continued into the 1950s and 1960s. Whitney, a fem of the younger generation, remembers that one or two held on to their aversion to oral sex: "When they would see mouthwash in somebody's bathroom, that person was automatically oral, and they were a dirty person."

The Winters' patrons had a more open, experimental attitude toward sex. They discussed it unreservedly and accepted the practice of oral sex. These women threw parties in which they tried threesomes and daisy chains. "People would try it and see how it worked out. But nothing really happened. One person would always get angry and leave, and they would end up with two" (Arden). Even if their sexual adventures did not always turn out as planned, the Winters crowd was unquestionably innovative. In this atmosphere partners talked together about sex, giving a little advice, "a little to left" (Arden). They did not, however, experiment with dildos or sex toys. No narrators from either Ralph Martin's or Winters had ever used a dildo, although most had heard that some people did. Arden did not feel that they were necessary for pleasure: "I thought it was silly. If a woman wanted the male apparatus she might as well be with men." Nevertheless, the Winters crowd was expanding the possibilities for women's sexual satisfaction and beginning to find and enjoy sex without love, a radical undertaking for their time. Arden reminisces that it was always a contrast to go home to the serene life of her religious family.

This greater freedom of sexual expression was developed within the framework of butch-fem eroticism. Mutual lovemaking was not part of this group's freer approach to sex. In fact, Dee, who states that the majority of her lovemaking was mutual, did not go to Winters and, like most patrons of Ralph Martin's, was conservative on sexual matters. She and her friends did not engage in discussions of sex, and she never tried oral sex until the 1960s, when she was introduced to the practice by a lover. In addition, she strongly disapproved of the sexual experimentation of the Winters crowd. She had been invited to some of their parties but never attended.[17]

> "[A friend] wanted me to go to this daisy chain gang on Lexington Avenue, and I was not interested. I have never been at all intrigued by multiple sex or sex orgies or groups of people having sex at the same time, because to me that is not love. It is reducing sex to an animal level and I consider myself above an animal. I love dogs, but I don't think I'm an animal, and to me sex should be intimate between two people with love involved. . . . I never went. . . . I just said, 'Thanks but no thanks.' I didn't go for that type of thing."

Inasmuch as pursuing lesbian sex itself implied a divergence from traditional social norms, the predominance of the more conservative sexual mores in this community indicates how hard it was for women to make a complete break with their upbringing. Just as for heterosexuals, lesbian sexual morality was in transition during this period. But the different sexual morals existed side by side arousing personal curiosity in some, moral judgment in others, but nothing more that might engender conflict or division within an otherwise homogeneous community. Lesbian culture was not yet at a stage where it was reaching out and educating newcomers. There was not, as yet, the assumption of a common culture that supported all women in exploring their sexuality.

Distinctive aspects of the Winters group shed light on the complex process of changing sexual norms for women. Arden emphasizes that these women were older; in her view they knew more and were less shy. In essence, she is assigning women in their thirties and forties a leading role in sexual innovation. This contradicts most of the dominant ideas about women and sexuality. Yet there is substantial evidence that at that time, and even today, women continued to expand their capacity for pleasure as they aged.[18] But age alone cannot explain the difference, since very few, if any, of the Ralph Martin's patrons became as sexually experimental as the Winters crowd as they aged. Other factors also shaped the sexual mores of the Winters group. Some of its members may have been exposed to the sex education available in middle-class marriage manuals.[19] The leader was a private secretary who had a little more money than the rest. She is remembered as a very charismatic person who talked a lot about sex. Her social position may have familiarized her with new middle-class attitudes about heterosexuality. In addition, this group had quite a few members who had been married and active heterosexuals. Arden identifies the married women as her best teachers. Perhaps through the process of leaving their marriages, these women gained enough confidence in themselves as sexual beings to create an environment that encouraged sharing information on sex among lesbians.

Given that most of the community did not discuss sexuality, and given that the lesbian community during this period did not reach out to or educate newcomers, how did lesbians become sexually active and develop themselves as sexual subjects? How did they learn about appropriate butch-fem behavior? The majority experienced their sexuality as something private and "natural," which did not need instruction. Butches took their own paths toward sexual expression, a difficult experience for some but not all. For fems it was easier, because they most often became sexually active with a more knowledgeable butch. In any event, when both were inexperienced the butch had the responsibility of knowing or figuring out what to do.

Arden and Leslie, the oldest butch narrators, who were teenagers in the early 1930s, were the ones who emphasize how difficult it was for women to become active sexually.[20] They did not have sexual relationships with women until their late teens and describe their early high school attractions as "innocently flirtatious" or "romantic." Leslie remembers that the objects of her affection would playfully encourage her: "[Two friends] and I would play a game. They would hold something over their heads and if I couldn't guess what it was I would have to go into the garage and kiss them." Although her interest in women was definitely sexual, the transition to having a sexual relationship was very hard for her. Since she was completely ignorant and inexperienced, she remembers being amused, when she first started going to the bars, by heterosexual women who were afraid that lesbians would attack them for sex: "It's funny I was kind of shy at that time. I did not know what to do anyway. It was hard for women, we did not have a sex education." She had no instruction and never had an affair with someone who was older or more experienced. But once she took the plunge, she had no difficulty. "The first time I was scared to death and then realized it was natural. . . . I did what I felt like doing."

Arden, who agrees with how difficult it was for women to know about sex, adds that her education was belated. "I had some good instruction at parties, but that was much later." Her instruction came when she joined the Winters crowd, and provides yet one more example of its distinctive attitude toward sex. She cannot rave enough about her two teachers who were both older than she was and had been married. She also takes great pride in herself, commenting: "I was an apt pupil." Her assumption that one needs to be a student of sex was unique to the Winters crowd during this period, although it became basic to lesbian culture during the next decade.

Dee, who was of this same age group, had her first sexual experience in a short-lived marriage and then had no trouble expressing herself as a lesbian. After leaving her husband, she had continued to date men. Then, without any contact with the lesbian community, her relationship with a woman friend whom she met through the bowling team at work easily took on a sexual dimension.

> "Well I was very fond of her. We started being friends in October when the bowling season opened, and New Year's Eve we had double dated, and the one fellow went home and the other one took me up to her apartment. We took her home, and he got drunk in the kitchen while we went to bed. And at that point I knew nothing about sex with a female, it just all came naturally. I hadn't read any books, I didn't know what to do, it just happened. . . . And after I got up we woke him up, we took a cab home. He lived a few doors up the street from me. Isn't that ridiculous? Heloise and I laugh about it to this day."

Narrators who were teenagers later, in the late 1930s and early 1940s, all became sexually active in their early teens, before they entered the lesbian community, and experienced no difficulties. The attraction to a woman led easily to sexual activity.[21] Debra knew what to do in a relationship that became sexual when she was thirteen years old. "I felt I knew exactly what I was doing. It was what I wanted to do, and I did it. And we did it the whole time I was there." D.J. became sexually active in a girl's reform school, but again with no real instruction, learning it as she went along.

> "The first, that goes way back. Well see, the main really right down to the nitty gritty, I was in Good Shepherd and I had the whole dormitory all by myself. There was no one else in there but me, and all the girls. I mean [no one] that was lesbian or homosexual, I was the only one. They thought I was a man running all through the place. And I had all the girls in the place! . . . Well as far as my dress, my haircut so forth and so on [they thought I was a man.] And you figure a dormitory as long as this house, beds on all sides and coming up the center, I had a good time. . . . I snuck out a few names, which you weren't supposed to. . . . Couldn't even use your own name there, we had different names they gave us. But I snuck out a few addresses and seen people afterwards. But that's really when I did everything right down to the works."

Before this she had only kissed girls, but she still had no trouble figuring out what to do when girls approached her.

"Well as far as kissing, put my arm around them and that, but the actual intimacy not till I got in there. . . . It just came natural. I woke up and some girl was leaning over me and that was that. 'Cause she thought I was a boy. . . . I don't know how the girls thought then, but they figured that was the closest looking thing to a man in the place. . . . She just leaned over and gave me a big smooch. And that was it. So I took over from there. . . . We used to sneak in the hall, and as I said news got around and there was quite a number."

When asked if any one of the girls had ever told her she was doing it right, she replies, in typical butch manner, by pointing to the successful results. "They seemed to enjoy it, so. . . . That was it. Everyone has their own way of doing things as far as that goes. . . . Satisfaction's there . . . you ain't gonna knock it." The ultimate test was her partners' pleasure.

This story illustrates that butch-fem sexuality often existed without women having had contact with a lesbian community. There is evidence to suggest that popular culture of the first half of the twentieth century represented sexuality primarily in terms of attraction between masculine and feminine. In this conceptual system what was anomalous about lesbian relationships was the gender inversion of the butch rather than the interest of a feminine woman in a masculine woman. The former's sexual interests were following gender prescribed sexuality.[22] Thus, when the young girl in the reform school leaned over D.J., she was not acting abnormally according to her cultural expectations, but responding to a masculine image that was familiar. Teenage passion allowed her to take the initiative, but did not fully break her feminine training. The young butch had already broken with feminine tradition, taking on more masculine attributes in her appearance and actions. Using a framework of gender roles, they nevertheless managed to transform the expectations of heterosexuality. They created a structure within which both could achieve fulfillment; the more masculine woman satisfying herself by becoming the active giver, and the more feminine woman, by being the receiver of pleasure.

THE SYSTEM OF BUTCH-FEM SEXUALITY IN THE 1950s

In the 1950s, the more experimental sexual mores of the Winters crowd came to predominate while those of the Ralph Martin's group virtually disappeared. Sex became a topic of conversation among all social groups. Oral sex became an accepted form of lovemaking, so that an individual who did not practice it was acting on personal preference rather than on ignorance or social proscription. In addition, most butch narrators for the 1950s recall having been teachers or pupils of sexual practices. Lesbian community and the resulting consciousness and pride had developed to the point where it could help all its members to leave their traditional women's upbringing and embrace these new sexual attitudes and practices. The new sexual mores had both a freeing and a repressive effect. They expanded and developed ideas about sexuality, and validated sexual feelings. At the same time they set rigid standards of correct sexual behavior for members of the community.[23] This is vividly evidenced by the developments around butch-fem eroticism. Social pressure to conform to the stone-butch ideal and to be consistent in following the butch-fem erotic system increased throughout the decade.

As in the 1940s, narrators from all social groups agree that the butch was the leader or the aggressor in lovemaking, and the fem was the focus of pleasure. This was true by definition. If a person's behavior were otherwise she would not be butch or fem. "Butch, . . . whatever, that's just a monogram, it's just a—you got to call it something. No really, this is how I feel. I mean you could call me a door, I mean it just doesn't matter. I'm an aggressive sort of person with a woman" (Sandy).

In the 1950s, the stone butch became a publicly discussed ideal for appropriate sexual behavior, and by the late 1950s it was the standard that young butches felt they had to achieve to be a "real" or "true" butch. In contrast to the 1940s, a 1950s fem who was out in the community would not have to ask her butch why she was untouchable and if there were others like her. She would have known it was the expected behavior for butches.

There is some disagreement in the community over the definition of a stone butch. In the intimate moments between two women, how untouchable was she? Some butches claim that they were absolutely untouchable. That was how they were, and that's how they enjoyed sex. When we confronted Stormy, who referred to herself as an "untouchable," with the opinion of another narrator, who maintained that stone butches had never really existed, she replied: "No, that's not true. I'm an untouchable. I've tried to have my lover make love to me, but I just couldn't stand it. . . . I really think there's something physical about that." Sandy, another stone butch, explains:

> "I wanted to satisfy them [women], and I wanted to make love—I love to make love. I still say that's the greatest thing in the world. And I don't want them to touch me. It spoils the whole thing. . . . I am the way I am. I'm not doing this because I'm pretending. This is my way. And I figure that if a girl is attracted to me, she's attracted to me because of what I am."

Other butches who consider themselves, and had the reputation of being, untouchable claim that it was, as a general matter, impossible to be completely untouchable. When asked if she were really untouchable, Vic replies, "Of course not. How would any woman stay with me if I was? It doesn't make any sense. . . . I don't believe there was ever such a class—other than what they told each other." Vic preferred not to be touched, but she did allow mutual lovemaking from time to time during her long-term relationships. A first time in bed, however:

"There's no way in hell that you would touch me . . . if you mean untouchable like that. But if I'm living with a woman, I'd have to be a liar if I said that she hadn't touched me. But I can say that I don't care for it to happen. And the only reason it does happen is because she wants it. It's not like something I desire or want. But there's no such thing as an untouchable butch, and I'm the finest in Buffalo and I'm tellin' you straight, and don't let them jive you around it—no way."

Vic's distinction between her behavior on a first night and her behavior in long-term relationships appears to have been accepted practice. The fact that some—albeit little—mutuality was allowed over the period of a long relationship did not affect one's reputation as an untouchable butch. Her perspective also indicates an undercurrent of pressure from fems to be permitted to make love to their butches.

In keeping with the ideal of untouchability, many butches did not take off their clothes in bed. Most butch narrators remember wearing a T-shirt and underpants to bed. If they were full-bosomed, they would take off their bra or binder, but they always wore a T-shirt. Little Gerry remembers: "If you wanted that close skin contact, you would take them off when you had sex. But you would put them on immediately afterwards. And you would not take them off every time."

The satisfaction stone butches experienced through pleasing their lovers was complex and not easily described. Since "friction" was no longer the dominant form of lovemaking, butches' genitals were not usually stimulated by direct physical contact. Many butches were and remain spontaneously orgasmic. Their excitement level peaks to orgasm while they make love orally or digitally to a woman. The nature of this orgasm is unclear. Some describe it as physical, while others think it is mental.[24] When asked if she had an orgasm while making love to her partner, Sandy said at first. "Not really, no. I'm satisfied, I'm happy. If she climaxes that's it for me." But pushed to describe her experience, she struggles to find the appropriate words.

"I experience something like that [an orgasm], but it's not—I don't know, it's really not a physical thing. I'm not lacking anything, don't want anything more. I can't say that I'm never satisfied, maybe not quite to what they [fems] want. . . . Like I feel a great excitement and a great joy. But not like they say they get. . . . I don't know how to explain. Like when they go off, like when it's there, I am just so enthralled, I just . . ."

The connection between her own sexual needs and those of her partner was so strong that Sandy does not consider physical satisfaction something which is necessary for herself. "And it's like when I'm in between affairs or whatever, oh what did this one girl say, 'Geez I haven't had it in so long I got to.' I don't have that, I don't need it. But if I meet someone I like, naturally I want to make love." Several other spontaneously orgasmic butches claim that masturbation gives them no pleasure. These butches' sexuality was completely defined in terms of pleasing their fem.

Being an untouchable butch became an increasingly important part of community values as the decade progressed. For those coming out in the early to mid-1950s, it was possible to be respected yet touchable. For women coming out at the end of the decade, being butch and being a stone butch became the same thing. Several narrators, both Black and white, who came out early in the decade, recognized the ideal of the stone butch but paid it little attention. This attitude did not affect their respected position in the community. They were unquestionably the aggressors in lovemaking and that sufficed for their butch identity. Their reasons for not following the stone butch ideal indicate the vitality of lesbian sexual expression at the time. Matty, a touchable butch, suspects that most of the butches she knew in the 1950s were not stone butches, no matter what they said. In her mind, relationships require mutuality to survive:

> "Once you get in bed, and the lights go out, when you get in between those sheets, I don't think there's any male or there's any female or butch or fem, and it's a fifty-fifty thing. And I think that any relationship . . . any true relationship that's gonna survive has got to be that way. You can't be a giver and can't be a taker. You've gotta both be givers and both gotta be takers."

Others, like Bert, who came out at about the same time, recognized the stone butch ideal, but left it behind for new found pleasures.

> "When it came to sex [in the 1950s] butches were untouchable, so to speak. They did all the lovemaking, but love was not made back to them. And after I found out how different it was, and how great it was, I said, 'What was I missing?' I remember a friend of mine, who dressed like a man all her life . . . and I remember talking to [her] and saying to her, you know you've got to stop being an untouchable butch, and she just couldn't agree. And I remember one time reaching over and pinching her and I said, 'Did you feel that?' and she said, 'Yes,' and I said, 'It hurt, didn't it? Well, why aren't you willing to feel something that's good?' "

Lonnie also questions the stone-butch ideal, emphasizing that people should do what they feel:

> "And these studs, talking about how 'I don't take the sheet.' You know what I mean, 'don't take the sheet,' don't you? That mean a stud make up to a fem all the time, a fem did not make up with a stud all the time. I don't believe in that. Don't nobody know what's going on when you close that door. If I kiss your body I want you to kiss mine, perhaps. You understand that?"

She goes on to point out how illogical it is to associate butchness and masculinity with not being touched, because certainly men like to be touched. "There's no such thing as stone. You touch me. Hey, a man likes to be touched doesn't he. O.K. then, so what's the difference?"

The social pressure for achieving the ideal of "untouchability" became greater toward the end of the decade. To be a respected leader in this younger set, a butch had to be untouchable. And all butch narrators for this period claimed to have been that way and butches were competitive with one another about it. To this day, narrators still make jokes about whether everybody who claimed to be untouchable actually was. The standard of untouchability was so powerful in shaping the behavior of those butches who came out in the late 1950s that some women who had experienced and enjoyed mutual lovemaking before entering the community felt they had to renounce it. Jamestown Gerry learned about sex in her early teens, before having any contact with the lesbian community, from a very experienced feminine woman. All their lovemaking was mutual, which she found extremely satisfying. "It is something I never had in my whole life. I found something in that bed I had never found in my life. I found the warmth and release from the daily tension." When she entered the bar community, however, she willingly adopted untouchability as her sexual posture because she saw it as a logical component of the butch role. Her interest in experiencing the other kind of release never truly left her, and in the 1970s she returned to mutual lovemaking.

The social ideal of the stone butch meant many lesbians of this period never experienced mutual lovemaking. For some butches untouchability has remained their personal style until today.

> "I just haven't changed, I have never changed. And I can say, I'll swear on this
> tape or on any bible you want, no girl has ever touched me. I mean the whole
> shot. . . . You know they say, 'Well what do you get out of this?' I say, don't
> worry about me. Because I'm happy when they are, that is my specific role
> and I do my best." (Sandy)

Others became more experimental in the late 1960s and 1970s when community norms began to change. The standard of untouchability was so embedded in their identity that the change did not come easily. Black, white, and Indian narrators all describe having to reorient their ways of feeling and thinking. For Jan it came as a pleasant surprise that she enjoyed being touched. "For some reason . . . I used to get enough mental satisfaction by satisfying a woman. . . . Then it got to the point where this one woman said, 'Well, I'm just not gonna accept that,' and she started venturing, and at first I said, 'No, no,' and then I said, 'Well, why not?' And I got to enjoy it." This change was not easy for a woman who had spent many years as an untouchable. At first, she was very nervous and uncomfortable about mutual sex, but "after I started reaching physical climaxes instead of just mental, it went, that little restlessness about it. It just mellowed me right out."

Piri describes that she had to rethink the way she viewed her role in order to make the change:

"It was always just something that I don't know, came along with the role. That I felt when I first started that I do the touching. They don't touch me, and then as I got older and got into it, I felt that it was really unfair to me. It just took a lot of thought a whole train of thought, to think about it, and deal with it."

Piri began to change only in the early 1970s. Consideration of her fem's desires were important in her decision.

"It was in the early '70s. 'Cause then I began to feel like the whole thing is a partnership. And if you denying her what she want to do, then the whole thing is not complete, and it's really unfair to her, . . . it's not right. I began to think about it that way, but at first no. . . . Over a period of time, like I had been with different ones, right? And they'd expressed their feeling and I said, 'No, no,' and then I began to think about it. Well, why not try it, 'cause I could imagine how I'd feel in the midst of making love and be denied what I wanted to do. . . . I just put myself in that position, to think about how I'd feel if I want to do this, and you say 'no'; so then I started thinking the other way."

The stone butches of the 1950s, both those who remained so and those who changed, offer explanations for their preference that provide valuable clues about the personal importance and the social "rightness" of untouchability as a community norm in the 1940s and 1950s. Some women, as indicated above, continue to view their discomfort with being touched as physical or biological. Others feel that untouchability maintained difference. If a fem were allowed the physical liberties usually associated with the butch role, distinctions would blur. "I feel that if we're in bed and she does the same thing to me that I do to her, we're the same thing." Toni, reflecting on the fact that she always went to bed with her clothes on, suggests that "what it came to was being uncomfortable with the female body. You didn't want people you were with to realize the likeness between the two." Still other butches are hesitant about the vulnerability implicit in mutual lovemaking. "When the first girl wanted to make a mutual exchange sexually . . . I didn't want to be in the position of being at somebody's disposal, or at their command that much—maybe that's still inside me. Maybe I never let loose enough" (Cheryl). Piri describes the rightness of untouchability as a matter of control: "It was an ego thing, that's all it was. I know that now 'cause I was that way for a long time. Hey man, we making love, I'm supposed to do that, that's my job, and you don't touch me. I stayed that way for years."

The unique sexual posture of the stone butch of this period, while encapsulating the desire to please a fem fully, resonates with the complexity of butch-fem roles in lesbian culture. This erotic stance relies on and fosters the differences between butch and fem that pervade the culture. It also identifies the butch as more active, more aggressive, more in control, which she was in public lesbian life. Finally, untouchability expresses discomfort with or at least ambivalence about the female body, which is consistent with the butch's pursuit of the masculine while remaining female.

How was a community able to monitor the sexual activities of its members, and how might people come to know if a butch "rolled over"—the community lingo for a butch who allowed fems to make love to her? The answer was simple: fems talked! A butch's reputation was based on her performance with fems. What went on in bed with the lights out was not always completely private. Fems "talking" today confirm that many butches were indeed untouchable, though certainly not all. "Let's say a couple of the butches, they're what you call untouchable. They would not allow to be touched. At all, even if you wanted to. So they did all the work" (Annie). Fem voices also convey the satisfaction achieved in lesbian sex during this period.

Black and white fem narrators recognized and accepted the standard of the butch as the doer, the aggressor, in lovemaking with the fem the center of attention. All fem narrators felt comfortable with this erotic system and liked being pleased.

> "I enjoy the feminine role better due to the fact it's not as much hard work; see, being a stud, that's a lot of work. I have a tendency to be kind of lazy. So I'd rather stay fem. Every once in a while I might want to act a little boyish and say 'Lay down girl it's my turn tonight,' but I couldn't stand a steady diet of that. No, that's kind of hard work. If [she's] anything like me, they gonna have a job. You just can't snap your fingers on me, boy. So I'm gonna stay like I am . . . a lady." (Arlette)

The idea that pleasing a fem requires hard work on the part of a butch is widespread among fems. Curiously, no butches articulate it, which suggests that statements about work were the fems' way of affirming their control in sexual relationships as well as expressing their appreciation of butches.

Fems were divided over the rightness or importance of the ideal of untouchability. Like the stone butches who felt strongly about not being touched, some fems really disliked taking the more active role in lovemaking. Bell remembers one of her first relationships, which did not work out well:

> "Well, she was trying to give me the impression that we were lovers, but she must have thought I was a real dumbbell or something, because it was like we didn't have sex too much, but it seemed like when she would want me to do something for her or when she would really need something, then we would have what she considered sex. It was like I would always have to do something with her, she never really seemed to want to do anything with me. [I had to be more] aggressive, yes I did, and I didn't like it."

Bell never became comfortable with more reciprocal sex. She particularly didn't like making love orally. In the 1970s this became a problem in her relationships, and she went to a counselor to try to resolve it. She wishes that sexuality had remained more role-defined because in the past she never had problems sexually.

> "I don't know if this is going to make any sense or not, but it seems like then that I had no problem with that [sex] because of the role-playing thing. I mean people seemed to know where they were at and I didn't have to worry about [it]. . . . A lot of butches were what you would call untouchable . . . and I was comfortable with that. It's not saying that I never wanted to touch them or anything like that, I just never really cared for getting into that oral sex thing. I just didn't like it. And [now] I [feel] uncomfortable . . . knowing, God, you know, I'm going to have to be doing this to these women. It isn't that I found it dirty or anything, I just did not like it. So I was very comfortable [with their untouchability]. . . . I feel like I'm a warm person and I have no trouble in that area at all."

Some fems did feel moved to make love to their butches on occasion, although none wanted to do so regularly. Annie ventured into making love to her butch and met no resistance: "She wanted me to. . . . No, [she didn't ask] but she didn't stop me, O.K." Annie was surprised at her butch's needs but felt she could accommodate them because she cared for her a lot.

> "Like the one girl I told you, she dressed very very butchy, she was an introvert, stayed very very much to herself, very nontalkative. She wouldn't mingle with the others, and tattoos on her arms, she really looked rugged. She looked rough. But when she got in bed she was just as feminine as any fem. . . . Well I happened to care for her, and naturally I wanted her 'cause I cared for her, so it really didn't bother me. It's not like something was pushed on me that I didn't want."

Arlette thinks of herself as quite flexible, and able to respond to different situations. In her experience many butches were not stone butches:

> "There are some ladies that are a little more reserved and naive than others and there's one that's more outgoing, so she'll probably play the come-on part more than the other girl. But in bed it doesn't make much difference as far as I can see. 'Cause I have associated with some so-called studs; they were more fem in the bed than they were fellas on their feet. They were wearing them boy's clothes but in the bed I damn near have to become the boy, so don't mean nothing. Then I have a turn, that I might even want to act like a boy that day. There is a role, but I've found a lot of stud boys I've found have been fem at one time and found they were so aggressive that they couldn't carry that fem part, so they carried the other part. And still in the bed it doesn't make any difference, once you close the doors, no matter who's who. It's what you feel like doing that night."

But all of these women who did make love to their butches were not critical of the stone butch. They appreciated the full attention focused on their own satisfaction. Arlette confirms this:

"I've had some that I couldn't touch no parts of their bodies. It was all about
me. 'Course I didn't mind! But every once in a while I felt like, well, 'Hey, let
me do something to you.' I could never understand that. 'Cause I lived with
a girl. I couldn't touch any part of her, no part. But boy did she make me feel
good, so I said, . . . 'All right with me!' It kept me back though, 'cause I felt,
'Hey, I want to do something to you tonight.' 'Nope!' Well O.K. Fine with
me. I don't mind laying down."

It is striking that our fem narrators' discussion of sexuality is quite self-
concerned. It does not express the kind of intense sexual passion for their butches—
the passion of response—that is conveyed in the essays and stories of fem writers
and activists such as Joan Nestle and Amber Hollibaugh.[25] In their life histories
fem narrators frequently and straightforwardly affirm their love for their butches.
But we have no description of what excites them about making love. There is no
fem equivalent to the statements of butches that describe how much they are
turned on by their partners. We suspect that the self-centered aspect of the fems'
sexual life is correct but comprises only one dimension of truth about the butch-
fem sexual dyad.

Many factors combine to create this imbalance in fem stories. Fems' socializing
together was not an institutionalized part of this culture. Fems might have had
individual girl friends, but there was no network of fem friendship akin to the
camaraderie of butches. Instead, there was a tradition of competitiveness. Because
of this, there was no safe and supportive place in which fems could share reflections
of their passion and learn from each other's joys and losses. By extension, the
interview sessions, conducted by women who are self-identified fems or who have
no role identification, might be suspect and might easily have set up a defensive
atmosphere surrounding delicate issues of sexuality.

Due to the absence of a supportive environment, fems may have lacked appropriate words. In reflecting on her relationships in the 1950s, Joan Nestle points
out:

"Fems may not have had a language with which to talk about sexual matters.
I don't remember fem women discussing sexual lust in the '50s. That was part
of butch play. . . . Public sexual language [for fems] was one of emotional need.
. . . I also think that fem language was always coded language. . . . The loudest
way of speaking was the offering of the woman's body to butch desire."[26]

Therefore, words of love, appreciation, closeness, and even flirtation could have
been coded substitutes for expressions of passion. Fems may only have spoken
about sexual passion for their butches, to their butches, in the privacy of their
relationships.

From the writings of Nestle and Hollibaugh we learn about aspects of fem desire
that might be applicable to Buffalo fems in the 1950s. A fem wants the feeling that
the butch's most sought after goal is to reach her femininity, the core of who she

is. The fem also wishes to validate the butch's existence by being responsive to her butch's desire. A fem's self-definition, insofar as it includes the conscious giving over of sexual control to ultimate desirability, is a major component of her power. Hollibaugh writes:

> My fantasy life is deeply involved in a butch/femme exchange. I never come together with a woman, sexually, outside of those roles. It's saying to my partner, "Love me enough to let me go where I need to go and take me there. Don't make me think it through. Give me a way to be so in my body that I don't have to think; that you can fantasize for the both of us. You map it out. You are in control."
>
>   It's hard to talk about things like giving up power without it sounding passive. I am willing to give myself over to a woman equal to her amount of wanting. I expose myself for her to see what's possible for her to love in me that's female. I want her to respond to it. I may not be doing something active with my body, but more eroticizing her need that I feel in her hands as she touches me.[27]

Fem satisfaction was at the center of the butch-fem erotic system. To give satisfaction was the butch's foremost goal, and the culture focused on her performance. There was social pressure for butches to attain the ideal of "untouchability" but no equivalent ideal of fem passivity. Fems upheld the standards of butch behavior in order to achieve their own satisfaction. This emphasis on their own fulfillment assured that fems developed sexual subjectivity, albeit differently from butches. It also balanced the power in butch-fem erotic relationships, making the pursuit of satisfaction legitimate for each partner.

In sexuality as in image, the 1950s community exerted strong pressure for consistent butch-fem role behavior. It had little tolerance for those lesbians whose sexual behavior was not consistently butch or fem. Such people were considered "ki-ki" (neither-nor), or more infrequently "AC/DC," both pejorative labels imposed by the community.[28] Not everyone in the community remembers such terminology, but all recall that those who regularly switched roles elicited negative comments and were the butt of jokes.

> "They used to make little wise cracks . . . you know, like, 'Well I wonder which way she's gonna go tonight.' Little smirks like that. 'Oh I see she's playing fem this week,' or 'Oh she's playing the big bad butch this week.' . . . But to be very honest with you, [the person I told you about] that's really about the only one that I knew that was like that back then, and is like that today. . . . She's still like that. And I told her, I said 'Hey, your time has finally come.'. . . I says, 'You're right in the ball park now, kiddo.' " (Sandy)

From the perspective of the 1990s, in which mutuality in lovemaking and the absence of roles are emphasized as positive qualities, it is important to clarify that ki-ki did not refer to an abandonment of role-defined sex, but rather to a shifting of sexual posture depending upon one's bed partner. It was thus firmly grounded in role playing. This culture could not imagine people without roles. Matty, in fact, defines ki-ki as "double role playing," and looks at it with much more sympathy today than she did formerly.

> "Yeah, they called them neither-nor, ki-ki. You find that now too, double role playing, that's all it is actually. . . . See, it isn't that they don't want to make a choice, it's that they're leaving themselves open to the occasion of whomever might come in that they could play either role. It isn't that they don't know what they are. . . . They don't want to pin any one thing on themselves for fear if they pin 'feminine' on themselves if they become attracted to a feminine girl, well that girl won't bother, you know. And I think that's the way it should be, you should be able to play either role. . . . 'Course I didn't know too many people back then that didn't play a role, there weren't that many when I came out. . . . But looking back now, if I knew then everything I know now that's the way I would have been when I came out."

The negative reactions in the 1950s to those who were ki-ki stem from the fact that such people disrupted the butch-fem social order. Those who maintained their roles felt that their own identities and reputations were threatened. Sandy remembers how she used to hate it if someone she was with became butch in another relationship. She didn't want others to think that she was fem. "I knew women who didn't know their role. I was with some when they were fems. When they came out butch, I didn't want anyone to get the idea that I rolled over." She explains that butches experienced this kind of role-changing as a personal betrayal. "You showed someone you cared. You let your defenses down, and then they switch roles and you feel betrayed."

Some fem narrators were also deeply upset by those who changed.

> "They swung like monkeys from one thing to another. . . . It was like one time, well I'm butch this week or this month and maybe I'll be fem the next month. . . . [They] totally disgusted me. . . . I feel that people should know . . . what they want. You've got to know where you're at. Like you're either butch or you're fem, you can't change a thing from one month to the next." (Bell)

A fem was not worried about her reputation, but rather that the person she was with would go back and forth in the relationship and not make the fems pleasure a priority. Bell continues:

> "I think most of your fems felt like I did and a lot of the butches, of course, they thought it was fun to fuck around and play around and change around. . . . Not a lot of them but some of them that I knew. But I didn't think that was too funny. . . . I didn't go to bed with them, but there was a friend of mine who had been with one of these particular people and she had thought that the party was quite fem in bed and other times very butch. It's confusing

and very hard to understand something like this. That's like someone having a split personality or something. I like someone who knows what they are and who stays that way. That fluctuating, whatever, I don't care for it."

The community's increased interest in setting standards for butch-fem eroticism in the late 1950s was partially related to the growing cohesion of the community and to the discussion of sexuality as part of lesbian culture. Butch-fem sexuality could not have been policed without a community to enforce norms through discussion and action. The social pressure for clearly defined roles also grew from the increasingly defiant stance of the community which was rooted in expressions of the butch role. This exaggerated the difference between butch and fem and demanded high performances from butches in defending their own and their fems' right to exist. The tough butch who could take care of business became idealized. Untouchability expressed difference from the fem, control over one's life, and ambivalence about one's female body, all characteristics of the butch persona. The strong concern for role-appropriate eroticism developed in creative tension with the culture's validation of female sexuality and emphasis on learning about and exploring new sexual practices. The butch was not only competent as a fighter, but also as a lover. In reaction to the dominant ideas about women needing men for sexual satisfaction, these butches projected themselves as better in bed than any man. Sandy explains what it meant to be an untouchable butch: "I didn't want to be a man, but I wanted to be treated like one, put it that way . . . right? I wanted to satisfy them and I wanted to make love." Ironically, the rigidification of roles and the openness about sexuality interacted to create an erotic system predicated above all on the sexual satisfaction of women.

LEARNING ABOUT SEX IN THE 1950s

Coming to sexual subjectivity was a different process for lesbians in the 1950s than the 1940s. For one thing, more resources about heterosexual sex were available to inform or misinform women about their sexuality.[29] More importantly, there was a different attitude within the lesbian community toward sexuality. Narrators for the 1930s and 1940s had described their sexual expression as "natural." Those narrators who came out in the 1950s approached sexuality as something they had to learn, making use of all the resources available. Although we might be tempted to say that acquiring sexual information and experience was easier due to a more supportive social context, such a statement does not capture the struggles of individuals to feel sexually knowledgeable.

The greater discussion of sexuality in society itself exposed lesbians to images of and ideas about sexual activities, albeit heterosexual ones. Many narrators transformed these to fit their own desires. Sandy remembers looking at her father's girlie magazines, and imagining herself with the models.

> " 'Cause then it was psss, psss, you know, whisper that shit. Read the books under the bed and things like that. . . . Sexual books, . . . pictures of nude women, I loved that. Oh God, I was crazy about 'em. . . . [I got them from] my father. Get them out of his room and go in my room. And he'd steal my comic books, wasn't that funny. He'd take my comic books and I'd take his girl books. . . . No, [it was] not real heavy stuff. I didn't know that much about it anyhow, so I wouldn't have known if it was heavy or not. I was really dumb when it came to stuff like that, 'cause I was never interested in it. You know, I never thought about relationships, like man and woman relationships. I'd look at the girls, pictures of women; put myself with them."

The incongruity of Sandy's statement that she was "dumb" about male-female relationships, and the fact that she knew enough to take her father's girlie magazines and enjoy them, reflects the ambiguous position of lesbian sexuality in 1950s society. The society moved toward increased openness about sexuality, even toward valuing sexual expression for its own sake, but at the same time it was ambivalent about women's sexuality and continued to outlaw homosexuality.[30] Many lesbians had to fight deep feelings of shame about being sexual. Vic, while reminiscing about how great her first sexual experience was, also recalls her embarrassment. "I was ashamed, you know, 'cause it wasn't the right thing to do." She attributes these feelings of shame at least partially to her family, remembering graphically the way her father humiliated her on his visits after he had her put in jail.

> "My father had me put in jail as a runaway, I was eighteen years old now, remember that. And I was told that, you have to live according to how your parents want you to live until you're twenty-one years old. . . . I was in jail for thirty days for doing this, and my father used to come and greet me every day and say, 'If that's how you want to be,' he used to say to me, 'I'll kick your teeth out and make your job easier for you.' I never had any idea what he was even referring to because I had never done anything like that to a woman, so I didn't know what he was talking about. Like I know now. But see, I guess that's what he worried that I was coming from. Which I wasn't aware of it. So I stayed in jail for thirty days and when I left out, that's when my friend and I went to Florida."

For butches, the actual coming to sexual subjectivity was a slow process, which they describe as moving from "bumbling" to excellence. The community was central in this process. In contrast to those of the 1940s, few butch narrators of the 1950s had their first full sexual experience before they had some contact with the public lesbian community, suggesting that women needed explicit social support to become competent leaders in lovemaking. Growing lesbian pride and the community's general willingness to reach out and educate newcomers meant that the community participated in sex education. The sources of instruction were varied.

As in the Winters crowd of the 1940s, the fem was an important teacher for butches. Bert, who had come out in the Army in the early 1950s, remembers a fem who tried to teach her, and although the attempt was unsuccessful, it made her curious to learn more.

> "The only thing I knew about—it took me a long time to come out as far as the overt sexuality—was necking and petting and I didn't know anything else. In fact I'll tell you a humorous story. It's very embarrassing but it's very funny. This one woman was after my body so to speak, so we went downtown and we got a hotel. And I guess I must have been pretty good at necking and petting, but I didn't know what you did beyond that. And she kept pushing my head and pushing my head, and I didn't know what the hell she was pushing my head for, and she got up and got her clothes on and got mad and left. So finally one day, [a few weeks later] there was ironically from California a woman, her name was Joan, we were in the shower and I told her what happened and asked her, 'What do you do?' and so she explained it all to me, . . . the many various positions. But I found out since I grew older she didn't know them all, I've learned a few since."

The woman who explained it to Bert had been gay before entering the Army and had a lot of experience.

Some fems were much more straightforward in their teaching. Sandy fumbled around for quite a while until she received explicit instructions from a fem partner. She had been strongly attracted to girls in high school but never knew what to do.

> "And I had crushes there [Girl's Vocational High] on about thirty girls, all without their knowledge of course. This was definitely a no-no, this was a horrible, horrible thing, like a leper. And so when I graduated from high school I decided I was going to join the service. I thought, well I heard so much that things like that go on there, maybe I could find something there. I really didn't know what to do or what you're supposed to do, all I knew was I wanted women. And so I went up to the Catskills to say goodby to my childhood friend. And we kissed goodby. Now, at seventeen you pretty well know what you're doing. That was all, there was never anything sexual. I don't know, just never was. I wanted it but you didn't know what the hell to do. You were filled with passion but you just didn't know how to go about this thing."

In the Marines she was too frightened to have relations with women, but when she left, she ran off with a Marine's wife. It took them a while to make love. "And then it happened. And all I can say is not because anyone told us, we didn't read books, we just went to bed and did whatever we felt we liked and enjoyed and I had sex." But later in her story she clarifies that this still wasn't complete in regard to sex. "Well it was but it wasn't. It wasn't all the way, it wasn't a complete affair. It was just the fumbling." She needed more education. She didn't want to ask other butches, however, because she felt it would contradict her tough image to appear ignorant about sex. "I didn't [talk much] anyhow. Because you were trying to have a good image of yourself, like you're tough, and you knew what the score was, what was what. . . . You couldn't talk about something you didn't know, and you didn't want to ask. So you just well, I got to peek or I got to find something."

Indirect learning—watching others and guessing what they did—cultivated mystery and excitement, if not knowledge, as captured by this narrator's humorous memories of her fantasies about the rubber gloves she saw when she went to a lesbian's home. After returning from the service, the first time she went to a gay bar, she met a woman she knew from the armed services who invited her to come over.

> "This was really funny. . . . We were talking about whatever, probably work, and her dresser drawer was open. Now this is how your mind can . . . I didn't know anything. There was a pair of rubber gloves there, in her drawer. Now I didn't know what they were for. . . . And I said, 'Oh my God, wonder what they use that for?' . . . And then I really thought, what am I getting into? What do they use those rubber gloves for? [I didn't ask.] I didn't want them to know I didn't know. Wouldn't I have been stupid if I had asked, 'What do you use those for? . . . [and she had answered], 'Oh I had a rash on my hands,' probably what it was!!!"

We asked her if she ever found out whether the rubber gloves were for something sexual or not. "No, I never found out. All I know is I don't need them!"

Finally, Sandy was with a fem who helped her out by giving specific instruction.

> "Well, I'd just been out a short time. And then I went with this girl that had been out for a while. She wasn't a new one. . . . So I guess I really frustrated the hell out of her, and she says, 'Sandy you start out but you just'—and she took a piece of paper and drew me a picture. She says, 'Now you get this spot right here.' . . . I felt like a jerk. I was embarrassed, because she had to tell me that, 'cause here I was trying to—you know how you like to look pretty great in people's eyes. Jesus, then you fuck up."

According to Sandy, the lesson helped, and she explains that, "I went on to greater and better things."

By the late 1950s many butches received their instruction from other butches, particularly if they were young and just entering the community. Since there was no longer a taboo on bringing people out, it was not uncommon for someone to have her first affair with a butch and learn from the experience that she wanted to be butch herself. This happened for both Black and white narrators. Piri remembers how she didn't like the role she assumed in her first serious affair with

an older butch. The experience confirmed what she had already known about
herself from playing around on the streets.

> "The first time I had ever had an affair with anybody it was with Jacki Jordan.
> . . . I was really fascinated by her 'cause she had all these women, and I couldn't
> figure this out. . . . I didn't know what this was about. I had been messing
> around with girls my age. But like Jacki Jordan's an older person. She's got
> all these broads and they go out and they make money and they come home
> and give it to her. . . . We wind up getting into it and I'm laying on my back,
> on the bottom and I say, 'Woman, this ain't about nothing. . . . I don't like
> this, uh uh, no." So I reversed it, which I was doing all the time, but at thirteen
> you don't know what you're doing. But with Jacki Jordan, I was really just
> fascinated by her and then when I got involved with her, I knew it wasn't the
> way I wanted it to go. Then we just became buddies."

Vic describes a similar learning experience:

> "The first sexual affair I had was with a bus driver, 'cause she let me use her
> car. I'm trying to think of how I could say it to you, 'cause I don't know now
> if you would call it a sexual affair. She used to drive the bus and she let me
> take her car while she was working. And I'd have to pick her up after work,
> and then I'd have to sit with her and we'd hug and kiss. But there was, gee
> how can I say it to you without feeling like a jerk. She was very butch, she
> was a very butch woman, masculine. She just used to tell me how nice my
> body was. There was never any clothes off at the time or anything like that.
> She was always fondling me but I could never touch her. Now how long, with
> me, can a relationship like that last? Car or no car, I can walk easier. That
> didn't work too well. [But the experience] was real to me, that was very real.
> You have to remember at that age you know, probably when that happened
> I was sixteen years old, and had never had any relationships with a man. That
> had to be very close to my first sexual encounter. . . . Who the hell, why would
> somebody want to be touching my boobs or my box, they got to be assholes.
> Then I realized well, maybe I could do it to other people and that's when I
> started doing it."

Knowing what she wanted to do and doing it were two different things. It was
at least a year before Vic actively began to touch a woman, even though she had
had relationships:

> "Well that's when I was going to . . . school. This girl that I was going with,
> we went in her car one time and I don't think that either one of us wanted
> the other one to know that they were attracted to each other. So whoever
> happened to be driving at the time, we were always drinking, and the other
> one would pass out conveniently on the other one's lap or breast or something,
> and then just kind of do all kinds of weird shit while you're passed out. You
> know how you might move your hand. . . . Neither one of us probably ever
> was passed out; we didn't have the balls enough to do anything straight. And

then, I don't know how to tell you Madeline. . . . I had never been with a naked woman till I came to Buffalo and was working at the lab. It was all like really stupid bullshit you know. . . . Yeah, but you got to sit here and say to somebody, 'Geez you mean to tell me you were eighteen or nineteen years old before you were ever with a naked woman?' and I guess that's what I have to say if I'm going to be honest with you."

The use of alcohol to deny responsibility for one's sexual interest is mentioned by other narrators, and is another indication of how difficult it was for women to become sexually active lesbians. After living with this partner, Vic finally touched her.

"We got an apartment together, possibly because we used to like to pass out on each other's boobs or box or whatever, I don't know. And then—I don't know, I just remember the first time I ever touched her and it was with my hand and she bled. And I don't know if she had her period or if she was a virgin, but for some reason I can't think of [her] being a virgin at the age of nineteen, so she must have had her period. But anyway, that [the touching] was like wow, the greatest thing in the world to me."

The 1950s also saw the advent of another completely new practice—experienced butches teaching novice butches about sex through discussion and support. This became more common at the end of the decade, particularly when the two parties socialized in the same group at the bars. The instructions were quite full and detailed. Sandy remembers that younger women frequently approached her with questions about sex: "There must be an X on my back. They just pick me out. . . ." She recalls when Ronni was first coming out and "had to know every single detail. She drove me crazy. Jesus Christ, y'know, just get down there and do it. Y'get so aggravated." Ronni, in turn, remembers the instruction vividly, and indicates that her older buddy was a very good teacher:

"And I finally talked to a butch buddy of mine. . . . She was a real tough one. I asked her, 'What do you do when you make love to a woman?' And we sat up for hours and hours at a time. . . . 'I feel sexually aroused by this woman, but if I take her to bed, what am I gonna do?' And she says, 'Well, what do you feel like doing?' And I says, 'Well, the only thing I can think of doing is . . . all I want to do is touch her, but what is the full thing of it . . . you know?' So when [she] told me I says, 'Really?' Well there was this one thing in there, uh . . . I don't know if you want me to state it. Maybe I can . . . well, . . . I'll put it in terms that you can understand. Amongst other things, the oral gratification. Well, that kind of floored me because I never expected something like that, and I thought, well, who knows, I might like it."

She later describes her first sexual experience. She had been chasing this woman, but was so scared that Sandy had to keep encouraging her. One day Sandy offered the use of her house, and finally shoved Ronni into the bedroom.

"So our first encounter was at Sandy's house. 'Cause I didn't have anywhere to stay with her. Finally Sandy says, 'Ronni, tonight's the night,' and I says, 'What do you mean?' and she says, 'Darlene wants to go home with you.' And I says, 'Oh, I'm not ready tonight—forget it—I changed my mind.' . . . I was still living at home with my mother. . . . So I went home to Sandy's apartment and Sandy was sitting around the kitchen drinking coffee with Darlene and myself. And I was getting very nervous because I knew Darlene really made up her mind that she was going to go to bed with me. 'Well,' I says, 'Sandy, I can't go through with it. I just can't. I'm too scared.' She says, 'You chicken. Get in there, you've been after me all this time, and you've been after her all this time. Now you're not going to leave here until you go in there.' So finally Darlene says, 'Well, good night.' She goes in the bedroom I says, 'Sandy, what am I gonna do?' I says, 'I'm leaving.' So she says, 'Ronni, you're gonna go in there.' So, I didn't expect my first encounter to be like this, but I finally got up to get something and Sandy started shoving me into the bedroom and I says, 'All right, all right, I'll go.' So Darlene says, 'Ronni, come on in here.' So I says, 'Yeah, just a second and I will.' And Sandy's shoving me. So Sandy gave me a good shove and I go sailing right through the bedroom door, and there's Darlene. Well, I expected first of all when you go to bed with a girl you kiss her, and you make love, and you both have your clothes on, and you let happen what comes naturally—which usually it does. There she was laying stark naked on the bed. Right on her back. Well, by that . . . I just, I was floored. I didn't expect that. But I got all my courage up, and I went right over to her. And I just flung myself on top of her, and I started kissing her— and that's something I wanted to do really bad. And everything happened naturally."

Once she got over her initial fear, Ronni performed well. She remembers that her partner, who was a prostitute and also had quite a bit of experience with women, thought she was quite good.

"She says, 'And you are a god damned liar, telling me that you've never been with a woman before.' I says, 'I haven't.' And she says, 'You're lying'. And I says, 'I'm not lying. If you want to believe I'm lying, go ahead.' We had an affair which lasted two and a half years and it was a very sexually active one. It was the most sexually active affair I ever had in my life, except for when Barbara came along, which happened over twenty years later. I had a dry run there for a while."

This new lesbian culture, which openly instructed butches about sex, did not completely replace the dominant society's conceptions about the privacy of sex, and the connections between sex and love, particularly for women. Some lesbians were still shy about sexual matters and could not bring themselves to ask openly for instruction. The other side of lesbian culture's willingness to instruct about sexuality was its monitoring and pushing of those who were hesitant to learn. Toni remembers that she was not fully sexual in her first affair and that the more experienced butches teased her about whether in fact she was a lesbian. She could not take the step toward a fully sexual relationship until she met someone with whom she was totally in love.

> "I didn't feel confident about myself as a lesbian, because, well, I didn't actually have sex with somebody until a few years had gone by. I had a girlfriend, oh, for about a year and a half, and I guess she used to flirt with a lot of people, and one of the people she flirted with was Iris. And one night, I guess whatever was going on between her and Iris I don't know, but me and this woman Arlene, we had never really had sex, I just couldn't get myself to really do anything sexually. And one night we were out drinking, I was with Arlene and Iris was there too, and we all ended up in the parking lot across from the Carousel. And Iris said to me, 'You're no more gay than that lamppost over there is gay.' And it kind of took me back, because I'd always respected her judgment and I knew she was gay and she knew I was gay. Well, the thing was that my track record, sexually, didn't prove I was gay 'cause I really hadn't had sex. I had like fooled around and necked and petted and stuff like that, but I knew inside me I was gay. So I couldn't buy that but it made me feel bad, that I hadn't proven myself, sexually, to be a lesbian. And it wasn't until I met someone that I fell very much in love with that then my fears dissolved. I didn't even remember my fears any more. But I needed that emotional feeling of being in love with someone, to carry you past the fear that I had."

Fems' memories of sex education, and the language they use to discuss it, are strikingly different from those of butches. Since, in the butch-fem erotic system, fems were the partners to be pleased, they did not feel the same degree of pressure and responsibility to be active and competent sexually. The butch's guidance and instruction of the less-experienced fem was generally satisfactory, though not always. Some fems, who went on to find sexual satisfaction, complain about the ignorance of their early lovers. Whitney took a particularly long time to feel comfortable expressing herself sexually, and her story makes an instructive contrast with those of the butches. She is aware of her own growth and movement toward becoming a good lover but does not express the journey as a quest. Rather the changes happened to her, catalyzed by her partners. Also, part of her growth entailed discoveries about her own body, something that is never mentioned by butches.

Her first sexual affair was with a man when she was sixteen, but she considers herself still physically and sexually undeveloped at the time. Soon afterward, she had several affairs with women, some of which she initiated. She remembers all of her early partners as sexually ignorant and her relationships as sexually unsatisfying.

> "Well Liz, one of the things when I was a fem, when I was twenty, twenty-one or so, women were not lovers, but then maybe most people of twenty are not lovers. But they sometimes would be very aggressive with their hands. . . .

> I had a hangup for many years about using my hands. I wouldn't do it. And poor Sonny, I said to her, 'Don't ever touch me with your hands.' Because I had a bad experience with butchie women and their hands, . . . just vaginal. They were just aggressive and they . . . didn't read anything, and they mustn't even have been hardly in touch with their own bodies. . . . I don't know how they had orgasms. So I just chose alternate things for myself to do. There are many themes and variations in making love."

She did not have her first orgasm until she was twenty-three and that was with an older, more experienced butch. It was an important event, which she marked by sending a note to one of the sexually ignorant butches she had been seeing. "It must have been about in June, I sent Gayle a note, and you can quote me. It said, 'Dear Gayle something happened to me last night that never happened before. Love Whitney.' So she sent back a card and the card said, 'Now you have something to crow about.'" The sex in this new relationship was hot and heavy for a while. "We had a really close, close, work-up-a-sweat, physical relationship." This was true despite the fact that Whitney continued not liking to be stimulated by her partner's hands.

> "And another thing I want to bring up about that too, Liz, was I told you I was a slow developer. Well when my nipples would be touched . . . it made me uncomfortable. . . . It was my body developing and I didn't know what it was. And so I'd say, 'Don't touch my breasts.' So poor Sonny . . . and when I think of it now I think, oh my word. If she slept with me now, I'm totally different. She would say, 'This isn't Whitney, who is this?'"

After a few years, the sex dropped off to nothing, which Whitney attributes to difference in age. In time, she started having affairs, one of which was critical in changing how she felt about her body and what she liked sexually.

> "Then when I was about twenty-nine I met a woman at a party, she thought I was nice and I thought she was nice. Some of my friends had told me that she had been quite heavy and she had lost a lot of weight, and I was really thinking she was kind of special. And she was interested in me and I was interested in her and we were both involved with someone else. So she told me that she masturbated, now I didn't know how to masturbate. So one night I was at her house and she was in bed with her lover and I was in their guest room, and I started thinking about her . . . and I masturbated. 'Hey I know I'm super great,' it's like your first orgasm, it's really brand new, it's super. Now if I hadn't had a relationship with someone else outside of the relationship with Sonny, I wouldn't have become as good a lover as I am today. Because I became in touch with my own body and I can be in touch with other people's bodies."

Some fems had extensive experiences with men before having relationships with women. This heterosexual experience, when combined with interest in a woman, did not automatically create sexually active fems. It often took time. Arlette pursued a young and attractive, though inexperienced, butch and it took them two years to make love. Her humorous memories of the early stages of this affair convey how dependent a fem, who is just beginning to explore lesbian sex, no matter how experienced she is in heterosexual sex, can be on the sexual confidence of the butch.

> "And the first person was Calley. She was young. I was driving around . . . and I saw her standing on Sycamore and Pratt. My girlfriend and I . . . were driving around Buffalo. . . . I had an Oldsmobile then. And I said, 'You know, that girl looks like one of those funny kind of girls.' She said, 'Yup'. She was really good-looking, short cut nice hair, light skin, she was cute. . . . We rode around the block to look at her again and she said, 'Hey, can I have a ride?' . . . We said, 'Yeah.' I was just bold enough. I said, 'Oh, if my nerve is up we going to find out about this.' And it's strange. She followed me everywhere I went, she went to my house and spent the night. But she would always get way on the other side of the bed and then I said, 'Well, hell, this isn't any fun.' . . . She never did anything. That went on for about two years. I ended up going back to Syracuse. She followed me to Syracuse. And I came back here again to Buffalo. I checked in to the Vendome Hotel. I'll never forget it, she walked in the bathroom while I was taking a bath. She was sitting on the side of the tub just talking. I thought, I don't understand this woman, I know she's weird, she's different. . . . She's not even trying to approach me. And funny thing about it though, when I stood up in the tub she looked at my body and fell in the water. Clothes and all. And it was a good year and a half before we had anything to do with each other. And we just kept messing around till one day she really got to me and that was it. Had somethin' on you and I was ruined.[31] From that day forward it was, ooh wow, 'cause I was going with a fella then."

After this relationship, Arlette became an active part of lesbian life, and affairs no longer took so long to begin. In fact she went on to instruct many young studs.

An experienced lover did not invariably make the transition to lesbian sexual activity easy. Annie's first encounter did nothing for her even though it was with a sexually experienced butch. Just like some butches, she needed to care deeply for someone in a warm, sustained relationship to feel the specialness of lesbianism.

> "That was a come-and-go thing. I was only with her that one night. . . . I couldn't see where the attraction was and anything. . . . Because, to really be honest I thought, well a man does the same thing. But it's more than just that. It's the softness, and where you don't feel like you got that iron hand over you or something. Where with a marriage, truly I feel as though it's like a job. I do. . . . A woman, I don't know, to me I think maybe it was . . . became exciting, different and new, curiosity."

Although in general fems tend to express their learning about sex more in terms of growth and self-knowledge than in performance, for those who attempted to take the more active role of making love to their partners orally, performance pressures did emerge. Even then, however, it is viewed as a specific part of pleasing a partner rather than generally upgrading one's sexual competence. Annie remembers feeling very ignorant the first time she made love orally.

> "Very stupid. . . . It's your first time around, you know. And you don't really know what it's all about. But I think you pick up this new fac[tor], oral sex. . . . It comes naturally too I think. . . . First you're shy or whatever . . . and the second time you're a pro. . . . I don't know. It's hard to remember how you felt afterwards, that's rather hard. . . . I just asked was it satis[factory]? Did I do all right or anything. And it's getting to know the body."

All of our fem narrators learned about lesbian sex from someone who already had some contact, even if marginal, with the public lesbian community. Sandy, however, suggests that this is atypical, and that it was common for fems to have their first affairs with women in their neighborhoods.

> "There's a lot that are having affairs with maybe their next-door neighbor or something, that have never been downtown. That have never been out. You know, and then when they do come out they know just about where it's at. Then there's the ones that just come out, and that's the one's that will be asking, that have never been with anyone. . . . I'd say the majority though, have had some sort of an affair before they come out. . . . I'd say seventy-five to eighty per cent, have had an affair. . . . That was just finding their space on the shelf, that's all."

Since many fems at this time had active lives as heterosexuals before—and also after—associating with lesbians, it would make sense that they might have their first affairs with neighbors, and that this experience would lead them to go downtown looking for other lesbians.

Our finding that lesbians talked and educated one another about sexuality during the 1950s has not been verified for other communities. In fact, some material exists to contradict our research. Phyllis Lyon, a very reliable source for lesbian history as co-founder with Del Martin of Daughters of Bilitis, states in her introduction to Sapphistry that her group of friends associated with Daughters of Bilitis never talked about sex.[32] Indeed, the topic of sexuality never came up in all the peer counseling that she and Del Martin did before 1968. She thinks this is because the topic was taboo, not because people didn't need help. To her mind 1968 is a turning point because of the founding in San Francisco of the National Sex Forum. The difference between Lyon's experience and that of Buffalo lesbians suggests that discussions about sex were predominantly a bar and butch-fem phenomenon. Those who left this community to form the DOB might not be familiar with the place of sexuality in bar culture, or might not have been open to considering bar culture's positive points along with the negative.

THE PURSUIT OF SEXUAL PLEASURE IN THE 1950s

As implied in the stories about sex education, this community valued sexual fulfillment, although that meant something different for butch and for fem. Lesbians created an environment in which sexual satisfaction was an acceptable and expected part of women's lives and in which sexual competence was encouraged. The assumed high quality of lesbian sex was expressed in a popular community myth: "But like they say, once you've been with a woman you'll always go back to a woman" (Annie).

The butch-fem erotic placed most of the pressure on the butch for attaining the competence that would lead to sexual satisfaction. Sexual performance was basic to the butch role. Sometimes when we would ask a fem narrator if a person she had just mentioned was butch, she would respond: "Yes, she was an excellent lover" (Bell). Butches also remark on the sexual expertise of their friends. Several butch narrators refer to Sandy as "the varsity." Sandy always set high standards for herself. "Sex is very important. I really try to be a perfectionist at it." Sexual competence did not consist of technique to the exclusion of feelings. Only one narrator did quite a bit of reading about sexuality. Typically, butches talk about experience as their main teacher, "on the job training experience" (Sandy), and the way their own feelings and their fems' responses served as their guidelines. "Wherever I felt this urge of excitement, I got right to it" (Sandy).

Butches did not discuss with one another particular fems' qualities as sexual partners. For old-time butches there was a protective attitude toward their fems. In addition, the performance ethic was so high for butches that, should fems not be enjoying themselves in bed, they assumed it reflected on their own performance. They felt a strong responsibility for their partner's pleasure. Vic attempts to clarify:

"You said there's sex and there's O.K. sex, I've never had that. All the women I've ever been with I could never say she was really great and this one was terrible. Women are good in bed, all women are, given the chance to be. . . . They're women. To me, first of all I enjoy being with them, you don't have to be, as you say, knock-out, drag-out sex. . . . They're good, if they're having sex with me they're good. How can a woman have bad sex? What do you do to have bad sex? . . . What's the difference between bad sex, good sex and medium sex? I don't know either. I want to know this myself, 'cause maybe I'm doing something wrong. 'Cause I'm the lovee not the lover or however you want to say it, and that can't be bad for me. . . . I could never, God, that's the highest insult you could give me when you say to me, 'dead lay.' I would never say that. . . . Now there's a difference between saying a woman is a bad lover and saying that I didn't get satisfied. I've been with a lot of women that I haven't been satisfied with, but I would still never say that they were bad in bed because of it."

The successful development of a sexual culture predicated on the butch's pleasing the fem can be measured by the rare occurrence of rape in this community. The butch's aggressiveness did not mean coercion, violence, or pain for her partners in the sexual realm. Butches' pride in their ability to fight straight men and to respond aggressively and violently if necessary, affected domestic life (as will be discussed in the following chapters on relationships) but not sexual relations. In fact, the more aggressive butches, the leaders in the community, were also those who were the most expert lovers. They wanted their women and felt it was their performance that was essential for success. The culture did not eroticize violence.

Two narrators report having been raped by women, but neither instance occurred within the context of community life. Whitney, who was not living in Buffalo at the time, brought another woman out and agreed to live with her. They did not participate regularly in the Buffalo lesbian community or any other. When Whitney was no longer interested in sex with her partner, she could not stop this woman's advances.

> "So I never had orgasms, right? And Grace was raping me regularly. . . . It was true. The thing is, these old people were in their house that we lived [in]. I couldn't make a hell of a lot of noise because we were gay. I couldn't . . . [yell] 'Get out of here' or slamming doors or I couldn't go through all those things, so I was like beating on her. . . . It was terrible. She had to be about a hundred and fifty pounds, and I was about ninety-five, a hundred. . . . There was no way I could physically avoid that. And she would just get into her cups and say, 'Great, a little Whitney tonight.' "

Whitney was not made cynical by this horrendous experience, and does not see it as typical lesbian behavior, rather, claiming like others, that it was extremely rare.

One butch was raped by her mother's lesbian friends when she was a young teenager. She had expressed interest in women and for whatever reason, they decided to "initiate" her, behavior that she does not understand or forgive to this day. In the interactions of mature women, such behavior was unknown. The aggressive aspect of the butch was tempered by the desire to be an excellent lover. Perhaps the community institution of fems talking about butch sexual behavior served as a check on the substitution of violence for sex.

This woman-centered, sex-positive culture was open to a variety of styles of lovemaking. Guided by feelings, butches developed their own styles and fems their particular preferences for sexual expression.

> "In fact I was really surprised, because as you're younger and you're seeing someone close to you, or if you have the opportunity to know someone that's

a lesbian—it's all in the curiosity. 'What do they do together? Oh my God, there's only one thing they can do together.' And that doesn't hold true. If they just happen to enjoy the female body, and they find their intimacy and that by dyking, and some others by oral. Or fooling around in your own little private way, whatever. But not everybody goes orally. . . . They do different things." (Annie)

Although oral sex had become quite common, dyking (tribadism) was still popular. Annie remembers with great affection some women who were exclusively dykers.

"I know of a butch that wouldn't think of having oral sex, would not think of it. Really. And I was involved with her, and strictly what you call a dyker. . . . She's my age, your age. . . . Same era but to have oral sex, no. She was strictly dyking, strictly. . . . What is dyking? It's when a butch and a fem, the fem plays the woman part and the butch plays the male part, and the male lays on the female just like a man would do to a woman, except for there's no intercourse. There's a very intimate feeling that goes on. It's like getting pressed together. . . . It does the same thing as the man would do except for you don't feel the penis inside of you. . . . Oh it's very beautiful. . . . Oh yeah, it's very intimate. It's more so than just having oral sex. . . . Oh yeah, I think you get much closer for a relationship and everything."

For the best moments, she thought it took a special partner plus working together. "Well it's the person that you're involved with number one, you just can't do it with anybody. And I don't know, it's a thing you work on, you build and you put your act together. . . . It is the full body. . . . Some don't even know how to do it. Theirs is strictly oral." Despite this fem's preference for good dyking, she did not experience it in all her relationships. The butch's style generally predominated. "I don't know. If it was there it was there; if it wasn't it wasn't. It's something that you have to, both parties, it has to come from both, not just one or whatever. And like I say, it's something that not everyone can do."

Within the framework of tribadism and oral sex, lesbians regularly tried new things, looking to expand pleasure. Sandy explains: "Might have discussed [sex with your partner] if you happened to fall upon some new discovery that really sends you somewhere. Say, 'Oh, you like that,' and here you just fell into that maybe by accident. And then you'd find out that that was what someone liked." But the culture also had definite limits. Sex toys and elaborate sex scenes were not a priority. Most narrators think that sadomasochistic sex was not practiced, or if it was, was kept very quiet, so others wouldn't know about it.

In the heterosexual world of this period, the penis was so central that sex could not be imagined without it. As a consequence, lesbians were stereotyped as unable to function sexually without using the dildo.[33] But since butches were masculine not male, lesbian sexual culture was built on altogether different premises. Butch-fem couples achieved sexual fulfillment through fully exploring the woman's body, and the dildo, if used at all, was a sex toy for enhancing pleasure. Butches did not ostracize those who used the dildo, but most thought it was unnecessary. When penetration was wanted, they used their hands. Their confidence in their own hands and their ability to please did not dispose them to think that a dildo would improve lovemaking.[34] Vic remembers her embarrassment when a friend, who had been a passing woman, excitedly showed her a newly acquired dildo.

> "[I never wanted to] dash out and buy a dildo or twenty years ago when they used to make them out of argyle socks.[35] Maybe you think I'm shitting you but I'm not. . . . Jamestown Gerry has a dildo that is totally unbelievable, unless you were married to a elephant. She called me in the bathroom at the Crescendo one time,[36] this was when she first got it. She says, 'You got to see this Vic you got to see it.' I didn't know what she was talking about. So she says, 'Come on, come on,' so we walk in the bathroom. Jesus, she whipped this thing out on [me]. . . . I'm supposed to be butch and my face felt like a neon sign. I could feel the embarrassment. How do you admire a dildo? No seriously, what do you say? 'Hey, wow, that's neat.' . . . She says, 'Look at it now, it's got veins, it's got everything, a woman can't tell.' 'Oh wow, oh wow. Maybe I ought to trade my hand in and get two.' I didn't know what the hell to say. Well what would you do if somebody did that to you? Well I tried to be cool about it, 'Heeeyyy. I want sequins on mine, that glows in the dark.' I know you think I'm shittin' you but I'm not. You got to meet her and then you'll just nod and you'll know where I'm comin from. 'Cause she's a trip. But nice, she's nice people."

Her attitude is not so much one of condemnation, but of incredulity. Fem narrators did not mention a desire for the use of a dildo, but we imagine that, just like some butches, some fems found it pleasurable and reacted positively to its use.[37]

Our discussion of lesbian sexual pleasure has been unavoidably flawed, because it treats sexuality in isolation, not sufficiently emphasizing the connections between sex and love. At this point it is necessary to indicate that, despite its open and supportive attitude toward sexual expression, lesbian culture did not completely separate the feelings of sex from the emotions of love. The discourse of sexual experience indicates it was about physical pleasure, beauty, intimacy, closeness, and caring. As can be seen from the quotations throughout this chapter, these words came up repeatedly in the discussions of sex. Lesbians of the 1950s had little trouble in explicitly discussing sex, but they did not value the physical as entirely distinct from the emotional. For most narrators, sex and love were intertwined as the basis for affairs and relationships, a subject that will be explored fully in the next chapter.

The place of sexual expression in lesbian life was innovative for women during the 1940s and 1950s. The culture validated women's desire for sexual satisfaction, providing opportunities for discussion and for experience.[38] In creating this culture, lesbians unquestionably built on the trend toward sexual liberalism in the larger society. But they also challenged heterosexual culture—particularly the repressive tone of the 1950s—in affirming lesbian sex, and by implication the sexual autonomy of women. Lesbian community was essential to creating a sex-positive culture, as it provided an environment for fostering alternative ideas and values. In the 1940s, positive attitudes about sex existed only in individuals and in small groups. But the consciousness and pride of the 1950s was strong enough to break down individual isolation and insure that sexual innovation was no longer the province of individual rebels. Lesbian community also provided a safe space for sexual experience. It contained no penalties—or very few—for sexual expression. In this context, lesbians' sexual subjectivity was nurtured.

The butch-fem erotic system was at the heart of the cultural ferment around women's sexuality. Lesbian culture drew on male-supremacist heterosexual models and successfully transformed them to create an erotic system that was gender defined but not governed by the penis. What emerges from our narrators' words is a range of sexual desires that shaped the framework of butch-fem sexuality, and in turn, was influenced by it. The definition of the butch's role to include both the aggressor and the giver of pleasure, and the defining of her sexual pleasure completely in terms of satisfying her fem, combined with the absence of penalties for sexual expression, created a culture in which women's sexual pleasure was central, but also defined this pleasure differently for butch and for fem. Butch-fem eroticism encapsulated a tension between the similarity among women and the differences between butch and fem.

In some sense, butch and fem each embodied complementary aspects of what feminists today would consider necessary for women's sexual autonomy. The butch represented woman's ability to initiate, act on, and realize sexual passion for another and to satisfy the other fully. The fem embodied woman's knowledge of and delight in her body and assertive concern for her own fulfillment. The butch-fem erotic system was organized around difference, but was flexible enough to let many lesbians develop sexual characteristics of both butch and fem, as long as roles weren't obliterated. Ironically, the ideology of the stone butch, which allowed the least flexibility, also pushed to the extreme women's potential for experiencing sexual passion and pleasure. The tough lesbians of the late 1950s, Black, Indian, or white, in a sense represented the beauty and illogic of this polarization among women. They did not foster similarity and mutuality between lovers, but they did establish a system for erotic satisfaction that was woman-centered and that distributed power evenly between partners.

This examination of lesbian sexuality during the 1940s and 1950s stands in contradiction to those feminist writings that posit women's lack of sexual subjectivity. Such theory maintains that women's sexuality has been completely colonized by a male-supremacist culture that defines women solely as the objects of male desire and enforces the system through violence.[39] The evidence is conclusive that these lesbians, in the context of a strong community culture, successfully sought to shape their own sexuality. To view their sexuality as male-defined fails to do justice to their accomplishment against tremendous odds. They created an erotic system that was woman-centered, albeit gender-defined. Their experience suggests that new forms of sexual expression come not simply from correct ideas but also from the ongoing activity of women in community.

In the varied and active sex lives of public lesbian communities, we can find the roots of a "personal-political" feminism. Women's concern with the ultimate satisfaction of other women is part of a strong sense of female, and potentially feminist, agency and may be the wellspring for the confidence, the goals, and the needs that shaped the later gay and lesbian feminist movements. In developing an understanding of the bar community as a predecessor to the gay liberation movement, the analysis must include sexuality. These lesbians actively sought, expanded, and shaped their sexual experience, a radical undertaking for women in the 1940s and 1950s. Lesbian sexuality was a harbinger of the sexual mores to be demanded by the radical feminist movement of the late 1960s and early 1970s.

"NOTHING IS FOREVER":
SERIAL MONOGAMY IN THE LESBIAN
COMMUNITY OF THE 1940s AND 1950s

Love came along and saved me
saved me   saved
me.
However, my life remains the same as before.
O What shall I do now that I have
what I've always been looking for.
—Judy Grahn, "Confrontations with the Devil in the Form of Love"

"I mean to me they come and they go. But I mean with me, you know, I've been with . . . like this girl right here [in that photo] we messed around with each other off and on for over twenty years. . . . And then like the girl that died, we lived together for nine years. I've had some short relationships. There's another lady. I just seen her picture. I messed around with her about twelve years. So sometimes you get into a whirlwind thing, then you find out after, it's not meant to be and then, you got to let go. But gay people, it's really odd to see a long-lasting relationship, you know, till death do us part. You don't find too many of those."

—Piri

Like Piri, all narrators had a series of relationships during the 1940s and 1950s, and afterward. To our knowledge, no historical research exists on the pattern of lesbian relationships that predominated not only in Buffalo but also in most other public lesbian communities of the twentieth century.[1] We think this absence is due in part to the fact that popular opinion assumes such relationships to be failed attempts at permanent coupling and therefore considers them insignificant, unworthy of serious attention. Deeply embedded in twentieth-century culture is the idea that lifelong marriage is the highest form of intimate relationship, and that inability to achieve it reflects immaturity and indicates failure. This idea is hegemonic, in that it is hard to discuss, or even imagine, other kinds of relationships as legitimate. Research on emotional bonding is deeply affected by this context.[2] We know this from first-hand experience because, to our surprise, we found ourselves beginning with negative judgments about the impermanence of lesbian relationships, which impoverished our ability to conceptualize an alternative framework.

On the surface, narrators also seem to judge their relationships by the standard of heterosexual marriage. They poignantly continued with the hope and intention of making each new serious love relationship last forever, despite the evidence, both perceived as well as experienced, that they wouldn't! "When I'm in a relationship, I think it's going to be forever. I feel that way now. I feel like it's going to be. I can't see it any other way. It probably won't be, but at this point I don't see it" (Phil). As our research progressed, however, we found increasing evidence that the framework of failure was not adequate to capture lesbian ideas about and experience of relationships. Narrators accepted serial relationships as part of their lives and did not present themselves as victims of impossible circumstances. They established their relationships with energy, and although they unquestionably suffered through breakups, they managed to maintain a sense of self-respect and autonomy. The tone captured in the opening quotation by "Then you got to let go" was typical.

These discoveries led us to hypothesize that the lesbian community created an alternate system of emotional bonding with its own logic and rules, a system we designate as serial monogamy. Lesbians might not have been able to articulate this alternate system fully, but they lived it. Narrators' lack of consciousness about a distinctive lesbian approach to relationships is in striking contrast to their willingness to discuss their independent views on sexuality. This suggests the power of the dominant discourse about the "maturity" and "validity" of lifelong marriage and how difficult it has been for lesbian culture to think of itself as separate from that discourse.[3] In identifying the lesbian system as distinctive, our goal is to delineate the social and cultural parameters in which individuals created, maintained, and ended their relationships rather than focusing on individual success and failure. We want to create a lesbian-centered approach to relationships, instead of one based on heterosexual norms and thus predicated on lesbian inadequacy. In addition we aim to construct a framework for comparing relationships in different twentieth-century lesbian communities.

As with the butch-fem image and sexuality, lesbian relationships both drew on the patterns and language of the dominant heterosexual society and also transformed them according to the imperatives of lesbian social life. The striking similarity between lesbian and heterosexual relationships of this period is the centrality of the gendered couple to the emotional and affectional life of both communities. This represents a radical departure from the nineteenth century, when the family was primarily an economic and reproductive unit organized for the maintenance of a household. Although love and sex were part of the husband-wife relationship in the nineteenth century, they were not the central foci of family life. Husband and wife oriented their social lives toward separate male and female spheres, and it was within these spheres that they developed their significant emotional ties. Many men also developed sexual liaisons with prostitutes and other women outside the boundaries of family.

By the 1920s, a new ideal of marriage came to predominate. It consisted of husband and wife being the center of each other's lives and focusing both their sexual desires and their emotional intimacy on one another.[4] In this context, some—particularly the Greenwich Village radicals of the 1920s—struggled to make a coupling of autonomous and independent women and men, but were not successful. A male-dominated and emotionally circumscribed version of the marriage relationship came to predominate throughout U.S. society by the 1930s. Social workers and sociologists of the time named this new form "companionate marriage," a term that was intended to convey that husband and wife were both sexually and emotionally intimate and meant everything to one another.[5] The trend toward the "companionate marriage" reflected the major changes in industrial capitalist and patriarchal society. The struggles of workers for a higher standard of living and more leisure time and the move toward a consumer economy led to the development of personal life as central to the family. Women's fight to enter the public sphere gave them more independence and autonomy and began to ease the sharp differences between men and women, but only served to reorganize rather than eliminate male supremacy. The modern lesbian couple obviously fits into these developments. They are involved in gendered relationships that combine sex and intimacy, and make emotional ties the focus of the relationship.[6]

Despite the centrality of the sexually intimate couple to both the heterosexual and lesbian worlds, there were significant differences in the nature of relationships in the two communities. Five aspects of lesbian relationships were unique and shaped the creation of serial monogamy.[7] First, lesbians could not marry. Though they might use that term among themselves, there was no church or state intervention in, or support for, lesbian relationships. To the contrary, severe oppression worked to undermine lesbians' self-respect and therefore their relationships. The continuity of relationships was based solely on interpersonal dynamics or on what this culture called "love."

The second distinct element of lesbian relationships was the fluidity of the power dynamic between partners, due to the marginal relation of lesbian culture to the institutions of male supremacy. Defining and understanding the precise nature of gender in lesbian relationships is a complex task, which will be a major focus of the next chapter. Here we will only briefly mention the aspects that are significant for understanding serial monogamy. Although, for reasons that we explained in preceding chapters, the lesbian couple was gendered, the butch role was not based on institutionalized male privilege and power. In most cases, the butch had no more economic or physical power than the fem. To make matters even more complex, the fem was less stigmatized than the butch by the dominant society and could more easily function within it, particularly if she kept her sexuality a secret. Therefore, butch-fem roles, unlike gender roles in a heterosexual marriage, did not make the feminine partner dependent on the continuity of the relationship for her economic survival and for the validation of her social identity.

The third distinct element was the priority both members of the lesbian couple placed on the pursuit of love and romance. The major goals prescribed for heterosexual men during this period were to marry and attain a good job or advance in a career, with the latter often taking priority over emotional commitments as they matured. Heterosexual women were to attain a great love and to build a home. In contrast, two lesbians came together with shared values about loving attachments. Because of similar socialization and because neither was distracted by greater job or career opportunities than the other, butch and fem alike were actively interested in love and willing to give a lot for it, a situation that fostered heightened emotional expression. The early and enduring feminist critique of love and romance as the basis of male supremacy, because of the ways in which they keep women tied into hierarchical relationships, was not applicable here.[8] Love was not more dangerous for one partner than the other. It was perhaps equally dangerous for both. The fourth distinctive aspect of lesbian relationships was the culture's integration of sex with love and romance. Lesbians—butch and fem alike—acknowledged having both serious and casual relationships in the 1940s and 1950s, and included sex as part of both. Lesbians recognized different intensities and qualities of romantic love and accepted the probability that many more than one important love relationship might exist in a lifetime. They did not reserve sex for their one or several true loves. Sex, unencumbered with the risks of social subordination or pregnancy, provided excitement and pleasure. Sex and love were not polarized on the basis of gender identity, with the butch valuing sex for itself and the fem, sex in the context of love.[9] Lesbians, butch and fem alike, appreciated and enjoyed love and sex, either separately or combined.

Fifth, the couple once formed did not radically change its social life. Very few couples during this period raised children, and without the responsibilities of parenting, couples did not abruptly have to move on to a different stage in the life cycle. Members of this community balanced their participation in the community with the building of intimate relationships throughout their lives. It was not enough for lesbians to build a love relationship. They also wanted to socialize actively in the community. They might go out less frequently when they had a partner, but they unquestionably continued to do so.

The contradictions created by the coexistence of these distinctive elements of lesbian relationships created the system of serial monogamy. The community's culture fostered and encouraged an atmosphere of romance, love, and flirtation. It also provided a setting in which people could date and find partners that might be either casual affairs or serious relationships. When true love was found, it led lesbians to want to live with one another and build a life together. Love was powerful and created strong relationships without the aid of institutionalized forces such as religion or the state.[10] At the same time, since members of the community continued to socialize and to value romance and sex, there was always the possibility of one partner developing romantic feelings or attraction for someone else, particularly since few lesbians subscribed to the concept of one true love. The role of romance was such that lesbians felt incomplete or deprived without it. The community provided ample opportunity for butch and fem to meet and establish new relationships, be they casual or serious. And when relationships ended, one partner was not automatically more disadvantaged than the other in the economic or social sense.

The system of serial monogamy was a constant throughout the 1940s and 1950s. When talking about bar life, butch-fem roles, and sexuality, narrators always emphasize how these had changed over the years, but when discussing relationships, they emphasize continuity. A typical comment is: "Are they that different now than in the past? The only difference I can see is that there is less difference between roles" (Leslie). As we listened to their life stories and focused on the information they furnished about relationships, we came to see that this perspective of little change is both true and not true. The form and content of lesbian relationships and of the system of serial monogamy remained fairly constant throughout the 1940s and the 1950s, with one exception. As the next chapter will discuss fully, in the rough bar crowd of the late 1950s and early 1960s, cheating, jealousy, and violence within relationships became prominent, and the length of time these relationships lasted was somewhat shorter than those of the previous decade.

Transformations in twentieth-century lesbian social life only slightly modified the content of relationships and did not alter their general contours. The changes that occurred were more in degree than in kind. For instance, in the 1950s, with the emergence of the tough bar lesbian, more lesbians, particularly butches, went out to the bars seven days a week, and bars became much more central to lesbian social life, but lesbians still had to balance socializing in bars with their romantic relationships. As the 1950s progressed, the community became much more accepting of casual affairs, but it also continued to value sex in the context of love just as lesbians in the 1940s had. These slight shifts in the content and meaning of community, love, and sexuality had little noticeable effect on the system of serial monogamy and therefore support the view that there has been little change.

To understand lesbian relationships on their own terms, rather than as an immature or failed version of the idealized heterosexual marriage, this chapter asks: What was the impetus for lesbians to form couples and what made those relationships end? We discuss the crucial place of romance and courting in lesbian life and explore the ideas and practices that comprise the connection between sex and love. Turning our attention to breakups, we examine the forces that led to separation, and the way lesbians survived these difficult times. Finally, we share narrators' views on the experience of a lifetime of serial monogamy, in order to consider how much serial monogamy is a response to oppression and how much it is an independent viable lesbian approach to relationships. Because narrators' emphasize continuity in the pattern of relationships, this chapter is not organized historically, but each section pays attention to historical trends.

COURTSHIP AND THE SEARCH FOR LOVE

Romance—the search for it, the delight in finding it, and the hope that it would be perfect—was at the heart of this community. Bars and house parties bristled with erotic tension. Lesbians developed crushes, pursued attractions, and courted. Jan insists that you never outgrow crushes: "Never, never, never. It's healthy, you're normal. I think. It's invigorating. Oh yeah, you got to dream, so oh Wow, you know." Lesbians unquestionably went out to be with their friends and to socialize with other lesbians, but they also went out "looking," butches for fems, fems for butches. The 1940s butches were notorious on their regular Butch Night Out. Dee, who was not sure of her role identity, remembers being made uncomfortable by their actions:

> "In fact, our crowd at that time, all of the butches thought that I was the butch, I don't know why, and wanted me to go to butch night, which on Friday nights was at Ralph Martin's. All of the butches would go down and stand at the bar in a row. I did it one time, the one time and I came home and said to Heloise, [my girlfriend,] 'That's not for ladies.' "

The active search for erotic partnerships was not limited to butches. Although fems in relationships were not expected to be interested in other partners, single fems, just by going to the bars, were perceived as actively "looking." Pearl, who entered the bars in 1945, but was heterosexually married and didn't settle down with a girlfriend until the mid-1950s, went out to the bars regularly. "Like I said, I got around a lot and I spent a lot of one-night stands. Like I was telling you the other day, I could not count them on my hands, on my fingers and toes, because that was the kind of life I led."

Part of the excitement of this erotic environment was the energy most lesbians—Black, Indian, or white—put into creating and displaying their good looks. Butch and fem went out in their best. They carefully cultivated their appearance, as evidenced by the butches' perfectly starched collars, perfectly creased pants, and the fems' latest-fashion dresses and hairstyles. They also were very conscious of self-presentation. Whitney remembers how an older, more experienced girlfriend had told her the colors to wear to be noticed.

"Sonny had a thing though, which I am passing along, this has to go down! When you go to a bar you always wear something very light, such as white. Because it's true, in the bar if you're wearing any other color, just about, people can't see you. You fade into the woodwork, but if you're wearing white you stand out. . . . You just look better. So you seldom see me in a dark color in a bar. I'm always wearing a white or yellow or light blue or something."

Butches as well as fems were conscious of becoming the object of desire. The artifice of the butch persona included projecting a striking image. The good looks of particular butches and fems were commented on many times in narrators' stories.

Butch-fem roles were the primary organizing principle for romance and courting. Butches were attracted to fems, and vice versa. Butches were not attracted to one another, nor were fems attracted to one another. These guidelines for attraction ran very deep.[11] Butch narrators of the 1940s insist they were never attracted to other butches. This same pattern continued into the 1950s. Toni remembers that she knew positively what she was looking for the first time she entered a gay bar.

"I wanted a girlfriend, a girlfriend that was more, like, femmy. And, in the beginning, the first women I was attracted to were always like real femmy, initially they were bleached blondes. That was what really turned me on was bleached blondes, and of course makeup and real femmy clothes, y'know, dresses and high heels and stuff like that. . . . And the first few relationships— the first several years of being gay these are the women I related to. They were like the extreme opposite of how I was."

Just as the butch was expected to be the aggressor sexually, she was expected to take more of the initiative in courting, to gaze boldly, to light a cigarette, to strike up a conversation, to buy a drink, or to ask for a dance. Pearl sees being pursued as part of her identity.

"I never had any question about [being feminine] I really never thought of any other way. . . . I just always liked to dress up and I always wanted . . . someone to pay attention to me. . . . I was not an aggressor. . . . The butch type was the aggressor, like a man would be the aggressor. To pick you up or want to take you out. . . . I would sit back and let them come to me."

Joanna mentions feeling uncomfortable in today's bar world where she sees everybody cruising. "And my idea of a butchy girl was one who cruised. So that is confusing to me [nowadays] to see a fem cruising. . . . You'd let someone know you like them, of course, but I always associated that kind of thing, [cruising] with a butchy girl." Courtship usually proceeded in a very romantic and highly stylized manner. Butches sent flowers, gave gifts, and took their dates out to dinner.

Despite the public prerogative of initiating relationships, most butches were cautious. As D.J. explains, they did not assume that they would be successful.

"If I would say, 'Would you care for a drink?' Now if she didn't accept, well you'd sort of back off. I would never press nothing. And she would have to be the first to make any move of any description of wanting to go out to dinner—through conversation or whatever—then I would pick up from there. But I would never—you can really tell through a conversation if someone is or they're not, or if they want to or they don't."

Some butches might have been more aggressive, but others were even more careful. Phil remembers the more intense butches:

"I've seen butches come on to fems, crazy, and pursue it. . . . You know, like [they] can't see anything else but that one person, and do everything and try everything to make out with her and meet her. No matter what they have to do, like get someone else to do something, and get their phone number through someone else, and pursue it that way. . . . There's a few that do have that— I don't know the word I want to use—confidence or that much macho, to do stuff like this."

Such butches were not in the majority. Quite a few butch narrators, from both decades and from all social subgroups, insisted that they never made the first move. Phil remembers vividly fems' overtures to her, most of which were not very subtle.

"Well I was bowling, and she'd be sitting back there watching constantly. Then she started to talk, and then—I don't know, they always say you have this feeling that you know, one knows the other, and we became friends and we went out. It just happened normally after that. . . . [Then] she just called up and said I have a key to a motel . . . on that order."

Jodi, a very handsome stud, in making fun of her own shyness gives the idea that most relationships began with mutual interest.

"I never made passes, I was too shy and nice. . . . [Butches] are supposed to, see I was a punk though. . . . I was a butch but I was kind of quiet and not very aggressive. . . . People just kind of drifted my way, what can I say. . . . I would just never overtly make a pass. I remember one time I . . . wanted to talk to this woman, so I went over to her, this was in a bar, I said, 'If a slow record comes on I'll be standing over here'; and I just walked away. So it was up to her if she wanted to ask me to dance. So if I was going to say something to somebody it was like that, backwards sort of. . . . That's the woman I was with for five years. . . . I let her call me up. But not just her, just everybody that I fooled around with. That's the way I did it, 'cause that's the kind of person I am. See I'm really a quiet person, and I don't have a lot to say, only when the tape is on."

The difference between the butch and the fem in initiating courtship was more a question of emphasis and style than a polarization of active and passive. True, fems rarely asked butches to dance, or bought drinks for butches. Nevertheless, they did not just wait to be chosen. In deciding with whom they would flirt, dance, and hold extended conversations, fems made clear their own choices and in doing so, shaped their own lives. A fem's approach entailed positioning herself correctly so that she could identify whom she was interested in and indicate it as she pleased.

> "I started going to this bar every night. I just felt like I had found something, I was really delighted and ecstatic with it. Here were all these women and I just knew in my mind this was the thing I wanted. But yet I wasn't too sure of how to go about anything. . . . I didn't drink too much, I used to sit at the bar and chew ice cubes. I always had this favorite spot at the end of the bar, and the bartender, whose name was Bingo, he was very friendly with me. . . . Because I've always had a friendly disposition, I became acquainted quickly with many different women. And I recall that one woman in particular was very interesting to me." (Bell)

No fem narrator was able to give us a description of how courting proceeded in the bars or house parties, probably because it was taken so for granted that it would be hard to retell. But Bell remembers the details of how she began a relationship in prison, and it is our guess that the butch-fem dynamics in the bars and house parties were quite similar. She saw herself as having chosen the butch she wanted. They both indicated their interest to one another nonverbally, then the butch took the first verbal step.

> "Well, I think basically that I was the one, I used to see her looking at me, like when we were having dinner. We worked in the kitchen together too, but she was in a different part. I used to catch her looking at me a lot but she was a very attractive girl, and I used to watch her too and I just felt a very strong gut desire within me that I would like to be with this woman. It's funny, when I saw something that I wanted or that I liked I would really pursue that and really try to get it. One night we were sitting in the rec room where they had the radio and the TV, and we . . . were sitting close together that night and she just kind of said real quietly, 'I would like to be with you some time, I find you very attractive.' And I said, 'Well, you know something Deena, I think I would like the same thing.' And she said, 'Well we'll decide when we can do it, when we can get together.' "

Because we have had at least social conversation with women who were out in the bars in the 1950s and early 1960s, we have been able to put together a composite picture of how a fem might go about catching the attention of a butch in the bars. Assuming the appropriate ambiance, things might have proceeded thus: After seeing someone she is attracted to, the first thing the fem would do is ask someone she already knew the name of her chosen butch and her status: "Is she going with anybody?" If she found that the butch might be available, a fem might get up from her seat and go to the juke box, making sure she crossed the butch's line of vision as closely as she could manage. She would spend quite some time staring at the title listing (even if she knew it by heart already!) and occasionally glancing in the butch's direction. She would then manage to play a song that might directly indicate her interest. If the butch was anywhere in range of the juke box, the fem would stay there and watch the dancers or hold passing conversation with other people she might know. She would always make sure, however, that she glanced often at the desired butch.

If the fem was noticed and the butch was interested, the butch would go to the juke box area and might either spend time staring at the titles or might ask the fem for her opinion on specific songs, the titles of which were indicative of attraction. The butch might mention that the bar was crowded, empty, quiet, noisy, anything to keep conversation going. If the fem wanted to dance, she might tell the butch that this was one of her favorite songs, to let the butch know she'd probably acquiesce to dancing to the number. If a fem was particularly bold, she might ask the butch if she ever danced—not if she would dance with her here and now—but only in a general, noncommittal way, so ego was not on the line. Any of these moves would let the butch know it was time to make her move and ask the fem to dance.

Once on the dance floor, things could progress more rapidly. After all, they would now be touching. They would be able to feel in each other's hands, bodies and voices—breathing patterns, ways of holding close, hands moving on backs, shoulders, waists, flirtatious conversation (like "I like the way you move.")—whether this was going to go further. Being able to touch one another was usually the clincher. If that was a successful erotic experience, the butch would usually ask to buy the fem a drink and later ask for a phone number and the courtship would commence.

Like the butches, some fems were more forward in their ability to express their desires, others less so. The culture encouraged them to develop their subjectivity, and offered no penalty for those who were more aggressive as long as they stayed within cultural boundaries and maintained their fem style: flirtatious, seductive, charmingly naive, or concerned, depending on their age and experience.

Whether the butch or the fem actually initiated contact, both had to deal with rejection. Although lesbians agree that it was not easy, they also articulate that it was inevitable, and therefore not worthy of too much upset.

> "Well, in between girls, of course, I get a crush on a lot of girls and I ask them out, if they're not interested they say 'no,' so I have to control my emotions, and I've learned to control my emotions and I just tell myself, 'Forget them', which I do. Because I have to put mind over matter, I can't sit in a bar and cry over one girl, what the hell, that's not healthy. So you move on to the next until you get somebody that's kind of attracted to you and then you have your mutual agreement." (Jan)

During this period, narrators pursued girlfriends in a variety of places. In both the 1940s and the 1950s, lesbians often found their lovers among the same set with which they were traveling. Vic recalls in the 1950s, "It was like a circle. . . . Everybody that you went with had already gone with everybody else. They'd break up and you'd start going with them and it kept going around and around." Other people went outside their circle, but stayed within the general community. In addition, butches often became interested in women they considered straight, who had no previous contact with the lesbian community and who returned to straight life after the relationship. They commonly met them while bowling, at work, in their neighborhood, or when such a woman made a trip to the bar because she was curious.

Narrators have vivid memories of the emotional and sexual explorations of courting and of finding and beginning relationships. Butch and fem had equal interest in this pursuit, though the fems' reflections in general seem to be less elaborate. Bell, who entered Bingo's in the mid-1950s, remembers her immediate interest in a woman tending bar.

> "Bingo's bar [was] the first bar that I ever went into. And once I started going I just couldn't stop, it fascinated me. In fact, the woman, one of the women who worked behind the bar, well it took about six years, kind of chasing her around and we kind of went through a lot of scenes, some good and some not so good. But we ended up as lovers."

Attraction and romance between bartenders and customers was quite common and added to the electricity in the air. In some sense the bartenders, butch or fem, were on display, deliciously visible and, by definition of their work, approachable. Ronni remembers when she was first coming out being thrilled by the feminine woman tending bar at the Carousel.

> "I had been to a couple of places. . . . And I found I was very attracted to very feminine women . . . to makeup and perfume and nice sweaters. I felt I was just looking for a really sexy-looking chick. And believe it or not, the barmaid [at the Carousel] absolutely flabbergasted me. She came on so strong. . . . I was just coming out. And I favored wearing khaki pants and flannel shirts and my hair short. I know even then I didn't recognize myself, what I was. But this girl apparently did because, oh boy, she put a real big make on me. I went back the following week with a bunch of girls from bowling, all straight. And meanwhile I was getting all these excited feelings about seeing this Aileen again. . . . She had dark hair, long eyelashes, nice body on her. So she waited on us, and secretly, I was getting a big charge out of this. So as we were all leaving to get back into my car, this girl runs out to my car, and I get behind the steering wheel and I'm just ready to turn the key, when the car door flings open, and the barmaid throws herself right at me and plants a big kiss right on my mouth and I said, 'Oh my god.' I didn't believe it. So after that incident I couldn't sleep, nothing. I couldn't eat; I was shaken and I went home. And that's all I could think of was her. And I finally started calling her up . . . started hanging around there every night and I started chasing this girl."

The most vivid memories are of early relationships, perhaps because the newness of lesbian life made them more exciting. Moreover, later relationships often began through one partner "cheating" in a previous relationship, so that the beginning had to be kept secret.[12] If a relationship began this way, the pleasure of the new relationship was colored by the difficulties of the breakup of the old. Nevertheless, lesbians in this community actively pursued romance throughout their lives, and remember this clearly.

The pursuit of a second love after a first or the third after a second was still exciting. People approached their later relationships with expectation and energy. Phil recalls the difference between her first and second relationships:

> "The difference was that the first one, it was a discovery of something that we both never had participated in before, so it was something new and exciting. And the next one, I mean I knew a little more about it, I knew what two girls did, so the excitement and the discovery of what you're about to do wasn't there. Although it was something that I felt, like I felt I was in love with her, and it was exciting because it was new"

Bell still remembers with pleasure her attraction to the woman who became her third or fourth serious relationship.

> "When I went with her she was fifteen and one-half years old. . . . She was very interesting. At that time she had a beautiful shape. Of course, at that time I was not heavy either. She was [slim], looked really good. I would say she was butch-looking but yet she was just something that appealed to me. She was very sexy and she was very attractive, just everything about her I liked. We spent most of our time in bed."

When asked if she—in her mid-twenties—was nervous about going with such a young butch, she replies:

> "No, no. I was kind of wild when I was younger, I think I, I was trying to find myself. . . . She was just it. As soon as I laid my eyes on her, she was a pretty woman. . . . She was funny, she was interesting, she made me laugh, she was excellent in all sexual areas, so she was everything that I felt that I really wanted and needed in someone."

Significant difference in age between partners in a relationship was neither the norm nor uncommon. Several fem narrators went with butches who were significantly younger, and butches went with younger fems. It was rarely referred to as anything significant.[13]

The active interest in pursuing romance in between relationships was strong enough to continue causing troublesome adventures as lesbians grew older. Debra remembers a scary incident that becomes humorous only with hindsight, when a husband walked in on her in bed with his wife.

"I had met him but I didn't know that he was [gay]. . . . And his wife liked me, and I kind of liked her just to go out with and I didn't, you know, keep it a going thing. And I was at his house once and I was in bed with his wife, and he came in and I'm telling you, I almost had a heart attack. Well you know, this guy is six feet five or something like that. And I was in bed with her and I heard the door click, and I happened to look around and he was coming through. Well he told me, 'Don't be afraid, I know what's going on.' But I couldn't do anything. I had to get up, really, and put my clothes on and I bet I was out of there within three minutes. But after that she called me and told me, 'You didn't have to go, he knows what's going on between us, he likes the guys. . . . ' I said, 'Why didn't you tell me all this before I came in?' I bet that['s] taken five years off of my life. Because if a guy walks in and you're with his wife, you never know what he knows. And I was just— absolutely petrified."

In this erotically electric atmosphere, within the larger context of severe oppression, excesses inevitably occurred. Pearl remembers how in her youth during the 1940s, she consciously fomented jealousy among her beaux.

"I don't know how I got away with all that stuff. I mean, they'd be fighting, arguing and fighting and then they'd be fighting with me and then I'd be lying to them, that kind of thing. I was not a very nice person, when I think back on the things I would do. I mean I was quite the liar. And I could do it with a straight face terribly. . . . Like I said, I didn't have many fems as friends. I just never got to be friendly with them, it was always the other way. I would lie to the butch and tell her that I would meet [her]. . . . And I'd be going out with different ones at the same time and I would lie about it. And it was not a nice way to do things, but that's what I did."

Sometimes the excesses developed into extreme situations, causing great anxiety and occasionally, fear. Matty, who was feminine in her early relationships and then became butch, recalls her first affair as a bizarre series of events starting with a kidnapping in the early 1950s.

"My first affair in gay life, I was kidnapped. . . . I wandered into [Pat's Cafe] one night and this girl became attracted to me and kept trying to buy me drinks. [The woman's friends said if I came with them to another bar and if the woman could buy me a few drinks she would stop bothering me.] So I said all right, got into their car and my car was left at the bar; the next thing I knew I was heading for Rochester. It was really bad. She had no intentions of bringing me back home either. In fact, she had to go to work, and she had somebody watching me so I didn't leave. And finally the girl went to the store and I made a phone call and I called home. [My parents were frantic and came and got me.]"

This suitor was persistent and she eventually won over Matty and her parents, despite the inauspicious beginning.

"She [the woman who kidnapped me] was a nice person but a little wild. [She kept calling but I rebuffed her.] It would be like St. Patrick's day and the doorbell rang and . . . this guy said to me, 'Does so-and-so live here?' And I said, 'She does, that's me.' And he looked out toward the street and said, 'Start bringing them in,' and I said, 'Start bringing what in?' And this other guy was in the truck out there and proceeded to bring in twenty-four dozen of green carnations and twelve dozen of red roses. The green carnations were for my mother and the twleve dozen red roses were for me, from this girl from Rochester. . . . We had green carnations all over the place! The girl also sent a complete backyard gym for my brothers and sisters. [She] kept doing things like that . . . and we got to be friends. I did have an affair with her, but it was more of a forced thing on me and it just wasn't what I was into."

The actual affair occurred after Matty had a fight with her parents. Her father hit her, causing her face to bleed, and she left home for a brief period. She stayed with this active suitor for a short while, because she provided a refuge from the trouble at home. In general, coercive behavior was not the norm and most people were not ensnared by it.

The lesbian culture of romance and love was very attractive to those who entered the community. Narrators frequently comment on the fact that gaining access to a public community presented myriad opportunities for the formation of relationships and therefore transformed their lives. Several butch narrators use the image of "a kid in a candy shop" to describe their excitement at entering the community and seeing the number and variety of women who were interested in them and who might potentially be their lovers.[14] Phil, who had been in a nine-year, relatively isolated relationship during the 1940s and who gradually found her way into the lesbian community in the early 1950s, describes her excitement about the new possibilities.

"She saw me and she pursued it, which at the time I wasn't even thinking about anybody else. You know it's like a kid that's never been in a candy shop. I only had the one and I really didn't know how it was outside that one. And then there were other girls. And the more I've seen, the more that were attracted to me because I have never once even approached a girl. I had never been the one to start anything."

Sandy, who had her first serious relationship with her teenage sweetheart, describes the cumulative impact of the community in a similar way:

"And then pretty soon we got into a nice necking session, I says, 'Wow, this is the top of the world, everything is coming true for me, this girl I have loved for so long. This is really it; I found my happiness.' And we stayed together for quite a while. Well then after her, I was with her about a year . . . I was really doing pretty well there, a lot of girls liked me. And this went to my head, I says, 'Wow'—so I started running around with the other ones because I couldn't get over it, 'Wow, Wow,' like a kid in a candy shop. And then after that we split up and it was really the first love; first breakup because I wanted to be with these other girls. And then after that 'go, go, go.' Now, I'm settled down—thirteen years with this one. Little hanky-panky here and there; we all do."

Lesbian community and culture nurtured the excitement of romance and the public expression of butch-fem eroticism. The continuous interest in love gave lesbian lives and relationships their distinctive character.

THE CASUAL VERSUS THE SERIOUS:
THE SEX-LOVE CONNECTION

All of the women we interviewed, butch and fem alike, entered the community with the hope of finding a perfect or great love, and many continued that search throughout their lives. In addition they expected and delighted in more casual sexual relationships. Narrators took for granted that, before finding their first "true love," or in between "marriages," they might go through any number of relationships seeking the right person. In this community there was no concern with virginity, and women did not feel that they had to "save" themselves sexually or emotionally for one or several true loves. Dating, therefore, had two dimensions that were not always distinguishable except in retrospect. First, it was goal-oriented, a testing ground for finding a lasting love. Second, it was fun in itself, providing experience, ego support, and fond memories. At the start, any relationship had potential to be either. Frequently, people's first relationships were motivated by love, and it was love that brought them together and helped them get beyond their ignorance of their own sexuality. Sandy says of her first affair with the Marine's wife with whom she ran off, "No experience, but in love." As women matured, however, they became more conscious of their intentions as they approached a relationship.

The community's language expressed both the ambiguous potential of any relationship and also the difference between the experience of serious and casual relationships. On the one hand, there is no name for a serious relationship as distinct from a casual relationship. The closest the community comes to differentiating them in its discourse is in the contrast between a relationship and an affair. However, "affair" is most frequently used for the practice of "cheating" while in a serious monogamous relationship, rather than to describe a casual relationship of a single person. Narrators who came out in the 1940s remember saying "so-and-so's going with someone" to indicate that two people were in a couple. There wasn't a different way to describe a relationship that was long lasting or one that was just beginning. They might say, "So-and-so was going around with someone but nothing happened." They might have indicated that something was just starting by using the word dating or courting, "That's when I was courting her." This language usage continued into the 1950s.

On the other hand, there were many ways to indicate the distinction between the feelings and intent in serious versus casual relationships. "But I'd say I cared for her an awful lot. As young as I was, I knew the difference between infatuation and love. I never threw the word love around unless I really meant it" (Reggie). Though the words vary, this distinction between infatuation and love emerges repeatedly. What this narrator calls love, others identify as "deep love," "true love," "marriage," a "steady relationship," "the love of your life," or they categorize this feeling as "serious." Infatuation is referred to as "hot pants," particularly in the 1950s, or is categorized as "casual," "less serious," appropriate for "playing around," or having an "affair".

The terms of address and reference that members of a couple used for one another tended to blur the difference between a serious and a casual relationship. In the 1940s, a woman most commonly referred to her partner as my "girlfriend," whatever her degree of specialness. This usage continued into the 1950s, except in the Black community. Drawing on straight language, a Black lesbian commonly referred to her partner in a serious relationship as "my people." These old-timers, white and Black, did not use the word "lover" and do not like it today.

> "To me when they say lover, that doesn't mean anybody specifically. That's whoever you're in bed with. That's your lover. But I find mostly in the Black kids, they don't use too much lover. They be talkin' about this is 'my woman.' There is a difference, it's a little more seriousness there. And if you're not their woman they'll say, 'This is Arlette.' That's lettin' somebody know that they ain't nothin' to me. That's a little message that some people can give to let you know, I'm not going with her, it's nothing serious, we're just out. And if they're really going they'll say, 'This is my lady,' or 'This is my love, Arlette.' Not lover. I never like the word lover. Anybody can be a lover." (Arlette)

Since lesbian language was ambiguous, and since any relationship had the potential of becoming a "true love," it would be possible to think that lesbians of this community did not actually conceptualize and experience casual relationships as distinct from those that were committed. Instead, the shorter relationships could be viewed as trial "committed" relationships. In many instances this was the case. Between "loves" or serious relationships, people often had a series of short, casual relationships. Dee recalls her behavior between two long relationships, one lasting thirteen years, the other, ten: "Then I had a little bit of drifting, playing the field. Nothing very serious, you know what I mean." Joanna describes the interim between two relationships in the 1950s in a goal-oriented manner:

> "And I dated other people in between, like I said nothing really . . . that was anything that lasted any length of time, mostly probably because I wasn't ready for it, and they, the person, was the wrong person or whatever, I don't know.

But it just wasn't the right time or the right place or the right person . . . and then I met Donna and I lived with her for five years."

When lesbians dated between relationships, they usually saw several people. Some were quite particular, preferring their independence to being with just anyone.

"Like if you were dating, I wasn't dating just one person. . . . I went out with many many people and I really didn't like anyone in particular, otherwise I wouldn't have been dating other people. They were all different. I really didn't want anybody to live with me. I didn't like anybody that well, to want to be with them, live with them. . . . I loved [being single]. Always had a dog. And I have a large family. They took up a lot of my time. . . . I don't think I could have just shoved another person down my family's throat." (Joanna)

Because of the stereotyped notion of women having little interest in casual sex, it is tempting to view all casual relationships as a testing ground for committed relationships. Our evidence suggests the contrary. Although there is no dating practice that is completely without goal orientation, as early as the 1940s the community's practice of dating show girls comes close. By the 1950s, most women sought out one-night stands for fun and with little ambivalence. Unquestionably, participants in this community dated for the excitement and adventure of romance and sex, as well as for finding a true love. Arden and Leslie remember meeting show girls at Eddie Ryan's Niagara Hotel. The hotel bar was regularly frequented by lesbians, and strippers stayed there because it was near the Palace Burlesque where they performed. Each of these narrators recalls her flings quite vividly. We asked, "What was a fling?" "It depended on how long their stay at the Palace lasted!" Arden once took a week's vacation for a fling. "Not often, because how much could you take? This one girl was there for a week and she moved in for a week. She had the wildest stories. She had a lover in every city." Arden recalls that her phone bill proved this fact, for it recorded calls to all over. "One time Mickey [this stripper's lover] from Dallas called and she wanted to speak to me. She asked 'What's going on there?' I said, 'Absolutely nothing, we're enjoying one another's company.' " In the interview we join her laughter because although the Dallas butch was very brusque over the phone, Arden could afford to be cool from 3,000 miles away.

Leslie had a colorful fling with Zelia who found Winters, where the two met. "She had wonderful stories to tell. . . . She was a wonderful woman and told stories about the problems she had when she was married and her husband was in jail. These show girls really get to know you. It is not as much getting into bed as you might think. She wanted to get to know you and you wanted to get to know her." Leslie remembers taking her to the depot and putting her on the train. "She turned around and said, 'Come with me, I'll take care of you.' I never regretted not going, though I thought about it. After all, she couldn't support me forever." One time

Zelia came back and called Leslie. She had her butch friend parked in a trailer and wanted them to all get together. "I didn't want to. I didn't feel it was proper. It would mean I would have to pretend I didn't, when I did. It wasn't right. It seems to be pushing your luck a little far. And after all, I didn't know how big she was!"

Although they acknowledge the fun and adventure of these relationships, when asked if they felt discomfort sleeping with someone who was sleeping with others, both Leslie and Arden answer "yes." Leslie recalls, "I felt as guilty as hell. It was going against religion and upbringing. You didn't do that." Arden comments that she remembered thinking to herself, "What the hell are you doing here? The fun can't go on forever. I had to go to work. I would feel guilty at work; not at ease." She normally felt quite at home with her fellow workers and thinks that she might have felt her actions were immoral. When asked if they thought *this* was immoral, didn't they therefore think lesbianism itself was also immoral, Leslie emphatically responds, "No. Because the romance [of lesbian relationships] was strong and you were with someone who loved you better. You then started making a home together and living together."

This discomfort with relationships that were clearly for fun and were unlikely to develop into lasting love relationships seemed to prevail through the 1940s. Phil, who came out in the 1940s, expresses difficulty with casual affairs in general.

> "Maybe because I feel that if you go to bed with someone it's because you really have the feeling that you're in love. I wouldn't go to bed with someone just because I was attracted to her. . . . I have had experiences where girls have wanted an affair and I have really wanted to but couldn't because I wasn't in love. . . . I've always envied . . . some of my friends. . . . They could pick up a girl that night and go to bed with them that night and then maybe forget it tomorrow . . . but I could never do that. . . . I really have to be into a relationship before I can do that.

At a subsequent part of the interview, Phil describes her participation in more casual affairs, underscoring the ambivalence narrators from the 1940s felt about relationships that were not specifically goal-oriented.

Narrators who came out in the 1950s express no ambivalence about going out with show girls or prostitutes or about casual relationships. They had regular contact with hookers and strippers in Pat's and the Mardi Gras. Dating beautiful women, whatever their occupation, was usually viewed as a feather in one's cap. Sandy recalls the flavor of contests between butches over dating in the 1950s.

> "Well then at that period we all were going through. . . . It was more or less a contest we had with each other. We didn't call it that but . . . what was the first one? The first one was show girls, that was it. One of us at one time or another happened to go into the Palace and happened to make out with a stripper. You get a stripper; I want to get a stripper. Vic and I especially, we always had something going; if she got, I had to get; if I got, she had to get.

So then we started and then everyone would look up, all the other butches. We'd come in with these dolls all really swinging, saying something; they were buying us clothes and holy Christ, so that was our niche. We stayed in that era for a while. Then we went to Dugan's, 'cause Dugan's was . . . right behind the Palace. And the show girls used to come in there and we'd grab 'em when they'd come in there and we'd make out like crazy."

The 1950s saw a variety of casual relationships. The one-night stand had become an expected part of lesbian culture. Most butch narrators for this period had been with more women than they could remember, and fems were only slightly more moderate. Vic cynically reflects on the place of one night stands in her life.

"Well, my first thing with a woman is if—if I can get your attention, and if I'm attracted to you, I'm gonna sleep with you, right? And I'm gonna try the best I can to be good. But there's never going to be a second time. 'Cause it's over as far as I'm concerned. Other than with the women I live with. These broads have fucked me once and are still waiting for the second time, and there isn't going to be any. And I'm not saying this to you like I'm all this fantastic. . . . But they want to do it. Maybe they care for me. And there's nobody that can treat you much better then I can if you're out with me. I can really make you feel like something even if you're a piece of shit. And they like that."

A variant on the one-night stand, which is even briefer, is the "bathroom" romance, having sex with someone you meet in the bathroom of the bars. Vic recounts with a bit of distaste:

"You meet somebody in the bathroom, do your thing, and then come out. . . . Butches stayed in there and waited. There were several of them around that would just stand in the bathrooms and wait for somebody to come in and hit on them in the shithouse. . . . Who knows what you did there, I'm not a shithouse romancer, but I'm sure a lot of them did. . . . I would bet some had more sex in the shithouse than they had in their bedrooms."

In the interview we mention that we had heard of such sexual liaisons in New York, but they were in the bathrooms of subways and parks, and the women brought paper bags for one to stand in to camouflage the second pair of feet.[15] Vic comments, "Well if you were doing it right, there would be but one set of feet showing in the first place. . . . If a lady gets her legs up high enough you don't need to worry about a paper bag."

Some lesbians also had casual relationships with straight acquaintances that they did not expect to go any further. Little Gerry had been to bed with the majority of straight women in her favorite beat bar of the late 1950s and 1960s.

"But my being the only real lesbian in that bar, these straight women used to come on to me all the time. I could tell you on a Sunday who I was going to go home with on Thursday. They all followed the same pattern, it all started at the [bar's Friday] baseball game. It was a real pattern. Madeline and I used to laugh about that. And it was simply because everybody wanted to experiment to see what it was like to sleep with a woman, and I didn't care. They wanted it, I wanted it. . . . Well, I wasn't looking for a relationship with any of these people, what I was looking for was sex. What they were looking for was not a relationship with me, they were looking for sex. And it never was detrimental to the way we related afterwards. One of my best friends, a woman that was a friend to me for years and years, we slept together within the first three months that we knew one another. No real big thing. We slept together and then we went on to be friends and she got married. . . . I didn't care, I didn't care if they were all straight or if they were all gay. I wanted sex and then they wanted the same thing. I agree [this is a problem] . . . if people would try to form some type of relationship and aren't honest, but these were people who were pretty much on the up and up. I ended up being friends with a lot of the women, a lot of their boyfriends didn't like me, but I was friendly with a lot of the women. Now you never missed a baseball game I'll tell you. I was at every softball game."

The pursuit of casual relationships did not necessarily mean that narrators unambivalently accepted sex for its own sake without the rationale of true love. We suspect, rather, that even in the 1950s, an important impetus for falling in love so frequently—for some every weekend—was to provide an acceptable framework for the sex that was part of their relationships. As Little Gerry comments sarcastically about her friends of the 1950s, "They didn't know the difference between hot pants and love." Furthermore, although lesbians in the 1950s practiced casual sex, they did not like it exclusively. Like Jan, many felt it was not as satisfying.

"I've always had the idea that a lot of girls are just out for the sexual part of it, where they could let loose sexually and know that they're not gonna get pregnant, but they're just out for sex. And that just isn't my idea of sex. . . . Sex is beautiful, but without emotion I don't think it's really that great. And I hated to ever get tied up [with] a woman that was just involved with sex. . . . No, believe it or not, [I've never been with that kind of woman.] I haven't been to bed with that many women, but the women that I've been to bed with was the ones I ended up going with for a length of time. Like these one-night stands, that's not my bag. I'm not saying I never did, but, you know, we all get weak. Well, it's probably a form of protection, because I really didn't want to get hurt, so I protected myself. In fact, I lived with this girl once for three months before we even had sex. . . . She was just afraid and I never pushed the issue until she was ready and felt it was worth waiting for. We lived together for three months. . . . No it was a little more than friends, kissing friends, but we never got into the act of sex. So finally, when she finally did, everything was beautiful. We had a beautiful sex life and everything."

The 1950s community was divided on how important sex—as contrasted with love—was to lesbians. Even Vic and Sandy, who set an example in the community with their interest in show girls and one-night stands, disagreed on this topic. Their thinking captures the varied opinions of the times. Sandy viewed sex as the best and most important thing in life. She is the woman who in chapter 6 states that she wants to be everything a man can be to a woman and more. "I wanted to make love. I love to make love, I still say it's the greatest thing in the world." Throughout her life story, she reiterates this point. As she talks with us about the pleasures of sex, she becomes sexually energized, "getting horney"; but this does not make her nervous. We suggest that we can change the subject. "No, that's all right, I just wanted to throw that in." This exchange underscores her pervasive concern with and appreciation of sexual matters.

Vic, who was equally popular in the community, and had as many one-night stands and live-in relationships as Sandy, nonetheless had her doubts about the place of sex in women's lives.

> "Well see I'm not into sex. To me sex isn't that important. . . . If I could go along with how you feel about it, if I thought that was really, that the woman was enjoying what I was doing to her, other than the fact that we care for each other and just to be close, I would probably have a very different outlook on it. But I don't believe that. . . . I'm not saying it's a terrible thing, but I can't see how you could put it [as the best thing]. . . . [Do] you ask all these people these same questions? . . . Well, when I read whatever you're putting out, then I'll know how many have told the truth and [how many] lied."

Rather than seeing herself as wanting to be desired like a man, Vic saw herself and other women as different from men where sex was concerned.

> "If I went to bed and I'm with my woman, then I can enjoy it. . . . But to me it's not like a man that sits around talking about it. Now like we've been talking about it, I don't have any desire to jump over on that couch and attack you. . . . Yeah, but if men were talking do you think it would be the same thing?"

Despite their differing views about the value of emotional closeness versus sex, 1950s lesbians all engaged in relationships that included both. They were not committed to separating sex from emotion. They adjusted the relative proportion according to situation and desire.

This analysis of love and sex in the public lesbian community of the 1940s and 1950s raises new perspectives and questions for women's history in general, as well as for lesbian history. Lesbians are no exception to the central role love plays in the lives of twentieth-century American women. Narrators pursued romance and engaged in the search for true love with energy, joy, and perseverance. Yet the lesbian search for love differed in significant ways from that of heterosexual women of the time. Lesbian romance completely integrated sexuality. The concept of "saving" oneself until one found true love was alien to this community and the celibate romance was uncommon. Although most lesbians were directed toward finding true love, their love and sex lives were not completely oriented toward this goal. They conceptualized infatuation and casual affairs positively and actively explored these alternatives. The culture did not polarize sex for sex's sake and sex in the context of love. Most lesbians had experienced both. This appears to be true for both butches and fems throughout the 1940s and 1950s, since we found no clear difference in their statements about love and romance.

From the perspective of lesbian history, women's pursuit of sexual/romantic encounters is severely repressed by the dangers male supremacy presents for women in institutionalized heterosexuality. In the heterosexist society of that time, women and men were obsessed by the sexual "goodness" or "badness" of women. Yet outside of these institutional confines, as early as the 1940s and perhaps even earlier, lesbians pursued casual and deep love relationships and integrated sex with both. We can either emphasize how creative and innovative this oppressed community was, or begin to contemplate how easy it is for women to express sex and love outside of institutionalized male dominance. It is breathtaking to realize this difference between the lives of lesbians and heterosexual women in the 1940s and 1950s.

FORCES LEADING TO BREAKUPS

In the context of their heightened sensibility to romance, participants in this community held a dual consciousness about relationships. They expected them to last forever, and at the same time knew that they wouldn't. As Piri comments, "And as much as sometimes people would like to think that their relationship with their mate will last forever, in dealing with reality we don't know if it will." Phil reminisces about the beginning of her second relationship:

> "I wasn't scared, no, that is not the word. I was apprehensive, I didn't really know if this was going to be a lasting relationship or not. I mean, every one I've had I feel like it's going to be that, the one I want to spend the rest of my life with, until someone else comes along, but it's always one at a time."

This complexity pervades most narrators' thinking, and even though they frequently articulated the desire to have their relationships last forever, they simultaneously had mixed feelings about lifelong relationships. Only one of the many narrators, D.J., invented her own marriage ceremony, and she remembers it with ambivalence.

"I liked the girl and everything, don't get me wrong. I used to hear about this all the time and I just more or less wanted to have the experience. . . . We had it right down in our [basement]. . . . We had a sleeping room, it was a good-sized one at that time. And I had a bridesmaid, a best man, and one guy played the minister. . . . To me it was more a farce than anything else. She wanted to go through with it see, and I said, 'Well, what have I got to lose? There's no papers signed, if I want to be out you're out. . . . ' They got a big cake and throwing rice and all the rest of it. So that's the first and only time I ever done it."

D.J.'s feeling that she didn't want to be tied into something she might not like is echoed by others. Arlette explains that she had never really wanted to get married in lesbian life.

"No. Well truthfully speaking, I don't know about going that far with anyone, 'cause I've never been with anyone that long. Because I don't know if it's my personality or how I am. Usually I can't go too far with them in the courtin' stage. To go to the marriage part. I think if I found a lady that was really mentally together, I probably would. What's the difference? If we could get along."

It is difficult to determine whether this attitude reflects defeatism born of oppression or the positive desire to maintain control over one's life at a time when, for women, marriage often meant subjugation. It is likely that both dimensions are true of lesbian relationships during this period.

We are regularly asked (and for that matter we ask ourselves) about the average length of relationships and which kind lasted the longest.[16] Since our method is oral history rather than the sociological survey with a representative sample, we are unable and unwilling to respond by presenting "averages." We can say no more than that the length of time relationships endured does not seem to vary significantly with the decades. Rather, it seems to have varied from individual to individual, with a tendency for lesbians to have longer relationships as they aged. Narrators who came out in the 1940s say that relationships during this period lasted about four or five years. However, it would be incorrect to generalize about the 1940s from this data because all our narrators were young at that time and we have no data on the relationships of older lesbians in that period. Even among the small number of narrators who were out in the 1940s, some did not create relationships that lasted this long during that decade or at any subsequent time in their lives. Others, who had four- to five-year relationships in the 1940s, went on to create even longer relationships in the 1950s. One narrator began a relationship in the late 1950s that has lasted until today as did several of her friends.

Narrators who were young in the late 1950s estimate that their lesbian relationships during that time lasted one to three years. The evidence suggests that their relationships were somewhat shorter than those of young lesbians in the 1940s and early 1950s. Nevertheless, most went on to develop longer relationships in the 1960s, some lasting as long as thirteen years. Others began relationships in the 1950s that lasted from six to thirteen years and continued this pattern.

Narrators offer different kinds of explanations for why breakups were such a regular part of lesbian life. By far the most common is that, in the process of socializing, one member of a couple found someone else or that a third party intruded on a relationship. (The third party could have been a man or a woman.) In addition, problems in the way the partners related to each other are sometimes mentioned as the cause of breakups. Several narrators also consider that the oppression of gay life created conditions unfavorable for lasting relationships. All three explanations are relevant for most breakups.[17]

Because romance, flirtation, and socializing publicly were important to this community, either member of a couple might meet someone to whom she was attracted, thereby threatening the relationship. The same conditions that fostered the pursuit of romance and the attainment of true love also endangered the longevity of relationships. Gay women were fully aware of this contradiction and had two solutions, neither of which really worked. The first was not to go out socially once one had found a true love. Narrators like Vic typically offer as an explanation for a relationship lasting that the couple did not go out: "They were home people, too, though, right? That's the whole thing right there, is they were people that stayed home, that did not frequent the bars most of them." And many narrators remember cutting down on going to the bars while they were in relationships.

> "The only time I really went out is like on my day off or something. But then when we would have dinner, have a couple of drinks, a lot of times it wasn't in a gay bar. It would be where we were having dinner, whatever. Then we'd step up to the bar or whatever, and have a conversation and that was the end of it." (D.J.)

The understanding that an established couple might need to have a less-active public life was accepted by most of the community. Some variation of the following was articulated by many narrators: "When you were out cruising, you were out eight days a week. And when you were in a relationship, you might have gone out one of the two week-end nights. Now you stayed home and played house" (Little Gerry).

Members of the community, by definition, could not completely follow the solution of not going out, since this community was centered around its social life. Matty remembers trying to explain this to her mother, who advised her to stay away from the bars when she was in a relationship:

> "She'd say that from what she could see, people who go into gay bars are people who are lonely and looking for someone. Or people who were trying

to break people up, . . . not because they want either one, but just to break them up. And she [my mother] always said, 'If you were happy and you had someone, why tempt fate?' But I used to tell her, 'Well you can't just stay in a house and not go out.' "

Going out not only meant having a good time, but it was also the only way a person could break down the isolation of being a lesbian and affirm her lesbian identity. In Vic's memory, she lost her first girlfriend as the price for ending the extreme loneliness.

"We probably would have stayed together for a long time if we'd have stayed in [Angola], where we started out, because you think there's no one else but you two. Which is a terrible feeling also. But when we came up here and found the bars and that there were other gay women, she dealt with it fine, but I didn't. Went nuts over it. . . . I was seeing other women that I knew I could be with."

The other solution was to trust one's partner, but it is the nature of trust that it lasts only as long as it lasts! "When you can trust the person you're going with, then you don't have to worry about that [your lover's being attracted to someone else] and it's got to be a mutual thing. . . . If you can't trust the person you're going with you're in bad shape" (Matty).

This tension between the potential for romance in socializing and its possible negative effects on committed monogamous love relationships pervaded this community's life. "Yes, and there always is a breakup because with lesbians there's a question of something new, or a new approach, or the sexual drive, that's the thing" (Dee). Arden comments that it was not so much that a person fell *out* of love with her previous girlfriend, but that she fell *in* love with someone else. The comradeship and fun that existed in the bars and house parties, therefore, had an undercurrent of competition for lovers. What is benign and exploratory from a single person's point of view may be destructive from the point of view of couples.

Competition among butches intensified significantly from the 1940s to the 1950s as indicated by increased fighting over lovers and the rise in jealous accusations.[18] The language of 1950s narrators expresses the destructive intent some lesbians displayed to others. Matty explains:

"Everybody would cheat . . . or tried to make a play for your girl. I still find that now; I don't think that will ever change. . . . There are people . . . in gay life who are not happy, who have not found their niche in life, and they'll be damned if they're gonna let anybody else be happy, and they'll try to break you up. There's the old saying, if you don't have anybody, nobody wants you, but as soon as you find somebody, everybody wants you. . . . It's not actually that they want you or that they want the person you're with, they just want to see if they can make you or the person, to break you up. And then you no longer have what they never had, and then they're happy. You're miserable but they're happy. I don't think that will ever change."

Arlette also warns against those who want to ruin your relationship:

"I have found that if you really find someone you want to be with, and want to try to make it with, you'll have to cut loose quite a bit of the crowd. [I'm] not saying everyone. I find some people just [go] too far, you just never see them. That is too boring to me. But I can realize that a lot of people, you know the troublemakers, you have to cut them out . . . if you're going to make it. Because there's always that set of people, gay kids, well even in true life, in straight life, there's always that home wrecker gonna come, or a person is gonna cause confusion. 'So-and-so said this,' or tell a lie, anything to keep you two fussing at each other, or doing wrong things."

Although some people were particularly known as trouble, everybody was a potential threat, particularly a single person.

"You don't hang around with somebody that has nobody. I have friends of mine that are mad 'cause now they've gotten together I don't come around. I said, 'Look, I don't have anybody, I don't think it's right for me to call you up and ask you all to go out, I'm a loner. . . . If you invite me over then I'll come, but I don't believe that I should be hanging around you two and I don't have anybody. . . . ' You really do have to kind of isolate yourself, if you want to stick together, you really do. And I don't get mad at any of my friends that do that." (Arlette)

In the late 1950s, competition existed among even the closest of friends.

"Somebody could be your best buddy, your best butch buddy, if you were a butch, and somebody that you went out on what they call the 'guys night out' and you draw them out to get drunk, and they could be your best buddy . . . don't leave your girl in their company or they'd try to make your girl, you know. Your friendship stopped where another female became involved. And I found that true." (Vic)

Sandy mentions that the most painful competition could come from an ex-lover.

"I've been with a girl and maybe done something or whatever, well anyhow we split up, 'cause I liked somebody else say. Now I'll be with someone else and she'll turn butch and come back and take that girl away from me. It kills you. I mean, there goes the one you were with, taking the one you love. . . . [She knows] your whole plan of action. So the only way she can get at you is that way and it usually works. Then you're alone. Here you had two, now you're alone and they're together. That happened to me."

Since many lesbians in committed relationships did have affairs, feelings of competition and insecurity were grounded in reality. It is important to add, however, that "cheating" did not necessarily lead to the end of a relationship, even when discovered. Joanna explains:

> "Not always . . . depending on how strong that relationship was. I think some-times if it was just for kicks or something, I think a lot of the girls didn't even know it had happened. . . . Sometimes relationships fall apart, sure, they didn't all stay together. But I think it was doomed anyway . . . it wasn't that it was so happy. And most of them stayed together because they were used to one another."

Discretion was a significant part of maintaining a committed relationship, as Whitney tells us:

> "The thing is, I don't have an ex-lover, affair, what have you, I don't have an enemy. I never had anyone come back to Sonny [my girlfriend] and say, 'Ooh whoo, I'm in love with Whitney,' and so on and so forth, because I got into relationships with people who felt the same way. That they were in a relation-ship or they realized that my relationship with Sonny was the most important thing. And so there was never any bad, any ill came out of that. I'm friends with people I ever was involved with. And Sonny was friends with [them]."

Since it is always hard to be completely discreet, discretion also relied on the complicity of others in the community. People did not always tell when they discovered someone cheating. If they really liked the fem and the butch they would ignore it. Annie remembers:

> "If you had any respect for the fem, no, you wouldn't squeal on her. 'Cause she would get it and the butch that she was messing with would get it. . . . [If the butch cheated] it all depended I think, really, on who the fem was, if she was a liked person or if she was disliked. [If she was disliked] then possibly they might say something, to stir up dirt or whatever. But if she was liked or whatever, [you wouldn't want to hurt her.]"

In a manner consistent with narrators' general view that socializing and the pursuit of romance threatened relationships, they also attribute the ending of specific relationships to the presence of a third party. Variations on "I met somebody else" or "my partner started seeing someone else" are the most common explanations narrators offer for why their relationships ended. Sometimes, the person left the old relationship on her own to be with someone new, but sometimes she was forced out because an affair was discovered. Pearl remembers giving her girlfriend, who had a propensity for cheating, an ultimatum, and she did end the relationship when her butch failed to respond.

> "I'm not running around or anything but she is, and she's bringing these people to the home, to the beaches, to wherever. And all of a sudden I said to her, 'Three times and you're out. . . . ' But she had two, at least two that I know of, that she brought home, in this area. And then when we went to [Albany]

I told her, no more. So she picked up with another one. See, then she'd moved out for a while . . . and yet she wanted me to be there when she wanted to come back. And that's the way it ended. And I'm still friends with her."

Several butches tell stories about throwing their partners out for sleeping with men.

"And then after, going on the tenth year, I happened to make a mistake and went into work when I was supposed to have off. Now this might have been going on for quite a while without my knowing it, but I just happened to come home. Go home and all the doors were locked. They were locked from the inside, and this had never been before. So I go around the side door, she's coming down in one of those see-through jobs, the shorty pajama type things, and I knew damn well she wasn't in 'em when the hell I left. So I knew right away something happened. I walked right around to the front door and there was some guy standing there, ready to go out the front door. . . . She went out and she stayed out. Never walked back in the house again, I wouldn't let her back." (D.J.)

This narrator is sure that it would not have made any difference if the affair had been with a woman.[19]

As we probed the history of relationships in this community, more often than not a third party was involved. It was very rare for people just to break up without one member of a couple already being interested in someone else. Many factors converged to make the third party such an important cause for breakups. In addition to the intense interest in romance, the competition that developed around it, and the related frequency of cheating, lesbians had a strong desire to be coupled and therefore were unlikely to end a relationship before they had met a potential new partner. Furthermore, the deep emotional ties developed within a serious relationship had a momentum for continuity, and were not easily broken without the presence of a third party.

The ideology that attributed breakups to a third party did not exclude paying attention to problems within a relationship. In this community, these two ways of thinking were closely interrelated, if not integral to each other. On the one hand, the idea of weakness in a relationship could provide a rationale for the third party either to move into the couple's territory or to make clear that she was available. Arlette recalls:

"I've seen a lot of studs I liked. They got somebody and I said, 'Well, maybe one of these days. . . . ' It's just somebody I liked, somebody I feel as though I could go with. But I don't like to be back-stabbing. I don't like that. But then if I see where you're not gettin' along too well, well I got nothin' to do with that, hey, let the best man win."

Little Gerry has similar memories:

"Like you never told anybody when you were having any trouble with the woman you were going with, because if they had any designs on her they

would move right in at that point. And the accepted thing was, well, she
wanted to be with me. . . . That was commonplace all the time. It doesn't
mean you didn't go to war over it, 'cause you would. But that's how it was."

Problems in a relationship also provided a justification for the more dissatisfied
member of the couple, if she pursued or accepted a third party. On the other
hand, acknowledging this weakness often provided a framework for the person
who was left to understand what had happened without simply blaming either her
own failings or the new couple. It also allowed both members of the couple an
opportunity to reflect on the internal dynamics of the relationship and to learn
better ways of handling their new relationships.

Common problems that led couples to break up in the 1940s and 1950s included
intense jealousy, a lover relationship evolving into a friendship, alcoholism, and
general incompatibility. The atmosphere of competition and the ever-present
possibility for discreet cheating or ending a relationship made jealousy a multidimensional problem in the lesbian community. Jealousy could explain breakups in
two ways. Philosophically, if women weren't so jealous they would have been able
to overlook one another's affairs and stay together. Several narrators expressed
that view, often negatively comparing gay women's possessiveness to gay men's
tolerance.

But jealous accusations in and of themselves could be so intense in both the
Black and white communities that they could be the basis for breakups, whether
or not affairs occurred.

> "Now just say if a girl would come up and ask me to dance. If the girl I'm
> with is the jealous type and she doesn't want me to dance, well naturally to
> keep the peace I may not dance. . . . It happened like that a lot of times, the
> girls, the fems would come up and ask the butch to dance. . . . As you
> know . . . there's some awfully jealous women out there. Believe me, I know.
> I had a girl once, when we'd go out she would want all of my attention, all
> of it. She wouldn't want me to dance with any[body]. She didn't even want
> me to socialize with people. So I didn't keep her very long because she was
> cramping my style. I couldn't be social." (Debra)

Fems disliked jealousy as well. Joanna recalls with distaste how her sociability was
limited by her partners and is convinced that this causes many fems to leave
relationships.

> "[Women are] too jealous. They're consuming. And I think this is bad. You're
> an individual, you eventually want to get away. It's too much like this
> togetherness. I have to be able to do my own thing, I can't stand a shadow.
> . . . Like where you're always together, forever. I think you get tired of this.
> I mean I think this is what happens in a relationship. But women . . . everybody
> I've ever known, that ever got away from anybody was because of this problem
> they couldn't stand it. [For me] especially with Renée, [she was] very possessive.
> And like, if you were out, say you're out for an evening, and I'd be talking to

someone. Don't forget, I had known a lot more people than she did in Buffalo. And she always would say, 'What do you find so much to talk about with so-and-so?' But it's because you've known somebody for so many years, you do have a lot to talk about.... I never felt that I was cruising or flirting or anything, I just like people.... If I like somebody I'm very demonstrative, I'm affectionate.... But as I said, women, they don't allow for this kind of thing and I think that's bad.... Everybody you talk to you don't have an ulterior motive. But guys [gay men] don't do this."

A very different kind of problem developed in relationships when lovers became close friends and therefore found it impossible to maintain romance and passion. The intimacy and closeness of living together had undercut the tensions around gendered difference required by their erotic system. Although only two narrators, a fem and a butch, explicitly mention this problem, they do so repeatedly. Since they were not close friends, it is our guess that this experience was fairly common.

"I think the first five years [with Renée] we were lovers. And then I would say the last three years we drifted further apart and became just friends.... And it wasn't that I was attracted to anybody. It just happened and ... it happened so quickly. It probably took a long time happening but to me it seemed like it happened so fast that I wasn't aware of it. But actually it was happening so slowly that I wasn't aware of it. You know each day was another day of ... where you know you were good friends, that's it." (Joanna)

This issue was extremely difficult for the couple to discuss, but when they did so, it became clear that the absence of romance was unacceptable, at least to Joanna's partner. "Well it became a problem because neither of us wanted to talk about it. And that's bad. But we eventually did talk about it.... I just said I couldn't do it.... Actually she was really more romantic than I was [and couldn't stay in the relationship without romance]." When questioned about why some of her lover relationships evolved into friendships she explains: "Because ... mentally they're no longer your lover, physically no way could they be. You start thinking of them differently. And you really do. You feel you enjoy going out with them, you enjoy living with them, but it would be like living with a roommate."

Another problem articulated by narrators was alcoholism. Many relationships suffered and a number broke up because one or both members drank to excess. Debra describes a relationship of the 1950s in which her partner's drinking was a major problem.

"Yeah. I went with Ernestine for three years but at the time I knew she wasn't drinking like she was drinking [in later years]. And that's why we quit, because she drank too much. She was a nice person. I don't think I could ever meet a girl no better than Ernestine, but I couldn't stand that drinking. When I met her, the first two years we were together, she didn't drink like that. And then she started drinking, heavy, and I told her, well I says, 'I can't put up with that. If there's anything I don't want it's an alcoholic.'. . . So she wouldn't stop, so we separated."

Bert ascribes many of the problems that led to the demise of one of her relationships to both her and her lover's drinking habits. "I think that our relationship . . . would have been different. Where we had our problems was 'cause we drank; we'd get into some knock-down drag-outs when we were drinking." Some narrators, like Melanie, analyze their breakups as having stemmed from incompatible lifestyles.

"We weren't getting along real good. Her life was altogether different from mine. She was up entertaining all night. And I had to go to work every morning. . . . She called me one day and said she wanted to break up. She went with some Black girls, she joined the James C. Strait show.[20] I took her to the train. She went on the road and I saw her a few times when she came back."

Frequently people see a combination of factors as leading to breakups. Joanna gives a complex analysis of a relationship that lasted for five and one-half years during the 1960s.

"After six years we became [friends], more like a kid sister. I think I felt differently towards her. I was more protective. . . . She was more vulnerable . . . I mean towards people. Like everything that happened she really and truly was a very bold type or irresponsible kid. . . . She was very different [from my previous partners] . . . not any less lovable or anything like that but very irresponsible. I mean nothing bothered her. I mean really, nothing really did bother her. And I think I became more protective. I became the stronger and . . . I didn't like [that] too well. I just felt that it was too one-sided. And she had a drinking problem . . . It wasn't anything that she could help. She was just a weaker person."

This case is a good example of how the presence of a third party and the problems within a relationship were both used to explain breakups. As clear as Joanna is about the evolution of difficulties in this relationship, at another point in her story, she also mentions a third party as the immediate factor that finally ended the relationship.

"Well, I had gone to [Florida] to visit my brother and when I came back, three weeks later, she told me that she had been out. . . . And that sort of made me feel kind of funny, and I thought, this is ridiculous, what am I doing in this situation? It's crazy. But actually as I said, we had become better friends than lovers, and I think that this was the start of it. I really didn't blame her because . . . well our relationship went from being lovers to being more like sisters. That is what happened. And we became very good friends."

When asked if she was hurt that her lover had become interested in someone else, she replies:

> "A little bit, but I can't honestly say that my whole life fell apart. I was hurt because I didn't expect it to be done when I was away. I don't know, maybe that was the point, that it was done behind my back. But as I said I don't really blame her, 'cause if I did I wouldn't be friends with her today."

Narrators who came out in the 1950s frequently see drinking in combination with cheating as leading to a breakup.

> "So but we did stay together three years. My heart was broke when we split up but there were just so many things. She was cheating on me at the end, she was seeing another woman. She was seeing someone who was the best friend of a friend of mine and that's like, you know, 'get out of that.' She was drinking a lot. We went through a lot. We started out good, we didn't end up so hot, it was heartbreaking. We were not friends for a long, long time. I was very bitter, I was nasty to her." (Bell)

Sometimes, multiple problems would cause the relationship to degenerate quickly. Melanie remembers how bad a relationship was that lasted only two years. "We lived together. That was a bad relationship, a horrible relationship. She liked to fight. She liked to fight physical. I don't know why, if because she used to drink a lot or because, because she wanted to be with Jill not with me. We didn't get along good at all."

What is striking about these analyses of the problematic dynamics of relationships is their lack of a psychological dimension. Identifying the ways an individual's personality contributes to the problems in a relationship was not part of working-class lesbian culture. Popular psychology, at the time, was hostile to homosexuals and to women. Its ideas were not attractive or relevant to lesbians. Few sought professional help and couples counseling was unknown.

Narrators' explanations are not limited to blaming the presence of a third party or reflections on the complex problems of a relationship. They also think that gay oppression and homophobia, even though they might not use these terms, put a strain on relationships and contributed to their dissolution. Participating in a public community not only brought lesbians together, but heightened the possibility of exposure to the outside world. D.J. remembers leaving her first serious relationship in the late 1940s to ease the tension in her girlfriend's family. "And I guess when they found out sister was involved with somebody else and not of the opposite sex, they started on her. So to save arguments and save her I just took off on that one. . . . I still cared for her. We seen each other afterwards, but [not] as far as the living [together]."

Arlette vividly describes the ongoing tension in relationships caused by the pressure to be more discreet.

"I would get mad with her because [I'd] say, 'Let's go out tonight and you dress up like a girl.' She wouldn't do that. Because there are a lot of clubs, they don't want you comin' in men's attire. And the clubs I worked in [in New York City], she'd like to come because all the top stars used to come there, like Sam Cook and all them. And once in a while they let her in, but then they got to the point where they didn't want her to come in dressed like that. And she would have the feeling that, well, if I can't go dressed like I want to I don't have to go. But it's not the point. . . . Her mother didn't know she was gay, and every time her mother came to the house she would rush back, 'Give me one of your outfits, give me one of your blouses, give me a pair of your slacks or give me your dress.' 'Well no. You don't care about how anybody else feels, let your mother see you in your men's clothes.' 'Cause I felt like this, you should have both kinds. . . . If you['re] going to an all gay place or all gay affair . . . that was fine. . . . But just every day and everywhere we go here you go in your men's clothes and then get indignant because they won't let you in. But yet still, when your mother or somebody comes, now you want to dress up like a girl. 'No. Uh uh. That['s] the way you feel about public, feel the same way about your family.' That's the way I feel, and I wouldn't give them to her. She got awful mad at me. She'd put mine on anyway."

Although in Arlette's relationship the tension over appearance did not lead to a breakup, in many cases it did. Sandy is particularly graphic about how her choice to be public about her lesbianism made life difficult for her partners and caused tension in her relationships.

"Relationships didn't last long, then, because there was so much against you that if one felt like, well I don't care if people know, maybe your partner did. Maybe there was a family situation or job situation, public situation, they couldn't be seen with you. . . . You had to sneak and hide and pretty soon you thought, well, what the hell, I want to be me. So things didn't last too long those days. The only ones that did last were the ones that, oh, didn't look gay, I'll put it that way. And there are still those today . . . I mean the majority, now I'm not saying one hundred percent but I'd say . . . ninety [percent]. Because sooner or later somebody would find out. If someone sees you, 'Oh, my God. We can't be seen together any more. Oh my boss saw me. I'll lose my job. Oh, we can't go in that restaurant, my brother goes there. I can't bring you home, you look funny.' . . . They [butches] wanted to be with a person; they wanted to prove that they are . . . whatever it is, take care of you, and then geez, she's embarrassed to let me see their family; she's ashamed of me. Go in this bar, oh I'm not ashamed but she is. I can't do this. I can't do that. I can't call her too often or someone's going to say 'What's going on?' And so pretty soon you say, 'Oh, the hell with it.' So you go and find someone else. You['d] be with them for a while, until they got nervous."

Gay oppression also led people to return to straight life, which in some cases meant breaking up relationships.[21] Joanna explains the breakup of her first relationship, which had lasted six years and was quite successful, by focusing on her guilt and the influence of her family.

> "Well . . . I really don't know what happened, honestly. I can't really put my finger on any particular thing. Many things. I probably sort of had a guilt complex, family-wise. I was really influenced by my family a lot. As I still am . . . and I just decided to go back and live with my mother. And that's exactly what I did."

She subsequently dated a man for one and one-half years and then decided to marry him, but it lasted only a short time.

Annie explains that desire for the security that gay life could not offer drew some women into straight life, including herself, for fifteen years.

> "All of a sudden one day as you start getting older you sit there and you think, 'Where have you been and where are you going?' and this is where a lot of kids, a lot of fems go straight, 'cause they want security . . . or they fall for the guy. You just can't get into a marriage and not have feelings as far as I'm concerned. But you have that security. While that lasts, as long as that lasts."

The marginal nature of gay life also meant that gay relationships had no support to help them weather difficult times. D.J. captures the lack of social incentives for staying together by expressing that gay relationships left no room for error. It was just too easy to leave.

> "Somebody does something wrong, there's no second chances. See there is not children involved where you have to stay together. . . . There's nothing written, you know. You can go wherever you want to go. And as soon as you do something wrong, or your partner, then that was it. Very rarely you sat down and discussed it; unless, at that time, you were one of the fortunate ones that owned a home together or had something material to keep you together. . . . You couldn't leave so much then."

Our narrators' understanding of the forces leading to breakups goes a long way toward explaining why their relationships inevitably ended. Their approach highlights the ways in which they created their own distinctive contradictions by valuing the pursuit of romance and social life, as well as lasting relationships in the context of the oppression of lesbian community and culture. Unlike gays or lesbians who came out since 1970, our narrators' explanations significantly underplay psychological factors.[22] Although the personal-development emphasis of contemporary lesbian culture unquestionably adds new and worthwhile perspectives, it may also deprive us of an understanding of the social forces that shape lesbian relationships and thereby link us unconsciously to an implicitly heterosexist model.

SURVIVING BREAKUPS

Although breakups were an integral part of lesbian experience in the 1940s and the 1950s, they were always painful. Arden expresses the opinion of most narrators that emotional pain caused by the dissolution of a relationship is one of the most difficult parts of gay life. "The hardest thing about gay life is the heartbreak. That can be very traumatic. That would always sour me for a while. Then I would begin to go out again and not look to the right or left, and finally, I would be all right again. But any of the bad breakups leave a mark" (Arden).

Leslie, who was present at this interview, responds: "I don't think that has changed much. I feel that I was lucky here, that Thea was the only one who walked out on me." Most narrators would agree that although both partners in a breakup experience pain, it is probably more difficult for the person who is left.

Bell remembers the painful loss involved in a breakup. In reminiscing about one of her favorite girlfriends she says: "Sometimes I think that I had wished that we could have stayed together forever. But nothing is forever and always is a lie." We asked her if she really believed that.

> "Well I don't know, I read a book that said that one time and it just seemed in my life that everything that I have ever really loved or really wanted was— I lost or it didn't last or it just wasn't meant to be or however you could term that. It seemed like we stayed together for a while and then we just split, it was just like gone with the wind."

In the rare instances where a couple raised children together and broke up while the child was young, the partner who was left without the child suffered tremendously. Ronni still feels the pain of her loss of a girlfriend's child in the 1960s, and argues that lesbian relationships must become legal so that lesbians have some concrete basis for continued contact with the children they help raise.

> "I almost had a nervous breakdown over living with a girl for almost four years, who had a little girl who I became so very fondly attached to, that when we broke up, it almost put me in a mental hospital. Believe me, I went completely berserk. I just thought that my daughter was torn away from me. . . . My little Rita left town with her mother, went all the way to California and I never seen her again. And even to this day sometimes when I think about her I cry because, it really ripped me apart. Now if I had been married to her, legally, and I was able to legally support that child, and be legally responsible for her, to this day I'd still be able to see her."

As one would expect, given the amount of emotional trauma involved, the majority of relationships did not end easily. Phil recalls:

"It's a lot of hassle and trouble, because I have never yet broken off a relationship without trouble except the very first girlfriend I had. . . . But everyone after that, a lot of troubles before they realized it was over. But it was never, 'Well I'm sorry it's over and good luck.' And they say good luck to you. No I've never been fortunate enough."

Sometimes in the pain of rejection a woman became vicious and went so far as exposing an ex-girlfriend as a lesbian at work or to her family. This was particularly problematic in the case of married women, who risked their relationships with their children. Phil remembers one ex-girlfriend: "She called my husband, told him about it. She called my sister, she called my daughter. She told everybody, gave [a] list of names that people were my friends. . . . She said that I was having a relationship with everyone." This led to an argument between Phil and her husband and Phil moved out.

"We broke up, and I was away from the kids for four days and I couldn't take it, couldn't stand it. I was willing to do anything. Luckily I didn't have to be the one to concede, he did. He called and said he wanted to talk and we talked and he said he was sorry he believed everything, he didn't really think it was true with me and all that. So I went along with that, just to be with the kids. And I maintained a sort of relationship, not like before, because he wasn't as trusting then. But it worked all right."

Another time, a jilted lover called this narrator's husband, but "by that time it was old hat," and the damage was minimal.

Division of the lesbian household at the time of a breakup was always problematic and did not seem to follow a set pattern, but rather depended on the emotional dynamics of the situation and the way household finances had been handled during the relationship.[23]

"I know one couple broke up and the butch just walked out of the house, left everything. I've heard of others breaking up, and one owes the other X amount of dollars for their share. I've heard of some that have walked out and took just some parts of the furniture, maybe the living room, and the other kept the refrigerator or they worked it out that way. . . . There's no set pattern on that. . . . It goes all the way back to the way you break up. I mean if you walk out and it's a violent breakup, maybe the other one won't even let you back in to get your clothes. If you break up in a friendly manner, you work things out. If you're the one that's doing the breaking up; you probably have a guilty conscience and leave everything. If you break up and you still love the person that you're breaking up with, you still want her to have everything." (Phil)

Although the emotional context is important, lesbians were also practical, thinking about what each had put in. When the butch paid for more, she was likely to want to keep more, whereas when butch and fem shared the expenses they were more likely to divide things equally. D.J., who had supported her girlfriend, even though the girlfriend worked, remembers how she kept what she wanted when she threw out her girlfriend for sleeping with a man. "She took what she wanted, but what I wanted it stayed there. No way in hell would she get it. 'Cause I said, 'You take out what the hell you paid for fine, but what I paid for stays right here.'" Vic remembers that, in her first relationship, she and her girlfriend had shared everything exactly, and they used the same principle in dividing their possessions when they broke up.

> "She's the first woman I ever lived with. . . . But we put our money together. Our money was right there together. I didn't pay and she didn't pay. The only thing that we had different was that she had a car at the time, and whenever she'd make a car payment that same amount of money would go into my bank account. And when we did leave each other, after many years, she took her car and whatever she had, and I had what was in the bank account, because I didn't have a car, she had it. . . . Well when we broke up I never got a set of lamps, because one she got and one I got."

In spite of the difficulties involved, all narrators survived the pain, most of them to go on to build other relationships. Right after the breakups people were often devastated. Toni recalls, "There were people weeping over their lovers and broken relationships, and the music on the juke box was a lot of the torch songs." She remembers that sometimes lesbians openly expressed their misery at the Carousel.

> "Occasionally there'd be people who'd slit their wrists out in the alley. Nobody ever died and nobody ever was in intensive care, it was more just the way people behaved then. That occasionally somebody would slice their hand or break a glass with their hand and bleed, or go in the bathroom and cut their wrist and go out in the back alley and bleed."

The despair passed, however. Not one narrator told us about remaining in love with an ex-lover for any period of time, although Joanna did describe the experience of a friend who could not seem to get over one particular woman. The story suggests that this kind of behavior was neither fostered nor encouraged.

> "The girl left her to go with someone else. And she carried a torch for many years for this girl, which I thought was odd. Because once somebody left me, I might carry a torch for a short time, but I don't think I would dwell on it. It wouldn't bother me that much. 'Cause I'd figure if she left me, I couldn't kid myself into thinking that I was any special kind of person to her. I don't think I could carry a torch that long. . . . But I don't think Marion ever faced reality. She probably blamed the other girl. I guess. She'd play records and cry and this kind of thing, and I thought, 'Oh God.' And I think this probably influenced [her next] relationship with Susan, which, I felt sorry for Susan."

The tradition of camaraderie and socializing that created the conditions for breakups also provided support in these hard times. Leslie and Arden agree that their friends supported them until they got over their hurt. "Friends would call you. Everybody knew everybody's business. You were a tight little group" (Leslie). When asked if people would support either side of a couple, she responds: "It was easier for the masculine side. They were more surrounded in camaraderie. Butches had a stronger support group while usually fems did not have lifelong friends." Joanna, when asked if people took sides when a couple broke up, gives a slightly different point of view, emphasizing the importance of enduring friendship, be it with a butch or a fem.

> "Everybody offers advice . . . y'know, on what you shouldn't have done or what you didn't do . . . but I don't really think they took sides. . . . I've known a lot of people that have gone with a lot of girls, and my friendship was never affected by it. I mean I never really took sides because I didn't have to. I mean my loyalty was always to one or the other in the beginning so when they did break up or went with someone else, I always stayed friends with the person I had been friendly with at the beginning. Because actually she was my friend."

Perhaps Leslie and Arden were responding to the fact that butch camaraderie was more institutionalized, while fem friendships were more individual. Joanna certainly had lifelong fem friends. "My one friend was married, also, for a short period like myself. . . . I met her when Ralph Martin's was open, now that's a long time ago. I've been friends with her since 1945 and we're still friends, we still see each other two or three times a week, at least two. [She] stays over. I go to her house." The same pattern of support existed in the 1950s, with butches having the more public friendship networks and fems having a few important personal friends.

Some women transformed their relationships with their ex-lovers into long-term friendships, thereby making their emotional loss less severe. Joanna felt quite strongly about remaining friends with her ex-lovers: "Because I think if you live with someone, you love them, and you have to like them. Something about them that's there and it just never dies. . . . Like if something happens to Renée or Leslie or Donna, I become upset. Like if somebody hurts them or if they're unhappy . . . it does affect me." Bell prides herself on being friends with at least some of her ex-girlfriends. She says of one:

> "To this day we are still friends. She's a lot of help to me right now in my life, in certain things, the problem that I am going through. . . . I still feel very, very, very good when I'm with her. She makes me laugh, she lifts my spirits. There isn't anything really that I could say about her that would be anything but a great person. Beautiful human being."

Sometimes these friendships still maintained an undercurrent of erotic tension, as indicated by Arlette, who includes her ex-girlfriends in her social life.

> "We remained very close friends, to the point that I still have some I used to go with will call me up. 'What are you doin'? Well let's go to a movie. Let's

go to dinner.' Maybe for a week and then I won't see them any more. I have some that make that a yearly thing, every two years. I get courted all over again. And then we don't go any further then. We talk about old times, go out to dinner, we might see [each other] for a week, have a good time, go to parties, and then I may not see them any more. They might call me on my birthday, or once every six months. 'I was think[ing] about you, how you doin'?' "

Since many of a butch's ex-girlfriends went back to being straight, maintaining friendships was more difficult for the butch. Joanna explains about one of her own ex's: "There's two ex-lovers of Leslie, and they're both married. They married fellas, and they have their families. . . . They can't be close friends 'cause they have different lives."

But it is not only the marriage of an ex that prevents a friendship. Many narrators feel that moving from a lover relationship to a friendship was and remains very difficult. Phil remembers marveling that some ex-lovers could, and only recently has been able to achieve this herself.

"I've seen it. I've seen a lot of it. I never thought I could be and I used to be amazed at seeing girls that had gone together and broken up and then meet each other with their other girlfriends at a place and be friendly. And I thought, gee, I don't think I could ever do that. I would be hurting too much. But I was wrong, you could be with, with certain [ones]. Depends how you break up. . . . See if you break up stormy and vicious and you hurt each other, or the one hurts you, well, no, you can't be. But [you can] if you break up like this ex friend of mine, my ex-lover and I did, in just a friendship state."

Lesbians had not found a foolproof method for maintaining friendships with ex-lovers, but they had certainly made some progress in that direction. The emotional closeness and intimacy that couples built with one another was, in many cases, strong and flexible enough to withstand a change in the definition of the relationship.[24]

There was no prescribed method for healing from the hurt of breakups. The community assumed that its members were strong enough to recover. Often the fastest and possibly most complete healing came through falling in love again, which most narrators did repeatedly throughout their lives.

EXPERIENCING A LIFETIME OF SERIAL MONOGAMY

Using the oral-history method, we have come to know not only the details about serial monogamy in the 1940s and 1950s, but also the reactions of lesbians to a lifetime of such relationships. This long-term view provides essential evidence for confirming our analysis, which posits that lesbians, despite extremely oppressive conditions, were not simply passive victims of circumstances that made it impossible to create lasting relationships. Instead, they created a system of relationships based in their own culture that offered a good deal of satisfaction along with the heartache.

Narrators' testimonies about the place of relationships in their lives over a period of thirty-five to fifty years suggests that lesbians have survived serial monogamy with dignity, energy, and a continued love of women. Some narrators have emerged from a life of serial monogamy with a consistent optimism, their self-confidence intact, ready to face the challenge of new relationships. Others have experienced emotional devastation for periods of time, but then have healed themselves in order to try again. Some have become cynical and protect themselves by not expecting too much. Only a very few have become disillusioned and have chosen to live alone or to try the straight life. As we stated earlier, some lesbians tended to establish longer relationships while others followed a pattern of shorter relationships. Quite unexpectedly, we found that whether people had a history of long or relatively short relationships had little or no bearing on their feelings about serial monogamy—either their optimism or their disillusionment.

Several narrators who experienced a series of long relationships continue to approach new involvements today with energy and excitement. Matty makes an eloquent statement of faith that serial monogamy can and does provide happiness:

> "I really love this life. . . . I've enjoyed it and I am enjoying it and I've had a lot of heartaches, but the good times outweigh the heartaches. . . . A lot of people come to me for advice now because I'm older, like if they're breaking up with somebody, and I can only tell them what I've experienced. You're with somebody who you love very very dearly, and when the time comes for you to part I don't think you or the other person has a choice in it. I think God is saying, 'You've been together for as long a time as you need to give each other what you have to offer. . . . Now it's time for you to go on to help somebody else who needs your help.' And you always think, 'Oh, God, I'm going to die. I love that person so much and I don't have them any more.' But God always provides, and the very next person that you do become entangled with you love so much more than the person you left. There's so much more feeling there and compatibility. And it just keeps going on. Each person seems to fit right into your pattern. And it isn't like that I go with a girl for two months, three months. . . . I go with a girl for five years, five and one-half years; I've been with one for six years, I've been with one for eleven years."

This kind of optimism also exists among narrators who experienced a series of shorter relationships throughout their lives. Arden, who talks in the previous section about the difficulty of, but necessity for, recovery from breakups, was a popular butch who had few if any relationships that lasted more than two years. She actively courted women until recently, but thinks she no longer has the sexual energy. "Well I'm seventy-five years, and its gone completely. I can tell you the last time I had sex." Leslie, who was at the interview, teases her by telling us, "Get out your notebook" to mark down this important confession by such a gallant and charming butch. Arden continues: "Let's see it was five years ago, I was seventy. But not any more. I couldn't perform any more." She had lived for the past twenty years with a dear friend who had been her girlfriend years ago. They provided each other with close companionship as they aged, and gave each other the opportunity to have relationships if they desired. The friend had recently died and Arden missed her greatly and was feeling lonely. Since this interview, we have heard that she has gone out to the bars several times, indicating that she is still interested in an active social life with lesbians.

Many narrators were not able to be this resilient, and had to take a break from relationships. Bert explains that after a thirteen year-relationship that ended in the early 1960s, followed by a three and one-half year-relationship, she lived alone for two and one-half years: "When I met Dotty, [I was] swearing that I would never get involved again. . . . because of bitterness. Just felt that I was tired of breaking up relationships." Six years later, at the time of our interview, she was still in this relationship.

Bell, who had a tenuous relation to gay life for ten years beginning in the early 1970s, is once again feeling positive about her relationships. After a series of short relationships, she became quite bitter.

> "During that time . . . I was very bitter and I just didn't feel like I wanted to be bothered with anyone. I felt like I could care less . . . if I ever had anybody again. Like this one friend asked me, 'Well do you feel like you want to go straight and get married or be with a man? or something like this?' I said, 'Well how stupid.' And they brought up the thing, 'Your friend Monica did.' I said, 'Well that's Monica, that's not me.' I said, 'I like women, and the fact still remains, and whether I'm alone, celibate or whatever I am I will remain the way I am. . . . ' Yes, I stayed by myself a long time. . . . There was quite a few years in between there. . . . Well, I had seen people in between, I had maybe slept with some of them . . . but nothing that's worth discussing really."

She actually considered going straight for a while, and attended a church that "was a ministry for people who want to be delivered from homosexuality," but left "because I'm comfortable with my sexuality and this is where I want to be."

In 1980 she met a young woman and began a satisfactory relationship, which renewed her faith in lesbian life. "Like I say, there have been times in my life when I have felt, 'God, what else? How much more can you take?' Like felt like I was just going nowhere and didn't know if I really wanted to be with anyone. But then I met this girl named Colleen." She liked this relationship and was not bitter when it ended. At the time of our interview, she was interested in someone her own age with similar life experience. Her state of mind combines a wistful longing for relationships that would last with a willingness to keep trying new relationships.

"I think this life in itself is tough enough, sometimes you really feel that you have found someone that's going to be there for you. I guess a lot of times I thought, 'Well, I'm going to be with this person for the rest of my life.' I think I felt that way about Gerry, I think I felt that way about Joy. I'm sure we've all been there and said, 'Well, I will never love another as long as I live.' But then we have to go back to the same thing, that after Joy and after Gerry there was another one."

For some narrators, their dissatisfaction and bitterness led to an extended break from committed relationships—fifteen or more years—before attempting another. At the time of her last interview, D.J. had been single for about thirteen years, and was lonely but uninterested in relationships. She claims to have given her all to them—holding steadfastly to monogamy, supporting her fem—and is still bewildered by her failures. Her negative experiences colored her entire view of gay life.

"See The Well of Loneliness can apply to every lesbian going or any gay boy or anyone that's in this life. Because the gay life in itself is a very lonely life. There's no security, very few really get along in years of relationships, it's a dead-end thing, it really is and I know it for fifty-three years. And you end up you have nothing. I have nothing to show for my fifty-three years of being homosexual. Outside of experiences here and experiences there, but nothing really to put my hand on and say, 'I accomplished something,' which I haven't. . . . You can go with somebody for a length of time, and then what have you got? Now this can happen in regular life too; in fact it's even happened in my own family. You can live with someone for a certain length of time, get divorced. But [gay life] is a different setup altogether, because you have too many obstacles to cover."

She does not contemplate leaving the gay life, but she does think that if she had her life to live over, she would lead it differently.

"If I wasn't gay to start with, or if I had acquired it later in life, I don't think very truthfully, I don't think I'd get married or have children, but I would never have indulged in it as much as I have, 'cause I say it's too lonely a life. You have very few friends, that really would understand the whole thing about it. . . . But if anybody that has any inclination of being not a lesbian, don't be. . . . It's too rough a life. . . . I mean I can't say it's all been bad. I really can't. There's times that I have enjoyed myself."

Several years after completing her interviews, D.J. started a new relationship with someone her own age whom she brought out, and she is ecstatic. The dramatic change in D.J.'s life is typical of these old-timers. We had to continually revise this section of the book as relationships ended and new ones began. Serial monogamy is indeed an ongoing system; relationships are not carved in stone.

Pearl, who was very discontented with a ten-year relationship that ended in the mid-1960s, was single for even longer—twenty years—than D.J. However, she did not feel lonely. Her relationships with her family were important to her. In addition, she developed close friendships, some with butch women, one with whom she lived for a short time. She missed having a love relationship but that was not a priority for her. "It's not that I was tired of it or anything, it's just that I [came] back to this area and I have family here and they've kept me pretty busy. [My children] and my sisters, they all live here. So it keeps me busy that way, and I have a granddaughter she's gonna be twenty-five." Recently, in her sixties, she started going out again, and felt she was at a point in her life where she could love a person even more deeply than when she was young, when she was running around too much.

> "Well I don't know, I think you could put it this way, people that I had met then . . . I could really like again. I mean there could be a relationship there again, that didn't get off to a very good start at that time. But you think about a person for years, and you remember them and then you meet them again and I think it could become a relationship."

Shortly after this interview she began a relationship with such a person, but it lasted only a short time.

A small number of narrators were so soured by their past relationships that they did not want to have any more to do with lesbian love. Debra tells of her sad experience with betrayal.

> "Well, my feelings were this. I had lost eight years. . . . Yes, I do feel that it was a loss and after that I didn't want to get in a long relationship. . . . A relationship fine, but not that long, and I wasn't even really particular about living with someone. But although I did live with someone after that, I didn't make it that long. . . . Well, the simple reason is the way we had broke up. If we had just broke up, and she went and got a guy, that would have been different. She started to fool around with the guy, and then when she and I broke up, she let the guy go. She did try to get me back, but I didn't want her back then. . . . I was interested in something else then. . . . In other words I didn't have the confidence in her, that I had once had. So I didn't want to get up and tie up some more years, and the same thing gonna happen over again. . . . I felt that it really soured the years that we had spent together. And especially after we did break up, I found out that she had been seeing guys the whole time we were together, not just this one guy. . . . Well, I felt this way, if she wanted a guy, wasn't no one stopping her from getting a guy. Why not leave the women alone and go on and get a guy? So that's why I felt it was a complete waste of eight years."

Her next relationship lasted three and one-half years and broke up because of her girlfriend's alcoholism. Then Debra dropped out of gay life, which was quite an extraordinary turn of events, given that she had been in the life since she was a teenager in the 1930s. "I never got out of the life until ten years ago. I did quit ten years ago. And I got disgusted behind a girl and I really quit." Melanie also developed relationships with men after she turned fifty.

"Since then [my last break-up] I haven't been involved with no women. . . . Well, I met a man that I liked, so, I don't know, I'll see how that goes. O.K. so far. . . . This is the first time. . . . Well, naturally, [it's] different than being with a woman, but I don't know. I like him, so I'll see how that works out. So far so good."

At the time of the interview, Melanie was hesitant about her relationship, but she has since married the man she was seeing. In most cases of women turning to straight life in their older years, they never completely sever their ties with past friends.

Some narrators were cynical about the possibilities for lesbian relationships due to the hurt, and lack of trust and understanding, but never gave up on them. Vic is one of these.

"You're talking to a cynic, you know. How can I say that to you? One time in my life I was ever hurt by a relationship, I could care, breakup, who cares. I've never been with only but one person that I ever loved. . . . Terrible thing to say, I know. That's a waste of love, but, that's the only one I ever did. Probably never will again."

The same attitude is expressed in Vic's comments about her current relationship and her prognosis for its future. "I don't know, but it doesn't matter, just keep truckin' down the line." But her cynicism doesn't come from simply feeling that others have betrayed her. She knows very well how her own active interest in the pursuit of romance shaped what happened in her life, and like many narrators, has no regrets.

"No, I would never change what I had in the 1950s, no. I love women, Liz. There's not any of them that I [would not have] like[d] to enjoy what I did with them, and what we did with each other. I don't regret nothing. . . . Let me put it this way, it was nicer than I thought. . . . I just like to be with women, I'm a real mean fucking machine, and I like to be with women. That's a fact."

Arlette's cynicism is also not rooted in the hurt of betrayal but rather in disappointment in the failed potential of understanding between women in a couple. "'Cause to me, really gay life to me is no different, there's not that much to talk about. As far as companionship and trust, you can forget it, I found." She challenges us to tell her what's special about gay relationships.

"What I don't understand, since you brought this tape in here, why . . . the idea of two women together seems to get lost? It gets to the point where everything gets out of its perspective. Lesbians are supposed to be together because of that fact that two women knew how they want to be talked to, how they wanted to be made love to, how they wanted understanding and how they wanted all this, but it doesn't end up being that way when it gets down to it. . . . Ain't nothing too much gay, if ladies know about each other, because most of them, it gets to the point where they're not thinking about how you feel."

Arlette is not sure what the future will bring, but is not afraid of aging, because she places exceptional emphasis on learning and growth, the qualities that make her a continuing leader.

"When you [were] a teenager you thought one way. When you got twenty-one a lot of things you thought [were] cool when you [were] a teenager you found out [were] stupid and you stopped doing that. Then when you got older and kept changing you found a lot of things you thought you couldn't cope with and you couldn't understand, you found out it was nothing to it. . . . But you find some people that do not mature at all. If you don't grow through life itself, then you are more retarded than a retarded person. It's all in developing your mind. Because I found that myself. People do worry about [aging], because I'm getting old, and I don't want to be alone. But I will if I have to."

The experiences of narrators makes clear that the system of serial monogamy did not give lesbians the certainty of a partner with whom they would age. Rather, most lesbians who were part of the public lesbian community during the 1940s or 1950s needed to keep looking for partners throughout their lives. In this situation, many lesbians relied on other sources of emotional support. For those who were part of the core groups at Ralph Martin's and Winters, their support network of friends continues until today. As the numbers decreased due to death and relocation, the Winters and Ralph Martin's group combined to strengthen their friendships. Leslie and Arden who are in their seventies keep in touch with one another weekly and go out with one another regularly. They also help one another if needed. They mentioned others from their group whom they see regularly as well. This friendship network is reinforced by the fact that some people within it had been lovers. Thus when Joanna was extremely ill, we were impressed by how all three of her ex-lovers took special care of her, going to see her regularly. In addition she had visits from other friends.

Those who were not part of these friendship groups that began in the 1940s managed to build other kinds of support systems. Some, particularly those who were married and had children, relied more on their families. D.J., the narrator of this period who expressed the most loneliness, was never part of the core forties crowd and went on to join the tough bar lesbian crowd in the 1950s. She, therefore, did not have a strong friendship group that functioned outside of the bars. Those narrators who came out during the 1950s are primarily fifty to sixty years old today so it is impossible to say how they will adapt to old age, and if they will be as lonely as the picture D.J. painted. It is our guess that they will be unless they have managed since the 1960s to develop supportive friendships.

Despite the fact that loneliness was not a recurrent theme in narrators' life stories, but in keeping with the uncertain future implied by serial monogamy, many narrators spontaneously mentioned the dream of creating an old-age home for lesbians. The existence of such similar visions among people who had not seen one another in years, or maybe had never spoken a word to one another in their lives, was striking. The desire for a lesbian old-age home seems to us to be rooted in and expressive of the values of serial monogamy. Lesbians wanted a permanent relationship that would support them in old age but did not have ultimate faith in achieving it. At the same time, they continued to value community—the possibility of socializing with others—until the end of their lives. An old-age home is an adaptation of bar life for the elderly lesbian.

By identifying serial monogamy as an alternate system of emotional bonding, we are able to draw attention away from stereotyped assumptions about failure or immaturity, and to focus on the complexities and accomplishments of lesbian relationships. This perspective also allows us to see that the public lesbian community of the 1940s and 1950s was more of a forerunner of contemporary lesbian-feminist relationships than is usually recognized. Although lesbian culture of the 1940s and 1950s did not include the concepts of autonomy and nonmonogamy so prevalent today, it nevertheless provided a relevant tradition of support for personal strength and independence.[25] It also affirmed the importance of community.

Living within the system of serial monogamy lesbians developed many positive character traits, and certainly cannot be seen simply as victims. Individuals' lives were seen as existing for more than the perfect relationship, and lesbians did not expect to lose themselves in a relationship to the point where they could not live outside of it. In addition, women actively pursued different kinds of relationships—both casual and committed—that included sex, and, at their best, had a vision of giving and gaining unique things from each of their partners. Furthermore, the breakup of a relationship did not necessarily mean estrangement and the emotional barrenness that comes from loss and discontinuity. Many individuals attempted successfully to build strong, lasting relationships with women who had been their lovers. Countering the stereotype of the sad, isolated "queer" who faces old age alone, many lesbians maintained a continuity of contact that provided a network of loving support in their later years.

Narrators' negative and positive comments—and all the shades in between—about serial monogamy make it difficult, if not impossible, to judge whether the system of serial monogamy is primarily a reaction to extremely oppressive conditions and the internalized homophobia they generate, or a freely created lesbian alternative. Given that oppression was inescapable, serial monogamy seems to have both components. Unquestionably, lesbians expressed a desire for life-long continuous relationships that they worked to build. However, it was not simply oppression that undermined them. Socializing with other lesbians and the ever present possibility of romance, which were at the heart of this community and gave its members a great deal of pleasure, strength, and autonomy, also worked against lasting monogamous relationships. Lesbians were aware that they could give up socializing and have a better chance at maintaining their relationships, but were not willing to do so. These two conflicting approaches to relationships have continued into the contemporary lesbian community. Some idealize life-long relationships and assume that without oppression and the resultant internalized homophobia, lesbians can achieve them. Others judge the committed monogamous couple to be based in patriarchy and unnecessarily restrictive. They, therefore, value socializing in community over any particular relationship and often practice nonmonogamy.[26] The unresolved debate between these philosophical positions suggests that there is a good deal of truth in narrators' comments that there hasn't been much change in relationships over time. It is perhaps too early to tell what lesbian relationships will be like if they are not formed in the context of an oppressive society.

8

"IT CAN'T BE A ONE-WAY STREET": COMMITTED BUTCH-FEM RELATIONSHIPS

"I'm glad some of my ex's weren't here [at this reading]. They always thought they did everything I said because they wanted to, they didn't know it was because I was bossy."

—Matty

my lady ain't no lady—

she has been known
   to speak in a loud voice,
   to pick her nose,
   stumble on a sidewalk,
   swear at her cats,
   swear at me,
   scream obscenities at men,
   paint rooms,
   repair houses,
   tote garbage,
   play basketball,
   & numerous other
   un lady like things.

my lady is definitely no lady
which is fine with me,

'cause i ain't no gentleman.
—Pat Parker, "My Lady Ain't No Lady"

The view that lesbian relationships are unfulfilling and doomed to fail extends beyond the social sciences, pervading Western culture with the power of myth. This is the way lesbian relationships have been consistently presented in literature, at least until the writings of Monique Wittig.[1] Cinema has hardly been better. The flawed relationship portrayed in *The Killing of Sister George* is a typical example.[2] Sister George, an "obvious" lesbian, jealously dominates the innocent Childie, who subsequently is saved by a sophisticated, calculating, closeted businesswoman, Mercy Croft. In analyzing the system of serial monogamy, it is tempting to focus disproportionately on the conditions that lead to discontinuity in relationships. It is equally significant and challenging, however, to understand the forces for continuity in butch-fem relationships and the dynamics of committed loving.

Despite their consciousness of the inevitability of breakups during the 1940s and 1950s, and without the institution of marriage or significant common property, butch-fem couples built strong intimate relationships. Narrators indicate two forces as important for continuity in a relationship. First is the love itself. To their minds, there is a distinct correlation between loving someone, caring for that person, desiring to share your life with her, and creating an enduring relationship.

> "Yes, I cared for her and she cared for me. I knew that. And I wanted to make it a long relationship. When you get into something like that and you love the person and everything, yeah, you think about it. Maybe this will last. . . . If you're in the life, and you like the life and you meet someone I don't see no need for running from here to there. You might as well stay in it. And you like the person well enough to share your life with them. You might as well stay in it." (Debra)

Second, at the same time that lesbians see a connection between a deep love and a lasting relationship, they also believe that they are more likely to create a lasting relationship as they grow older and settle down.

> "I got one now. I want this one to last. I don't want to get into it and then have to do a whole switch-around, and try to find someone else and get off into that. I think when you are younger it might tend to be a whirlwind thing, you know, off this day and on the next. But I think when you get older it's just like with any relationships, with a heterosexual relationship." (Piri)

Whitney tells us about a deceased girlfriend, who used to worry when she was younger that there were no older lesbians in the bars, until she realized they were home in relationships.

> "When she was younger and she first went into the bars she said. 'But where are the older people?' But then I realized . . . that older people make homes; they make long-lasting relationships, and they meet other people socially through their friends, people with like interests . . . and they take trips and they do all the things that other people do."

The absence of older people from the bars because they were home with their lasting relationships is such a pervasive part of people's memories that we have a quote from Leslie that virtually replicates this one.

Implicit in this discussion of the relative longevity of older lesbians' relationships is the routinization of love in the context of a satisfying home life. Committed relationships unquestionably had a momentum for continuity, so much so that for some they were difficult to leave. When asked about how long a relationship lasted, Bert responds: "It was almost thirteen years. I remember I always said eight years of happiness and five years of hell." This kind of comment, which suggests that a relationship lasted longer than it should have, is fairly common. Whitney reflects on the difficulty of leaving her relationship even though she recognized herself as the cause of the problems. "When you love somebody . . . when you get 'married,' for richer for poorer, for better or for worse, you don't even have to say those words, because if you have a commitment with someone it's there, and you can't walk away. Even if you're the pain, even if you're the agony . . . you can't." When pressed, Whitney adds that people stay together because they really love each other and because, "It's family. Your lover is your family." Committed relationships developed some of the complex ties and dependencies, the stickiness and messiness, that characterize U.S. kinship.[3]

When we began studying relationships we assumed that the distinction between deep and casual relationships would manifest itself in the length of time a relationship lasted. We have come to understand, however, that this judgment derives from a heterosexual model, which assumes that we will all have one serious relationship—marriage—in a lifetime, or if we are less lucky, two. Such an approach does not take into account that some lesbians tend to have longer relationships and others shorter, yet both groups tend to judge their relationships as equally important. Nor does this view validate young lesbians' relatively brief relationships, which in the heterosexual world of the 1940s and 1950s would have been preparatory to marriage, but in the lesbian world were not. Time is a subjective and relative phenomenon. "I said to Sonny [my girlfriend] one time, 'I went with her [a previous lover] a long time.' She said, 'How long?' I said, 'Three months!' 'Cause when you're twenty, three months is a long time" (Whitney).[4] The quality of feeling—its depth, its intensity—was as important as time in a person's judgment of the significance of a relationship. Commitment also was essential in determining its seriousness. "An affair I think is something you have, a relationship is something you're committed to" (Little Gerry). This variation in the longevity of lesbian relationships has led us to designate the important relationships in people's lives as "committed" rather than "long-term."

What kind of committed relationships did butch and fem couples build in the 1940s and 1950s without the support of society, and certainly outside of its conventions? What were relationships like that were gendered but lesbian and hence not fully integrated into the dominant society's system of male supremacy? When narrators describe the couple relationship, their first reference is often to it being like that of husband and wife.[5] The similarities they highlight are the gendered nature of the interaction, the living together, and the seriousness of the connection. Unquestionably, the butch-fem dynamic emphasized gendered difference between partners, with the butch being the more aggressive and more active in the public lesbian world, and the fem taking leadership in the home, providing a comfortable refuge. However, also relevant to daily life, although less talked about, almost taken for granted, was the similarity of goals among women. Butch and fem shared a desire for love, intimacy, and a good home life, all priorities held by women in general in the twentieth century. In addition, both butch and fem usually worked outside the home in a labor force that discriminated against women. The resulting power balance in the relationship is hard to define, particularly since there was no economic support for butch power and authority, and since fems were less vulnerable than butches to stigmatization as lesbians.

In discussing relationships, most butch narrators, Black, Indian, and white, emphasize their bossiness, but also the need for appropriate limits. Debra attempts to capture this balance in her description of the dynamics of the butch-fem dyad.

> "Well actually, it means that the butch is the boss. It's just the same if you have a husband. The husband is the boss. The butch makes the rules. . . . But it doesn't always work that way, as you know. . . . We'll just say how it was back there, it was just like it is now, as they want it to be now. But it doesn't always work the way the butch wants it. And any relationship, if you're going to be a success in it, it's give and take. That's the way I've always felt about it."

D.J. also describes the circumscribed nature of butch control. "To me a fem . . . then had to be a woman, had to be a lady. She had to conduct herself as such. In other words, you [the butch] had to be a boss to a degree, but not down to everything. . . . You just had to have a little more bossiness about you. It was being domineering without . . ." Her voice trails off as she searches for a proper analysis.

In a slightly different vein, Vic explains butch aggressiveness in terms of the harmony to be found in complementary gender roles.

> "There's got to be the loved and the lover, and the hunter and the hunted, so somebody has to be one or the other. I don't think that two people that are equal right down the line—they wouldn't be together. I think there has to be a more dominant one, not necessarily physically, but there has to be somebody that's gonna lead the show. You know, you can't have two nimbos together and then you can't have, you know, two people that are gonna be killin' each other together."

Fems see the butch as stronger and more aggressive, but usually limit the areas about which this was true and complain about butches who were too controlling. Joanna had quite a bit to say about the suggestion that butches might be emotionally and/or physically stronger than fems and her views are common. "Well, that's a fallacy—I wouldn't say in every case, but I would say in the majority of cases, the ratio of stronger fem girls is much larger than those of the butchy girl, I think. [A butch girl identifies herself by] her clothing, her dress, her mannerism. . . . But certainly not the stronger." Several fems thought butches were stronger, more powerful, and liked it that way, but they are ambivalent about their control.

"I feel that, back then, role playing was very important. I still feel and always will that someone should be the more aggressive person in a relationship. I would say that I'm more of a type that is not a leader but a follower. . . . I'd like someone who would be a stronger person in the relationship, in terms of maybe managing the finances or stronger sexually also. . . . I prefer women who would be, not dressing real mannish, but just someone who would be a stronger person and sort of someone that I would be able to lean on and depend on." (Bell)

Nevertheless, she indicates later in her life story how much she valued her independence, and expresses her discontent with butches who asserted too much control.

"The only thing I didn't like about her was she was so damn possessive. I've always kind of been the type of person who likes to be very independent. I like leaning on someone for decisions, I like someone stronger in the sexual area of things, but I don't like being told what to do. I accept things better if someone will suggest to me, 'It would be nice if you would do this or better if you do this,' not say, 'You have to do this.' Because it seems like from very early in my childhood I was being told, . . . 'You've got to do this' and shoving me here and pushing me there, and to this day I rebel against that very strongly, I can't stand it."

Butch-fem relationships encompassed these two contradictory impulses: the tendency toward butch control and the tendency toward cooperation. Most narrators look back with pleasure at their relationships and feel good about the closeness and time shared. There is an undercurrent of complaint, however, in the stories of fems about the bossiness of butches, especially their jealous control over fems' socializing outside the relationship and their selfishness. The tension was resolved differently in different historical periods, but also by different individuals within any one period. In some cases, the conflict led to personal growth and stability in the relationships, in others to extreme pain and, in some relationships of the late 1950s, to violence. The instability created by the contradictory power dynamics between butch and fem might be part of the reason for the avid interest of some of these butch-fem couples in the feminist movement of the 1970s. Its critique of gender offered insight into an ongoing, and often troublesome, issue in their lives.

In order to reclaim the history of lesbian relationships, this chapter examines the social basis of the dynamics of love in committed butch-fem relationships, focusing on the organization of domestic life and the tension between shared power and butch control. Given the continuing oppression of lesbians, we try to resist the temptation to uncritically praise or denigrate lesbian relationships. We look at expressions of closeness, caring, and understanding as well as at cheating and jealousy, and pay particular attention to the conditions that gave rise to increased violence in the late 1950s.

LIVING ARRANGEMENTS AND THE ORGANIZATION OF DOMESTIC LIFE

Committed relationships usually developed within the context of living together. Joanna expresses the connection between loving someone and living with her.

> "I think I'd have to really like someone before I could . . . not before I could go to bed, not that part. But before I could really want to live with them, like to share my life with them, and that's important to me. But I think it starts out by liking someone as a person, respecting them, and then I think you fall in love. But I don't think you fall in love first before you know someone. I think that that's different."

D.J. indicates that living together was a step toward recognizing the seriousness of a relationship. She wouldn't know right away that she loved someone she was courting. It was a process. "Each one was for a while and built up, and I said, 'Hey, move in.' It wasn't an overnight thing, no, no, I cannot say that." In general, narrators moved in with their deep loves within a year of beginning the relationship. One fem narrator, for instance, moved in with one girlfriend after a month and with another after six months.

Lesbians not only chose to live with their girlfriends, but preferred living with them exclusively. Sometimes a friend of one person might join a couple, but this never lasted more than a short time. Or two friends might be living together, but when one found a serious relationship, she usually moved out. In the early 1960s, a group of single lesbians, mainly butches, developed a supportive living arrangement in a building at the western end of Days Park, which came to be known as "homo haven." The building had apartments of one to two rooms with a kitchen, and occupants shared a bath with the several other apartments on the floor. But most lesbians moved out when they formed serious relationships. "When they came there, they came alone, and then if you met somebody . . . you'd bring [them] home. . . . If you've been with somebody let's say six months or so and you see it's pretty sure, then you'd look for an apartment" (Sandy).

In only a few situations did gay women of this period not live with their steady girlfriends. Young people who hadn't yet moved out of their parents' houses and women who were living at home taking care of aging parents had serious relationships without living together.[6] In addition, married women frequently did not live with their girlfriends.[7] Pearl remembers, "I had lasting relationships even when he was around, but I never really lived with anyone until the late 1950s, when he left and went [out West]." It was difficult to manage relationships under these conditions, but Pearl did it.

> "[My girlfriend] was living with her mother, her family, when I first met her. And then she decided she wanted to get an apartment of her own because she didn't have enough privacy with her family. Although I had gone to her house

with her mother and father and everything, she decided she wanted to move. So she got an apartment, and then I would go to her apartment, and spend the night. I always would go at night and I'd make sure I got up early in the morning and go home. That used to be terrible to get up and go home. . . . I would be home when they [my kids] got up."

Her girlfriend only stayed at her house when her husband was away.

The desire to live with one's girlfriend was so strong that some married women worked out an arrangement whereby they would have their girlfriends stay in the same house as their husbands, while keeping the nature of the relationship a secret.[8] The unmarried woman often became an aunt to the children of the marriage, and the husband considered the woman a friend of the family. Although not easy, such an arrangement was workable, as Phil explains:

> "Well there has to be some problems, but it seemed to work out all right. I didn't have the kind of husband that [was very demanding] to start with, so it sort of worked out all right. . . . [And] she [my girlfriend] walked into it like that and she expected it. . . . There were days that we had together, children were in school and he was working, we had our time."

It was very important for Phil to keep her family together.

> "She [my girlfriend] lived with us. . . . He [my husband] didn't know the relationship. . . . And it wasn't anything we flaunted either. It was like two lives I had to lead, without hurting one or the other. I had to stay sort of in the middle. It wasn't easy, but it's something I felt I had to do because I had children. . . . It was my family first and she understood that and went along with it. . . . I had to do [it] to keep the kids with a father and mother, and not disrupt their lives at all, because nothing is worth doing that."

Taking care of their children was an overwhelming priority for married lesbians. No narrators contemplated a divorce while their children were young, although all divorced after the children grew up. Despite the restrictions of their discreet social lives, they continued to find ways to go out, form committed relationships, and survive the breakups.

Lesbians without husbands only rarely lived with and raised their children alone or with lesbian partners during the 1940s, but the practice became more common as the century progressed. Not one narrator raised children without a husband until the late 1950s. Debra, who had a child from a brief marriage in the early 1940s, gave him to her family to raise until he became a teenager. Lesbians raising children outside of marriage was possible even at that time, however. Several narrators remember a woman who raised her daughter during the 1940s. She was the same woman who organized the picket of Ralph Martin's and everyone agrees she was ahead of her time. She even took her daughter to Ralph Martin's to celebrate after the child's graduation, and when the mother left Buffalo to join a girlfriend, her daughter went with her. In addition, several narrators, Black and white, were themselves raised by mothers who lived as lesbians for some period of their childhood during the 1940s and early 1950s.[9] During the 1950s, Marla chose to have her child raised by her family while Piri chose to raise her own daughter. Although a heavy stud, Piri was unquestionably mother to her children, even when living with fem partners. D.J. helped to raise her fem's son during the 1950s. In the early 1960s, Charlie raised her baby with her girlfriend and the couple stayed together until the child was grown. And, several of the tough bar lesbians, Little Gerry, Ronni, Vic, Sandy, as well as others, went with women who had children, and helped to raise them.[10]

In the case of most narrators, butch and fem alike, living with a partner allowed them to actualize their strong desire to make a home. Leslie remembers, "We used to talk about the difference between gay girls and gay boys. Girls used to look at each other, kiss and then make a nest and start buying stuff. But not the boys."[11] When reminded that that wasn't true for one of her friends who had taken a long time to settle down, she replies: "That's because she did not have to make a nest. She had a nest with her [family].[12] I didn't have anything, not a home or anything. I had to make one." Making a home was a goal of narrators in the 1950s as well. "Having a nice home had always been important to me. Not because I was into materialistic things. But to have a comfortable home—which it still is—[was] important" (Bert).

Living in their own apartments or houses was a big step for women during this time period. It indicated separation from family, and subjected such independent women to disapproval. Narrators who came out in the 1940s noted the proscriptions against unmarried women leaving their parental homes and establishing residences of their own.

> "At that time, girls leaving home, was most unusual. Now it's an accepted thing, [then] it was a catastrophe. . . . Well my mother went to bed that day and she was very ill, and I was leaving her. Of course you see, my . . . father, dying when I was [young], and then mother not remarrying until I was [in my twenties], she and I had been very, very close all those years. So for me to want to live someplace else, it was a very traumatic thing for my mother. But then she got used to it, too, my living with different girls." (Dee)

After another narrator left home, her family did not talk to her for a year. Nevertheless, all of them did set up homes with their girlfriends in their maturity, and this task became easier as the century progressed.

Lesbian residences were dispersed throughout urban Buffalo and neighboring towns. At different times, some lesbians clustered together in particular houses. In the early 1940s, several white lesbian couples lived in a building on Elmwood Avenue near Allen Street, in the "artsy" section of town, and had other friends who lived nearby.[13] In the early 1950s, a group of white lesbians lived in an apartment building on East Utica Street between Michigan and Masten. This was a predominantly German and Jewish section, just beginning to have its first Blacks take up residence. "[The apartments] were small with a living room, kitchen, bedroom, bath, and closet. You shared a washing machine" (Leslie). A couple would share such limited quarters. "Remember, we were much poorer then." For a time in the mid-1950s, several Black lesbians had rooms and apartments in the same house on Michigan across from the Lincoln Club in the heart of the Black section. In the late 1950s, the lower West Side, a working-class Italian neighborhood, particularly attracted the lesbian population. All of these neighborhoods were either within walking distance of the downtown area or were on a bus or streetcar line. The bars were therefore relatively accessible to lesbians seeking a social life in the community.

Inevitably, making a home together not only drew criticism from family, but also subjected couples to the judgments of neighbors. Because narrators were role-identified and therefore easily recognized as lesbian couples, this contact was always potentially dangerous. The way two women set up their household could be scrutinized by neighbors for clues about their living situation. Although some couples were careful and maintained two bedrooms, one of which was for "show," others, not caring about appearances, had only one bedroom. "We always had one bedroom and I never thought anything about it. Until one person brought it up one time; I said, 'Well, it doesn't bother me. Let them think what they want' " (Bert).

In the 1950s, the increased visibility of the tough bar lesbians made acceptance by neighbors a definite challenge. Maintaining the property with care—usually the butch's job—was a common strategy for winning neighbors' respect and promoting friendly interactions. Matty describes with pride how she handled neighbors in a West Side Italian section in the early 1960s:

> "[The neighborhood was] really macho, man, y'know. And we got this really nice apartment there and people automatically . . . y'know, two girls moving in and they took for granted what we were and that was fine with me. And it would be when we'd go out, like in the morning . . . I'd say, 'Hello'; the wives would snub me, but the husbands would say, 'Hello'. . . . Well one day we were out there trimming the bushes . . . and the people next door to us were trimming their bushes and the guy came over and he said, 'You know something, you girls got this place looking beautiful. . . . ' And his wife wandered over and she came up to me and said, 'Yes, the bushes really do look beautiful. . . . ' and I completely ignored her and kept right on trimming the bushes. And Barbara [my girlfriend] was shocked and she said, 'Matty, that woman is talking to you.' And I turned and looked at Barbara and said very loud so that woman could hear me, 'Yes, Barbara, but I've been talking to her for two months and she's ignored me. I want her to see how it feels.' And the woman came up to me and took my hand and said, 'I'm sorry.' She apologized."

Butch-fem roles were important to the organization of a couple's domestic life, in the sense that they symbolically and ideologically associated the butch with the public world, the world of the streets and bars, and the fem with the home. D.J. describes the butch-fem relationship in a manner that was typical: "A woman in the house . . . it's her place to be the boss. Out in the public, taking care of the woman, that was the butch's business." D.J. had lovers who held jobs outside the home, and she saw this as acceptable. "As long as she came back in the house and lived her life the way it was supposed to be lived in the house." The division of labor by gender had meaning primarily in relation to the way a couple socialized in the community.

The butch's role was, above all, that of the protector, both in terms of fending off harassment from the outside world, and in limiting passes from other butches. These women were living in an environment that was extremely hostile to lesbians. Men would make passes at fems, sometimes even at butches, and men would verbally and, in the 1950s, physically attack lesbians. The protector role was therefore crucial and was one element that allowed the community to socialize and grow. Offering this protection was an institutionalized part of the butch role, one way of showing respect for a fem. Vic took exception to D.J. who, in their joint interview, implied that the most important way to show respect was by being monogamous. Vic felt it was by offering protection to fems.

> "I don't think that's a fair statement to make. I don't think anybody loved a woman and cared for her any more than I did mine. It's just I wasn't capable of being that sincere, but as far as respect . . . I respected every woman I was ever with. As far as letting somebody hurt them or bother them or something like that. . . . Any time I did anything, I certainly didn't do it to degrade the person I was with. But if you were really heavy into being a truck driver like I was back then, when I went out, you'd sit there, that's Vic's lady, now you don't mess with her. Now half the women I was with, people wouldn't even talk to them. Or if they were with Sandy or Iris or somebody that they knew, that that was hers. Those were the butches that you just did not mess with their women. And people knew that and they didn't do it."

Fems wanted and expected this kind of protection. It made them feel comfortable going out. For Arlette, the appropriate role as protector was more important than proper sexual behavior.

> "My choice is, I like the kind of hard-type-appearing stud. Mannish but not man dressing. I like that cause I'm gonna be the lady, that's why. I don't care what she likes when we get in the bed, but when I go out, yeah, I want her to be able to say, 'Listen this is my lady and leave her alone.' 'Cause there are times when you have to . . . protect them. 'What the heck is this? I got to protect you? I should be the stud. But you sittin' up there lettin' people mistreat your woman.' I've had that happen to me. You're supposed to be my stud and here's another stud threatening my life and she's sittin' up there picking her nose. [If] I got to stand and fight, I don't need her. . . . Because if I could do the fightin' and stuff I might as well be by myself."

At the same time fems didn't want protection to be overdone. Arlette continues:

> "I don't like that, any time somebody says something, [they start up]. . . . You like me, so what's gonna stop somebody else from liking me? But now it's up to me to handle that, you don't handle it for me until it gets to the point where I say, 'Baby, I keep telling this party I don't want to be bothered with him, they're bugging me.' Then I expect you to set them straight. 'Cause nine out of ten your woman knows how to keep somebody off of her. . . . So they like me, so what. What am I supposed to do, not speak to them, don't dance with them? I know how to carry myself. But if it gets to the point where they get too outrageous and I tell them to stop and they don't want to, . . . then I expect that so-called stud to get up and say, 'Listen,' you know. Because as long as I got to do it I don't need her."

As a result of the butch's protector role, fems did not develop an extensive social life without the butch. This was symbolized in the 1940s by Butch Night Out. Without such a custom in the 1950s, fems' socializing was nevertheless limited. Vic expresses her preference for a close relationship in which the fem is either with her or at home. She preferred her woman to have only a few outside interests.

> "Well because if you have to be with one person, the person you're living with and your life revolves just around them, you know, it can get pretty tight. For you and them. You must have outside activity. Like my old lady might go to bingo, but she's very limited in what she can do. . . . She was limited when I met her. Otherwise I wouldn't be with her. If she was a big gadabout and into all these projects and that, I wouldn't be with her."

Despite this powerful distinction between the public realm of the butch and the domestic realm of the fem, but in keeping with the fact that the fem was normally part of the work force, butch-fem roles did not rigidly determine the assignment of work. In the dominant male-supremacist society, gender was key for organizing work, but this was not an essential aspect of butch-fem roles in the lesbian community. Either because butch and fem both wanted to work or wanted the autonomy that comes with supporting themselves, or because one woman's salary was rarely enough to support a couple, or because couples rarely raised children, the butch's role was not primarily that of breadwinner. Not surprisingly, given the emphasis on the masculine responsibility for earning in the dominant society and the great deal of attention paid to masculinity in the lesbian culture, there was an undercurrent of feeling on the part of some butches and some fems that the butch should support the fem. But this was not a culturally validated norm and did not frequently happen in practice. Jan recalls that some fems expected the butch to support them, just like they expected the butch to be the aggressor. "She expected you to support her, like a man would, which I do not believe in, not whatsoever. If you're a woman and I'm a woman, then let's pay half our share. Tit for tat." This reaction is quite typical.

There were no rules about the division of work in the home that the community found important to uphold. A number of couples who were out in the 1940s shared the expenses of living together and the housework. Leslie remembers doing all the housework in her relationships, but not the cooking. Arden recalls sharing all the housework, and also cooking. "I liked to cook." This was true despite, or because of, the fact that she never cooked until she left home. To her mind, certain jobs were butch jobs, like "cleaning the bathroom, washing the kitchen floor, vacuuming." Butches of this group did not expect the fem to take exclusive care of the house. Leslie remembers sharing the work and the expense when she joined the household of another butch friend and her girlfriend. All three put in money for the food and rent. The two butches cleaned and the fem did all the cooking. When asked if the fem was like the wife and mother, Leslie comments, "She didn't do much work, she was a professional woman, she didn't have time. . . . She cooked, and [my friend] and I did the housecleaning." It is important to emphasize that these butches, although they did housework, were extremely masculine. Their masculine identity did not exclude domestic work.

Joanna, who worked outside the home, concurs that expenses and housework were shared. She remembers that domestic life became easier in the 1950s. She describes her partner of the 1940s as "frugal." They did not go out to eat and they did all their own housework. In the 1950s, however, she and her partner went out to eat frequently and hired someone to clean for them.

> "It's a lot easier, don't forget, when you come home after a whole day, especially like if you worked overtime or if you had a bad day, who the heck feels like cleaning? A lot of times we ate out. . . . The whole concept of gay life to me had changed. I mean we had a cleaning woman; we're eating out more. It was different, very different."

It is not completely clear if the reason for this change was the atmosphere of the 1950s, which allowed lesbians to go out more to restaurants or to feel more comfortable in hiring someone to come to their house, or whether the economic conditions of these particular individuals allowed this level of comfort. We do know that Joanna and her butch in the 1940s were both just entering the work force, and in fact, for some of this period the butch was still in school. In the 1950s, she and her butch both made comfortable wages.

Other lesbians who were out in the 1940s organized their relationships differently, following the classic heterosexual model more closely. "To me, all mine were on the order as a man and woman getting married. . . . And it was the thing that she would take care of the house, whatever, I would work, support and so on, and she'd take care of the house for me. . . . You were mine" (D.J.). This was the arrangement, despite the fact that the women D.J. went with worked.

"Oh yeah, yeah, they worked. They had jobs. . . . But as I say . . . I took care of the rent, gas, electric, phone, or whatever, and food went on the table. . . . Well that's the way I always lived, I was in that position, [like] a marital status, that's the way I lived. I always supported a woman. . . . If she wanted something extra around the house or whatever, I'd say, 'Go do your thing,' so she'd go and buy it. . . . If she needed something different for her son, he ended up living in the house, . . . she'd go get it and bring it herself. That's the way I always did it. . . . [I bought her clothes] on holidays or whatever. The same way she'd buy me gifts. But if she wanted a pair of shoes or something she'd buy it out of her own money. And then she'd always buy me a little gift on the side. It was a nice relationship."

Her paying the bills was based on her vision of the butch role and did not reflect a higher income than her fem's. "No, I was working at the hospital, I mean hospitals weren't making that much money, and rents at that time were a darn sight cheaper than they are now. Right now, I couldn't do it." Her fem not only used her money for herself, but also for special things for the couple. "When we took a vacation or whatever, she'd put in for gas; and [when] we went to a restaurant she'd say, 'Well it's time for [me] to buy the meal' and whatever it cost us. On vacation times or whatever, buy a gift or something, it was nice."

Pearl describes yet a different pattern of domestic organization for a relationship in the 1950s that also was used in the heterosexual world. Both butch and fem shared expenses, but the fem managed the housework and the finances.

"In a way it was like, you know, you do all the cooking, you do all the washing, you control the home. You take care of the money, you know what you're gonna buy. . . . Well this is the way it worked with me anyway I handled all the money. I worked, the other woman worked, and I had most of the money. She would give me her paycheck, and she would take so much for herself for her own expenses. If we went out, then we would say, 'Now we're gonna spend so much.' I would give her the money so it wouldn't embarrass her for me paying, but it would come from what we had at home. . . . But I had control of the home. And then of course, her going out and doing what she wanted, that was different. But it's like I said, I only lived with one person."

Pearl giving her butch money so she could pay when they went out was quite typical. It is consistent with the view that the butch is in charge, and has leadership in the couple's public life.

Narrators who came out in the 1950s also had a variety of approaches to dividing housework, although there seemed to be a tendency for fems to do more of it. Bert remembers that her fem did "the majority of the [housework]. But that was because she wanted to. She kind of spoiled me in that way. She used to say she enjoyed keeping house. In fact when we first met she didn't know how to clean house and she didn't know how to cook." Bert, however, did part of the cooking. "Oh, I cooked, that's one thing I've always done, my share of cooking. . . . I was very sympathetic about her not knowing how; I didn't get angry or anything, 'cause I realized that some people, their mothers or their family would never let them do it."

As the 1950s progressed, the ideology of the rough, tough butches clearly assigned fems responsibility for the housework. However, Arlette remembers that, in practice, the housework arrangements changed depending on whether she was working or being supported.

> "I felt like this. If I am the lady in the house and if my stud is working and I'm at home, I feel like that's my part to do. But I don't want her to feel as though she's not supposed to do it, just because she's the stud, which some of them feel like, that's your job and that makes me mad. 'Cause I tell them right quick: 'We both wear sanitary pads. I may not feel like cooking today, you can have all them pots and pans. . . . ' Don't put me in a position where I got to. 'Cause I feel as though if I'm working, too, then baby it's who gets home first and we all got a job. But if I'm staying at home I don't see anything wrong with me being the lady of the house. I think it's proper. Because I'm sitting at home, well what am I supposed to do? Nothing? And I want to have her food done, how she likes her bath, whatever she likes she gonna get it. Because I'm sitting at home being taken care of. Whatever she likes to eat supposed to be there at all times. I really believe in that. I don't care what I'm doin', 'Hey, my baby's comin' home, I got to get this food on.' "

The flexibility of rules about domestic work and finances appears to be related to the fact that in most cases both butch and fem expected to work outside the home. This was particularly true in the 1940s. "Very seldom you meet anyone that . . . meet two people they both wasn't workin' " (Debra). This pattern of butch and fem working changed somewhat in the 1950s, with the rise of the tough bar lesbian, who projected a butch image twenty-four hours a day and whose job opportunities were therefore limited. "There were a lot of butches around, if you remember, that the woman took care of them. A lot of them. 'Cause they couldn't work or didn't want to because they looked so butch and all of this, so the woman supported them" (Vic). Working fems gave many tough lesbians the freedom to live the way they wanted.

> "I started drinking every day, and the Memorial Day weekend came along. I got fired from my job because I didn't want to get out of bed. I was having such a nice morning there . . . and when I did finally go in the next day I was handed my walking papers. So I ended up on the streets, having Aileen support me. She was stealing money off the bars. She, without my knowledge, turned

tricks a couple of times and she always had money on her, so I didn't have to worry right then and there." (Ronni)

Sometimes, in these relationships, neither partner was steadily employed and both hustled.

"We went through a lot of hard times. Neither one of us really were working, we didn't have a lot, but those two years were good. We made it. . . . There were times when we had very hard times and then there were times when I felt like, well, I was just on top of the world. We loved each other a lot, we went through a lot together. But somehow we always managed to pay our rent and keep our head above water." (Bell)

Vic remembers that in such a relationship, she didn't worry about whose money it was. "Didn't matter if she's got it or I got it or who's got it, it's our money." The fluidity of domestic arrangements is typified by Vic, who experienced three different kinds within the period of several years. In her first relationship, before she had extended contact with the lesbian community, she and her partner both worked and shared absolutely everything. Once she was out in the community and developing her butch persona, she worked a good job and supported her fem. And then, when she felt working interfered with being her butch self, she quit her job and was supported by her fems, many of whom hustled.

Very few narrators, no matter the decade, were ever in a relationship where the butch worked and not the fem. If the fem did not work, she usually had children.

"Yes, I always had [to] hustle . . . go out and make a dollar. And I definitely don't like my lady to work for me. Go and dress, [go] out and have your good time, whatever, but don't come in here and bother me. She [my current lady] wants to work. . . . She's a licensed beautician. . . . I don't want her to though. That's where our biggest fight[s] come. . . . That's about the only one I've had that really wanted to." (Lonnie)

Not surprisingly, Lonnie is one who always looked for women with children.

Since lesbian couples did not usually prioritize the butch's work, it was not functional to the relationship for the butch to pay most of the bills, nor for the fem to do most of the housework and cooking. They had to negotiate their own solutions based on upbringing, temperament, role identity, and work conditions. They worked these out satisfactorily, at least to the extent that in people's memories domestic work is not a significant point of conflict.

The juxtaposition of the cooperative aspect of butch and fem in working to maintain the couple, and the controlling aspect of the butch's role as protector of the fem represents the contradiction that underlies and determines the dynamic of committed relationships. The material conditions of danger pulled in one direction, the material conditions of work pulled in the other, just as the ideology of difference enforced one tendency while the reality of similarity enforced the other. Together, these contradictions created the unique character of committed relationships in this butch-fem culture.

GIVE AND TAKE: SEXUAL INTIMACY, EMOTIONAL WARMTH, AND CARING

Members of a lesbian couple developed strong bonds. Some felt that, in the absence of the institution of marriage, it was important for the emotional ties to be even stronger than those of the heterosexual world. "Yeah, very tight, very tight. . . . It was ownership, that's what I'm saying to you. Like say if two women could get married now, you have it on paper. We had a—there was a bond, you know, they really respected each other a lot. You and your lady were just very tight" (Vic). This bond was built on a bedrock of sexual intimacy, emotional warmth, and caring that facilitated cooperation and mutual respect between partners. The gendered nature of the couple was part of this closeness and sharing, but also was a source of tension within it.

As lesbians of this period searched for the "loves of their lives," many looked for attributes in a girlfriend, in addition to looks, that would allow them to build a fulfilling relationship and make them happy. For most, finding a constructive person with whom they would be safe and perhaps could better themselves was particularly important. Joanna, who prized her independence, was always grateful for her first girlfriend, particularly since their meeting was by chance; this butch was the first to approach her on her first night in a lesbian bar. "She could have really been a rat, really a fink. But thank God I met someone who was really nice and a [steady worker], a nice person who was good and was not going to lead me [a]stray." For her second relationship, she wanted to stay in that set, although she didn't do so. "I was interested in that set because. . . . I think I was spoiled because they were a really nice group. They liked theater, they liked . . . movies. They did a lot more things, rather than going to bars all the time." It was not simply the kind of job her butch had that she valued, because later in her life she went with a factory worker. She is concerned with character and values. The friend who took her to that first gay bar had her first relationship with a very destructive woman, and Joanna feels that's why her friend didn't remain a lesbian.

> "I think she had a very bad experience with a girl she went with. She turned out to be kind of a loser, really not a very nice person, made a lot of trouble for her, for her family, etc. which . . . [really does] put it down a little and I don't think after that she really trusted anybody. I mean it's too bad, because she introduced me. . . . I'm sure I would have found it myself eventually but it just speeded up my entry into the gay scene."

Concern about character was very common, because most lesbians wanted to build decent lives for themselves. Pearl was in a relationship but never divorced her husband, even though her children were grown, until she met someone she trusted.

> "Now I was going with this other girl, she never could get me to get the divorce. I don't know what the difference was. I think the difference was, I knew what kind of person she was and I didn't want to really get that involved. . . . I knew she went out on Friday night and picked somebody up for a one-night stand, I knew all this about her. So I didn't really trust her enough to get a divorce and move in with her. Where the other girl, she was different in that respect in the beginning. And then after I got the divorce and everything, then's when she started the other stuff. So she was the one that really got me to get the divorce."

The tough bar crowd of the late 1950s and early 1960s sought excitement and ego support rather than security and upward mobility. Vic remembers the women who made her feel most worthwhile:

> "If I could have a date with any girl I have ever been with, it would be with Diane. I found her the most fascinating girl I was ever with. And to this day, if I could be with her I would. . . . I really thought she was like really neat people. She's one of the few people who ever made me feel like I was a person. *Made* me you know. . . . And I think that's probably why I spent any time at all with Selena. I thought it would be the same way, and you know, it wasn't. I thought it ran true to form with people that had any kind of intellect, but I was wrong. . . . I was like hung up for a long time on educated people. . . . I really thought Diane, was like you know, very stable, very intelligent, and I really just liked her type of woman, and I thought it went with that, with education and all that, and it doesn't."

Lesbians also had individualized preferences. As Lonnie's love for children led to her preference for women with children.

> "I used to wouldn't even talk to a woman unless she had kids. 'Cause I love kids. I love them. I love to spoil them. But I like for them to move when I say move. Boys or girls. Don't care what color they are, how they act, how they look, still love them, somebody's children. I just wouldn't talk to no girls unless they had babies."

Committed relationships began with or soon developed a satisfying sexual component that was expected to continue. Of the many relationships we learned about, only two or three were not sexual before the couple moved in together, and these became sexual in time. Joanna attests to the importance of compatible sex for lesbian relationships:

"I don't think that it's the biggest thing in the world, but I think it's darn important. . . . To be able to go to bed with somebody and enjoy them, that's very flattering. For both parties, really. You, because you want them, and they because they want you. . . . It's nice to be wanted. . . . You know, it's nice to have someone be affectionate with you. . . . And I think two women . . . are much more affectionate than a man and a woman. There isn't that closeness with a man. . . . There are things you can't discuss with a man. . . . There are a lot of things that I'd never discuss with my husband, never. Like your feelings. . . . And I think with a woman you can talk about sex more freely, you know, it's not something that just happens when you go to bed. I think you should be able to discuss it out of bed, if you have problems especially. . . . I know . . . because I've done it."

Both butch and fem expressed a continuing interest in sex in a relationship. However, the fem acted more indirectly, just as she did during courtship. Despite Joanna's statement above that she could talk easily about sexual matters with a butch, there were some limits. When asked if her fems ever directly asked for sex, Leslie replies, "There are ways of promoting things without asking directly, like squeezing up, or running her hand on the back of the head, subtle things like that." And from her point of view, she was always ready.

Sexual problems are not prominent in the memories of this community. Only two or three narrators mentioned them.[14] There was an assumption, however, that sexual interest would diminish as the relationship continued. Vic, with her usual cynicism, describes the situation bluntly. "Yeah, and to get a kiss goodnight after two years is like pretty tough." The community was divided about the degree to which sexual activity waned in committed relationships. Many did not experience much of a decline. D.J. feels that she maintained warmth, intimacy, and sexual expression throughout her long relationships.

"Even at the beginning I would never do it every night in the week, and until this day I still don't. I feel that I have more pleasure in waiting a while, and then let it all come at one time. Even up until [the end], we still had our thing. Now I would be working, and there were days sometimes I'd be so god damn tired at night, and she'd be working and I'd just fall asleep on the couch. But there was times, like on my days off, maybe we'd have a couple drinks around the house and then we'd just do our thing. But it was not an every night occasion."[15]

The waning of sexual interest, when it occurred, was not treated as a problem to be solved, but rather was accepted philosophically as a part of life. Leslie felt that it depended on how physical the partners were to begin with. Others feel the decline was related to the transformation of a love relationship into a friendship and a subsequent romantic interest in someone else, or a combination of the two.

"Anybody that I had a long relationship with I didn't enjoy sex any more from the first year than I did the fiftieth, that was still there. . . . It wasn't something that wore off, that you just didn't want to be bothered. Like you say, you didn't do it as often, but when you did have it it was the same. . . . It wasn't like you got so used to each other that they weren't your lover any more, now they're your friend. That happens a lot in gay relationships, I think lovers change to friends and therefore your sex drive is [lower]. Now you're going to find someone else." (Vic)

Little Gerry gives yet another analysis: Because butches had so much responsibility for initiating and leading sexual activity, after some time in a relationship, the idea of sex often became burdensome and even boring. Although no other narrators offered this explanation for the decline of sexual activity, when presented with this theory, many agreed.[16]

When sexual activity diminished in a relationship, it did not automatically mean that the relationship ended. Joanna tells the story of a friend who was in a relationship without sex for at least fifteen years.

"Laura was living with a girl for sixteen years and I think for fifteen and a half years they had not had sex. She told me this, and I thought that was funny. Well, I think the other girl was very inhibited, I mean more so than Laura. And it wasn't like a young relationship . . . it wasn't like they started out when they were kids. . . . Oh, I think if it bothered them I think they kept it to themselves. I don't think it was openly discussed. I don't think these two have ever discussed sex. Laura, as I said, Laura and I were very close and if she could tell me this, this is difficult to tell somebody you're living with. And I said, 'Did you ever broach the subject, you know, when you were talking some time?' And she said, 'Oh, she clams up immediately.' It's almost like it never happened. It's almost like they just lived together as friends. Funny."

Both butch and fem expected each other to be monogamous in their committed relationships. In some sense, fidelity was viewed as the test of whether a person was deeply in love or really cared. Phil expresses this:

"I think it's the person I like not what they do or how their lifestyle is. I mean if she felt like going with one person and going the next time with another one, all the more power to her. If I like her I didn't question her lifestyle, the way she lived and what she did. And I've known a few like that. But eventually they settle down for a while. I think if you're not serious with one person why stay with one person? As long as they accept the fact that you're seeing others. But when you fall in love deeply, then you don't do that. You don't want to."

Annie expresses similar ideas about herself.

"My relationships, I always had a very close relationship. There wasn't [an] agreement, well, you sleep with me Monday, Tuesday, Wednesday and Thursday, and then you can go out and have the weekends. . . . I don't think I could go with that type of an agreement. If I did, I know myself, it's because I really didn't care."

Monogamy also meant showing respect for your true love since you gave yourself only to her. D.J., who is adamant that she never cheated on her steady relationships, explains:

"But I can say myself and the relations I've had, not one, I never cheated on them. Not once. Wholeheartedly, . . . never cheated. I came home from work and that was that. . . . Because I happened to think that meant I didn't have much respect for her. I thought that much of her. Just didn't want to be with anyone else. That's the only way to show true love, is being with that person and not somebody else."

The exclusiveness implied by monogamy also had a dimension of possession. D.J. reminisces about how she ended a ten-year relationship when she found her fem in bed with a man: "If you're living with me, under my roof, and I'm taking care of you wholeheartedly, you are mine and not everybody else's." In the late 1950s, among the rough and tough lesbians, the concept of ownership was frequently used to describe the sexually exclusive nature of the relationship.

The emotional power of loyalty is expressed poignantly in Whitney's story of how the terrible sexual difficulties in her relationship led her to change her religion. She had hoped this would ease her frustration and reduce the temptation to have affairs.

"So here I was, twenty-three, right?—orgasms—and Sonny is into menopause. So I thought, it will pass, it will pass. . . . I didn't want to cheat and I was going crazy, crazy, and she was not interested in any physical activity whatsoever. And she would say to me at night, . . . 'Get into bed' and I would be all brushed and everything else, you know, and she would pat my shoulder and she would say, 'Honey, go to sleep. You're tired.' And because I had her on a pedestal, it was my problem, . . . I couldn't turn around and say, 'I'm not tired. . . . ' I couldn't say to her, 'No, I wanna make love. . . . ' And I was lying there in knots, seething, angry, angry, and it was nothing to do with homosexuality. It had to do with being able to express anger and I couldn't express anger. We went together five years and I thought, well, it's not getting better and I don't want to cheat, and I knew that in the Catholic Church for people of the same sex to have sex together was a sin, so I said, 'Fine. . . . ' So I converted to Catholicism so that I wouldn't want her."

Conversion worked, but only for a while.

For those couples in which the fem was a prostitute, the standard of monogamy still applied between women. Both butch and fem viewed turning tricks as a job, so the butch did not interfere. Sandy remembers, "I never wanted to know much about it." Annie confirms that butches looked the other way.

"They had to accept it. That was a thing that you wouldn't even look at or discuss. Afterwards you wouldn't talk about it, and you'd just go on and live your normal life. . . . It was a thing that had to be done. You didn't think of it as the part of the sex, whether you enjoyed it with a man or that. You went there for the money. . . . It was like a job. . . . A lot of guys knew all the gay kids, both butch and fem, and would buy both a drink but still would meet the fem around the corner, to go to a hotel with her. And it was never discussed afterward, what went on in the room. I think they were very mature in that respect. Even though we were young you still had a great understanding . . . of the difference, the separation. Whereas today, depending on the butch, I don't think a few of them would tolerate that."

The bond of intimacy was built on warmth and closeness as well as sexuality. Some narrators emphasize closeness as more important than sex for women. Vic and D.J., friends from different generations, discuss this issue, trying to sort it out. Vic: "I'm just saying that it [sex] is not first and foremost. I don't think that women that stay together for any length of time stay together because their love life is terrific." D.J. disagrees because she has a broader definition of love to include affection as well as sex.

"In other words, if you sit there and just put your arm around her. If you're watching television, the gentle things, not the get into the bed bit. There are all [different] ways of showing affection . . . just holding hands, watching television or anything you think of. Just to be close, just show that you care for each other. Makes a lot of difference. . . . Not just to hop in bed and do your thing. It's a twenty-four-hour romance. You got to get up in the morning and sit at the table and have a cup of coffee and be, 'Hey, good morning, how do you feel?' You know, gentle conversation that makes you close. . . . Because there's 365 days a year. There's sometimes I go to bed and would want nothing. I could go a week. But it was this thing that I'd sit on the couch alongside of you, you could lean up against me, hold me, be watching television, just a niceness together. . . . I think it's being tight with somebody more than being in love with somebody, the closeness. Reaching out and touching someone's hand and let it run through you. . . . [I mean] people are in love with each other, but I don't think that they have to sleep together every night of the week or have sex every night of the week for that relationship to grow."

In all narrators' minds, the closeness of a love relationship was different from that of a friendship. This distinction is quite striking when contrasted with the contemporary lesbian-feminist assumption that lovers are each other's best friends, and appears to be rooted in the maintenance of a gendered erotic system.[17] Phil tries to explain the difference between a friend and a lover:

"I think you can talk to a friend much more intimately than you could with your lover, I really do. To me, a friend is there when you need them, to talk or to do something. . . . On the other hand, a lover is one that you're with

> especially if you're living with them. You're living with them and you're
> intimate and you have sex and you go out, you go to parties. . . . A friend is
> . . . there when you need them. . . . I do have a lot of friends."

Joanna does not draw the line so clearly between friend and lover.

> "But I say if you love someone you have to like them, you couldn't just, not
> be friends with them, you know. And I never really pushed the friendship. I
> don't think I was obnoxious about it. It just happened. We just happened to
> be good friends, and we're still all good friends today. It's funny . . . because
> I don't think you could do this with husbands. . . . I don't think so because [I
> am not] my husband's friend nor is he mine."[18]

Even Joanna, however, as mentioned in the previous chapter, judges that friendship
can never predominate in a lover relationship. She suggests when your lover turns
into your best friend, the relationship is over.

> "I honestly couldn't put my finger on how or when it changed. But it did. I
> really honestly don't know. Except as I said we became better friends than
> lovers. You know, it gets to that point. . . . It's amazing. Then you start thinking
> of them as your friend and they're no longer a lover and it's very difficult to
> go to bed with your friend. It would be like going to bed with your sister."

This dichotomy between friendship and love continued into the 1950s and
became even more exaggerated among the tough bar crowd, a few of whom went
as far as to suggest that liking someone had little to do with a lover relationship.
Vic insists, "I've never been with anybody because they were nice people. I've
always been with somebody because they were either a pretty girl, or sexy to me.
I have people that are my friends that I really like, but I've never been with a girl
that I really like." Jodi remembers that her main objective was to find a "piece of
ass" when she was coming out in the late 1950s. "[A relationship] always starts
out as a piece of ass, let's face it." Although these are extreme statements they
remain in the genre of the more attenuated distinctions between friendship and love
that pervaded lesbian culture. We suspect that the importance of this dichotomy lies
in the opposition of sexuality and friendship, something hinted at in all of the
quotes on this topic. In fact, Vic, who insists she did not like her girlfriends,
mentions at another point in her story that she is friends with all her ex-lovers,
suggesting that for her, once the sexual relationship was over, friendship is possible.

The butch-fem erotic system required the tension of gendered difference, and
maintaining it worked against envisioning lovers as best friends or sisters. Butches'
and fems' similar valuation of love did not seem to undermine the erotic tension,
but their commonality as woman friends and the similarity it implied did so. This
interpretation is consistent with the fact that the distinction between friends and
lovers became exaggerated in the late 1950s. It was in this period that the rough

and tough lesbians' confrontation with the public was more aggressive and the differences between butch and fem became more exaggerated and rigid.

A concrete way in which a couple expressed intimacy and affection with one another—and a way that is easily recorded for history—was by giving presents. A great deal of care and thought went into choosing the gift that was appropriate for a girlfriend. Whitney had special guidelines for her presents; for instance, at Christmas, she always gave her butch a gift for each of the five senses. Although gift giving on special occasions like birthdays, anniversaries, Christmas, and Valentine's Day was reciprocal, butches gave fems special presents throughout the relationship, almost like a continuation of courtship. The presents were rarely reciprocated in kind. An understanding of this dynamic helps to capture the gendered emotionality of these relationships. When asked if she courted her women by sending flowers and candy, Leslie replies, "Of course. I brought them even after, once the relationship started, I don't forget." In the interview when we ask if fems also gave these special presents, we are surprised to learn, that they did not. Arden searches her memory only to find one exception. "Once a show girl . . . bought me a shirt. It was a lovely blue shirt, really beautiful."[19]

To help us better understand the dynamic of gift giving, Leslie goes on to clarify: "When I give a gift I get pleasure from that giving so it wasn't just the recipient who got the pleasure." She also thinks that this custom might have been true for her and her friends because they went with the real "damey dames," the real fems. This pattern of butches giving gifts continued into the 1950s. Little Gerry remarks that you can go into people's houses and see the special gifts a fem has received in her life. She feels it is important to explain, "I didn't give presents because I was buying the person. I gave presents because these women deserved it. It was a special thing to do for a special person. . . . A butch got from her fem something that she couldn't get anywhere else, the feeling of being an important person."

Fem memories confirm this pattern of gift giving. When asked if the differences between butch and fem years ago meant that butches looked down on or patronized fems, Joanna insists not and goes on to praise the old-fashioned approach to romance.

> "They were from the old school. . . . I really think that they were more romantic and there was much more chivalry. . . . They used to, like the guys would come [into the bar] and sell flowers, and they'd buy you a flower. . . . Even when you were living with someone for five years. . . . That's kind of, just cute I think."

This pattern of gift giving and the attitudes surrounding it parallel closely butch-fem sexuality—that of the butch as the doer who gets pleasure from giving pleasure—and adds yet another dimension of meaning to the complex dynamic. In some sense, for butches the giving of gifts was an ongoing wooing. But it was more than that. It expressed a deep appreciation for the unique validation they received from their fems.

Each member of a couple was also expected to take care of the other, and they prided themselves on doing it well. Making sure that one's partner looked good was a concrete manifestation of this caring. Vic explains:

> "See in those days, I don't know if D.J. will agree with me, and again we're back to if you're bar people or if you're not, it was a pride thing, you know. You were very proud of your woman and the woman was very proud of her butch. The woman took care of her butch in the way she always looked good. If the butch looked bad it was your fault if she did. . . . And you were proud of your woman. You wouldn't take your woman out with a rag on her head and no makeup on, she'd keep her at home if you looked like that. And you didn't leave the house without her saying you look good. There was a very deep pride there. With women that you were with, I don't mean a fly-by-night fem, who cares. I don't know if it's the same way now, I don't think it could be 'cause I see some pretty dumpy-looking people around. Really!"

Vic underlines that being attractive was not the issue. Butch and fem helped one another to look their best out of respect, and, true to the rough, late-1950s culture, this took on a tone of competition.

> "Good-looking doesn't have anything to do with it. . . . You always knew when somebody walked in the bar, like that's so-and-so and her old lady. You knew. You could tell just by looking at each other what the fem thought about her butch or what the butch thought about her fem. I'm not gonna take my lady out and she's gonna wear jeans from Norban's when this one's taking her lady out and she's got jeans from A. M. & A.'s, it's not gonna happen like that.[20] My lady's gonna look as good as yours if I have to sell my soul to do it. And it would be the same thing with the butches. My collar always had as much starch in it as the one sitting next to it, it was always just as clean and white. That was important. And when those things don't happen, then there's something wrong there. You don't care about your people, that's how it was put to you."

It is in this area of caring for one another that the absence of legal marriage especially thwarted committed relationships. Aside from emotional support, all resources for helping each other in times of trouble, such as medical insurance or life insurance, were denied lesbian couples. Leslie laughs at the naiveté of herself and her butch buddies who in their youth would try to arrange to take care of their fems: "We would swear if anything happened to one of us, the other would see that the girlfriend who was left would eat. You know it was really buddy-buddy stuff." From a lifetime of frustration, narrators repeatedly bring up how important it is for lesbian relationships to win legal recognition so that members of a couple can take care of one another:

"I feel like, that if two girls could get married—like I have a really good job, I feel that if I ever [again] really fell in love with someone, and I wanted to marry her and I wanted to support her, and if I should die or get killed, this person that I love very much I figure should be entitled to whatever I have." (Ronni)

Within the framework of emotional and sexual closeness couples attempted to build the kind of understanding that would allow a relationship to last:

"I find that the first year is the easiest, because you're in bliss, you're in heaven, you're still exploring and experimenting. And the second year is the test of whether or not you can relate to one another and what your feeling level is, when your life starts to fall into a pattern. . . . And then when you get into the second year you start thinking, oh my God, there's gas bills and electric bills, reality sort of slaps you in the face a little bit. The first year you knock yourself out with sex, you're screwing all the time." (Little Gerry)

The goal of the couple was for each to maintain her own individuality in an atmosphere of cooperation and communication. Many butches were committed to achieving common understanding and to establishing give and take in their relationships, as expressed eloquently by D.J.:

"Well it's just a feeling that two people have together and as I say, you got to talk, you can't scream at each other. Now say in your house you would like something in a different position or whatever. . . . I know a couple of [people] even a roll of toilet paper they can't stand a certain way. But if you went in there and you put an extra roll on it and you put it on a different roll, they'd have a fit. [You can't have a relationship like that.] Shit no. Like your TV, maybe I'd like it someplace else, maybe you like it there, and you just have to sort of get together on it."

At another point in her interview she returns to this same theme:

"It can't be a one-way street, no way in hell. You have to give a little to receive a little. You have to sit down and talk without screaming your brains out. 'This is wrong and that's wrong, you're doing this wrong.' You have to talk things out, that's what we used to do. And then after a while, if they got to the point [where resolution was impossible] you'd just drop the subject, that's all. We had problems, I never hit one. There was arguments, whatever, not that I'd knock her around the house or anything. I'd bust up the house first. Think I hit a woman only once, but I learned from it. . . . I don't know, it was just an argument, I just hauled off and hit her. But I had to buy quite a few dishes at times."

Little Gerry, who is younger, echoes this same view of relationships but also mentions how her selfishness would get in the way:

"Relationships require a lot of work, you have to put a lot of time into them. There's a whole lot of giving and taking. You have to give up things and you have to take things. At least that's what I've always found in relationships that I've been in. . . . [There were] a lot of things that [were] necessary for me to give up, so that the relationship [would go somewhere]. I have always basically been selfish, I always wanted my own way. If I didn't get it I took my football and went home."

Quite a few butches who came out in the late 1950s mention not being able to give or take in relationships when they were young, then learning in time.[21] Jodi recalls her early years:

"All those years that's the way I was and I thought that was it. . . . A lot of stuff just became kind of cruel, I couldn't believe that I had done some of the stuff that I had done all these years, and the ways that I acted and how I treated people. Just really cold and unfeeling. I just could not believe that I had been that way for so long to so many people. In fact, this past Christmas vacation, I used to go with this woman in Albany . . . and I read her letters. . . . I don't know what I was doing to her, God it must have been traumatic. I guess I did some really fucked-up shit to her, and this was like 1970. . . . So I wrote her a letter, told her I was sorry, for some of the stuff, and I felt better. It was real clear, because the person I broke up with [recently] was trying to say that I was doing this stuff to her, and I did. . . . That's just how I acted, it wasn't that I treated her any different, I was just a cruel person. . . . I thought I didn't need [affection]. I thought I didn't need a lot of things that I found out this fall that I need. She used to tell me that I needed them, I said, 'No, I don't.'"

Most fems wanted a relationship based on give and take. They struggled to have their interests heard, but unfortunately were not always successful. Arlette speaks eloquently of how she was fed up with butches who always put themselves first:

"If we have an argument and you know I'm mad, send me some flowers, box of candy or something. Or call me up and talk sweet. Don't call me up and keep on arguing 'cause if I'm near you I'm gonna try to knock you on your head. That's not gonna help the situation. I'm like this though, when I'm with somebody and I can tell we're having a misunderstanding, I believe in talking. And then what I hate is, they don't want to talk to you. And then when you try to talk they want to get nasty. . . . When I say, 'Baby, something is wrong, what is it? If it's something I'm doing tell it.' But I'm like this. If I'm with somebody and I like them, every time they do something I don't like, I'll say, 'Look, I don't like that.' I try to tell you what I don't like. Then if I jump on you don't tell me you don't know why. If I keep on telling you I don't like this, then I can understand a fight jumping off. But I don't want to go out with somebody that will snatch on me every time I say something about it. . . . Tell me you don't like it, then we'll talk about it, 'cause I'm not gonna change myself entirely for you and I don't expect you to change yourself entirely for me. But I think we can compromise. And I find that you can't do that with a lot of these ladies. They want everything their way. Not if you're gonna be my woman. . . . 'Cause we're not going to make it. It's not always *their* way, it's *our* way, if you're together. Well this is the point to me of two women together. But I find a lot of them don't even know anything about that. This is where the gay ladies part jumps really out of pocket as far as I'm concerned. . . . If we're two ladies and we like each other, let's see what we can do. It's not like, 'Well *I* want this and *I*,' '*I* nothing. If you start *I-ing* me too much, what about *we*? What are *we* gonna do? *We* like to do this, not what *I*.' Well then 'Hey, if that's the way it is. You go along *I* and I'll go along *I*. *I'll* go upstairs and then *I'll* get it myself and you want that you get yours yourself.' That's not being together. And that's nothing."

The tension between open communication and butch control in relationships pervades the culture, as can be seen from a disagreement between Vic and D.J. about why couples stayed together. D.J., who is older, feels the important ingredient was "common understanding." Vic feels relationships lasted because the fems were "scared to death. Some of it was like that, with the people I was around, anyway. The fems just toed the mark, they didn't dare do anything." Together these two views describe the realities of lesbian relationships during this period; some based on understanding, others on fear, and still others on a combination of the two.

BUTCH CONTROL: CHEATING AND JEALOUSY

Coexisting with closeness and mutual give and take in a committed relationship was the butch's attempt to control her fem. Although this was subtly present in the 1940s, it became obvious in the 1950s, when butches supervised their fems to the point that fems in the tough bar crowd could not go anywhere or do anything without their butches' permission. In this culture, cheating was common for both partners, but the repercussions were more severe for fems. Jealousy pervaded the community, but accusations were strongest against fems. Furthermore, in the late 1950s, butches sometimes used violence to control their fems. These developments seem to be rooted, on a social level, in butch solidarity and aggressiveness, which comes from their position as defenders and protectors of their fems and their community, and, on a psychological level, in the attraction of male privilege and in the insecurity born from the stigmatization of being butch. Fems, who never ceased to act on their own initiative, in some contexts were defined as other, as not really lesbian, because of their traditional feminine looks or their active heterosexual pasts.[22] In these complex conditions, it is understandable that some lesbians remember their relationships as based on communication and free exchange, whereas others remember control and fear.

Control over a partner's social and sexual life was a major issue in this community, because the other side of the strong standard of monogamy was the common practice of cheating. The meaning of cheating, however, is somewhat different from its meaning in the heterosexual world.[23] If we are identifying the lesbian system of serial monogamy as distinct, the phenomenon of cheating also needs rethinking. Although monogamy was unquestionably the articulated ideal for the lesbian community of this period, it was not backed up by legal, religious, or family sanction. In practice, sexual exploration with other than one's primary partner was not uncommon and did not necessarily lead to disastrous outcomes.

In keeping with the community's emphasis on romance, both butch and fem, once coupled, did not completely give up pursuing attraction to others, but instead had secret affairs that were not supposed to be known to their partners. Members of the community did not openly condone cheating, yet everyone recognized that it occurred, and most narrators could discuss cheating from first-hand experience. "I would say, from my own opinion, of my own knowing, my own experience, I'd say maybe twenty percent—that's a long haul in fifty-three years—twenty percent that I would say stuck together without messing around. 'Cause when the butches went out, any girl at the bar, you know. And this I can truthfully say" (D.J.).

Butch Night Out in the 1940s was conducive to cheating. Butches might not have found an affair every time they went out, but they often did. Pearl, who was single for a good portion of the 1940s, remembers the cheating vividly:

> "They were always out looking for something, something different. . . . And like I said, they would have girlfriends home, but it didn't mean anything. I don't know what they told their girlfriends, but they were out there joking around anyway. . . . I don't know how I got away with it, because I would be friends with these people, and yet I'd be going out with their girlfriends. . . . The first girl I ever went with, I knew her girlfriend, she lived with a girl, she had lived with her for years, I would go to their home. And I would be treated very nice. And yet we would meet outside. And [I] wasn't the only one, she wasn't just meeting me outside. . . . She had other ones besides. . . . I don't know [if her girlfriend knew.] I wondered about it lots of times, but of course I wasn't gonna ask her."

Butches did more "running around" and were more obvious than fems. In a manner consistent, however, with fems' interest in exploring sexuality, they also cheated.

> "It was mostly the butch that would run around. . . . Sometimes both, but you were apt to see—if the fem ran around she was more discreet. You didn't see her out in these places with somebody else as much as you saw the butch out

there. You'd see them out finding an all-night stand, or just out drinking to have a good time." (Pearl)

Joanna confirms that fems cheated at that time. When asked whether people cheated, she says:

"It [playing around] hasn't changed, no. It hasn't increased or decreased. . . . Oh I think you always say this. . . . 'Oh I'll love you forever. I'll never fool around, I'll never do this,' but you do. You pledge a lot of things, some of them come true, some of them don't. I mean, nothing is forever, let's face it."

When asked if she had ever cheated, she replies:

"Yes, you might see somebody tomorrow that appealed to you, isn't that true? And just the day, the right time, the right day, whatever. You know like all the stars and things are in your favor. But did you ever say to someone, I don't care for so-and-so, all of a sudden one day, she really is a nice person. She really looks good to you. She looks entirely different in your eyes. And I think this happens. I think this is what happens with romances."

What is striking about the quotation above is Joanna's emphasis, not on seeking out a secondary deep love relationship, but on lesbian life's inclusion of an active component of fleeting romance. Butch narrators confirm that fems in relationships had affairs on the side. Arden, while reminiscing about her youthful charm, remembers how she had been approached many times by fems for lunch and to have affairs. These women were in couples, "not of the kind I came to know later, where people had a home and intended to stay together. These people were living together, but I assume not too happily. I never knew another group like it." The affairs would last only a short time.

Cheating continued to be common in the 1950s. The 1950s butches, without the institution of Butch Night Out, still had ample opportunity to cheat, particularly those in the rough crowd of the late 1950s, who were underemployed. Butch and fem narrators alike relate stories of their own or others' outside affairs. For many butches, cheating was a way of life. Vic remembers her inability to remain faithful even to an ostensibly monogamous partner, and her various partners' unwillingness to accept this. "I've been with people two and three years. I do believe that they've been sincere and I haven't. . . . And if they could have dealt with how I was, I probably would have stayed with the first one I was with. But see they didn't deal with it either. . . . That's weird." Annie remembers the manipulative dimension of cheating.

"They [fems] would cheat. If they knew they had a butch that was going out on the town; if they knew what she was doing, they had a line out for another butch. There was always one in the, what you would call it . . . in the wings? . . . If we were fighting I would go out. But to leave her home and to say I had to go somewhere or do this or that, to purposely go out and cheat, no. . . . It's an ego thing, and it's a thing that's all in maturing."

Despite the prevalence of cheating, monogamy remained the endorsed standard and continued to imply the special importance of the relationship. Annie is still pleased with the specialness of her relationship with Sandy, her butch of the late 1950s.

"Well let's face it, there has been cheating since Adam and Eve. What you don't know don't hurt you. That thing. I mean I've asked Sandy, 'Did you ever cheat on me? You cheated on everybody else, did you ever cheat on me?' I've even asked her today. Not today, but recently. [She] says, 'I have never cheated on you.' 'Well, you cheated on everybody else you ran around with, how come? Why not me?' So we just have that little tie, like a chemical thing."

On some level, she is aware that her butch's loyalty might be a fiction, but that doesn't matter. The romantic illusion remains important.

Although both butches and fems had affairs, all narrators agree that when caught, fems were subject to more social disapproval than the butches. Annie, like most fems, expresses discontent with the unfairness of this system.

"I think there's more disapproval of a fem. . . . And I still think that holds true today. Really. I don't know [why], but it does. To me if anybody cheats on me, I can play the same game . . . 'cause I think if you really look at it, I think they're playing the part. They think they're playing the part of a man, and they think maybe, deep in the back of their mind, that men do it to women in the straight life. Where sometimes little do they know, that there's a lot of men that are very very devoted to their wives. Very, very devoted. You can't look at one man and judge all men by one man. Or you can't look at one butch like [she's typical]."

Her association of the greater freedom of the butch with a masculine identity seems correct on some level. Butches frequently appropriated familiar male prerogatives. But a psychological explanation is not sufficient. As will become apparent later in this section, customs giving butches control over fems became institutionalized and helped enforce different standards for butch and fem loyalty.

The contradiction between the strong standard of monogamy, and the known cheating in the community created jealousy between members of a couple as well as accusations directed toward others. Joanna contrasts the gay-male culture with that of lesbians on the basis of the tension over affairs.

"They're not as serious as the girls, and maybe that's what makes them different. Maybe they don't get so involved, you know, that everything is a big catastrophe that happens, and they're probably happier, because they don't get that emotionally involved. I'm not saying that some of them don't of course, but they're more liberal in their relationships. You know yourself, if two guys that live together, they still go out and date, they trick, but they stay together, the two original are together. . . . Women are too possessive."

In the 1940s, expressions of jealousy were not yet institutionalized and had little place in public life. Arden remembers a lot of jealousy, but says of herself, "I was too busy having fun, so I didn't pay as much attention," a feeling that others echo. On further reflection, however, she adds that people didn't show their jealousy in public, but she is sure it came out in the privacy of their homes. She knew she didn't want to make a scene in the bars. "[We] were always well-behaved. [We] didn't want to be thrown out of the places because they were the only places left to go." She remembers being jealous over two specific women, and thinks that butches were more jealous than fems, although if one hit the other, "I think it was maybe the feminine one taking a swipe at the butch one, if the butch was looking at another girl." Fems also remember jealousy during the 1940s, attributing it to both butches and fems. Joanna recalls that in her group, the fems were the most jealous. "Because some of them, the butchy-looking girls, were really good-looking girls. Really." In Joanna's experience, she feels that it is usually the butches who are the problem, though not her own girlfriend of the 1940s. This butch was not as bad as her later girlfriends. "[She] was a little more liberal than—she wasn't as consuming and as possessive. [But] in her own little way she was."

Jealousy and the violence associated with it is prominent in all narrators' memories of the 1950s.

> "The butches would walk in and they'd see another butch talking or having their arm around the shoulder, whatever, and they'd just take the arm down and [pow!] there you had it. Then the girls would be dragged out. . . . That was mainly the reason for the fighting. 'Cause you didn't want your girl messing around and your girl didn't want you messing around. So she would get in fights too with girls. In other words, if my girl came in and seen me with my arm around you, now she might be hollering at me, but there's always two to tango, so she'd either take a punch at you or a punch at me, one of the two. That's the way it used to work." (D.J.)

Most narrators confirm that fems as well as butches would make jealous accusations and that they would also get into fights.

> "They'd both fight, or sometimes just the butch would beat up the fem. Or the two butches would fight, and the fem would stand there screaming. You know, 'Get away, stop, stop'. . . . [If a butch got caught by her fem], same thing. The fem would get very mad and be fighting with her butch. . . . Sometimes [it was physical]. Most often it was just hollering and screaming." (Pearl)

Jealousy was so much a part of this community that its absence could make a lover feel unwanted. Bert, reminiscing about the problems in her thirteen-year relationship, identifies this as one of them.

"I remember her last words when she saw me. . . . People always used to say, 'Bert, if you ever break up with [Gail] I'd sure like to go with her.' And I'd say, 'Oh I'll tie a red ribbon around her and you can have her,' and I meant it in jest. She told me that one of my faults was that I never showed any jealousy. She said she got tired of me giving her away with a red ribbon tied around her."

Jealousy created an undercurrent of suspicion and competition that powerfully shaped the social life of the 1950s, influencing the way couples related to one another when they went out, as well as the way a butch and a fem socialized. Although both butch and fem experienced jealousy and acted on it, making accusations and starting fights, the 1950s culture with its emphasis on the butch's protective bravery put butches in the controlling position. The institutions of socializing were built on the presupposition of butch control. All narrators who came out in the 1950s make some statement like the following:

"In those days, if you were a butch, you went to the bar with your fem and sat her down at a table and she didn't move till you said, 'Get up.' This is going to be hard to believe, but in those days, the fem even asked the butch if it was O.K. if she went to the john . . . and the butch went with her to make sure nobody made a pass at her." (Matty)

The custom of accompanying one's fem to the bathroom existed in the 1940s, but it was not universally practiced and is remembered as the only institutionalized restriction on fem behavior at the time. It served principally as protection from danger. One narrator of the 1940s remembers that the bars were quite rough. There might have been some straight men who would bother the women on the way to the bathroom, and also there were a number of butches whom "the fem girls made quite a pretense of being afraid of. . . . They [the butchy girls] swaggered around" (Arden).[24] The possessive dimension of this custom might have existed, but it was not yet fully developed.

By the 1950s, the customs governing the socializing of butch-fem couples served both to protect and control the fem. Many of these 1950s bars, particularly the street bars, were rougher than those of the 1940s, so that the butch's protection was still wanted and needed. Since part of a butch's reputation was built on her effective bravery in difficult situations, she publicly demonstrated her competence in protecting her fem from advances and harassment. But showing control over her fem to others in the community also was important. The limitations on a fem's behavior went beyond protecting her from danger. She could not freely move around the bar, talk to or dance with others without her butch's permission. These rules aimed to keep a fem tied to and dependent on her butch, while preventing her from establishing liaisons.

The customs for socializing governed not only fem behavior, but also that of butches. Butches followed rules for socializing with one another's fems that showed respect not simply for the fem, but for her butch. An etiquette existed in the 1950s that recognized butches' rights to their fems, respected their territory, so to speak. "Or how can you let your girlfriend stand at the bar and talk to so-and-so, well don't they respect you? Would somebody dare, would I walk over to [Annie] and say to [Annie] while [Sandy's] sitting there, '[Annie], would you dance with me?' You wouldn't do that shit. You'd ask [Sandy]" (Vic). This culture not only required a butch asking another's permission to dance with or even talk to her fem, it also frowned upon a butch visiting a couple's house if the fem was home alone. Toni recalls:

> "I know that, with some couples, if the butch wasn't home and a friend who was a butch came to the door and only the fem was there, you were not supposed to go in the house. It just wasn't done. To borrow something—you weren't supposed to go into the house. If she could hand it to you, that was O.K., but you really shouldn't go in that house."

If she did, she was risking a fight. "And a bad reputation too. . . . If you got a reputation that it wasn't safe to have you around people's girlfriends . . . see you could get a reputation like that. That you would steal someone's girlfriend; flirt with someone's girlfriend" (Toni).

By the late 1950s, a butch's control over her fem had become so important that younger butches wouldn't blame the offending butch if there was trouble.[25] If a butch "approached you to go out, put her hands on you, kiss[ed] you in the back room," it was always the fem's fault:

> "See that's like really putting somebody down, that if I would ever have to come to you and argue with you over my lady, that would be about the most degrading thing I could do. 'Cause I can't control her apparently. . . . No, the butches hit on their women. . . . I'm going with *you*, whatever happened shouldn't have happened. See I don't go with her. She approached *you* and *you* did something wrong, you're the one that's gonna be hit. 'Cause I go with *you*, I don't go with her, I don't care what she thinks." (Vic)

The extremes of the late-1950s butch's desire for control and the jealous violence that accompanied it are apparent in Vic's disturbing story about testing.

> "The big thing was they used to leave notes, 'Meet me at the juke box at 10:15.' Butches used to have somebody give their fem notes to see if they would get up and do it. And everybody would sit and [wait]. . . . Say like I was a pal of D.J.'s, right? I'd walk over to her fem and say, 'Here, somebody told me to give you this.' And [it] would say, 'Meet me at the juke box at 10:15,' or something. And then everybody'd sit back and say, 'Oh God, she's not gonna do it. 'Cause she's gonna get a beating if she does.' And a lot of them did, they got right up and went to the juke box. . . . And then she could go ahead and go to the juke box and I'm two steps behind her. You got it. . . . Yeah, it was tests, it was all these tests. . . . Or you'd put it under the

windshield wiper. I could tell you a girl that took a terrible beating at the Midtown Grill because she got up, and Sandy was right there also. We sat there and said, 'Oh God, if she don't make her move, and didn't she.' And the worst part is the bitch doesn't even know who the note came from. But is her ego affect[ed] that much that she had to find out? 'Cause she knew she was gonna take an ass kicking. . . . She would get up to the juke box and go and her butch would be right behind her and knock the shit right out of her. . . . But with the fems, they were tested all the time, all the time. At home, on the phone."

From the point of view of the butch offering respect to her fem in exchange for control, Vic can understand a fem's response to these notes only in terms of fem ego. And she doesn't find that satisfactory. "Well see, the weird part is that you think that they would have learned by then. They had stature, like you said, if they were sitting with me. . . . They just get their ass kicked. Why, if somebody handed you a note you would hope your hands fell off." In the interview, we suggest that maybe fems didn't want to be owned, but that was outside the boundaries of the way she conceptualized relationships. Ownership was an integral part of being in a couple at that time. If fems didn't like it, "Well, then they should have just got up and got out."

The proper behavior for the fem in a situation like this would have been to hand the note over to the butch. She was expected to report all incidents of butch attention, including those that occurred when her own butch was not around.

"Because that would have to be a butch that was an asshole, that didn't respect me. And to do that to her didn't respect me, and she's my lady and she loves me, she respects me. . . . What if somebody else in the bathroom or wherever it was, seen somebody hitting on my old lady and my old lady didn't come and tell me, and someone else told you. So to protect herself or whatever [she had better tell]." (Vic)

The reporting demonstrated not only the fem's sexual loyalty to the butch, but the respect she wanted her butch to receive from others. The two were inseparable. If a butch was respected, control over her fem was acknowledged by other butches in treating the fem as if she were forbidden property.

Fems would also be jealous of their butches. Such behavior was expected, in fact. "It wasn't just butches fighting, the fems fought a lot among themselves." But fems' jealousy was very different from butches' in the 1950s because they were not expected to, and had none of the social institutions that would help them control their butches' behavior. They had no equivalent of the tests that butches used, because it would be impossible to find anyone to deliver the notes for them. There was no strong solidarity among fems, and butches were too comradely to participate in one another's undoing. Butches might be strongly competitive over fems, but they also had a structure of solidarity based in the necessity of working together to create and defend a lesbian world. In addition, some of the customs of respect helped to quell the competition. Fems had no equivalent structures for building solidarity. Therefore, all they might resort to were bad temper and harsh words.

Butches were suspicious all the time, particularly in the late-1950s crowd.

> "I guess the butches had more freedom. It was like expected that you would, oh, maybe go out and get drunk with your friends in the afternoon or something. . . . But I know that I never wanted anyone I was with to step foot in a gay bar without me. That just, you know, was not really supposed to happen; and I wasn't really supposed to go in there alone myself, but I know I didn't want anybody I was with going in there without me. It frightened me. . . . What did she do? Of course she had to flirt with somebody. And then I would get so jealous, it would be awful." (Toni)

Vic says the fact that fems did not look like lesbians and had more freedom of movement increased the feelings of insecurity.

> "See fems could go wherever they wanted to go and they could do anything they wanted to do and the butches couldn't. I didn't go out a lot even during the daytime, because I didn't want to have to deal with the neighbors and things. You know, I'd wait till night to go out. She could go any time she wanted to go, and I guess it's resenting the fact that she could do this and I couldn't. I mean, if you're gone to the store for a half an hour does it take you half an hour to get a quart of milk? Now what were you doing? Did you make a phone call, did you see somebody? I'm not saying all of them, but I bet you if they're honest. . . . [I was like that] terribly, I still am. I just can't get rid of it, you know, the fact that there's always somebody there that's gonna try to do it to you."

Their own experience could do little to calm these fears. Most butches had had an affair with a fem who was in a relationship with someone else. Relationships that started in this manner did not exactly breed trust. Vic remembers that the fems she had been with came from a variety of situations.

> "Some of them weren't involved with other people, some of them had broken up relationships, and some of them were cheating. And that's probably why a lot of the jealousy came about is because you'd wind up going with a girl that had been with somebody else, and you knew damn well they cheated on them, so you think they're not gonna do it to you?"

D.J. agrees, "Well this is what I just said before, you don't trust. You can't trust. And 'cause you've seen what they did to the last person, who they tell you they were insanely in love with."

Butches were not simply victims of fems cheating. In many cases they encouraged it to prove that they were irresistible.

"I never seen a couple in all the time that I was out that, and this is gonna sound like a probably very self-centered thing to say, but I've never seen a woman that can't be made, and I don't care how much in love she is with her [girlfriend] I've never seen one yet. Because I've done it, I've done it, and I don't deny it." (Vic)

Even though many paid each other respect, butches could not always offer one another a sense of security. Vic remembers having to be suspicious of her friends in the late 1950s.

"I used to have good conversations with Toni, you know who I'm talking about. I guess we had kind of a respect for each other, and then we got turned off to each other. One time I asked her something, and I don't know who took more offense to it, her or myself, but I said, 'If I had to go somewhere and I had to leave my girlfriend with you, could I trust you with her? Do you think you'd make advances?' And she said to me, 'Yeah, I probably would if I was attracted to her.' You know, that kind of blew my mind right there. 'Cause I would never do that. No matter how attracted I was, I had that little bit of—help me with the word. . . . Well I'm a very honorable person, believe it or not. I couldn't do that."

Fems were also quite suspicious, but with different results. From their position of control, butches did not simply complain, but manipulated to take the offensive. They frequently blamed fems' accusations for driving them to activities they would not otherwise have thought about.

"But then sometime you can have a woman that she would drive you to do things. They nag you. They accuse you of doing things that you're not doing, give you an idea, and so if you're going to get accused of it you might as well go on out there and do it. Like the woman I had in New York, and she was much older than me, she should have known better. She was jealous, oh boy, she was really jealous. If I left the house and says, 'Well, I'm going to the show or any place,' say if I went to the show, she would figure up every minute of those two features that's playing, and if I [was] five minutes late she'd want to know where those five minutes went. So a person like that will really drive you to do things, because you are being accused of it and it's not even in your mind to do anything. So what the hell, I might as well go on and do it." (Debra)

In the 1950s, the bravado of butches was such that many narrators remember saying, "If you're gonna have the name, you might as well play the game" (Little Gerry), a perfect excuse for doing what they wanted to do anyway.

The tendency toward butch control in committed relationships was unquestionably irksome to fems. In some part of their interviews, *all* fems object to butch bossiness or jealousy. Some found the limitations placed on them by the butches extremely unpleasant, and are filled to this day with anger. Joanna comments on what she considered the excessive constraints of her relationships in the 1940s and 1950s, due to jealousy.

"If two girls live together there's no such thing like you can say to someone, I'm going to stop and have a drink after work, with the people you work with or something. There's that routine of coming home, . . . it's too domesticated, you know. I mean you become so involved, it's like being married then. This is what I fought against, I felt like I had never escaped my marriage and that was one thing I hated about my marriage, I felt like I was trapped."

Charlie is eloquent in her complaints. She loved a girlfriend dearly and they were together many years, but she still becomes angered by the jealousy.

"The difference in now and twenty-five years ago is twenty-five years ago anybody who was butch wanted to put you under their finger or thumb and they were extremely jealous. They gave you no room to breathe. It was almost like a prison. And even though some people could be happy in those conditions and arrangements, it wasn't as it is now. Now, anything I want to do, I do. If somebody doesn't want to do it with me, I do it. I don't mean I do anything that's bad. . . . I was told I was in love with the principal, I had a child. . . . I couldn't go to the PTA meetings, I couldn't go to school because I said the principal was a nice little guy, and he was. . . . Just like you would say [of] somebody on TV, 'Gee, isn't he a nice-looking guy?' So I was told that I was in love with the principal and I got so I was afraid to go in the grocery store, 'cause I didn't want to make any waves or any problems or troubles, but I didn't feel free. And if I had felt free I would have been a lot farther ahead today. Not to do anything wrong, but to be able to—like now I have a lot of men that call me for business reasons only, and there's no problem. I have meetings with men, I have lunch with men, you know, my life, everyone's life, consists of men, the men own the world. . . . Like in the last ten years I've just seemed to have come a long way, because nobody is telling me, 'Hey, you're in love with the principal,' or 'You can't go to the PTA meeting.' I couldn't even go to my best girl friend's wedding because I was told we were making love over the fence, 'cause she lived right next door. And it wasn't true. We're still to this day real good friends. And she got married and no, no, no, we had a big argument about the wedding. Is this being recorded too?"

These two fems were not actively part of the tough lesbian crowd and did not spend the majority of their time in open house parties and bars; nevertheless, they object to the possessiveness of butches. Curiously, fem narrators who were part of the tough street culture are no more critical of butch control, and, like the older fems, they emphasize their dislike of the possessive jealousy. A common complaint is about studs who stick too close so that the fems couldn't have any fun when they were out. Arlette still gripes about going to a new bar in Rochester that she had heard a great deal about, but not having a chance to enjoy it because she had to be so close to her butch.

"I don't like those kind of studs that feel like every time I step out the door [they] gotta go too. I don't need no shadows. We weren't Siamese twins. You take me out and expect I'm supposed to sit and look at you all night long. I feel like this, I had a girl I used to go with, take me all the way to Rochester to the Pink Panther. I heard so much about the Pink Panther. I get to Rochester and I said, 'Umm, very interesting, let's see what these kids are like here.' The first day she came out to tell me, 'Look at me.' [She wanted me to spend the whole evening looking at her. I could have been home.]"

In fems' memories, the possessive jealousy combined with the bossiness and sometimes violence created a difficult situation, something that fems would like to have changed about gay life.

"Oh no, I knew the situation I was in. I knew I had a [child] and I knew who I was with and I thought the world of her. But I didn't like the jealousness and I didn't like the bossiness. And then after going through it for all these years, now if you meet somebody who is bossy you just want to give them one punch and that's it, goodby. And the one I'm with now is such a doll, she only hollers once a year, and she hollers real loud then." (Charlie)

Despite their complaints, most fems evaluated their relationships positively. They were not sorry they had been in them, nor did they think they should have left them. Only a few look back on their relationships and can't understand why they ever stayed in them, given the unpleasant nature of the bossiness, jealousy, and cheating. They did not recall having gotten anything else out of the relationship.

"I don't know. I really don't know what made it last to tell you the truth. It was nothin.' When I think about it now, she was very demanding, she was very bossy, and I don't really know why I stayed with her as long as I did. She was one that had girlfriends, two or three girlfriends . . . and I'm still home, I'm still staying home." (Pearl)

For the majority of fems, the jealousy and bossiness were just an unpleasant side of an otherwise good relationship that they valued and cherished. Charlie explains that at the time she didn't know any better.

"Just like I was a wife. Well, first of all, she wouldn't let me work, which I wanted to work because I wanted to make money, but I did have my [child]. She still had a [child], and we bought this house and she was like the husband, she went to work, she brought home the pay. She was very demanding and commanding but we still got along. I didn't know any better or any different, I think that's what you'd call it. I think it's nice that people should be jealous, but not to the extreme."

Her girlfriend was very helpful and supportive to her, emotionally and financially, while she raised her child. To her mind, she was and still is a wonderful person.

"To this day she's one of the most wonderful people in the whole world. I see her [frequently. She] . . . tries to run my house. . . . Still tries to tell me what to do. . . . I mean you just can't take it out of her, that this remains in there, that she is the father. Demanding and commanding and bossy, but . . . she only has about an hour and a half to do it. But she's really a wonderful person."

Fems from the rough and tough lesbian crowd also evaluate their relationships positively, appreciating the caring, closeness, and respect between butch and fem. At many points in her life story, Annie favorably compares her experience of being in a butch-fem couple to that of being married. To her, everything is better about the butch-fem relationships, but she particularly likes the cooperation and freedom.

"A husband is like a job. . . . It's like a nine-to-five job. Where with the same type of sex [in the gay life] you're more freer I think. Not that you're gonna cheat on them or that, but you just feel more relaxed about it. If you both want to go somewhere or do the same thing, or whatever, you both will do it. Where with a husband, they don't want to always do things. . . . To me it seems more like a reporting thing. . . . Well here you do [have to tell] too, but it just doesn't seem to have the same pressure as far as I'm concerned."

BUTCH CONTROL: VIOLENCE IN LESBIAN RELATIONSHIPS OF THE LATE 1950s

Just as the public expression of jealousy increased in lesbian life in the 1950s, so did the violence, and, in narrators' minds, they are frequently connected. No narrator, butch or fem, remembers violence as part of her own relationships in the 1940s, nor did they know of it in other relationships. It might have existed in relationships, but was hidden.[26] However, throughout the 1950s, in keeping with the prominent role of violence in community life, violence became fairly common in relationships and it increased markedly in the rough and tough lesbian culture at the end of the decade. This escalation of butch violence toward the fems with whom they were involved is puzzling and distressing to contemplate. On the one hand, butches hitting fems evokes everything that is wrong with male supremacy. It has been the quintessential example for contemporary feminists of why this gendered lesbian culture has nothing to offer and should be dismissed from our heritage. On the other hand, once we digest the evidence that such physical abuse occurred in a limited historical period of butch-fem culture, under specific social conditions, this history opens up new perspectives on the complex connections among gender, power and violence.

Butch narrators who came out in the early 1950s, like those who came out in the 1940s, do not recall hitting their partners, but we know from fems that some butches of this period did use violence. Pearl remembers that her butch of this age group had beaten other partners, and had tried to beat her once:

> "Well, one time I heard that the butch went around saying that she beat me up, but she didn't. I came home drunk and she slapped me in the face and I slapped her back. She slapped me in the face and I slapped her back. . . . She never beat me up, but she said she did. . . . I know she did with other ones. In fact, one of the girls she went with is still a very good friend of mine and she used to beat her up. . . . But she never did with me because I just wouldn't let her. I mean I wasn't gonna stand there and let her slap me. Who did she think she was? And I told her so, I says, 'You don't slap me,' and I kept slapping her back till she finally decided to stop. My husband never beat me up and I couldn't see any woman beating me up."

All narrators, butch and fem alike, remember and talk about the violence in relationships of the tough crowd in the late 1950s and early 1960s. It was a public part of community life. This does not mean that all butches of this crowd and period hit their fems. In fact, we know some who did not. But the possibility of using violence was integrated into the culture. Butches not only talk about others' violence, but openly acknowledge their own, although they have neither the words nor the stomach to discuss it fully. "And there was also violence. There was a lot of violence. . . . What will I talk about? Do you want to sit around and talk about, you know, the girl that you punched in the face because she did something wrong, you don't want to say all that. But it was very violent" (Vic). Violence in relationships is not only taken for granted as part of the fabric of late-1950s social life, but also is dramatically marked in people's memories. Little Gerry, hearing a draft of our work, urges us not to cover up the violence, and immediately shares a vivid and unpleasant memory of "a butch taking her fem by the hair and bashing her head down on the bar. It was not nice."

In keeping with the autonomy of fems, violence was not limited to the butches. Some fems fought back and many were tough. In some cases, the fem's use of violence limited her butch's attack. In others, the violence escalated. Vic remembers with pain a particularly difficult relationship. "Those were rough years then. It was a very intense thing then . . . very violent. 'Cause she was the type, like D.J. said, you didn't just slap her in the mouth and that was O.K. She'd slap you back. And then the battle would be on and you'd fight, and the bar would." Sandy says some fems even initiated physical violence. "There were a few, but not too many mean fems." Narrators remember that drunkenness played a prominent role in exacerbating violent behavior in butches and fems.[27]

This culture did not articulate a prohibition against violence in relationships, as long as it did not go too far. Violence was integral to the entire way of life. There was an expectation that if a fight became too ugly, friends in the bar would intervene. And it never happened that other butches would join in to help a friend beat up her fem. The general feeling of narrators was that the violence rarely led to serious physical harm. Their memories reveal only one or two butches who were known for badly bruising their fems. Only one fem narrator, Bell, was badly beaten and by only one of her partners, who was her pimp who used force to keep her working.[28]

> "And she became forceful at times with me. . . . One evening she came into the bar and I was sitting and she was very angry that I was sitting down in the bar. She felt that I should be home getting dressed to go out and do this hooking that she wanted me to do. And we got into an argument because I really didn't want to do this stuff. And she dragged me out of the bar by the hair on my head. This was Bingo's bar. And I don't know what the people in the bar thought, at this point they didn't really know what was happening, but I knew what was happening. And they figured we were just having a lover's fight I guess. So a lot of times people did not step into things, but then there were times when your good friends did jump in and fight for you or with you. I was just tired of this thing, because it was constant with us that she was trying to make me do this hustling."

When Bell finally broke away, she was frightened that her pimp would find her.

> "In the meantime, I still wasn't too happy and my friend still had not found me. But I felt in my heart, that she was looking for me and she would find me. And it did happen. I would say about two weeks after that she did find me and we had a terrible, terrible argument, and I thought that she was gonna beat the living shit out of me. . . . She did hit me, and I had a black eye. When she hit me it was like in the center of my nose here. She didn't break my nose, but it like gave me two black eyes and my face was all swollen."

After this violent confrontation, the two no longer had anything to do with one another, and Bell was not beaten in her subsequent relationships.

The threat of violence meant that at least some fems at some times lived in fear in their relationships. Pearl was somewhat impatient with other fems for complaining about the violence, yet staying in the relationships. She thinks, however, that they may have stayed out of fear.

> "Oh yeah, they would cry about it, but they'd still go back to the same person again. They would still stay with them. And I believe, if that's what you want, you know, I can't see it myself, but that was just my opinion. . . . I don't know, I couldn't understand why they would stay in a situation. They would say that they liked the person so well or they loved the person so much that they would stand for it. And yet they would cry about it and complain. They might have been like I was with my husband, afraid to leave."[29]

Although violence had the effect of keeping some people in relationships, its effect was not long-lasting. In the rough culture of the late 1950s, when relationships were most violent, most relationships were relatively short, one to three years. And even relationships that lasted longer inevitably ended.

Because this community was not completely tied into the dominant system of heterosexual male supremacy, violence did not function in lesbian relationships in the same way as in heterosexual relationships: physical violence had a limited effect in terrorizing fems. Most important, the use of violence by butches was not a secret. At this time, fems were neither isolated in their relationships nor ashamed of the violence. Most fems talked with others about violence and did not live under the threat of serious repercussion should they tell the truth; the "truth" was known. Since people went out regularly, any serious violence in the home was apparent to the community. Many fights actually took place in public, in the bars. Not only were there witnesses, but also observers would usually step in and interrupt a fight that got too bad. Ironically, lesbian feminist culture of the 1970s, by adopting the ideology that only men were violent, created an atmosphere in which violence in lesbian relationships needed to be kept a secret and many women lost the protection of community limitation.

In addition, very few fems were totally dependent on their butches. Most supported themselves and knew that they could make a life for themselves. Furthermore, both butch and fem knew that the relationship would not last forever, that there was no social support for its continuity. Vic, with the benefit of distance and experience, points out that the use of violence hastened the end of a relationship. "When you hit your woman, that was like really bad to do that. Because then in a way you were losing control. And that was like the first thing before a breakup, when you started slapping your woman around." Should a fem leave, there was little impetus for the butch to keep harassing her. Community values and institutions emphasized the excitement of a new romance, rather than the necessity of continuing the old.[30]

Fem narrators from the tough street crowd object more to the jealousy than to the violence. They see the former as the cause of the latter. Their overlooking of the problems associated with violence could reflect a tendency on the part of those who have been beaten to underplay or deny their experience. Of our fem narrators, only Bell mentioned having been battered. We know that Arlette was never beaten, because she had the reputation of ending a relationship when a butch raised a hand to her. For the others, it is difficult to ascertain their experiences. It is possible that much of the violence directed toward fems was disparate instances of aggression, not a developed pattern of abuse, and that in the context of this rough street life, where butches and fems fended off attack from the heterosexual world, fems took expressions of violence for granted.[31]

A variety of factors created the increase in violence in lesbian relationships throughout the 1950s. Fem narrators most frequently explain it in terms of the butch's pursuit of the masculine persona. "Yeah, there was quite a few [who were violent]. It was quite a fashionable [thing], to be the strong one, supposedly. They figured they were the man" (Pearl). But the rise in violence cannot be understood simply in terms of maleness, because 1940s butches were as masculine as those in the 1950s. It was the tough masculine culture—the violence, jealousy, and solidarity—of the 1950s bar crowd that was crucial. "You know the butches were trying to be really tough. . . . 'I'll show you I'm boss. I'll give you a smack' " (Sandy). Butch solidarity and aggressiveness, whether it be in protecting fems and the community or in testing their fems' loyalty, supported this assertion of butch control and power.

Vic remembers learning to hit her fem as part of the cultural package of becoming butch, like how to dress.

> "When you ask that question, where do you think that people, like myself, that came out in the '50s, where do you think I learned how to act and how to deal in the bar? . . . From the butches that were around from the '40s and early '50s, that's where I learned. I seen them. They were gods to me. And I seen how they treated their people and I did the same thing that they did. They were the ones that would, you know, 'Fems, don't let her do that, you tell her to sit down, and that's it. . . . ' Well how would I know, I was just coming out, how would I know that? Hit my girlfriend, I would never hit her. She might leave me and she's the only one in the world. But then they taught me, you wear your hair short and you dress like this and your woman does this and that. They're the ones that showed me how to—what I should be like, to be right up there with them."

Vic is adamant that the violence that was part of her life must have existed earlier. She was incredulous when D.J. said she had only hit a woman once. "You can say that you've only hit one woman in your life?" Under interrogation, D.J. modifies her position slightly: "The ones that I've lived with is what I'm talking. Oh I've hit other women." Vic takes this as a sign of D.J. reneging on her original position and becoming more honest. The strength of her views reflects the fact that violence was so embedded in this culture by the time she entered the bars that it is hard to imagine its absence a decade earlier. Unquestionably, she learned violent behavior from older lesbians at the bar, but then she went on to be an active participant in the culture of the late 1950s and early 1960s, which pushed the use of violence to the extreme.

Why would the violence and the solidarity that was central to the lesbian confrontation with the straight world be turned inward toward fems? This aggressive and confrontational culture placed the butch in the vulnerable and stressful position of defender of the community and promoted the fem as the highly desired, but unreliable, refuge or source of security. As the decade progressed, the butches' full-time masculine persona isolated them completely from society, to the point where many could not hold down jobs. Their confrontational approach to straight society gave rise to a consistent challenge and danger from straight men. And, of course, the increased time in bars promoted greater alcohol consumption. Such a situation promoted self-hatred and insecurity. Sandy identifies the reasons for violence in relationships as the guilt complex she and her friends had about living off their fems. "A lot of times you get to feel like, when a girl was working—you get like a guilt complex. Like, 'Why can't I make the money?' So you even would start a fight." Vic attributes the violence to tremendous insecurity.

> "Most relationships were very violent at that time. And I think that's what happened to most people. I don't think it was money or jobs or society or anything else, it was just a very insecure time that you were going through. When you loved somebody you owned them, it was an ownership. This is my woman. . . . She knew that. When a woman got in a relationship with a butch she knew she belonged to them. And that's how it was."

In this situation, fems were the only source of beauty and joy in butches' lives. But in this culture, which was expanding its boundaries, fems, by definition, were unstable "possessions," who had to be watched carefully and defended rigorously, lest they be lost. Their sexuality was in question in basic ways due to their heterosexual pasts and also to the association of many with prostitution, not to mention their active sexual lives in the lesbian community. Butches, many of whom had little of material value, including good jobs, warily protected all that they saw of import in their lives—their fems and their relationships.[32]

In an atmosphere that constantly threatened lesbians' self-worth and undermined their self-image, violence became central in some lesbian relationships. Butches regretted it and apologized for it, but they continued to act it out. Tragically, it never achieved the end it aimed for, but rather often served to undermine the relationships and cause these butches to lose the very thing they sought to secure. From the perspective of the 1990s, when for at least two decades the feminist movement has organized to combat violence against women, it seems curious how matter-of-factly these lesbians speak of the violence in their past relationships. Although tough lesbians of the late 1950s banded together to fight the overt oppression of the straight world, they had little analysis of the dynamics engendered by male supremacy, homophobia, and self-hatred, the recognition of which, in later years, created the tools for women to confront and resist violence in relationships.

This research shows that the publicly violent relationships of the late 1950s and early 1960s are representative of only a limited time period and cultural group in lesbian life, in which certain tendencies of pre-feminist and pre-gay liberation lesbian culture were carried to excess. Although nothing can excuse the jealousy and violence, they do need to be understood as having developed in the context of the severe stress and pressure created by the attempt to publicly validate lesbian life and to claim more space for lesbians. The self-hatred of these particular public lesbians, born of extreme stigmatization, took a toll on personal life. To single out their relationships as representative of working-class lesbian relationships of the period makes it difficult to focus on the strengths of the majority of lesbian relationships—their accomplishment in fostering the expression of love between women in extremely oppressive conditions. Moreover, to isolate them from the tradition of lesbian relationships that preceded them highlights only their violence and underplays dimensions of caring and closeness.

The committed relationships of the tough street crowd are neither typical nor anomalous in lesbian history. They must be seen in the context of a tradition of butch-fem relationships built on contradictory tendencies within the culture. On the one hand, these committed relationships fostered warmth, closeness, intimacy, romance, caring, cooperation, and exchange. They also frequently supported personal growth. On the other hand, they encouraged butch control, which manifested itself in protectiveness, possessiveness, bossiness, and aggressiveness. Narrators' insistence that lesbian relationships have not changed much over time indicates that they didn't see the behavior as different enough to mark it as a separate period. Furthermore, the grievances of fems from all decades about butch bossiness and aggressiveness provide strong evidence that the confrontational culture of the late 1950s was only extending the already existing tendency toward butch control of fems.

The ugly stereotype of lesbian relationships as destructively jealous and of the masculine woman as harmfully controlling has some truth. The oppressive social conditions—the lack of validation for lesbians, the necessity to fight for one's dignity, the vulnerable identity of the fem—did combine to bring tyrannical jealousy to the fore. But this is only one limited aspect of lesbian relationships in public communities. The framework of serial monogamy allows us to hear and acknowledge the voices of lesbians who express pleasure about the place of relationships in their lives, and see the positive aspects of relationships. In addition, by taking a larger view, we are able to see change in the expression of intimacy over time and therefore to identify specific social and cultural conditions that give rise to violence in intimate relationships.

From this perspective, butch-fem couples should be respected not simply for their heroism in confronting heterosexual society, but also for the passion, loving, and commitment they shared under extremely oppressive conditions. Recognizing these accomplishments does not negate the difficulties of lesbian relationships in the past—the painful break-ups, the jealousy and, in the late 1950s, the violence. It provides a more accurate, balanced picture. It is time to let the full history of lesbian relationships enter the social record and become the broader basis for mythmaking in lesbian consciousness.[33]

"IN EVERYBODY'S LIFE THERE HAS TO BE A GYM TEACHER": THE FORMATION OF LESBIAN IDENTITIES AND THE REPRODUCTION OF BUTCH-FEM ROLES

At least for a woman, wanting to become a man proves that she has escaped her initial programming. But even if she would like to, with all her strength, she cannot become a man. For becoming a man would demand from a woman not only a man's external appearance but his consciousness as well, that is, the consciousness of one who disposes by right of at least two "natural" slaves during his life span. This is impossible, and one feature of lesbian oppression consists precisely of making women out of reach for us, since women belong to men. Thus a lesbian has to be something else, a not-woman, a not-man, a product of society, not a product of nature, for there is no nature in society.

—Monique Wittig, "One Is Not Born a Woman"

If sexual desire is masculine, and if the feminine woman only wants to attract men, then the womanly lesbian cannot logically exist. Mary's real story has yet to be told.

—Esther Newton, "The Mythic Mannish Lesbian"

The preceding chapters have documented changes in the content and meaning of butch-fem roles over time, and have emphasized growth and transformation in the way those roles have functioned in the community. Nevertheless, the prominence and tenacity of butch-fem roles resonates with the idea that masculine and feminine emotional, psychological, and behavioral traits transcend time and culture, and are biologically based. Such thinking always lurks under the surface in twentieth-century Western culture, inviting the interpretation that butch-fem roles, and even lesbianism itself, develop because some women are genetically or hormonally more male than the norm. The tension between biology and culture or continuity and change raises questions about the nature of lesbian identity and the way butch-fem culture was reproduced over time. Did people come to the community with butch and fem as part of their identities, or were the roles learned in the community? At what age did people come to their lesbian identities, and was that different for butch or fem identities? What was the boundary between lesbianism and heterosexuality? Were fems as well as butches perceived as lesbians?

We have left the discussion of these complex issues of butch, fem, lesbian and gay identities to the last in order to explore them in the context of changing forms of community and culture. We aim to illuminate the degree to which lesbian identity changed through history. As yet, little research exists on gay and lesbian identity in the early and mid-twentieth century. Ironically, the assumption that modern homosexual identity came into being in the late nineteenth century, while so fruitful for historical research on the development of gay and lesbian communities and political action, has tended to obscure and deemphasize changes within twentieth-century gay and lesbian identities and to rigidify the boundaries between homosexuals and heterosexuals as distinct kinds of people. Most historians assign an influential role in shaping lesbian and gay identity to the late-nineteenth and early-twentieth-century medical writings and the sexologists that built on and popularized this work. These sources were the first to name and discuss in print homosexuals as distinct kinds of people. They also defined as a disease what had been heretofore either a sin or a crime, usually identifying the cause as some constitutional flaw. In this early writing, gender inversion rather than choice of sexual partner defined homosexuality. The masculine woman was the homosexual. Her partner, who followed appropriate gender guidelines in appearance and behavior and was attracted to the masculine if not to the male, was not thought to transcend the boundaries of normalcy, and consequently received little medical attention.[1]

Esther Newton and George Chauncey both caution against seeing a direct relationship between medical models and the formation of gay and lesbian identities. At the turn of the century, when society viewed women as without sexual interest, Newton argues that lesbians created a masculine identity in order to be able to pursue their sexual interests in women.[2] Chauncey in his study of the 1919–1929 Navy trials of gay men in Newport, Rhode Island, found no evidence of gay men's or heterosexual people's familiarity with the medical writings, even though both groups' understandings of gay identity resembled the medical model.[3] He therefore suggests that working-class gay men had created their own identity through community, and it was this that the medical profession was attempting to catalogue, describe, and explain. Chauncey's and Newton's interpretations assign gays and lesbians agency in shaping their own identities and lives, albeit in an extremely oppressive context. In this framework, the medical profession did not impose a gender inversion model on a lesbian and gay population that already had an idea of "same-sex" love. But rather lesbian identity based on gender inversion and that based on the choice of sexual partner were shaped by lesbians in the context of resisting the limitations imposed by a hostile society. Recognizing that gays actively formed the identity of "sexual inversion," rather than having had it imposed on them by "professionals," highlights how greatly homosexual identity has changed over the past ninety years.[4]

Chauncey's masterfully intricate analysis of working-class gay male identity in 1919 and the ways it began to change is a useful starting point for analyzing Buffalo butch, fem, and lesbian identities. In the Newport, Rhode Island homosexual subculture, gender inversion, not sexual behavior, was the determining factor in homosexual identity. This homosexual subculture was well known throughout the Northeast and centered around a group of effeminate men who were sexually passive and who identified themselves as "queer." The "queers" pursued sex with sailors and townspeople. Those heterosexuals or "straights" who would have sex with them were called "trade" and were not considered "queer" or different from other heterosexual men. The Navy wanted to rid the area of "queers" and felt free to gather data on them by recruiting volunteers to entrap and have sex with them.

At the beginning of the ensuing trial, neither the Navy nor the decoys themselves considered the decoys tainted with homosexuality because they had engaged in sex with the "queers." Gender was so identified with sexuality that it was not choice of a partner of the "same sex" that indicated homosexuality, but the taking on of the role of the "opposite sex" in the pursuit of sexual relations with the "same sex." During the course of the trial, these ideas began to change. Due to irregularities in the case, there had to be a retrial. At that time, the defense changed its approach, introducing the idea that the decoys not only solicited the gay men, but enjoyed the sex they had with them, and were therefore homosexual themselves. Thus the idea that the homosexual is defined not by his (or her) gender behavior, but by his (or her) choice of sex partner began to engage the popular imagination.[5]

The specific date of the transition from a definition of homosexual identity based in gender inversion to the contemporary one based on object choice is difficult to ascertain. Rather, the idea that a homosexual was someone who was attracted to a person of the "same sex" became slowly and unevenly incorporated into medicine, popular culture, and gay and lesbian culture. We put "same sex" in quotation marks to remind the reader that this concept is a modern cultural construction.[6] The first of Freud's *Three Essays on the Theory of Sexuality* published in 1905 is a landmark in this process, though Freud remains ambiguous about the nature of lesbian identity.[7] Officially by World War II the Army, in the examination of recruits had made the change. Nevertheless, they still looked for effeminacy, as well as interest in the opposite sex.[8] Kinsey's *Sexual Behavior in the Human Female* unequivocally assumes homosexuality to be a sexual relationship between two people of the same sex, as clearly stated in the opening sentence of the chapter on homosexuality: "The classification of sexual behavior as masturbatory, heterosexual or homosexual is based upon the nature of the stimulus which initiates the behavior."[9] By the founding of the homophile movement in the 1950s, object choice was the primary definer of homosexual identity.

Our research indicates that Buffalo's working-class lesbian community was in the midst of the transition from gender inversion to object choice during the 1940s and 1950s. In the 1940s, the identities of community participants still had a lot in common with those described by participants in the gay-male subculture of 1919, in the sense that the community was strongly gendered and the butch was unmistakably "homosexual" or "queer," while the fem was not; ideas of "same-sex" love, however, were also present in the articulation of lesbian identity. This historical context allows us to understand that the ambiguous position of the fem is not rooted, as feminists often assume, in misogyny or antifemale sentiment, since in the gay-male culture the identity of masculine men was equally ambiguous, but rather in the understanding of what it is to be homosexual. By the 1950s, lesbian identity had undergone a significant shift. Most women who came out during this period based their identity in attraction to women, and fems as well as butches considered themselves gay, if not lesbian. This change had significant implications for lesbian culture and social life. It increased the similarities between butch and fem at a time when gender roles were becoming ever more stringent, and changed the way boundaries were drawn between heterosexuals and homosexuals.

The primary reasons for change in the nature of lesbian identity would seem to be the increasing separation between gender and sex as the twentieth century progressed, due to the struggle of women for greater autonomy and the expansion of consumer capitalism and its drive to use sex to sell goods. As we will argue in this chapter, Buffalo lesbians were actors in this process. The increased sexual awareness of women in their teen years allowed women to develop an identity based on sexual feelings and replace the masculine as a badge and marker of difference. In addition, it seems that the actual growth and stabilization of the community itself affected the formation of identity, and that in turn, this affected lesbian culture. In order to explore these connections between identity and community organization and culture, this chapter documents the meaning of butch, fem, lesbian, and gay identities for individual narrators. It is organized by decade to highlight the process of change.

BUTCH, LESBIAN AND GAY IDENTITIES IN THE 1940s

Butch and fem identities were significantly different during the 1940s. Butch identity was deeply felt internally, something that marked the person as different, while fem identity was rooted in socializing with and having relationships with gays. Fems did not experience themselves as basically different from heterosexual women except to the extent that they were part of gay life. Within this general pattern there was significant variation in the form and content of the identities of both butches and fems. Also, the connection between butch and fem identities and gay identity varied.

Butch identity was based in various combinations of masculine inclination and sexual interest in women. Some version of the late-nineteenth-century invert model that defined a lesbian as a masculine woman was used by most. In the 1940s it was overdetermined that feeling different, being lesbian would be expressed in terms of masculinity. The concept "lesbian" was not yet known by the average young woman. Instead, masculinity readily expressed a sense of autonomy and an erotic interest in women. In addition, for most women, sexuality was still so embedded in gender that ungendered sex would be hard to imagine.

In the case of many butches, their masculinity indicated their difference when they were quite young; for others, their masculinity is apparent to them in retrospect, and came to consciousness at the same time as their interest in women. The early and clear recognition of masculinity seems to correlate with a strong need to build gay community, for all such butches were central to that process. For other butches, interest in women was the primary definer of who they were, but was rarely completely separated from masculinity. These women spent long periods away from the bar community and some married. This would seem to confirm the theory that taking on masculine attributes was very important for women to be able to announce their sexual interest to other women, and to find others like themselves. In addition, the use of the term "gay" as a marker of identity was not common for those who identified clearly and strongly as masculine. For them it was more of a descriptive term. Those whose interest in women was the predominant marker of their identity more often used the term "gay" as a definition of who they were.

Arden and Leslie are quite typical in their early appropriation of masculine behavior. Arden, like several other narrators of this period, remembers that she preferred to play with the boys because "the straight girls were too picky." In the street when she was young, she projected a masculine image—"had that air about myself"—and didn't care what others thought. Leslie gives many examples of her desire to take on masculine characteristics early in life. She remembers reveling in the boyish shoes her father made her wear because she was so hard on her shoes, and related a humorous tale of getting her first short haircut in the 1930s.

> "Then the boy's bob came out. My father took me to a barber he knew, and he got carried away and was telling the guy how to cut it up around the ears. My mother screamed, 'What happened to your hair?' [Then] I used to take a scissors into the bathroom and cut my hair, and my mother would say, 'How come your hair doesn't grow?' I would say, 'Gee, I don't know!' "

She still marvels at how she knew so young that her interests were "wrong" and could only be expressed with caution and subterfuge.

Leslie's masculinity was coupled with an aggressive attraction to women at an early age. She couldn't remember a time when she wasn't "after the girls. . . . A father caught me rubbing against his daughter, standing on the running board of the car. I was sent home and forbidden to play with the girl again." When asked if she was consciously initiating sexual contact, she responds, "Definitely."

Family disapproval and discipline of their unruly behavior did not deter either of these young women. They consciously went out as teenagers to find other lesbians. Arden had a few gay friends in her neighborhood and through them found Galante's in 1932. Leslie had a harder time and remembers thinking in high school in 1936 that she was "the only one on earth." They both read *The Well of Loneliness* before actively participating in bar life, and both identified with Stephen. They did not have to learn a butch identity when they entered the bars, but simply learned appropriate ways to express their already developed identities.

Debra's butch identity developed early with sexual experience being more prominent in her memory than masculine interests, although they were closely intertwined. The two are difficult to separate for these butches because sexual interest in women was taken as a sign of masculinity. In her first sexual relationship at the age of thirteen, she played the more masculine role, carrying her sweetheart's books, but also being more aggressive sexually. She felt at the time that there was something different or unnatural about the relationship, but it did not deter her. When her family sent her up North, thereby ending the relationship with this woman, she was unclear about what she wanted in life. In Buffalo, she continued to meet lesbians and also, due to pressure from her family, began to date men. She married, but knew immediately it wasn't for her and took off for another city.

> "I didn't have a boyfriend, and they [my family were] always saying to me, 'Why don't you get a boyfriend, have a boyfriend like the other young girls?' And I'd always tell em, 'I don't want to, there's plenty of time for that.' So anyway they kept after me and kept after me, and then I got married. But the first day, the marriage lasted one day, I knew that wasn't for me. . . . I told him I didn't want him, he wasn't for me. . . . Well at first he thought I was crazy. But after, later on, he found out why I didn't want him. . . . I'm afraid he never understood that."

From her one-day marriage she became pregnant and had a child who was raised by a sibling, but whom she saw regularly. She feels that lesbians can be good mothers, perhaps better mothers because they "know the ropes."

The kind of independence Debra asserted by leaving her marriage and creating the life that she wanted was characteristic of many butches of this period. They did not intend to define themselves through marriage, but rather to work and build their own lives. They developed an extraordinary sense of their right to be who they were and an ability to affirm this for themselves. Debra still feels this strongly today, despite the fact that a few years ago she left lesbian life because she was disgusted with the way her relationships had gone. She has no regrets. "I didn't try to live my life to suit somebody else. I lived mine to suit myself. So I have nothing to regret, because I did exactly what I wanted to do."

Although masculinity was prominent in these three women's identities from an early age, it meant significantly different things to each of them. Leslie would have preferred to have been a man, and live a heterosexual life as a husband to a woman and the father of children. Arden had no such desires. Her masculinity did not pervade all aspects of her identity, to the extent that for brief periods in her life she was interested in being a mother, and at one time had discussed the possibility with a friend, but decided that she did not want to sleep with a man. Although Debra was an extremely masculine butch, and was considered very good-looking by fems who knew her, she did not see her masculinity as an immutable or rigid part of her identity. She understands identity to be something which is continually created. "If you're in gay life, you're in gay life, whichever—if you want to play the fem or be the butch, you certainly have to go out and find it, one way or the other, what part you are going to play." Though strongly butch-identified, she lived her life with considerable flexibility. She permitted herself to mother, and then entered the straight life in her later years.

D.J., slightly younger than these other three butches, was the only one to have any contact with the medical profession, and this definitely affected her understanding of herself and her identity. When asked how old she was when she came out, she responds in terms of medical diagnosis. "Well according to [the] doctor . . . I was born that way, so from the day I was born I've been homosexual." She also had clear categories of who and what was normal. She remembers going to the doctor because "I wanted to make sure one way or the other. Not that I was out of my mind, but I mean as far as my feelings, emotions, I knew at the time being with a girl was not normal."

D.J. knew she was different from the time she was ten or so, because she was definitely interested in girls. Since she did not get along with her stepmother, she left home, which allowed her to explore her feelings. She cut her hair short and dressed as a boy for protection on the street. In time, she ran into trouble with the law.[10] After reform school, she tried to sort out who she was, and was recommended by a family friend to see an expert at E. J. Meyer Memorial Hospital.[11]

> "And she asked me if I'd like to talk to someone, [that] this is her field, and I says, 'O.K. I ain't got nothin' to lose.' And I figured, 'Hey, if I am I am, if I ain't I ain't.' One way or other I gotta know. So I went up to the Meyer Hospital at the time, the clinic, went through all the tests. And he came at the end and he told me, he says, 'You're one of the unfortunate ones that are born that way.' He said, 'You have to learn to live with society. You have to learn to control your emotions when and where they suit you.' So in other words, when you are working you don't make out with the girl alongside of you. When you go to your own places, then you do your thing. You can't mix business and pleasure."

Although the doctors were confident in their diagnosis, they also suggested one last test.

"Now the doctor said that I had to find out one way or the other for my own peace of mind whether or not I was or I wasn't. So they made one suggestion. . . . 'Go out with a man, and see whether or not you did or did not like one way. . . . ' See you have to try both. . . . Try to see whether or not I was completely or, as they would say, the bisexual bit. This got just so far and that was it, ended the whole deal."

D.J. never found it necessary to go back to the doctor, and he did not propose her returning for treatment. "Well, he said there was nothing else he could do, that you have to learn to live with it in public. It's something you're born with and can't change it, and that was it. He says, 'As far as the tests are and everything, flying colors, you're not nuts.' I said, 'Thanks. Thank you.' "

Ever since D.J. received confirmation that she was "abnormal" and also that she was born that way and couldn't help it, it has been imprinted in her mind. Others might have occasionally thought these things about themselves, but it was not so prominent in their consciousness. Of all narrators for this period, D.J. most regrets being a lesbian, and wishes she could have been different. It may be that the medical profession, by intervening in lesbians' lives, naming their condition as a disease that is inborn and cannot be escaped, made lesbians feel sorry for themselves and regret who they were, rather than helping them feel in control of their lives and goals.

The clarity these butches have about their early identities encourages the idea that they were born that way, and they merely had to learn to interpret behavior that started earlier. Several of them actually understand their lives this way. But butch identity is more complicated than this, as suggested by Debra, who sees lesbians as creating their butch identity. In fact, not all butches were aware of their identities from an early age. A surprising number came to their butchness, and to lesbianism, through a relationship, or through chance contact with the lesbian community after being actively heterosexual. Significantly, however, none of these butches built their lives around socializing in the public lesbian community. In all such cases, sexual interest in women is the more prominent marker of lesbian identity, but nevertheless masculinity plays a surprisingly important role.

Dee did not think of herself as gay until in 1938, after a five-month marriage to a man who turned out to be alcoholic and abusive, she met and fell in love with a woman from work. Once this happened, she could look back on earlier signs of being gay. With hindsight she remembers being interested in traditionally masculine things and having crushes on older girls.

"When I was twelve years old I had this very, very mad crush on a gal who at that point was twenty. I used to play violin all over town, and Rita would always drive me. Rita would let me drive her car. Rita would take me out for ice cream sodas and sundaes, and one night we were coming home from somewhere, and she kissed me on the forehead and said, 'Read *The Well of Loneliness* when you get a little older and I don't want to see you until you're eighteen.' And I was heartbroken. I worshipped the ground this gal walked on. . . . In fact, I was on crutches due to a dislocated knee, my cousin would drive me up to Buffalo General Hospital, that's where she was, and from the Buffalo General Hospital I would walk home . . . on crutches, that is how madly I was in love. Well this broke my heart, and for days I was actually distraught. Well the time, that Halloween, the first time that Heloise and I walked into Ralph Martin's, Rita was sitting there with a girlfriend. And she looked up at me and she said, 'I figured I'd see you here one day.' "

She did go out and find *The Well of Loneliness* as Rita had recommended. Nevertheless, her masculine interests, her crushes, and the book did not combine to give her consciousness about being different or gay.

"They used to in those days have lending libraries, for three cents a day you got a book, and the drugstore had a lot of books, and I was an avid reader. And so when I was about fourteen I read it once. . . . Well I didn't make any sense out of it, at that point. And then when I was seventeen or so I read it again, and I still didn't connect it with me. As I said, I got married when I was eighteen. . . . It was after Heloise and I started going together, then I read it again and then I realized how it made sense, how it applied to me."

For Dee, lesbian identity, or as she would say being gay, was more central than being butch. In her own mind, she didn't believe in roles, and did not live her life according to them. Although she was more butch in her first relationship, she was more feminine in several subsequent relationships. Then she was more butch again in her second long relationship. When she dated again she was feminine in several relationships and in her third long relationship she was the more feminine. Dee did not have a preference.

"I would respond to whichever relationship I was in. . . . It depended upon the individual. No, I think by nature, because I built a house and wired it and because I . . . like Sunday, when Gloria's furnace went off, I crawled in and tried to light the pilot, but it wouldn't stay lit cause it needed a thermocouple which I didn't have. I mean, the average woman doesn't do that sort of thing. So I think. . . . I had more masculine than feminine tendencies, but I also like to clean house and cook. I love to experiment in cooking. So as I said, I pretty much respond to who I'm with. Now Heloise was very completely fem, little dainty, long fingernails and polished. Claire was [fem] so I was the more masculine one of that group. With Ellen she is the more masculine, she's big and brawny. And with Marcia, the one gal that I went with during the war off and on, the one I said with the lunch bucket and the men's dungarees bit, which in those days even the men didn't have men's dungarees, I was the more feminine. I guess I sort of fell between. Not that I am knowingly sitting down and saying, 'O.K., they got more masculine tendencies, therefore I'll be more feminine, or they have more feminine tendencies and therefore I'll be more masculine.'. . . This is quite unconscious on my part, it's just this is how

I respond to people. It depends on *their* outstanding traits compared to mine, and I give."

Dee's philosophy about roles went along with this flexibility in relationships and was quite similar to some contemporary feminist thinking. As mentioned in chapter 5, she believes all humans have masculine and feminine potential, and considers lesbianism to be based on women's erotic interest in women. Once she had her first relationship with a woman, Dee remained gay throughout her life. Masculinity plays a contradictory role in the formation of her identity. On the one hand, throughout her life story she takes her "masculine" interest in mechanical things as indicating that she was born gay. For instance, when asked what helped her accept all sides of herself she replies:

> "Well I don't know, I guess I just realized I am what I am and I can't do much about it. I think I was gay from when I was born, because when I was five years old my mother gave me one of those little automobiles that you peddle— I think I told you this, didn't I?—and with the first spring day I had it in fifty million pieces 'cause I wanted to see what made it work. And then I put it back together again, and I forever was taking things apart, radios, and hot water tanks and you name it."

On the other hand, she thinks everyone has masculine and feminine characteristics and should act on them as they desire. The idea that a lesbian was a masculine woman was so powerful that she could not let it go even though she lived her own life according to different ideas.

Reggie's butch identity is firmer than Dee's. She was butch in all her lesbian relationships, but she never felt herself as butch as others, and for periods of her life she was confused about whether she was gay, which resulted in a twenty-year marriage. Reggie was not consciously aware of being different until her first trip to Ralph Martin's with her fiancé. On that night, when an attractive fem asked her to dance, she learned that she was butch.

> "I never danced, never, not even at proms. I danced, let's face it, but I didn't follow good; so I got out and it was just a natural thing. I grabbed her and I led. She was tiny and cute, and she says, 'You're gay.' I says, 'Oh yeah, I'm happy,' and I meant it. It was sincere. She thought I was pulling her leg. And of course you're always going to try to act older because of where you are. And she said, 'No,' she said, 'I knew you were a butch when you walked in the door. I don't care if you've got long hair or what.' And I said, 'Oh, I'm engaged to be married.' She said, 'I don't care if you're engaged, got long hair, I know you're a gay butch.' I says, 'Oh, no, I'm going, Oh God.' Well we finished our dance and I joined her group."

Reggie remembers crushes on neighborhood girls when she was young, but as with others of this generation, that in itself was not enough to form her gay identity. Memories of her masculine inclinations are also significant. In her case, it was not mechanical interests but sports that indicated her masculinity. "Like my father used to say, 'Can't you play with girls?' 'Cause I always used to play with the boys as far as sports." She also idealized her brothers, watching and mimicking their every move. The place and meaning of masculinity in her life is a question that runs throughout her life story. "But yet I'm different. . . . There's some times I haven't been recognized in gay clubs because I looked too feminine to them. Or, I look too, say, [straight]. . . . Whereas when I'm around straight people that I know, they know I'm a little different. So it's been offset both ways." Although she did not appear as severe as the older butches at Ralph Martin's, or act as rough as the butches she met in reform school or in the 1950s bars, nevertheless she was actively gay and masculine in the bars, in the reformatory, and upon release in New York City.

After a series of disappointments with family, work, and love, she decided to marry. She describes herself as being unsure about her sexual interests at the time.

"Of course, as I say, I didn't really know about myself. So one time he asked me to marry him. I said, 'I can't marry you.' 'Why?' I said, 'I just can't, because I don't love you.' I said, 'I love you, but I don't love you that way.' He said, 'Well love grows.' I said, 'Yes it does, but I don't think it will ever grow that way.' That kept up until one day he asked me, and I said, 'O.K.' The good part was I came out and I told Bernie about it. I don't know if I told him to be honest with him or to scare him away. But I know I had to be honest with him, I said, 'I'm not too sure, but I know I like women.' [He said,] 'That's in the past.' I said, 'I was like this for years Bernie, forget it.' Well anyway we got married."

They married and had two children whom they raised together. She maintained gay relationships on the side, but never allowed them to disrupt her home life. "My life was at a level that I was more free than the average married woman. Within reason. I had obligations as far as entertaining, going to couples' homes, straight people." She met women through work, bowling leagues, the trap club, and sometimes in the bars, where she went sporadically. She also maintained lesbian friends who would come to the house. She didn't have an active sexual life with her husband. "We didn't have too much to do with each other. I know basically we have two kids, yes, we had to do something. But like a normal husband and wife we did not have."

There were a few periods when her marriage became rocky but they both did what was needed to help repair it because they wanted a secure and pleasant home for themselves and their children. After twenty-three years, when their children were fully grown, she left. She now wanted to live her life the way she wanted. "In my heart I had to leave. He was starting to pressure me in front of the [kids]. He was all right until he knew I wanted one specific person." Still, she did not leave him for any particular woman, but for herself.

"It was my life that I had to make a decision for. My [children] were getting older. It was an obligation, 'cause we weren't having anything for so long,

Bernie and I. He wasn't a person I could talk to then. It interfered because he loved me in a way and yet, I can't explain it, I don't understand it. Like I say, we have a better relationship as far as friends now and we talk, and of course through the girls."

Reggie thinks of herself as having been gay all of her life, despite her marriage and the uncertainty she felt at times regarding her identity. She always felt more masculine in image and sexuality, but acted that out visibly only for short periods of her life. She was a devoted mother, and unquestionably looks at her children as one of the more fortunate things in her life. Her butchness is not as central to her identity as her gayness, but still plays some part in how she understands being gay.

Phil is unique among the narrators who came out in the 1930s and 1940s in that masculinity plays no part in shaping her consciousness of being different. Today, we experience her as unquestionably butch, an image she has projected quite strongly since her divorce. Nevertheless, she saw her masculinity as inconsequential to being a lesbian, something that had been with her as a heterosexual as well.

Phil thinks that she married because it was expected of her, but is not sorry for having done so. "If I had to be married, I'm glad it was the someone I married. Very nice man, very good father, good husband, etc." After having several children, she began her first lesbian relationship in the early 1940s. This relationship was with a woman at work and it was the first for both of them. Phil had realized that she was gay a little earlier in her marriage, but "did nothing about it." It was primarily her feelings toward women that indicated to her that she was gay.

"I always felt differently toward women, but never really knew why, until after I was married. And I did have some woman approach me when I was like twelve, but she wouldn't say or do anything except to say, 'When you're older I'll tell you how I feel about you and you'll understand more.' . . . I was excited, I didn't know why but . . . I knew I wanted to be with her . . . going to the show with her and taking walks with her. And naturally my mother didn't like it. . . . She didn't think it was a very good relationship, a twelve-year-old girl and a nineteen-year-old woman that was married. . . . But she never tried anything, until maybe four or five years after I was married. But you know, that was like more or less the start. . . . I knew I was different. I didn't mind it a bit either."

Since her first relationship, Phil has always been the more masculine partner. But this didn't disrupt her role in her marriage, as she was just being herself. She thinks it was not masculinity, but "sportiness" that characterized her way of being. "No, I have always been me, I have not been strictly masculine. More so after I was divorced, but then I was just me. I dressed sporty because that's how I've always been, even before I knew that I was gay. So it didn't really change me that much."

Phil was very comfortable being gay from the beginning. She never felt confused or guilty. Like several other narrators, she was indignant at the label "queer," which she thought was more appropriate for the behavior of some heterosexuals.

> "I mean I've heard pro and con on it, after, and I never felt that it was bad. I never felt it was a sin, I never felt it was something wrong. I never liked the word 'queer,' that used to send me up the wall. 'Cause to me straight people are queer, I mean they're really bent. I mean that's how I felt, when I've seen a lot of the stuff I've seen with married couples. Any woman that will take what I've seen some women take. They're weird. So I never had a hang-up about it, never, I never wanted to be any different. I never tried to change."

Despite her acceptance of being gay, she was very cautious about announcing it to others, including her children. She felt that this was related to her desire to protect her family. She did not want to hurt them, given how unacceptable gayness was and remains.

> "We've had discussions about that, about how to act in public. I, for one, never wanted to flaunt it to society. Mainly because of my family and mainly because I knew that society has not accepted it, and still hasn't really. I've talked to girls that asked me if I were ashamed of being gay, and that's not the point at all. I was never ashamed. I mean, if I could live in a society where they accept me, then I would be very happy about that. I've had a lot of discussion about that, and some have said I couldn't because of my job, it would hurt my mother, you know, a million reasons why people can't, even though they'd like to."

She has continued to keep her gayness from her children despite the fact they are married. "I don't want them to know. . . . No, not from me. I would never say 'Yes.' They've never asked, but I'm sure they have an idea." The role of mother and that of lesbian were hard to integrate, even by this woman who accepted her own gayness.[12]

In a society that hates and fears lesbians, most narrators who came out during the 1930s and 1940s had internalized some degree of stigma as part of their butch identity, as part of being different. This is evidenced by the use of such terms as "homo" or "abnormal"; but on the whole we were struck that stigma, though present, did not dominate their consciousnesses. Of all narrators of this period, Phil was the only one who felt no ambivalence about the goodness or rightness of being gay. Her situation raises interesting perspectives on the relation between stigma and butch identity. Phil was the narrator who was the least public about her gayness. She did not become conscious of her difference as a child and therefore did not come into conflict with her family while she was young. As an adult during the 1940s and early 1950s, she led a married life and raised children and did most of her socializing as a lesbian in small private groups. In addition, Phil had no contact with the medical profession, which seemed to promote the abnormality of being gay, even if at the same time it certified a person as normal in other aspects of her life. Phil's Italian upbringing may also be significant. A good number of Italian-American narrators did not seem to have guilt feelings about sex with women, perhaps because close relationships among women were common in their families. Furthermore, some narrators who were raised Catholic remember that their early training was filled with admonitions against fooling around with boys. Intimacies with women were so far from their parents' minds that they never received warnings about sexual relations with girls.

Phil's experience strongly suggests that the degree of internalization of stigma by butches seems to be directly correlated with the degree to which a person was drawn into confrontation with the heterosexual world through her "obvious" appearance or behavior. This illuminates an interesting aspect of living in the closet. Lesbians were in the closet not so much for shame or guilt, which they may not have felt at all, but because of a realistic assessment of what they would lose by coming out. Their suffering came from living in constant fear of exposure and knowing the severity of the consequences. Ironically, due to the context of severe oppression, those who were more obvious, intending to change the world's evaluation of lesbians and homosexuals, in the process internalized the stigma of being "homo" or "queer."

FEM, GAY, AND LESBIAN IDENTITIES IN THE 1940s

Fem identity was different from that of butches. In general, it was not based in strongly internalized feelings of difference, but rather in the commitment to a different way of life—socializing in the gay world and having a relationship with a woman. Whereas butches had two indicators of identity—attraction to women and desire to appropriate masculine characteristics—fems had only one; logically, femininity did not set them apart from other women. Fems had to have contact with a lesbian community or a lesbian relationship to develop awareness of their difference. Most fems spent some time in the heterosexual world and attempted to be happy, but it didn't work out. Moreover, they had more fun and better relationships in gay life. Although they consider themselves gay, their gayness is dictated more by setting and circumstance than by a sense of fundamental difference. Being gay is what they like, sexually and emotionally. They remember that years ago gay was more of a descriptive term than a marker of fem identity. In the past, it was more likely that they would have been considered and referred to as fem, not gay.

Joanna had no conscious sense of being gay, lesbian, or different until a friend took her to Ralph Martin's on a night they had intended to go bowling. For two years, beginning when she was eight, she had had an intense erotic friendship with a girl two years older, but she had never interpreted it as a sign of being "different."

> "Because when I was quite young, like about eight or nine, there was a girl in my neighborhood and we played little games together. Didn't even know what we were doing. However, we were attracted to one another. . . . My mother knew there was an attachment, but she didn't know what kind and she'd say, 'Why are you always hanging around with her?' And I said, 'We have a lot of fun together.' I knew that it was the kind of thing I could not tell my mother at eight years old. Couldn't possibly tell my mother that we were necking and fooling around. We used to take baths together. . . . Maybe that you would do with a kid sister. . . . I knew it was a different kind of feeling that I felt for my family, [or] for any of my other acquaintances. It was a tremendous attraction."

Joanna did not think at the time that she was different from other girls, or that she would not have the same feelings for boys later. "I really thought I was going through a slight infatuation. But I really couldn't fathom this. . . . I knew that it was not the thing that should be; however, I couldn't stop it and it went on for a couple of years."

When Joanna went into Ralph Martin's the first time, she immediately made the connection with her past experiences.

> "And then [my friend] told me when we got in, she said, 'Do you like it?' And I said, 'Oh yeah, I do.' I liked everything. I loved watching everybody. I thought that it was great. . . . I didn't think it [being gay] was odd so it really didn't strike me funny. Because don't forget I've already had that experience. . . . I thought that's what I felt for her. I never knew what I felt for her, except a lot of affection, admiration, and whatever that goes with someone you love."

When she saw butch-fem roles in the bar, she also "never thought that was odd." She knew right away that she was fem. "I mean how do you know what you feel? You know how you feel." Unquestionably, she "preferred it," and she stayed with that preference all her life. She remembers that same constancy was true for her friends, a core group in the bars of the 1940s.

> "I have to tell you something. In this group that I first met, none of them ever changed. . . . Ever! That's funny. You know that you would think like maybe one of the girls who had been attracted like to another girl [who] had a little more masculinity in her. No. I never never have known one that changed. And as I said I'm still in contact with almost all of them that I was close to."

After eight years, Joanna left her first relationship and returned to live with her mother in an attempt to try heterosexual life. She attributes this partly to guilt generated by her family, who did not approve of her being a lesbian. She also thinks she was influenced by fear. At one point in her interview, she mentions that people have been afraid to tell the story of gays and correct misconceptions, and includes herself as a person who has been afraid. "I was one too, I was afraid. Job, pain, whatever. . . . I was married a short time, you know. I was afraid."

In time, she met a man at work whom she was initially hesitant about marrying, but then changed her mind.

> "I met this fella and I was working at [the Army Corps of Engineers]. He was an inspector, my age, and [we] started going out. Basketball games, sporting events, whatever, and he asked me to marry him. And I thought about it and I thought, oh that's a bad idea. I went with him for, oh, about a year and a half and just dated, you know. I went home to my mother, you know, each night and, and then [all of a sudden] I said, 'Well maybe this is my salvation, you know. Never tried it, why not?' . . . Lasted two and a half weeks. And I just couldn't. I knew that I had made the biggest mistake of my life. As I said if [he] had maybe been a different person but he was not the right person. He was a very weak person, which you don't discover until you're around someone. Then I said 'Oh no, this is not my bag.'"

Several of Joanna's friends indicate that she was married slightly longer, more like six months, jokingly saying that every time she tells the story, the marriage gets shorter.

After Joanna left the marriage, she went back to her mother. "I just resigned myself to the fact that I'd made a mistake, but I felt badly because I really did screw up his life, let's face it. . . . He's never remarried." At that time, she wasn't looking consciously for a man or a woman. "Because it really didn't make any difference. I think this is just the right person. There was no preference to gender, you know. I think it was just, I needed someone, I needed a friend. . . . I just needed someone that I could talk to and go out to dinner or whatever, you know, and enjoy."

The year her mother died, she started a relationship with a woman that lasted eight or nine years. She remained in the gay life from that point on, although a woman who knew her fairly well says that after a painful breakup, later on, she went out with several men again for a short period. She certainly was not opposed to such behavior. When imagining a future world where gays are no longer oppressed, she mentions there would be more gays, but, based on her own interests, she thinks there would still be heterosexuality.

> "I don't think of a completely gay world as being utopia either though. . . . I think you should have your choice, why not? I certainly wouldn't want to see a completely heterosexual world or a completely gay world. I think we need the balance. . . . Because I think the reproduction is good, and I think relationships with, like even say men you work with, isn't that obnoxious to me."

Although Joanna's identity was strongly feminine, she was not interested in having children. She is not supportive of lesbians raising children because she thinks children need a stable home life. If a woman who has children separates from her husband, Joanna thinks that ideally she should keep the child but not be actively gay; she should not live with a woman and have her friends over.

Joanna is very sure that she was not born gay, although she is aware that most butches thought that they were, especially the first two she was involved with:

> "All of a sudden, my whole system changed, my whole chemistry changed, my body chemistry did. But I never felt as strongly about being gay at that time. . . . I thought that was something that happened to me. . . . But she [my first relationship], I know that she was gay from the time she was a little child. As far back as she can remember. She always liked boys' clothes and she was attracted to little girls."

Still, she doesn't really believe that they were born that way, but rather interprets their early feelings of masculinity in terms of family dynamics.

> "I never felt that I was born that way. Because I know when I was little I didn't think that way. Maybe because I was around so many boys, with brothers, my thinking may have been different. And if I had been an only child like Leslie and Renée. Both were only children. Maybe they weren't influenced by the male and both of them, their fathers had left their mothers when they were very young. And so they weren't around that many men, you know."

Joanna's gay identity is clearly based in attraction to other women. Although she was happy in her relationships, she had a struggle with living a life outside the accepted norms of her family. In addition, she had fleeting interests in men. Despite this, she lived most of her life socializing with the gay community and having gay relationships, and, in her mind, she was unquestionably gay. She was generally satisfied with this choice. "Let's face it, the gay life is not so terrible."

Pearl's gay identity also seems to come more from socializing in the gay community and taking part in the gay life than from strong feelings of difference. She was taken to her first gay bar by her husband, who thought she might be interested.

> "My husband took me down there, and he left me and said he'd be back to pick me up later. . . . See, it was during the war, right around when they were making airplanes, and I was working at Curtis and I would go into the ladies room, and then I would tell him about this woman asking me if I would want to go to Berger's.[13] She was asking me questions like, 'Wouldn't you like to go out for dinner?' or 'Wouldn't you like to go here or there?' And [my husband] was quite a few years older than me, and he had been associated with this type of thing before. He is the one that knew about Kleinhans corner. . . .[14] And when he took me downtown and all these girls are walking around and I didn't know what to make of it, but I enjoyed it. . . . I was frightened at first. But after that I would go down there by myself."

When Pearl's husband took her to Ralph Martin's, it was as much due to his interest in exploring ménages à trois—her bringing a woman home or his picking up a woman and all three having sex—as to sensitivity to her feelings.

At first she had no interest in going to Ralph Martin's; the trip was entirely his idea. "The reason I was there was because my husband, I think he realized more than I did that that's what I should be doing. That that's what I would like. I don't know why he thought that. I never asked him. . . . Whatever way he ever figured it I don't know." After she started going to the bars regularly, she did reinterpret some of her earlier life, recognizing that she had had some interest in women, although never consciously. "Certain persons that I would like I would think, 'Oh gee, I wish I could get to know her better.' Or I used to have a girl friend that we would stay all night together, you know, I'd stay at her house and we'd sleep together and everything. And then I thought back at things like that."

Even though she began to enjoy gay life and frequented gay bars regularly, she doesn't think people thought of her as gay, but rather as the feminine type. "I don't think we ever discussed it, to tell you the truth. They just figured me as a fem, that was what they would talk about me. They never really have said I was gay, no." She isn't sure whether she considered herself gay. She was just having a good time.

> "You know, I didn't really know. I just knew that I enjoyed the women's company, I enjoyed going to these places, I enjoyed their company better than men. I enjoyed the gay boys' company, I used to quite often go out with them, go to their homes and everything. But I don't really remember whether we discussed it. I never thought about it. I was doing what I wanted to do, what I liked to do. As time went on I got to be going out more, being with more people, having longer relationships away from home. I mean it wasn't always that I brought them home with me, most of the time I went to their homes. Most of them had apartments of their own."

Her husband did not view her relationships with women as threatening. "He always said, 'I don't care what you do with women, but don't do anything with men.' That was always what he would say."

While active in the gay community, she continued to have sexual relations with her husband, even though she no longer wanted them. She sometimes took women home for the two of them, and he sometimes picked women up. In the beginning, she was indifferent to these activities. "I was very passive, maybe. I mean I just didn't care. I had no feeling either way. It didn't make any difference to me." Later, she came to dislike them, but as soon as Pearl offered any resistance, he threatened her with taking away their children. In time, the relationship became unbearable, and she became more adamant about not wanting to be with him. The problems in their relationship were not simply sexual. He was seeing other women regularly. In addition, he offered no economic security as he did not work steadily, and the money he got he spent immediately. Finally, she decided she wanted him to leave. "He stood in my way quite a bit until the 1950s and then I started to decide I didn't like his ideas anymore, I didn't like what he was doing. . . . I wanted to do my own thing, I wanted to live my own life. Even though I told him I would never leave him, he would have to leave, and finally he left." She wouldn't leave him, "'cause if I left then he could get me on desertion with his kids. And forget it, you know, I ain't leavin'."

Pearl never went back to a heterosexual life, and, when not in lesbian relationships, was happily busy with her siblings, whom she raised. She never told them the details of her life, but she thinks they knew anyway.

> "We've never discussed it and I've never discussed it with my family, and yet, they all know. They all accept anyone I bring home. They all accept my way of life, they never question me. . . . They were brought up with it. . . . I had different friends coming to the house and my sisters and brothers were growing up with it, so it doesn't bother them."

Today, Pearl definitely considers herself gay. Like Joanna, she seems to derive identity from the way she lived her life, how she spent her time and with whom, rather than some deeply felt constitutional difference. There is no question that she liked women—socially and sexually—but she does not feel that that marked her as different. Her problems with her husband were not based simply in dissatisfaction with sex, but with his entire way of life.

Charlie represents a slightly different variation on this same fem pattern. She was unaware of her attraction to women until she was sixteen, when a woman expressed interest in her.

> "She used to call me jailbait. And because she was in the service and I guess I was younger than eighteen, it was just a fling, nothing happened. She went back into the service and that was the end of that. . . . It was exciting. But she came up after she liked me, and told me she liked me. She kind of ran away because of the fact that she was in the service and I was jailbait. It probably would be different now."

She never thought much about the fact that it meant she was unusual. She just knew she was having a good time. "No, I didn't know. I didn't know really what it was. It was fun."

Her first real gay relationship occurred when she was in her twenties, already married.

> "But naturally in everybody's life there has to be a gym teacher . . . yeah, she was cute. And I think that's where it began, but I also was married at the time. . . . And then it was the big run and chase. She was real nice to me. I went out with her for about three years. Well I was married and that also broke up, being married. But then she met someone else."

At this point in her life, Charlie was interested in both men and women. The desire to marry and have children was strong, as was the interest in women. "I guess I was still interested in both sides, I don't know. . . . Naturally I guess I still wanted to get married and have children. I was married, I got divorced. She was very nice, very nice to me, also very nice to the person that she wound up with." During this period, Charlie went to quite a few gay bars and was out looking for a good time, drinking, and dancing. She rarely went with her gym teacher friend, whose profession forced her to be cautious about being exposed. After they broke up, Charlie went to Florida and hung around quite a few gay boys, going to their shows, including the Jewel Box Review, but she remained unclear about her own sexual preference.

When she returned to Buffalo, she met a man whom she married. This marriage also did not work out, and she became interested in women again.

> "I got an apartment with two friends, two straight girls, who were very nice. We all worked downtown and we all shared the same car, my car, and we had a good time. And then I met this fella that started to wine and dine me and roses and champagne. . . . So I thought, well, should I or shouldn't I? and I did. And like the day after we got married everything was different. He thought I was his mother and his maid and his cleaning lady and it didn't last too long. So he was tending bar in the bowling alley and he was talking to me one night and said, 'They have these bunch of lezzies that bowl on Monday night or Tuesday night'. . . . And I said to myself, 'Oh, oh, I'm going.' I naturally didn't discuss this stuff with him. So I went to the bowling alley and I met the whole group. And there was one person there that I liked. And he and I weren't getting along at all, anyway . . . so I started seeing this person. Well, then I found out she lived three blocks away from me. And she invited me to her house to have dinner with her and her husband and her family, and I went. She wouldn't admit to me anything. Her appearance I knew . . . but she wouldn't admit it, and I wasn't gonna admit it, 'cause I was married to the bartender, which was a big mistake. So this began a fifteen-year friendship and love affair, and everything else you can think of."

When Charlie's fifteen-year relationship broke up, she began another stable and lasting relationship with a woman.

Charlie considers herself gay, but implies that fem is the more accurate term. "No, even in the group that I know now I'd never say, 'You're fem, do you think you're gay?' You just don't ask this. Mostly you'd probably look at what they're wearing and well, she's gotta be a butch or she's gotta be a fem, even today." Despite the fact that she spent a portion of her life as an active heterosexual, she would not label herself bisexual. "Well I had . . . I've had both, I don't know. I guess it's what you're doing at the time you're doing it." She thinks that one is what one is living. Rather than her sexual identity being deeply ingrained, it is something that is informed by the way she is living her life.

In keeping with narrators' varied experiences in finding their identities, the community did not have—nor does it now have—a hegemonic view about how to draw the line between the homosexual and the heterosexual. Many narrators see the butch lesbian as the true lesbian. Other narrators consider anyone who stays with women and is part of the community a lesbian. Leslie and Arden, who were conscious of their difference at an early age and were core members of the lesbian community during the 1940s, disagree with one another on the subject and their argument, which they think was quite common among members of the community in the past, eloquently explores the central issues of who is a lesbian.

During the interview, Leslie took the position that only butches are lesbians. She is a lesbian, and is never attracted to another lesbian, but always to a more feminine type. Arden, on the other hand, thought that all women who stay with women are lesbians, butch or fem, as long as they don't flip back and forth between being with men and being with women. Each tried to convince the other of the rightness of her position. Leslie asked Arden about two women who had been Arden's instructors in sex. These women had been married. Didn't Arden consider them bisexual? Arden: "No, they didn't go back and forth. Once they were in the crowd, they stayed. It was good fun and they liked it." The friends then discussed the women who had started seeing lesbians during the war, while their husbands were away. Some of these women went back and forth, while others did not. Leslie again did not agree with Arden that those who stayed with women were lesbians. Arden then remembered a feminine woman, Ramona, with whom Leslie had gone years ago. Since Ramona is still out and has never been with a man, Arden thought this case would surely indicate to Leslie the flaw in her thinking. But this was not so. Leslie's rationale was that she had strongly influenced Ramona, who was sixteen and in high school when they met. Ramona's life was shaped by her attraction to Leslie and might have been different if Ramona had been twenty-five with more experience when their relationship began. The two friends admitted that it would be impossible to come to an agreement.

At another interview, Leslie and Arden continued their disagreement on a different level, with Leslie emphasizing the pressures of heterosexual life that might influence a woman who is not a lesbian to turn to gay life. "But women of all kinds get involved in the fun of gay life. They like the fun and freedom of gay life, and it has nothing to do with sexual preference." Arden countered, emphasizing the forces that encouraged lesbians to pursue heterosexual marriage. "But also there is another side. I think that there were many women who liked being with women, who preferred women, but who get the Mrs. because they wanted that status."

Although they disagree, Leslie and Arden both are astute observers of the social forces that influence a woman to cross the boundaries between heterosexuality and homosexuality. Each analysis can be supported by evidence from the period. On the one hand, fem narrators mention liking the fun of gay life. Fems and butches alike also remember many women during the war who would go to the bars to have a good time without getting pregnant. On the other hand, fems and even butches also mention the pressure to get married. With ample evidence for both positions, it is their different interpretive frameworks that lead each to evaluate the evidence differently, and ultimately come to a different understanding about what defines a lesbian.

Leslie's idea that only butches are true lesbians bears a striking similarity to early medical theories of inversion, which were popularized through *The Well of Loneliness*. But her thinking is also similar to some elements of the Kinsey reports, which were published after she came of age.[15] Like Kinsey, she is using a continuum model in which there are "true lesbians" who have sex only with women, and fems, whom she considers bisexuals, who can have sex with either men or women. In fact, she believes that the majority of the world is bisexual. Arden bases her analysis primarily on whom one chooses as an erotic partner, an idea that is also prevalent in Kinsey's work. But she does not go from here to develop a concept of the purer or truer lesbian. For Arden, if women spend time in the lesbian community and consider themselves lesbians, they are lesbians, whether they are butch or fem. The key factor is whom they stay with, and, by extension, their participation in lesbian life. In her view, people are what they are doing at the moment, as long as they don't regularly go back and forth between men and women. Leslie's position clearly separates the experience and identity of butches and fems, emphasizing fems' participation in heterosexuality, whereas Arden's view focuses on the common erotic interests and social life of butch and fem. Leslie draws a firm boundary between the heterosexual and the homosexual by excluding the fem, or putting her in an intermediate position. Arden draws a less firm boundary, one that takes circumstances into account and includes the fem.

Other butch narrators who were part of the 1940s community agree with one or the other of these positions and some hold parts of both, suggesting that this was a time of transition for ideas and concepts about lesbians. For instance, D.J. sees herself as having gone with straight women, women who had been married, while Phil, who also went with previously married women, considers her partners gay.

Most fems simultaneously hold both positions on who is a lesbian, thereby resolving the contradictions of their relationship to the lesbian community. They recognize both the similarities and the differences between the butch and the fem. When asked if she considered herself a lesbian, Charlie replies, "No, I considered myself gay." Joanna refers to herself as gay throughout her story, but uses the word lesbian only for the butches. She regularly refers to the two people in an old-time couple as a lesbian and her girlfriend. This indicates that to the fems, the lesbian *was* the masculine woman, the butch, while gay was a term that referred to all women who had relationships with women. None of the fems considered

herself bisexual. "You were either gay or straight. . . . I never even heard the word
bisexual (Joanna)." Because of our guidelines on whom to interview, all fem
narrators had been in the gay life for a long period of time, and this may account
for why they are so confident that they were gay. It is possible that many fems
who spent a short period of time in gay life might not have considered themselves
gay. They may have seen themselves as quite different from their "lesbian" partners,
a difference butches frequently mention, particularly those who see themselves as
the true lesbians.

Two contradictory conditions seem to be at work in supporting the continuity
of the old view (based on gender inversion) and the development of the new.
During the war, many butches in the bars met women who were honest about
their heterosexual interests, but went to the bars for a good time.

> "There were quite a few feminine girls . . . maybe five or ten percent of the
> people that made up that clique that hung around the bar were married and
> had their husbands in the service, and when their husbands came out, you
> never saw them again. . . . They made no bones about it. They didn't say that
> they were unattached, you know. . . . As soon as somebody told you that, you
> think, oh she doesn't want to get pregnant, this is why she's hanging around
> girls. . . . One girl admitted it. Because she already had a couple of kids, didn't
> want any more. . . . I think it's a terrible thing to do to somebody, don't you?
> . . . take allotment checks and then go out, go around to gay bars. . . . The one
> girl was married and was going with another guy and he had no family or
> anybody and he used to send her his check. Do you believe this? She had two
> checks coming in. Didn't have any trouble. I remember her. Nice-looking
> girl." (Joanna)

Since fems were living heterosexual lives before and often after their relationships
with women, it is hard, in such a situation, to call them "gay." A system that
polarizes sexualities cannot properly conceptualize them. When asked to explain
why she called a woman from her bowling league with whom she had an affair
straight not gay, Reggie challenges us to provide a better term before going on to
explain her logic.

> "Oh you mean when I say a straight woman? . . . I don't know, how do you
> separate it? All right, there are women that never been with a girl, that
> probably never had any experience until then. But they fall in very easily. . . .
> Maybe one time in their life they did. But I know up until the time I met 'em
> they were strictly married women going with guys. I refer to them as straight,
> they aren't gay. I don't know, it's screwy."

At the same time that fems developed tangential relationships to the community,
the community was growing, becoming more public, so this gave fems more and
more of an opportunity to identify as gay, either by hearing about gay people, or
by participating actively in a gay circle.

BUTCH, FEM, AND LESBIAN IDENTITIES IN THE EARLY 1950s

Those women who came out into the lesbian community in the 1950s hold a subtly different understanding of lesbian identity from women of the 1940s. Despite the fact that the 1950s community more actively enforced butch-fem roles, masculinity was less significant as an indicator of lesbian identity for butches than in the preceding decade. And 1950s fems, more so than the older fems, saw themselves as unquestionably gay as well as fem. By the end of the decade, for both butch and fem, sexual interest in women became the key indicator of lesbianism. Furthermore, in a manner consistent with identity's being marked by attraction to women rather than by gender inversion, but within a social framework that absolutely required roles, many women switched roles, until they found what they liked for themselves.

Of the five narrators who entered the lesbian community in the early 1950s, one of the butches formed an identity quite similar to that of butches of the 1940s. It was created from an interweaving of masculinity and interest in women. The other four represent a distinct departure: they based their lesbian identity primarily on their interest in women and considered being gay or lesbian distinct from being butch or fem.

Masculinity had little or no part in Matty's recognizing her lesbian identity, even though she has been a butch leader since the mid-1950s. In her mind, recognition of her lesbianism is correlated with developing an intense, erotic, but not explicitly sexual relationship with a nun. In retrospect, Matty feels it began in the third grade, although she was not conscious of it at the time. "I did silly things like deliberately failing third grade . . . so I could stay in her class." Matty and the nun discussed their relationship some time later.

> "I was in eighth grade. Well, we had a very close friendship, I used to go and see her all the time; there was nothing sexual between us. And the night I graduated, when I left the school after the graduation, she asked me if I would please come to see her at the convent. And I said, 'Yeah, I would'; and I went home and my mother had this big huge party, and I said, 'Mom I have to go visit the sister.' 'Not tonight, you're there every night, you're having a party.' I said, 'I have to, I promised her I would.' And she wanted me there because she was telling me that she was leaving Buffalo. I got very indignant and told her she wasn't going anywhere. How do you feel when you're that old, you know, the person you believe that you're so madly in love with is telling you that they're gonna leave? And I started to cry and she walked away and looked out the window, and she started to cry. And she turned around and came over and put her arm around me and said that everything would be all right. That I would find my way. And she did leave but she wrote to me all the time."

When the nun returned to Buffalo several years later, she invited Matty to visit her at the convent.

> "[She] threw her arms around me and kissed me right on the mouth. And it shocked me more then, you know. . . . It was the summer I had graduated from high school. And she was really happy to see me. And then we saw each other and talked for a while, and she told me how disappointed she was. See I had told her when she left that if I had to join the convent to be with her I would. And she had gone to the Mother House in Philadelphia and she said every time they had new girls coming in she'd go down 'cause she thought sure I'd be there. At this time I was thinking of joining the service and I talked to her about it. And she said, 'No,' she said, 'I know now it would have been a mistake for you to come into the convent and [it] would also be a mistake for you to go into the service.' She said, 'When you feel the way you do about women, you don't go where you're surrounded by nothing but women.' And I said to her, 'That's if you're trying to fight it, I'm not trying to fight it.' I mean I had nothing to fight, it was my life, I realized that."

From here, Matty went on to find her way into the lesbian bar community of the late 1940s and early 1950s. In several years, she had her first relationship, which was not really of her choosing; she was aggressively pursued and she acquiesced, and in that relationship, which did not last long, she was fem. In her second relationship, she began as a fem, but tension developed between her and her partner, and, on her mother's advice, she and her partner switched roles, which helped. She remembers affectionately that her mother had more insight into her developing role identity than she did herself.

> "She [my second relationship] was on the masculine side but I was very attracted to her, and so I naturally took the feminine approach. We started to see each other, and then we started to go together, and we really loved each other but we weren't making it, we were constantly hassling and fighting and arguing. And I talked to my mother and said, 'Gee I don't know what it is I really like her.' . . . And my mother said, 'Maybe you're not happy in the way you're living your life with her.' I said, 'What do you mean?' She said—my mother would get embarrassed when she tried to explain things in daylight—and she said, 'Before you met [Joan] you used to dress a little different, you wore slacks and that. Now you're in dresses all the time and you put makeup on. You don't seem like you're happy. Maybe you should go back to what you were and let her be a little more feminine.' I kind of thought about that and I talked it over with this girl, and do you know that that relationship lasted for six years?"

Although in her youth Matty had defied the traditional female socialization, she had not identified her difference in terms of masculinity. It was necessary for her mother to help Matty interpret her life in a gendered framework. And even though

Matty switched to the butch role, she never adopted the idea that the butch was sexually untouchable.

The switching of roles was not unusual in the 1950s. Although lesbians only rarely switched roles during a relationship, it was common for people to change their roles after their first relationships. Such a change was associated with coming out and a woman finding her place in the community and her sexual preferences. Coming out fem and then becoming butch was the usual direction of this early change. There was a common saying among butches in the lesbian community, "Today's love affair is tomorrow's competition." Another narrator explains this switching as due not only to inexperience, but to the kind of vulnerability required of fems. "Some would start out real fem and the minute they got hurt by a butch . . . the next time you'd see them they'd be real butchy. . . . They'd be dressed up really butchy. . . . Usually the butches broke up with them. They'd start getting really butchy too. I don't know if they think butch is better."

Matty's lesbian identity is very modern, completely based on her romantic and sexual interest in women, with masculinity playing no part as an emblem or marker. Nevertheless, she is confident that she is truly gay and that she has been gay all her life. Interestingly, she does not explain this continuity in terms of biology. She tells a humorous story about why she is gay, which captures the impossibility of knowing, yet the certainty with which she feels her identity.

> "People ask me . . . when I tell them I've been gay all my life . . . 'How did you get to be gay all your life?' And I tell them the story. I say, 'Well you see, when I was born the doctor was so busy with my mother, it was a hard birth for her . . . that it was the nurse that slapped my ass to bring that first breath of life into me. And I liked the touch of that feminine hand so much that I've been gay ever since.'"

Throughout her life, Matty's sexual interest has been in women only. She likes men, and gets along with them, but not sexually. "If I wanted to have sex with a man, I would have sex with a man. I'm not even curious; even out of curiosity, I'd have done it years ago, but I'm not curious about it. I'm perfectly content."

For Matty, gayness is a central part of one's being, present from the beginning, which people—butches and fems alike—have to find for themselves.

> "I don't think that anybody gets to be gay. How can you get to be gay, you're either gay or you're not. . . . See in my case it was brought out very early, I don't remember any other life but being gay. But even like there are people who have lived a straight life and who have had sexual relations with a man and boom, all of a sudden it hits them, 'I'm not happy in this relationship,' and then they become gay. I don't think that person is getting to be gay. They have been gay right along but they haven't realized it. It took a while for it to dawn on them."

This framework divides the world quite neatly into the truly straight, the truly gay, and those who are mixed up or still finding themselves and is quite similar to the categories of gay liberation.

To say that masculinity was not at the core of Matty's definition of herself as a lesbian is confusing, because it was central to the way she handled herself in the lesbian world. On the surface, one could never tell that she was any different from the women in the 1940s, to whom masculinity was central. Once she changed roles, her appearance was extremely masculine, and she was always attracted to very feminine women. Her thinking that lesbianism was about being attracted to women didn't mean she was less committed to roles. She remembers her mother asking her why roles were important if being a lesbian was about loving women. Today, she agrees with her mother, but at the time she did not.

> "I don't tend to wear a lot of boys' clothes now like I used to, back in those days, but I've come to realize that one does not have to appear mannish to achieve your goal in your gay world. My mother tried to stress that in my head years ago and I just wouldn't listen to her, but it's the truth. She used to say to me, 'What difference does it make what you wear? I thought, the way you explained it, the whole idea of gay life in the girls' world was one woman who loves another woman, so what difference does it make, why do you have to dress like a man?' And she's right, the times change and I've changed with the times."

Lonnie who came out later than Matty has a more mixed basis for her identity. Although, like Matty, she definitely thinks being lesbian is about attraction to women, like many of the 1940s butches she appropriated masculine characteristics from childhood on. "Nine years old, I knew. I used to beat up boys; girls—I would just treat them like little doll babies. But I never cared for a doll. . . . I had two brothers and a sister and my younger brother used to get cap pistols, trucks and things, I got dolls. . . . I used to beat him up and take his trucks and cap pistols and give him my dolls." Despite her masculine interests, she was not clear from her youth that she was a lesbian. She first experimented sexually with a woman at nine, and had her first full sexual affair at thirteen. But under pressure from her family she also dated men and was engaged three times. During this period she had a child, and later always went with women with children whom she helped to rear. Lonnie never accepted the ideal of untouchability for butches.

Like several other narrators who had been masculine-identified since childhood, Lonnie thought for a while that she "got mixed up in the wrong body." When she was older, she contemplated having a sex-change operation.

> "I wanted to change, I even—when John Hopkins Hospital first came out in the States with this changeover—I sent and I got an application. Yeah, I wanted to go all the way. And then I got to thinking . . . I grew up religious,

my family and everything; I said, 'God really really did it, He can't make a mistake.' And then I got to thinking, maybe He did."

But in the end, after a lot of thought she decided not to have one, and has been completely satisfied with her decision.

Although Matty switched roles, and Lonnie did not religiously follow them in regard to sexual expression, they were both completely comfortable in them, while Bert and Marla coming out in the early 1950s were much more ambivalent about gender definitions and conformed to roles only inasmuch as their social life required. The first time Bert consciously thought that she was a lesbian was when someone in the Army kissed her and she liked it.

> "Well, I can' tell you exactly how it happened. I guess we can all remember that. I was very [averse] to drinking in those days, and of course everybody drank. And I remember there was a woman that was in the Army at Fort Sam Houston, and she used to tell me, "You shouldn't hang around with us.' In fact she was up for being discharged. We were coming back from being in town on a Sunday night, and she told me that she was a very impulsive person and she always did what her impulses told her to do, and then she leaned over and kissed me and said, 'That was like I had that impulse.' And my only reaction to it was, that was really neat, I like it, and I accepted it right there. I didn't go wow, or shocked or anything like that. I like it, and that was the beginning."

She explored this new interest in the service and, in time, began a relationship. During this process, her socializing with gay people helped her realize she was gay.

> "When you asked me previously about was I aware of my gay feelings earlier, and I think the reason I wasn't was because I wasn't around any gay people and didn't have a chance to have them brought out. I think it's being around gay people, you're put in a situation where you're comfortable to come out. Because there are other people like you, you're not the only one."

She is certain that she had no idea about being gay before entering the Army. "Not that I was aware of. And I don't know if it's because I wasn't subjected to gay people. . . . But I knew [I] was different." Like many other narrators, in retrospect she can identify signs of being lesbian early in life. Her memories include not being turned on by *True Story* magazine, and having a crush on a camp counselor. In addition, she remembers her interest in boys' things—bikes, clothes. But in her mind, it was her nonconformity rather than her masculinity that marked her as different.

In no area did she experience a deep proclivity toward masculinity. When she was young, she had the expectation of getting married and having children. "I used to say, when I was younger, I wanted to get married young and have my children—grow up with my children." After she came out, she still wanted to be a mother, "or at least have a child to raise. I think that's why I was so happy in the job working with the [kids]. They were my kids for two years. I've always loved children." After she had been out fifteen years, this led to a marriage of convenience with a gay man for the purpose of having children, but it did not work out on any level.

Once she was in the lesbian community, on the surface she appeared butch, and always took the butch role in her relationships; she viewed this, however, as something she adapted to, rather than a core definition of herself. "I think on the surface I identified . . . when I was involved in the gay community, you either had to be butch or fem. And I was always the, I guess you'd say, the butch appearing one—back to the days when D.A. haircuts were popular." But she was never too serious about roles, making jokes even at a time when rules were strict and serious.

> "Thinking back I can remember one of the things I used to say, people would say, 'Are you butch or are you fem?' And I used to say, 'Well, the only difference to me between the butch or a fem is when you get up on the dance floor, so you don't have to argue who's going to lead.' And I have another saying since then, 'My biggest decision when I get up every morning is whether to be an aggressive fem or a nelly butch!' "

In keeping with her view that a lesbian is a woman attracted to other women, Bert considers both butch and fem to be gay. And, in fact, most of the feminine women Bert had relationships with have remained lesbians.[16] She remembers teasing a doctor in California, who was unnecessarily prying into a friend's life, about all the queer fems in the services.

> "He was a big-mouth guy, never crude, and I remember him saying, 'Miss [so-and-so] I heard you were in the Navy, and I heard that fifty percent,' he probably said 'girls,' '[of the] girls in the Navy were butch.' And I remember saying to him, 'You know doctor that's very right, but you've been really misinformed. Most people think that the [other] women in the service were prostitutes, well fifty percent were butch and the other fifty percent were fem.' And I added, 'We were all queer.' "

Marla, like Bert, came out in the armed services, and despite the fact that she has been athletic all her life, she does not have memories of early tendencies toward masculinity. In retrospect, she does remember her early attractions to women.

> "I just would always want to be around this one counselor, all the chance I could. Like we used to have campfires and I'd go sit by her. Or else try to sit . . . like you sit on the sand legs parted, I used to sit in between her legs with my back up against her, just to be sitting that way. Her name was Patty, I'll never forget. That was the first recollection I ever had."

At this time, however, Marla did go on some dates with men, although not too many because her father was very strict and didn't allow them. In college, she studied physical education and got very close—hugging and kissing—to some of the women, particularly a roommate, but they never talked about what they were doing.

The Army rules against lesbianism were her first explicit knowledge of lesbians. "And then it was brought out in basic, 'cause two girls couldn't sit on the same bed with each other. Or . . . two girls couldn't dance together. And that was brought up then little by little. It might have been mentioned before in my life but I just wasn't [aware of it]." It was several years before she actually had a relationship, because of the restrictions of basic training. And also, as a Black woman in the South, she did not have as much freedom to maneuver as did whites. She could not easily accompany white women when they went out.

Throughout her service career, Marla played sports—softball, basketball—and through this she made most of her friends. Her developing active life as a lesbian got her into trouble. She was spied on and harassed by the Army and finally discharged. "By this time I was really in the gay life and that's all I wanted. Be around girls and that's where I stayed."

Both in the service and at home in Buffalo, role playing was very important, but it did not suit Marla to be overtly butch or fem. "Well everybody used to think I was a big bad butch and I wasn't see, that's the only trouble that I had because I was a tomboy. I played sports a lot and anybody that was in sports was supposed to have been [butch]." Being fem was not right for her either. "You'd sit down. You know [butches would] pick you up and take you out on a date, you had to sit there. The only thing with me, I didn't like it 'cause I could never sit still long enough for anybody to pin me in." In some of her relationships, Marla has been more butch, in others more fem.

She was not uncomfortable with others' choosing roles; they just didn't suit her. Although people assumed Marla to be butch, they never pressured her into that role. "I really don't remember anybody forcing you to be a part, but if you ended up with a girl that was that way you had to play the opposite role." She interprets the times that butches would dress up in feminine attire as a sign that people didn't require roles.[17]

Matty's, Lonnie's, Bert's, and Marla's experiences are testimony to how effective butch-fem culture was for organizing lesbian resistance and lesbian eroticism. In the early 1950s, despite the new understanding of lesbianism as based in attraction to women rather than gender inversion, butch-fem roles remained extremely powerful. They worked and people followed them. The increased pressure in the 1950s to adhere to roles was possibly a response to the fact that gender was becoming less fundamental to lesbian identity.

BUTCH, LESBIAN, AND GAY IDENTITIES IN THE LATE 1950s

The increased pressure as the decade progressed to follow butch-fem roles makes it much more difficult to sort out the basis of lesbian identity for those who came out in the latter part of the decade. The temporary return to the strict enforcement of gender roles in the society at large during the 1950s—the period when these women came to adolescence—gives gender a central place in their identity formation. What we see is that for some butches a form of masculine identity emerged early on, but its meaning is somewhat different from that of the masculine identity of the 1940s butch. Others did not link gender and lesbianism until they participated in the community. For all women who came out in this period, however, attraction to women is the strong force in understanding themselves as different. Gender inversion was no longer the true marker of lesbianism. Thus the real, the pure lesbian became the one who had never slept with a man. The change in thinking is such that some women even define their interest in masculine clothes as transvestism, and their sexual interests as lesbianism.

The identities of the two most noted leaders in the white community of the late 1950s represent the two major types of that period. For one, Sandy, masculinity was a strong part of her identity, along with sexual attraction, from the time she was young. The other, Vic, did not take on masculine identity until she entered the community, although at that time it felt completely comfortable to her. Her entry into lesbian life came from erotic interest in women.

Sandy remembers feeling different very early. "I did in grammar school. I knew it from when I could know, that there was a difference. I mean I didn't know [what it meant]." When she was with her grandparents in the summer, she developed a close bond with her grandfather and went with him wherever he went. She had to wear skirts to school, but otherwise was allowed to dress as she wished. "I always wore pants. I wore cowboy outfits for years and years. Finally they didn't make any to fit me any more. You know, when you're about twenty-five. . . . I was Roy Rogers." She loved cowboy movies and "identified with Roy Rogers," clarifying, "I think I loved his horse, not him." In high school in Buffalo, she did not befriend either the boys or the girls. The girls she wanted to spend time with were the ones on whom she had crushes. By this time, she was fully conscious of her sexual interest in women. Eventually, she made friends with another tomboy, whom she met again years later in the gay bars.

At the time she was unaware of other lesbians, so finding a way to express her difference was more important to her future than thinking about work. When asked if she thought about what kind of job she would like, Sandy responds:

> "I pushed those thoughts away, I wouldn't let them interfere with me. . . . I was afraid of it. Not afraid, but it was written that you grow up, you go to school, you learn a trade, whatever you had, and you go out and you work in this trade, you get married and have kids, and that's it. So I just wouldn't think about those things. That wasn't gonna be me. . . . I'd cross that bridge when I come to it."

The military was attractive to her. "I thought of the service a lot of times . . . because I identified with that, like war, adventure. I liked all that. I liked the military. I still do today." As soon as she finished high school, she signed up with the Marines, "The toughest, the best." She excelled in the service and relished her masculine accomplishment. She sought out and enjoyed open competition with men. "You know I'm better than a lot of those that had been in twenty years. I'm not saying all of them. I excelled in those things."

This willingness to compete with men on their own terms was definitely part of the culture of rough and tough lesbians, but it is interesting to see it as part of this lesbian's consciousness before entering the community. None of the narrators about the 1940s expressed this. It is possible that 1940s women had this feeling when young, and have just forgotten it as their community did not encourage it. But it is also possible that we are seeing a fundamental shift in the meaning of gender roles in the 1950s. While the roles were becoming more restrictive on the surface, more and more young women were challenging their legitimacy.

At this point in her life, Sandy gave military accomplishment a priority. She did not endanger it by pursuing erotic relationships with women, and therefore had no trouble in the Marines. After her three years, she left with the same powerful determination that characterizes most butches' lives. She knew she had to make a life for herself with women.

> "I guess it's all part of growing up. That was my first time that I ever did anything on my own. And that period of eighteen to twenty-one, I was also told what to do. . . . I loved it, 'cause there was no responsibility on me. And when my enlistment was up, and I thought, well hell, now I'm going to get out and, I *knew* I had to be with women, and I couldn't be that in the service. And besides that I wanted to do something on my own, and so I left the service. It's too bad, I'd still be in today if it was as liberal then as it was today.[18] . . . It wasn't. See all this shit, like jobs you couldn't have. There was a military career you couldn't have, 'cause you were gay. So many things you were denied because you were gay. It's a bitch."

Sandy objects to the modern lesbian use of the concept of "role playing." In her mind she was not "playing" the butch role, she was being herself. "I look gay, but not because I'm dressing this way to play a role. If I wasn't gay I'd be dressed like this. This is the only way I know, it's the way I was raised. I always dressed this way." She is also the woman who said: "Butch, fem, whatever, that's just a monogram, it's just a—you got to call it something. No really, this is how I feel. I mean you could call me a door, I mean it just doesn't matter. I'm an aggressive sort of person with a woman." On one level, this is a statement like that of some women of the 1940s that being butch is just being who they are. But the way she phrases it is no longer in a framework of gender inversion. She is able to imagine looking masculine and not being gay. She can imagine aggression being other than solely a male trait.

This pattern of identity formed around attraction to women combined with strong masculine inclinations when young was quite common but had many variations. Toni, one of the youngest narrators, was underage when she entered the bars in 1957, and is the most articulate about separating masculinity and lesbianism. Her understanding clarifies the fact that even if, on the surface, the connection between gender and lesbianism seems as strong in the 1950s as in the 1940s, this was not the case conceptually. Toni was conscious of being different, being a homosexual at an early age.

> "But I knew, before I put a concept or a word to it that I was gay. When I looked up that word at about ten or eleven, I was looking for some confirmation of my identity, and all I found was something that was very derogatory. . . . It horrified me; that wasn't me, but yet I knew I was what they were talking about. And I had a friend at the time; we used to talk about how we were different and how we liked girls and we had crushes on girls."

She also had had masculine inclinations since she was young. "I was under ten when I was wearing [my brother's] clothes when nobody was around. I always felt that I was in drag in women's clothing even as a child." And, like Sandy, she had fantasies of being a cowboy.

> "I was heavy, I was a compulsive eater as a child, so I was a little bit chubby, and they were always after me about being heavy. So, when I was in fifth grade . . . I used to have this fantasy that . . . I was a cowboy. . . . This excess weight I had was just sort of like props that I had on my body, and when I would leave the classroom, and sneak out the side door, and take off this excess weight, [I'd put on] my cowboy suit and get on my horse and ride away."

Even though both masculinity and lesbianism were important to her identity, she does not see them as inextricably connected. "I had to live out pretending I was male in a sense, which doesn't detract from my being a lesbian or alter or change it." She understands her masculinity as something rooted in her rebellion against gender roles in the family.

> "The reasons why I'm never sure of. I've tried to put the pieces together, but I grew up telling myself that I was a boy. And I think it was because of the horrible position I saw women, females, girls in as a child. And I couldn't imagine myself being in that position. It actually repulsed me. It was like less than human, submissive. It seemed like just there was no freedom to being in that role of a female. My brother got my mother's love and I didn't get it, so I always wanted to be like him. I would wear his clothes, and I guess to feel that I was important, I felt I was male. I knew I wasn't but I still told myself that I was, in my mind, in my fantasies. . . . I related to myself as a male."

Although Toni's masculinity is important to her lesbianism, it is not the key or defining feature. While she feels she has to explain why she was masculine, being a lesbian, a homosexual, was something natural; it was how she was.

"I was still a Catholic. I remember I had a medal around my neck, I still thought that this Catholic God was very powerful too. I was so angry [at] what I was, and I had to accept what I was or else I'd be lying . . . to myself and I couldn't do that. I had an idea of what was in store for me. I didn't want to face anyone, but yet I knew I had to go through with this. And I remember—I ripped the medal off my neck and I threw it on the floor and I just thought, 'Fuck you God, just fuck you. Just to be who I am, now look what I gotta deal with.' My brother and his friends, it would be humiliating for everybody, and it was hard for me to face people. And yet I had to do what I was doing, because I felt that it was real for me."

The clarity and forcefulness of these women's early perceptions of their butch identities were not universal for butches. Other narrators did not know their gender role until they entered the community, and still others had difficulty finding the appropriate role for themselves. Vic became aware of her attraction to women when she was in the eighth or ninth grade. "I can remember when I had the girls' names written on my dungarees when other girls had guy's names written on them. I used to sit in my grandmother's bedroom window and watch the baby-sitter across the street. You know, I was about twelve or thirteen years old then." Despite this consciousness of difference, she did not have a strong feeling that she wasn't supposed to be like that.

"I never knew I wasn't supposed to be. . . . I had to be seventeen years old before I really realized what I was supposedly doing was wrong according to society. Not even society, fuck society, with my family, like threw it in my face. 'What are you doin?!' I says, 'Nothing. What am I doing? I'm not doing anything. . . . ' I never thought of myself as any other way. I never realized that my friends thought anything about me until like when my mother died and I saw some of my classmates at my mother's funeral, and they told me how that they used to be afraid of me. But I never bothered them, so they never said anything about it. Which totally crushed me because I had no idea of that until that time. I was like thirty-five years old then. . . . One of my best friends in high school told me right in my father's house after my mother's funeral, 'Well we knew you were like that, never bothered us, so.' 'You knew more than I knew then 'cause I didn't know anything myself.' Which is strange. And I'm glad now that I didn't know. It really hurt me when she said it to me. I really thought we were friends and no problem."

Her parents attributed her becoming gay to joining a women's baseball team, but Vic identifies her relationship with a nun as a critical turning point. The relationship lasted several years, and ended with Vic's being thrown out of school when she was seventeen.

"[At a dance] my English teacher . . . was taking coats at the door. . . . When we were leaving she was giving the coats out and she says to me, 'Victoria, are you coming back?' I didn't even know what she meant. She says, 'Are you going to stop back because I'm going to be down in the home economics room doing some work.' I went back. Now I can't tell you why, because I don't know why myself. I guess it was a feeling that I had that she was saying something to me, or it was just the way she approached me. . . . That was my first affair that I ever had. . . . It wasn't like a sexual affair. It was like kissing and caressing, and you know to me that was like kissing and caressing the Virgin Mary. 'Cause I was brought up to think that they were so holier than thou, that I tried to tell my girlfriend about it and she didn't want to listen. The first person that knew about it was my girlfriend because she bet me, and I remember it to this day, a tuna fish sandwich, that Sister Estella wasn't like that. So we went down there again one night and I had to kiss Sister Estella in front of her to win my tuna fish sandwich, and I did it. . . . Well [I] went with her, I bought her a ring and she wore it over her habit on a chain to all her classes. . . . She taught class even with hickies on her neck. I'm telling you now, you can buy it or sell it, I don't give a shit. And I went through that with her up to my junior year, when the principal found out and I was put out of the school."

Vic went to a psychiatrist because her parents forced her to, but the several sessions did not leave much of an impression. Her parents also took her to the Monsignor and she remembers the visit clearly because he was supportive of her.

"The only one that ever impressed me is that my mother took me to Monsignor at our church, and thought I guess that he would put the fear of God in my mind. He was an old man and I was really terrified of him. And he told my mother, 'If she lives a good life, let her live it any way she wants to live it.' Which really blew my mind, because I really thought he was going to condemn me to hell 'cause he was such an old pious bastard. And when he said that I think that kind of threw my mother back on her heels. She didn't just know how to deal with the situation. She had lost control by that time anyhow, nothing she could do. . . . At that time the man was probably in his late sixties or early seventies, and like really a pious man. Even as I think of him now, I know I can't say, 'Oh maybe he was a faggot,' because you know, I can't even think that."

When she left home to go to school, she had to drop out before finishing because, "I was more into being with women than going to school. I had finally found, I guess you would call them weird people at that time, because I don't think too many people called anybody gay. I was introduced to gay bars, introduced to being masculine."

Although she did not define herself as masculine until she entered the community, from that time on she became completely comfortable with this understanding of herself. "I can't even relate to myself as being feminine." She was unquestionably respected by the community as one of the best-looking and most courageous butches. The fact that she had not consciously developed this masculine identity when young was irrelevant to her adult behavior. She has maintained her butch style until the present, even at a time when gay and lesbian life does not require it.

Little Gerry, who was definitely butch from the late 1950s on, also says she did not know about butch-fem roles until she entered the lesbian community. But she clarifies that it was not so much that she did not have masculine interests when she was younger, but that she did not polarize the masculine and feminine until entering the community, which was most likely true of many other women, including Vic.

Little Gerry knew she was interested in women from the time she was seven, when she had an intense crush on her sister-in-law. In fact, she can't remember a time when she wasn't interested in women. By the time she was thirteen, she was involved in an active sexual relationship which lasted for several years, with a woman who was two years older. At the time, Little Gerry thought that they were the only two like that; she did not learn the word for what they were until high school. She was sexually forward in the relationship because she knew that was what she wanted. She was also a tomboy, and felt comfortable in blue jeans. She thinks it was not so much that she was boyish, or that she wanted to be a man, rather, it was a rebellion against the restrictions of womanliness. In high school, Little Gerry actively pursued relationships with women, which led to her being expelled. She also tried a few relationships with men, and found them lacking the spark she found with women. "I kept waiting and waiting for all the bells and the fire engines and the sirens and it just never—none of them ever rang or whistled or anything."

When Little Gerry was eighteen, she found her first true love, and they went together for five years. They patronized the beat bars and although Little Gerry was more masculine and her partner more feminine, they did not follow roles. But when Little Gerry entered the lesbian bars she became unambiguously butch, aiming to be one of the best.

A comparison between the butches who came out in the late and early 1950s confirms the idea that the intensity of open conflict with society correlates directly with the degree of internalization of stigma. Sandy and Vic as leaders of the late 1950s crowd and, therefore, in the most open conflict with society, express extreme pride in being gay, but they also express the most pain over being queer. For Sandy, being honest and sticking to who she was is a source of pride. She feels sorry for those who didn't come out until later.

> "It's a long process. You just go and you're looking for whatever, you're looking for a place that you belong, where you're comfortable. And I feel so sorry for those that never come out. I wouldn't even be alive today if I didn't just go ahead and fumble on through until what I just wanted to be, and be stubborn about it and take my knocks like the rest. I'd come out now I'd be a forty-five-year-old shaking creep looking around saying, 'What do I do now?

How do I get introduced?' Well who the fuck wants to know you? You got to come out and make a name for yourself."

Despite her pride in recognizing who she was, she also has internalized a great deal of stigma with her identity. She frequently describes herself as queer and conveys all the pain and bitterness that accompanies such stigmatization. "And nobody would respect you being queer." As a leader during this period, she pushed her challenge to heterosexual society to the limit. Her only support came from the community, which respected her, but its support was somewhat limited by the stiff competition among butches.

Vic feels that being gay is her natural way, and if she had her choice she would lead her life again this way, perhaps being less butch, because of the isolation it causes.

"If I was, let's say twenty, 'cause that's a fairly decent age, I would definitely be gay, but I wouldn't be as severe a butch. I wish I didn't come out when there was roles. Only because I find myself confined and I like people, but I can't be around them. I would like to be able to be with people of my own kind and talk with them, like you and I are doing. But see I'm in the butch role, I can't do that, see, 'cause people won't talk to me."

Her pride, like that of other leaders, is tempered with feelings of self-hatred, born from the intense condemnation of society and family. She is always conscious of how much her "queerness" is despised.

The life histories of other narrators indicate that support by family and religion can mitigate the internalization of stigma. Matty's identity as a lesbian was unusual among 1950s butches in that she did not internalize being gay or butch as a stigma. It is true that as an older butch she was not involved in constant, violent confrontation with society, but she was publicly out. She was also the only narrator who was completely accepted by her family and by her religion, which suggests how important these were in creating a positive self-identity. As mentioned in chapter 3, after coming out to her family, she was able to maintain warm and close relationships with them. Furthermore, she has continued to go to church and to confession, but, on the advice of a priest years ago, does not confess homosexuality. At that time, she had a long discussion with him that culminated in his asking her if she thought homosexuality was a sin.

"I said, 'No.' I said, 'I've been this way all my life so God must have made me this way, I mean this is the way I was put on this earth.' And he said, 'If you think something is a sin and you do it anyway, then for you it's a sin, but if you don't think it's a sin, then it's not. . . . ' He told me not to confess it anymore, and from that time on I never have."

She did confess it one more time, when she was very ill in the hospital, and the priest was silent for a while and then said, " 'Now would you like to tell me your sins?' And that was the last time I ever confessed it."

Most narrators did not have the solid support from their families that Matty did. Although it is difficult to judge how the degree of acceptance affects the extent of internalization of stigma, it is our impression that it makes some difference. For instance, Little Gerry, who was never forced to break off her relations with her family, has internalized little self-hatred about being gay despite her openness. She never told her family directly that she was gay and they never aggressively set about discovering it.

> "I can't remember how old I was, eighteen, nineteen, twenty, somewhere around there, my mother had said to me one time. . . . Well she used to tell me all the time that I got too close to my friends. And one time when I was really upset about something that was going on . . . she had mentioned that I was particularly close with this one woman, and that I was acting strangely, was this friendship more than a friendship? And I said, 'Yes.' And she asked me if I wanted to talk about it, and I said, 'No.' I didn't know how to talk about it. And she never brought it up to me again, and I never brought it up to her, so I don't know what her response would have been to my saying that I was gay. And then she died, when I was in my twenties, so it was a conversation that we never had."

Later, her siblings found out, but only one reacted badly and stopped talking to her. The others accepted it quietly.

Most narrators also did not have the support of their religion. Although Little Gerry, like many of the Catholic narrators, felt no guilt about loving women, the first and only time she mentioned it in confession, she was severely reprimanded; that drove her from the Church. "When I went to confession I just happened to bring it up. Oh my God, the priest went into a tirade. So that started to introduce my first [doubts about the Church]. I just didn't like the idea of being told I was never going to be able to do something again that I found so enjoyable." Many more butch narrators were ostracized than accepted by their religions and therefore did not have this important source of support.

Throughout the 1950s, butch identity did not preclude the desire to raise children. Butch narrators were divided on their interest in having children. Some were not at all interested, but a surprising number were. For those who were interested, oppression of gays and lesbians seems to be the main factor affecting the realization of their desire. In keeping with Matty's positive attitude about being gay, she feels that lesbians could be good mothers, depending on the individual. She would have been interested in adopting a child.

> "I think it [raising children from a previous marriage] can be healthy, just like I also believe that gay women should be able to adopt children. I would like to adopt a child. I wouldn't particularly like to have one, or never had the desire to have one. But I think it's very healthy to think that even though I'm gay, that I could raise a child up healthy and normal and have them grow up

and go out into the straight world and become an individual. And when they get old enough to realize that I am gay, they make up their own minds. Not to force anything on them."

Despite her prowess as a butch, Vic was very much interested in having her own child. She thought about it seriously during the late 1960s and early 1970s, but then decided against it, because she didn't feel she could provide the kind of care a child needs.

> "I went through it maybe ten years ago, that I really thought I was missing something 'cause I didn't have children. And I thought, 'God, how can somebody that [is] supposedly as butch as I am have a child? . . . ' I wanted to have my own. . . . [It]] was really like something that was in my head for a long time. And then the more I thought about it, I thought, geez, are you doing this maybe to prove to yourself that you're a woman or are you doing it because you want the child, or what? I really went through a lot of changes, Madeline, and then I realized that you don't just have it and look at it and say, 'O.K., I had you, thank you and good evening.' And I could never deal with this. Like if I went out tonight and got raped and got pregnant behind the rape, I would have to keep it because I could never give it up. And what would I do then? . . . I like children, but could I cope with it for however many years you have to do that, and I don't think I could. It bothered me for a long time."

Part of the reason she did not feel confident in raising a child was that she did not think a lesbian environment was good for children. "Probably if I would have been married or something before I came out, I probably would have had children. And then I wonder would they be with me now? Couldn't be. I could never have children with me now. I would never want them to be raised in the environment that I live in." She not only sets high standards for herself, but for other lesbians. In this society, under these conditions, she is against lesbians' choosing to have children, because lesbians are still too stigmatized. From the perspective of the lives of 1950s butches, it seems fair to say that the contemporary lesbian interest in having children has a long tradition; the gains of the gay and lesbian liberation movements in lessening oppression have allowed those lesbians who so desire to actualize parenting.

These 1950s butches, who based their lesbian identity on sexual attraction to women, and who were part of a culture that required gender identity, draw the line between heterosexual and homosexual somewhat differently than those of the 1940s. Homosexuality was now identified by practice and by the person to whom one was actually attracted. To draw the line clearly between homosexual and heterosexual, this culture developed the standard of the true lesbian, the true butch—one who has never had sexual relations with men—to which all butches should aspire. Some butches tried to police the behavior of others in this area, to keep the reputation of butches high. This framework created the same kind of disagreements as occurred in the 1940s about whether fems were lesbians. Some, like Lonnie, feel that all women who sleep with women are lesbians, butch or fem.

> "I think all of them [studs and fems] are born gay deep within. And who knows whether we should be with men or not, who knows this? We don't know this, we're going by a book. Weren't none of us there. Who knows? So we go by how we feel inside. I like the softness of a woman's body next to mine. A man, you know, it just couldn't be."

She recognizes that many fems go back to men, but counters this by saying that many butches are bisexual as well. She uses as her proof that some butches get pregnant, which other narrators also point out frequently. "I know quite a few studs have come up pregnant while they was with their ladies. I know quite a few studs that go out with fellows, all except bona fide stud broads. . . . Because a stud could be bisexual just as well as a fem, but they don't want to admit that." Even with her idea that butch and fem are both gay, Lonnie can't escape the prevalent concept of the true butch. For her, the boundaries are muddy and difficult to set, no matter which way she looks at it.

Toni uses the test of time in gay life to determine if someone is gay, so includes fems in her definition.

> "Well, I know that there were women that I saw in the bars then that were a little bit older than me, 'cause they were like mature women, and they were real fems. Now I just ran into one of those women just a couple months ago, and she's in a relationship today with a woman who was a butch way back then. I don't know if she still defines herself like that or not, but this is over twenty years, so this woman must have been all along in gay life. Some of them dropped out, they didn't stay a lesbian."

This sensible view has the drawback of requiring hindsight to judge whether a fem is a lesbian.[19]

Others are much more suspicious of fems. Many butches, particularly the leaders who aggressively expanded the space available to lesbians, experienced fems as not remaining in gay life. They knew first-hand of having gone with women who were straight and having been left by these women when they went back to men. Some say that these fems did not consider themselves lesbian. Sandy articulates the view of many: "There was always that . . . jealousy. If you'd see [a fem] looking at a man, you'd think, 'What are you looking at him for?' You couldn't think of them as a lesbian—a lesbian wouldn't do that." When pressed further she adds, "They're not as true as we are. . . . I bet mostly all of the old [butches] feel that way."

FEM, GAY, AND LESBIAN IDENTITY IN THE LATE 1950s

Corresponding with the shift in the definition of lesbian toward a basis in attraction to the same sex, fem identity as gay or lesbian became firmer in the

1950s. All fem narrators, without hesitation or qualification, considered themselves as gay, and some even felt comfortable calling themselves "lesbian." Just as in the 1940s, the formation of fem identity followed a path distinct from that of butches. In general, fems experienced less of an imperative to live the gay life, raising interesting questions about their choices. They usually did not experience gender conflicts at an early age, and contact with the community was essential, therefore, for forming their identity. They went through a long process of questioning if they wanted to live the gay life, often with actively heterosexual interludes.[26]

Arlette was and remains an important and respected leader in the Black community. Before coming out she led an active heterosexual life. Although she was aware of lesbians from childhood because one lived in her neighborhood, and in retrospect, she can identify being attracted to women in adolescence, if not earlier, in her youth she never considered herself different or gay. In her twenties, she became curious about gay women, and had her first affair with her boss, who was a lesbian. At the time, she was afraid because of all the negative things she had heard about lesbians, and therefore always got drunk.

> "I thought it was terrible that women went together. I talked about her [my employer] like a dog. Oh hell yeah. You couldn't even convince me that was anything right about that. Because I used to talk about her bad when these lesbians used to come and pick her up, I said, 'It's ridiculous, it's terrible.' . . . But [my boss] ended up seducing me; she used to get me drunk off of some good Gordon's gin. Every time we turned out we would just about kill the whole bottle. And the next thing I know something happened, but I never knew what happened. Next time I came to her house she told me, 'You know, I'm getting tired of this drunk action from you,' and I drank some more. 'Cause I would always get out of my mind so I didn't know what was going on. . . . I was curious, more than anything else. 'Cause they always told me lesbians would kill you. They were the wrong people to associate with. So I had a fear of lesbians. I forgot, the first time I walked in the club in [Detroit] it was the Club Rendezvous, this girl approached me in the ladies bathroom and demanded to kiss me. She scared me to death. And I didn't want to kiss her. She grabbed a whiskey bottle like she was going to hit me with it. And another girl snatched her out of there; and that was my first encounter with a gay lady. . . . I said well, I really thought they were crazy. She was drunk out of her mind. That same woman ended up killing a couple of people, though. . . . But it wasn't women, it was men she killed. . . . She was high in the bathroom. . . . And I said, 'Oh my god, they're really like that.'"

Because Arlette was drinking, she doesn't consider this a full introduction to gay life. "I was always loaded . . . and like if you drink, you get loaded, you don't care what you do, but I always could never remember." Her curiosity continued after she moved to Buffalo, "But this time I tried to be a little sober." After her second relationship, which was with a young butch, she has primarily been with women, except for work, and maybe some short flings. She has periodically had an urge for a man, and thinks that is not exceptional. She appreciates partners who understand this.

Arlette is not sure what makes her gay. She can understand why other people can't understand gayness, because she herself finds it perplexing.

"Yeah, well, nobody's gonna understand that gayness, 'cause I couldn't understand it myself. But I realized when I was a kid, I'd think back, that if I saw a nice-looking girl, or a girl that attracted me, I could never understand, 'Why am I attracted to this girl? Something's wrong with me. Why do I like her?' When I was coming up I liked fellows too, but there was some girls that I just had a funny feeling, that urge that I wanted to do something. And it was always pertained to sex, and I would shake my head, say, 'What's wrong with you, you don't think like that.' I can't say, if I always was gay or not, because maybe it was because that lady [in the neighborhood] used to come through my shortcut. But a lot of people try to make like family [is the cause]. No, couldn't possibly be family had anything to do with it. And then it could be because my family was really strict, too strict, that I could always be around girls but I couldn't be around no fellows. They were so old-fashioned. At that time . . . my grandmother had to go to a party with me. . . . I had to have an older person take me some place at all times. . . . I always had to be chaperoned. I could go to a girl's house and spend the night if she had no brothers."

Consistent with not feeling different from straights at an early age, Arlette thinks that everybody has some homosexual inclination and therefore they should not be so judgmental about gays. She does not draw the line sharply between homosexuals and heterosexuals. When asked what is the most important thing we should tell people in this book, she responds:

" 'Cause Phil Donahue['s] show, those women made me so mad when they stood up and talking about, 'Well I think it's terrible.' I wanted to say, 'You are a liar.' If I was private you couldn't tell me you haven't looked at a woman or felt something for a woman, or you haven't ever had some type of experience. If you [were] in elementary school, you had a best girlfriend and you all used to play with each other. 'Cause we had a club like that and I didn't even know what we [were] doin', but me and my best, the only girl I was allowed to be 'round, we used to play with each other. Didn't know what we [were] doin' but we [were] doin' it. In fact, wait a minute, come to think of it, I had a very good friend of mine and I used to pick her up going to school every day. She grabbed me in the bathroom one day, she said, 'Arlette, come in here with me,' and threw me down on the floor and jumped on top of me, and she was getting her pubic hair for the first time, it was kind of sharp. And she leaped on me and just rubbed away. I said, 'What are you doing?' Sometimes I think about her, I wonder where she is and what's she's doin'. And I'd like to go over, run across and say, 'Hey you, come here, we've got a job to finish here.' "

Despite the certainty with which Arlette considers herself gay, she does not consider herself lesbian. When first asked for an interview, she sent the message back that she is not a lesbian, but gay. In her mind, lesbian means the sexual aggressor, so she reserves that term for butches. This is true despite thirty years in gay life instructing many butches in how to behave. She claims that many fems feel this way, and many of the butch narrators remember the same. Her distance from the term lesbian seems a way of dissociating from the stigma. Arlette's thinking strikingly resembles the gender-inversion model, emphasizing the difference between butch and fem. But she also knows the similarities between butch and fem as gay women. She does not see the inclination to be butch or fem as based in physiology, but as a role someone chooses. "I don't know how they get their role because, I think it's a matter of choice, what they feel like they want to do, I suppose. It's hard to say. Because sometime, I feel like I might want to turn stud. Really!" She also knows that it is not only fems who sleep with men, either as prostitutes or by inclination.

> "Like some of them end up, they don't want their woman talking to nobody, but they end up pregnant. How did you get pregnant? You supposed to be the stud. Can't no man speak to me but here you are gonna hand me a baby. . . . And you're telling me can't no guy touch me, you don't want no guy around, but you come home tellin' me you got a tumor and find out it's a nine-month tumor. Seen that happen too. These guys, most of the gay studs have the babies and the fems don't have no kids, and the studs are going around with the babies. One girl told me she had toilet paper and cotton in there. I said, 'All that and you got pregnant? Don't tell me that. How did the man get in if you had toilet tissue and cotton in there?' 'I have a tumor.' The tumor came out with heads and legs. And I found a lot of that. You see a lot of studs, they got four or five kids, three or four kids, and the lady, where are your kids?"

Arlette thinks that for those who remain in gay life, motherhood can be good. Being butch or fem was not the key to good or poor mothering.

> "I've seen some [children] that couldn't cope. But it was their parent's fault, because she wanted to be so hard, so much boy, she wouldn't even go to school to see about her child because she didn't want to put on a dress. . . . But I have experienced quite a few ladies I know that had children that are well-adjusted. . . . Now I don't give a darn if the child is five years old, give them respect, because you're gay you don't have to flaunt it in your kid's face. At least be mother at home. And when you get ready to step out, be your gay self."

She never gave birth to nor raised a child, but she did take care of many young gay women.

Bell's identity as a fem was somewhat different from Arlette's. She was the only fem narrator who felt from adolescence that she was different, who did not cultivate a feminine appearance, who had several children, and who was repelled by sex with men.

"I always knew or felt that my thoughts and my feelings were different. Like when I was going to school, instead of wanting to be like other people and having dates with guys and stuff, I was looking at women and seeing things in women that really interested me. Or carrying women's books or things like this here. It was kind of an early age, around when I was even twelve or thirteen years old."

At seventeen or eighteen, she started going to Bingo's. "I knew I had to try to determine and decide within myself that this was what I really wanted . . . this type of lifestyle . . . if I would be comfortable with it." She had difficult relations with her family, which she thinks made it easier to come out, because she did not have to worry about their acceptance.

Although unquestionably fem, Bell did not appear traditionally feminine. "I've had many people, though, that have taken me to be a butch because I do not like dressing really feminine, and I feel that I do have some butch ways that have led people to believe that I just might be a butch. I'm not real feminine acting." Feminine appearance and mannerisms were less important to her identity than sexual interests and her need to be dependent on someone "strong."

After coming out, Bell was introduced to prostitution. This remained a source of income on and off for ten to fifteen years. She was never interested in men and was repulsed by much of the work. After several years, she was no longer working on the streets, but had special clients. While a hooker, she had six children. One of her special clients was the father of two of her kids, and he wanted her to marry him.

"I just didn't feel like I could marry the bastard. If I'd have known that he was going to croak, maybe I would have married him just to get the money, because he worked on the railroad and the pension would have been great. It would have been maybe a thing for security and that. . . . It was aggravating me being with these men and stuff. But it seemed like the money was good and that was the only, the sole reason that I did this."

Bell has mixed feelings about being a mother. She is not sure it was appropriate for her.

"I do have kids, and I can't say that I regret it. But I don't really feel that I was cut out to be a mother. Sometimes I feel that it was the wrong thing for me because I'm not a person that has good discipline; I never did. It was hard for me to discipline my kids, because I was beaten a lot as a child. And it's hard for me to hit my daughter, especially now, the last one. . . . But then she'll get me so angry or push me to the point where I'll haul off and knock her head off for her."

Bell's life has been very difficult, but she has always persevered with the hope of finding something better. For a while, she was very confused about herself, bitter about the fact that her lesbian relationships didn't last, and she briefly thought of leaving gay life. She sees herself as having a lot to offer because of all she has learned.

> "I think it was a very mixed-up, wild life. If I had the ability or knew how to do it, I really think that I would like to write a book on a story of my life. It would have to start from . . . very early in my childhood where there was so much. . . . And I think it would be a best seller, really. Lot of things happened to me in my life. . . . I wouldn't want to go back and do them over again but I do not regret them, because they have given me a lot of experience, experience on how to deal and how to cope. For a while it made me bitter, but I don't feel really bitter any more about it because I've learned a lot of things, and experience is the best teacher."

Life for fems in this rough and tough crowd was very difficult, with few cushions. They might have been less subject than butches to harassment as lesbians, but they were often abused as women in a misogynist society—raped, beaten, and forced to raise children without adequate support. Bell stuck with it, keeping her head above water, and eventually came to feel good about herself.

Annie also worked as a prostitute while she was in the lesbian community during the late 1950s and early 1960s. Her identity is slightly different, yet again, emphasizing the element of choice for fems, and the internal strength they have for finding and creating a good life for themselves. She grew up with a butch sister, so she had some idea about gay life, but she never thought about it for herself while she was young.

After she became a prostitute, she went with well-known underworld figures who controlled her strictly. To get away from them, she started hanging around a gay bar. She remembers being frightened the first time she entered, because of the stereotypes she had of gay women and their sexual appetites. "The first time, if you're straight going into a gay bar, you're petrified, everybody is. 'Cause you think that's all they want, is that they're like vultures, in which case they're not, right?" She was not thrilled by her first affair, but nevertheless continued going to gay bars. "They were always trying to make out with you, but I didn't want no part of it, 'cause I was straight." In time, however, she met other women. "That's how I got started. I'd periodically stop back into the bar. I wasn't gung-ho right at the beginning." She started to meet more women and fell in love with one.

After five or six years as a lesbian, she decided to get married. She left both the lesbian life and prostitution for fifteen years. It was a change she made for security and she thinks fems commonly make such decisions.

> "I think I enjoy the gay life now, more now, that I'm older, than I did when I was younger. Because when I was younger, you really don't know if you want to get married, settle down, or what you really want, and you're very unsure at that point. Whereas a butch usually is butch and they usually stay butch. And you don't ever see them getting married. Where with fems, they'll

be in the gay life for a few years or whatever, especially if they're young, and you can't really blame them. And then they decide to get married and have children, some of them. Or they'll marry for security. That's what they'll look for in a man is security."

While she was actively socializing with lesbians, she didn't think about the limitations of her carefree and exciting life, but slowly different goals surfaced. She didn't feel that she could achieve the kind of security she wanted with lesbians.

"I had to, I was young and I had to see what life was really about. I wasn't going anywhere fast, and I was getting older, and I wanted to do something with my life. . . . It's not that I couldn't do it [with women], I think I was looking for security. . . . Maybe because none of us worked. . . . We weren't looking forward or that. . . . No goals. So I went to beauty school . . . and I had a beauty salon for five years."

After making her way in straight life and doing the things she wanted to do, Annie came back to gay life. She prefers it, but she wouldn't rule out marrying again if the conditions were attractive.

"I might get married again, but he's got to be at least eighty . . . have to give him his vitamin pill in the morning and a sleeping pill in the evening. And at that point they've outgrown their jealousy and all that bit, and they just want companionship. And that's what I would want out of a marriage. . . . It would have to really depend on the circumstances. If he slept in his own bedroom, I had mine, and strictly for companionship, why not. No sex, why not?"

Despite the fifteen years in straight life, Annie feels she was a lesbian when she was younger in gay life, as she is now. When told that some people in the community feel that fems aren't real lesbians, Annie is at first incredulous: "Well what would you call them? I mean actually, . . . if a woman's having a sexual affair with another woman, she's just as much a lesbian. . . . They're two lesbians, I would say." Annie has a modern gay consciousness that bases identity in same-sex attraction. Like the butches who consider all women who are attracted to women as lesbians, she went on to introduce the concept of the "purer" lesbian.

"Oh yeah. Not as much as, let's say, an untouched butch or a virgin butch. Now maybe that's where you're getting it from, these butches I'm assuming are the ones that you interviewed and said that they're the lesbians and a fem is not a lesbian. Right. Maybe because they've never been touched by a man. Maybe this is in the back of their minds. . . . Because with a fem woman, somewhere along the way, she's either had or will have, sex with a man."

She thinks butch and fem are not fundamentally different kinds of lesbians. If a fem didn't have sex with a man, she would be as much of a pure lesbian as a butch. "I would say she's very much a lesbian. Very much. Wouldn't you? . . . And she's always been involved with the same sex, I would say she's very, very, very lesbian."

Annie thinks that gender identification, rather than sexual interest, does make a difference in a person's life, and that is what makes it more likely for fems to go with men.

> "I think with butches, I think this is something that overpowers them at a very young age, as far as being more masculine than girlish. Acting more tomboyish, than more girlish, that's what I'm trying to say. And I don't really think this ever really grows out of them, and when they start growing up and they become that in their early teens and they start saying, 'Gee she looks good, he doesn't look good but she looks good.' And they start recognizing their problem. And I think with a butch, I don't think they could actually really take the domineering husband. Or the husband that wants to be the husband. You know what I mean. Where a fem is really adjusted to it. They're girl girl, and you find that it's very easy for them to adjust to a marriage more so than a butchy girl. Cause they've played the lead role all their life. . . . And then for them to step into a marriage and have a man rule them, there'd probably be imprints in the wall. There would be the man's imprint."

In Annie's mind butches resisted female socialization while fems did not. Nevertheless, her clarity about the choices she made highlights the strength of fems and their will to live with women, despite the barriers against them.

Throughout the 1940s and 1950s, it was a problem for both butches and fems to articulate the construction of the fem identity in the lesbian world. Although fem identity has received little scholarly attention heretofore, it raises some of the most interesting questions about lesbian community. Most fems grew up feeling little difference from straight women in terms of their position in society. They realized their attraction to women at varying ages and did not feel that this made them either male or unfeminine. It also appears that they did not strongly internalize the stigma of being sexually different. Some were attracted to men for periods in their lives, others were never interested in men. Most had some heterosexual sex, at least in their younger years, and were conscious of making clear choices about how they would live their lives, rather than being led by some internal or biological imperative. They also shared a determination to be with the women they loved, to establish a viable place for themselves in lesbian society, and to defend their right to help structure a world that could comfortably accommodate the relationships they desired.

The gender-inversion model for homosexuality which was still prevalent in the 1940s postulated a radical dichotomy between butch and fem, denying the latter a lesbian identity while making masculinity central in lesbian identity. The move toward an identity based on "same-sex" attraction had different meaning for butches and fems. For butches, masculinity became less a marker or emblem of difference. Lesbian identity became based on sexual attraction to women, rather than on masculinity. "Same-sex" attraction also came to mean that fems could begin to claim a lesbian identity for themselves. The development of community was critical in this because it presented a lifestyle around which fems could build their identities.

This analysis illuminates two important issues in lesbian history. First, it clarifies what is meant by the social construction of homosexuality. Despite the similarity of woman-to-woman sexual relations, lesbian identity meant significantly different things in different decades, and even to butches and fems at any particular time period. On the surface, gender played a similar role in the identity of the 1940s and 1950s, but in reality it did not. By the end of the 1950s, masculinity and lesbian identity were no longer merged. This separation of gender and sexual identity is difficult to identify without listening carefully to lesbians' words, because it occurred at precisely the time that the lesbian community required increasing obedience to gender-defined behavior, giving the appearance that gender was even more central to the formation of identity. The radical change in the nature of sexual identity over the last ninety years suggests that such change continues today. That the sexual politics of the future will be framed around yet a different understanding of sexual identity, perhaps one where "object choice" is no longer important and technique comes to the fore. We are likely already in the midst of an historical process that makes identity less fixed and loving less polarized.

Second, the complicated relationship between gender identity and lesbian identity during these two decades confirms once again, though from a different perspective, the social power of adherence to butch-fem roles. The fact that some butches did not polarize masculine and feminine when young, that some butches and fems switched roles after entering the community, and that some butches and fems adapted to roles only enough to be accepted in the community indicates that roles were learned, rather than being inborn, and for many involved an element of conscious choice. Thus, the diesel dyke, bull dyke, or truck-driver lesbian of the 1950s, infamous for her masculine excesses, might not have had a masculine identity until she entered the community. It was a stance she adopted because it offered her a way of announcing, encouraging, and supporting her erotic love of women.

The reproduction of butch-fem roles involved community instruction and pressure as well as complex issues of psychosocial identity. As the preceding chapters have documented, lesbian life during the 1950s involved a variety of ways for educating newcomers, including role modeling and explicit instruction. Furthermore, the culture in the 1940s as well as the 1950s was imbued with the logic of gender polarity, on all levels, but particularly in regard to the erotic. Finally, butch-fem roles "worked" for organizing a stable culture of resistance and lesbians followed them. The powerful presence of butch-fem roles in the 1950s, despite the new understanding of lesbianism as based in attraction to women rather than gender inversion, is testimony to how effective butch-fem culture was for organizing lesbian resistance and lesbian eroticism. Lesbians chose to follow and reproduce it, whether it coincided or conflicted with their personal identities.

We have argued in Chapter 5 and 6 that the increased rigidification of butch-fem roles was not simply a reflection of the larger society's return to polarized gender roles. Rather, it was rooted in the increased repression of the 1950s and the heightened resistance based in the butch's confrontation with the heterosexual world. The butch was so central to the methods of resistance that she required sharper rules of behavior for defense and offense. This chapter adds yet another dimension to the process. Since gender identification was no longer central to lesbian identity during the 1950s, yet the entire strategy of resistance was built around gender, it became more imperative that gender rules be clearly enforced.

10

CONCLUSION

If we are the people who call down history from its heights in marble assembly halls, if we put desire into history, if we document how a collective erotic imagination questions and modifies monolithic societal structures like gender, if we change the notion of woman as self-chosen victim by our public stances and private styles, then surely no apologies are due. Being a sexual people is our gift to the world.

—Joan Nestle, *A Restricted Country*

One aspect of heterosexual oppression is to make a negatively defined homosexuality central in our lives. Our recent progressive response to that negation has been to make a positively defined lesbian and gay identity essential. But some of us are now beginning to think about more radically transcendent responses, those which both affirm our feelings and acts, and begin to go beyond the old hetero/homo polarity.

—Jonathan Katz, *Gay/Lesbian Almanac*

Boots of Leather, Slippers of Gold traces the roots of gay and lesbian liberation to the resistance culture of working-class lesbians. Butch-fem roles coalesced an entire culture into the prepolitical, but none the less active, struggle against gay and lesbian oppression. Working-class lesbians had a key role in shaping their history, transforming their social life, sexual expression, relationships, and identity. Together these changes created the consciousness of kind necessary for the boldness that was to characterize gay liberation. The civil-rights, women's, and antiwar movements did not generate gay liberation, but rather served as a catalyst to bring together and transform two different political tendencies already existing within the working-class lesbian community. On the one hand, the homophile movement, which was relatively small in number, used accommodationist strategies in order to develop dialogues with the straight world, thereby supporting lesbians' entrance into the political arena. On the other hand, the tough bar lesbians, who were many in number and came from various racial/ethnic groups, refused to deny their difference, and used confrontational tactics to deal with the heterosexual world.

In the late 1960s their pride and boldness, when meshed with the homophile strategies and organizations, generated a powerful movement.

At the moment there is not enough research on lesbian communities to allow for a detailed comparison between Buffalo and other cities. As we argued in the introduction, there is good reason to believe communities similar to that of Buffalo developed in most middle-sized industrial cities in the U.S. during the 1940s and 1950s, with regional variations depending on racial/ethnic makeup of the area, state laws, local police policies, and so forth, but this must await further research by community activists as well as scholars. In this conclusion, therefore, we want to reflect more broadly on some of the general issues raised by this study. First, we give a narrative summary of the development of the Buffalo lesbian working-class community and consciousness, establishing a framework for understanding how the various dimensions of socializing, sexuality, and relationships relate to the formation of consciousness and resistance to oppression. We then turn to more speculative matters. We address whether these butch-fem communities should be considered as part of the feminist project, a vexing question that has appeared throughout the manuscript. Comparing working-class lesbian and gay-male communities, we next raise questions about the differential effect of gender hierarchy on each. What does it mean that lesbians are oppressed as both women and homosexuals while gay men are only oppressed as the latter, except of course for race and class oppression should they be relevant. And finally, we use this research as a starting point to illuminate contemporary issues around identity politics and the future of the gay and lesbian movements.

TWENTIETH-CENTURY LESBIAN SOCIAL LIFE: AN ARENA FOR RESISTANCE

In order for a mass movement of lesbians to have developed in the late 1960s and early 1970s, lesbian consciousness had to move from the self-image of an isolated and perhaps sick or evil individual to the self-image of a participant in a proud group whose members help one another and expect that society treats them well. What we learn about this crucial process from studying the Buffalo working-class lesbian community is the way that social life, sexuality, relationships, and identity formation are intertwined through the cultural system of butch-fem roles. The process of generating self-esteem and solidarity is multidimensional and depends on the activities of members of the community itself as well as of the state.

The distinguishing feature of twentieth-century working-class lesbian communities and what makes them such important contributors to lesbian history is their claiming of social space, the breaking of silence around lesbians. Working-class lesbians of the 1930s, 1940s, and 1950s acted upon an irrepressible urge to be with others of their kind, to pursue sexual liaisons, and to have a good time. During the 1930s in cities like Buffalo, some working-class lesbians managed to locate one another, socialize together, and have fun in speakeasies and later in bars—in some cases the back rooms of heterosexual bars—and house parties. World War II dramatically expanded the possibilities for lesbian socializing. With so many men in the service, women had greater freedom of movement on the street and could easily go out with one another to dinner, to bars, and to parks. The dress code for women also relaxed, allowing lesbians to wear clothes which expressed their erotic interests. White lesbians in Buffalo had two favorite bars, Ralph Martin's and Winters, and Black lesbians went to house parties and the Black entertainment bars, although some as individuals went to the white bars. In these locations lesbians gathered with dignity and developed positive feelings about themselves. The friendships that formed in the bars and parties extended to socializing beyond them—theater, concerts, parks—and lasted a life time.

In the 1940s, butch-fem culture was an integral part of the growth of lesbian community, culture, and consciousness because it announced lesbianism to the public and organized lesbian desire. Butches had a special leadership role in forging lesbian social life. In creating and experiencing themselves as different, as "homos"—neither traditional men nor traditional women—they needed to find others like themselves. Their carefully cultivated masculine appearance advertised their difference and indicated a woman's explicit sexual interest in another woman. At this point in history the image of the butch, or the butch-fem couple, was the only distinct marker around which a community could be built. By going out regularly, butches found new bars, talked to people, built social ties, and began to develop a sense of community and a common culture. Because of their appearance, butches were stigmatized as "homos," and subjected to ridicule, ostracism, and hatred. Their strategy for managing this oppression centered around making a firm division between their social lives and their work and family lives. They moved out of their family homes and socialized in gay and lesbian bars only on weekends.

Fems, whose identity was not based on strong internal feelings of difference and, therefore, did not feel urgency to look for others like themselves, could not serve as a marker for community. They were not by definition as central to the public aspect of forging community as the butch. Nevertheless, they were essential to its continuity. One of the ingredients for having a good time was the expression of erotic interest, which was always between butch and fem, and one of the goals of lesbian life was to find and stay with a partner. Fems were not passive participants in this process. They decided that sex and/or relationships with women were what they wanted, and took themselves to bars or house parties, sometimes becoming active participants in lesbian community. Since the appearance of butch and fem together in a couple was the most explicit announcement of sexual activity between women that was available at the time, many fems suffered stigmatization, although it was not as continuous as that of butches. Also like butches, fems had to negotiate difficult relationships with their families.

The search for sexual partners might have been the reason for interest in finding community, yet at the same time the formation of community had a powerful impact on sexual expression. In the context of a safe space, butches and fems actively expanded the sexual possibilities for women. Courting had an explicitly erotic dimension and relationships quickly developed a sexual component. In addition, although butches and fems appreciated romance and love within a sexual relationship, both were able to separate love from sex. Butches, though they might have felt a bit uneasy, pursued flings with "show girls" who were on tour. And fems, though they marvel at their behavior today, did not pull away from fleeting affairs. In the area of sexuality the still-formative nature of 1940s lesbian culture is most apparent, highlighting the importance of a stable women's community for the development of sexual autonomy and subjectivity in women. Rather than a general lesbian culture of sexuality, radically different sexual mores existed in different social groups.

Lesbians' active social lives created a distinct form or system of relationships, which we suggest be designated as serial monogamy. Lesbians in the public communities of the 1940s had few, if any, relationships which lasted for a lifetime. Butches and fems formed committed relationships, living together, going out together, and caring for one another which gave them pleasure and satisfaction. While building relationships they continued to socialize regularly in bars and parties in order to temper the isolation and stigma of being lesbian. Loving relationships gone sour did not have to continue due to isolation and fear. Butch and fem remained somewhat autonomous and enjoyed socializing and pursuing erotic interests. The culture of romance fostered in the bars, however, generated excitement about new love and frequently led to breakups.

These 1940s lesbians who went out to bars and parties regularly had an independent and nonconformist strategy for living as well as a concern for community among lesbians. They pushed the boundaries of permissibility for women generally, not just for themselves as individuals. They indicated their difference through appearance, through avoiding marriage, and through making a home with women. They fostered sexual exploration and autonomy among women, and pursued satisfying and lasting relationships. They often led adventurous lives, including social trips to other cities. Their social lives effectively countered feelings of isolation and stigma created by society's oppression of gays and lesbians. Together these accomplishments shaped the lesbian community of the 1950s.

In the 1950s, lesbian culture and community took on a different character caused by the confluence of the developing tradition of community among lesbians and the severe state persecution of lesbians and gays. In Buffalo, and most likely throughout the U.S., the lesbian community became class-stratified. At one extreme were the explicit "queers" who were tough enough to hang around the street bars frequented by the sexual fringe; they were not willing to compromise their behavior to gain heterosexual approval, and therefore had to work in blue-collar jobs if they worked at all. At the other extreme were the more upwardly mobile who were circumspect about their lesbianism in order to find better jobs and to move ahead. The community also became racially mixed. Black lesbians desegregated the bars of the rough and rebellious white lesbians at the same time that two lesbian bars opened in the Black community which some whites visited. Blacks also continued the tradition of socializing in house parties. Those who lived through these changes had no question about their significance. Narrators from the 1940s never felt comfortable with the rough crowd's violence and aggressiveness nor the upwardly mobile crowd's unwillingness to claim a lesbian identity.

Growing solidarity and related feelings of pride created by the tradition of lesbians acting together to build community were key for the developments of the 1950s. Butch-fem roles continued to be integral to the growth of lesbian culture particularly for the tough rebellious lesbians, both white and Black. In the tough crowd, the new feelings of unity and pride led butches to take the offensive in relation to the heterosexual world. Butches began to discard 1940s rules of discretion. They challenged the double life, going to the bars as often as they could and wearing men's clothes as much of the time as possible. Not to do so was experienced as a compromise of self. If necessary they were willing to resort to physical violence to protect their right to socialize, walk the street, and be with women, thereby expanding the places where lesbians could congregate. They also banded together when in trouble and recognized as their leaders those who looked out for and took care of members of the community. For the first time lesbians could protect their own and the bars began hiring lesbians as bartenders and bouncers. Masculinity was central to this aggressive stance, but butches usually did not go over the line and become or pretend to be male. In fact they rather scorned men, rarely spending time with them—gay or straight.

Fems might not have directly created this confrontational culture but they were attracted to it and willingly participated in it. They too were regulars at bars and house parties, sometimes tending bar. Furthermore their support and love, the only validation that butches received, was critical. Some fems represented the voice of compromise, arguing that it was not necessary to advertise lesbianism all the time. But all appreciated and admired their butches for the protection they offered in a hostile world.

Solidarity and a developing consciousness of being lesbians together were also necessary for the desegregation of the bars. Although Blacks were not at first welcomed by whites, they persevered until they made friends. In time Blacks and whites began to socialize outside of the bars, going to Black after-hour joints and house parties, and some interracial relationships formed. Despite the fact that white and Black butches of this rough crowd were ready to fight at any provocation, the tension between Blacks and whites rarely erupted into open conflict, a strong testimony to the existence of a consciousness of being lesbians together. In some contexts the Black and white lesbian communities were unquestionably part of one larger community, in others they were distinct, due to racism in the larger society and their distinct traditions.

Pride, if not solidarity, also helped to create the more upwardly mobile group who came to believe that they were not very different from straights and were entitled to the same benefits in life. They, therefore, concentrated on finding good jobs and building a private social life that decreased the risks of exposure. Nevertheless, they did not completely hide their lesbianism. They continued to go out to "reputable" bars, even if only once every week or two. Although this group most likely represents the kind of social consciousness that formed women's homophile organizations in large metropolitan centers, in Buffalo, a blue-collar town, they had little impact on shaping lesbian politics. In Buffalo it was the tough and rebellious lesbians who were the expanding force. They envisioned the lesbian community as encompassing all lesbians, yet at the same time their strategy and tactic of putting an end to secrecy and hiding inevitably divided them from those who emphasized discretion in order to keep good jobs and a respected social position.

In the context of the antigay witch hunts of the 1950s, the increase in lesbian self-esteem indicates that lesbians themselves were important actors in setting the direction and possibilities for change. The openness of working-class lesbians in this very hostile environment was based in the emerging strength and solidarity of a culture that was able to take care of its members for an extended period of time. Years of socializing together, of dating and forming relationships during the 1940s, supported the development of a consciousness of kind. The change is represented graphically by the fact that in the 1940s lesbians rarely reached out to newcomers. But by the early 1950s, despite the hostile environment, lesbians introduced one another to the bars and helped ease newcomers' entrance, a process that became more and more institutionalized as the 1950s progressed, to the extent that young lesbians considered their elders role models by the end of the decade.

Increased community solidarity and pride supported lesbians in the development of sexual subjectivity. Unlike many straight women who didn't talk about sex at all or straight men for whom sex was power and a dirty joke, lesbians openly explored and expressed desire. In the 1950s sex was a common topic of discussion, and butches in particular saw themselves as students of sex. Fems participated in teaching their partners to be good lovers and demanded and appreciated a high level of performance from their butches. Butches were firmly committed to making sex good for their fems while fems were enthusiastic about enjoying it and had confidence that their lovers thought they were terrific. This atmosphere fostered a sense of female agency that in turn furthered the establishment of community.

Although the severely antigay environment of the 1950s did not stop the development of lesbian solidarity and consciousness, it did sharply mark their form, giving the culture of the tough lesbians in the late 1950s and early 1960s an extremely defensive tone. The pleasure of socializing with other lesbians and the difficulty of this accomplishment pervade all narrators' memories. The forms of resistance which were based on constant confrontation with the heterosexual world without conscious long-term strategies and tactics took a tremendous toll physically and emotionally. Although butches could rely on each other when challenged by the heterosexual world, their relations with one another were tinged with competition to be the best and did not provide emotional support or nurturing. At the same time, fems' active sexual interest in butches and their contact with the heterosexual world combined with the isolation, insecurity, and aggressiveness of butches to make relationships increasingly brittle and violent as the decade progressed.

Without the support and strategy of a political movement late-1950s rough and tough butches were not able to immediately achieve their goal of creating a better world for lesbians and gays. They did, however, succeed in forging the consciousness that was to become, a decade later, central to gay liberation—that gays and lesbians should end hiding and demand for themselves what they deserve. This consciousness in the large lesbian and gay subcultures throughout the country provided an environment for the rapid spread of gay liberation and in many cases actually provided some of the impetus for the movement. In a city such as Buffalo, where police harassment of the bars was intense during the 1960s, many of the bar lesbians who came out in the late 1950s went on to form the first gay organization in the city, which soon became part of the gay liberation movement. In lesbian and gay mythology the first person to take a swing at the police in the Stonewall Riots, thereby igniting the street battle, was a lesbian.[1] Assigning a rough and tough lesbian a primary role in the launching of gay liberation is completely in keeping with her character. Her fighting back would not be the isolated act of an angry individual but would have been an integral part of her culture.

FEMINIST INCLINATIONS OF THE WORKING-CLASS LESBIAN COMMUNITY

Because of the centrality of butch and fem roles to the organization of Black and white working-class lesbian communities, feminists have been hesitant to claim these communities as central to lesbian and women's history. Unquestionably they raise vexing questions that have appeared throughout this study: Do these communities challenge or weaken male power and claim more for women, or do they reproduce male hierarchy and division among women?

The working-class lesbian community did not have a conscious relation to feminism. In the woman-hating 1950s, the assertion of a powerful identity as women was difficult for both butches and fems. In general they did not challenge gender polarity or the devaluation of women. Furthermore, they were not motivated to make a better life for women, but rather a better life for lesbians. It was in the process of achieving the latter that the former was accomplished.[2] What they particularly appreciated about the rebirth of the feminist movement of the late 1960s was the ways it taught them to value themselves as women as well as lesbians. In a misogynist society the idea was electrifying and changed many of their lives. Nevertheless, in the absence of a mass feminist movement in the 1940s and 1950s, butch-fem culture represented some elements of an untutored feminism; butches by claiming male privilege for women on the streets and fems by living as feminine women without men. Certainly one dimension of contemporary lesbian feminism's platform has been to equip women to learn how to take care of themselves and live self-sufficiently, something which butch-fem couples had definitely accomplished.

As we have suggested throughout, there is no simple explanation for understanding the progressive or conservative role of gender in working-class lesbian communities. We have argued that in the process of lesbian resistance butch-fem culture both drew on and transformed the dominant society's male supremacist and heterosexual uses of gender. A fundamental ambiguity pervaded these communities. The butch identity was masculine not male while the fem identity was feminine but not heterosexual. Therefore butch-fem community and culture was based on a tension between the similarities of women and the differences, sometimes hierarchical, of gender. Butches did not have access to institutionalized male power in the economic and political sphere. Nor did they have male bodies with which to support whatever power they claimed. Fems unquestionably chose to be with women, not men, even if these women had a masculine image.

The forces for mutuality between butch and fem were strong, and therefore gender difference did not necessarily always mean hierarchy. This is typified by the gender-polarized erotic system, which created an intriguing balance between butch and fem rather than a rigid hierarchy and allowed women to explore and understand their own sexual desires. Although butches were aggressive in their pursuit of women, this did not limit fems' sexual expression. Fems were reactive and responsive, rather than passive. Many enjoyed and encouraged the pleasures of the body and their passion was the butches' fulfillment. Butch-fem sexuality was successfully built around the female body and made pleasing the fem absolutely central, the focus of sexuality.

It is in the area of committed butch-fem relationships that the contradictions inherent in lesbians' building a gender-polarized culture were most apparent. Butch and fem couples continually negotiated the tension between the mutuality of women together and the potential for hierarchical differences. Economic power was distributed fairly evenly between butch and fem. Because of this general economic balance, neither one was more vulnerable to being left than the other.

Fems had the advantage of not being severely stigmatized by the heterosexual society, which gave them considerably more freedom of movement and more possibility of social support outside of the lesbian community; in some cases it also meant they could earn more money. However, butches, by their very masculinity, seemed to project an aura of prestige, which many also earned by protecting and fighting for the community. In keeping with this, butches also tended to have stronger and more reliable social networks within the community. In the 1940s this was manifested by Butch Night Out, in the 1950s rough crowd, by the "gang," who banded together to take care of business. Butch prestige and networks often tipped the balance of power in relationships giving butches more control. Most fems, no matter the era in which they came out, complain of butch jealousy, possessiveness, and attempts at control. This domineering behavior was particularly exaggerated in the 1950s rough crowd, when some butches used violence in their relationships with their fems, as well as in defending the community at large.

Despite these tendencies toward gender hierarchy, we still argue that the lesbian community transformed gender for its own purposes. To underestimate the degree of transformation is to seriously misjudge the difficulty of the feminist project of overcoming hierarchical gender divisions. Recent feminist writing cumulatively indicates the intransigence of gender—the difficulty of eliminating its hierarchical categories.[3] These realizations place in perspective the challenge faced by butch-fem communities of the 1940s and 1950s, particularly when we consider the advantageous position of today's lesbian feminists. In the 1940s the dominant society did not foster the separation of gender and sex, while today we can easily conceptualize attraction among women in an ungendered context. We think this ability is possible partly because of the struggles of butch-fem communities of the past for women's sexual autonomy. A helpful way to understand butch-fem culture is to see its participants as facing and trying to solve the same issues with which lesbian theorists of today still grapple. How can women live without gender in a culture that is committed to its reproduction? Seen in this context butch-fem communities offer rather creative and interesting solutions to the contradictions of gender and sex.

THE RELATIONSHIP BETWEEN THE SUBCULTURES OF WORKING-CLASS LESBIANS AND GAY MEN

Our analysis of the development of lesbian consciousness, community, and politic suggests that the histories of working-class lesbians and gay men have a great deal in common, but also are significantly different.[4] In Buffalo the similarities and differences between gay men and lesbians were represented concretely by their interaction in the bars. Gay men and lesbians frequented most of the same bars during the 1940s and 1950s, yet they each had some bars that were primarily their own. Although there was no ideological commitment to separation and many friendship groups included both lesbians and gay men, there was unquestionably some difference in culture and consciousness, as expressed most clearly by the rough and tough lesbians who had little to do with gay men.

Working-class lesbian history raises new questions about consciousness formation for gay males as well as lesbians. Unquestionably working-class lesbians and gay men in the 1930s, 1940s, and 1950s both sought out places to meet others like themselves, often congregating in the same locales. Through this socializing gays and lesbians developed a distinct culture and consciousness of kind, which allowed them to generate a distinctive subculture, the homophile movement, and later gay liberation and lesbian feminism. However, the kinds of social life lesbians and gay men built were significantly different reflecting the gender hierarchy in the general society. Gay-male history is shaped by the privilege of men just as lesbian history is by the oppression of women. Lesbians not only had to resist lesbian oppression in order to have erotic relationships with women, but also had to struggle to function autonomously from men.

That lesbians are oppressed both as gays and as women is obvious but difficult to grasp. Gay scholarship has tended to look only at the oppression of homosexuality, not gender, while much lesbian-feminist discourse has focused primarily on the oppression of women, at least this was true when we started this study. Now at the end of our research, in part due to struggles within the movement to which we have contributed, some lesbian feminists have come to appreciate the similarities between the oppression of gay men and lesbians as sexual minorities, almost forgetting the oppression of women.[5] The answer to the question, who is more oppressed in history, lesbians or gay men, differs significantly according to whether or not one understands the double nature of lesbian oppression. From the seventeenth- and eighteenth-century British laws which required death for sodomy, to the twentieth-century police raids on bathhouses and public parks, gay men appear to have borne the brunt of homosexual oppression. This is a popular view held by many narrators. However, we are arguing that such a view does not take into account the lesbian fight for the right to congregate and develop a sexual subjectivity independent of men. The violence against women that kept women off the streets and under male authority has to be seen as part of lesbian oppression. That Queen Victoria could not even imagine lesbianism and therefore did not think it had to be mentioned in the penal code, simultaneously offered freedom to women by not legally circumscribing their behavior, while maintaining the male-supremacist fiction that women were not autonomous beings.[6]

This study suggests that the double nature of lesbian oppression marked the formation of lesbian community, requiring that first and foremost it create a protected environment where women could form erotic attachments, free from the interference of male power. This fundamental need gave priority to building a protected community life and therefore to the butch role. In the first half of the twentieth century lesbian culture developed in bars and house parties while gay-male culture developed in these two sites as well as in public places such as parks, beaches, and baths. Until World War II it was not easy for women to negotiate the streets and to go to bars by themselves. For women to pursue sexual interests with other women outside of a protected environment such as a bar was likely to be misunderstood as "coming on" to men, or to provoke violent reactions from men, including rape. In the context of the sexual repression of women, women needed a supportive environment in which to explore their sexuality. The lesbian's need for a protected and supportive environment led to a strong community from at least the 1940s on, which served as the basis for the development of pride and group consciousness among lesbians. This history suggests that the basis of solidarity and pride might be quite different in the lesbian and gay-male communities. Furthermore, it is possible that bar lesbians of the 1940s and 1950s were less resistant than men to overriding feelings of individual stigma and developing a consciousness of kind. The relatively greater space for gay-male sexual expression might have created a less-effective counter to the dominant society's understanding of gayness as an individual defect.[7]

Contrary to popular stereotypes our analysis shows that lesbians, like gay-men, were explicitly interested in exploring sexuality and took risks far beyond what was expected of women. However, where the lesbian and gay-male communities differed was that men have institutionalized enjoying sex for sex's sake, while lesbians have not. Although most lesbians during the 1940s and 1950s had experienced the fleeting affair, the majority did not do so regularly, and tricking was not an established part of lesbian culture. There is not enough evidence to indicate why this should be the case, and that which does exist allows for contradictory interpretations. On the one hand, we could say that the community's emphasis on protection suggests that oppression and repression have affected lesbians' expression of sexuality, and when the oppression of women lessens lesbians are likely to engage in more sex for sex's sake. On the other hand, the pleasure lesbians take in romance, and the way the integration of romance and sex has so fundamentally shaped their system of relationships, suggests that for the majority of lesbians the two are not likely to separate even if women's oppression lessens. We don't yet understand the kinds of social conditions that lead to the integration or separation of love and sex.

The working-class lesbian project of building a protective community has numerous implications for creating differences in the social life of lesbians and gay men. Gender roles seem to have greater persistence as organizers of social life and sexuality for working-class lesbians than gay men. If solidarity was unimportant to gay men's expression of sexuality, they might not have needed gender, or any other consistent system, to organize social relationships. It is our guess that at one point in the twentieth century, gender roles were as important to gay-male eroticism as they were to lesbian eroticism of the 1940s and 1950s, and that masculine men went with feminine men exclusively, as suggested by George Chauncey's analysis of the Rhode Island Navy trials.[8] This raises numerous questions for understanding the nature of gay and lesbian social life and consciousness. Were the 1940s the time of transition from a model of homosexuality based in gender inversion to one based on same-sex attraction for both gay men and lesbians, or did it occur earlier for gay men? Did women hold on to gender polarity in relationships longer than men because gender polarity was more central for building their culture and community? Did the repression of women's sexuality in society at large make it more difficult to give up an erotic system based on gender polarity?

A striking but little-discussed difference between gay-male and lesbian communities was the high development of camp in the former and its almost complete absence in the latter. A corollary is that queens (feminine-identified gay males) were experts in camp while butches were not. From her study of female impersonators Esther Newton identifies three elements which together constitute camp—incongruity, theatricality, and humor.[9] If we assume that camp humor is based on juxtaposing incongruous extremes, certainly it should flourish in the lesbian community as well as in the male-homosexual community. In gay-male culture the queen constructs her identity around being male yet being feminine. The butch identity is also based on gender artifice, that of being female but masculine. But anyone who talks to these old-time butches is not struck by their campy sense of humor, as one is when listening to or reading about old-time queens.[10]

The difference between the queen's and butch's relationship to camp can again be located in the effect of gender hierarchy on men and women. Queens based their strategy of resistance on wit, verbal agility, and a sense of theater and used these to create a common culture. Such tools were not on their own adequate to meet the challenges lesbians faced. In the context of the history of the working-class lesbian community in Buffalo, we see that the butch persona centered on physically taking care of lesbians—butches and fems—and protecting and defending women's right to live independently from men and pursue erotic liaisons with women. In most situations, therefore, there was nothing really humorous or theatrical about butch artifice. Butch effectiveness was based on concretely usurping male prerogatives in order to assert women's sexual autonomy and to defend a space in which women could love women. In this woman-hating society, and in the dangerous environment of the bars, the butch had to be able to assert and defend herself. The butch persona, unlike that of the queen, carried the burden of twentieth-century women's struggle for the right to function independently in the public world. Camp was not designed for that task. The perspective of lesbian history suggests that more work is needed to understand how the development of camp is embedded in institutionalized gender hierarchy and what it means that the queen's camp was key in building gay-male consciousness while the butch's aggressive protection shaped the formation of lesbian consciousness.

IDENTITY AND THE POLITICS OF LESBIAN AND GAY LIBERATION

The history of twentieth-century working-class lesbian resistance tantalizingly includes two different ways of conceptualizing lesbian identity. On the one hand, the prominent role of the visible butch in the prepolitical resistance of lesbian subcultures suggests that twentieth-century lesbian consciousness was based on a fixed identity: something that was set at birth, stable, and continuous. On the other hand, the existence of different butch images in different subcommunities, and most importantly, the differences between butch and fem identity, suggest that lesbian identity is multiple and changes according to particular historical conditions. The coexistence of fixed and changing aspects of identity parallels contradictions faced by the contemporary gay and lesbian liberation movements: In an oppressive society, gay and lesbian activists need to struggle for gay and lesbian rights, and this is aided by the affirmation of a fixed lesbian and gay identity. At the same time, a radical platform for lesbian and gay liberation envisions a world where sexuality might not be polarized around homosexuality and heterosexuality, and individuals might be free to pursue their sexual attractions without a fixed sexual identity. This history suggests that these contradictory impulses are historically part of twentieth-century working-class lesbian culture.

From the perspective of indicating a new social grouping that came into being in the twentieth century, it is correct to talk of the development of a lesbian community. In other contexts, however, the concept of one community is a distortion. In fact several lesbian subcommunities emerged in the twentieth century, each with its own culture and consciousness. Minimally we could document three public working-class subcommunities in Buffalo in the 1950s—the upwardly mobile, the tough Black crowd, and the tough, primarily white, bar crowd. In some situations these subcommunities saw themselves as one lesbian community, in others they experienced themselves as separate and acted accordingly. The prominence of these separate communities in the 1950s suggests that in the process of creating gay liberation and lesbian feminism, the public definition of gay and lesbian became homogenized. In the particular setting of the late 1960s and early 1970s, a lesbian politic that was based on a unified sense of identity actually severed existing ties between different lesbian subcommunities; "the lesbian" became white and middle-class. Black and white bar lesbians might have had more contact with one another in the 1950s than Black and white lesbians do today in Buffalo, despite the past twenty years of struggle to diversify the gay and lesbian movements.

Further problems in the concept of a single lesbian community is further revealed by the lack of a common consistent usage of the word lesbian, or any equivalent, during the 1940s and 1950s. Rather than there being a unitary group of lesbians there were butches and fems, who sometimes grouped themselves together as gay, but not always. Butches and fems had distinct identities, different roles in building a "lesbian" community.

The key element in creating the butch's identity was an active recognition that she was different—aggressive, autonomous, and/or interested sexually in women—and taking the step to represent herself as such and to build a life that accommodated that difference. Difference was not a core part of the fems' identity, and not something they experienced or struggled with while growing up. Most had lived comfortably at least some of their lives as heterosexuals. Their identity was first and foremost feminine, and they did not identify as lesbians in the same way as butches. The use of the category lesbian was situational, describing with whom and how they spent their time. Fem identity was always somewhat ambiguous. The participation of fems in the community affirmed the possibility of lesbian community as well as its fragility. They indicated it was possible to build a meaningful life through loving women; at the same time they were always suspect because they might be interested in loving men.

Fem identity raises provocative questions that have been largely ignored by contemporary gay, lesbian, and feminist scholarship: for instance, what drew fems to lesbian life? The antigay environment of our times combined with a theoretical framework which favors drawing a clear demarcation between heterosexuals and homosexuals in search of fixed lesbian identity is not conducive to comprehending the position of fems. Fems could and did function in the heterosexual world, but for myriad reasons preferred not to. However, in a homophobic society the concept of preference is always too simplistic and is generally dangerous in the analysis of lesbian culture. It encourages the idea that lesbians should be punished for capricious and immoral behavior and forced to conform. In protecting ourselves from the impact of such conservative visions of sexuality, we rob fems of some of their past dignity. Fems made a profoundly nontraditional choice even though they were not driven to it by deeply internal feelings of difference. The challenge lesbian and gay scholars face is to imagine sexual expression not as something that is immutably fixed at birth, or in childhood, but less flexible than a simple choice between equal alternatives. Only then will we have a better framework for understanding the determinants of fem life.

The difference between butch and fem identities is further complicated by the fact that the meaning of each has changed significantly during the twentieth century. In the early part of the century gender inversion was the basis for most lesbians' identities, so that the butch was the lesbian. But from the mid-1950s on, women's attraction to women was the dominant way of defining and expressing lesbian identity, establishing commonality between butch and fem.

By pointing out that butch and fem identity were formed differently in relation to heterosexuality, no matter the definition of lesbian, we do not intend to cast suspicion on fems and valorize butches as being more serious lesbians. We know from narrators' life histories and debates that some butches moved in and out of lesbian life, just as some fems spent the majority of their lives in the gay community. Based on life histories and the information they provide on identity, we find it helpful to conceptualize twentieth-century lesbian community as having two different sorts of members: one can be characterized as persistent and the other as fluid.[11] Both ways were critical to the development of community. Those butches and fems who were persistent were sure of their identities and what they wanted, and played a leadership role in building the community. Without their consistent presence, the development of community consciousness and pride would not have been possible. Many women, however, had a more fluid relationship to the community. At times some built a separate, more isolated lesbian life and others participated for periods in the heterosexual world. They refused to have their sexuality completely ordered by social categories. While making it hard to draw the boundary between the heterosexual and homosexual worlds, they complicated the picture of twentieth-century sexuality and expanded the numbers of women touched by the lesbian community. In general the butch role was more consistent with persistent lesbian identity and behavior, and the feminine role with more fluid lesbian identity and behavior, but this was not always the case.

In keeping with the finding that working-class lesbian communities are crucial for the development of twentieth-century lesbian consciousness and politics, the history of working-class lesbian culture suggests that sexual identity is much more fluid than the dominant conceptual system allows us to entertain. The boundaries between heterosexual and homosexual have always been difficult to draw. The gender-inversion model made the boundary clear by excluding fems, or women who might function, or appear to function, in both the homosexual and heterosexual worlds. The gay-liberation model made the boundary clear by categorically including every woman who is attracted to a woman. But throughout the twentieth century there have been women who have spent some time in the heterosexual world and some in the homosexual world. Frequently the women's movement is blamed for bringing out women who were not real lesbians and who in time went back to the straight life. But in fact women's interest in joining and leaving the lesbian life is part of lesbian history. There have always been historical events which have loosened the hold of patriarchy on women's lives and have allowed them to explore other alternatives. Most narrators were aware of these ambiguities and took them into account by speaking in terms of bisexuality, or the pure versus the less-pure lesbian.

We have before us the challenge of thinking of new ways of drawing the boundaries, free from nineteenth-century moral imperatives, that capture the full complexity of human sexuality.[12] This history shows clearly that to develop gay and lesbian politics solely around the concept of a fixed identity is problematic, for it requires the drawing of static and arbitrary boundaries in a situation that is fluid and changing. The challenge we face—to organize a movement that both defends gay rights in a homophobic society on the basis of the assumption of a fixed gay identity, and envisions a society where sexuality is not polarized into fixed homo/hetero identities—is difficult but worthwhile. The complexity entailed is not a contemporary phenomenon, but is part of working-class lesbian history. We need concepts that will take into account the persistent and the fluid, the butch and the fem, and the Black, the white, the Indian, the Hispanic, the Asian-American lesbian. Playing with the idea of multiple identities, while understanding the dramatic changes lesbian resistance has attained in lesbian life, identity, and consciousness throughout this century, begins to lay the groundwork for creating a world where "who we love and how we love them is a matter of aesthetics."[13]

NOTES

Preface

1. Carroll Smith-Rosenberg, "The Female World of Love and Ritual: Relations between Women in Nineteenth-Century America," *Signs* 1.1 (1975): 1–29; Jonathan Katz, ed., *Gay American History: Lesbians and Gay Men in the U.S.A.* (New York: Crowell, 1976); introduction by Gayle Rubin, to *A Woman Appeared to Me* by Renée Vivien (N.p.: Naiad Press, 1976); Blanche Wiesen Cook, "Female Support Networks and Political Activism: Lillian Wald, Crystal Eastman, Emma Goldman," *Chrysalis* 3 (1977): 43–61; reprinted in *A Heritage of Her Own: Toward a New Social History of American Women*, ed. Nancy Cott and Elizabeth Pleck (New York: Simon and Schuster, 1979), 412–44; Jeffrey Weeks, *Coming Out: Homosexual Politics in Britain from the Nineteenth Century to the Present* (London: Quartet Books, 1977).

2. One project was the Lesbian Herstory Archives in New York City. In addition to creating its own archival collection, it has offered ongoing support to researchers, in many cases initiating research projects itself and publishing an occasional newsletter. The San Francisco Lesbian and Gay History Project produced several extraordinary slide tapes—"She Never Chewed Tobacco" and "Resorts for Sex Perverts." The Boston project created a slide tape on the history of lesbians and gays in the Boston area.

3. We had gotten to know Michelson and Edwards when they were Masters students in the Department of American Studies/Women's Studies at the State University of New York at Buffalo.

4. For discussion of the development of the field of gay and lesbian history, see Jonathan Katz, "Introduction," *Gay American History*, 1–9; John D'Emilio, "Introduction," *Sexual Politics, Sexual Communities: The Making of a Homosexual Minority in the United States, 1940–1970* (Chicago: University of Chicago Press, 1983), 1–6; and George Chauncey, Jr., Martin Duberman, Martha Vicinus, "Introduction," *Hidden from History: Reclaiming the Gay and Lesbian Past*, ed. Martin Duberman, Martha Vicinus and George Chauncey, Jr. (New York: New American Library, 1989), 1–13. For a discussion of the complex relationship of gays and lesbians to the history profession see John D'Emilio, "Not a Simple Matter: Gay History and Gay Historians," *Journal of American History* 76.2 (1989), 435–43. For a discussion of the development of the field of gay and lesbian studies see Jeff Escoffier, "Inside the Ivory Closet," *Outlook* 10 (Fall 1990): 40–49.

Chapter 1

1. We single out these three racial/ethnic groups because they were the important actors in Buffalo. We imagine in other areas of the country different racial/ethnic groupings were important.

2. See Frank Caprio, *Female Homosexuality: A Psychodynamic Study of Lesbianism* (New York: Citadel Press, 1954); Dr. George W. Henry, *Sex Variants: A Study of Homosexual Patterns*, (New York: P. B. Hoeber, 1948); Jess Stearn, *The Grapevine* (New York: Doubleday, Manor Books, 1964); Betty Wysor, *The Lesbian Myth* (New York: Random House, 1974); Artemis Smith, *The Third Sex* (N.

p.: Universal Publishing, 1959); Ann Bannon, *Beebo Brinker* (Greenwich, Conn.: Fawcett, 1962); Sheila Jeffreys, "Butch and Femme, Now and Then," in *Not a Passing Phase: Reclaiming Lesbians in History 1840–1985*, ed. the Lesbian History Group (London: The Women's Press, 1989), 158–197.

3. The concept of prepolitical comes from Eric Hobsbawm, *Primitive Rebels: Studies in Archaic Forms of Social Movement in the Nineteenth and Twentieth Centuries* (New York: Praeger, 1963), 2. By using this concept we don't mean to override the feminist tenet that the personal is political. We are rather working on a different level in a more traditional framework, in order to make distinctions between different kinds of resistance. In this framework, political actions are part of distinctly defined political institutions. Prepolitical activities are social acts of resistance that haven't yet crystallized into political institutions as opposed to isolated individual acts of resistance.

4. John D'Emilio, *Sexual Politics, Sexual Communities: The Making of a Homosexual Minority in the United States, 1940–1970* (Chicago: University of Chicago Press, 1983), 1–2.

5. Of the upper-class lesbians in Paris, London, and New York, the only one who had a lasting impact on working-class lesbian lives was Radclyffe Hall, whose novel *The Well of Loneliness* (1928; reprint, London: Transworld Publishers, Corgi Books, 1974) was well publicized in the U.S. because of the censor's attempt to ban it in 1929. See "1929: The American Reaction to *The Well of Loneliness*; 'On behalf of a misunderstood and misjudged minority,' " *Gay American History: Lesbians and Gay Men in the U.S.A.*, ed. Jonathan Katz (New York: Crowell, 1976), 397–405. Today many lesbians who have achieved some security in earning a living as a result of the lesbian and gay-liberation movement, and are not immediately threatened by exposure, are rediscovering and valuing upper-class lesbians' view of the world; see, for instance, Blanche Wiesen Cook, " 'Women Alone Stir My Imagination': Lesbianism and the Cultural Tradition," *Signs* 4.4 (1979): 718–39.

6. See Vern Bullough and Bonnie Bullough, "Lesbianism in the 1920s and 1930s: A New Found Study," *Signs* 2.4 (1977): 895–904, for a good example of this kind of consciousness. For many of these women, the secret was part of the experience of being gay and they did not want to violate it. The San Francisco Lesbian and Gay History Project reported to us that they had a hard time finding people to interview because for many women keeping the secret was part of their identity. They did not see coming out as a benefit. Kennedy had a moving and enlightening experience when meeting a teacher who was interested in being more public. This woman described being a lesbian, living with a partner for more than twenty years. They were best friends with a gay-male couple for this entire period, but the two couples never once discussed among themselves being lesbian or being gay.

7. For an overview of this work, see D'Emilio, *Sexual Politics, Sexual Communities*, chapter 8, section 3, 140–144. Important sources not mentioned in that overview include: Mary McIntosh, "The Homosexual Role," *Social Problems* 16.2 (1968): 182–92; Nancy B. Achilles, *The Homosexual Bar*, M.A. Thesis, University of Chicago, 1964; Ethel Sawyer, *A Study of a Public Lesbian Community*, M.A. Thesis, Sociology-Anthropology Honors Essay Series, Washington University, St. Louis, 1965. Esther Newton's *Mother Camp: Female Impersonators in America* (Englewood Cliffs, N. J.: Prentice-Hall, 1972) was submitted as a dissertation in 1968. Focusing on the female impersonator, Newton creatively analyzed the key elements of gay culture and gay identity, using these to learn not only about homosexuals, but to glean insight into American culture in general.

8. Research in newspaper archives uncovered an upper-class, woman-defined—perhaps lesbian—community in Buffalo in the 1920s. One narrator gave us the obituary for an upper-class woman that mentioned the friend with whom she had lived. From this, we were able to discover a set of articles in the newspapers of the 1920s about this woman and her friends, who founded Buffalo Musical Arts, Inc. We did not thoroughly pursue information on upper-class women, as we determined from our narrators that the paths of upper-class and working-

class lesbians rarely, if ever, crossed. (The newspaper clippings are on file with the Lesbian Herstory Archives; we also have a set in our own files. They were the starting point for Candace Kanes' "Swornest Chums, Buffalo Women in Business and the Arts, 1900–1935," M.A. Thesis, State University of New York at Buffalo, 1992.) The existence of an upper-class woman-defined community suggests the possibility that a working-class community existed during the 1920s but we have no way of knowing. It is difficult if not impossible to find documents on working-class lesbian life; so we are limited primarily to oral history. The only evidence we could find relating to working-class lesbians for the first two decades of the century was for a small community of passing women who worked on the railroad and spent time socializing together in Buffalo during the first decade of the twentieth century. See "1903: Edward I. Prime Stevenson (Xavier Mayne, pseud.); Harry Gorman," in Katz, *Gay American History*, 249–250. We found one of the passing women, Harry Gorman, listed in the city directory but could go no further.

9. We have chosen to use the spelling "fem" rather than "femme" on the advice of our narrators. This is the spelling they have always used. They also feel that "fem" is a more American spelling and that "femme" has an academic component that is too high-toned for their liking. For reference to butch-fem roles in pre-1970s communities see, for instance, Del Martin and Phyllis Lyon, *Lesbian/Woman* (New York: Bantam, 1972); Audre Lorde, "Tar Beach," *Conditions* 5 (1979): 34–47; Joan Nestle, "Butch-Femme Relationships: Sexual Courage in the 1950s," *Heresies* 12 (1981): 21–24; reprinted in *A Restricted Country*, (Ithaca: Firebrand Books, 1987), 100–109; D'Emilio, *Sexual Politics, Sexual Communities*; Esther Newton, "The Mythic Mannish Lesbian: Radclyffe Hall and the New Woman," *Signs* 9.4 (1984): 557–75; reprinted in *Hidden from History: Reclaiming the Gay and Lesbian Past*, ed. Martin Duberman, Martha Vicinus and George Chauncey, Jr. (New York: New American Library, 1989), 281–93. Butch-fem roles also are apparent in twentieth-century novels and pulp fiction. For an example of the former, see, for instance, Gale Wilhelm, *We Too Are Drifting* (New York: Random House, 1935); and, of the latter, Ann Bannon, *Beebo Brinker* (Greenwich, Conn.: Fawcett, 1962).

10. See Jonathan Katz, Introduction to "Passing Women, 1782–1929," in *Gay American History*, 209–211.

11. Jeffrey Weeks, *Coming Out: Homosexual Politics in Britain from the Nineteenth Century to the Present* (London: Quartet, 1977), 88–92.

12. Newton, "The Mythic Mannish Lesbian." George Chauncey adds yet a further dimension, suggesting that at the turn of the century sex and gender were so intertwined that men, and presumably women, could not imagine sex outside of a gendered context (George Chauncey, "Negotiating the Boundaries of Masculinity: Gay Identities and Culture in the Early Twentieth Century," paper presented at *Constructing Masculinities* sponsored by Rutgers Center for Historical Analysis, December 8/9 1989). The lesbian dyad therefore had to include both a male and female persona. We explore this idea more fully in chapter 9.

13. Our perspective on butch-fem roles is highly controversial. Perhaps the most articulate critic has been Sheila Jeffreys, who argues that roles are an anathema to feminism in that they institutionalize hierarchy and dominance in lesbian relationships. See "Butch and Femme, Now and Then." The next section of the introduction indicates the specifics of our disagreement with such a position and this theme is further explored throughout the book. Here we want to clarify that the terms "authentic" and "world of their own" do not mean an ideal or pure vision of lesbian culture, but simply a culture created for and by lesbians. We also do not mean, as Jeffreys assumes, that lesbians who create a culture without butch-fem roles are inauthentic. There can be many authentic lesbian cultures. Our point is to show that butch-fem culture is created out of the specific conditions of lesbians' lives and is not simply an imitation of heterosexual society.

14. "Straight" is the gay and lesbian community's term for heterosexual.

15. We do not mention anthropology as influential for our questions, because at the time we began there was relatively little anthropological scholarship on lesbians and gays. Anthropology was essential in shaping the form of this study, that is, our intent to write an historical ethnography about working-class lesbian social life and culture.

16. For a full treatment of passing women, see section 3, "Passing Women: 1782–1920," in Katz, *Gay American History*, 209–81.

17. Carroll Smith-Rosenberg, "The Female World of Love and Ritual: Relations between Women in Nineteenth-Century America," *Signs* 1.1 (1975): 1–29; reprinted in Carroll Smith-Rosenberg, *Disorderly Conduct: Visions of Gender in Victorian America* (New York: A. A. Knopf, 1985), 53–76.

18. Blanche Wiesen Cook, "Female Support Networks and Political Activism: Lillian Wald, Crystal Eastman, Emma Goldman," *Chrysalis* 3 (1977): 43–61; reprinted in *A Heritage of Her Own: Toward a New Social History of American Women*, ed. Nancy Cott and Elizabeth Pleck (New York: Simon and Schuster, 1979), 412–44.

19. Women in the late-nineteenth century were aware of the implications of this different sexual identity. For instance, in her autobiography, Mary Casal, who explicitly acknowledged the sexual component of her love for the woman with whom she lived for many years, nevertheless saw the two of them as distinct from a small group of women in Brooklyn during the 1890s who seemed primarily concerned with their erotic interest in women. As she expressed it: "Juno and I always felt out of place among the people who were 'different,' we felt so secure in our love for each other and so out of their class; yet we kept in touch with them in a degree ever curious." Mary Casal, *The Stone Wall: An Autobiography* (Chicago: Eyncourt Press, 1930), 183.

20. See Jonathan Katz, ed., *Gay/Lesbian Almanac: A New Documentary* (New York: Harper and Row, 1983); and Weeks, *Coming Out*. At least in the U.S., this direction of thinking was very much influenced by the accomplishments of feminist history, which brought into focus changing forms of private life.

21. D'Emilio, *Sexual Politics, Sexual Communities*, 11; Katz, *Gay/Lesbian Almanac*, 137–74; George Chauncey, Jr., Martin Duberman, Martha Vicinus, "Introduction," *Hidden from History*, 8–9. Randolph Trumbach dates the emergence of modern gay and lesbian identity earlier in the 18th century; see, Randolph Trumbach, "The Birth of the Queen: Sodomy and the Emergence of Gender Equality in Modern Culture," 1660–1750; *Hidden From History* 129–40; and Randolph Trumbach, "The Origins of the Modern Lesbian Role in the 18th Century: From Three Sexes to Four Genders," (Paper delivered at Fifth Annual Lesbian and Gay Studies Conference, Rutgers University and Princeton University, November 2, 1991).

22. For a strong statement on the need to conceptualize discontinuity, see Jonathan Katz, "General Introduction, Lesbian and Gay History—Theory and Practice," *Gay/Lesbian Almanac*, 1–19. For a good picture of the debate, sometimes characterized as essentialism versus social constructionism, see the first three articles in Duberman, et al., *Hidden from History*, 17–54. For further refinement of the social-constructionist position see Gayle Rubin, "Thinking Sex: Notes for a Radical Theory of the Politics of Sexuality," *Pleasure and Danger: Exploring Female Sexuality*, ed. Carole S. Vance (London: Routledge and Kegan Paul, 1984), 267–319; and Carole S. Vance, "Social Construction Theory: Problems in the History of Sexuality," *Homosexuality, Which Homosexuality*, Dennis Altman, Carole Vance, Martha Vicinus, Jeffrey Weeks, et al., eds. (Amsterdam: Schorer Press, 1989), 13–34.

23. See Jonathan Katz, "The Invention of Heterosexuality," *Socialist Review* 20.1 (1990): 7–34.

24. This explanation is put together from a variety of sources, most importantly, Ann Ferguson, "Patriarchy, Sexual Identity, and the Sexual Revolution," part of "On 'Compulsory Heterosexuality and Lesbian Existence': Defining the Issues," *Signs* 7.1 (1981): 158–172; Katz, *Gay/Lesbian Almanac*, particularly "General Introduction" and the introduction to part 2, 1–19, 137–174; John D'Emilio and Estelle Freedman, *Intimate Matters: The History of Sexuality in America* (New York: Harper and Row, 1988), particularly chapters 10 and 11, 222–74.

25. See D'Emilio and Freedman, *Intimate Matters*, 222–74.

26. The earliest references to lesbian bar communities appear in French fiction, Emile Zola's *Nana* (1880) and Guy de Maupassant's "Paul's Mistress" (1881). For a discussion of these sources, albeit a negative one, see Lillian Faderman, *Surpassing the Love of Men: Romantic Friendship and Love between Women from the Renaissance to the Present* (New York: Morrow, 1981), 282–84. For a reference to lesbian socializing in dances and bars in 1890s New York, see "Dr. Charles Terrence Nesbitt: 'Sexual Perverts,' " in Katz, *Gay/Lesbian Almanac*, 218–22. For other early sources, see Barry D. Adam, *The Rise of a Gay and Lesbian Movement* (Boston: Twayne, 1987), 10.

27. Faderman, *Surpassing the Love of Men*, 369–73; Shari Benstock, *Women of the Left Bank: Paris, 1900–1940* (Austin: University of Texas Press, 1986); Gayle Rubin, "Introduction" *A Woman Appeared to Me*, by Renée Vivien (N.p.: Naiad Press, 1976), iii–xxix; Adam, *The Rise of a Gay and Lesbian Movement*, 17–45.

28. See all the sources in the previous footnote, and also: Karla Jay, *The Amazon and the Page: Natalie Clifford Barney and Renee Vivien* (Bloomington: Indiana University Press, 1988); Delores Klaich, *Woman plus Woman* (New York: Simon and Schuster, 1974), 161–215; and Frances Doughty, "A Family of Friends: Portrait of a Lesbian Friendship Group, 1921–1973," slide show presented at *Wilde 1982: a Conference on Gay History*, Toronto, July 1982.

29. In her forthcoming book on Cherry Grove, Esther Newton documents the existence of a lesbian community in the U.S. from at least the 1930s (Esther Newton, *Cherry Grove: Pleasure Island, Gay and Lesbian U.S.A., 1930s–1980s* [Boston: Beacon Press, 1993]).

30. Colette, *The Earthly Paradise* (New York: Farrar, Straus and Giroux, 1966), 144–50.

31. Eric Garber, "A Spectacle in Color: The Lesbian and Gay Subculture in Jazz Age Harlem," in Duberman et al., *Hidden From History*, 318–31; and Lillian Faderman, *Odd Girls and Twilight Lovers: A History of Lesbian Life in Twentieth-Century America* (New York: Columbia University Press, 1991), 72–79. A buffet flat was an after-hours spot in someone's apartment where illegal activities, including gambling, drinking, prostitution, and sexual pleasures were available. Such flats grew out of the tradition of African Americans needing private accommodation because hotels would not give them nightly accommodations.

32. One of the lines reads: "B.D. women sure is rough; they drink up many a whiskey and they sure can strut their stuff," in Garber, "A Spectacle," 320. Other sources on lesbians and the blues include: "Chris Albertson; Lesbianism in the Life of Bessie Smith," in Katz, *Gay American History*, 76–82; Hazel Carby, " 'It Jus Be's Dat Way Sometime': the Sexual Politics of Women's Blues," in *Unequal Sisters: A Multicultural Reader in U.S. Women's History*, ed. Ellen Carol DuBois and Vicki Ruiz (New York: Routledge, 1990), 238–249.

33. Bullough and Bullough, "Lesbianism in the 1920s and 1930s."

34. "Pat", in *Word Is Out, Stories of Some of Our Lives*, eds. Nancy Adair and Casey Adair (San Francisco: New Glide Publications, 1978), 61–62. Other sources that mention 1940s bars include: Allan Berube, *Coming Out under Fire: The History of Gay Men and Women in World War Two* (New York: The Free Press, 1990); and Faderman, *Odd Girls and Twilight Lovers*, 118–38.

35. "The Old Moody Garden Gang Reunions, Another Chapter in the Women's Herstory of Lowell, Mass.," *Lesbian Herstory Archives News* 7 (1981): 9–10.

36. The Lesbian Herstory Archives is a rich source of material, with a particularly moving set of papers on Columbus, Ohio. The lesbian and gay research projects across the country in Boston, Philadelphia, and San Francisco, have all found bars for the 1950s. Julia Penelope Stanley mentions the bars in Miami during the 1950s in "My Life as a Lesbian," *The Coming Out Stories*, ed. Julia Penelope Stanley and Susan J. Wolfe (Watertown, Mass.: Persephone Press, 1980), 195–206. Faderman, *Odd Girls and Twilight Lovers* makes ample reference to 1950s bars, 159–87.

37. Buffalo had a distinct African-American subcommunity. We would expect cities like Minneapolis or Albuquerque to have Native-American or Chicana subcommunities rather than African-American, due to the demographics of their states.

38. *U.S. Bureau of the Census. U.S. Census of the Population: 1900*, vol. 1. Population: Part 1. Washington, D.C., U.S. Government Printing Office, 1901, Table 22 p. ixix; and *U.S. Bureau of the Census. U.S. Census of the Population: 1950*, vol. 3. Census Tract Statistics. Chapter 8. (Washington, D.C.: U.S. Government Printing Office, 1952), Table 1, 7.

39. Mark Goldman, *High Hopes: The Rise and Decline of Buffalo, New York* (Albany: SUNY Press, 1983). Richard Brown and Bob Watson, *Buffalo Lake City in Niagara Land: An Illustrated History* (Woodland Hills, Cal.: Windsor Publications, 1981).

40. In 1930, the Buffalo labor force totaled 239,161, of which 58,235 were women. In 1940, the labor force totaled 247,385, of which 66,882 were women. *U.S. Bureau of the Census. U.S. Census of the Population: 1940*, vol. 2, Characteristics of the Population. Part 5: New York. (Washington, D.C.: U.S. Government Printing Office, 1942), Table B–41, 153.

41. Henry Louis Taylor, Jr., ed., *African Americans and the Rise of Buffalo's Post-Industrial City, 1940 to the Present*, vol. 2 (Buffalo: Urban League, 1990), 23.

42. See Jeffreys, "Butch and Femme, Now and Then"; Wysor, *The Lesbian Myth*.

43. Alice Echols points out that, from its origin in 1970, the notion of woman identification had the purpose of underplaying sexuality between women in the building of the feminist movement; *Daring to Be Bad: Radical Feminism in America, 1967–1975* (Minneapolis: University of Minnesota Press, 1989), 215–19.

44. Shane Phelan argues in *Identity Politics: Lesbian Feminism and the Limits of Community* (Philadelphia: Temple University Press, 1989) that in a society as steeped in liberal politics as the U.S., the temptation for radicals to build a politics on individual identity is great, because of the abstract nature of the individual in liberal thinking. In this framework, the developments of lesbian feminism in the 1970s and 1980s that generated the sex wars, (the term graduate students now use to discuss the debate around sexuality and representation that raged in the feminist movement during the 1980s) can be understood as the defining of a lesbian-feminist identity around which to build a movement. The new politics was rooted in affirming and asserting that identity. Lesbian history was inevitably drawn into and used in this process and the debate that ensued, because gay and lesbian radicals assumed that knowing one's past is important for effective action in the present.

45. Adrienne Rich, "Compulsory Heterosexuality and Lesbian Existence," *Signs* 5.4 (1980): 631–60.

46. Phelan in *Identity Politics* sees this as a weakness in identity politics. It cannot provide a constructive framework for dealing with difference. It could not deal with difference among white lesbians, much less respond flexibly to women of color.

47. Martha Vicinus, "Distance and Desire: English Boarding School Friendships, 1870–1920," Duberman et al., *Hidden From History*, 212–29.

48. D'Emilio and Freedman, *Intimate Matters*, particularly chapters 10 and 11, 222–76.

49. Two comprehensive volumes represent this direction in scholarship: Ann Snitow, Christine Stansell, and Sharon Thompson, eds., *Powers of Desire: The Politics of Sexuality*, (New York: Monthly Review Press, 1983) and Carole S. Vance, ed., *Pleasure and Danger*.

50. A helpful overview of the debate is "Forum: The Feminist Sexuality Debates," *Signs* 10.1 (Autumn 1984): 106–25.

51. The debate resonated with definitional problems faced by historians about what is a lesbian. On the one hand, to identify the relationship of passionate friends as lesbian has the benefit of drawing attention to deep erotic attraction and connection between women in a society that denies it. On the other hand, such a definition underplays the role of explicit sexuality in women's lives, and might also violate such women's historically specific sense of their own identity. See, for instance, Katz, "General Introduction," *Gay/Lesbian Almanac*, and Leila Rupp, " 'Imagine My Surprise': Women's Relationships in Mid-Twentieth Century America," in Duberman et al., *Hidden From History*, 395–411.

52. At presentations during the mid-1980s, we would grit our teeth waiting for the inevitable

hostile comments from the audience or later in the feminist press about how we were antifeminist, antiwoman, and dangerous in our "glorification" of gender roles and hence of the patriarchy. We also received thanks from many young lesbians for giving them a glimpse of what lesbian life had been like before gay liberation, and from older lesbians who had lived through that period for capturing and validating their experiences.

53. Faderman, *Odd Girls and Twilight Lovers*, 166–67.

54. Judy Grahn, *Another Mother Tongue: Gay Words, Gay Worlds* (Boston: Beacon Press, 1984); Audre Lorde, *Zami, A New Spelling of My Name* (Trumansburg, N. Y.: The Crossing Press, 1982); Joan Nestle, *A Restricted Country* (Ithaca: Firebrand Books, 1987).

55. The phrase is the title of a song by Madeline Davis, the lyrics of which are printed on the frontispiece.

56. Our analysis has been attacked by Sheila Jeffreys in an article entitled "Butch and Femme, Now and Then" for romanticizing butch-fem roles, and offering dignity and respect to butch-fem culture. We think that she seriously misreads our work. The point is not to glorify butch-fem roles, but to understand them from the perspective of someone who is inside the culture. Our goal is to understand the conditions that generated them, and the strengths that perpetuated them. This is not to say that some lesbians weren't hurt by butch-fem roles. They were. But they were the only vital alternative for working-class lesbians, and through roles lesbians began to develop pride and solidarity. Jeffreys quotes Julia Penelope Stanley extensively as a source for how destructive roles were. There are others who were critical of butch-fem communities, but also understood their profound importance. Lorde writes in *Zami* of not partaking in butch-fem culture but recognizing that it offered community which, no matter how limited, was better than nothing; see 178–79, 180–81, 186–87, 205–6, 220–26, 241–47.

57. The common assumption, particularly in the communist/socialist tradition, that lesbianism and homosexuality are primarily upper-class phenomena most likely results from the class-based nature of lasting evidence.

58. We found a variety of sources helpful for learning about issues and problems of oral-history research. They include the special issue on Women's Oral History, *Frontiers* 2.2 (1977); Willa K. Baum, *Oral History for the Local Historical Society* (Nashville, Tenn.: American Association for State and Local History, 1974); Michael Frisch, "Oral History and *Hard Times*: A Review Essay," *Oral History Review* (1979): 70–79; Ronald Grele, ed., *Envelopes of Sound: Six Practitioners Discuss the Method, Theory, and Practice of Oral History and Oral Testimony* (Chicago: Precedent Publishing, 1975); Ronald Grele, "Can Anyone over Thirty Be Trusted: A Friendly Critique of Oral History," *Oral History Review* (1978): 36–44; "Generations: Women in the South," special issue of *Southern Exposure* 4.4 (1977); "No More Moanin,' " special issue of *Southern Exposure* 1.3, 4 (1974); Peter Friedlander, *The Emergence of a UAW Local, 1936–1939: A Study in Class and Culture* (Pittsburgh: University of Pittsburgh Press, 1975); William Lynwood Montell, *The Saga of Coe Ridge: A Study in Oral History* (Knoxville: University of Tennessee Press, 1970); Studs Terkel, *Hard Times: An Oral History of the Great Depression* (New York: Pantheon Books, 1970); Martin B. Duberman, *Black Mountain: An Exploration in Community* (Garden City, N.J.: Doubleday, 1973); Sherna Gluck, ed., *From Parlor to Prison: Five American Suffragists Talk about Their Lives* (New York: Vintage, 1976); and Kathy Kahn, *Hillbilly Women* (Garden City, N.Y.: Doubleday, 1973). At the time we were finishing this book two books were useful for rethinking the potential and pitfalls of oral history. Michael Frisch, *A Shared Authority: Essays on the Craft and Meaning of Oral and Public History* (Albany: SUNY Press, 1990); and Sherna Berger Gluck and Daphne Patai, *Women's Words: The Feminist Practice of Oral History* (New York: Routledge, 1991).

59. Our thinking about the goals of feminist research and the problems with complete relativism have been helped by the writings of Sandra Harding, especially the Introduction and Conclusion of *Feminism and Methodology: Social Science Issues* (Bloomington: University of Indiana Press, 1986), 1–14, 181–90; and Evelyn Fox Keller, "Feminism and Science," *Signs* 7.3 (1982): 589–602.

60. The majority of the interviews were done by the two authors. However, some were done by

Madeline's class as discussed in the preface, and Avra Michelson and Wanda Edwards did a few while associated with the project.

61. Although up until now in this book we have used the terms African-American, European-American, and Native-American to indicate the significant racial/ethnic groups in Buffalo, from this point on we will use the terms Black, white, and Indian. We think the former method of designation is more appropriate analytically, and reflects the past twenty years' thinking on the subject. But since the latter terms are used by our narrators in their interviews, we have decided to use them as well.

62. We did not look for balance among the white ethnic groups represented because the issue of white ethnicity never came up in our work as will be discussed in chapter 4.

63. We speculate, based on interviews with younger Hispanic women, that the Buffalo Hispanic community was still too small at that time to provide Hispanic lesbians with the anonymity they needed to socialize as lesbians; any local lesbians would have migrated to New York City. The U.S. census reports that there were 2,176 Puerto Ricans in Buffalo in 1960, of whom 1,386 were born in Puerto Rico. *U.S. Bureau of the Census, U.S. Census of the Population and Housing: 1960*. New York. Census Tracts Final Report, PHC(1)–21 (Washington, D.C.: U.S. Government Printing Office, 1963), Table p–1, 15. A local study of the same period generally confirms the census, finding that there were 2,240 to 2,330 Puerto Ricans in Buffalo in 1961. (Thomas P. Imse, "Puerto Ricans in Buffalo," Study for the City of Buffalo, Board of Community Relations (unpublished) July 20, 1961, State University of New York at Buffalo Archives). The U.S. Census indicates that there were far fewer Indians than Puerto Ricans in Buffalo, in 1960, only 920. *U.S. Bureau of the Census. U.S. Census of the Population: 1960*, vol. 1. New York. Characteristics of the population. Part 34, table 21, 102. On the surface this would appear to contradict our theory about how a racial/ethnic group has to achieve a certain size in order for its members to be able to have anonymity while socializing as lesbians. In fact it does not, but rather reflects different patterns of migration. Most Puerto Ricans migrated to urban areas with families and desired to create strong family bonds. Most Indian families in western New York remained located on the reservations in the countryside. Indian lesbians, therefore, did not need a large urban Indian population to gain anonymity. Most were not born in the city and their families did not live in the city. They migrated to Buffalo to gain anonymity while still maintaining strong ties with their rural families. To the best of our knowledge, there was not an Asian-American community in Buffalo at the time.

64. Although Wanda Edwards, a young Black woman hired on a small grant in 1981, stayed on as an advisor to the project, she was not at that time well known in the Black lesbian community and therefore was not able to help us acquire more Black narrators.

65. We were the only people who listened to the tapes. Narrators could get a copy of their own tape, but no one else's. Although they could authorize a friend or a lover to hear their own tape, that never happened. The agreement with all narrators is that at some future date these tapes will be turned over to an archive, where they will be available for educational purposes.

66. In 1986, the Supreme Court issued the Hardwick decision upholding Georgia's state statute criminalizing sodomy. This is one indication of the conservative and therefore dangerous temperament of the times. (*United States Reports* vol. 478 , October term, 1985, Washington, D.C.: U.S. Government Printing Office, 1989, 186–220.) In New York State, there is currently no law that criminalizes sodomy. (*United States Reports* vol. 467, October term, 1983, Washington D.C.: U.S. Government Printing Office 1983, 246–252.) However, very few municipalities prohibit discrimination against gays and lesbians in employment, housing, and/or public accommodations, and the state provides only limited protection for gay and lesbian employees; therefore, knowledge about homosexuality can present prejudicial circumstances.

67. Although in the book we only use pseudonyms, we gave all narrators a choice of taking a pseudonym or using only their first names in their actual oral histories in order to respect

some narrators' desire not to hide. Those who had been relatively open throughout their lives felt that not using last names gave them adequate protection.

The archive tapes are filed by first name, real or pseudonym, and if a name is duplicated, a last initial is used. These are the only records we have on our work. The effectiveness of this system for achieving anonymity for those who chose pseudonyms was proved to us when we almost made the mistake of initiating contact twice with the same woman. She had taken a pseudonym when interviewed several years earlier, and in the intervening time we had completely forgotten her true identity. Only in the process of making contact with her did we realize that we had already interviewed her.

Even a simple procedure like asking narrators to sign release forms, a standard procedure in oral-history work, became a challenging problem. Release forms are necessary to maximize the rights of the narrators concerning how we use the information they have contributed, and to protect us from any future challenges about whether we had the right to establish an archive of tapes or write a book based on the oral histories. But release forms require a signature, and since we were not using last names anywhere in the project, we had to find a substitute. After a great deal of legal research, we decided to have our narrators read a release statement into the tape recorder at the beginning of a set of interviews.

68. Most of those who had used their own names for their oral histories were satisfied with our policy of employing only pseudonyms in the book. Even the few who were ambivalent about our decision appreciated our reasoning: that a project as large and as public as this book must try to protect narrators from possible anti-lesbian bigotry.

69. Every photo has been modified by computer to disguise the faces, unless we had express permission to use the image as is.

70. In most cases we interviewed people singly; however, two friends wanted to be interviewed together, and that worked out very well. In another case, we had interviewed two friends separately, but then wanted information on a particular topic and set up a joint interview. In general we were satisfied with joint interviews and might pursue more of them in the future.

71. We are grateful to members of the San Francisco Lesbian and Gay History project at a presentation in 1980 for first suggesting that we were more reluctant to hear these painful stories than our narrators were to tell them.

72. "Letting the data sing" was a concept that Liz developed for explaining how a researcher identifies a good interpretative framework. We were both struck by how closely this idea resembles those expressed by Barbara McClintock about her own research in her biography: Evelyn Fox Keller, *A Feeling for the Organism: The Life and Work of Barbara McClintock* (San Francisco: W. H. Freeman, 1983), particularly chapter 12, 197–207. Good research is more than a rational process. It requires a total immersion in the data, which generates "a feeling for the organism" from which comes analytical and theoretical insight.

73. For a helpful discussion of memory, see John A. Neuenschwander, "Remembrance of Things Past: Oral Historians and Long-Term Memory," *Oral History Review* (1978): 46–53; many sources cited in note 25 also have relevant discussions of memory; in particular, see Frisch, *A Shared Authority*; Grele, *Envelopes of Sound*; Friedlander; and Montell.

74. See, for instance, Joan Nestle, "Esther's Story: 1960," *Common Lives/Lesbian Lives* 1 (Fall 1981): 5–9; reprinted in *A Restricted Country*, 40–45; Nestle, "Butch-Femme Relationships"; Lorde, "Tar Beach"; and Audre Lorde, "The Beginning," in *Lesbian Fiction*, ed. Elly Bulkin (Watertown, Mass.: Persephone Press, 1981), 255–74. Lesbian pulp fiction can also provide insight into the emotional and sexual life of this period; see for instance, Ann Bannon's *I Am a Woman* (Greenwich, Conn: Fawcett, 1959) and *Beebo Brinker*.

75. To improve the flow of the written statements, repetitive phrases and comments have been eliminated without any indication. We have also eliminated tangential ideas, and some of our questions. This is indicated in the text by an ellipsis (. . .). We have not edited the order of

a narrator's words, or combined statements on similar topics recorded at different times. Several narrators who read chapters edited their own quotes to clarify meaning and make the spoken word more suitable for print. We are impressed that no narrator ever wanted to change the content of what was said. Following the lead of those narrators who read the manuscript, we did some minor editing of quotes to make the grammar more suitable for the printed page. We made perhaps fifteen such changes in the entire book, and like all other additions by us they are indicated in brackets ([   ]).

76. We were alerted to the folk-tale quality of these memories by the repetition of both factual material and language. Sometimes we would ask a narrator a similar question two years later, and her response would resemble the original in detail and phrasing. For a helpful discussion of the importance of stories in cultures of survival see Alexis De Veaux, *Concealed Weapons: Contemporary Black Women's Short Stories as Agents of Social Change, 1960s to the Present*, Ph.D. diss., Department of American Studies, State University of New York at Buffalo, 1992.

Chapter 2

1. Useful studies of straight bar life include: Sherri Cavan, *Liquor License: An Ethnography of Bar Behavior* (Chicago: Aldine, 1966) and Julian B. Roebuck and Wolfgang Frese, *The Rendezvous: A Case Study of An After-Hours Club* (New York: The Free Press, 1976).
2. Radclyffe Hall, *The Well of Loneliness* (1928; reprint, London: Transworld Publishers, Corgi Books, 1974), 439–53. It is possible that at the time Hall was writing bars were not centers of resistance. It is also possible that class factors shaped Hall's portrayal of bars. It might have been difficult for an upper-class woman to be part of a working-class culture of resistance.
3. See, for instance, Ann Bannon, *Odd Girl Out* (New York: Fawcett, 1957), *I Am a Woman* (New York: Fawcett, 1959), *Women in the Shadows* (New York: Fawcett, 1959), *Journey to a Woman* (New York: Fawcett, 1960), and *Beebo Brinker* (New York: Fawcett, 1962); Ann Aldrich, *We Walk Alone* (New York: Fawcett, 1955), and *We Too Must Love* (New York: Fawcett, 1958).
4. Nancy B. Achilles, *The Homosexual Bar*, M. A. Thesis, University of Chicago, 1964.
5. Ethel Sawyer, *A Study of a Public Lesbian Community*, M.A. Thesis, Sociology-Anthropology Honors Essay Series, Washington University, St. Louis, 1965.
6. Kathy Peiss uses the concept of heterosocial to parallel the concept of homosocial. The latter means a social life organized around one sex, the former, a social life organized around the interactions of men and women. Kathy Peiss, *Cheap Amusements: Working Women and Leisure in Turn-of-the-Century New York*, (Philadelphia: Temple University Press, 1986), 183–84. Her use of the term heterosocial is helpful because it highlights just how gender and class interacted to create heterosexual culture as we know it today, and thus contributes to an understanding that heterosexuality as well as homosexuality is created. For further discussion of this topic see, Jonathan Katz, "The Invention of Heterosexuality," *Socialist Review*, 20.1 (Feb. 1990): 7–34.
7. Peiss, *Cheap Amusements*, 114.
8. Ibid. 28–29.
9. Allan Berube, *Coming Out under Fire: The History of Gay Men and Women in World War Two* (New York: The Free Press, 1990), 113.
10. "Women Drinking at Bars Declared Cause of Vice," *Buffalo Courier-Express*, Feb. 27, 1944, sect. 5, 1, and "City Will Ask Legislation Banning Girls from Bars," *Buffalo Courier-Express*, Feb. 29, 1944, 1.
11. John D'Emilio, "Gay Politics and Community in San Francisco Since World War II," in *Hidden From History*, ed. Martin Duberman, Martha Vicinus and George Chauncey, Jr. (New York:

New American Library, 1989), 458–59; John D'Emilio, *Sexual Politics, Sexual Community: The Making of a Homosexual Minority in the United States, 1940–1970* (Chicago: University of Chicago Press, 1983), 22–39; and Berube, *Coming Out under Fire*, 98–127.

12. Berube, *Coming Out under Fire*, 126.

13. For figures on the size of the women's branches of the service in 1943 see Berube, *Coming Out under Fire*, 28; and D'Emilio, *Sexual Politics, Sexual Communities*, 29.

14. The process of identity formation is quite complex and will be dealt with in detail in chapter 9.

15. After hours of microfilm research, we have not been able to find any mention of these raids in the newspaper.

16. Susan Ware writes: "During the 1930s, women's softball and basketball teams flourished." Susan Ware, *Holding Their Own: American Women in the 1930s* (Boston: Twayne, 1988), 174.

17. The daughter of a well-known local sports figure shared with us her mother's photo collection that included pictures of Eddie's. The daughter suspects that her mother was a lesbian but she lived a heterosexual life. She also has good reason to suspect that many of her mother's friends were lesbians.

18. The reasons for the difference will be discussed later in the chapter.

19. Butch consciousness and fem consciousness were somewhat different, as will be discussed in detail later in the book.

20. Our analysis is consistent with and furthers that of D'Emilio, *Sexual Politics, Sexual Communities*, 29; for another discussion of lesbians and World War II, see Lillian Faderman, *Odd Girls and Twilight Lovers: A History of Lesbian Life in Twentieth-Century America* (New York: Columbia University Press, 1991), 118–38.

21. According to Allan Berube in a phone conversation, February 1989, the WACS paid less than defense industries, about $20.00 per month plus room and board.

22. Allan Berube mentions the discreet male bars at posh hotels in the dowtown section of major metropolitan centers like "the Astor Bar in New York's Times Square, the Top of the Mark at the Mark Hopkins in San Francisco, and the Biltmore men's bar just off Pershing Square in Los Angeles" (*Coming Out under Fire*, 114). This is an example of a discreet woman's bar in a downtown hotel. Although Eddie Ryan's Niagara Hotel was not as elegant as the Mark Hopkins, it was respectable.

23. This fact contradicts the findings of Nancy Achilles in her early study of the homosexual bar in San Francisco. She says, "Homosexuals rarely infiltrate an already established bar and make it their own, a gay bar is gay from the beginning" (*The Homosexual Bar*, 65). It could be that San Francisco was different from Buffalo. It is also possible that she was using a framework that did not encourage her to assign full agency to gays and lesbians, and therefore hid homosexuals' activity on their own behalf.

24. The relevant law is Subdivision 6, Section 106 of the New York State Alcoholic Beverage Control Laws. From *New York Consolidated Laws Service, Annotated Statutes with Forms*, vol. 1, 1976, 1950. We are grateful to George Chauncey for clarifying our understanding of the law in a telephone conversation, January 1989.

25. We had difficulty finding information on the activities of the State Liquor Authority in Buffalo during this period. Our information comes from a telephone conversation with George Chauncey, January 23, 1989. According to his research on gays in New York City the State Liquor Authority was very punitive. In the 1940s and 1950s the legal strategy of most bar owners was to deny the presence of homosexuals. They did not fight the policies of the State Liquor Authority until the 1960s. Chauncey is currently completing a social history of gay male life, *Gay New York: Gender, Urban Culture and the Making of the Gay Male Worlds of New York City, 1890–1970*, to be published by Basic Books in 1994.

26. According to George Chauncey, most of the gay and lesbian bars in New York City had some relationship to the Mafia (personal communication, January 1989). The reason for this difference awaits further research.

27. This view is backed up by evidence of some conflict between the State Liquor Authority and the Buffalo police in 1944. See "State Cancels Liquor Permit of Night Spot," *Buffalo Courier-Express*, April 7, 1944, 11.

28. After hours of microfilm research, we were unable to find a reference to this raid in the newspapers.

29. In the 1940s the mayor ordered all taverns and bowling alleys to close at 11 p.m. due to fuel shortages. This must have increased the popularity of after-hours clubs. *Buffalo Courier-Express*, Feb. 2, 1945, 1.

30. These parties were not necessarily all Black. Debra had a racially mixed group of friends and often went to mixed parties. A white woman's desire for discretion could have led her to socialize primarily at small parties, rather than bars.

31. These two women were friends and were not gay, but "were making money on the gay girls" (Arden).

32. The population of Buffalo Blacks was 4,511 in 1920, 13,563 in 1930, 17,694 in 1940, 36,745 in 1950, and 70,904 in 1960. Henry L. Taylor, Jr., ed. *African Americans and the Rise of Buffalo's Post-Industrial City, 1940 to the Present*, vol. 2 (Buffalo: Urban League, 1990) 23.

33. For a discussion of race relations in Buffalo, see Lillian Serece Williams, *The Development of a Black Community: Buffalo, New York, 1900–1940*, Ph.D. diss., SUNY/Buffalo, 1978; Lillian Serece Williams, "To Elevate the Race: The Michigan Avenue YMCA and the Advancement of Blacks in Buffalo, New York, 1922–40," *New Perspectives on Black Educational History*, Vincent P. Franklin and James D. Anderson, eds. (Boston: G. K. Hall, 1978), 129–48; Ralph Richard Watkins, *Black Buffalo 1920–1927*, Ph.D. diss. SUNY/Buffalo, 1978; Niles Carpenter, "Nationality, Color and Economic Opportunity in the City of Buffalo," *The University of Buffalo Studies* 5 (1926–27): 95–194.

34. Reggie, who spent several years in New York City during the 1940s, remembers that bars in Greenwich Village were racially mixed. Berube, *Coming Out under Fire*, 116–17, reports racially mixed bars in New York and Chicago, which suggests that desegregation of the gay community occurred earlier in large metropolitan centers.

35. St. Clair Drake and Horace R. Cayton, *Black Metropolis: A Study of Negro Life in a Northern City* (1945; New York: Harper and Row, 1962), 608–9; David Lewis, *When Harlem Was in Vogue* (New York: Vintage, 1982), 107, mentions rent parties that were open to the public and attended by lesbians.

36. Half of the narrators for this period finished high school and half did not. Working-class is probably not the term narrators would use to designate themselves today, because it now has derogatory connotations, and in general they feel proud of who they are.

37. See Esther Newton, "Sex and Sensibility, Social Science and the Idea of Lesbian Community," unpublished paper, for a provocative discussion of homogeneity in the lesbian community today. She relates the diversity in the male community to its sexual institutions—fuck bars, baths, tea rooms, cruising areas, and all-male porn movie houses—and suggests that the eroticization of power differences might undermine as well as uphold power structures.

38. The Deco Restaurants were popular coffee shops in the Buffalo area that advertised "Buffalo's best cup of coffee." They served low-priced meals and were "hangouts" for students, neighborhood residents, and workers.

39. The term "the club" was used in the 1950s and we suspect also in the 1940s to denote gay and lesbian bars without having to specifically name them. This method was employed prior to the advent of gay liberation and may still be used by some today.

40. According to narrators who had some knowledge of prostitution, it was common for women

who became involved in a prostitution ring to work a circuit that included Pennsylvania, Ohio, Washington, D.C., and West Virginia. They would work in a different house each week and would be off the week they were menstruating.

41. Our narrators think that the famous Erie, Pennsylvania, annual gay summer picnic might have started as early as the mid-1940s.

42. See, for instance, Williams, *The Development of a Black Community: Buffalo, New York, 1900–1940*; Carpenter, "Nationality, Color, and Economic Opportunity in the City of Buffalo"; Chester W. Gregory, *Women in Defense Work during World War II* (New York: Exposition Press, 1974); U.S. Department of Labor, "Women Workers in Ten War Production Areas and Their Postwar Employment Plans," *Women's Bureau Bulletin* 209, 1946; U.S. Department of Labor, "Negro Women War Workers," Women's Bureau Bulletin 205, 1945.

43. Sending a daughter to jail was relatively uncommon in the 1940s, and putting a daughter into a mental institution was unheard of. Not one narrator knew anyone who had been hospitalized. In part, this had to do with the working-class suspicion of psychiatrists, but also the working class did not trust state institutions with their children.

44. This raises the possibility that Black families, even if they disapprove of a member's gayness, continue to value, or at least be loyal to, that member despite his or her choice of life style. Thomas B. Romney, "Homophobia in the Black Community," *Blacklight* 1 (1980): 4, argues exactly this point. He states that homophobia is strong in the Black community, yet individual Black families "tend to be very accepting of family members who identify themselves as sexual minorities." In contrast, most Black lesbian intellectuals write about the severity of the oppression of lesbians in the Black community. See, for instance, S. Diane Bogus, "The Black Lesbian," *Blacklight* 1 (Sept./Oct. 1980): 8; Evelyn C. White, "Comprehensive Oppression, Lesbians and Race in the Work of Ann Allen Shockley," *Backbone* 3 (1981): 38–40; Ann Allen Shockley, "The Black Lesbian in American Literature: An Overview," *The Black Women's Issue, Conditions* 5 (1979): 132–42; Anita Cornwall, *The Black Lesbian in White America* (Tallahassee: Naiad Press, 1983), 5–34; Audre Lorde, "Scratching the Surface: Some Barriers to Women and Loving," in *Sister Outsider: Essays and Speeches by Audre Lorde* (Trumansburg, N.Y.: Crossing Press, 1984), 45–52; and Cheryl Clarke, "The Failure to Transform: Homophobia in the Black Community," in *Home Girls: A Black Feminist Anthology*, ed. Barbara Smith (New York: Kitchen Table: Women of Color Press, 1983), 197–208. The Black narrators of the 1950s hold divergent opinions on whether the Black community is more accepting of homosexuality than the white. Some are adamant that it is, while some think it is even more oppressive than the white community. Perhaps the approach of separating the community view from the actions of individual families helps to explain these differing points of view. Perhaps also different churches foster different views.

45. For this narrator, a lesbian is a butch. Her conceptual system will be explored more fully in chapter 9.

46. We are indebted to Judy Grahn's *Another Mother Tongue: Gay Words, Gay Worlds*, (Boston: Beacon Press, 1984), 207–11, for pointing out vividly how much lesbian social life is affected by the male objectification of women.

Chapter 3

1. John D'Emilio, *Sexual Politics, Sexual Communities: The Making of a Homosexual Minority in the United States, 1940–1970*, (Chicago: University of Chicago Press, 1983), 58, 102.

2. In fact, the founders of Mattachine in 1951 envisioned it as an organization for a distinctive minority who were struggling to achieve their own freedom, but their leadership was defeated

in 1953 and replaced by those favoring an integrationist position. For a full treatment of this subject, see D'Emilio, *Sexual Politics, Sexual Communities*, chapters 4 and 5, 63–91.

3. D'Emilio, *Sexual Politics, Sexual Communities*, 115. In addition to Los Angeles/Long Beach and San Francisco, the cities that had Mattachine chapters during the 1950s were New York, Boston, Denver, and Philadelphia, and for a brief period, Detroit, Chicago, and Washington, D.C. In addition to San Francisco, there were DOB chapters in New York, Los Angeles, and Chicago, and for a short period, Rhode Island.

4. "To Russell the bars were 'just slightly removed from Hell, I would like to see a better meeting place for those who wish more from life than a nightmare of whiskey and sex, brutality and vanity, self-pity and despair,' she wrote" (D'Emilio, *Sexual Politics, Sexual Communities*, 106–7).

5. The use of decades as a marker in lesbian history is a somewhat arbitrary imposition. We do not know the exact year that tough bar lesbians became numerous in the lesbian community; rather we are speaking of general trends. Narrators who entered the bars in the early 1950s already found a vital, tough bar social life that did not exist in the heyday of Ralph Martin's and Winters in the mid-1940s. The important role of the tough bar lesbian continued into the 1960s and didn't decline until the founding of gay liberation organizations and the rise of the women's liberation movement in Buffalo in the late 1960s.

6. These tough bar lesbians were most likely the basis for society's enduring negative stereotypes—dyke, bull dagger, and diesel dyke—epithets that capture their aggressive, male-imitating style, and also convey their association with lower-class, seedy bar life. However, like most stereotypes, they have only a limited basis in fact. They fail to recognize the way in which these women were important historical agents in the lesbian struggle for public recognition and dignity.

7. Tribadism is sexual intercourse achieved through rubbing clitorises, when one woman is on top of the other.

8. Elaine Tyler May, *Homeward Bound: American Families in the Cold War Era* (New York: Basic Books, 1988), 20, 5–7.

9. Ibid. 15, 36.

10. Ibid. 11.

11. John D'Emilio, "Gay Politics and Community in San Francisco Since World War II," in *Hidden from History: Reclaiming the Gay and Lesbian Past*, ed. Martin Bauml Duberman, Martha Vicinus, and George Chauncey, Jr. (New York: New American Library, 1989) 459. For a full discussion of the persecution of homosexuals in the 1950s see, John D'Emilio, "The Homosexual Menace: The Politics of Sexuality in Cold War America," in *Passion and Power: Sexuality in History*, ed. Kathy Peiss and Christina Simmons with Robert A. Padgug (Philadelphia: Temple University Press, 1989) 226–40. See also, May, *Homeward Bound*, 92–96.

12. This is a truly original insight into the 1950s, and is the argument of her whole book, *Homeward Bound*.

13. Most narrators attribute the closing of Ralph Martin's to the owner's illness. We have confirmed that Ralph Martin died on November 7, 1951. Some suggest that the closing of Winters was due to the owner's drinking. People are less sure about what happened to the other bars, where they spent less time. Probably the forces that created the changes in the community itself led to the closing of the bars.

14. Testimony in a court trial about the closing of a bar in the early 1960s refers to this as the homosexual area. A section of the summary of the owner's testimony reads: "He testified that prior to going into business at the present location that he was familiar with the general type of people in such location and that it is an area frequented by homosexuals and that some of these individuals are white and others are colored. He stated that the type of patron which visited the licensed premises hasn't changed for a period of eight years. He stated also that the licensed premises were located in an area which is known as a business area and not a resident-

type neighborhood" (*Cases and Points* 3258–1, State of New York, Executive Department, Division of Alcoholic Beverage Control, Erie RL 7803 case against John DeSimone, Exhibit C annexed to Amended Answer, Sect. 98, June 21, 1960, 33).

15. The One Thirty-Two at the corner of Oak and Genesee Streets was primarily a lesbian bar and had two large rooms. The back room had tables and a dance floor. Narrators remember large crowds on weekends and many people dancing.

16. Between 1940 and 1960, the Black population grew from 17,694 to 70,904, 3.1% of Buffalo's total population to 13.3%. Henry Louis Taylor Jr., ed., *African Americans and the Rise of Buffalo's Post-Industrial City, 1940 to the Present*, vol. 2 (Buffalo: Urban League, 1990) 23.

17. It is possible that for some, their interest extended beyond money, at least once their bars were threatened. The owner of Johnny's Sixty-Eight, who we know had a gay relative, fought the closing in the courts, perhaps indicating that he believed that lesbians and gays should be allowed a place to congregate.

18. See Ralph Lee Smith, *The Tarnished Badge*, (New York: Crowell, 1965) ch. 4, "See Nothing, Know Nothing—The Police in Buffalo," 41–64.

19. "Reports to Commissioners on Suspected Premises," *Buffalo Evening News*, July 6, 1960, 26.

20. "City Nabs 7 in 237 Complaints," *Buffalo Courier Express*, July 7, 1960, 4.

21. According to Smith, "Pitsburgh Books" were used to register the details of crimes that were not entered in the official record books at police headquarters. Crimes not officially recorded did not have to be followed up, relieving officers of the work of dealing with certain cases. The "Pittsburgh Book" was kept particularly for the purpose of answering information requests from insurance companies in cases of robbery and to supplement personal police files for future reference if precinct officers wanted to consult it. "At public hearings the chief of the communications bureau was queried about an entry in the 'Action Taken' column of the third precinct complaint log, 'Note in Pitt. Book.' " It was known by precinct officers that the book received its name as "a wry suggestion that the crimes were committed not in Buffalo but in far-away Pittsburgh" (Smith, *The Tarnished Badge*, 55).

22. Neither Bingo's nor the street bars had dancing; the former was too small and the latter had a substantial straight clientele.

23. Although Sandy assumed that Marla was butch due to her short, curly hair and her athletic demeanor, Marla identifies herself as more fem in later interviews.

24. The average wages for women decreased significantly after the war. See May, *Homeward Bound*, 76.

25. For a discussion of the increased persecution of gays and lesbians in the military during the 1950s, see D'Emilio, "The Homosexual Menace," 229–30.

26. Most of the tough bar lesbians either completed high school or received a high school equivalency diploma. Some, like Bert, also acquired special training beyond high school in the Army or in technical school.

27. These white working-class families exhibited the same attitude of acceptance of individual homosexual children, if not tolerance of homosexuality in general, that has been noted for the Black community as discussed in chapter 2 note 44. Class might be as important a factor as ethnicity in determining treatment of lesbian daughters.

28. We will discuss prostitution in more detail later in the chapter.

29. This is a manner of speaking. She must mean here that she cannot go into a straight bar and drink as she wants. She has to be confined to a lesbian bar. As we said earlier in the chapter, there were no arrests in gay and lesbian bars during the 1950s.

30. For a discussion of the forces that led heavy industry once again to hire women in what were exclusively male jobs at this time, see Alice Kessler Harris, *Out to Work: A History of Wage-Earning Women in the United States* (New York: Oxford University Press, 1982), 311–18.

31. We will discuss street harassment further in chapter 5.

32. The Stage Door was a night club that featured women performers, and in the 1960s, strippers, many of whom dated our tough lesbian narrators.

33. The connections between lesbians and prostitutes have a long, still unexplored history. For a good beginning see Joan Nestle, "Lesbians and Prostitutes: An Historical Sisterhood," in *A Restricted Country* (Ithaca: Firebrand Books, 1987) 157–77.

34. Straight men who were interested in oral sex with lesbians were so common that they had a distinct name, "fish queens."

35. For mention of several examples of female-female prostitution, see Nestle, "Lesbians and Prostitutes," 167–69. In addition, several times when we were presenting papers, members of the audience told us about "well-known" female-female prostitution rings in their cities. Because of this, we probed our narrators' memories carefully on this topic but got no further information. Since at the moment the evidence on female-female prostitution is scanty and fragmented, it is not possible for us to make a comparison between the Buffalo situation and others.

36. One white butch narrator did discuss being a pimp—albeit in another city—and afterward withdrew her tapes.

37. D'Emilio in *Sexual Politics, Sexual Communities*, 129–48, documents the shift in the public perception of gays in the 1960s and argues that this was essential for setting the conditions for the emergence of a mass movement. It would be hard to imagine this change without the visible bar culture that became an important focus of media stories and pulp novels. Scholars concerned with understanding gays and lesbians in a social context also directed attention to bar culture.

38. For instance, Lillian Faderman argues that the 1940s were relatively hospitable to lesbians while the 1950s "were perhaps the worst time in history for women to love women" (*Odd Girls and Twilight Lovers: A History of Lesbian Life in Twentieth-Century America* [New York: Columbia University Press, 1991], 157).

Chapter 4

1. bell hooks, "Homophobia in Black Communities," in *Talking Back: Thinking Feminist, Thinking Black* (Boston: South End Press, 1989), 120–26; and Gloria Joseph, "Styling, Profiling and Pretending: The Games before the Fall," in *Common Differences: Conflicts in Black and White Feminist Perspectives*, by Gloria I. Joseph and Jill Lewis (Garden City: Anchor Books, Doubleday, 1981), 188–94.

2. We have little information on the historical depth of this semiautonomous Black lesbian community. The one Black narrator who was out in Buffalo in the late 1930s socialized in small house parties that were racially mixed. We have heard from other narrators about some older Black lesbians who have been central to the Black lesbian community for years, suggesting that there was an independent Black lesbian community as far back as the 1940s and perhaps the 1930s. However, we were unable to interview these elder lesbians, due to their failing health, among other things. As a result, we do not have adequate information on the nature of the Buffalo Black lesbian community before the mid-1950s.

3. The tradition of Black parties is relevant because white lesbians in Buffalo did not create the same kinds of pay parties. For a brief description of the culture of the earlier rent parties, see Joseph, "Styling," 182–86; and Eric Garber, "A Spectacle in Color: The Lesbian and Gay Subculture of Jazz Age Harlem," *Hidden From History: Reclaiming the Gay and Lesbian Past,* ed. Martin Bauml Duberman, Martha Vicinus and George Chauncey, Jr. (New York: New American Library, 1989), 318–31.

4. For a brief description of the impact of the Supreme Court decision against separate education for Blacks on a Black lesbian's consciousness, see Audre Lorde, *Zami: A New Spelling of My Name* (Trumansburg, N.Y.: The Crossing Press, 1982), 172–73.

5. The Crystal Beach amusement park was one of the few public places shared by white and Black youths at the time, although the beach proper was still all white. The investigations of the Canadiana incident indicate that it was definitely about race relations even though the community leaders tried to deny it. The events of the day started on the midday run of the Canadiana when a Black youth struck a white soldier after a racial slur. Conflict erupted in the park later and continued on the 9:15 p.m. run of the boat, which held about 1,000 persons, the majority of whom were Black teenagers. A white patron on the boat remembers being "approached by a Black youth asking the question, 'What color am I?' If you'd say 'well, you look brown,' they'd say 'I'm not Negro or a coon, I'm Black.' It was the first time I'd heard the word 'Black' " (William Graebner, *Coming of Age in Buffalo: Teenage Culture in the Postwar Era*, an exhibit presented by the Buffalo and Erie County Historical Society (The Buffalo and Erie County Historical Society, 1986), 73–79).

6. Lorde, *Zami*, 176–256.

7. There was a small upwardly mobile or perhaps middle-class Black lesbian community, but we did not interview any of its members. According to Arlette, these lesbians owned bars and shops and were very discreet, never socializing together in public places.

8. For a discussion of the integrationist writings of the 1940s see Jonathan Katz, *Gay/Lesbian Almanac: A New Documentary* (New York: Harper and Row, 1983), 161, 591–95, 597–604, 647–51. For a discussion of the importance of reclaiming lesbian and gay humanity, see John D'Emilio, *Sexual Politics, Sexual Communities: The Making of a Homosexual Minority in the United States, 1940–1970* (Chicago: University of Chicago Press, 1983), 79.

9. Clerical work expanded continuously for women from 1890 to 1970, but especially after World War II. During the postwar period, Black women for the first time entered clerical jobs. See Teresa Amott and Julie Matthaei, *Race, Gender and Work: A Multicultural Economic History of Women in the United States* (Boston: South End Press, 1991), 178–79, 335–36.

10. There was a substantial Indian population in western New York, which is the home of the Iroquois Confederacy, but to our knowledge there was not a separate community of Indian lesbians. The two Indian narrators and others we have heard about socialized primarily in the white communities. There is a growing body of literature by or about Indian lesbians and gay men; see, for instance, Paula Gunn Allen, "Lesbians in American Indian Cultures," Duberman et al., *Hidden From History*, 106–17; Evelyn Blackwood, "Sexuality and Gender in Certain Native American Tribes: The Case of Cross-Gender Females," *Signs* 10.1 (Autumn 1984): 27–42; Walter Williams, *The Spirit and the Flesh: Sexual Diversity in American Indian Culture* (Boston: Beacon Press, 1986); and Will Roscoe, ed., *Living the Spirit: A Gay American Indian Anthology* (New York: St. Martin's Press, 1988).

11. The use of "Indian" as a descriptor, like any other, is only partially convincing. Other than the two Indian narrators we interviewed for the 1950s, no other narrators were referred to by ethnic appellation. There are no narrators called "Polish" or "Italian". Therefore we have to deduce that being Indian was something of a marked category. The only narrator called "Black" was, in fact, a white woman who was a dark complected Italian. We will discuss ethnic consciousness in this community in the last section of this chapter.

12. There is a myth that interracial couples in the lesbian community are usually composed of white fems and Black butches; see, for instance, Calvin Hernton, *Sex and Racism in America* (New York: Grove Press, 1965), 113. Audre Lorde's experience at the Bagatelle in New York City supports a version of this myth. She writes that Black fems were not popular due to the society's racist standards for beauty (*Zami*, 224). However, this is not borne out by the Buffalo

lesbian community where it was equally common for Black butches to go with white fems as it was for white butches to go with Black fems. Some Black fems were renowned for their beauty.

13. People remember more racial fights at the Havana Casino, a bar that opened about 1963 with a fairly balanced white and Black clientele.

14. Women were part of the racial conflict on the Canadiana. Some sources even suggest that, "Most of the trouble was caused by gangs of Negro girls who walked the deck, attacking and molesting young white girls" (Graebner, *Coming of Age*, 75). We know that at least one Black lesbian was on the Canadiana that night. This was a woman we contacted for an interview, but she kept putting us off until we lost contact. We did manage to have lunch with her, which was when she told us about the Canadiana.

15. Only one Black narrator disagrees with this assessment of the patrons at the Two Seventeen and the Five Five Seven. Piri, who is quoted above about how important a mixed community is to her, claims that it was more equally divided between Black and white. It is possible that she moved in the most interracial set and that whenever she was at these bars, therefore, they had a more interracial atmosphere.

16. Lorde, *Zami*, 180–81, 204–5.

17. A similar phenomenon seems to have happened in the women's liberation movement. There were African-American feminists writing in the early women's movement—Francis Beal, Flo Kennedy—but in the development of the movement they are rendered invisible and the movement becomes "white." Basing politics on a simple concept of identity seems to encourage racial hierarchy; as suggested by, among others, Shane Phelan, *Identity Politics: Lesbian Feminism and the Limits of Community* (Philadelphia: Temple University Press, 1989).

18. The discussion of social life in the Black community is relatively truncated because we had fewer Black narrators than white. For instance, we do not have enough data for a discussion of complex topics such as friendship patterns. A Black narrator criticized a much earlier draft of this work, saying that we didn't capture the liveliness and fun of the times. We hope at least to have begun to do that.

19. We briefly interviewed a straight Black man who regularly went to these parties. His memories corroborate the descriptions given by lesbian narrators.

20. hooks, "Homophobia," 120–26. Cheryl Clarke in "The Failure to Transform: Homophobia and the Black Community," in *Home Girls: A Black Feminist Anthology*, ed. Barbara Smith (New York: Kitchen Table: Women of Color Press, 1983), 197–208, discusses the homophobia in the radical Black movements of the 1960s and 1970s. It is possible that this legacy gives white feminists the false impression of deep-seated homophobia in the Black community.

21. The film *Paris Is Burning* suggests that the title "Mother" is used throughout the Black gay and lesbian community for those who show leadership in nurturing others.

22. The tradition of self-activity continued beyond the 1950s. In the mid-1960s, Black lesbians created the first lesbian social organization in Buffalo, the Royal L's, which sponsored social events. "They would give you door prizes and whatnot; little tickets just like a club would give. They would have their picnics. I have a friend in Rochester . . . she would hire buses . . . clear from Buffalo, Syracuse, and a whole lot of places, and she would transport you to the picnic area. . . . They used to have gay banquet shows where you would pay ten dollars or twelve dollars for a ticket. You had dinner and a show and you had a dance" (Arlette).

23. We guess that the expanding presence of the young, tough lesbians forced this change.

24. Carol, whose real name was Carolyn Rose, was married and most narrators claim she was not interested in women. A very few say she was, but this is hard to evaluate and could just be rumor.

25. The Washington Market, also known as the Chippewa Market, was an open air market of produce stalls located on the block bounded by Washington, Chippewa, Ellicott, and St. Michaels. It attracted shoppers until it closed in the mid-1960s and was sold to the Buffalo

Savings Bank, which razed it to construct a parking lot. See "Washington Market to Close July 1," *Buffalo Evening News*, Jan. 11, 1965, 21.

26. In general, the women from the 1940s who had completed high school degrees or more felt this way about Bingo's, while those with less education felt more at home with the tough bar lesbians and made them the center of their social life. One fem from the 1940s crowd felt at home with both groups and changed whom she socialized with according to the preferences of her lovers.

27. Although all working-class lesbians had contact with the bars, many middle-class lesbians never went to the "downtown" bars. Some of them spent their time in women-oriented organizations such as the Girl Scouts and local women's sports teams where their lesbianism was not acknowledged, while others, particularly professional women, had no contact with a community of women.

28. Men had several popular bars of their own at that time.

29. Lillian Faderman, in *Odd Girls and Twilight Lovers: A History of Lesbian Life in Twentieth-Century America* (New York: Columbia University Press, 1991), 163–67, discusses alcohol as one of the dangers of lesbian bar life. Some narrators who are recovering alcoholics share this view. Most alcohol researchers accept that the rate of alcoholism is significantly higher among lesbians than heterosexual women. One estimate is twenty-eight percent versus five percent (Lee K. Nicoloff and Eloise A. Stiglitz, "Lesbian Alcoholism: Etiology, Treatment, and Recovery," in *Lesbian Psychologies: Explorations and Challenges*, ed. Boston Lesbian Psychologies Collective (Urbana: University of Illinois Press, 1987), 283–93.) Since ours is not a statistical study, we cannot give specific data on the number of women who were alcoholic in these communities. However, from our interviews we want to share the following observations. First, although the rowdy behavior of the tough bar lesbians suggests that they abused alcohol more than the upwardly mobile crowd, we have not found this to be the case. Second, given that bars and parties were the only ways that lesbians had to socialize before gay liberation, the percentage of alcoholics seems comparatively low.

30. Del Martin's talk at the round table, "Daughters of Bilitis—First National Lesbian Organization: An Oral History by Women Who Were There," at the Seventh Berkshire Conference on the History of Women, Wellesley College, June 19–21, 1987, Wellesley, Mass., made us aware of the importance of dialogue in homophile politics. She emphasized the Daughters of Bilitis's concern to open up dialogue with the straight world, no matter the cost.

31. In fact, very few professional women were involved in founding Daughters of Bilitis. John D'Emilio writes, "The founders and leaders of DOB were for the most part white-collar semiprofessionals disenchanted with a bar subculture, whose population included many women who labored in factories and appeared butch in dress and behavior" (*Sexual Politics, Sexual Communities*, 106).

32. Since we are using the method of oral history, it is difficult for us to be precise about the ethnic composition of these communities. We base our statements on the fact that our narrators themselves are a mixed group—Irish, German, Italian, fourth generation American WASP—indicating the diversity of ethnic experience represented in the community. For reasons we do not quite understand, we have no Polish narrators. We don't believe this reflects the composition of the community, given that we have often heard narrators refer to women with Polish names, particularly in the more upwardly mobile group. One narrator, when asked, suggested that there were few Polish tough bar lesbians because Polish values stressed steady work and the tough bar lesbians did not. In addition, we have no Jewish narrators, and our narrators have never mentioned Jewish lesbians. From other sources, we know that there were some Jewish women in the upwardly mobile group in the 1960s.

33. Faderman, *Odd Girls and Twilight Lovers*, documents class distinctions and discusses them as class wars, emphasizing division and hostility (181–87). We are arguing that the forces for unity were also strong, particularly from the perspective of the rough and tough lesbians. Also, we

see tensions around class as primarily about differences between strategies of resistance. It is possible that the women Faderman refers to as middle-class do not hold the same social position as those we call upwardly mobile. In particular, they might not have roots in the working class. Further research is needed on this topic.

34. By straight bars, Sandy is referring to the street bars that had a substantial straight clientele.
35. For references to the closing of the Club Co Co, the One Thirty-Two, Pink Pony, and Leonard's see "22 Bars Penalized for Girl's Drinking," *Buffalo Courier-Express*, May 26, 1961, 1, and "23 Taverns and Hotels Penalized for Serving Girls," *Buffalo Evening News*, May 26, 1961, 29. For an earlier raid on the Club Co Co, see "Right Key Sets Up Club Co Co Raid, Aided by K–9 Corps," *Buffalo Evening News*, November 18, 1960, 27. For reference to the closing of the Carousel, see "SLA Crackdown Upheld in 2 Restaurant Cases," *Buffalo Evening News*, December 1, 1961, 22. For discussion of the appeals relating to the revocation of the liquor license for Johnny's Club Sixty-Eight see "DeSimone vs. New York State Liquor Authority," Supreme Court, Appellate Division appeals Feb. 23, 1961, March 9, 1961, and June 30, 1961, in *211 N.Y. Supplement, 2nd 481*, Court of Appeals, Appellate Div. All appeals were denied. This was one of the first cases in New York State where the owner acknowledged that he served homosexuals and challenged the State Liquor Authority on what consituted disorderly conduct. The decision was precedent setting. The findings focused on such things as the female attire of some male patrons, men dancing together, and men fondling and kissing one another. In the testimony questions were also asked about a woman dressed in male attire who worked behind the bar. (Research on SLA license determinations and articles on bar closings was done by Avra Michelson.)
36. In the Polk *Buffalo City Directory*, Bingo's is listed until 1959, but no longer has a listing in 1960.
37. For reference to closing of the Carousel see "SLA Crackdown Upheld in 2 Restaurant Cases," *Buffalo Evening News*, December 1, 1961, 22.
38. Serving alcoholic beverages to minors was a charge used against many bars and restaurants during this time period, including Howard Johnson's. "SLA Suspends 6 Liquor Licenses," *Buffalo Courier-Express*, August 30, 1950, 15.
39. There is some possibility that the degree of overt male sexual behavior increased in Buffalo at this time. We had never heard women comment on it when reminiscing about the 1940s and 1950s.
40. According to Arlette, the owner of the Five Five Seven became ill with cancer and the new owner was not able to keep the business going. The Two Seventeen continued well into the 1960s.
41. These memories support the analysis that it was a lesbian who started the rebellion at the Stonewall Inn, 1969. See D'Emilio, *Sexual Politics, Sexual Communities*, 231–32.
42. Although nationally Mattachine societies are homophile associations, Buffalo's organization began much later and therefore its politics resembled that of the gay liberation movement.
43. Frank Kameny came to Buffalo in 1969 to talk to gays and lesbians about organizing. His presentation was instrumental in the founding of the Mattachine Society of the Niagara Frontier. John D'Emilio records the first example of the merging of the developing gay movement and the bar subculture in San Francisco in the early 1960s. In this situation a number of forces coalesced: the harassment of the police and the nonconformity of the beat culture, plus the politics in the city (D'Emilio, *Sexual Politics, Sexual Communities*, 176–97).

Chapter 5

1. The same unanimity exists in all observers of pre-gay liberation public lesbian life during this century, as mentioned in chapter 1.

2. Most feminist scholarship which uses the concept of gender roles comes from the tradition of the empirical social sciences and has been concerned primarily with issues of the division of labor in order to illuminate the socially constructed nature of gender hierarchy. Therefore, the framework for talking about gender roles is most often one that gives primary importance to work. Work is not a particularly helpful framework for examining gender roles in the lesbian community. Why work should have been relatively unimportant in the lesbian gender system will be considered in chapter 8, while this chapter and the next will make increasingly apparent why image and sexuality were the important indicators of butch-fem roles.

3. Chapter 9 will treat the development of butch and fem identities, and how individuals came to their roles.

4. For a recent and explicit critique of butch-fem communities, and one that addresses our work directly, see Sheila Jeffreys, "Butch and Femme, Now and Then," *Not a Passing Phase: Reclaiming Lesbians in History 1840–1985*, edited by the Lesbian History group (London: The Women's Press, 1989), 158–97. For general disapproval of butch-fem communities, see, for instance, Blanche Wiesen Cook, " 'Women Alone Stir My Imagination': Lesbianism and the Cultural Tradition," *Signs* 4.4 (1979): 718–39; Adrienne Rich, "Compulsory Heterosexuality and Lesbian Existence," *Signs* 5.4 (1980): 631–60. Many activists in the feminist antipornography movement are critical of butch-fem roles as represented in the leaflets distributed at the Barnard Conference, "The Scholar and the Feminist, Toward a Politics of Sexuality," Saturday, April 24, 1982. The feminist antipornography movement's ideas about sex are represented in Robin Ruth Linden, Darlene R. Pagano, Diana E. H. Russell, and Susan Leigh Star, eds., *Against Sadomasochism: A Radical Feminist Analysis* (East Palo Alto, Calif.: Frog in the Well, 1982). Although the book is in general a critique of sadomasochism, two essays refer particularly to butch-fem roles: Jeanette Nichols, Darlene R. Pagano, and Margaret Rossoff, "Is Sadomasochism Feminist? A Critique of the Samois Position," 137–45, and Diana E. H. Russell, "Sadomasochism: A Contra-Feminist Activity," 176–83. The authors see them as reproducing patriarchal power relations between women.

5. Simone de Beauvoir, *The Second Sex,* trans. H. M. Parshley (New York: Alfred Knopf, 1953), 404–24.

6. Joan Nestle, "Butch-Femme Relationships: Sexual Courage in the 1950s," *Heresies* 12 (1981): 21–24; reprinted in *A Restricted Country* (Ithaca: Firebrand Books, 1987), 100–109; many other essays in this collection are also relevant. Esther Newton, "The Mythic Mannish Lesbian: Radclyffe Hall and the New Woman," Signs 9.4 (Summer 1984): 557–75, reprinted in *Hidden from History: Reclaiming the Gay and Lesbian Past*, ed. Martin Bauml Duberman, Martha Vicinus and George Chauncey, Jr. (New York: New American Library, 1989), 281–93 is also an important part of this tradition.

7. As will be discussed in chapter 9, most of these women considered themselves butch or fem, not lesbian.

8. The division between what is dealt with in this chapter and the next is somewhat arbitrary but required by attempts to discuss complex social reality. The logic of this division derives from this culture's implicit priorities of creating space for lesbians and finding the love of one's life.

9. In addition to work pants, some narrators found ladies' pants meant for casual sportswear—roller skating or bowling.

10. These women performed at such places as the Palace Burlesque and might be in Buffalo for only several weeks during the year.

11. The D.A.—the letters stand for "duck's ass"—was a popular hairdo for working-class men and butches during the 1950s. All side hair was combed back and joined the back hair in a manner resembling the layered feathers of a duck's tail, hence the name. Pomade was used to hold the hair in place and give a sleek appearance.

12. Esther Newton in a personal communication, 1988, recalls the butch image in New York City. "The look as I remember it from one summer in 1959 in New York was much as your narrators describe it, except many white butches bleached their D.A.'s—though a disproportionate number were actually Jewish or Italian, many, many were bottle blondes—and, although they didn't wear makeup, they assiduously plucked their eyebrows, which of course most women did then (for some reason it made butches look even tougher). They also—to the best of my knowledge—shaved their legs and under their arms, a practice continued by most all lesbians in Cherry Grove today, working-class, upper-class or whatever." Several narrators recall Buffalo butches bleaching their hair, but are absolutely certain that none plucked their eyebrows. Toni remembers noticing butches' plucked eyebrows immediately upon her first trip to New York City. She thought it made them look a little more "effeminate and classy." Some Buffalo butches did shave their armpits and legs; others did not.

13. Esther Newton in a personal communication, 1988, says: "This is so true—still today the purse of course is the core of feminine symbology. All these men's pants the butches wore—and still wear—had pockets. Fems' pants do not. This is a deep problem in butch-fem relationships. [A butch] gets sick of carrying all her [fem's] things in her pockets. And it ruins the line." Madeline adds that by the same token, fems get tired of carrying their butch's wallet, change, extra cigarettes and lighters, etc. in their purses because they weigh too much. The controversy continues!

14. Polly Powell and Lucy Peel, *50s and 60s Style* (Secaucus, New Jersey: Chartwell Books, 1988) 32.

15. She was arrested for an incident in relation to prostitution.

16. Seeburg's was a men's clothing factory outlet on Genesee Street in the downtown area. Kresge's was part of a chain of stores on the order of J. C. Penney's and sold a moderately priced line of men's clothes. It has since become K-Mart.

17. This development parallels an increased male concern with physical toughness in the society at large as documented in Donald J. Mrozek, "The Cult and Ritual of Toughness in Cold War America," *Rituals and Ceremonies in Popular Culture*, ed. Ray B. Browne (Bowling Green, Ohio: Bowling Green University Press, 1980), 178–91.

18. We don't think she meant that everybody modeled themselves specifically on Italian men from the West Side. Rather she is using the Italian image to represent a typical working-class man. Although she is Italian, many narrators were not. Italian culture was not predominant in lesbian culture. It is worth noting that narrators did not compare their looks to that of juvenile delinquent boys, an assumption made by many people who have heard our papers. In narrators' minds, the image was of mature males, not of youths.

19. Nobody explained the difference between the appearance of the more upwardly mobile white lesbians and the tough Black lesbians. Perhaps because of the racial difference, narrators and we ourselves unconsciously assumed difference and didn't think it needed explanation.

20. The muted differences in butch-fem roles suggests that the upwardly mobile lesbians might have had a developing understanding of feminism, and therefore underplayed gender divisions. But from our own research we cannot confirm this. Rather the issue of discretion seems to be the overwhelming priority. Studies of *The Ladder* suggest that Daughters of Bilitis began developing an explicit feminist understanding of the world in the mid 1960s. See Rose Weitz, "From Accommodation to Rebellion: The Politicization of Lesbianism," *Women-Identified Women*, ed. Trudy Darty and Sandee Potter (Palo Alto, Calif.: Mayfield, 1984), 233–249.

21. The lack of use of the masculine pronoun for butches was noted as early as 1941 by Gershon Legman in "The Language of Homosexuality," which was a glossary of homosexual slang included in the first edition of Dr. George Henry's *Sex Variants: A Study of Homosexual Patterns*. Selections of the piece are included in Jonathan Katz, ed., *Gay/Lesbian Almanac: A New Documentary* (New York: Harper and Row, 1983), 571–84. The lesbian and gay-male communities differ

significantly in the use of pronouns. The queen, the gender-crossing figure of the gay-male community, is usually referred to by a feminine pronoun. The persistent use of female pronouns for butches is perhaps part of the way butches distinguished themselves from the tradition of passing women. They wanted to gain male privilege while being female. In addition, the contrasting use of gendered pronouns in the gay-male and lesbian communities is probably related to more fundamental differences between the communities, like the absence of a developed tradition of camp in the lesbian community, which we will consider in more detail in the conclusion of the book.

22. This was the only beating of lesbians we recorded for the 1940s and does not necessarily counter our generalization that violence against lesbians was limited in Buffalo during the decade. It took place in New York City and also followed an act of defiance. It is significant that most Buffalo narrators did not respond this brazenly during the 1940s; however, during the 1950s, when such responses would have been more common, a lesbian could expect her friends to come to her defense. To have witnessed this kind of event and not have gone to help would have been unheard of in the 1950s in Buffalo.

23. Gay Rights for Older Women (GROW) and Country Friends are two women's organizations in Buffalo today that offer support for women coming out and organize ongoing social activities. These organizations are fairly discreet and do not use or advocate confrontational politics. This narrator is comfortable with such an approach and is active in the organizations.

24. We want to be clear that we are not implying that those who were more "obvious" were more courageous. On the contrary, the purpose of the book is to show that, under different historical conditions, lesbians developed different forms of resistance.

25. This competitiveness also might have been true among Black lesbians, but we have no evidence either way.

26. William Graebner, "The Containment of Juvenile Delinquency, Social Engineering and American Youth Culture in the Postwar Era," *American Studies* 27.1 (1986): 81–97. Graebner presents a telling incident about the politics of dress. After the death of one of the cult figures of youth, Buffalo teenagers began wearing black T-shirts to school. The mayor was so convinced of their danger that he outlawed the sale of black T-shirts in the city (90).

27. Appearance was also a marker for beat culture. "A beat style of dress emerged. It was surprisingly forward looking, consisting of largely black clothes with glasses, and for men, an obligatory beard. . . . The standard beat girl might wear black stockings, a short skirt and duffle coat, and would sport pale lips and long, loose hair" (Powell and Peel, *50s and 60s Style*, 48).

28. Op. cit., 90–93. Another dimension of the program, the way it involved students in setting the standards, was a new attempt at social engineering and was also part of the program's appeal.

29. We have not been able to find a New York State law about what constitutes male or female impersonation, despite the unanimity of narrators on the subject. According to Professor Nan Hunter of the Brooklyn College Law School, no such law exists (personal communication, January 1992). It is her guess that a judge in a particular case made a ruling that two or three pieces of clothing of the "correct" sex negated male or female impersonation and that set a precedent used by law enforcement agencies. Without doing extensive research, she has not been able to find such a ruling. Male and female impersonation have been prosecuted in New York State in two ways. (All laws about "masquerading" or "impersonation" are state laws.) An 1845 vagrancy law defines a vagrant as a person who disguises herself in order to prevent identification. This law was adopted in response to antirent demonstrations by farmers who masqueraded as Indians and served as the basis for criminalizing cross-dressing until 1967. After 1967 the police prosecuted cross-dressing under the loitering law which prohibits disguise in public places. In 1974 the courts found such prosecution outside of the intent of the loitering law and all arrests on cross-dressing have ceased in New York State. See Nan Hunter, "Gender

Disguise and the Law," unpublished paper presented at the Eighth Berkshire Conference on the History of Women, Douglass College at Rutgers University, June 1990.

30. The slang term "to whack off" usually refers to male masturbation; see Paul Beal, ed., *A Concise Dictionary of Slang and Unconventional English* (New York: Macmillan, 1989), 498. In this context it would mean to say something demeaning or insulting. Little Gerry comments, "This would be a frontal assault to Sandy, like being hit. It was something she'd have to respond to."

31. To "go down" in this context means to fight or "go to the mat" in boxing or wrestling terminology.

32. Judy Grahn, *Another Mother Tongue: Gay Words, Gay Worlds* (Boston: Beacon Press, 1984) 133–62.

33. We did not find the same degree of self-hatred and bitterness among stud narrators. We are not sure if this indicates a significant difference in the communities, or if it is a false difference created by having fewer narrators for the Black community, and the hesitancy on the part of those we did have to show their feelings to complete strangers from a different racial group. We think, however, it is possible that the studs really are less bitter about the costs of their lives as butches. Racial discrimination meant that none of them had expectations of better jobs that were squashed because of their commitment to being butch. Also, of the two undisputed white leaders of the late 1950s who are quoted here, one has been underemployed for the last twenty-five years, and the other unemployed. In contrast, all of the studs we interviewed were working. Their job situations were more stable at the time of the interview than they were thirty years ago. Furthermore, none of the studs mentioned being beaten up or harassed by Black people in their own neighborhoods; the harassment and violence came from either the law or whites. They were therefore less isolated from a larger Black community than the white narrators from a white community. The Black community might not have approved, but they did not violently attack them during the 1950s.

34. The founding of gay liberation is usually taken as the Stonewall riots, and, as such, glorifies gays' commitment to fight off the police. For a good overview of the roots of gay liberation in the 1960s, see John D'Emilio, *Sexual Politics, Sexual Communities: The Making of a Homosexual Minority in the United States, 1940–1970* (Chicago: University of Chicago Press, 1983), 129–250.

35. It is impossible to know based on this evidence whether "coming out" was used in Buffalo prior to gay liberation. John D'Emilio indicates that the concept of "coming out" predates gay liberation, although it had a very different meaning (D'Emilio, *Sexual Politics, Sexual Communities*, 235). This leads us to suspect that "coming out" was used in Buffalo in the 1940s and 1950s. That people do not remember it indicates just how radically the meaning of the term has changed. Also, it is likely that "coming out" was not a central concept to the pregay liberation culture, and therefore was not used frequently, while in contemporary lesbian and gay culture, it is a core concept.

Chapter 6

1. Our thinking on lesbian eroticism owes a great deal to Joan Nestle's courageous work on butch-fem roles.

2. Several narrators note that there was more divergence between appearance and sexual posture in the larger metropolitan lesbian communities of New York and San Francisco than in Buffalo, suggesting that the butch-fem system of meaning was even more complex in these communities. In the section on gay men and roles, Karla Jay and Allen Young's *The Gay Report: Lesbians and Gay Men Speak Out about Sexual Experiences and Lifestyles* (New York: Summit Books, 1979), 365–75, indicates that at least in the contemporary community, appearance and sexual performance do not always correlate for men. Personal communication with George Chauncey suggests that

this lack of correlation existed in the past too, suggesting that the strict correspondence between image and sexual desire is something unique to the lesbian community, particularly those away from the large metropolitan centers.

3. John D'Emilio and Estelle Freedman, *Intimate Matters: The History of Sexuality in America* (New York: Harper and Row, 1988), 267–68; Atina Grossmann, "The New Woman and the Rationalization of Sexuality in Weimar Germany," *Powers of Desire: The Politics of Sexuality*, ed. Ann Snitow, Christine Stansell, and Sharon Thompson (New York: Monthly Review Press, 1983), 159–60; and Margaret Jackson, " 'Facts of Life' or the Eroticization of Women's Oppression? Sexology and the Social Construction of Heterosexuality," *The Cultural Construction of Sexuality*, ed. Pat Caplan (London: Tavistock, 1987), 52–81.

4. This idea comes from Peter Murphy, "Review Essay: Toward a Feminist Masculinity," *Feminist Studies* 15.2 (Summer 1989): 356, where he is discussing Emmanual Reynaud's, *Holy Virility: The Social Construction of Masculinity*.

5. The importance of thinking about lesbian eroticism without using a phallocentric model is pointed out delightfully by Marilyn Frye in "Lesbian 'Sex,' " *Lesbian Philosophies and Cultures*, ed. Jeffner Allen (Albany: SUNY Press, 1990), 305–16.

6. These attributes of butch-fem sexual identity remove sexuality from the realm of the "natural," challenging the notion that sexual performance is a function of biology and affirming the view that sexual desire and gratification is socially constructed.

7. Alfred C. Kinsey, Wardell B. Pomeroy, and Clyde E. Martin, *Sexual Behavior in the Human Male* (Philadelphia: W. B. Saunders, 1948) and Alfred C. Kinsey, Wardell B. Pomeroy, Clyde E. Martin, and Paul H. Gebhard, *Sexual Behavior in the Human Female* (Philadelphia: W. B. Saunders, 1953). Numerous sources document this trend; see, for instance, Ann Snitow, et al., *Powers of Desire*, in particular, the introduction, section 2, "Sexual Revolutions," and section 3, "The Institution of Heterosexuality," 9–47, 115–71, 173–275; and Jonathan Katz, *Gay/Lesbian Almanac: A New Documentary* (New York, Harper and Row, 1983), 222–74.

8. D'Emilio and Freedman, *Intimate Matters*, 222–74.

9. See Elaine Tyler May, *Homeward Bound: American Families in the Cold War Era* (New York: Basic Books, 1988).

10. D'Emilio and Freedman, *Intimate Matters*, chapter 12, "Redrawing the Boundaries," 275–301.

11. Grossmann, "The New Woman," 169. Although Grossmann is writing about Weimar Germany, she sees it as relevant to the U.S. This quote is specifically about women on this side of the Atlantic.

12. There is a growing body of writing by African-American women on sexuality; see, for instance, Rennie Simson, "The Afro-American Female: The Historical Context of the Construction of Sexual Identity," in *Powers of Desire*, ed., Ann Snitow et al., 229–236; Hortense J. Spillers, "Interstices: A Small Drama of Words," in *Pleasure and Danger: Exploring Female Sexuality*, ed. Carole S. Vance (Boston: Routledge & Kegan Paul, 1984), 73–100; and Hazel V. Carby " 'It Jus Be's Dat Way Sometime': The Sexual Politics of Women's Blues," in *Unequal Sisters: A Multicultural Reader in U.S. Women's History*, ed. Ellen Carol DuBois and Vicki Ruiz (New York: Routledge, 1990), 238–249. More research is needed on the nature of black lesbian sexuality and the impact of race/ethnicity on lesbian sexual expression.

13. These two women who did not adhere strictly to the norms about butch-fem sexuality were the same two who were mentioned in the preceding chapter for not projecting a severely butch appearance. This suggests a certain internal consistency in a particular person's approach to roles.

14. This comment raises the question about how much leeway butch and fem had before they were considered to be breaking out of their roles. It is impossible to know for the 1940s when sex was not widely discussed. We address this fully in the next section while discussing butch-fem sexuality in the 1950s.

15. The use of the term "conservative" here always needs to be taken within the context of the fact that, as lesbians seeking erotic satisfaction from other women, these women were all pioneering radicals.

16. Pearl remembers a butch, in fact her first lover, who practiced oral sex. But she also said this was uncommon. And in fact she does not to this day have a word for oral sex. This community's preference for friction over oral sex differs significantly from the Kinsey findings, which give the following figures on the techniques used by the women in their sample who had extensive lesbian experience: manipulation of the breast and genitalia was nearly universal; deep kissing was used by 77%; oral stimulation of the female breast, 85%; oral stimulation of the genitals, 78%; and genital apposition, what our narrators called friction, 56% (*Sexual Behavior in the Human Female*, 466–67). Since Kinsey's study includes all lesbians in the population while our study focuses only on working-class women in a bar community, this suggests that class background is a factor in determining lesbian sexual practices.

17. The dissociation of gender-free sexual behavior from sexual innovation is one other instance which confirms the usefulness of distinguishing gender and sex analytically. Sometimes they have a different history.

18. For instance, Kinsey's discussion of masturbation shows that, between age fifteen and age thirty-five, there is a steady increase in the number of women masturbating to orgasm. The numbers continue to increase after that but at a slightly slower rate (*Sexual Behavior in the Human Female*, 142–43). Two factors seem to be camouflaging older women's roles as sexual innovators. Popular culture assumes that this century has moved steadily toward sexual liberalism, and therefore automatically deduces that it is the younger generations that are always more liberal. This error is compounded by the fact that popular models for sexual activity are all based on the male experience of youth as the time of high sexual activity.

19. D'Emilio and Freedman, *Intimate Matters*, 265–74, document the availability of information on sex to middle-class women during the 1930s and 1940s. The marriage advice manuals used mainly by the middle-class had come to be very explicit about the importance of sex in marriage and the ways a couple could achieve mutual satisfaction. One study even showed that a majority of middle-class women felt they knew what they needed to know about sex before they got married. This was less true about working-class women at the time.

20. The numbers are too small to generalize about whether becoming sexually active became easier as the decade progressed. Individual factors like access to private space might be as important as age.

21. It should not be surprising that some women move to being sexually active so easily. Kinsey's study of masturbation shows that 58% of women learn to masturbate by self-discovery, while 28% of men learn this way. Most men learn through contact with verbal and printed sources or observation of others (*Sexual Behavior in the Human Female*, 138). The figures suggest that some women can come to sexuality with very little outside help.

22. In chapter 9 we discuss in detail the idea that in the early twentieth century lesbians were identified by gender inversion not by choice of sexual object. Here we just want to provide some evidence for this position. George Chauncey's research on New York City fairies indicates that working-class culture conceptualized homosexuality on the basis of cross-gendered behavior rather than by object choice (George Chauncey, Jr., "Negotiating the Boundaries of Masculinity: Gay Identities and Culture in the Early Twentieth Century," paper presented at *Constructing Masculinities* sponsored by Rutgers Center for Historical Analysis, Dec. 8/9 1989). Hence, there was nothing anomalous about the men who had relationships with fairies because they were attracted to the feminine and maintained masculine behavior. It was the fairy who was perceived as the homosexual, not because of his object choice, but because of his combination of masculine and feminine characteristics.

23. This is consistent with recent writing in the history of sexuality, which challenges the idea that Western sexual history progresses from sexual repression toward sexual freedom. Rather sexuality is always constructed with different periods of history having different sexual systems.

See, for instance, Michel Foucault, *The History of Sexuality*, part 1 (New York: Vintage, 1978) and D'Emilio and Freedman, *Intimate Matters*, xi–xx.

24. Modern sex research claims that all orgasms have the same physical source. The attempt to distinguish the two on the part of several of our narrators does not contradict this. Rather it expresses that orgasms were experienced differently depending upon the kind of arousal.

25. See, for instance, Joan Nestle, "Esther's Story" and "The Gift of Taking" in *A Restricted Country*, 40–46, 127–30; Amber Hollibaugh and Cherríe Moraga, "What We're Rollin' Around in Bed with: Sexual Silences in Feminism" in Snitow et al., *Powers of Desire*, 394–405.

26. Personal communication with Joan Nestle, January 11, 1992.

27. Hollibaugh and Moraga, "What We're Rolling Around in Bed With," 398.

28. For indications that ki-ki (pronounced kī kī) was used nationally in the lesbian subculture, see Katz, *Gay/Lesbian Almanac*, 15, 626. This usage of AC/DC is different from current jargon in which AC/DC means bisexual. Lillian Faderman associates ki-ki with middle-class culture which was not true in Buffalo (*Odd Girls and Twilight Lovers: A History of Lesbian Life in the Twentieth-Century* [New York: Columbia University Press, 1991], 179). It is likely that ki-ki meant different things in different cities.

29. D'Emilio and Freedman, *Intimate Matters*, describe the increasing presence of sexually explicit magazines and paperbacks in American culture during the 1950s and the consequent crusades against smut. This situation led the Supreme Court to redefine what was obscene in the 1957 *Roth* decision. The publication of the Kinsey reports in 1948 and 1953 also affected the public discussion of sex (275–88).

30. See D'Emilio and Freedman, *Intimate Matters*, chapter 12, "Redrawing the Boundaries," 275–300.

31. "Had somethin' on you", means "Had your number" or knew what you were all about, in Black English.

32. Phyllis Lyon, "Introduction," *Sapphistry: The Book of Lesbian Sexuality*, by Pat Califia (Tallahassee: Naiad Press, 1980), xi–xii.

33. See Delores Klaich, *Woman plus Woman* (New York: Simon and Schuster, 1974), 48–52.

34. Confidence in one's ability to give pleasure without a dildo seems to be widespread among lesbians. See Klaich, *Woman plus Woman*, 49–50.

35. This comment on argyle socks refers to some lesbians creating the illusion of having a penis by stuffing socks with tissues and putting them into their underpants. When we told Vic we thought it might have referred to a sexual device, she laughed and said no, but she thought the idea was intriguing!

36. The Crescendo was a predominantly lesbian bar of the mid-1960s located on Elmwood Avenue at the corner of Huron Street.

37. For a New York City fem who enjoyed the dildo, see "Jul Bruno," *The Persistent Desire: A Femme-Butch Reader*, ed. Joan Nestle (Boston: Alyson Publications, 1992) 195–98.

38. Discussion and therefore language are still important for supporting lesbian sex today. "Most of my lifetime, most of my experience in the realms commonly designated as 'sexual' has been pre-linguistic, non-cognitive. I have, in effect, no linguistic community, no language, and therefore in one important sense, no knowledge" (Frye, "Lesbian 'Sex,' " 311).

39. This line of thinking is most eloquently laid out in Catharine A. MacKinnon, "Feminism, Marxism, Method, and the State: An Agenda for Theory," *Signs* 7.3 (1982): 515–44.

Chapter 7

1. For instance, this was the pattern of relationships among Margaret Anderson's group of friends; see Frances Doughty, "A Family of Friends: Portrait of a Lesbian Friendship Group, 1921–1973," slide show presented at *Wilde 1982: A Conference on Gay History*, Toronto, July 1982.

2. In the late 1970s and early 1980s—when we began this research—even the best sociological and psychological research on contemporary lesbian communities, although recognizing the satisfaction found in lesbian relationships, often considered the recurrent breakups as failures that could have been remedied. See, for instance, Jo-Ann Krestan and Claudia S. Bepko, "The Problem of Fusion in Lesbian Relationships," *Family Process* 19 (September 1980): 277–89.

3. Throughout the U.S. in lesbian communities of the past twenty years, issues of sexuality have been the center of discussion and debate, whereas issues of relationships have received relatively little attention. In the middle 1970s discussion of monogamy versus non-monogamy was heated, but this did not continue. Since 1988 there seems to be a growing interest in analyzing relationships as evidenced by a burst of publication. See, for instance, D. Merilee Clunis and G. Dorsey Green, *Lesbian Couples* (Seattle: Seal Press, 1988); Carol S. Becker, *Unbroken Ties: Lesbian Ex-Lovers* (Boston: Alyson Publications, 1988); Susan E. Johnson, *Staying Power: Long Term Lesbian Couples* (Tallahassee: Naiad Press, 1990); Becky Butler, ed., *Ceremonies of the Heart: Celebrating Lesbian Unions* (Seattle: Seal Press, 1990). This writing seems to have successfully freed itself from the view that repeated breakups in relationships indicate failure and immaturity. However, the last two books unmistakably validate the lasting relationship. The cover blurb on *Staying Power* states: "*Staying Power* is the book about the one goal that most lesbians express as an ambition; the creation and nurturance of a lifetime love affair."

4. See Ellen Kay Trimberger, "Feminism, Men, and Modern Love: Greenwich Village, 1900–1925," in *Powers of Desire: The Politics of Sexuality*, ed. Ann Snitow, Christine Stansell, and Sharon Thompson (New York: Monthly Review Press, 1983); John D'Emilio and Estelle Freedman, *Intimate Matters: A History of Sexuality in America* (New York: Harper and Row, 1988), 265–74; and Christina Simmons, "Modern Sexuality and the Myth of Victorian Repression," in *Passion and Power: Sexuality in History*, ed. Kathy Peiss and Christina Simmons with Robert A. Padgug (Philadelphia: Temple University Press, 1989), 157–77.

5. It was unquestionably male-dominated and did not represent independence and autonomy for women. Women's interests were subordinated to men's, and women's sexual subjectivity was defined in the service of men's sexuality. See the references in note 4.

6. This should be no surprise, because the forces that led to the development of twentieth-century marriage forms are the same forces that led to the development of a modern lesbian identity. They both require sexuality and personal life to be central to the culture. See, for instance, John D'Emilio, "Capitalism and Gay Identity," Snitow et al., *Powers of Desire*, 100–13; and Jeffrey Weeks, "Capitalism and the Organization of Sex," in *Homosexuality: Power and Politics*, ed. Gay Left Collective (London: Alison and Busy, 1980), 11–20. This connection between the rise of modern lesbian identity and the modern couple relationship brings into focus the need to look at changes in capitalism as well as in patriarchy in the study of lesbian history. A primary concern of Lillian Faderman's influential, *Surpassing the Love of Men: Romantic Friendship and Love between Women from the Renaissance to the Present* (New York: Morrow, 1981) was on the changing institutionalization of heterosexuality in the early twentieth century, which undermined women's autonomy and woman-identified relationships. Such a focus highlights the contrast between the powerful women's communities of the Progressive Era, which developed around public institutions and the stigmatized, role-defined, and relatively isolated lesbian couples of the 1920s and afterward. To understand this shift as primarily due to the reorganization of patriarchy so as to undercut women's power and autonomy does not tell the whole story. Modern women, heterosexual and lesbian, fought for a sexual subjectivity, in a way that was not central to women's communities of the Progressive Era. This process in itself undermined the extended family and public communities and, in the context of a capitalist and patriarchal society, made the romantic couple primary.

7. It would be enlightening also to contrast lesbian relationships with gay-male relationships, but there is not enough research at this time to permit such a comparison.

8. See, for instance, Shulamith Firestone, *The Dialectic of Sex: The Case for Feminist Revolution* (New York: Morrow, 1970), 142–75.

9. A study by Winston Ehrmann of the dating behavior of male and female college students during the 1940s and 1950s suggests that the values of each group about sex and love were so different that two separate subcultures existed (D'Emilio and Freedman, *Intimate Matters*, 262–63).

10. Most lesbian couples of this community did not hold significant common property or share in the raising of children.

11. John D'Emilio, in his comment on "Pat Loves Mary, Loves Joan, Loves Louise: Lesbian Relationships in the 1940s and 1950s," at the Seventh Berkshire Conference on the History of Women, Wellesley College, June 1987, suggested that this set of proscriptions functioned very much like an incest taboo, indicating in which group you found social allies, and in which group you found "marriage" partners, thereby fostering solidarity among the former. Such a system may have helped the lesbian community attain some stability by designating some relationships as free from the transitory and impulsive effects of romance. This interpretation is supported by the fact that, as we will discuss in the next chapter, this lesbian community made a sharp distinction between lovers and friends.

12. "Cheating" will be discussed again later in this chapter and more fully in the next chapter.

13. From the perspective of trying to understand the ways in which the butch-fem dynamic is similar to and different from heterosexual gender roles, it is noteworthy that older butches did not pursue or fall in love with teenage fems, but teenage butches did pursue and were pursued by older fems. Butches did not consolidate their power as they aged, nor did they value fems only for youth and beauty.

14. Although entering a community provided opportunities for expanding one's social horizons and forming new relationships, participation in the community also increased the possibilities for intrusion on and dissolution of existing relationships. We shall treat the latter issue fully in the section on breakups.

15. Personal communication from Joan Nestle, 1984 and 1992.

16. Those with an investment in upholding the normalcy of heterosexuality want the numbers in order to prove the negative aspects of gay relationships. Lesbians want numbers in hopes that they will be inspired by others' lasting relationships and insecurities will thereby be quelled.

17. Becker, *Unbroken Ties*, presents an analysis of why contemporary relationships break up, which is not radically different, 32–46.

18. The reasons for the increase will be discussed in chapter 8.

19. Curiously, we have no stories about a butch ending her relationship when she found her fem in bed with another woman. This might suggest that such situations were always more complex than when a man was involved. Or it could indicate that the anger over a partner's sleeping with a man was so strong that the incident is emblazoned on people's memories, waiting to be told.

20. The James C. Strait show was a circus and midway operation that traveled among small towns and cities at least in the Northeast. It featured entertainers, side shows, rides, games of chance, and food concessions.

21. All our instances are of fems. Butches, of course, also felt the pressure of gay life. One eighteen-year-old butch left gay life for a marriage that lasted one day, but she did not leave a particular lesbian relationship to do it. Another butch left lesbian life for fifteen years and got married, but she was not in a relationship at the time. The pressures of gay life, which demanded that butches be more public and take on a more deviant identity, probably made it less likely that they were still unresolved about gay life after being deeply involved for a number of years. The different relationship of butch and of fem to gay and straight life will be discussed more fully in chapter 9.

22. For instance, contrast these narrators' statements with those in Susan Krieger's *The Mirror Dance: Identity in a Women's Community* (Philadelphia: Temple University Press, 1983), 67–80.

23. The ways in which lesbian couples handled domestic finances will be discussed in more detail in chapter 8.

24. Becker, *Unbroken Ties*, shows how the pattern of becoming friends with ex-lovers has continued into contemporary lesbian life.

25. This observation is indirectly supported by Letitia Anne Peplau, Susan Cochran, Karen Rook, and Christine Padesky, "Loving Women: Attachment and Autonomy in Lesbian Relationships," *Journal of Social Issues* 34.3 (1978): 7–27. The authors of this study express surprise that autonomy and equality were the same in traditional lesbian relationships and in those affected by the feminist movement.

26. For a period in the 1970s radical feminists expressed alternate visions for relationships. See, for instance, Jeri Dilno, "Monogamy and Alternate Life-Styles," *Our Right to Love: A Lesbian Resource Book*, ed. Ginny Vida (Englewood Cliffs, N.J.: Prentice-Hall, 1978), 56–63. Krieger's *The Mirror Dance*, 67–80, captures how one feminist community seems to value the group over individual relationships. Their relationships were often nonmonogamous and relatively short-lived. Karla Jay and Allen Young in *The Gay Report: Lesbians and Gay Men Speak Out about Sexual Experiences and Lifestyles* (New York: Summit Books, 1977), 301–2, criticize the "self-avowed 'radical' lesbians" for their criticism of couple relationships. Their survey shows that most lesbians value coupling and that lesbians are about equally divided in practicing monogamy versus nonmonogamy. Recent writing seems to value the lasting relationship; see for instance, Johnson, *Staying Power* and Butler, *Ceremonies of the Heart*.

Chapter 8

1. See Elaine Marks, "Lesbian Intertextuality," *Homosexualities and French Literature: Cultural Contexts, Critical Texts*, ed. George Stambolian and Elaine Marks (Ithaca, N.Y.: Cornell University Press, 1979). She writes of the corpus of texts that use the Sappho model and present lesbian characters: "Perhaps the most tenacious and pernicious element in this creation, reiterated by almost every writer, female and male, with the exception of Monique Wittig, is that lesbianism implies a nostalgic regression to the mother-daughter couple and is therefore not viable" (377).

2. *The Killing of Sister George*, Robert Aldrich, 1968, starring Beryl Reid, Susannah York, and Coral Browne.

3. David Schneider, *American Kinship*, (Englewood Cliffs, N.J.: Prentice-Hall, 1968).

4. The relativeness of time is still true today. Recently, a twenty-three-year-old lesbian was talking to one of the authors, Liz, about how serious her relationship with her ex-lover had been, and how long they had been together. Liz asked how long, and the twenty-three-year-old replied, "fifteen months."

5. Not one narrator actually attempted a religious or legal marriage, or knew of anybody during the 1940s or 1950s who did. This opportunity was not available at the time, and the oppression was too great for people even to consider it. "In the first place, I know I wouldn't have never did it here in Buffalo, when most of my family's here. And they'd get out. They always thought I was a little crazy anyway. And I know they would absolutely have me committed, if I did anything like that" (Debra). The first lesbian marriage ceremonies narrators remember were in the mid-1960s, and they were rare in both the Black and white communities. None of these marriages lasted for a lifetime; like other committed relationships, they ended too, as narrators readily point out.

6. There was one exception among our narrators and probably more in the community at large. Her first girlfriend came to live with her in her parent's home for a brief period in the late

1930s, before they decided to move out to get an apartment. They shared a room and were very discreet.

7. Narrators say that women involved in marriages of convenience didn't live with their girlfriends either, although none of them had had first-hand experience with such an arrangement.

8. This kind of arrangement was more common than we expected. Two narrators had lived this way for a period in their lives. These women knew others in the same situations, as did most of the other narrators. Why some married women would choose not to live with their partners and others to live with them is hard to tell. In the cases of the two women, one butch and one fem, who did not live with their partners, their husbands knew of their lesbian interests so it would be hard to camouflage a relationship with a live-in friend. In two cases of those who lived with both their husbands and partners, the husbands were unaware of their wives' lesbian propensities. In both of these cases, the women were Italian, with Italian men. It is possible that the closeness among women in Italian families made the arrangement less suspicious. As one said: "Well I brought her around as a friend of mine. I've always had friends. Even before I had a relationship I always had one good friend, and they were more or less used to that, my family, my immediate family, and my relatives. So it really wasn't anything unusual to them" (Phil).

9. Since we have not talked to any of these women directly, we don't know how they organized socializing, having committed relationships, and raising children.

10. There might be a significant difference between white and Black narrators in the raising of children. At least among our narrators, Black lesbians were more likely to have had children outside of marriage or in a brief marriage when young, and let their families raise them. White lesbians with children were more likely to feel compelled to keep their marriages together for the sake of their children. This difference would seem to follow differences in white and Black working-class family patterns. Black women were more likely to have the support of an extended family that was willing to raise other family members' children—see, for instance, Joyce Ladner's *Tomorrow's Tomorrow: The Black Woman* (Garden City, N.Y.: Doubleday, 1971)— while white women had to rely primarily on the nuclear family they created once they were married. In addition, and perhaps most important, Black narrators have proportionately more experience with raising children than white narrators, which is particularly striking given that we have interviewed so many more white narrators. This suggests that mothering played a more important part in Black lesbian lives of the past than in white lesbian lives. But the evidence is too scanty in numbers and the cultural statements too limited to make any firm generalizations about ethnic or racial difference in lesbian mothering.

11. This comparison with gay men is provocative. Why should it be more important for women than for men to build a home with their partners? Is it conditioning? Is it that men don't need a partner to have a good home life due to help from mothers and sisters, and higher salaries that allow them to buy more services?

12. This woman lived in an unusual situation with several female relatives who were fairly tolerant of her independence, so she had the space to develop her life as she wanted without leaving home. She denied having a home with her family, but she didn't move out until she was in her thirties, which was late compared to other narrators.

13. Dee, the narrator who lived in the apartment on Elmwood, took it in 1938 and paid twenty-five dollars a month including utilities. She was earning about fifteen dollars a week at the time, working in a technical job at a factory. She was able to buy furniture, and she and her girlfriend had a car, which was unusual for single women of that period.

14. One of the instances is discussed in detail in chapter 6 as part of a fem's story about coming to her sexual subjectivity.

15. The claim by some that sexual interest remained active throughout their relationship seems to go against recent studies of lesbian couples that show that lesbian sex falls off dramatically

after two years. The best-known study is Phillip Blumstein and Pepper Schwartz, *American Couples: Money, Work, Sex* (New York: Morrow, 1983), 195–206. Margaret Nichols in "Lesbian Sexuality: Issues and Developing Theory," *Lesbian Psychologies, Explorations & Challenges*, ed. the Boston Lesbian Psychologies Collective (Urbana: University of Illinois Press, 1987), 97–125, confirms the Blumstein and Schwartz findings based on experience in her practice and her life and relates this to the sexual repression of women. Marilyn Frye makes a humorous and insightful criticism of the idea of the frequency of sex in "Lesbian 'Sex,' " *Lesbian Philosophies and Cultures*, ed. Jeffner Allen (Albany: SUNY Press, 1990), 305–15. Despite this research, we think it is possible that many old-time couples who socialized in bars and parties did maintain active sex lives. As we argue in chapters 6 and 7, the culture of bars and house parties encouraged lesbian sexual expression, thereby supporting women to counter sexual repression.

16. This situation might be seen as a "catch 22," since mutuality, which many butches would not allow, might have been able to ameliorate the burden of responsibility.

17. It is tempting to say that the difference between a love relationship and friendship derives from following the heterosexual, male-supremacist model of marriage. This explanation is too simple, however. On the one hand, the dominant ideology of the companionate marriage, which presented husband and wife as each other's best friend, already was well established in this time period. On the other hand, there is evidence that the dominant ideology had little effect in working-class white and Black culture; see, for instance, Ladner, *Tomorrow's Tomorrow*, and Lillian Breslow Rubin, *Worlds of Pain: Life in a Working-Class Family* (New York: Basic Books, 1976). We argue here that there were also imperatives in lesbian culture itself that led to the sharp cultural distinction between friends and lovers.

18. Joanna was married for a short period in the early 1950s.

19. Gift giving is influenced by the domestic arrangements of the couple. This pattern was common when couples shared expenses. But in those where the butch paid the household expenses, and the fem kept her money for herself and for vacations, she also bought regular presents for the butch.

20. Norban's was an inexpensive clothing store, a national chain, and A. M. & A.'s, Adam, Meldrum and Anderson's, was and is one of Buffalo's higher quality department stores.

21. As mentioned in chapter 5, this narrator was affected by the feminist movement. It is therefore possible that the feminist movement as well as age was significant in changing her behavior. The same could be said for several other narrators.

22. A full discussion of fem identity, and how it differs from butch identity, is presented in chapter 9.

23. We are grateful to Joan Nestle for pointing this out.

24. To this narrator's mind, these butches' roughness was for show. They weren't really rough like the women of the Mardi Gras and Chesterfield during the 1950s. She reminds us that until the war, these women wore skirts, just as she did.

25. We will discuss in more detail why jealousy should have increased throughout the 1950s in the next section as part of our explanation of the increase in violence.

26. Here we are trying to talk about the institutionalization of violence as part of a culture. We cannot deal with the psychological factors that predispose particular individuals to use violence in love relationships more than others, such as how individuals were treated as children.

27. Alcohol unquestionably exacerbated the tough crowd's tendency to use violence in relationships; however, as we explained in chapter 4, lesbians of all groups consumed significant amounts of alcohol, so alcohol in and of itself could not create the tendency toward violence. It is possible that because many rough and tough lesbians did not work, they drank more than older lesbians, or than their upwardly mobile contemporaries, but the difference could not have been significant enough to cause the rise of violence in relationships.

28. This stud left town shortly after this incident so we don't really know how her behavior was accepted by community members over time.

29. She was not afraid of physical violence with her husband, but was afraid he would take the children.

30. Kerry Lobel, ed. for the National Coalition Against Domestic Violence Lesbian Task Force, *Naming the Violence: Speaking Out about Lesbian Battering* (Seattle: Seal Press, 1986) is the major text available on lesbian battering and we found it very helpful. We were particularly struck by the statement: "As a lesbian community, we identify with the power, control and anger of lesbians who batter. We identify ourselves as potential batterers. We do not recognize that we risk being the targets of abuse in our relationships, that we deny our vulnerability, and that we are like battered women who stay in relationships with an abusive person despite the violence" (14). We are not sure that we agree with such a statement, but found it thought-provoking. The book does not deal directly with violence in bar communities. In the preface, Barbara Hart suggests that the victims of violence in contemporary bars are as terrorized and controlled as battered women in traditional male-female relationships (11). However, she does not analyze bar violence, nor do any of the essays in the book, which are primarily about hidden domestic violence. In a later essay in the same book Barbara Hart indicates that individual acts of violence do not constitute battering, rather battering " . . . is that pattern of violent and coercive behaviors whereby a lesbian seeks to control the thoughts, beliefs or conduct of her intimate partner or to punish the intimate for resisting the perpetrator's control over her" ("Lesbian Battering: An Examination," 173). From this point of view some violence in butch-fem couples might not have been battering, whereas some clearly was.

31. In a public reading of a draft of this chapter in Buffalo, butch narrators who had not been violent in relationships expressed discontent with the righteous judgment that contemporary lesbians make of the use of physical violence in the late 1950s. They feel that today there is a lot of verbal abuse that goes unnoticed. They also suspect hidden physical violence in relationships. Although they do not excuse physical abuse, they feel that contemporary lesbians are not making an effort to place the expressions of violence in the context of extreme oppression.

32. This examination of the rise of violence in lesbian relationships has interesting implications for violence in heterosexual relationships in the way it highlights the importance of social conditions in creating and condoning masculine violence toward feminine partners.

33. Marks in "Lesbian Intertextuality" points out that the lesbian tradition has built its myths—oral and written—by incorporating the lives of real women. This has been partially responsible for the focus on immaturity. From the perspective of our analysis, this process has been distorted by focusing only on discontinuity, meaning failure, rather than on the depth and meaning of love in committed relationships while they lasted.

Chapter 9

1. Helpful discussions of this work include: George Chauncey, Jr., "From Sexual Inversion to Homosexuality: The Changing Medical Conceptualization of Female 'Deviance,' " *Passion and Power: Sexuality in History,* edited by Kathy Peiss and Christina Simmons with Robert A. Padgug (Philadelphia: Temple University Press, 1989), 87–117; and Lillian Faderman, *Surpassing the Love of Men: Romantic Friendship and Love between Women from the Renaissance to the Present* (New York: Morrow, 1981), 239–53.

2. Esther Newton, "The Mythic Mannish Lesbian: Radclyffe Hall and the New Woman," in *Hidden*

from History: Reclaiming the Gay and Lesbian Past, ed. Martin Bauml Duberman, Martha Vicinus, and George Chauncey, Jr. (New York: New American Library, 1989), 281–93.

3. George Chauncey, Jr. "Christian Brotherhood or Sexual Perversion? Homosexual Identities and the Construction of Sexual Boundaries in the World War I Era," ed. Duberman et al., *Hidden from History*, 294–317.

4. Once the sexologists' discourse was formulated and disseminated, it of course did directly affect the formation of lesbian identities, at least among middle-class women, who came to recognize their lesbianism after reading some of the medical texts. See, for instance, Ruth F. Claus, "Confronting Homosexuality: A Letter from Frances Wilder: Archives," *Signs* 2.4 (1977): 928–33.

5. Chauncey, "Christian Brotherhood."

6. For a discussion of the development of the idea of "same-sex" relations, see Jonathan Katz, "Introduction," Part 2, "The Modern United States: The Invention of the Homosexual, 1880–1950," in *Gay/Lesbian Almanac: A New Documentary*, Jonathan Katz, ed. (New York: Harper and Row, 1983), 247.

7. Sigmund Freud, "Sexual Aberrations," *Three Essays on the Theory of Sexuality*, trans. James Strachey (New York: Basic Books, 1962), 1–38.

8. Allan Berube, *Coming Out under Fire: The History of Gay Men and Women in World War Two* (New York: The Free Press, 1990), 8–33.

9. Alfred C. Kinsey, Wardell B. Pomeroy, Clyde E. Martin, and Paul H. Gebhard, *Sexual Behavior in the Human Female* (Philadelphia: W. B. Saunders Company, 1953), chapter 11, "Homosexual Responses and Contacts," 446.

10. She did not want to share what had led to trouble with the law, but did say it wasn't theft.

11. Although it was not common for working-class families to use psychiatrists as a helpful resource, it was not completely unknown. Jo Sinclair's *The Wasteland* (New York: Harper & Brothers, 1946) is a novel of the 1940s and tells the story of two children, one of whom was a lesbian, in a Jewish working-class family who went on their own to see a psychiatrist.

12. Gay activists who came out in the 1950s have had similar difficulties in merging the role of parent and gay. We have heard many say that they would find it hard if they learned now that their parents are gay. Several radical heterosexual students of Liz Kennedy who were willing to accept their friends' homosexuality had a problem in accepting that of their parents when they learned about it after having grown up.

13. Berger's was one of Buffalo's most expensive women's clothing stores on Main Street downtown.

14. Kleinhans clothing store (for men) was located on a corner of Lafayette Square downtown. According to Pearl, this area was a notorious pickup spot for men interested in men, as well as for men and some women interested in women.

15. Kinsey, *Sexual Behavior in the Human Female*, 468–76.

16. Unfortunately many of them had left the city, living in other parts of the country, so we did not interview them.

17. The butches themselves did not see their behavior this way as discussed in chapter 5.

18. The rash of discharges of lesbians and gay men and law suits against the military in 1992 indicates that the armed forces are not yet accepting of homosexuals.

19. When Toni read the manuscript through, she told us that she has since found out that this fem was heterosexual for a number of years and then returned to gay life.

20. There is very little research and writing on fem identity. See Mary Louise Adams, "Disputed Desire: The 'Feminine' Women in Lesbian History," paper presented at the Eighth Berkshire Conference on the History of Women, Douglass College, June 1990. In addition see Joan Nestle and Amber Hollibaugh's groundbreaking writing: Joan Nestle, *A Restricted Country* (Ithaca: Firebrand Books, 1987); and Amber Hollibaugh and Cherríe Moraga, "What We're Rollin Around in Bed With: Sexual Silences in Feminism," *Powers of Desire: The Politics of Sexuality*, ed.

Ann Snitow, Christine Stansell, and Sharon Thompson (New York: Monthly Review Press, 1983), 394–405.

Chapter 10

1. John D'Emilio's research supports this assertion. "A few minutes later, an officer attempted to steer the last of the patrons, a lesbian, through the bystanders to a nearby patrol car. 'She put up a struggle,' the *Village Voice* reported, 'from car to door to car again.' At that moment, 'the scene became explosive. Limp wrists were forgotten. Beer cans and bottles were heaved at the windows and a rain of coins descended on the cops' " (*Sexual Politics, Sexual Communities: The Making of a Homosexual Minority in the United States, 1940–1970* (Chicago: University of Chicago Press, 1983), 231–32). The Stonewall was a bar frequented by many men of color, but at this stage of research we have no idea of the racial/ethnic identity of the lesbian who started the fight.

2. Nationally, Daughter's of Bilitis was one of the few groups which fostered a feminist consciousness but not until the mid-1960s, and some of the more upwardly mobile lesbians in Buffalo did have such a consciousness. Rose Weitz, "From Accommodation to Rebellion: The Politicization of Lesbianism," in *Women-Identified Women*, ed. Trudy Darty and Sandee Potter (Palo Alto, Calif.: Mayfield, 1984), 233–49; see also, Elizabeth Smith, "Butches, Femmes, and Feminists: The Politics of Lesbian Sexuality," *NWSA Journal* 1 (1989): 398–421.

3. Teresa De Lauretis suggests that feminism, by focusing so much on gender difference, can be a source of the reproduction of gender, even when trying to escape it (Teresa de Lauretis, "The Technology of Gender," *Technologies of Gender: Essays on Theory, Film, and Fiction* [Bloomington: Indiana University Press, 1987], 1–27). Monique Wittig has shown the difficulty of writing as a lesbian who lives outside gender. The task requires minimally a total revamping of language; weak attempts to change the spelling of woman to "wymyn" or "wimmin" do not begin to scratch the surface. Monique Wittig, *The Lesbian Body*, trans. David Le Vay, (Boston: Beacon Press, 1973). Thanks to Carolyn Korsmeyer for coining the apt phrase "the intransigence of gender" in one of our writing-group meetings.

4. To our knowledge there are, as yet, no microstudies of twentieth-century working-class gay-male culture except for Esther Newton, *Mother Camp: Female Impersonators in America* (Englewood Cliffs, N.J.: Prentice-Hall, 1972). Thus our comparisons are of necessity tentative. Two relevant studies are nearing completion and will be published shortly: Esther Newton, *Cherry Grove: Pleasure Island, Gay and Lesbian U.S.A., 1930s–1980s* (Boston: Beacon Press, 1993); and George Chauncey, *Gay New York: Gender, Urban Culture and the Making of the Gay Male Worlds of New York City, 1890–1970*, to be published by Basic Books in 1994.

5. For an interesting comment on this trend see Biddy Martin, unpublished paper presented at *Homotextualities*, SUNY/Buffalo, November 1992.

6. Marilyn Frye cogently explores the oppressive aspect of invisibility in "Oppression," *Politics of Reality* (Trumansburg, N.Y.: The Crossing Press, 1983), 1–16.

7. It is perhaps no accident that scholars of twentieth-century gay life, who have tended to take gay-male experience as central, have not examined the role of gay-male bars, clubs, baths, etc. for developing gay consciousness. Instead they have looked to outside sources. Eric Garber has suggested that gays' and lesbians' consciousness of themselves as a minority group is rooted in contact with the Harlem Renaissance. ("A Spectacle in Color: The Lesbian and Gay Subculture of Jazz Age Harlem," in *Hidden from History: Reclaiming the Gay and Lesbian Past*, ed. Martin Bauml Duberman, Martha Vicinus, and George Chauncey, Jr. (New York: New American Library, 1989), 318–32). John D'Emilio has argued the importance of Harry Hay's experience in the Communist party for shaping a consciousness of gays as an oppressed group which would

allow for political action (*Sexual Politics, Sexual Communities*, 57–74). We would agree that both of these had an important impact on the development of gay politics, but at least in the case of lesbians, it was in interaction with the material conditions of community life.

8. George Chauncey, Jr. "Christian Brotherhood or Sexual Perversion? Homosexual Identities and the Construction of Sexual Boundaries in the World War I Era," Duberman et al. *Hidden from History*, 294–319.

9. Newton, *Mother Camp*, 106.

10. Sue Ellen Case argues that camp does exist in the lesbian community in "Towards a Butch-Femme Aesthetic," *Discourse* 11 (Winter 1988–89): 55–73. This is a topic that demands further research and analysis. In any case we don't mean to imply here that butches had no sense of humor, they did, as is apparent in many of the quotations used throughout the book. But their humor is not to our minds like the camp humor associated with queens. The nature of butch-fem humor awaits future study.

11. We are grateful to Peter Stallybass for the concepts of persistence and fluidity. Several conversations with Liz at the University of California at Riverside Conference, "Unauthorized Sexual Behavior," May 1991, helped bring into perspective the importance of both types of relationship to the lesbian community.

12. Jonathan Katz beautifully delineates this challenge in *Gay/ Lesbian Almanac: A New Documentary* (New York: Harper and Row, 1983), 172–74.

13. Katz, *Gay/Lesbian Almanac*, 18.

GENERAL INDEX

INDEX OF NARRATORS